MAN'S BOOK

ROAD BLOCK
Hillary Waugh

★

FAITH HAS
NO COUNTRY
R. Vernon Beste

★

THE MAN WHO
OWNED THE WORLD
Charles Eric Maine

★

also
TRAIL CREW
a short story by
Jack Schaefer

ODHAMS PRESS LIMITED
LONG ACRE, LONDON

S.162.S.N.

MADE AND PRINTED IN GREAT BRITAIN BY ODHAMS (WATFORD) LTD. WATFORD, HERTS

CONTENTS

ROAD BLOCK

Hillary Waugh

*"Road Block" is published by
Victor Gollancz Ltd.*

The Author

Hillary Waugh is a writer whose earnings with the pen enabled his wife to go to college. While he was busy writing his best-selling thrillers, Mrs. Waugh was working her way through Smith, one of America's most famous women's colleges. But it wasn't all one-sided—in return she provided her husband with background material for his collegiate thriller *Last Seen Wearing,* his fourth mystery story and his last before *Road Block.* Hillary Waugh lives in Northampton, Massachusetts.

CHAPTER ONE

Thursday, October 8

THE room was poorly furnished. There was a wrenched couch, a frayed rug, a narrow, sheet-covered table by the front windows, and a scattering of chairs. A doorway on one side of the sofa led to the tiny entrance hall and staircase and through to a dining room beyond. A doorway on the other side opened into the kitchen and a third door led into a through hall, the side door, and the back stairs. Dark window shades were pulled below the sills.

Two men were in the room. One sat at a wobbly card table under the light fixture playing solitaire by the gleam of two naked bulbs. He was about thirty-five years old with black hair and a harsh face. His eyes were dark and cold, his cheeks sallow, and he turned over his cards with long nervous fingers. A blue-black suit coat hung on the back of his chair and the trousers he wore matched the coat. His shoes were black but they were not matching shoes. The left one had a built-up heel and an inch and a half thick sole and the foot, in repose, rested in a crooked and unnatural angle. Beside him on the table was an empty glass that had contained milk and an ash tray filled with butts. A burning cigarette hung on the edge of the table.

The other man was taller and heavier, though still slender. He too had black hair but his skin was darker and there was a bluish cast to his cheeks and chin where the beard showed through. He was older than his companion, but still short of forty and his brown eyes were softer. A spread of newspaper was on the couch beside him and he worked with a rag and a small can of oil cleaning the dissembled parts of a Smith and Wesson .38 revolver with the tenderness of a stamp collector mounting a specimen.

At the table, the first man swept his cards together. He was outwardly impassive but the violence of his hand movements and the harshness of his voice gave him away. He banged his glass on the table and said, "Hey, Pete!"

A third man appeared from the kitchen. He was the shortest

of the three, thin and sandy-haired, with the obsequious manner of a dependent relative or expendable hireling. "Yeah, Lloyd?" he said.

Lloyd held out his glass. "Get me some more milk."

"Sure, Lloyd."

The other man looked up from the oiling of his gun. "When the hell do we eat? Do you know what time it is?"

"Yeah," Pete said. "Quarter of eight."

"I been here since six o'clock. How the hell long does it take you to get a meal?"

"It's ready. I was waiting for the others."

"The hell with the others. I want to eat now."

Pete said, "Yeah. O.K., Deacon. I'll get it."

He went back to the kitchen and Deacon, without troubling to lower his voice, said to Lloyd, "You must be pretty goddam hard up to drag him in on this. That two-bit heister ain't up to a big-league operation."

Lloyd, shuffling his deck with the speed and precision of a professional gambler, started laying out cards again. "He put us on it," he said without looking up. "That's why he's in."

"He'll chicken or go haywire. He'll louse us up sure."

Pete re-entered the room, a fresh glass of milk in one hand and a steaming plate of brown, semi-liquid paste in the other. It was a concoction that obviously had a canned bean base but it had been doctored by indeterminate additives. Pete, aware of protocol, delivered the milk first and then handed the plate to Deacon.

Deacon shoveled a forkful of the paste into his mouth and made a face. "Who the hell told you you could cook?"

Pete was unhappy at the censure. "Nobody. I ain't a cook. Lloyd said——"

"Lloyd's on a milk diet. He don't have to eat this slop."

Lloyd, not looking up from his cards, said quietly, "You don't like the food, you cook."

Deacon lapsed into sullen silence. He made a face and took another mouthful. "Scram," he ordered.

Pete wet his lips. "Yeah. Sure, Deacon."

Deacon watched him go. He swallowed another mouthful and eyed Lloyd playing his quiet game. "Whaddaya mean Pete set you onto it?"

"Just that," Lloyd said without interrupting his turn of the cards. "He met a guy."

"What guy? Where? Will you, for Christ's sake, tell me what the deal is?"

Lloyd reached the end of his game and started to gather in the deck once more. "I ain't gonna tell it twenty times," he said irritably. "When Chick and Lido get here we'll go over all of it."

"You got Lido for driver?"

"That's who I got. Any objections?"

"Not me. What would I be objecting for? He's only the best in the business." He watched Lloyd start another game, scraped up more food, and looked around. "But Christ. It's almost eight o'clock. Where the hell are they?"

Lloyd said, "I ain't a fortuneteller."

Deacon sat forward, resting his elbows on his knees, holding his plate. "It's a hundred grand, huh?"

"I don't know what it is."

"I thought you said——"

Lloyd looked up sharply. "It's a week's pay for a thousand men. Now shut your face. You get on my nerves."

Deacon sat back, grumbling defensively, and there was silence while Lloyd played another game of solitaire. From the kitchen a tinny girl's voice spoke suddenly. "Car one. Calling car one. Over."

There was a staticky, garbled voice in reply. "What do you want, Doris?"

"Got a complaint, Bill. Mrs. McKinley. Twenty-two Farnsworth Street. There's a cat in her tree."

"Tell her to put a steak under it."

"You tell her. It's not her cat."

"Roger, wilco, and out," the staticky voice sang.

Lloyd looked up angrily and said to Deacon, "Tell that god-damned Pete to turn off the radio."

Deacon got up and took his plate into the kitchen. A portable short-wave was set up on the table and Pete was sitting by it sipping a cup of acrid, steaming coffee. "Shut it off," Deacon snapped.

"What the hell," Pete complained. "I get nervous sitting around."

"Lloyd says to shut it off."

Pete sighed and twisted a knob and the empty hum of the radio stopped. He smiled. "The cops got a cat up a tree. Maybe tomorrow they'll have something else on their hands."

"Yeah." Deacon paused and pointed at the cup. "Gimme some of that mud."

Pete hastened to oblige, pouring a serving from the large enameled pot on the stove, getting milk and sugar from an old refrigerator by the hall exit.

Deacon said, "What the hell do you keep sugar in the ice-box for?"

"I don't want it to spoil."

"Sugar?"

"Well, how do I know what spoils and what don't?" He slumped into his chair sullenly.

Deacon, facing him, leaned forward. "What's the story, Pete? What's the whole thing about?"

Pete sat straighter, pleased. "It's like this, Deacon, A couppla months ago things got hot for me in the big town and I decided to lam out for a spell. I got an aunt and uncle, own this place, so I come out for a visit till things cool off.

"There ain't nothing to do here, so I took a look around the burg to see if there wasn't a few stores or gas stations around that was careless the way they took care of their money. So I was in this bar on Municipal Street taking in the lay of the land and cooling my throat. So what do I find in there but a guy lapping up the booze and groaning and complaining to the bartender. I'm bending an ear in his direction and what he's talking about is he works at the plant here in town. The Grafton Tool and Die Company. It's on Grafton Boulevard a mile, two miles out, and it's a big place. It's got close to a thousand guys on the payroll. So he's complaining about how the armored truck brings out the payroll every Friday and his job is helping stand guard and doing things to keep everything safe. One of the things he's supposed to do is lock a certain door. It's the door outta the room into another room and that's supposed to be kept locked when the pay envelopes are being handed out. So what's happened, he's been careless and forgetting to lock that door and that morning—it was a Friday—somebody accidentally opened that door to come in. Well, the guards pulled their guns and the guy almost got himself shot and the guards, they had a hemorrhage from fright and the whole place was in an uproar all because this guy'd forgot to lock this particular door.

"So what happened, they called the guy on the carpet and they docked his pay." Pete smiled with pleasure at the recollection.

"The bawling out, that didn't bother him none. That was O.K. But docking him ten bucks, that was in the old breadbasket. The guy makes eighty-two fifty a week, see? Eighty-two fifty, and he's got a wife and four kids and his wife is ailing and she's been having to go to the doctor. And besides that, he's got payments on an icebox and a television and a brand-new car, and he's working tight up to here and that ten bucks is a big wallop. So he's complaining fit to be tied.

"Well, I'm listening and I'm getting all this and I'm thinking to myself, 'Whaddaya know. Here's a plant that still pays its guys in cash insteadda check and if a certain door don't get locked and if a guy should come through it with a gun on purpose insteadda by accident, it could mean a nice piece of change if the right man did it'."

Deacon rubbed his chin. "Yeah," he said, and sipped his coffee.

"I started talking to the guy," Pete went on quickly, trying to hold his audience. "I thought it was a small shop I might take almost by myself, but then I find out it's a big plant and a real big payroll. See? So I buy him a couple of drinks and pump him and he starts crying on my shoulder. He's burned about the ten bucks, see? He tells me it ain't fair because so what if the door ain't locked? There ain't nobody could hold up that payroll anyhow. He says it just couldn't be done.

"So I'm thinking more and more and I decide this is the kind of operation's gonna need a real big-time heister, a guy who's got brains, a guy who'll know just how to handle jobs that need planning and timing and all that sort of skill. So I'm right away thinking about Lloyd Ragan and how a job like this would be a pushover for somebody in his class. I ask the guy what the payroll is—how much dough is in the sacks those armored-car men carry into the joint and he guesses there's maybe close to a hundred grand, only he don't know. So I tell him he's cockeyed if he thinks that payroll couldn't be snatched 'cause I know personally a guy who could steal the whole kaboodle if that one door was left unlocked.

"So he's staring at me like I'm some real bigshot or something, knowing somebody like that. And he says, 'You do?' kind of awed like. So that's when I hit him. I say I not only know such a guy but that same guy would undoubtedly be willing to pay five grand to a fella if all that fella did was happen to forget to lock that door. In other words, instead of getting fined for forgetting, a fella'd get five thousand dollars."

Pete grinned. "I guess I ain't no dummy, Deacon. Five grand was more'n that bird'd make in a year. It was so much money he couldn't even believe it. He sat there shaking his head and saying, 'Five thousand dollars just for forgetting to lock a door?'

"So that's when I hit him again. I pointed out that it's not like being a crook, forgetting a little thing like that. The only difference was that instead of forgetting for nothing, like before, he could forget and collect all that change."

Pete, trying to increase his stature, glowed with pride. "I could see the lug was taking the bait, but then he started getting a conscience. He thought it was pretty fine but if the payroll got stolen, he said, the men wouldn't get their pay, or the company'd be out all that dough. He didn't want the company to lose all that dough even if they had cheated him outa ten bucks. So I pointed out to him that maybe the men wouldn't get paid that day but they'd get every penny that was coming to them and the company wouldn't be out anything on accountta payrolls are always insured and the insurance company would make it good.

"So he was pretty well sold and I told him what I'd do was get my friend down to talk to him in case there was any problem about the thing that was worrying him. I called up Lloyd right away and I guess after he talked to the guy a while, he decided I wasn't calling him up here on any wild goose chase. No, sir. I guess he decided Pete Gudge knows what's what. He was only too glad to take over the operation."

Deacon tried the coffee again. "So Lloyd has me and Chick Morell for guns——"

"And me," Pete added.

"——and Johnny Lido for driver."

"That's right. A top driver and top guns and, of course, you know what Lloyd can do. It's a lead-pipe cinch."

Deacon said dourly, "There ain't no lead-pipe cinches. Them guards are armed, ain't they? You go against a gun and you can get shot."

"Yeah, but with Lloyd——"

"Nobody cops a hundred grand shooting ducks in a pond, stupid. And after we get the dough, how do we know some blabbermouth won't——"

"The guard can't talk, Deacon. He's in it with us."

"What about your aunt and uncle?"

Pete laughed. "They're down in Florida. Lloyd give 'em a free vacation. Don't worry, Deacon. He's thought of everything."

"Has he thought about what's gonna happen if Chick and Lido don't show?"

At that moment the knocker on the front door tapped and Pete straightened. "There they are now. Everything's gonna be all right, Deacon. You'll see."

CHAPTER TWO

IT WAS Deacon who went to the door, on an order from Ragan, but the man on the outside step was not Chick Morell. This was a short, stocky man of fifty with a brownish mustache, a heavy face, and gray, brooding eyes. He was wearing a tacky winter overcoat, open arctics with his pants stuffed inside, and an olive-green visor cap.

Deacon glared at the man. "Who the hell are you?"

"George Krulevich," the shorter man said importantly.

"Go to hell," Deacon started to close the door.

"But I want to see Mr. Ragan."

"He don't want to see you."

Pete came into the hall. "Oh. It's you, George. Oh."

"This man won't let me in," George complained. "I want to see Mr. Ragan."

"It's O.K., Deacon. He's O.K."

George entered, taking off his hat. At the card table, Lloyd snapped, "What do you want?" and made a move in his solitaire game.

George glanced around. He saw the dissembled gun spread on the paper and he didn't look happy.

Behind, Deacon looked over George's balding head at Ragan. "Who's this joker, Lloyd?"

"He works in the plant. He's the key man in our plans."

George's feeling of importance at being a key man had largely vanished at sight of the gun parts. Until this moment, the holdup was a nebulous thing, a future act that had no connection with reality. The gun brought it down to earth. The gun said it was actually going to happen. The gun was a weapon that could kill and it was going to be pointed at somebody. George had been persuaded that on the morrow everyone would gain and no one would lose except that impersonal, vague organization, the insurance company. Now, suddenly, it occurred to George, as it had to Deacon, that it isn't easy to take a hundred thousand dollars, even from an insurance company, and that certain risks were involved, that someone else might lose something too.

Lloyd repeated his question impatiently and George, hat in hand, pulled his eyes around. He hemmed and hawed uncertainly and Pete, struck by the hesitancy, said wildly, "Something's gone wrong. Ain't that right, George? The truck ain't coming tomorrow."

George shook his head. "No. That ain't it."

Lloyd said, "Speak up. What *is* it?"

George twisted his hat. "It's like this, Mr. Ragan. My wife's back in the hospital. The doctors say it's diabetes. And one of my kids is sick."

"So what?"

"I want my five thousand dollars now."

Ragan didn't answer right away. He went back to his game, played a card and moved a pile over, giving himself a space. He looked at the next card and laid it down. "Getting greedy, aren't you?"

George said a little desperately, "I got to have the money."

"You'll get it after *we* get it."

"But I want it now!"

Lloyd snorted. "You think I'm a jerk, maybe?"

George edged up a step. "Look, Mr. Ragan. It's like this. Tomorrow the banks are open. I can go put the money in. But after the robbery I got to wait till Monday. I'm stuck with five thousand bucks and nothing to do with it."

"You'll be at the plant when the bank opens, you liar."

"All right, I didn't think of that. But look. I'm a hostage, see? Now what kind of a hostage am I if I get turned loose with five thousand dollars in my pants? You gotta pay me now so I can put the money away."

Ragan laughed harshly. "Yeah. I pay you five grand now and tomorrow the door ain't unlocked and there's an army of cops waiting for us. You're a real comedian, Krulevich."

"I wouldn't pull nothing like that on you, Mr. Ragan."

"You're damned right you won't."

George twitched nervously. "Half now and half when the job's done. That's fair."

"You get nothing till after the job's done! Go on home. You bother me."

Krulevich didn't like being talked to in that tone and he didn't like not getting some money. "Listen, Mr. Ragan. I'm pretty important. Without me, you can't get anything."

The front-door knocker interrupted. It banged with a cheerful clatter and some of the strain went out of Ragan's face. "That's Morell," he said to Deacon. "Let him in."

It was Pete who ran for the door. He pulled back the catches and threw it open, and in walked a blonde.

She was a big girl of something like Amazon proportions, a good five-nine in height and, in her heels, she towered. Her bleached yellow hair was thick and long and painstakingly coiffured, her shoes were green satin spikes, her wrap-around coat a gorgeous silver fox. She strode in, complete with pendant earrings and queenly aplomb, looked down at Pete and said, "Hello, little man."

The other three stared at her, Deacon and Krulevich standing by the card table, Ragan sitting behind it. She entered with a swaying walk and paused dramatically in the doorway. "Don't bother to get up," she said to Ragan. "I'm not Mrs. Eisenhower."

Behind her came Chick Morell with two suitcases which he thrust at Pete saying, "Here, waiter, take milady's things to the boudoir." He came in around the girl and waved cheerfully at the others. "Hail, hail, the gang's all here." In height he was as tall as the girl in her heels, slender but not thin, and he was a good-looking, sandy-haired man in his middle thirties, decked out like a fashion plate.

Ragan was not amused. He jerked his head at the girl. "Who the hell is this?"

"Ah," Chick smiled. "But of course. This is Lela Trojan. Lela, meet the boys. That's Lloyd Ragan, this's Joe Deacon, the butler is Pete Gudge—and this guy is"—he gestured at Krulevich—"J. Edgar Hoover."

Lela leaned against the doorway with a hand on her hip. "What an array of talent."

"What's she doing here?" Ragan snapped.

"Well, Lloyd, old boy, you told me to bring what I needed to stay a few days." He gestured grandly. "I brought her."

"Get her out," Ragan exploded angrily. "Flop her in a hotel or something but get her out!"

The fire came up in Lela's eyes. "Listen, small-change, who do you think you are, Friar Tuck? I'm with Chick."

"Get her out," Ragan told Chick, ignoring her.

Chick shrugged. "Honey, I don't think we're welcome here. And after such a long trip too." He flipped his hand carelessly at Ragan. "See you around, Lloyd."

"Where do you think you're going?"

"Baby and me, we've got plans."

"You're staying here."

Chick turned without malice. "I gotta tell you. Lela's my A-number one love life. I can't hardly get along without her. Now you went and hurt her feelings, Lloyd. Telling her to leave is like telling my right arm to leave. If it has to go, I have to go."

"Don't be a fool," Ragan said. "You ain't gonna throw down a big job for a tramp, are ya?"

Lela said, "Chick, this guy never heard of Dale Carnegie."

"It's like this," Chick said lightly. "I don't mind taking orders from you on a job, Lloyd, on accountta I got respect for your brains. But when it comes to my private life, my respect just don't stretch that far."

Ragan said, "This *is* a job and I'm running it and business and pleasure don't mix."

Chick laughed. "Hell, I wasn't planning on taking her with us, Lloyd." He patted her rear. "She's going to sit home here and wait for papa."

A young boy of eighteen came through the front door unannounced. He was short and slender, clad in a black motor-cycle jacket and his dark hair was combed pompadour-style with long sideburns. He had narrow eyes, a tough curl to his mouth, and a freshly lit cigarete dangling from his lips.

Ragan stared and exploded again. "Who's this punk?"

The kid pushed between Chick and the girl and took a stand with his feet spread. He gave Ragan his toughest stare.

Chick said, "That's Ed Trojan. He's Lela's brother."

"What's he doing here?"

"You told me to get a driver."

"I told you to get Johnny Lido!"

"Johnny's in the hospital. He cracked up last month."

"You're a goddam liar!"

Chick shrugged. "What do you want, an argument? He's in Bellevue Hospital with one leg and one arm in a cast and a police guard at the door. Call 'em up."

Ragan put his hands over his face. "Jesus H. Christ. So you bring in some punk."

"He can handle a car. He hit eighty-five on the parkway coming out."

"What else did he hit?"

The kid took the cigarette out of his mouth. "Listen. I don't have to take that from you. I can drive a car through the eye of a needle. I can handle a gun too. You don't have to worry when I'm around."

Ragan glared at him. "You ever drive on a job before?"

"No, but I been on jobs before. You don't have to worry."

Ragan groaned. "That's what we got around here. This is supposed to be a big operation and we've got a country club. A hundred-thousand-dollar payroll and we're going to try to cop it with a dame and a punk."

Morell laughed shortly. "Damned if I don't think you're losing your grip, Lloyd. Don't you like the risks any more?"

"Only a fool likes risks, you jerk. Why do you think I plan the jobs instead of you? Because I don't like chances. Because the guys who work with me know I don't like chances. Because they know I'll figure it to give us all the odds. How many times have you been in jail, Chick? I was only in once, for six months, and that was when I was nineteen. I didn't like jail, Chick. When I was serving my time, I swore I'd never go to jail again. I tripped myself up that time on a stupid blunder. I took a chance I shouldn't have had to take. I assumed something I shouldn't have assumed and I swore I'd never tackle a job again until I had every possible angle covered. And I made it my business to check everything personally and then I made it a point only to work with top men, men I could depend on to do their job. Now you've got me stuck with a driver I don't know how he's gonna go. You're sticking our necks out, Chick."

Morell said, "Listen, the kid can drive. You can check on that yourself."

"I'll check, don't you think I won't." He turned to the boy. "What'd Morell offer you?"

The kid said out of the side of his mouth, "Seven fifty."

Morell said, "If it was Lido, I'd've offered fifteen C's like you said, but not for an inexperienced guy like Trojan."

"Seven fifty," Ragan said to the boy. "If you do a good job."

"I'll do a good job. Don't worry about that."

Ragan snorted in contempt. Then he rubbed both hands over his face and sighed in resignation. "Well, it's too late to do anything about it now. We'll have to play the hand Morell dealt us." He looked up and gestured, "Pete, give 'em all some food. Get 'em fixed up and then we'll go over all this."

CHAPTER THREE

"Doris," said a voice on the short-wave.

"Yes?"

"Doris. This is Bill. Will you call the fire department?"

Chick Morell came in from the kitchen. "What's Pete trying to do, poison us?" he asked Ragan. "What's that stuff he cooked?"

"I don't know. I been living on milk "

"He musta seasoned it from the medicine cabinet."

From the kitchen the radio voice said, "—it's not, Doris. The cat's there, but it's Tom. He's stuck. He can't get down."

Ragan, shuffling his cards again, said, "You don't like the food, you cook."

"I got a better idea. Hereafter I'm gonna have Lela cook."

Ragan snorted. "That dame?"

"She's a good cook. Her ma made her stand over a stove all the time when she was a kid."

"Her ma shouldda put her *in* the stove."

Lela came into the room. She had shed her silver fox and stood revealed in a green wool dress two sizes too small. It had stretch wrinkles and clung too tightly for anything to be underneath. "I heard that, lean-and-ugly," she said. "What are you going to do for friends when your brain gives out?"

"What're you gonna do for friends when you add about three more pounds?"

Morell said wearily, "Will you two, for Christ's sake, cut it out? We got business. Come on, Lloyd. How about opening up?"

The radio voice said, "—be back?" and Doris answered, "I guess any time. That grass fire started at six."

Ragan gestured. "Get those bums in here away from the radio and we'll go over it." He got up, opened a large atlas lying on the table by the windows, removed a folded packet of papers and brought it to the card table. Lela sat down on the couch and watched while he put away the cards, opened the packet and sorted through several large sheets for the one he wanted.

The men came in, Krulevich looking sullen, Deacon pessimistic, Ed Trojan with a put-on expression of blasé toughness, and Pete excited. Chick Morell grinned as he took his stand with the rest of them around the table and he caught Lela's eye with a wink.

Lloyd Ragan opened his paper and spread it before him. "This is a map of Stockford," he said. "Now I'm gonna explain it to you. This is the center of town, right here. This little triangle is the green. The street on the bottom of the green here, running east and west, is Center Street. North and south on the left-hand side is Meadow Street. The diagonal is Park Street. On Park Street, right here, dead center facing the green is the Town Hall. In the basement of the Town Hall is police headquarters."

Lela said, "You sound like a sight-seeing guide."

Ragan ignored her. He stuck his hands in his hip pockets and looked around. "The chief of police is a guy named Fred Fellows. There is a detective sergeant named Sidney Wilks, two desk sergeants named Gorman and Unger, and fifteen other men."

"Men who get caught up in trees chasing cats," laughed Morell.

Ragan scowled. "Don't go knocking this police force. The worst thing you can do is underestimate the opposition."

"It's smart opposition. Almost as smart as a cat."

Deacon said, "Chick's right. Never mind the police force. Get to the plan. A bunch of hick cops, forget it."

Ragan's voice was heavy with sarcasm. "This hick chief you're laughing at solved a murder last March they're still talking about. He's no dummy. Get that through your thick skulls. He's smarter than the lot of you put together. Much smarter."

Morell grinned. "But not as smart as you."

Ragan shot him a look and lighted a cigarette. "All right. The force has two police cars, black Plymouth station wagons. They operate one or two men to a car, usually two in the day and one at night. They range the limits of the town which has an area of roughly twenty-five square miles. As you hear tonight, they're both equipped with two-way sending and receiving sets."

"So they can get cats out of trees in a hurry," Morell said.

"Two cars," Ragan went on. "We've got to watch out for them."

Deacon said, "We can send them to the other side of town on phony calls."

"That's what we're going to do."

Chick said, "We can tell them a cat's in a tree."

Ragan snapped, "If you were half as good as you are funny, you could cop this payroll all by yourself. Now make up your mind. You gonna listen or talk?"

He bent over the map once more. "These sections north-west and north of the center of Stockford are housing developments, middle-class areas. This is the railroad. It lies to the south and just south of it, this area here is factory district."

Pete said, "That's where I run into George Krulevich. In a bar on Municipal Street."

"Now," Ragan went on, "this street running east from the factory district is Grafton Boulevard. Here's the Grafton Tool and Die Works, one mile out. This trunk line connects it to the railroad. You got it so far?"

Pete rubbed his hands. "There ain't nothing around it. It's in the wilderness. How about it? Did I pick it?"

"Shut up, Pete," Ragan said, but not severely. "That's our target." He pointed at an "X" he'd made on the map. "And here's where we are, down south of this ridge. The distance from this house to the gate of the plant is five and nine-tenths miles. The best route there is to take the dirt road out front east to County Road, follow that north to Edgewood Farm Road, here, right on that and go left on Grafton Boulevard. The distances are as follows: on the road out front, one point seven miles to County Road. North and west on County Road one point nine miles, north on Edgewood Farm Road one point one miles, and west on Grafton Boulevard one point two miles. The best time I've been able to make the trip, and that's at night, was eleven minutes and thirty-six seconds. Johnny Lido could maybe knock a minute off that. I don't what this kid can do.

"Now about these roads. The one out front is dirt and winding. You don't have to worry about traffic, there ain't any. Outside of a new house up near the corner, there're only three farms on the whole of it and this is one of them. The other two have gone almost as much to seed. The most you'd ever find along here would be a beat-up truck carting vegetables to town.

"County Road, that's blacktop, a wide two lanes, white stripe in the middle. The turns are shallow and you can hit sixty on the straightaways if it's clear. There is some traffic, however, and that will probably slow us down.

"Edgewood Farm Road winds more than the map shows. It's blacktop, but a narrow two lanes. You can hit forty but you can't maintain it on the curves and there's also traffic. A guess is you'd meet two cars and catch up to one on that mile stretch.

"Grafton Boulevard is straight as string, most of it. It's three lanes wide and lightly traveled. You can hit and maintain your top speed here."

Deacon leaned forward and put a finger on the map. "How about this road?"

"Massasoit? That's a good road, blacktop, little traffic."

"Why not take that instead of Edgewood Farm? There's less of it and you can stay on County longer."

"It'd save a few seconds," Ragan said, "but it's got one disadvantage. Anybody at the plant could look straight up the boulevard and see us turn on it. Grafton Boulevard makes a turn after that and nobody can see what we do at Edgewood Farm Road. The chances are they'll figure we've kept to Grafton and set up their road blocks ahead. Grafton's the logical speed route out of the area. In fact, it and County Road are the only fast routes east and south in that direction."

Deacon said sourly, "So we sacrifice speed for deception. I think we'd have a better chance running for it. The hell with tricks. Get out fast before they can block us off."

Ragan, a finger on the map, looked up sharply. "Deacon! You know about the Bergen bank job where the bank in the middle of town was robbed of fifty grand two years ago?"

Deacon said grudgingly, "Yeah, I heard about it."

"Well, I managed it. The State Police had road blocks up on all routes less than twenty minutes after the alarm went out. All routes, Deacon, in less than twenty minutes. And all they grabbed was air. The same is true of the jewelry store holdup in Pittsfield, upstate a ways. Seventy thousand dollars' worth of gems. That was four years ago and they had road blocks up all over the place. So you just listen to me, Deacon, and you'll be O.K."

He picked up the map and folded it slowly. "Now have you all got the picture clearly in your minds? You know the layout of the town and where the plant is?" He looked around at nodding heads, laid the map aside and brought the next paper over. "Now

I'm going to show you a map of the grounds. Krulevich couldn't get me any blueprints, so these drawings ain't gonna be absolutely accurate. They're as good as I could do from photographs I took of the place."

Morell laughed. "What'd you do, Lloyd, walk in and take pictures?"

"Nothing that brave or that stupid. There's high ground on the south side of the boulevard. Nothing but dried grass and dirt and shrubs. I took pictures from up there through a telephoto lens."

On the couch, Lela shook her head. "This thing sounds like the invasion of Europe."

"And that," said Deacon, "is why he's planning the job."

"I thought you just walked in and said, 'Stick 'em up'."

Ragan looked over at her. "That's for gas stations, drug-stores, and penny ante stuff. That's the way Pete makes his living. In the big leagues you play Class A ball."

She waved airily. "O.K., Ragan. Shoot your breeze. I'm for you just so long as you make a pile for my boy Chick."

He allowed a faint smile for the first time. "We'll all make a pile." The smile disappeared immediately and he spread his new chart on the table, a meticulous pen and ruler layout of the factory area drawn to a scale of one inch to twenty feet. The men leaned over it, obviously impressed. Morell said, "Are you sure it isn't one inch to twenty-one feet?"

"It's not perfectly accurate," Ragan said. "I had to estimate it by the size of people against the buildings."

"That's pretty smart, huh?" Pete said. "That's using the bean, huh?"

"All around the plant there's a ten-foot wire fence with a barbed-wire top. The fence goes all the way to the freight car loading platforms here by the tracks. They come in there against the side of the building. Only the loading platform is out in the open."

Morell laughed. "What are they making? The H-bomb?"

"They made bombsight parts during the war. The government put the fence round it then."

Lela said to Chick, "Ask him anything. He's the original encyclopedia."

"There is a gate," Ragan said, "right here. It's the only gate in the fence. It's a double gate that swings in. This little thing beside it on the left is a guardhouse. The guardhouse is tended by a watchman. He don't spend all his time there, that's only his headquarters. In fact, most of the time he's never there. But he *will* be there when we're there. It's part of his job to stand by the gates the whole time the payroll truck is inside. One thing I haven't been able to find out is how strong the catch is on the gate, whether a car could snap it or not. So we'll assume a car couldn't get out if that gate is closed. It's therefore our business to see to it that that gate doesn't get closed while we're on the grounds."

"How does the gate operate?" Deacon wanted to know.

"By hand. The day watchman relieves the night watchman at seven in the morning. The night watchman opens the gate at quarter of. The gate stays open until quarter of seven at night. It's the first thing the night watchman does, close and lock the gate. He chain-locks it."

"Just so long as there's no automatic switch."

"No. There is a siren alarm system, though, and if that goes off, the first thing the gateman does is close those gates. The gateman is an old geezer and I estimate it would take him at least half a minute after the alarm sounds to get those gates locked. Now the kid is going to be stationed behind the administration building with the motor running. The distance from there to the gate is about five hundred feet. The car should cover the distance in twenty seconds."

"That's after we get *in* the car, right?" asked Deacon.

"Once the car starts to move."

"That means if that siren sounds we got only ten seconds to get in the car and start moving, huh?"

"*If* the siren sounds," Ragan said. "But the siren ain't gonna sound."

"You hope!"

Morell laughed. "Don't listen to Worryguts, Lloyd. If he escaped to South America with the whole of Fort Knox, he'd worry about catching some disease he'd have to come back to see a doctor about."

"He don't have to worry about this," Ragan said. "There're only two alarm switches in the administration building, one in the accountants' office and one in the president's office and nobody's gonna be pulling them because nobody's gonna know anything's happening until it's over. Now let's get on with this.

"This area to the right when you go in is the parking lot. It's dirt with paved lanes. The visitors' area is this part right here, front left and closest to the ad building. It's a walk of about two hundred feet to the front door and the reception room.

"This large building back here is the plant itself. Beyond it, off here, is the garage. Back here, near the warehouse, is the lab and various outbuildings. None of those concern us. The only thing that counts is the ad building and, fortunately, it's nearest to the gate. Follow me?"

There were sounds of agreement and Ragan straightened up, lighting and inhaling deeply on a cigarette. "Now we get down to the facts of life. The office force and the workers are paid on Fridays for the preceding week. And they're paid in cash. As I understand it, they started paying off by check three years ago and immediately all the bars in town started up a check-cashing system at ten cents each and all the workers were cashing their checks in bars and having a few drinks at the same time. It got to be a regular Friday habit and the wives began to bitch to the company about their men blowing some of their pay and coming home loaded every week. So the company tried to operate a check-cashing system by having an armored truck come in with funds Friday afternoons. The men still went to the bars and the wives still complained. They complained to the union and the union complained to the company, so the company went back to paying most of the help in cash except the big executives whose salary gets banked to their accounts.

"The whole situation is this. Company pay accountants go through the records the first of the week figuring out who gets what. Then along about Wednesday or Thursday they make out a check for the full amount and take the money out of the bank —only the money don't leave the bank. They go into a special room in the vault and stick money in envelopes for each guy. When they got that all done, they put all the envelopes into two canvas bags and padlock them and store them in the bank safe.

"On Friday morning, come nine o'clock, the armored car pulls up at the back of the bank and takes on the two canvas sacks full of envelopes and drives to the plant. The truck arrives at the plant between nine twenty-five and nine-thirty. I've timed its arrival for five Fridays and the earliest it got there was nine twenty-six and the latest, nine twenty-nine."

Ragan took another deep drag on his cigarette. "There are two men in the truck. All right, that payoff is made in the stock room in the ad building. The accountants have their office but it's a hole in the wall and it's right off the main office room where the girls are batting their typewriters. The stock room is the perfect answer for them. It's at the back of the building with a direct entrance to a loading platform and it's plenty large."

Regan folded his layout and put it aside, bringing out another drawing, this one less accurate. It was a floor plan of the ad building drawn from information supplied by George Krulevich. He pointed to the entrance and said, "Here's the front of the building, the reception room, and switchboard. From the reception room you enter the main office space. It's full of secretaries and typists. A couple of offices are on the right. Now, at the end of this area there's a U-shaped corridor. It goes right, then straight, then left, then right. That U business is a detour around the president's office. There are small offices here, across from his.

"After the U, you will notice, the corridor leads straight to the rear of the building. That U is just what the doctor ordered. It shuts off the whole rear corridor and makes it private. There's only one office, here at the beginning on the left. That's the purchasing agent's office. That will be occupied by the agent and his secretary. Next to that is the dispensary. There's an outer waiting room, a little hall around a closet, and an inner room. There's a nurse on duty there at all times and a doctor is there for an hour in the morning and another hour in the afternoon. Ten to eleven and three to four. Next to the dispensary is the stock room where the pay envelopes are handed out.

"The other side of the corridor is a blank wall. The rooms behind it are rooms for the board of directors and are only used when directors' meetings are held, which is once a month. Any questions so far?"

Lela raised a hand and said, "One question, Professor. How did you find all this out?"

"That's neither here nor there."

Pete said with admiration, "Ain't he terrific? I couldn'tta done this in a million years."

Even Morell was interested now. "Let's get to the heart of the matter, Lloyd."

"All right, a few more points first. At the end of the corridor, at the back of the building here, there's a door with a bar lock. It can be opened from the inside but not the outside unless the bar is hooked down. From the door there are four steps to the ground. To the left of the steps, right here, is a loading platform about three feet off the ground. From the loading platform there is a set of double doors opening into the stock room. They're the same as the corridor door. They can be opened from the inside but not the out. There are two other ways to get into the stock room. One is this door here into the corridor and the other is this door over here into the treatment room of the dispensary."

Ragan pointed out the three entrances to the vital room, snubbed out his cigarette, and stuffed his hands in his hip pockets. "The armored truck," he said, "comes through the gate and drives around to the loading platform at the rear of the building. When the truck comes through the gate, the watchman is at his post at the guardhouse protecting the gate. Meanwhile, inside the ad building, the two paymasters and Krulevich go into the stock room. Krulevich locks the door to the corridor and is supposed to lock the door to the dispensary. He's also supposed to make sure that the corridor door to the outside is set so nobody can come in.

"The paymasters open the doors to the loading platform and one guard brings in the two bags while the other stands guard. I might add that the area must be cleared of any loiterers before this happens. Nobody is allowed to come anywhere near the truck. The bags are brought in one at a time and the truck is locked between trips. Meanwhile, the paymasters stand by the doors where they can lock themselves in if anything goes wrong."

"They must expect to be robbed every week," Morell said.

"This is the system that's been worked out to keep them from being robbed. They've been doing it this way for years, since before they tried paying off by check. There's never been an attempt made. In fact, a guy walking through a door Krulevich forgot to lock is the biggest scare they ever had. It's likely they're sloppy. It'll help us if they are, but I'm only telling what's supposed to happen when the payroll is delivered.

"All right. Both bags are inside now. There's a big table set up in the stock room. It's a permanent fixture. The paymasters are the only ones with keys to the bags. They close the platform doors and latch them when the second bag is brought in and the man on guard comes in too. So now we've got, inside that room, five men. The two armored truck guards, the two paymasters, and Krulevich.

"The paymasters open the bags and put the envelopes in piles by departments and alphabetically. They've been arranged that way at the bank so it's only a case of distributing the different piles. When they're ready, Krulevich opens the corridor door." He leaned forward and put a finger on the paper. "This one here."

Morell said, "And then the payoff starts!"

"That's right. The time is now twenty minutes of ten. They start handing out envelopes and continue until roughly one-fifteen. That's how long it takes to pay off a thousand guys. And during this whole time the guards remain on duty in that room.

"When the job is done, then the guards pick up the empty sacks and leave in the truck. The paymasters take any extra envelopes to the pay office with them and lock them in the safe. Krulevich unlocks the dispensary door, and everything's back to normal."

Deacon said, "I don't see no loopholes in that," and Morell said, "So far, great. Where do we come in? When do we make our move?"

"Obviously," Ragan said, "before they start handing out any envelopes. When all the dough is right there in the stock room."

Morell laughed. "And a thousand men are in the corridor waiting for it?"

"They don't line up, Chick. That's the point. Payment is made by departments and each department has its own schedule for being paid off. If you don't collect during your department's time, you can't get paid until afterwards." He looked around. "People here," he said and put the flat of his hand on the paper, "get paid first. Department heads have top priority. Their time is nine-forty to nine-fifty. Then comes secretaries and assistant personnel, from nine-fifty until ten sharp. At ten, the typists line up. At ten-fifteen it's the low echelons, office boys, janitors, maintenance people in the administration building. By ten twenty-five they're all done and the first group from the factory comes over. Or maybe it's the lab people, I'm not sure. It doesn't matter. Anyway, there's a set procedure. No more than one employee can enter the room at one time. They line up outside and when George here opens the door, the first man gives Krulevich his name and comes in. George repeats the name and while the man is advancing to the table, one paymaster locates his envelope and the other checks his name off. When he leaves the room, the next man gives George his name and comes in, and so on. Now that's the whole story of the payroll operation and I give it to you only so you'll know the complete background, so you'll be familiar with the whole operation. Actually none of this should concern us at all. Our job is to get that payroll as soon after the money gets inside the stock room as we can."

Chick grinned. "And you've got it figured out how we can do that, huh?"

"I didn't call you up here to this hole to tell you what I know about payrolls."

CHAPTER FOUR

"The key to the whole operation," Ragan said, "is right here," and he put his finger on the door to the dispensary. "If that door is left unlocked and a couple of guns come through, there shouldn't be any trouble getting the jump on the guards because their attention is focused on the corridor door. Well, tomorrow that door is going to be left unlocked and tomorrow a couple of guns are coming through."

"Whose guns?" asked Chick.

"Yours and mine."

Chick raised his eyebrows.

"You and I are handling that end. Pete and Deacon back us up in the corridor."

"Only the corridor door is locked," Chick said dryly.

"Keep your pants on, will you? What's the matter, you scared?"

"I just want to make sure we don't have a rooting section getting cut in on what you and I work for."

"When we come through that door, Krulevich will be already stationed by the corridor door ready to unlock it when the time comes. That's his normal position, see? Well, tomorrow he's gonna assume his normal position as soon as the paymasters sit down with the bags. He'll be right by that door when we come in with our guns. What's gonna happen is he's gonna get so frightened the first thing he thinks about is escaping and, seeing as how we come in with our guns trained on the guards, he's gonna think he sees his chance. He unlocks the corridor door. The key's already in the lock, see? He turns the key and opens the door and in come the reinforcements to back up the play. We got 'em four against two because the paymasters don't carry guns. Only the guards."

Deacon said, "Is Krulevich gonna open the door to the back steps? Is that how we all get in?"

Ragan said in disgust, "You guys sound like a bunch of amateurs on your first job. If I was gonna blast my way to the payroll, I'd hire myself a bunch of punks. I got you guys because I want finesse and you're supposed to be pros. You sound like punks yourself. Suppose you wait until I explain the operation and then ask your questions."

The men stood silent and Ragan, mashing out his cigarette, lighted still another nervously. He swallowed once or twice. "Tomorrow morning at exactly twenty after nine, Chick and I are gonna drive into the plant and park the car in the visitors' slot. I'm gonna get out and walk into the reception room and he's gonna stay behind and rustle around like he's busy with papers. That's in case the gatekeeper's noticing.

"I'm going to introduce myself to the receptionist as John Logan, a salesman, and I'm gonna ask to see the purchasing agent. Now the purchasing agent is the only guy who's got an office in that back corridor, but I ain't gonna get to see him on accountta the receptionist is gonna tell me he don't see nobody before ten o'clock. This is because it's Friday and he don't see anybody Friday until after he gets paid. His ten-minute pay period is nine-forty to nine-fifty and he don't want to have to interrupt conversations to run out and collect his envelope. See? This is information I already found out. So the girl will ring his office and she'll tell me he's tied up till ten and do I want to wait and I'll say yeah.

"I'm gonna sit there and thumb through magazines and meanwhile Chick is staying in the car looking busy.

"When the armored truck comes in the gate, Chick will get out and he'll come over to the reception room too. When he shows up, I'll know the truck has arrived and gone around to the back."

Ragan turned to Morell. "Now here's the thing, Chick. You're gonna come in with a briefcase like you're there on business too, only you're gonna come in doubled over and clutching your stomach. You're gonna say to me and the receptionist, 'It must be something I ate,' and you're gonna put on a great act about being sick. In fact, you're gonna be so sick you can hardly stand up. I'm gonna help you and we're gonna play it that way until the receptionist gets alarmed and says you should go to the dispensary.

"You're gonna be so sick you can hardly go yourself and I'm gonna help you get there. When we get into that back corridor, I'm gonna take the opportunity to set the bar on the back door so it can be opened from the outside. Then we'll get you into the nurse's office back there and you'll fake the sickness and I'll stand by, checking the corridor and keeping an eye on things. When everything is ready, then I join you in the dispensary and we open the door."

"What about the nurse?"

"Oh, yeah. This we're gonna have to play a little bit by ear. You're gonna try to persuade her all you need to do is lie down. If you can, you get her out of the back room and into the front room or, better yet, out of the office entirely. If we have trouble with her, there'll be a lot of adhesive tape handy and we can tie her up. If we show her a gun, I don't think she'll be interested in screaming but you never can tell about women, so I don't want to get her upset more than I can help."

Chick said, "How about bringing her in with us as a shield?"

Lloyd stroked his chin thoughtfully. "Now that's an angle I ain't thought of. That might solve both problems. Trouble is, it slows us up a little and speed's important. We've got to have the jump on those guards before they can draw."

"I think it's the deal myself," Chick said.

"All right. If she's there, we'll use her. If she ain't—if she's out of the room somewhere, we'll let well enough alone." He paused, considering, then nodded as if it were settled. "All right, now the cars. What kind have you got, Chick?"

"A black, four-door Olds, nineteen fifty-seven. Trojan stole it this afternoon."

"It'll hold six?"

"Easy."

"That's two cars, not counting an old jalopy in the barn. Mine is an unregistered Pontiac and I ain't used it here at all. Pete did the shopping and picked up Deacon in the jalopy. The Pontiac is the car Chick and I go in. The rest of you—the kid, Deacon, and Pete—you go in the Olds. Now look at this map." He unfolded once again the area map of Stockford and laid it on the table.

"Here's the bank," Lloyd said, putting his finger on the center of town. "The distance from here to the plant on the route the truck takes is just under two miles. The truck generally leaves the bank at twenty after nine and makes the run in seven to eight minutes, depending on the traffic and the lights. The route the truck takes is this. It heads west on Center Street to the light at Center and Meadow, turns south on Meadow, goes over the railroad tracks here and turns east on this street in the factory district.

This is Begley Street. Begley goes here and then angles and comes into Grafton Boulevard and the truck goes on to the plant.

"On this triangular block where Begley comes into Grafton there's a gas station. You are going to be parked on Grafton just short of that gas station. That gives you a good view. You're going to wait there for the truck, but you ain't gonna just sit. I don't want some gas attendant wondering what you're waiting for. Keep busy. Study a road map or walk around the car or do something. But don't put up the hood and act like you got trouble or that attendant'll be sure to come over. You make it look like you got business that just happens to end when that truck goes by. Then you get in your car and follow.

"Now one thing, Deacon. Don't let that kid get too fast a start. That armoured truck doesn't hit more than thirty even on the straightaway. If you end up poking along behind, the guards in that truck are gonna wonder about you. Give 'em plenty of room. When the truck goes by, take your time about getting started. The speed limit on Grafton Boulevard is forty. You should be able to go forty and still not get to the gate until at least twenty seconds after the truck goes through. It's better if it's a minute. One thing, though; don't lose sight of that truck. Deacon, this is your responsibility. When that truck goes through that gate, you start timing. It takes the truck twenty seconds to pass out of sight around back of the ad building. You give it twenty-five. That way the guards will never know you're there.

"I got Krulevich to time things from the other end. He says they sound a horn when they pull up and see that the coast is clear and then the boys inside open the stock-room doors. Krulevich timed it each week since I been in here—how long it takes from the time the horn sounds to get all the money inside and the doors bolted again. The fastest was one minute and fifty seconds and the slowest, two minutes and ten seconds. Add twenty-five seconds for the trip from the gate and you've got it that in two minutes and thirty-five seconds after the truck turns through the gate the guards and the money are inside the stock room and the doors are bolted. From that time on, any car can drive around back there and nobody will know it." Ragan pointed at Deacon. "The timing is up to you, Deacon. Don't go around in back of the building less than two minutes and thirty-five seconds after the truck goes through the gate, but go around there as soon after that as you can. How you stall is up to you. If you get to the gate too soon, drive straight down to the warehouse and go around the factory. Do whatever you want so long as you don't make the gateman suspicious and so long as the guards in the truck don't see you."

Ragan lighted another cigarette from the butt of the last. He mashed out the old one, smoothed his hands on his shirt, and rubbed his face. He sighed and said, "All right. You've come around behind the ad building. The only people who could see you are workers in the factory building back here. The chances are nobody there will, because they're supposed to be working and the chances are they wouldn't do anything if they saw you march up the steps with machine guns. But you ain't gonna do nothing like that. You're going to pull up like you've got business there. Deacon, you and Pete are gonna get out and walk up the steps to the back corridor door. It'll be unlocked and the hall's gonna be empty because nobody's allowed to line up for a pay envelope until nine-forty and the time's gonna be about nine thirty-two.

"While you're going inside, the kid here is going to turn the car around and open the doors on that side so there won't be any delay getting away. You come in and get your guns out and wait by the stock-room door, wait for Krulevich to open it. When he does, you come in.

"If all goes well, we'll already have the drop on the guards. Chick and I will chase the paymasters away from the table. You, Deacon, are going for the canvas bags. Any envelopes the paymasters have put out on the table, you're gonna shovel back into the sacks. Pete is going to take the guards' guns. Pete, you know what you do before that?"

Pete said, "The first thing I do is relock the door."

"That's right. You relock the corridor door and you take their guns. By that time we should have the sacks. Deacon, you're gonna carry them. They're pretty heavy, so Pete can help you. We go out the platform doors, you two first. Chick and I keep guns on the people in the room until you've got the bags in the car. Then we tell Krulevich to come with us. We're gonna make everybody think we're taking him hostage. We get him down in the car. We hand him over to you; then we follow and get moving. Any questions?"

Chick said, "What about the other car? The one you and I go in?"

"We leave it there. We ain't gonna lose time trying to take the other car. That stays."

"Six men in one car. That oughtta be easy for the cops."

Ragan put out his cigarette. "I'm forgetting one thing." He sorted through his papers and found a slip. "I forgot to mention one thing. That filling station where you wait for the truck—there's an outside phone booth there. One of the things you're gonna do while you're waiting is put in two phone calls. Pete makes one and Deacon makes the other. Both calls are to the Stockford police station. Make notes of this, both of you. Pete, you're going to say you're a Mr. Hildreth who lives on River Road. Fourteen River Road. That's up here." Lloyd put his finger on the development northwest of the center of town. "You're going to say there's something funny floating in the river. That's here. You're going to say you aren't sure whether it's an animal or what, but you think they ought to know about it."

Pete said, "Why don't I tell them it's a body? Then they'll be sure to come."

"You're not going to tell them it's a body. You're gonna tell them what I tell you to tell them. You're going to say it's something strange. You don't know what it is but you thought they ought to know. And if they ask your name and address, you tell them Hildreth, John Hildreth, and you live at Fourteen River Road. Deacon," he said, turning. "Five minutes after Pete calls, you call them and say there's been an auto accident at the corner of Center Street and Old Town Road." He pointed to a junction two and a half miles northeast of the town. "Center Street and Old Town Road. That's here. Your name, if they want to know, is Carter Blake and you live on Old Town Road, just off Center, between Center and the railroad tracks. Those calls are to be made at nine-fifteen and nine-twenty. Got it?"

Chick said, "Why don't you have them say there's a cat up a tree?"

"Dry up," Ragan snapped. "I ain't in no mood for humor. Now alla you guys got all this?"

The men nodded and Ragan said, "I don't see anybody making no notes. I suppose you got such great brains you don't need no notes or nothing."

Chick said, "While we're talking about brains, what about that car you're going to leave behind? You gonna leave a bunch of prints around for the cops to find out who it was who pulled the job?"

"My car's already been wiped. There ain't no prints in it and we're all wearing gloves. Don't ask stupid questions."

"Here's one that's not so stupid. If you aren't going to swap cars and if you aren't going to have a second car, tell me how you expect six guys in one car to get through road blocks that are looking for six men in a car."

"We ain't gonna meet any road blocks."

"You're a real optimist."

"We ain't because we ain't going anywhere. What do you think I was talking about when I told you to come ready to stay a few days? We're coming right back here."

"Hide out under their noses?"

"That's right. We come back here, the six of us, and we hide the car in the barn. Then we divide the money and sit around listening to the radio set—what the hell did you think I brought the set for? So when the heat's off and the cops have decided we got away and they take away the road blocks, then we drive off, split up, and we're on our own."

"What about Krulevich?"

"We turn him loose. He's going to walk till he gets picked up and he'll say he was held prisoner some place a two-hours' drive from here."

"And nobody found him until he walked all the way back?"

"Relax, will you? The whole thing's gonna be set up right. Only that ain't important right now. The important thing is what we do before we get back to the house, not after. You all got gloves?"

The men nodded.

"You're gonna wear them all the time in the car. I don't want any fingerprints anywhere."

Deacon jerked his head at Krulevich. "There're a couple of important things that're going to happen after. So that guy comes home. So they question him about us. He knows our names."

"He's gonna forget our names. He's gonna say he's been blind-folded most of the time and he don't know much what we look like and he's going to misdescribe us. The cops ain't gonna get anything from him."

Deacon said, "They'd better not," and the slow, dark way he said it made Krulevich wince. "Don't worry," the stocky man said, trying to grin. "I know how to take care of myself."

"It's how you take care of us I'm interested in."

Ragan said, "Stop worrying, Deacon. Krulevich knows what happens to guys who rat. He knows what happens to their families." He turned to the man. "All right, Krulevich. Go on home."

Krulevich left quickly. He said no more about an advance. Ragan turned to the others. "Now," he said, "all of you go out and wipe down that Olds. Outside and in. I don't want so much as a smudge on it."

Chick said, "Hey, the hell with that, Lloyd. That's the car we'll be keeping. The cops won't get that one."

Ragan's voice came up. "I'm running this, ain't I? I'm planning this. You do what I tell you."

"Let the kid do it."

"I don't trust the kid. All of you do it and do it right now."

The men grumbled but they went out, leaving Lela and Ragan alone in the room. She watched as he puffed jerkily on the cigarette. "It's a great life you lead if you can stand the pace," she said.

"I don't know what you're talking about."

She laughed lazily. "You don't eat, you drink milk. You smoke like a cigarette's an oxygen tube and you're fresh out of air. You snap like a dog that's been tied to a tree and beaten every hour. For what?"

"For about forty thousand dollars. That's for what."

"What're you gonna do with the dough, buy yourself a new stomach?"

Ragan said irritably, "What are you supposed to be, a comedian?"

Lela took a cigarette out of her purse and lighted it with a small gold lighter. She crossed her legs and her skirt showed her knees. "You're snapping again," she said.

Ragan snubbed his cigarette and took another himself. He looked at it with sudden awareness and laid it on the table before him. "It's easy for you to talk, Miss Relaxation. You're a dame and dames can make money without doing any work. I gotta struggle for my dough. I got to worry about punks like your brother. I got to plan jobs and rely on people like that Krulevich to see they come off. I got to sweat out accidents, all the kind of incidental things that can go wrong and louse up a perfectly planned job. How do you think I can relax, huh?" He looked down at the cigarette, snatched it up and put it in his mouth.

She shook her head. "Seems to me a smart guy like you could make money without so much strain."

"Not forty thousand bucks. You don't make that in one haul without strain. Nobody does." He stalked into the kitchen with his slight limp, snapped on the radio and hunched over it. After a few moments, Lela followed. She looked at his bent back and then at the sink with its scattering of dirty dishes. Without a word she started to wash them.

A voice on the radio said, "Doris?"

"Yeah, Bill," was the tinny response.

"Call the fire department again, will you? Tell them to send over a scaling ladder."

"What's the matter? They were just there."

"The cat's on the roof."

"Isn't there a skylight?"

"Yeah, but the roof's steep. I don't want to go on it without a scaling ladder."

Doris said, "I don't know why you don't leave him there. He'll come down when he wants to."

"The old bag—I mean the lady says his howling gets on her nerves. She won't be able to sleep."

Ragan snapped off the radio and turned around. "Hey," he said to Lela. "That ain't for you. That's Pete's job."

"I might as well contribute something to this family gathering," she said, running the water. "Besides, I'm used to it. I've been doing it all my life."

"Dames oughtta be decoration. They ain't oughtta work," he said, but he let her continue.

Lela laughed. "So that's what you want the forty thousand for. You want to decorate some dames."

"Dames I ain't got much use for," Ragan said, coming over. "They don't go for a guy, they go for a guy's money."

Lela dumped in the dishes. "Maybe you know the wrong kind of dames."

"I ain't ever met any other kind. You get a guy like me. All a dame'd look at about me would be the bankroll."

"What's the matter? You sensitive about your foot or something?"

Ragan's voice got hard. "You lay off about my foot."

"O.K., O.K. Don't get touchy."

"Besides, I don't bother with dames. The hell with 'em. All

you can buy is their bodies. That ain't very satisfying after a while, y'know what I mean? I mean when a man passes a certain age he ain't so interested in just bodies any more."

Lela snorted and rinsed a dish. "You ain't any older'n Chick and if you think he ain't interested, you don't know Chick."

He looked her over. "Well, a dame like you, you really got one."

"I ain't no different from any other dame, really," she said, obviously pleased. "I'm bigger, maybe——"

"Bigger in the right places."

She laughed and put the last dish aside. "Yeah. Especially here," she said, smoothing her hips. "I don't wear anything underneath and I get my dresses as tight as I can but I'm still too big. You wantta guess what I weigh?"

"Naw. Whatever it is, it's just right for you."

Lela wiped her hands. "You know, you're a lot different when you aren't under pressure."

"Ain't we all?"

"What're you going to do after? I mean after tomorrow?"

Ragan shrugged. "I don't know. Take it easy for a while. Depends, of course, on whether the cops are looking for me." He searched her eyes briefly. "You know, that's one thing about this foot. I mean you can't disguise yourself so good. Most of the time I been lucky. I mean I don't limp much and people are all excited and they ain't very accurate in their descriptions. Most of the time they don't notice I got a limp and the cops never figure it was me who did it. I been walking around now for five years saying hello to cops and they still don't know who pulled the Bergen bank job or the Pittsfield jewelry store holdup, or any of the other things. I mean I been questioned now and then but they ain't had no proof, especially when none of the witnesses could say anybody limped."

Lela poured herself a cup of coffee and sat down at the table. She said, "I don't know what you got to be nervous about. You got it made."

"You ain't never got it made, Kiddo," he said, sitting opposite. "No matter what you get, somebody can take it away from you. You always gotta be watching what you got and grabbing what someone else ain't watching. It's the only way to get along."

"You don't think much of people, do you?"

Ragan shrugged. "People ain't no different from animals. They got brains, that's the only difference. And all they use the brains for's to do the things animals do, only do 'em better. The guy with the most brains gets the lion's share, but that don't mean he's got it made. Even lions very seldom die of old age."

The others came in then, led by Chick who said, "Well, ain't this a pretty party."

Lela jerked her head at him. "See what I was telling you about him? I mean he's even jealous of my shadow."

Chick said, "Honey, anybody who ain't jealous of you ought to have his head examined."

Ragan got up. "All right. I'm taking the kid out for a ride. Get your gloves on, Kid. And while we're gone, the rest of you are gonna get out paper and pencil and write down exactly what you're supposed to do and exactly what time you're supposed to do it. When I come back we'll go over it again."

CHAPTER FIVE

Friday, October 9

AT seven o'clock the next morning, Lloyd Ragan came down the back stairs of the house. There was a fragrance of coffee in the air and the aroma of bacon and eggs but, if anything, the odors wrinkled Ragan's nose. He was disheveled and unshaven, his clothes looked slept in but he looked sleepless.

Lela was in the kitchen at the stove. She wore an orange and gold-figured robe, tied with a sash at the waist, and the subtle variations of light and shadow as her body moved beneath it indicated that, as with her dress, she wore nothing underneath. The robe gaped as she bent but she seemed oblivious, her concentration being on the production of breakfast.

Ragan stopped in the doorway wincing. "What are you doing here?"

She looked up. Her hair was well brushed and her face had a fresh and carefully prepared look, a Hollywood version of a farmer's wife. "I thought everybody'd want to eat."

"Where's Chick?"

"Sleeping like a rock." She shook her head. "I swear. He's got no more nerves than a lobster. I tossed and turned. I don't think I slept two hours."

"I know. I didn't sleep either."

"You ought to've slept," she said with concern. "I mean you ought to be right on your toes."

He waved a hand and slumped into a chair at the table. "I can't ever sleep the night before a big job. It ain't like I'm doing it all by myself. I got to depend on other people. I got to hope they don't make a slip. One false move by somebody and the whole thing's in the fire."

She said, "I know," and set some coffee things on the table, then returned to the stove. Ragan watched her go as if seeing her for the first time. Women had little place in his life but her imperfectly clad figure was impinging on his senses and on his brain in a way that made him temporarily forget even the pot of gold at the end of that day's rainbow. He licked his lips lightly and watched as she laid the bacon aside. "You oughtn't to be doing something like that," he said in an even tone.

"I like to," she said. "I want to. It makes me feel useful."

"A doll like you oughtn't to lift a finger."

She came back with the pot of coffee and poured two cups. "It's a funny thing about a woman," she said, pushing a cup across to him and sitting down at her own. "I developed early. I was getting whistles from the drugstore cowboys when I was twelve years old and back then I loved it. I used to dress for it. I even used to detour to go by the ice-cream parlor where the bigger boys hung out just so I could hear them whistle. You know something? When I was thirteen, my measurements were thirty-eight, twenty-two, forty. I know because I used to measure myself every night. My big ambition was to change it to forty, twenty-two, and thirty-eight. I got the forty all right, and then some, but the hips never went down. But even so, I was proud of myself. I knew I had something the boys wanted and I liked the power it gave me. I liked the fact I could get things for it. The first time I let a boy feel me it was for a banana split. I ordered the most expensive thing on the menu. I figured I might as well get what I could for it."

She stirred some sugar and milk into her coffee and stared at the liquid as she swirled it with her spoon. "I'm twenty-six now," she said. "I've had thirteen years of parlaying what I've got into the little luxuries of life but it's not the same any more. I don't want to be just one thing to a man any more. I don't want to sit around cooling my heels waiting for whenever Chick decides he wants me. I want to give a man something else, something more. You know what I mean?"

Ragan nodded. "Sure I know."

Lela shrugged. "Maybe I haven't anything more to give, but I keep thinking I do. I've read a lot of stories about love. I don't know what it really means, not the way poets and people write about it, but it sounds great. It's what I mean. A man needs a woman for other things, and she needs him too, not just for a new coat or something but for——" She hesitated and then took a quick gulp of coffee. "I guess I sound sappy."

Ragan said, "I don't think you sound sappy at all. I think you're a hell of a girl."

She put down the cup. "I don't think so—much—any more. But that's why I came downstairs and started breakfast. You're all going out. You've got a big job to do. I don't want to do nothing. I want to be useful. I want to feel like I'm contributing something, even if it's only breakfast."

Ragan, ignoring his coffee, lighted a cigarette. His hands were twitching a little more obviously than they had the night before. He poured himself a glass of milk. "Sure," he said, looking over at her, his eyes dropping once to the V of her robe, "it's a partnership. It's a man and a woman having things in common, working for something together. It's not like you and Chick. That guy don't need nobody but himself. I'm surprised you ever tied up with someone like him."

Lela shrugged. "Chick's a good egg. He don't understand what we're talking about. If I ever told him what I just told you, he'd think I was off my rocker. But he's really decent. He ain't never pushed me around and, you know, he's really fun to be with. He gives me comical kinds of presents sometimes, and he plays tricks, only they ain't mean tricks, they're funny tricks. I like him a lot. I guess I even kind of love him—I don't mean like the poets say where you lose weight and can't eat and get sick if the guy don't come around, but I sure like him better than anybody else I ever been with."

"Chick's all right," Ragan said, staring moodily into his glass, "but you're right. He don't understand you."

"He doesn't have brains like yours. I mean I think I have a better brain than he does."

"You do," Ragan assured her. "I don't like dames as a rule because I want more from them, like what you were saying. That's why you're different. When you first come in last night, I thought, 'Oh, another dame! She'll do nothing but get in the way.' But you're different. You made me change my mind."

"You're different too. I can tell. Maybe it's because you suffered."

"Well, I had a tough life. Being crippled, you know. You know something? I ain't never talked about being crippled to anybody but you."

She nodded soberly. "I know. I've been telling you things too. Say, don't you want your coffee?"

He shook his head. "I can't. I got this ulcer. It gets really acting up when I'm on a job. It's been getting worse now for the last six weeks. I got cramps in my stomach all the time."

"Gee, that's tough."

"I don't admit it to anybody else but I guess I can tell it to you."

She smiled. It was a warm and flashing and personal smile. "I get a lot of compliments on my looks, but I think that's the nicest thing that's ever been said to me. It makes me feel kind of special, like I mean something."

Ragan nodded and got up, picking up his coffee. She rose and took it from him. "Here. You sit down." She carried the cup to the sink and he came up behind her. "You are something special," he said softly. He put his hands around her waist and slid them up over her breasts. "You're the most special thing that's ever happened to me."

She pulled away like a flash. "Hey, cut that out."

He caught her arm. "Relax, Baby. It's like you say. We've got something for each other."

"Not this. I'm Chick's girl and I don't cheat."

Ragan was ardent now. "The hell with Chick. He don't understand you like I do." He pulled her to him and kissed her roughly. His hands yanked at her robe.

She tore her lips from his and clawed four red scratches down the side of his face. He let her go like a hot iron and grabbed for a handkerchief, his face white.

"You cheap hustler," Lela said, holding herself from shouting. She jerked the robe angrily together and retied the sash. "Just another line. Just another man."

Ragan mopped the streaks of blood from his cheek. "I'll kill you," he said hoarsely, looking from her to the tiny red spots on his handkerchief.

There were footsteps on the stairs and Chick came in. He was fully dressed even to his tie and jacket. He took one look and suddenly a gun was in his hand. "So, right behind my back," he snarled at Ragan. "What'd he do to you, Lela?"

"Nothing," she said sourly.

"What're you trying to pull, Ragan?"

"Nothing."

Chick advanced and yanked the handkerchief from his hand. "Blood." He looked at Ragan's face. "She scratched you. You goddam bastard!"

"I ain't done nothing," Ragan said. "It's just what I told you. You come around bringing these damn bitches in here when we've got work to do. I told you women get in the way. I told you to get her out of here."

"Nobody tells me anything, Ragan. I said that before. And I'm going to tell you if you touch Lela again I'll give it to you right here," and he jammed his gun into Ragan's stomach enough to make him grunt. "And don't think your bossing this job will stop me. A hundred grand or no hundred grand, I'll kill the first man who lays a hand on my girl."

"I wouldn't touch your girl with lead gloves," Ragan said, raising his voice. "I wouldn't let my worst enemy come within fifty feet of the Jonah."

Chick said over his shoulder, "You want him to apologize for that crack?"

Lela shook her head. She had recovered and her manner was nonchalant to the point of disdain.

"You want us to pack and leave here right now?"

She sat down in the chair and crossed her legs. "Not on my account, Chick. You can leave the guy alone just so long as he understands what's what around here."

Chick said to the other man. "You get that straight, Lloyd, or the next time I'll use this gun." He tucked it back in its shoulder holster and sat down at the table in Ragan's seat. Lela poured him a cup of coffee.

Ragan stalked off up the stairs.

CHAPTER SIX

At eighteen minutes past nine, Lloyd Ragan drove through the gate of the Grafton Tool and Die Company in a green Pontiac

sedan, Chick Morell in the seat beside him. The gatekeeper's
booth was by the entrance but the keeper wasn't in sight. Off to
the left, centered in a well-kept lawn, stood the low, whitewashed
administration building, a paved road running along its right
side, a turnaround area to the left in front. The road ahead ran
past the factory building down to the warehouse at the end, eight
hundred feet away. The labs were to its right, opposite the factory,
and they too were surrounded by lawns. Nearer, on the right, was
the vast parking area with room for five hundred cars and Ragan
headed to it, swinging in at the near corner where a five-space area
was marked "Visitors".

Ragan shut off the motor and put the car keys in his pocket.
He was wearing his dark suit, a knitted tie, and a brown felt hat
in the latest Ivy League style. The day was cloudy but the weather
was hot and muggy enough to make a coat unnecessary and Ragan
wore none.

He picked up a shiny new leather briefcase from the seat beside
him, the kind salesmen carry their papers in, but this briefcase
contained an oiled and loaded .38 revolver.

As he opened the door and stepped out, he looked every inch
the salesman making a call on a company purchasing agent except
for one small detail. He was wearing a pair of white cotton gloves.
It was a defect that was quickly remedied. He pulled them off and
tucked them in his briefcase as soon as he closed the door. Then
he leaned on the sill, being careful not to touch the car with his
hands, and said to Chick, "You got everything straight?" It was
the first time he'd spoken to Chick since they'd started.

"What do you think I am, a dope?" Chick retorted. He too was
well dressed, but his clothes didn't show the same quality of taste.

"If, by some fluke, that purchasing agent lets me in, you're on
your own on that sick business. I'll keep his office door open and
wait for you to come down that hall."

Chick said irritably, "For Christ's sake, will you quit worrying?
You're like an old mother hen."

"I want to make sure you don't goof it up."

"If you thought I'd goof it up, what'd you call me in for?"

"O.K., O.K. But when we leave, you get in the back seat. There's
a shotgun and a couple of revolvers on the floor of the other car.
You handle the shotgun if there's trouble." Lloyd looked around
and muttered, "There's the gatekeeper. He's heading for his
booth." He picked up his briefcase and strode with only a slight

limp across the pavement toward the administration building.

The reception room inside the glass swinging door was small. Six chairs faced each other in sets of three with walking space between to the receptionist's window. The receptionist herself, a dark-haired girl with glasses, whose name was Miss Mayweather, was on the other side of the partition in a small room of her own. She had a telephone switchboard, a little counter, and a book she was reading. When Lloyd approached, she looked up and said brightly, "Can I help you?"

"Yeah. Yes, ma'am. I'd like to see Mr. Gordon, the purchasing agent."

"May I ask your name?"

"Logan. John Logan. I'm with the Morris Company."

She suggested he take a seat and plugged in her line. Ragan sat, putting the briefcase between his legs, taking a chair that faced the frosted inner door and the electric clock on the wall beside.

Miss Mayweather said some words into her mouthpiece and unplugged the line. "Mr. Gordon's busy until ten o'clock, Mr. Logan. Would you care to wait?"

Ragan looked up at the clock. The time was nine twenty-four and a half. "I think I will." He reached for a magazine on a small metal table beside the chairs.

The girl went back to her book. The switchboard buzzed and she pulled out a line and resumed reading. Ragan folded over his magazine, a back issue of the *Saturday Evening Post*, and pretended to engross himself in one of the articles, but an eye was on the clock. The red second hand crept slowly and the black minute hand seemed to move not at all. He lighted a cigarette and started to look for the cartoons. He smoked the cigarette fiercely, taking deep drags, and though he tried to make his movements casual and offhand, the drags were frequent.

At a little after nine twenty-seven, he was down to a stub, debated a moment, then lighted a fresh one from the butt. He sat a little straighter and made a conscious effort to stop jiggling his knees. He reached down and touched the briefcase, took a few more puffs on the new cigarette, made himself lay it aside, and changed magazines.

The glass door beside him swung open suddenly, making him jump. He retrieved his cigarette casually and looked up and this time he almost jumped again. The man who had come in was tall and plump, wearing a brown suit and mopping a perspiring brow. It wasn't Chick Morell.

Ragan instinctively slid his left foot behind the briefcase. He wet his lips and sneaked a glance at the clock. It was just past nine twenty-eight.

The new man went to the window and said, "Hi, Angel. You look gorgeous today. Tell that bum Gordon I got a real bargain on the Brooklyn Bridge."

The girl laughed. "Mr. Gordon's in a conference right now, Mr. Jayware. Do you want to wait?"

"Hell," boomed the salesman. "A conference? He's pulling your leg. When's he through?"

"Ten o'clock. But this gentleman's ahead of you."

Jayware turned around and looked at Lloyd. He sighed and said, "Well, I'll see." He said to Ragan, "You going to be with Gordon long?"

Ragan put out his cigarette and glanced at the clock as he brought his gaze around. "I hope for an hour."

"Hell, that's no good." The big man set down his briefcase, wiped his hands on his handkerchief and worked his mouth. Then he said with more enthusiasm, "My name's Jayware. Horace P. Jayware," and held out his hand.

Ragan shook hands from his chair. "Logan," he said shortly.

"Who're you with, Logan?" Horace P. Jayware asked, easing down in a facing chair.

"Morris."

"Morris?—Morris?" He wiped his round cheeks and tucked away the handkerchief. "Which Morris?"

Ragan fixed him with a cold eye. "Pennsylvania," he said. "Anything else you want to know?"

The man flushed a little and said nothing. He fidgeted uneasily in his chair, uncertain whether to stay or go. Ragan sat back with his magazine, an angry scowl on his face, but inwardly he was as tight as a spring and perspiration was starting to form on his own forehead. The time was nine-thirty and Chick hadn't come.

Across from him Mr. Jayware picked up a magazine and that didn't help matters. The man was going to stay, after all. Ragan lighted another cigarette, an act which caught Jayware's attention. Lloyd went back to the magazine, conscious that Jayware was still watching. It was the kind of study that impressed a face and Lloyd didn't like it. He looked up slowly and the other man averted his eyes. He looked higher, up to the clock. Another minute had passed.

He mashed out his cigarette before he became aware he'd hardly smoked it. He wanted another but didn't dare. He wanted to get up and look out the door but he didn't dare do that either. Jayware was only pretending to look at his magazine, as if feeling the tension in the little reception room, as if he could sense an aura of taut waiting.

Ragan forced himself to be nonchalant. He idly skimmed over his magazine, turning pages, ignoring the man across from him. He sneaked a glance at his wristwatch and another at the clock. The times jibed within twenty seconds but the times of both were in the nine thirty-three range. Chick should have come through the door five minutes before.

Ragan took the last cigarette from a pack, crumpled the wrapper and let it drop into the ash stand beside him. He smoked the cigarette as slowly as he could manage, trying to make it last, trying to tell himself Chick would come in before he finished.

Chick didn't and the clock said nine thirty-five. In five more minutes the first department would be lining up in the back corridor for their pay checks. It was no good. It was already too late. There was nothing to do but leave quietly. He mashed out the cigarette and started to rise.

The door opened and Chick came in carrying a briefcase and holding his stomach. He looked dazedly at both Ragan and Jayware and half staggered to the window.

Ragan sat back down and the tension inside him snapped tight again. Across from him Jayware leaned toward the newcomer. "What's the matter, son? You sick?"

Chick nodded and leaned heavily on the counter at the window. "You got a place?—It just came over me. Something I ate."

Jayware pushed himself out of his chair. "Let me take him to the dispensary, Gloria. I know where it is."

Gloria started to agree but Ragan was back in action. "I'll take him," he said, coming to his feet. "This guy's a friend of mine." He put an elbow in the fat man's belly as he shouldered his way between and it gave him a momentary advantage. The big man grunted and almost collapsed in a seat.

Ragan led Chick around, snatched up his briefcase and hat, and helped the doubled-over man to the door. Miss Mayweather said, "But you don't know where it is."

"I'll find it," Ragan assured her, pushing the door bar with his elbow.

Then Jayware recovered once again. "I'll go with them. I'll show them." He started for the door Lloyd was getting Chick through but Lloyd turned and stopped him in his tracks.

"You're staying here," he snapped. "You ain't beating me to Gordon, so sit down." Jayware, startled, took a backward step and Ragan let the door swing shut in his face.

Inside, there were rows of desks tended by busily working typists, most of whom didn't bother to look up. Chick, letting himself be assisted toward the rear of the room, whispered fiercely, "What did you do that for? You made him suspicious!"

"I'm not gonna let that punk come along, you stupid jerk. Double up more. You're sick."

"I don't have to be sick in here."

"Be sick. What the hell held you up? Do you know what time it is?"

"Ask what held the truck up. It only just came."

The awkward walk of Chick was attracting attention and now all the girls were noticing. One at a nearby desk got up and said, "Can I help?"

"It's all right," Ragan said. "Something this man ate. I'm taking him to the dispensary."

"It's that corridor there. Near the end of the building."

Ragan, ignoring her, got Chick into the hallway and around the turn. In its privacy, Chick shook him off. "Come on. Don't overdo it."

"You're sick. Stay sick even if nobody's looking. You're supposed to be a pro."

Chick made a face but continued his doubled-up hobbling walk around the rest of the turns and into the straight stretch at the rear. The right wall was devoid of doors and there were only three on the left, the purchasing agent's, which was open, revealing an outer office with a secretary and a doorway to a well-furnished inner sanctum; the dispensary door and, beyond that, the stock-room door, both solid panels.

The dispensary door was narrow and the word was painted in gold across its face. Ragan let go of Chick in front of it and dug into his briefcase. "Quick. Get your gloves back on."

"Not me. I can't handle a gun with gloves."

"Wear gloves, you damned fool. You want to leave your prints all over everything?"

"I won't touch anything. I can't wear gloves."

Ragan pulled on his own, swearing under his breath and seized the knob. It didn't turn. He tried again, giving it an almost frantic wrench. It held firm and he cursed.

"The genius," Chick muttered. "Thinks of everything. Now what do we do?"

"Shut up!" Ragan pounded on the door more heavily than he intended. He looked at his watch desperately. It was nearly twenty of.

The door opened and the nurse stood there. She was a stocky, middle-aged woman in a white uniform and nurse's cap, a woman with a rolling walk and sharp eyes hidden behind steel-rimmed glasses. She held a cardboard coffee container in one hand and didn't look happy about the interruption. "Yes?"

"It's my friend," Lloyd said. "He's sick. Something he ate."

She let them into the small anteroom. There were glass-faced cabinets with red crosses on the panes and sterile white appurtenances inside, a small white table and two chairs. The narrow passage to the room behind was at the right.

"Something he ate?" the woman said. "I guess we can fix him up."

She showed no inclination to take them into the rear room, so Lloyd said, "He wants to lie down."

"Oh. All right. In there." She pointed at the hall and Lloyd took Chick through. The rear room was equally small. There was a window and a reclining table and more cabinets, these with instruments. On the right was a door. It was the door that was to be unlocked, the door to the stock room.

Chick got up on the cushioned table and looked dourly at the vital panel. "What do you want to bet that's locked too?"

"If it is, there's gonna be a guy who'll wish he was never born." Ragan put down his briefcase and hat and walked out past the nurse who had her back to him taking something out of one of the cabinets.

In the corridor he looked around, then went to the door at the end, pushed down the bar and locked it. As he turned back, the purchasing agent and his secretary came out of their office and started toward him. It was twenty minutes of ten and the first departments were due to be paid.

Ragan was ready. He walked toward them and halted, planting his hands on his hips. "And where do you two think you're going?"

They stopped in surprise. The agent said, "I beg your pardon?"

"I'm talking to you, Gordon," Ragan snapped. "Why aren't you in your office working?"

"This happens to be payday."

"The time's been changed. Don't you read the notices around here? You're one of the people who's causing all the trouble in this plant. You go into the president's office and wait there for me." He turned to the girl. "You too. You're in this too."

The mention of the president's office carried some weight. Gordon paled a little. "I don't understand," he said. "Who are you?"

"I've been hired to find out why this plant is so inefficient and you're one of the men I've had my eye on. I thought you'd pull something like this. Now you get into the office. I have things to say to you."

Gordon, white-faced, turned around and, followed by his secretary, went back. At the corner they encountered two girls and a man just arriving. They gestured and the three, taking one look at Lloyd and two at Gordon, disappeared with them. Ragan returned to the dispensary.

The nurse was with Chick, presenting him with a glass of colorless liquid. Chick was objecting, saying he'd be all right, and the nurse was insisting, saying he wouldn't.

"Go ahead and drink it," Lloyd said maliciously. "It's good for you." Under his stony gaze, Chick angrily took the glass and sipped.

"Gulp it down," the nurse said. "Get it down as fast as you can."

"It's great," Chick said, sitting up straight. "One sip and I'm good as new."

Lloyd went back to the corridor. No one else had dared show his face, but Pete and Deacon weren't there yet. He looked at his wristwatch for the thousandth time and his own stomach hurt. It was almost quarter of ten.

Then the rear door opened and Pete came in nervously, followed by Deacon who eased the door to behind him. Lloyd went to them. "What's wrong?"

"Nothing's wrong," Pete whispered. "Trojan's outside. He did fine."

"You call the cops like I said?"

"We called them. Their cars are way the hell on the other side of town by now."

"This is the door. Keep your gloves on and get ready but don't show your guns. Some bastards may come down the corridor. If anybody shows, order them into the president's office."

Pete stared. "And have the president——"

"Don't argue. You'll only be here half a minute." He stepped back into the dispensary. The nurse was still in the back room. He could hear her urging Chick to finish his glass.

Lloyd closed the dispensary door and pushed the knob lock. He went through the passage and caught Chick's eye over the nurse's head. He nodded at him and opened his briefcase.

CHAPTER SEVEN

THE nurse's back was still turned when Lloyd took out his gun. She was mothering Chick, the recalcitrant sick child who seemed remarkably recovered from the dying man who had come in. Her first warning that things were not as they should be came when Chick put his glass on the window ledge and kicked his feet over the side of the table. His hand went inside his coat and came out with a revolver.

She was startled but before she could speak, Lloyd jammed his gun in her back and seized her roughly. "All right, Grandma. One sound and I'll kill you. Turn around. We're gonna take a walk." He twisted the frightened woman around with one hand and shoved her up beside Chick who was already at the door. "Let's go," he said.

Chick quietly turned the knob. The door was not locked. He threw it open and burst into the room. Behind him, Lloyd pushed the nurse.

It was a large room with stock shelves jutting into it. In the middle was the table with two men starting the process of spreading envelopes. Against the opposite walls were more shelves but it was the deep shelves by the dispensary door that caused the trouble. They blocked a view of the whole room and when Chick came through, he had to take an extra step to get clear of the obstruction.

He said, "Get 'em up, everybody," and then realized he was only seeing one guard. That guard was standing by the table sipping coffee. The other guard, the one he didn't see, was near the door, a figure in uniform he mistook for Krulevich. When he spied Krulevich on the other side, he realized his error, but he had lost precious time. He swung around as the guard drew and at that moment, he was bumped from behind by the nurse Lloyd was pushing.

Lloyd fired at the guard and missed. The paymasters threw themselves on the floor. The guard with the coffee flung it away and jumped for safety behind the shelves near the platform doors.

Lloyd couldn't get off another shot. The first guard was already pulling the trigger. His gun jumped and Chick cried once in pain. He sagged against the shelves, blood running down his face. There was bedlam in the room, but one man didn't move. Krulevich, by the door, stood frozen.

Lloyd tried another shot as the guard dove for the table but the struggling nurse made him miss again. Then Chick fell against them both, his gun cluttering to the floor. The collision pushed Lloyd off balance against the side shelves and the other guard fired his first shot. Lloyd yanked the screaming nurse in front of him again and still Krulevich hadn't moved. "Open that door!" Lloyd shouted, waving his gun at the stricken man.

The table came over, crashing to the floor, spilling envelopes and the two canvas sacks. One guard and two paymasters cowered behind it.

"Open that door or I'll kill you," Lloyd shouted at Krulevich and this time he got through. Krulevich moved woodenly to obey.

"Drop your guns," Lloyd shouted, but another shot whistled over his head from the guard behind the shelves. Lloyd put a bullet into the heavy table and someone behind it screamed. Then Chick crashed to the floor, face up, a gaping red-rimmed hole over his eye. He landed at the nurse's feet and she fainted in Lloyd's arms.

Lloyd struggled to hold her in front of him, but he had to use his gun hand. The guard behind the table put his head and gun over the top. "Drop it," he ordered. But Krulevich was turning the key that unlocked the corridor door.

Deacon was firing as the door flew open. His first bullet caught the guard behind the shelves, knocking him to his feet. The second caught him full in the chest. The guard dropped his gun and slid down the wall. Pete aimed at the guard behind the table, a position completely open from the door. The bullet missed its mark but it told the story. The guard dropped his gun and raised his hands. One terrified paymaster did likewise, shrieking, "Don't shoot. Please don't shoot." The other paymaster lay quietly on his back beside him, his breath coming in short gasps, his shirt stained red.

Lloyd let the nurse fall, dumping her onto Chick Morell's body. "Up against the shelves," he shrieked at the guard and paymaster in a high-pitched, unnatural tone. The gun shook in his hands and his face was pasty. The two backed up quickly and flattened themselves, hands high. Lloyd kicked at the loose envelopes as Pete grabbed up the guard's gun. "Get busy. We'll have the whole office force on us!"

Pete and Deacon leaped to obey. Lloyd went up to the guard and rammed the muzzle of his revolver in the man's stomach. "Draw on me, will you?" he said in his high-pitched wild voice. "Kill Chick will you?" There was a muffled explosion as he pulled the trigger and the guard's mouth popped open.

Lloyd stepped back and let him fall, a stream of curses pouring from his mouth. Deacon, shoveling envelopes into the open sack with Pete, leaped up. He grabbed him and shook him. "Lloyd! What are you doing?"

Ragan pushed him away. His face was clearer and his eyes had lost their light. "Don't maul me," he snapped. "I'm running this. You got the money?"

"It's all in the sack but——"

"Pete. Get my hat and the briefcases out of the dispensary. Hurry!"

Pete ran out. Lloyd turned on Deacon again. "Grab one of those sacks. You know your job."

Deacon lifted the heavy locked bag and started to the platform doors. Pete came back with the hat and cases, his gun still in his hand. Lloyd took them. "Grab the other bag." He turned to Krulevich and waved his gun. "Come on, you. Get over to the door." He followed behind, one threatening eye on the paymaster, frightened and stiff against the shelves.

Deacon was first at the doors. He kicked the bar with his foot, throwing them open, took a step outside and turned white. There was nothing out back but the gray, tightly locked, armored truck. "The car's gone," he gasped and his knees buckled with shock.

"That lousy punk!" Ragan shrieked. "That lousy kid!" He wheeled on Pete. "Search the guards. Find that truck key!"

Pete loaded the heavy pay sack into Lloyd's arms and started to turn. At that moment the siren whistle cut loose. It brought the men up straight. Deacon said, "We're trapped!"

"My car," Lloyd shouted. "The parking lot! Run for it." He led the way, leaping from the platform, trying to sprint under the weight of the sack, briefcases, hat and gun. Deacon followed and Pete shoved Krulevich off the platform. "Run like hell," he yelled at the man and Krulevich, moving as if in a coma, went after the others, puffing and panting, his short stubby legs, long unused to the effort, taking him along at a trot.

The four men ran, trailed out in a line, alongside the building and into the open, Ragan in the lead. Around them the siren screamed like a banshee and out by the road, the keeper was obeying its signal. He had already half closed one of the gates and was going after the other.

Lloyd shouted at him and fired a wild shot. The explosion brought the man around but it didn't cow him. He took one look and redoubled his efforts. Lloyd stopped dead in the road and took aim. The distance was a hundred yards, still too far for a hit, but this time the gatekeeper could hear the whine of the bullet and that made him pause.

Deacon caught up to Lloyd and dropped his bag. "Get the car. I'll get him."

Ragan loped on again, burdened with his load, and Pete picked up Deacon's sack and staggered after Krulevich. The gatekeeper was still the only man in sight and he backed off slowly in the face of Deacon's advance.

Ragan threw his bag on the front seat and clambered under the wheel. Pete, laboring under the weight of his own sack, boosted Krulevich into the back with a kick and followed as Lloyd started the engine.

The car squealed in a U-turn, slamming the door, shot out and screeched to a stop beside Deacon near the gate. Deacon yanked open the front door and was pitched against the seat climbing in as the car leaped forward again. It roared through the gate with its door open, narrowly missed a car coming from the east, turned left as Deacon fought the door closed, and went up the road like a jet.

At the wheel, Lloyd gradually relaxed his grip and let the white go out of his knuckles. His face was dripping perspiration and a pain like a knife was in his stomach.

Deacon, looking back for signs of pursuit, said, "God, what a mess. Everything went wrong."

Lloyd said grimly, "I'm gonna kill that Trojan punk."

"Poor Chick."

"It serves him right for bringing in that yellow bastard and that painted bitch. He never had any brains."

In the back seat, Krulevich said numbly, "Mr. Perkins is dead."

Lloyd growled, "The only thing that could go wrong that hasn't is for this damned car to break down."

Deacon said, "What do we do, give Chick's share to the girl?"

"That bitch gets nothing. We split his share."

"He mightta wanted her to have it."

"He ain't in this any more. She didn't do a damned thing. She don't get nothing."

Krulevich said, "Mr. Perkins is dead. You told me nobody'd get hurt."

"What d'ya think this is," Pete said, "high tea?"

"But I knew him. And you killed the guards. You didn't say anybody'd get killed."

Pete snapped at him. "It's their own fault for firing at us. What d'ya think we're gonna do, stand there and get shot?"

Deacon leaned close and muttered to Lloyd, "I think that bastard's going to pieces."

"Don't worry about it," Lloyd said. "I told you I figure everything."

A car was behind them well in the distance, a car that had been coming along when they turned onto Grafton Boulevard. They left it out of sight rounding the slight bend in Grafton and when Lloyd swung the car off onto Edgewood Farm Road, only an oncoming car a mile ahead was in view. He took the curves at reckless speed, passed the intersection of Uphill Road, got around a car in front of him, sped by the entrance of Grandma's Lane and made a fast left turn onto County Road. Deacon checked his watch. "Jesus, it's not even ten o'clock. It feels like noon."

Lloyd slowed the car suddenly and made a quick turn onto a narrow blacktop wooded road that came in from the left. Deacon said, "Hey, where're you going?"

Lloyd didn't answer. He stopped at the side a hundred yards in and jerked on the emergency. He got out quickly and yanked the back door open. When he did, his gun was in his hand. "All right, Krulevich. Get out."

Krulevich stared at him wide-eyed. "Me? What for?"

"Get out or I'll put a bullet through you. Move!"

Krulevich moved, but slowly. "What's the matter, Mr. Ragan? I'm supposed to go with you. Don't you remember?"

"There's been a change of plans." Lloyd seized the man roughly and gave him a shove toward an opening in the woods. "Walk!"

Krulevich started along a small trail, leading the way. "But Mr. Ragan. I don't get it."

"You will."

Something in Lloyd's tone penetrated the other man's stalled brain. He said in a quavering voice, "What are you gonna do, Mr. Ragan? Listen, Mr. Ragan. You wouldn't shoot me?"

"All right. This is far enough."

Krulevich turned around. His knees shook and his jaw sagged at the cold, merciless face in front of him, the deliberate pointing of the gun. He sank to his knees and clasped his hands. His eyes, fixed on Lloyd's, were pleading and desperate. "Mr. Ragan, Mr. Ragan," he said in a voice that wouldn't function properly. "Please. Please, Mr. Ragan, have mercy. I did like you said, Mr. Ragan. I got a sick wife. I got four kids. I'll give you my money. I'll give you everything I own. Please don't kill me."

CHAPTER EIGHT

CHIEF of Police Fred C. Fellows was having coffee at the main desk with Detective Sergeant Sidney G. Wilks when the call came through. An excited voice said, "Police! Robbery! We're being robbed!"

Fellows, an elbow on the desk, said, "Who's we?"

"Grafton Tool and Die. It's the payroll. A car full of gangsters!"

Fellows looked up at the clock. It was seven minutes of ten. "When did it happen?"

"Just now. They just went out the gate."

"Which direction?"

"East on Grafton."

"How many?"

"Three men, and one of our men. They took him hostage."

"What kind of a car?"

"A sedan. A green sedan. The watchman might have got the number."

Fellows held out the phone. "Take this, Sid. The Grafton payroll's been stolen. Get anything you can on the car and bring it to me." He got out of his seat with remarkable alacrity for a big man and hurried into his office behind the main desk.

His own desk was an old roll top against the end wall near the door under a collection of calendar girls looking down at the scene over their naked bosoms. The top of the desk was a clutter of papers and Fellows pushed them around to find a road map in their midst. He pulled open the left top drawer and sorted quickly through for another paper. He half ran from the room, out a door on the left, and along the basement corridor to a small room whose head-high windows looked out onto the dirt yard in the rear.

It was the communications room and the large short-wave sending and receiving set was tended by a young, dark-haired girl reading *Lady Chatterly's Lover* in unexpurgated form. Fellows ignored her, pushing a phone connection into a direct line to the State Police. She closed the book and said, "What's happened?"

"Armed robbery. A big one. Open up this map, will you?" Into the phone, he said, "This is Fred Fellows. The Grafton Tool and Die Company has just been robbed by three men. They've got the payroll and a hostage and escaped in a green sedan. Have you got that?"

He laid his slip of paper on the map the girl had spread in front of him. "Here's what I want," he went on. "Road blocks as follows —never mind, I don't know yet. I'll give you the license if we can get it. It's a green sedan with four men in it, three robbers and one hostage. Remember that. They've got a hostage. I want road blocks as fast as you can get them up in the following places—call all the local police departments in the area. Get a man going on this while I'm talking. They left the plant no more than three minutes ago. I want the Weston entrance to the Merritt Parkway covered by eight minutes after ten. Get that done somehow. They can't make the Merritt before eight after ten. If you can't cover it by then, get on it and patrol it. They're probably making for the Merritt. I want the entrances to the Connecticut Turnpike in the Westport area covered by eighteen minutes after. Alert the Norwalk toll station. Alert them all but get that one first. I want road blocks in Redding Ridge and Redding by quarter past ten. Set one at the junction of route fifty-eight and U.S. two-oh-two by twenty-three minutes after. Intercept everything going through Wilton by eight after, and if you miss times there, get Norwalk set up by sixteen minutes after. I don't think they'll try through Ridgefield but we need that to seal off the area, so get a road block set up there by ten after. And, lastly, seal off the roads in and out of Danbury. That's got to be done by sixteen after, too. You got all those times and places?" Fellows nodded. "Good, but get the word out. There isn't much time." He looked up as Wilks came in and said into the phone, "Hold it. More information."

Wilks said, "It's a green four-door sedan. The guard thinks it's a Chevrolet. He says it's a New York license——"

Fellows said into the phone, "Four-door sedan. A Chevvie. New York plates."

"The plates," Wilks said, "end in numbers three-eight-four."

"The last three numbers on the plate are three-eight-four."

"One of the robbers was killed," Wilks said. "Also both payroll guards. Another man wounded. They got away with the whole payroll."

Fellows said into the phone, "And listen. They're not just robbers, they're killers. Warn your men. And call me back the second those road blocks are up. I want to know what the times are—I know I'm asking a lot but the sooner we can get them up, the fewer we need." He hung up and sighed as if winded. "They killed two men, huh?" he said to Wilks.

"At least two. Maybe three."

"That's tough."

The girl said, "You want me to call in the cars?"

"I guess you'd better. What are they out on?"

"Harris is on River Road investigating something unidentified floating in the river. Henderson's investigating an accident at Center Street and Old Town Road."

Just then the speaker came alive. "Grace. You sure it's Center and Old Town?"

Grace picked up her mike. "That's right, Larry. A Carter Blake called in."

"I talked to him but he doesn't know about any accident."

Fellows' eyes widened and he picked up the mike. "Forget it, Henderson. It's a false alarm. The Grafton Tool Company's been robbed. Stay where you are and flag every car. We're looking for a green sedan with New York plates carrying four men, but you stop every car. And watch yourself. They've killed two men. Harris. Can you hear me?"

Another voice came in. "Yes, Chief. I got that."

"Go to the corner of Center and Old Town and help Henderson. Do a spot check of all drivers' licenses and registrations. They might have switched cars or they might have broken up. There wasn't anything floating in the river was there?"

"No, sir."

"All right. On your way." He gave the mike back to Grace and gathered up his papers.

Wilks said, "Phony phone calls to send us off in the opposite direction?"

"That's what they were."

"Then the robbers certainly won't go that way."

"I don't think so, but there's a chance they might double back, figuring we'd have called them in by now."

"Robbers aren't generally that smart."

"Not generally," Fellows said, starting back to the headquarters room. "But I'm not going to be caught napping by one who might be."

"And that road block stuff. Road blocks in Danbury by sixteen minutes after ten. What's all that?"

"If they made a beeline for Danbury it would take them at least twenty-three minutes."

"How do you know?"

Fellows smiled as he re-entered the room. "I don't work on model trains like you, Sid. With four kids I can't afford it. So I guess my only hobby is the police department. It's not a twenty-four-hour-a-day job running this force as you know, so I kind of spend my spare time working out problems. You know—what to do if—? So, just for the heck of it, I tested how long it would take a car driving from the bank to get to all the places we could intercept it. I didn't figure the bank would be robbed, but it was something to do. And, because Grafton was the only other place in town a big robbery might take place, I adjusted the times for that place too." He entered his office, tossed the road map back on his desk and replaced the paper in his drawer.

Wilks said, "And what happens if they can't get Danbury set up by sixteen after ten? Suppose it's seventeen after?"

"The chances are still good. The times I gave were absolute minimums. If the road blocks can be set up by then, we *know* the car hasn't gone through. For every minute more it takes, the chances they escaped go up." He returned to the main room and made a phone call. "Unger," he said. "Get down here right away and take over the desk. Wilks and I have to go out. And as soon as you get in, call all off-duty men. I want the whole force out. There's been a robbery. Send Ed Lewis and four or five others out to the Grafton Tool and Die Company. Get them there as fast as you can and tell them to bring fingerprint equipment. Put the rest of them out patrolling the roads. I want all the super-numeraries out patrolling too. Map out the area when you get down here. I want every road covered that's on the map on my desk. Have them report in every half-hour. Follow up anyone who doesn't. You got all that? . . . Good. Now they're looking for a green four-door sedan, probably a Chevvie, with four men in it, three armed men and a hostage. Don't take chances, they're dangerous. The last numbers of the license are three-eight-four. Any questions?"

After that call, Fellows made two others, one to Hank Lemmon, photographer for the *Stockford Weekly Bulletin,* and the second to James MacFarlane, the medical examiner. MacFarlane, he was told, had already been called. He hung up and said, "Well, Sid, I guess the next thing to do is go out there."

CHAPTER NINE

THERE was chaos at the plant when Fellows and Wilks rolled up in front of the administration building at ten minutes past ten. A plant guard at the front door was keeping workers from other parts of the plant away and, inside, the office force was nothing but a mass of gibbering talkers, held in their own rooms by other guards. Little production and no paper work was being accomplished that morning.

Fellows and Wilks, in their gray shirts, sun helmets, and dark trousers, got out of the car and spoke to the first guard. "I don't know much," he said. "I'm on duty at the plant. They called me to take over here."

"What about the wounded man?"

"They've called an ambulance, I think. I don't know much else."

Inside the front door, Horace P. Jayware was pacing the tiny reception room floor. Fellows stopped him to ask who he was and he introduced himself, mopping his perspiring face. "Are you the police?"

"We pass as such around here, Mr. Jayware."

"The guard outside wouldn't let me leave. I've got other calls to make. If you want a statement, could I give it to you now and go?"

"You know anything about this?"

He nodded. "The man was right here. One of the robbers was here. He said he wanted to see Gordon, the purchasing agent. I can tell you just what he looked like. Both of them."

"I'll want to talk to you, but not just yet, if you don't mind." Fellows pushed the inner door open and looked around at the gathered groups of typists standing, smoking, talking excitedly. One of them was saying, "—it must be a hundred thousand dollars."

A second guard was at the back of the room at the entrance to the corridor. He waved the policemen over and directed them on. They met Otis Overbridge, president of the company, in the hall and he led them the rest of the way.

The three doors to the stock room were all wide open. A guard stood inside the room at the dispensary entrance, another patrolled the loading platform, and a third held back a group of people at the corridor door. Inside, it looked like a massacre. Chick Morell lay where he had fallen near the nook to the dispensary. Blood was all over his face and shirt, and in trickles and pools around him. His arms were outstretched, palms up, his legs straight, the toes of his shoes pointed out. One payroll guard lay on his side with his legs doubled up in the corner of the shelf projection near the platform doors. The other was crumpled on his face, his arms clutching his stomach, in front of the shelves.

The upset table had been moved aside to get to Perkins, the wounded paymaster. He was in shirt sleeves, lying on his back, one knee flexed. Someone's coat had been folded for a pillow and his shirt had been opened. A man was kneeling beside him, holding his pulse. He was the only outsider in the room and he looked up when Fellows stepped through the doorway. "He's hurt pretty bad," he said.

The chief knelt on the other side and put a large hand on the victim's damp white forehead. The wound was in the chest and it was welling blood slowly.

"He was shot through the table," the man said. "There were splinters of wood on his shirt." He gestured helplessly. "I don't know what to do for him."

"You the doctor?"

"I'm the purchasing agent. My name's Gordon."

"Isn't there a doctor around?"

"A nurse." He nodded at the dispensary door. "She's in there. She's suffering from shock. She and Broderick, the other paymaster."

Fellows got up and nodded at the wounded man. "See if you can get something to put over him until the doctor gets here." He went back to Wilks and Overbridge. "Sid, go out to the car, would you? Find out about those road blocks, then bring the car around to the back by that platform." He turned to the president and took out his notebook. "What can you tell me about this, Mr. Overbridge?"

Overbridge shook his head. "It's astounding. The first thing I knew about it was when I heard the shots. I was in my office and I heard the first shot. I couldn't imagine what it was. Well, the second shot was right on top of it, one and then two and then there were some more. Well, I went to the door to tell my secretary to find out what was going on and there was Gordon, my purchasing agent, sitting there. Not only him, but his secretary. I couldn't imagine what they were doing there and I said so. Well, he said the new efficiency expert had told him to report there and wait. 'What efficiency expert?' I wanted to know and he said, 'The one down the hall.' Well, that was where all the noise was coming from and I went out and around the corner. I didn't have any idea it was a robbery and those were guns I was hearing. Such an idea simply never occurred to me. I wanted to find out who this self-styled efficiency expert was and who he thought he was ordering my employees around, and what that racket was.

"Well, when I saw the door to the stock room open and heard the noise coming from there, then I realized what it was. By then the shooting had stopped but I wasted no time. I ran back to my office and sounded the siren which would signal all the guards in the place and would let the gatekeeper know he should lock the gate. I thought that way we'd be sure to stop it. I hurried over to the office opposite and saw the robbers running across the grounds and they had one of my guards with them, fellow by the name of George Krulevich. I hurried over to the front to see the gate and poor Amos Greene, he was trying to close the gate but the robbers were shooting at him. I was afraid they'd kill him too and I couldn't do anything to help him, so I came back to my office right away and called you. They hadn't even got out the gate by then, but I did see the car they were getting in. It was a green sedan."

"A Chevrolet, I understand."

"I guess so. I wouldn't know. Gordon was with me. He stayed at the front windows and as soon as the car got away he ran out to talk to the guard and he brought me the information I told your Mr. Wilks."

"You saw them run across the grounds? Can you describe them at all?"

"Not too well, I'm afraid," Overbridge said. "They were sort of dark figures, but I did recognize Krulevich."

"I'd like to talk to the gatekeeper if I may."

The gatekeeper came forward. He was an old man with hunched shoulders and the olive drab uniform was ill-fitting. "I tried to get those gates closed, sir, but they shot at me." He added proudly, "but I didn't stop. I didn't figure they could hit me. But one of the men came running towards me. I stood my ground long's I could, but he wasn't fooling and I had to back off else he would've killed me." He rubbed a finger under his nose and his eyes were bright. "But I got a good look at 'em, I did. And I damned near got the whole license number."

"A green four-door sedan?" Fellows said. "You sure it was a Chevrolet?"

"Nope," the man said. "Can't swear to that. I don't know all these new cars. All look alike to me. But if I had to pick something, I'd say it was a Chevrolet."

"And what about the men?"

"They come running across the roadway from around this building. The siren'd already started and I was trying to get the gate closed and soon as I saw 'em, I figured it was a robbery. The front man, the first fella who shot at me, was wearing a dark suit and carrying a white sack. I guess it was the money bag. He was running but he kindda limped, like he twisted an ankle or something. He took one shot and then he stopped and took another.

"The second fella was taller and he was wearing a dark suit too. He had another money bag but he dropped it and come running at me. I quit trying to close the gate when he was close enough to hit me, but he was still too far away for me to get a good look at his face. I just let go of the gate and run off to the side and he stayed there till the car come by and picked him up.

I ran back when he went out the gate to see the license but I couldn't get too good a look."

"What about the third man?"

"Well, sir, that third man was chasing George along. He was kind of short and he wore a brown suit and he had brownish hair. He picked up the other money bag and he climbed into the back seat with George. The first fella, the one with the game leg, did the driving. The one who came after me sat in the front seat with him.

"They went streaking off down Grafton Boulevard towards Georgetown and I ran out in the road to watch 'em go till they was out of sight. Then Mr. Gordon came running out to ask what I saw and I told him and he went back and told Mr. Overbridge."

"You see those gangsters come into the place?"

Amos Greene nodded knowingly. "I'll tell you, Chief. I shouldda suspected something right from scratch because of the funny things going on. First off, the truck was late and I was standing at the gate for maybe ten minutes and there's not a soul around. Then the truck comes through and the minute it goes by the parking lot, a man gets out of the green sedan and goes into the front door of this building. That struck me funny right then. What's the guy been sitting in the car for all this time?"

"Which of the men was that?"

"I dunno. I wasn't paying too much attention, I guess. But then, a couple of minutes later, through the gate comes a big black sedan. A young kid is driving it and two guys are sitting with him in the front seat but I can't tell you which ones they were because I didn't get that good a look. That car goes around back of this building, following the truck, and I guess I shouldda smelled a rat but, you know, you never think about anything like a robbery. So then I hear the shots, only I don't know what they are. I thought it was something at the plant but all of a sudden, back comes the black car like a bat outta—excuse me, Chief, I mean tearing out of the place and it whips through the gate and turns right, toward town and only the kid's in it. And then, right after that, the siren sounds."

"I don't suppose you got the license on that car, did you?"

Greene shook his head. "I'm pretty dumb, I guess, but I didn't tumble that anything was wrong. Can't tell you the license or what make car it is, 'cepting it was big, four doors, and black."

Wilks came in through the back door with Hank Lemmon and

his camera equipment. He said, "Grace wants to talk to you."

Fellows nodded and looked into the stock room. "How's Perkins?" he asked Gordon. Gordon, who had spread a coat over the man, said, "The same."

"What's that ambulance doing?" Fellows fretted. "Coming by way of China?" As if in answer, the sound of a siren was heard in the distance and some of the lines went out of his face. "All right, Sid. You want to handle things in here? Have Hank photograph the bodies as they lie and get the room." He went to the door, pushed it open, paused and observed that the bar had been locked down. He went down the steps to his car, drawn in behind the armored truck and blocked by Lemmon's sedan. He sat down on the front seat, one leg out the door and picked up the mike. "Grace, this is Fellows. Go ahead."

"Chief, we've got reports coming in. The Merritt Parkway's covered. They're stopping all cars at the Weston entrance, east and westbound. The Turnpike's blocked off at the Norwalk toll station."

"What times?"

"One trooper was at the westbound Weston entrance at two minutes of ten. Another took over the eastbound entrance three minutes later. That's ten-oh-one. They're stopping all cars for a spot check of licenses and registrations. Westbound cars at the Norwalk toll booth have been checked since ten minutes after ten."

Fellows nodded and depressed the mike button. "That's good. Anything else?"

The wail of the siren drowned out Grace's reply as the ambulance came around to the back of the building and pulled in by the armored truck. Two white-uniformed men got out quickly and ran around to the back for the stretcher. Dr. James MacFarlane and an interne passed it out and climbed down after. Fellows called, "What the hell kept you, Jim?"

"Another call. We've only got one ambulance."

"Let's have that again, Grace," Fellows said into the mike.

"Three State Police cars are patrolling the Turnpike between Westport and Norwalk, checking all entering vehicles."

"Well, you pass the word along, will you, for everyone to be on the lookout for a black four-door sedan driven by a kid, a young punk. He's in this thing, but he got frightened and ran. I want him picked up if possible, but I can't tell you the make of the car or the license. It's probably a New York car and it's black."

"All right, Chief. I'll notify all stations."

"Meanwhile, anything on the other road blocks?"

"Not yet. They're being handled by local police."

Another voice cut in. "Harris to headquarters. Harris to headquarters. I just got that message. Are we to stop all cars or just green and black sedans? Over."

"Check all cars," the chief said. "They might have split up or switched." He put down the mike, got out of the car and climbed the steps again.

In the stock room, MacFarlane and the interne were kneeling over the wounded man. Gordon was standing by, and Hank Lemmon was taking pictures with his flash equipment. The hall outside was milling with the curious, eager to see and to give their stories. Fellows said, "All right, people. Let's be a little quiet here if you don't mind. There's a man pretty badly hurt. Let's give him a break." He turned to Wilks. "Listen, Sid, that guy Jayware out in the front room. See what he's got to say, will you, while I talk to some of the people around here?"

Wilks went off and Fellows called Gordon into the hall. "Mr. Gordon, you talked to this man. You want to tell me what happened?"

Gordon related the experience, how he'd come to get his paycheck and been chased off by the stranger. "Maybe I shouldn't have believed him, but when he told me to wait in the president's office, I thought he must know what he was about."

"It's probably a good thing for you you did what he said, Mr. Gordon. The man didn't have any intention of letting you interfere with a robbery this big."

"Yeah, but I might have talked to Mr. Overbridge. I might have asked him what the score was."

Fellows went on. "You said the man told you he'd had his eye on you. He act as if he knew you?"

"He did. He called me by name."

"And you'd never seen him before?"

"Never."

"He called your secretary by name too?"

"No. I don't think he knew her name. I don't know how he could have found out who I was, though."

"You don't keep it any secret, do you?"

"No. It's on the door, come to think of it. The man might have noticed it as he went by. Except the door was open. I suppose he could still have seen it, though."

"What'd the man look like?"

"Narrow, close-set eyes, black hair, widow's peak. A rather nasty and evil face."

"Can you be a little more specific? How about height and weight and face structure?"

"He was about six feet tall, I guess, moderate build, and he was wearing a charcoal-gray suit and no hat. I'd guess he was forty to forty-five years old. His face was narrow and long and his voice was rasping."

Fellows made notes in his book and MacFarlane came out. "Fred," he said, "you want to help with the stretcher? We want to let the man off the platform."

Fellows said, "Sure," and put his notebook away. Perkins was on the stretcher now, still unconscious, and the chief took the stretcher bars at his feet. "Lift with me," the attendant at the other end said. "Don't let him tip."

Fellows nodded and raised it evenly. The interne and other attendant led the way onto the platform, jumped to the ground and carefully took the stretcher from there. Fellows watched with his hands on his hips as they put it into the rear of the ambulance. MacFarlane came out beside him. "The bullet lost some of its force going through the table," he said, "but it still got him pretty bad. It's in his lung."

"He got much of a chance, Jim?"

"Fair to middling. It's shock and loss of blood right now. Lots of blood collecting in his chest cavity. It's a job for Dr. Spears."

The attendants slammed the rear door and ran around to the driver's seat. They threw the ambulance into gear and turned a tight circle, swaying the interne in the rear. The siren started and they raced away.

Fellows said, "I guess I respect a hero as much as the next man, Jim, but I can't help wondering what was accomplished by the armored truck guards trying to shoot it out with the thieves. Three men are dead and one near death. Since the payroll's insured, I wonder if it's worth it."

CHAPTER TEN

WHEN Wilks returned from his interview with Jayware, Hank Lemmon had gone and Fellows was back in his car getting the latest road block news. The detective sergeant went down the steps just as the chief got out and they stood together in temporary privacy while they swapped information. "The robber introduced himself as Logan," Wilks said. "John Logan. And he asked the girl for Mr. Gordon by name. Gordon sent word he was in a conference until ten, so the man waited. Then Jayware came in. That was about nine-thirty. According to him, Logan was surly. Anything but a salesman type. He claims he was suspicious from the start."

"He give you a good description?"

"Logan was short and skinny, sallow face, dark blue suit, new hat, new briefcase that had a bulge in it. He thinks Logan kept his gun there."

"He thinks so now, you mean."

"Well, you can't blame him for not thinking so then. Who's going to expect a payroll robber to be quietly sitting in some anteroom waiting to see the purchasing agent?"

"Then what?"

"After about ten minutes another man came in claiming he was sick. He had sandy hair and was kind of flashily dressed, a natty suit——"

"Sounds like the one who was killed," Fellows said. "I haven't taken a real look at him yet, but the clothes fit."

"Then it doesn't help much. Anyway, here's what happened. He came in holding his stomach and wanted to lie down. The receptionist, Miss Mayweather, told him to go to the dispensary and Jayware offered to take him, only this Logan character butted in and said he'd take him, said he was a friend."

"I guess he was," Fellows said.

"And that's it at that end. They both came in here and next we know, Logan is alone in the hall chasing Gordon to the president's office." He looked over at the car short-wave which was quiet. "How're the road blocks?"

"Danbury and Ridgefield reported. They're on time."

"But nobody's intercepted anybody?"

Fellows shook his head. "That's the trouble. If they were all set up on time, those crooks would be caught in a double ring. If they got past a first, they'd still hit a second. It's half past ten. It should have happened by now."

"Which means they weren't set up on time?"

"I don't know. Since those crooks sent our cars north, I have to guess they went south. It's a New York car and the odds are all in favor of their making for the Merritt or the Turnpike heading west. Those places were reported blocked off on time."

"Which means Logan figured that's what we'd figure and he went in a different direction."

Fellows said glumly, "He'd expect us to throw up road blocks but he couldn't expect us to get them up before he could make the parkways. If I were doing it, I'd plan to ride the Merritt or Connecticut for a while and then turn off."

"And the Merritt rather than the Turnpike. He wouldn't want to hit all those toll stations."

Fellows heaved a sigh. "Well, I can't figure it. Let's take a look at the dead man. Maybe we can get an idea who planned the thing."

MacFarlane was in the stock room examining one of the dead guards. The robber's body was undisturbed and Fellows knelt beside it. "Sandy hair. It's the guy who was supposed to be sick, all right, but his face is a mess." He looked up at the open door to the dispensary, now devoid of the guard, and said, "Want to get a towel from there, Sid, and see if we can't wipe off some of this blood?"

Wilks went in the door and Fellows searched quickly and deftly through the dead man's pockets. There was a box of shells, a handkerchief, some keys, a pencil, and a wallet with six hundred and eighty-four dollars in it and no name. Some loose change lay around him. Wilks came back and helped with the search. He said, "The nurse is in there with another man. They were witnesses."

"They able to talk now?"

"They've come around."

Fellows nodded and put the wallet aside. He wiped the man's face with the wet towel roughly, getting it fairly cleaned of blood. "Well," he said. "I don't recognize him, but I guess that doesn't mean much."

"They might have his photograph and fingerprints in Hartford or New York."

"That doesn't help us right now, unfortunately. Did Jayware notice whether Logan limped or not?"

"He didn't mention any limp."

"Neither did Gordon, but he was definitely limping when he ran for the car. Maybe he twisted an ankle jumping off the platform."

MacFarlane came over and said, "You want anything done, Fred?"

The chief got to his feet. "I don't know, Jim. Last rites from a priest is all I can think of, in case either of them was Catholic. There's no question about cause of death or anything like that?"

"No. I guess you won't need an autopsy."

"I'll want one of the robber. Never can tell what you might find —some disease or something we could trace. And take good care of his clothes. We'll have to try to trace them too. I think the main problem's going to be one of identity."

"The ambulance will come back after it gets the wounded man to the hospital. I'll take them away then. Anybody call the guards' families or Perkins?"

"I don't know. Mr. Overbridge might have."

MacFarlane said, "I'll ask him. Want me to make the calls if he hasn't?"

"I'd appreciate it, Jim. And you'd better call Krulevich's home. He's the hostage they took."

MacFarlane went out and Fellows stepped into the dispensary. The nurse was lying on the table with a wet rag on her forehead. Broderick, the other paymaster, was hunched in a chair smoking a cigarette and not looking up. The plant guard was leaning against the wall and two young smartly dressed typists were helping, one wringing out a compress, the other brewing some coffee on a small electric burner.

The nurse struggled up at the chief's entrance, holding the compress to her forehead. "It was just terrible," she said. "Just terrible. I thought I was going to be killed for sure."

"You were a witness, Miss——"

"Caldwell. You're the police?"

Fellows nodded. "You feel like talking about it?"

The girl handling the compress took it away and tried to replace

it with another but the nurse waved it away. "It was just terrible,"
she said. "I was in here alone, having a morning cup of coffee,
when there was this terrible pounding on the door. I thought it
was an emergency. I opened the door and there were these two
frightful men. Beasts they were. One said he was sick. He wanted
to lie down. I didn't dare not let them in, they were so frightful
looking, especially the one with him. I'll dream about that face
to my dying day."

"What'd they do?"

"The other one lay down and I got him something. The hideous
one, the one with the frightful face, went out again but he came
back. I should have locked the door on him but I didn't dare.
I was afraid he'd kill me. He came back while I was trying to
get the sick man to drink something but he wouldn't drink it.
Then suddenly the frightful man put a gun in my back and the
other man had a gun and he got his gun out and the terrible man
grabbed hold of me and warned me on pain of death not to make
a sound. Then they opened the door and shoved me into the room
where everybody had guns. I was looking right into the mouths of
guns. Then everybody started shooting and the sick man fell down
dead at my feet and the next thing I knew, someone was sprinkling
water on me."

Fellows said, "Can you describe the man who held you?"

"He was just terrible," Miss Caldwell said. "Very dark hair and
a widow's peak. He looked like the devil incarnate. Very evil eyes.
They bored holes right through you."

"About how tall was he?"

"Very tall and very big."

"Taller than the other man?"

"Oh, yes. Much."

"The other man looks close to six feet. He's even taller?"

"Oh, yes. Two or three inches taller."

"How heavy?"

"Muscular, very muscular. He handled me as if I didn't weigh
ten pounds. He was a tremendous man."

Fellows got out his notebook, jotted down the information and
scowled at the other notes he had. "There seems to be quite a
lot of disagreement about his size, Miss Caldwell."

"Well, I certainly ought to know what I see."

"He held you from behind, didn't he?"

"That doesn't mean I didn't see him. I saw him supporting the other man when they came in. He handled him like a baby too. He's a tremendous and terrible man."

"How many people were in the room when he pushed you in?"

She shook her head. "Oh, there must have been seven or eight. The room was full of people, all with guns, all shooting."

The small man, hunched over his cigarette, said, "I didn't have a gun. I wasn't doing any shooting."

Fellows turned. "You're Mister——"

"Broderick." He looked up. "It's that Krulevich. It's the second time he didn't lock this door."

"That door is supposed to be locked?"

"That's right. Krulevich is supposed to lock it every Friday before the truck comes. Twice he didn't lock it and twice people came in. Hell, maybe he never locked it. He was supposed to, though. I guess right about now he wishes he had. Serves the bastard right, their taking him with them."

"It's a pretty severe punishment for an oversight."

"They didn't punish him enough last time. The lousy bum. If he'd done his job, it wouldn't have happened. Perkins wouldn'tta been shot."

Fellows said, "What happened the first time?"

"The doctor came in. The medical supplies are right near the door and he came in to get something. It was about noon, when he was here, and those guards drew their guns so fast they almost shot him before they saw him. He musta lost ten years of his life. It was just a mistake because, if the door'd been locked as it should have been, he couldn't have come in that way and if he wanted something, he'd have had to go around to the other door and ask permission to get it. So Krulevich got a dressing down and a fine for forgetting that door. It was part of his job to lock it before the truck came and unlock it after the truck went away again."

The girl at the Silex poured coffee into a white china mug and took it to Broderick. She offered some to Miss Caldwell who refused and to Fellows who accepted. He stirred in milk and sugar and said, "Can you tell me what happened today, Mr. Broderick?"

Broderick sipped his steaming black coffee. "The truck came late today. Perkins and I were in the room with Krulevich waiting for it. The two guards brought in the money sacks and Perkins and I were just starting to get out the envelopes when the man who was killed came in with a gun and the other man came in behind him, holding Miss Caldwell. I put up my hands but one of the guards drew his gun. After that, the bullets started flying. I don't know what happened next except that I found myself under the table with Perkins. Then one of the guards dove under the table with us and tipped it over. Perkins and I hid behind it and the shooting kept on. Then Perkins screamed and fell over and then two more men came through the other door and killed the other guard and stuck the rest of us up. They lined me and the guard against the wall and the man who had Miss Caldwell came up and killed the guard in cold blood. He just came up to him and shot him."

"He give any reason?" Fellows asked.

"Yeah. He said it was for killing his pal."

"He mention his pal's name?"

Broderick shook his head. "I don't think so, no. I think he said, 'That's for killing my pal.' Something like that."

"Did anybody mention any names?"

"Not that I recall."

"Where was Krulevich at this point? Was he lined up with you?"

"No. He was by the door."

"They didn't line him up against the wall too?"

Broderick shook his head. "They didn't bother. I guess they forgot about him. He was like a statue."

"Then what happened?"

"They picked up all the money. It couldn't have taken more than a few seconds. Then they waved a gun at Krulevich and told him to come with them and they all went out the back doors."

"The ones leading to the platform?"

"Those are the ones. And they were very angry because somebody was supposed to be there with a car and wasn't. They decided to take the truck keys off one of the guards but the siren started up, so they jumped off the loading platform and started running. Then I went to see how Perkins was. Then Mr. Overbridge came in and Mr. Gordon and he looked at Perkins. He said he was still alive. I thought he was dead. Then I felt pretty weak and came in here and sat down."

"Any of the men limp that you noticed?"

Broderick shook his head.

"Were they wearing gloves?"

Broderick pursed his lips and the nurse said, "No. Definitely not. The one who was killed—I gave him a glass. He didn't have any gloves."

"I noticed that. None of the others did either?"

Broderick said, "No. I think she's right. They weren't wearing gloves."

"That should help." Fellows sipped his coffee and looked thoughtful. "Was this door here the only one that was supposed to be locked?"

"Naw. They were all supposed to be locked until we had the envelopes ready." He looked up suddenly. "You mean——?"

"Yes, I mean how did the other two holdup men get through the door from the corridor?"

"Jesus. Krulevich must have forgotten to lock that one too. I hope they cut his guts out."

"Either forgot, or opened it. He was standing right there didn't you say?"

"The whole blessed time. You mean he deliberately opened it?"

"He might have been ordered to, at gunpoint. You remember anything about that?"

"I only remember there was a lot of shooting and a lot of shouting."

Wilks came to the stock-room entrance. "Ed is here and some of the others, Fred. And Grace has more reports on the road blocks."

CHAPTER ELEVEN

A GRAY, secondhand sedan had joined the armored truck and the chief's car in back of the building. It belonged to Joseph Dzanowski, one of Fellows' police officers, and it contained four other uniformed patrolmen, Daniels, Cassidy, Wilson, and Lambert, as well as Ed Lewis, the force's plainclothesman. Fellows came down the back steps with Wilks and said, "Ed, I want you to get inside and interview some of the people I haven't talked to. Three men escaped with the payroll and a hostage. Get everything you can from anybody who saw them. Dzanowski, I want you to monitor this short-wave. Take down everything Grace tells you for me. Cassidy, you and the others go in the stock room, there. Fingerprint the dead holdup man and fingerprint the whole room. Keep everybody else out." He slid into the front seat of his own car and picked up the mike. "This is Fellows, Grace. Let's have the latest." He let go of the button and got out his notebook.

"Wilton reports," the girl said, "road block set up at nine minutes after ten. Norwalk has blocked off route seven since thirteen minutes after. No report on Redding Ridge, Redding, and the intersection of fifty-eight and U.S. two-oh-two. Over."

"Any cars been picked up?"

"None reported."

Fellows depressed the button again. "Better warn the State Police to have every man report in periodically and check on any who don't. The holdup men may try to shoot their way through."

"Roger, wilco."

"Has Unger come in yet?"

"He's here on the telephone. He's calling supernumeraries."

Fellows hung up the mike and got out of the car. "It's yours, Dzanowski." He walked with Wilks to the steps again. "Wilton was four minutes late," he said.

"That's not good. That was an important spot."

"I don't know that the car could have got through there."

"With four minutes leeway?"

Fellows paused as he opened the door. "Ten-oh-eight was the minimum time if they went down route seven through Ashmun and Cannondale. They were heading east when they left the plant. That means they'd have to cut south to County and go over Cloverdale Road to get there. That's dirt and winding. I don't think they'd do it in those four extra minutes. Besides, Norwalk was covered in time and that backs up Wilton."

Wilks said, "But the Merritt wasn't covered. They get through Wilton and they've got the Merritt."

"Maybe, Sid. But they'd have to be awful fast. My own hunch is we've got them bottled." He went into the hallway again and looked in the door of the stock room. Sheets from the dispensary had been spread over the bodies and the fingerprint men were starting to work. He went past Lewis who was interviewing three people, and entered the dispensary. "I want to look at that door to the stock room," he told Wilks. "This whole thing has a very fishy smell."

He examined the door, turned the knobs, and looked for marks. The nurse, Broderick, and the guard were still there but the typists had gone. Fellows said, "You have a key for this door, Miss Caldwell?"

"No, sir."

"How did you get supplies when you needed them?"

"We just opened the door and helped ourselves. It wasn't ever locked except when they used the room to give out wages."

"Is that the way they handle supplies? Everyone helps himself?"

"Oh no. There's a stock-room clerk. You fill out requests and get them signed by some authority. You hand it to the clerk and he gets the things for you."

"But you don't have to do that?"

"It's my own office, the doctor's and mine. If we need something, we sign our own. We're the authority. We give him the chit and help ourselves. It's easier than having him try to find things for us. We're the ones who order and put away our own supplies."

"Who'd have a key to this door besides Mr. Krulevich?"

"There're keys to everything in Mr. Overbridge's office. Maybe the night watchman would. I don't know."

Fellows thanked her and went out. "Their stories jibe," he said. "That door wasn't jimmied. It just wasn't locked today. Do you begin to smell a rat?"

Wilks said, "A rat named Krulevich?"

"We'll know better after we talk to Mr. Overbridge."

They found the president in his office with MacFarlane. The doctor said, "I called Perkins' wife. She's on her way to the hospital. And I tried to get Krulevich's wife but all I got was one of his kids who's home with a cold. He said Mrs. Krulevich is in the hospital. I didn't quite get what was wrong with her. The kid called it diarrhea." He smiled faintly. "That doesn't sound quite right."

"What about the guards?"

MacFarlane sighed heavily and stared at the floor. "I've been trying to find out who they are. I guess I haven't been trying too hard. I guess I'm something of a coward."

Fellows said, "My men are in the stock room. They might have an identification."

MacFarlane nodded and went out. Overbridge looked up at the chief from his chair back of the desk. "You won't catch them, of course. I only pray they don't harm poor George."

"We're going to try to catch them, Mr. Overbridge. How much was in the payroll?"

"Ninety-three thousand, four hundred and eighty-two dollars, give or take a few dollars' overtime."

"You want to tell me what safety precautions you take regarding that much money?"

"Gladly. The armored truck brings it out with two armed guards. The guards stand by while the payments are made. We let no more than one man at a time into the stock room."

"What about locking doors?"

"All doors are kept locked. Krulevich opens the corridor door when they're ready to make payments. Otherwise all doors are kept locked throughout the period of pay."

"How about the back door to the outside steps?"

"That too. They're all Krulevich's responsibility."

Fellows nodded. He said, "How long has Krulevich worked for you?"

Overbridge looked up scowling. "Now hold up, Chief. Are you trying to suggest he helped commit this robbery?"

Fellows met his eye. "The man called Logan came into the reception room about twenty-five after nine. He was on edge. Then his cohort, the man who was killed, came in pretending to be sick and Logan helped him into the dispensary. It was not a coincidence, Mr. Overbridge, that the second man got out of his car and entered the building right after the armored truck went by, nor was it coincidence that a black sedan with three men in it went through the gate a minute or two after the truck and drove around the back of the building. The driver of that car fled the moment the shooting began, but that's the only unforeseen thing that happened to those robbers. The men in the dispensary knew they could get through the door. The men in the black car knew they could get in the back door to the corridor. Both of those doors Krulevich is supposed to have locked."

Overbridge shook his head. "I think you're wrong, Chief. He must have forgotten to lock the dispensary door. He's forgotten before. As for the back door, that's kept locked all the time. I refuse to believe he would have deliberately unlocked it. One of the robbers probably did that. The one who sent Gordon to my office. He was near that door when Gordon saw him."

"That may be," Fellows said, "but they knew the dispensary was next to the stock room. They knew the whole layout of the plant. They knew the dispensary door would be unlocked. That means they got to somebody inside this plant, Mr. Overbridge, and the evidence says it's Krulevich."

Overbridge spread his hands. "Krulevich has been with us for over fifteen years, Chief. In all that time he hasn't stolen so much as a pencil. He was a trusted guard. He's one of maybe two or three men who has keys to every door in the whole plant."

Fellows said, "He not only didn't lock the dispensary door but he also either didn't lock or unlocked the corridor door. He stood by while the money was picked up——"

"Do you think he's going to risk death over a payroll that's insured? Do you think he wants to cash in the ten thousand dollar company policy on his own life? That doesn't make sense."

"The holdup men," Fellows went on, "didn't line him up against the wall with the guard and your paymaster. And he's the one they took as a hostage. I think that's the way they mean to pay him off, either with money or a bullet. If he comes back unharmed, Mr. Overbridge, it's my guess he'll have his pockets lined with stolen payroll money."

"He wouldn't do a thing like that," Overbridge said. "He's a reliable man."

"Reliable? I thought he forgot to lock the dispensary door."

"A mistake. He was punished for it."

"How?"

"He was bawled out and fined."

Fellows pursed his lips and looked over at Wilks. "How did he take it?"

"Not very well. I think he thought it was harsher than he deserved. But we weren't harsh, Chief. The doctor almost got killed. It was a serious error."

"But he didn't like the punishment. He was resentful?"

"He was," Overbridge admitted. "Particularly about the fine."

"When did it happen?"

"About two months ago." He checked his paper. "August fourteenth to be exact."

Wilks said, "A resentful guy might be a soft touch to a slick approach."

Fellows said, "He's right, Mr. Overbridge. Know anything about Krulevich's hangouts? His friends?"

"I'm afraid I don't."

"Who would?"

Overbridge pressed a buzzer on his desk and ordered the file on Krulevich from his secretary. "Name," he read when she brought it to him, "George Herman Krulevich. Address: Twenty-four Sully Street. Married. Wife's name: Anna. Four children.

Has been in our employ since November 1942." He looked up. "I didn't realize it was that long. Seventeen years. I guess he came in when we organized for war production." He looked through the rest of the records. "I don't seem to have anything that would help you about his friends. I presume it would be people in the neighborhood. Oh. Here's something. His wife was one of those who complained when we started paying wages by check. He was cashing checks in bars and drinking some of the proceeds before going home." He pushed the records aside. "We had a lot of complaints like that. That's why we went back to paying cash."

Fellows jotted down the information. "And his wife's in the hospital and he's got four children. What's his pay?"

Overbridge referred to the papers again. "Eighty-two fifty a week."

"A fine, a sick wife, and four kids. That adds up."

Overbridge shook his head. "I hope you're wrong. I'd hate to think George could be responsible for something as terrible as this."

CHAPTER TWELVE

THE ambulance returned at ten minutes of eleven to remove the bodies and Fellows and Wilks, coming back from the president's office, stopped at the stock room to oversee the process, making sure it didn't interfere with the fingerprinting. When satisfied, they went down the back steps with MacFarlane, leaving him to go to the car. The chief picked up Dzanowski's notebook and read the last reports. Redding had been blocked off at 10:16, Redding Ridge at 10:19, and the intersection of 58 and U.S. 202 at 10:28. No suspicious cars had been intercepted.

"I don't like it," Fellows said. "They could have got through there."

"How much are they off?" Wilks asked.

"Redding by a minute, but the others by four or five. That's the way they were heading, too."

"They'd get stopped in Danbury."

"If they went west. If they went east to Newtown and Sandy Hook, they got away."

"It's a New York car, Fred. They'd be almost certain to head west."

"They'd be almost certain to head south and west, Sid, but they don't seem to have done it." He rubbed his chin. "I wonder if they'd have a short-wave in the car, listening in to our calls."

"More likely they switched cars and split up."

"And ditched Krulevich? He had a uniform. He'd stand out."

"There isn't much to do but wait."

The ambulance moved quietly away, leaving the armored truck and two cars, Dzanowski's and the chief's. Around them things seemed to be quieting down. Fellows leaned past Dzanowski and picked up the mike. "This is Fellows, Grace. What are the State Police doing?"

Grace came in. "They've got everybody out patrolling. All local police departments in the state have been alerted for a green Chevrolet with four men in it, New York plates ending in three-eight-four."

"Sandy Hook and Newtown been alerted?"

"They've all been alerted, Chief."

Fellows rehung the mike. He stared up at the overcast muggy sky and wiped perspiration from his brow with the back of his hand. "You know what this reminds me of, Sid? The Bergen bank robbery and the Cathcart jewelry store job."

"What are they?"

"Two of Connecticut's unsolved crimes. Fifty thousand cash from the bank and seventy thousand in stones from the jewelry store. They threw a net around both places and they never caught a thing."

Wilks smiled. "What are you, a walking encyclopedia?"

"Like I say, I can't afford model trains."

"Well, they didn't get the nets up as fast as you did. They didn't have police chiefs who spend their time working out the hows, wheres, and whens of road blocks."

"They got them up in time, Sid. Not as close to home as we did, but they got them up where they could catch them."

"If they took main routes, but you go out from the point of the robbery very far and you have such a network of roads it's impossible to cover them all." He said, "You're just fretting because you've got nothing to do. They won't get through yours."

"They're probably through already." Fellows made a face. "I've had this plan worked out and ready for over five years and the one time I can use it, it breaks down on me."

"Give yourself time, Fred. Don't throw in the towel yet."

Fellows laughed dryly. "You remind me of the father of a little boy I got a story about. Seems the boy lit a giant fire-cracker on the Fourth of July and the thing didn't go off. Well, that father wouldn't let that little boy go near it for fear it would blow up. You know what happened? That firecracker lay on the ground all winter before anybody picked it up again. Time's time, Sid, but how long do you think it'd take the holdup car to run into a road block around these parts?"

Wilks said, "The trouble with you, Fred, is your diet. It makes you sour. You need to go back to headquarters where the coffeepot is."

"We'll go after I check on what Ed's got. But I think we'll go via the factory district. Krulevich was in on that robbery, Sid."

CHAPTER THIRTEEN

ED LEWIS was still interviewing but he had no further information that would help. Fellows listened and then told Lewis to take Dzanowski with him when he was through and check out Krulevich, find out everything he could about him. After that, he left with Wilks to do a little checking on Krulevich himself.

There was a bar called Frank's on the corner of Municipal and Dennis Streets, one block from Sully, and Fellows, cruising slowly, pulled in at the curb. "What do you think, Sid? This would probably be his hangout."

Wilks nodded. "If Krulevich dealt with crooks, he'd probably meet them in a bar."

"You doubt that he did?" the chief asked, getting out.

"No, but I doubt he'd take them to a bar in the neighborhood."

It was, nevertheless, the easiest place to start and the two men pulled open the door and walked into the almost black interior. The bar itself was on the right, booths on the left. The booths were occupied by a scattering of people, mostly old men whose interest in life ran little beyond the confines of the tavern. They munched sandwiches the bar advertised as lunch, and drank beer. Two colored women, one with a large shopping bag at her feet, dallied over a similar spread alone near the door, and all looked up at the appearance of the police. The bartender, an Irishman of forty, lean and lined and with fading red hair, edged over to them.

Behind, in one of the booths, a man made a Bronx cheer with his tongue and lips.

The chief didn't look around. He hitched his hip on one of the bar stools. "You know a fellow named George Krulevich? Lives around the corner on Sully Street."

The bartender nodded. "I guess I do."

"Know him well?"

"Pretty well."

"He hang out here much?"

"Sometimes. Not too much."

"Did you hear about him getting bawled out and fined at the company a couple of months ago?"

The bartender leaned an elbow on the counter. He was carefully being neither hostile nor warm. "Yeah. I remember that. I forget why it was, but he was pretty sore."

"Think hard now. Since that time has he ever come in here with people who are strangers to you?"

The man didn't think very long. "Nope," he said.

"Did he ever meet or talk to strangers in here?"

"Listen, I don't keep track of who people talk to in here. I serve 'em drinks."

"Do you get many strangers?"

"A few. Mostly it's local clientele, but people are in and out all the time."

Fellows tried a shot in the dark. "When he got fined that time, he came in here and told you about it?"

"Yeah. He kind of sopped it up that afternoon."

"You happen to know if he told anybody else in here about it?"

He shrugged. "He probably did. He was in a mood to tell anybody who'd listen. I couldn't remember though."

Fellows thanked him and walked out with Wilks. Another Bronx cheer from a man in one of the booths followed them. "My guess," Fellows said on the way to the car, "is somebody heard him complaining. He wouldn't go out deliberately and look someone up. He wouldn't know how. Somebody came to him. Somebody heard him bitch and got after him."

"You don't have to say 'somebody', Fred. You mean one of the gang."

"That gang is a bunch of somebodies to us. 'Logan' is the only name we've got and ten to one it's a phony." He paused before getting into the car and stared down towards Sully Street. "His wife's in the hospital. I don't suppose she'd know anything about it."

"And his kids are in school and I don't think they would either."

"One of them's home sick, but all right." Fellows smiled. "You want to go back to headquarters. We'll let Ed take care of it."

Grace had no news for them when they returned and checked the communications room. "I keep tuning in State Police calls but they don't say anything. Sergeant Unger might have heard from some of the supernumeraries. They're supposed to call in every half-hour."

"He hasn't heard anything," Fellows told her and went back to his office. He opened the road map and spread it on top of his papers. "I don't get it, Sid," he said, shaking his head. "They had to go somewhere."

"Sure," Wilks said, putting a finger on Redding. "Right through there before they got the road block up."

"But what the devil would they go that way for? Where would they be heading?"

"Newtown and Sandy Hook. It has to be."

"And what the hell do they do there?"

"Try to get lost."

"That would take a lot of doing. All the cops up there are looking for them."

"Well, they sure as hell wouldn't go through Wilton and grab the Merritt, Fred. That's the last way they'd go."

"Why?"

"If they want the Merritt, they'd take the fastest route to it and that's through Weston. To get to Wilton they'd have to go over Cloverdale Road. They'd lose too much time."

"That reminds me of a British commander who was celebrating Christmas Eve at a big party with his men. He figured he could indulge himself because George Washington couldn't possibly be dumb enough to lead the Americans across the Delaware in the freezing cold at night in small boats. But I guess you've heard that story, Sid."

Wilks looked up and smiled. "You fancy yourself a military strategist, Fred?"

"I'm just a cop, but in a thing like this, there's an element of strategy involved, wouldn't you say?"

"I'll tell you what I'd say. The man who led that robbery isn't George Washington."

Fellows pulled his notebook from his pocket and flipped the pages. "Interesting thing about that robbery, Sid. We've got a pretty vague description of Logan. He's anywhere from five feet eight to six feet four inches tall. He's got dark hair, a lean face, and a build that ranges from a skinny ninety-seven-pound weakling to Charles Atlas. I guess we don't have much idea as to what he looks like, but we do know how his brain works."

"He plots his robberies carefully."

"He plots them more than carefully. He plots boldly."

Wilks threw up his hands. "Here we go."

"What's the matter?"

"Up in the stratosphere. You're off again. You're going to start analysing this guy's character down to what he eats for breakfast."

Fellows sighed. "Here's the thing, Sid. If we can learn something about how his mind operates from what he's already done, we might be able to figure out what he's going to do."

"I can tell you what he's going to do, Fred. He's going to escape. Anybody who's got his holdup plot so well planned that it goes through when things go wrong is going to have his escape laid out so well you aren't going to pick him up even if you do get all the road blocks up on time."

"What's he going to do, disappear? You've got him better than old G. Washington."

"He'll have some back roads we've never heard of picked out. Or he'll have a short-wave radio in his car and he's listening to our calls."

Fellows said, "Sid, you're a damned pessimist. He can stay on back roads till the cows come home but those roads end somewhere. They come out onto bigger roads. You can't go very far before you're going to run into civilization and civilization's supposed to be laying for him."

"They weren't in Redding or Wilton."

"Those places have been backed up by now."

"I still think he's gotten through, Fred. Otherwise, as you say, we'd have had a call. It's noon. What's probably happened is, they had two other cars stashed away somewhere and they split up. If you want my view, the only thing we can do is wait until Krulevich shows up and then pump him."

Fellows shook his head. "I'll tell you, Sid. I think the best thing we can hope for is some long-range clue. What Krulevich could tell us would help, but I have a feeling we aren't going to see him again."

"You think they'll kill him?"

"Either that or he's joined up permanently with the gang. If he can tell us anything that could help us catch them, I don't think Logan is going to let us get our hands on him. I don't hold out much hope on that score. No, what I'm thinking about is some clue, like identifying the man who got killed or finding a set of fingerprints somewhere. And there are things like informants. Some crook in New York might be a little flusher with his money than usual and the cops might hear about it. That's the main hope and it's maybe not too good a one, especially if Logan is the same man who pulled off the Bergen bank job and the jewelry store robbery I mentioned. Nobody's ever had a whisper about who did those. But, anyway, since there isn't much for us to do around here, we might as well think about the case. We might as well try to dope out what kind of a man this gang leader is and what his technique is for avoiding capture. It won't hurt us any."

Wilks nodded. "O.K., Fred. He's bold. What else do you deduce?"

Fellows rubbed his stomach and sat up in his chair. "You know, Sid, I didn't eat any breakfast this morning and it's after twelve. Let's send Unger out for a hamburger and some coffee. I think better on a full stomach."

"You ought to eat breakfast, Fred. You can't go through a morning without a big hearty meal."

"I gotta try to, Sid. I'd hate to tell you what I weigh."

The phone rang in the outer room and Unger answered. He said a few words and then called, "Chief! It's Jack Pebble. He's found something."

Fellows was on his feet in a flash. He went out to the main desk in three strides and took up the phone. "Yeah, Jack?"

"Hello, Chief. Listen. I'm calling from a farmhouse on Two Mile Road. You know where it is?"

"Yes, I know."

"Well, down at the south end of it, right near County, I found a car half hidden in the bushes. It's a green Pontiac and it's just sitting there, keys in the ignition and everything."

"Anybody around it?"

"Not that I could see. I know we're looking for a Chevrolet but this is pretty funny."

"I'm not looking for a Chevrolet, Jack; I'm looking for anything green with four doors."

"This one has four."

"New York plates ending in three-eight-four?"

"They end in three-eight-nine, but they're New York plates all right."

"Two Mile Road, just off County," Fellows said, motioning to Unger to write it down. "Get back there but don't touch anything. We'll be right out."

CHAPTER FOURTEEN

PEBBLE was waiting by the car when Fellows and Wilks arrived. It had been pulled off to the side, heading into the woods that overran the area, but no particular pains had been made to conceal it. Fellows walked all around the car carefully, looking it over without touching it. It was a green car all right, but it was dusty and dirty and had not been washed for a long time. The chief put a hand on the hood when he reached the front but if the motor had been running, it had long since cooled. The license plates, like the rest of the car, were dirty and hard to read and when Fellows had completed his circuit, he came back to Wilks who was peering through the windows and said, "If this *is* the car, that watchman's got good eyesight."

Wilks said, "He's about the only one at the plant who kept his head at all. I'd guess his description of the men would be the most accurate."

"I wonder about Logan and his limp. Did he twist an ankle jumping off that platform, or did he limp when he came in?"

"No one saw him limp before. He probably twisted an ankle."

"No one seeing him limp doesn't mean much, judging from the way the descriptions read. Half a dozen people give half a dozen different pictures of the guys."

"Well, what are we going to do here, wait for Unger to call the fingerprint men or are you planning to do some looking around?"

"I'll tell you what I'd like you and Pebble to do. Go up this road, Pebble in his car and you in mine and inquire at all the houses you come to. I want to know who's seen this car here and who drove by before this car was here. I want to find out what cars were parked here before this one. They made a switch and we've got to find out, if we can, what they switched to."

It was a promising project and the two men went off. As for Fellows, he reached through the driver's window and, touching the handle as little as possible, got the door open. There was no question in his mind that this was the getaway car but he sought some evidence that would prove it. There was nothing on the floor of either the front or back seats that he could find; not so much as a thread or loose hair. Nor was there any clue in the glove compartment. Nothing was in that but dust in the corners. Next he took the key from the ignition and opened the trunk but that too contained nothing that to his educated eye would help.

When he was through, he slammed the trunk lid down, then sat on the back bumper, bit off a piece of chewing tobacco, and looked with appreciation at the fading but still green foliage around him. A car came by and paused, the driver leaning out to say, "You in trouble?"

Fellows shook his head. "Not exactly. You been down this road earlier today?"

"No."

"Then I guess you can't help. Thanks all the same."

The car went on and the chief had fifteen minutes of patient waiting before Dzanowski's gray Plymouth turned in from County Road and disgorged Daniels and Wilson with fingerprint equipment.

The chief got up then. "You finished at the plant?"

"We got a lot of prints," Daniels said, "but they're probably all employees. None of the people there could remember the robbers touching anything except a glass and that was handled by the dead man."

"Try this car, inside and out," Fellows told him. "If there's a print, I want it."

"You're sure this is their car?"

"I'm not sure at all. The way she's turned off the road makes it look like she came from County but the crooks were last seen driving out Grafton. I suspect, that's all."

The men got to work with the chief supervising. Almost at once it was discovered that the door handles bore no prints. "Wiped," Daniels said. "Looks like this car's been cleaned."

Fellows nodded. "I guess that answers the question about who it belongs to. Well, don't give up. They may have missed a print somewhere."

The men opened the car doors and started dusting the inside. Wilks came back in the chief's car with Pebble behind, and he pulled in at the side of the road. The chief strode over. "Anything come through the radio while you had the car?"

"Nothing except that there was nothing. I got the information you wanted, only you're not going to like it."

Fellows smiled. "Try me."

"There's a Mr. Husher up the road who came by here with a load of apples for the cider mill in Weston and he swears there were no cars at all here when he went, but this one was here when he came back."

Fellows arched an eyebrow. "None at all? What time was that?"

"About nine-thirty. And this car was here when he came back at ten-thirty."

Fellows spit tobacco juice into the grass and rubbed his chin. "Well, that kind of puts a different complexion on things, doesn't it? What would they be stopping here for and where did they go without a car?"

"Maybe they've got a place in the woods somewhere. Maybe they're hiding out."

"Maybe. But why wouldn't they hide the car?"

"Or maybe somebody came down the road and they ditched this car and took his."

"I don't know," Fellows said. "This guy Logan doesn't leave it to chance for a car to come along and this seems planned to me."

"A police car," Wilks said.

Fellows' eyes widened. "I didn't think of that. If some cop flagged them down, they might have——" He said slowly, "That car's been wiped clean, Sid. It's theirs all right, and the fact that they stopped to wipe it shows they weren't being pressured in any way." He turned and waved at the others. "You men want to leave off the fingerprinting a little? I think we'd better take a look around these woods. Let's fan out in a circle and work our way in a couple of hundred feet. Look for any kind of a sign someone's been around: matches, butts, broken twigs, anything."

Wilks muttered under his breath, "including a dead policeman."

The men dropped their work and started the operation without question. Fellows had Pebble stand guard at the car and he and Wilks joined in the hunt.

It didn't take long. Five minutes after Fellows gave the order, Wilson yelled. Fellows, who was closest to him, was the first to arrive at the little clearing, but he was quickly joined by the others.

In the middle of the small area, lying with his mouth open and two red stains on his olive-colored uniform, was George Krulevich.

CHAPTER FIFTEEN

AT quarter of two the ambulance, making its fourth trip of the day, arrived at the scene and disgorged Dr. MacFarlane and the usual two attendants with their inevitable stretcher. By that time Otis Overbridge had been called to the scene to identify the body as that of his trusted guard, and Hank Lemmon had come back with his camera and tripod for more pictures.

Fellows met the doctor at the edge of the road and led him to the body which had by now been moved. "He walked, he wasn't dragged," the chief said. "Shot twice, and the bullets are still in him. We'll want the bullets of course. I don't expect much but they might be on record somewhere."

"Killed their hostage, eh?" MacFarlane said, looking down at the corpse whose uniform had now been opened revealing a bare and clotted chest.

"If he was a hostage. I think he was in it with them."

"So he couldn't talk?"

"The body can't talk so far. You might be able to make it say something. But I'm afraid it won't be anything we can't already guess. Death would be around ten o'clock, I'd say. If you make it much later, we're going to have to rearrange our thinking."

"Cold-blooded, first degree murder?" the doctor said, putting down his bag and kneeling by the body. "His family know about it yet?"

Fellows shook his head unhappily. "Not yet. I guess the poor guy thought he could make himself enough to pay some bills." He sighed. "I guess I'm elected to go to the hospital and talk to the wife. At least the plant insured him. Maybe she can learn to snuggle up to ten thousand dollars in bed this winter."

The chief left the doctor and the attendants at the body and went back to his car. Wilks was there, minding the radio. "No fingerprints on the Pontiac," the detective sergeant said. "No clues, no nothing."

"One clue," Fellows corrected. "They didn't get through Redding, Redding Ridge, or Wilton before the road blocks were set up. That's for sure."

"Not dallying around here they didn't, but what does that tell us? Where are they now?"

"The way I see it is this. They stopped here to kill the guy and somebody came driving by. That somebody might have stopped to offer assistance just the way it happened to me while I was waiting here, and that somebody heard the shot in the woods and the robbers decided to keep that somebody with them. So what happened is they all took the new car and left this one behind."

"Which means it's going to be four people in a car, any kind of a car. They could probably slip through our road blocks that way. They make the guy drive and if he's questioned, he's got his own registration and everything else. They'd be passed right through."

"That's what I'm afraid of. Of course those cops are supposed to stop *all* cars and I've sent the word out that they're no longer in a green sedan, but the human element isn't too reliable. Logan was pretty good at bluffing Gordon out of getting his pay, so he could probably bluff a cop on a road block pretty good too." He paused as the stretcher came into view and the body made its litter trip to the ambulance. "I don't know," he said. "If it was just money they took it wouldn't eat at me like this. But it was lives. Three lives, and maybe more. For a hundred thousand dollars life seems cheap to a lot of people. They got rid of one hostage but I'm afraid they've got another. I don't know what we're going to do about it."

Wilks said, "We ought to try to find out who, Fred."

"Yeah. We'd better go back to headquarters and call the local radio and television stations to put in some announcement that we think the holdup men have kidnapped someone. That might give us some help."

They drove back to the Town Hall in thoughtful silence and walked in through the side door from the steps to the yard. Unger was there talking to two reporters and the men turned to the chief for further details.

"There isn't much to say," Fellows told them. "They killed the hostage and left his body in the woods. I guess the sergeant told you that. We think they hijacked another car, probably with the people in it. We haven't had any reports on that."

They asked a few questions but the chief turned them over to Wilks for details and went into the communications office to make his appeal to the radio and TV stations on the phone there. When he came back, both Wilks and the reporters were gone.

He went into his office then and sat down at his desk, spreading the area road map out on top of the papers for study. Wilks returned in fifteen minutes with a couple of sandwiches and containers of coffee. "Here," the detective sergeant said, "you haven't eaten."

Fellows smiled. "Come to think of it, neither have you."

"I've got my own here too. The roast beef is yours."

Fellows looked at it. "Three hundred calories at least. Well, gaining weight isn't the worst thing that can happen to you, I guess. Not after what I've seen going on today." He unwrapped the sandwich and started to munch as Wilks sat down at the table behind him. "The way I see it, Sid," Fellows said over his shoulder, "is, Logan wanted to get down to the parkways. He ran out of sight along Grafton to throw pursuers off, then cut over to County, made a stop to kill Krulevich, and kept on going. They must have been heading for Weston and the Merritt."

"But we had that blocked off."

"That's right. And we didn't pick them up. Now one thing went wrong with their plans. They didn't escape in the car they intended to. We don't know what they had in that car, a short-wave, a proper registration, a couple of machine guns. In that car they might have been able to get through the road blocks some way. In the Pontiac, perhaps they figured they couldn't. Perhaps that's why they hijacked this other car. Maybe they thought this could get them through."

"And, if so, it worked and we're out of luck."

Fellows raised a hand. "Not so fast. That's a pretty risky gamble. Judging from the care with which Logan plans, it's my guess they'd also have an alternative plan."

"Which would be what?"

Fellows shrugged. "Maybe they have a hideout somewhere."

Wilks said, "Of course they have a hideout somewhere. They cased the plant pretty thoroughly and I don't think they commuted from New York to do it."

"The question is," Fellows mused, "where would they stay? An inn? A motel?"

"If so, they'd hardly go right back there."

"No, they wouldn't. But they might have some cave or something set aside for an emergency."

"Maybe they rented a house."

Fellows smiled. "A short-term lease from Frank Restlin?"

Wilks grinned back. "Something like that."

Fellows said, "I don't know. It'd be kind of easy to trace."

"They wouldn't be expecting you to try to trace it."

"And," Wilks went on, "it'd be to the south of town. County Road would take you in that direction."

Fellows shook his head. "You don't give him credit for any brains at all." He went to the door and said, "Unger. Call up every real-estate agent in the area. Get a list of all rentals for the past couple of months." He took out his notebook. "From August fourteenth to be exact. Get the dates and the locations of the houses, the names of the tenants and any description you can on them."

He came back and sat down to his sandwich. Wilks had finished his and was sipping his coffee. "The trouble is, Fred, it's impossible to figure out which of any ten or twenty moves the guy could have made and we can't follow them all."

"What you're saying is, you don't think he rented a house?"

"He might have. He must have done something to stay around this area. He might have rented something, probably a room. But it's a waste of time trying to find it. He used the hijacked car to talk his way through the road blocks, Fred. He'd never stay around in the area. It's too risky."

"That reminds me of the guy who sold his house and everything he owned to go prospect for oil, Sid. He went out and prospected for twenty years and he never had any luck. So finally he came back to the old home town, tired and broke and lo and behold, where his house used to be was a big mansion. Seems the people he sold to found oil in the back yard."

"So?"

"So I think we shouldn't overlook our own back yard."

Outside, in the main room, Unger's phone calls to area real-estate agents were interrupted by a loud male voice. Fellows went to the door and looked out. A man in overalls and sweaty plaid shirt, with the hard-lined face of a worker in the soil, had entered the room. At sight of Fellows he headed for him. "You gotta do something. You're a cop. It's my wife. She's been kidnapped."

CHAPTER SIXTEEN

UNGER, hanging up the phone, said, "What?" but the chief stayed where he was. "You're sure?" he asked quietly.

"What do you mean? Of course I'm sure. What d'ya think I'm doing here?"

"Don't get excited. That won't help things a bit." The chief moved into the room and pulled a chair from the table. "Here. Sit down and tell us about it."

The man wouldn't sit. He paced back and forth in front of the chief. "I just got it on the radio ten minutes ago that those robbers kidnapped somebody and it's my wife they took."

"How do you know?"

"She was supposed to come back for lunch but she didn't come back yet."

"Where had she gone?"

"To visit her mother. She was supposed to be home for lunch. My wife's supposed to get lunch for me. She ain't back yet."

"You call her mother?"

"I didn't waste time doing things like that. If my wife ain't back it means something's happened to her. My wife knows better than to do something I don't tell her to."

The chief picked up the phone. "Want to tell me your wife's name and your mother-in-law's phone number?"

"My wife's name is Edith. Edith Carson. Her mother's name is Brown. I wouldn't know the number."

"What's her full name and address?"

"Letitia Brown. She lives on Widow's Way."

Fellows dialed the operator and asked for the information and a connection. "What time did she leave this morning?"

"About eight or nine. Somewhere around there. I don't know. I was out in the orchard."

"Where do you live?"

"Plain Farms Road. This side of Indian River. I heard about it on the radio when I was loading the truck and I dropped everything and come right on in."

"Plain Farms Road to Widow's Way? What would your wife be doing on Two Mile Road? That's way out of the way."

"I don't know Two Mile Road. I only know my wife's gone."

Fellows said, "Thank you," into the phone and dialed a number. He listened a long time and got no answer. "Your mother-in-law live alone?" he said, hanging up.

"Yep. Ain't nobody in their right mind'd live with her, including her husband. Now you see? She's kidnapped."

"I don't get any answer. Would your wife and her mother go for a ride someplace?"

"How would I know? You're supposed to tell me the answers."

Fellows looked over at Wilks. "I don't know about this, Sid. Widow's Way isn't too far from Two Mile Road. What kind of car was your wife driving?"

"A Ford—1940 station wagon."

Fellows said, "Sid, you run things from here, will you? I think I'll ride with Mr. Carson out to his mother-in-law's. You might put it on the wires to watch out for a 1940 Ford station wagon, just in case."

Carson went huffily out of the door with the chief, saying, "I don't know what you think going to the old hag's home's gonna do," to which the chief replied, "We kind of want to stay away from false alarms, Mr. Carson. We want to make sure if we can."

They drove out in Fellows' car with the man complaining about his wife and how she wouldn't dare go off with her mother without asking permission and therefore she had to be kidnapped. "Her and her mother," the man grumbled. "They gab on the phone every other day and if my wife doesn't get a call, she has to go see what the matter is."

The house was empty but the doors were open. The station wagon wasn't in sight. The two men wandered through the house, Carson heedlessly. Fellows looking carefully, though quickly, at everything. "See?" Carson said. "They ain't here. I told you that. I don't know what you had to come out here for."

"Your mother-in-law have any neighbors who drop in?" Fellows asked, stopping by the sink in the kitchen to examine half a dozen dishes with hardened food on them.

"That old hag hasn't a friend in the world."

Fellows picked up a dinner plate with bits of dried hamburger and caked potato on it. He looked at an old cereal dish and then around at the otherwise spotless kitchen. "There a phone here?"

"Yeah. In the living room."

Fellows went back through the house to it and dialed a number.

He got an answer and said, "Did a Mrs. Letitia Brown check in there today?"

He listened to the answer, said thanks, and hung up. Carson said, "What's that all about?"

"Your mother-in-law's in the hospital," Fellows said. "Your wife's there with her. She found her sick and called the ambulance."

Carson was somewhat taken aback. He said nothing and Fellows opened the door. "I'll take you back to your car. I think we'd better go. I've got a lot to do."

CHAPTER SEVENTEEN

THERE was another man at headquarters when Fellows dropped Carson at his car and came back down the steps. He was a man in his thirties, a nice-looking executive type, and his name was Lary. He turned anxiously at the chief's entrance and Wilks, standing beside him, seemed equally concerned. "What about it, Fred?"

Fellows shook his head. "False alarmist."

"Then this doesn't sound good. This is Mr. Lary."

Fellows hung up his helmet. "What is it, Mr. Lary?"

"My wife went out this morning with our little daughter. She was going to spend the day with a friend, a Maureen Cole. They planned to go shopping in Hartford, but my wife never arrived."

"Can you tell me some times? When she went? What route she would take?"

"This I don't know exactly. Maureen lives on County Road between here and Weston. We live on Crestwood Drive. That's in Floral Acres. I don't know when Helen was supposed to go there. I was at work. At any rate, she didn't come and she didn't come and Maureen called the house several times but didn't get any answer. So she didn't go to Hartford and half an hour or so ago, she heard about the robbery on the radio and that there was probably a kidnapping. She called me at the office and I came over here." He said with a slight edge of panic in his voice, "Do you think something like that could have happened to my wife?"

"I don't know," Fellows said grimly. He moved on into his office and bent over the road map. Then he shook his head and straightened. "I'm going to be frank," he said. "Her quickest route would probably be out East Street and down Highland Road to Grafton Boulevard, back on Grafton to Two Mile Road and down to County Road. Of course she could have gone through Stockford Center to pick up County Road but the point is she didn't arrive at Mrs. Cole's house."

"You think something's happened to her?"

"I think something has to have happened to her to keep her from getting to her friend's. Whether she's been kidnapped or not is a different question."

Wilks said, "I don't think you should butter him up, Fred. I don't think there's any question about it."

The man said numbly, "But, my God. They'll kill her and my daughter. She had our daughter with her. What'll they do? What'll I do?" He turned around in a tight circle. "It can't be. It can't happen like this!"

Fellows watched him. He said, "Tell me the kind of a car she drove, what your license number is. Tell me about her and your daughter."

The man stopped. "It's a 1956 Buick, four-door sedan, two-tone blue. The license is—is—AM9687. My wife is twenty-seven, dark hair, brown eyes, and she's pregnant. My little girl is blonde, not quite three. I don't know what either of them would be wearing. If my wife has a coat, it'll be a light tan one."

"She have your car registration?"

"It's—we keep it in the glove compartment. She knows where it is."

Fellows said, "Sid, you want to take that information into communications and get it out? We want to know if three men, a pregnant woman, and a small girl in a blue Buick were remembered at any of the road blocks."

Wilks hurried off and Sergeant Unger held out three sheets of paper to the chief. "These are the houses that were rented. You want anything done about them?"

Fellows nodded.

"I want them all checked out. How many are there?"

"Eight. Three are on one-year leases. The rest are longer."

"I want at least two men to a house, Unger. They're to proceed with caution in each case, but I've got to see who's in those houses."

"We don't have any men."

"We'll send out the day-shift men.' He turned. "I'm sorry, Mr.

Lary. These things have to be done. Let's go into my office now. I guess you want to know what we think's happened."

The chief closed the door and gave Lary the chair by the table. He sat down at his desk, looked hungrily at the half-eaten sandwich and the cold coffee, and sighed. "Could I get you something, Mr. Lary? Coffee?"

"No thanks."

Fellows, with an effort, turned his back on the remains of his lunch. "We know this much. A gang of four men robbed the Grafton Tool and Die Company of a hundred-thousand-dollar payroll this morning at quarter of ten. One of the men was killed. The other three escaped with the money and with one of the plant employees as a hostage. They drove east on Grafton Boulevard, south on Edgewood Farm Road, south-east on County to the next road which is Two Mile Road. They turned in there and parked and one of the men took the plant employee into the woods and shot him. Along about that time your wife, if it was your wife, came down the road. Now I don't know how this happened, whether they held her up or whether she stopped, or whether they thought she heard something or what, but they got her car stopped and got in with her and went on. Where, we don't know. That's what we're trying to find out right now."

"She stopped," the man said. "If she came along and saw a car parked, she'd stop and ask if they were in trouble. That's what she'd do. She's a trusting woman. She's very naïve that way. She'd want to help them."

Fellows shook his head ruefully. "That may be it, Mr. Lary. She might have stopped to offer them assistance and heard the shooting and the two men guarding the car would be afraid she'd spread the alarm. They might have felt they had to take her—them—with them."

"What will they do to her, Chief? She never hurt anybody in her life." He made a face of pain. "I don't suppose many people would think she was pretty, but I think she was beautiful. She—she—what would they do?"

Fellows said, with more confidence than he felt, "I think the chances are they won't do anything to her. They'll use her to protect themselves. They might use her to get through the road blocks and to keep the police from opening fire on them but when they don't need her any more, they'll probably just put her and your daughter out of the car."

"But they're killers, Chief."

Fellows nodded. "They're killers. But I'll tell you, Mr. Lary. Even people like them, who don't put much premium on human life, don't go around and kill just for fun. They especially don't when it would handicap them. Only a madman does something like that, and these people seem to be reasonably sane. They won't hesitate to kill if something stands in their way, but they don't kill indiscriminately."

"They killed that plant employee, you said. What could he have done?"

"We think he was in with them, Mr. Lary. It's not the same thing with your wife. It would be easier, when the time comes, for them to stop the car and put them out than it would be to stop the car and try to do something to them. You see what I mean?"

Lary nodded. "I see, but you don't make me feel much better. They might be afraid she could identify them later or something. They might do things to her and my daughter for all kinds of reasons."

Fellows said soberly, "I'm not going to try to say they wouldn't, Mr. Lary. You're not a fool and I'm not going to kid you. I told you what I did to try to show there are a lot of reasons why they wouldn't harm your wife and daughter. I don't want you to give up hope."

Wilks came in and looked from one to the other of the two men. Then he said to the chief, "The word's gone out. The reports will be in pretty soon. Is there any question about the kidnapping?"

Fellows worked his lips. "Not as far as I can see," he said flatly.

"Then I'm afraid they got through." Wilks looked uneasily at Lary and the man said, "Go ahead. I want to hear everything, the bad and the good. And I don't want to be lied to."

Wilks looked at Fellows for a sign of confirmation and said, "All right. Let's say they expect road blocks. If they make her drive and one of the men sits in front with her and the child, posing as her husband, and the other two sit in the back seat, they can probably get through. She'll show the cops her license and car registration and one guy will have the child on his lap and she'll call the man 'dear' or whatever they make her do, and the cops will wave her through. It's a blue sedan and everything's in order. It's not what they're looking for at all."

"They could have, Sid. I guess I have to admit that."

"And don't expect anybody to remember it, Fred. They'd have gone through nearly six hours ago."

"Well, Sid, if they had, they wouldn't be still keeping Mrs. Lary and her daughter hostage."

Wilks glanced again at Lary. He said, "That's right."

Fellows got up. "It's three-thirty, Sid. Time for muster."

They left Lary in the chief's office and moved into the main room where patrolmen Daniels, Cassidy, Wilson, Lambert and Dzanowski were gathered for roll call, along with Sergeant William Gorman who handled the desk from four to twelve.

"You don't have to be quite so blunt, Sid," Fellows said under his breath. "I can add two and two and so can Lary. There's no point in upsetting him more than necessary."

"You said he wanted the truth. If they got through a road block this morning and no word's been heard about Mrs. Lary, the truth isn't pretty."

"He may say he wants the bitter truth, but no man really does. All right," he said to the men. "Fall in."

The six men came to attention and Sergeant Unger came out from behind his desk to call the roll and hand out assignments. Fellows stood by while that was done and then briefed them himself on the latest developments in the robbery, which consisted of the discovery of the apparent kidnapping. He told them to keep their eyes open and phone in anything they saw and make sure they reported promptly on their rounds.

He went on into communications then where Doris Norton was getting ready to take over for Grace. Grace told him no black sedan driven by a youth and no blue Buick with three men, a woman, and a little girl were remembered at any of the road blocks.

"I don't hope much on the black sedan," Fellows said. "I'm afraid that's long gone. But I did kind of hope a little on the Buick." He asked her to summon in the police squad cars and returned to his office.

At four o'clock the cars were back and so were the foot patrolmen of the daytime shift. The three patrolmen had been informed of the robbery during their routine check-ins but they had seen nothing and came in confidently expecting to go off duty. The chief had other plans for them, however. He assigned Harris and Manny to one of the squad cars, Wade and Kettlemen to the other. "Here's a list of eight houses," he said. "There's a bare possibility the gang that robbed the Grafton plant rented one of them. I want them checked out with that in mind. That means talk to the people in each house. I want only one man to go to the house. The other's to stay in the car at the radio. If anything develops, I want an instant report. These men are armed and dangerous. They'll kill you as soon as look at you, so watch your step. Here're their descriptions. I've written them down for you as well as the descriptions of the woman and child we think they've got with them. And here's the information about the people who've rented those houses, their names and whatever else the real-estate agents could tell us about them. Compare the two. I want the houses canvassed in the order listed and I want a report radioed in when you get to a house and when you both leave it. If anything goes wrong and we don't get a call from you, I want to know when and where it was. You understand that?"

The men nodded and Fellows said, "You can arrange between you who will go to what house, but one of you stays in the car with the mike in his hand the whole time the other's asking questions. All right, now do it as fast as you can. If you're suspicious about anything at all, try not to let the people know it. Hide it and report to headquarters immediately. And, if anything starts, remember there's a woman and child held hostage so don't do anything on your own initiative. Do only what I've told you and if there's any question, you call here for instructions."

He dismissed them and turned back to his office. Lary was waiting for him in the doorway, a drawn and anxious man. Fellows clapped him on the shoulder and edged past to his desk.

CHAPTER EIGHTEEN

THE reports that came in between four and five were discouraging. None of the rented houses was either empty or inhabited by gangsters. No blue Buick was seen nor a black sedan, nor, in fact, were any clues at all developing in the area. Two newspapermen sat at the main table in headquarters playing gin rummy; Sergeant Gorman made phone calls to inns and motels; and Mr. Lary took turns around the room, reading all the items on the bulletin board, watching the rummy game, going into the communications room at eight-minute intervals to question Doris on latest news, then repeating the process.

In the chief's office, behind the half-opened door, Fellows sat at his desk, hunched over his road map. Some of the time he looked at it but for the most part he stared without seeing it. It served no purpose except the psychological one of making him feel he had things at his fingertips. The coffee and sandwich had been consumed at last and the remnants were in the wastebasket. It wasn't much of a lunch but his mind wasn't on his stomach.

Wilks sat in the office with him, staring for the most part into space. Both were phlegmatic and both could indulge in long periods of inactivity. Little was said between them. They were waiting without expectation, waiting because there wasn't anything else to do. Had a woman and child not been taken, the two men would have long since gone home, for reports could easily have reached them there. The kidnapping lent an urgency to the case, however, made Fellows struggle a little harder for a solution, made him reluctant to quit the drab confines of his office. Now, were he so moved, could he very well go home with Mr. Lary pacing in the next room. It might not be lying down on the job but it would look that way.

"I didn't think they'd rent a house," he said at last. "That leaves too many tracks."

"It's a motel or an inn somewhere, or tourist cabins," Wilks said. "It has to be."

"Well, Gorman may find the place and we'll probably get fingerprints if he does. That may give us the identity of the gang, but it's not going to do Mrs. Lary much good, I'm afraid."

"I'm afraid," Wilks said, lowering his voice, "that Mrs. Lary's already beyond being done any good for."

"What I want to know is," Fellows said, resting his chin on his palm and staring again at the road map, "how did they manage those road blocks. There isn't a single place they could have got through without being stopped. How did they snow the cops?"

"They made Mrs. Lary talk for them. Her car, her registration. And she says she's driving someplace with her husband and child and a couple of friends. They can't arrest every car that comes 'long with three men in it."

"I don't mean that," Fellows said. "What was their original plan? How were they going to work it if they'd taken the other car and if they hadn't picked up a couple of hostages?" He sat up. "Maybe that's one reason they killed Krulevich. He had a guard's uniform. That would ruin them sure. And they'd know cops would be looking for four men in a car, one wearing such a uniform. Killing him cuts it down to three. That's part of their plan, I'm sure of it. What's the rest of it?"

"Separate cars. They had two or three stashed somewhere, Fred. Not where we found the Pontiac, not where they shot Krulevich, but some other place. They split up."

"How, for example? Remember, they left one of their number behind."

"What of it? They have two other cars, Fred. They were going to split two and two. Now it's two and one."

Fellows wiped his face with his hand and swung his chair around. "That reminds me of the young couple who had a very rich uncle. Well, they wined and dined him every time he came to town and sent him expensive presents and waited on him hand and foot. Then when he took to his bed in his final illness, they wouldn't let him hire nurses. They moved into his house and slaved to make his last days as pleasant as possible. I can't say their motives were the purest, of course, because they were the first to arrive when it came time to read the will. So what did the old man do? He left his fortune to his dog."

Wilks said, "You lost me in there somewhere."

"I'll tell you, Sid. I don't know much about honor among thieves and all that, but if I'd been in on that payroll robbery, I'd kind of hate to see that money ride off in a different car from the one I was driving. I don't know how well thieves' honor can withstand a hundred thousand bucks."

"With three people? I think I'd kind of work to be the one who drives alone."

"You're trying to complicate things, Fred. The leader would drive alone with one bag and keep it. The other two men would take the other bag and split it."

Fellows nodded. "That's what they might have done at the end, but in the beginning there were four men. There were, in fact, five. We're forgetting the driver of the getaway car who chickened out. Where does he come in? And why a getaway car and driver if they're going to split up anyway? I don't know. I don't quite like that."

Doris came through the other room, protesting to Lary that she had nothing. She pushed open the chief's door and said, "A report just came in. The New York Motor Vehicle Department says the license plates on the Pontiac belong to a Judson Stitch of 654 East Fifty-third Street. He owns a Cadillac which was reported stolen nearly nine months ago."

Fellows nodded. "Thanks, Doris." She went out and he said to Wilks, "They'd have to have phony registrations for all those cars you have them using. They couldn't get through the road blocks without them and that's quite a job right there. I didn't find any in the Pontiac."

"Which is probably why they held up another car."

Fellows said, "All we can do is sit. I wish to hell I could figure out where they'd be by now."

"In some New York City hideout counting the dough."

"And what about Mrs. Lary and the little girl?"

Wilks shook his head. "I don't want to make any guesses about that."

They lapsed into silence again and finally Fellows heaved himself to his feet and went out to where Gorman was phoning. "Any luck?"

Gorman, the phone at his ear and the classified section of the phone book in front of him, shook his head and put a finger on the page showing where he was. There were three to go.

Fellows stayed on to listen as Gorman said, "This is Sergeant Gorman of the Stockford Police Force. There was a payroll robbery here this morning. We want to know if anybody answering the following descriptions is or was registered with you. First——"

The chief listened idly to the descriptions, watching the reporters going about their gin rummy game. The reply from the motel was negative and Gorman dialed another number. Fellows said, "You trying all the tourist homes too, Bill?"

Gorman nodded and started his spiel again. Wilks came out of the office and left the room, heading for communications. Fellows went to the door and switched on the overhead light. "You fellows will ruin your eyes playing in the dark like that," he said to the card players. They finished a hand and one sat back. "Jesus, the thing I hate about this business is the sitting around. Nothing's gonna happen. There isn't going to be any news. Gorman's going to finish the calls and so what? But we got to sit somewhere and wait. As long as those road blocks are up, we're stuck here."

Fellows said, "So am I."

"Why don't you call off the road blocks, Chief? Those guys are on the outside sitting back and laughing at you."

"Or," said the chief, "they might be sitting on the inside just waiting for me to give up."

"So they'll wait. You can't keep them up forever."

"I can at least keep them up until they make plans to spend the night."

"And some motel owner will call in? Fat chance."

Wilks came back from communications with Lary and said, "Nothing, except the cars are getting backed up at the Turnpike toll stations. Friday night week-end traffic. The State Police are getting a little worried."

Fellows said, "We'll keep it up a little longer. I'm going out and stretch my legs a little. Who else wants coffee?"

CHAPTER NINETEEN

AT five minutes of six Fellows brought a container of coffee to Doris Norton who was monitoring the State Police broadcast frequency, switching between that and Stockford's. She thanked him and said, "There's a big bottleneck at the toll stations on the Turnpike."

Fellows swigged some coffee from his own container. "I know. I guess I'd better let the road blocks go. They're probably through anyway."

Doris switched back to the State Police frequency and almost immediately a voice said, "Weston Barracks, this is unit four. Over."

"Unit four. Come in."

"A black sedan, New York plates, just crashed the road block at the Weston entrance to the Merritt, going west. Am giving chase."

"Right, unit four. Attention all units. Attention all units. Be on lookout for black, New York sedan, traveling west on Merritt Parkway. Right now between Weston and Wilton parkway exits. Intercept."

"Keep that on," Fellows ordered. He turned and walked down the hall to the headquarters door. "Sid!" he said, putting his head inside.

Wilks, sipping coffee at the desk, came out and followed him back. So did Lary and the two reporters. They arrived in time to hear one of the other troopers say, "—turning around to intercept."

The first voice said, "This is unit four. Traffic. Traveling seventy-five. Have him in sight but can't catch him. Passing Wilton exit." His voice was tinny and hard to hear over the sound of his siren.

A new voice came in. "This is unit three. Proceeding west on Merritt, passing Darien turnoff at forty miles an hour. I'll herd him in when he gets to me."

There was silence for perhaps a minute. Then the first voice came back with a dying siren for background. "Weston Barracks, this is unit four. Send an ambulance. He jumped the esplanade and rammed another car half a mile past Wilton. Send the ambulance. It's a bad one. Out."

Fellows didn't wait for more. He nudged Sid and said, "Let's go."

They took the chief's car and sped down route seven, through Ashmun, Cannondale, and Wilton to the parkway, Fellows touching the siren button when necessary. Two policemen, flagging down cars just south of Wilton, waved them through.

Traffic on the parkway west was heavy, but moving. On the opposite of the divider it was very light and the ambulance that shrieked by had the double lanes almost to itself.

The accident was at a slight bend. Two police cars were parked on the narrow strip of esplanade grass with a second ambulance near by. The wrecks were a twisted jumble over at the far side while a double line of cars, backed up behind, extended out of sight around the next bend. A trooper was directing them, one at a time, through a narrow space of cleared road. Beside the passable lane two bodies, covered with sheets, lay on the warm pavement in the fading light.

As Fellows pulled up onto the esplanade and got out, the ambulance men crossed the far road with a stretcher and prepared to load one of the corpses. A trooper came out of nowhere to look Fellows over. "You the law around here?"

"I'm Chief Fellows of Stockford. This is Sergeant Wilks."

"I'm Halas." He turned to look at the wreck. "You think he was one of the men?"

"That's what I want to find out. You chase him?"

"I was the one. He was doing seventy-five and the traffic was pretty heavy. This road isn't made for that kind of speed. He got crowded at the turn and shot through here. You can see the marks where he stripped the bushes. There were a lot of cars coming the other way. There wasn't a chance he could miss them."

"How many dead?"

"Three. Man, woman, and child in the car he hit."

"How about him?"

"Still alive, but it won't be for long, I don't think. This is the worst one I've seen." He growled suddenly, "The lousy son of a bitch."

"Find out anything about him?"

"I got his wallet in my car. Guy by the name of Trojan."

Fellows wanted to see it and the trooper led them over and picked it up from the floor of his front seat.

The wallet was wet and slippery with blood. Fellows flipped open the tan cowhide folder, counted fourteen dollars in bills, and pulled out some wet, pink-stained papers. There was a driver's license issued to an Edward J. Trojan, 823 West 115th St., New York, N.Y., his birth date listed as 1941. There was a sales slip from a liquor store in New York, a plastic comb, and an I.O.U. for something less than ten dollars. The paper was so wet the amount and the signature were illegible.

"That's all," the trooper said, "except he'd been drinking. He got thrown clear, about fifty feet up the bank, and when I bent over him, I could smell it."

"You looked at his car yet?"

"Only to call in the license."

Fellows and Wilks gave back the wallet and headed across the esplanade. The second trooper was holding traffic so the stretcher could be brought across the road and the two policemen detoured around the bearers and around some scattered puddles of bright red blood to the cars.

One, the family's, was a twisted mass. The black sedan had hit it on an angle just forward of the driver's seat, had torn the hood off, sprung all four doors, ruptured the cushions, and rammed the shattered steering post through one of them. Red stains were all over the upholstery.

The sedan itself was in better shape, but not much. Its front end was destroyed, its engine ripped loose and the body wrenched out of line. Both front wheels were gone, the driver's door was open and jammed and the steering wheel was broken, the post at an angle. But the seats were in place and the back doors worked.

Fellows bent in over the front floorboards. A right shoe lay there and the pieces of a broken pint bottle. He climbed across the seat and tried the glove compartment. It was locked and he took the key from the ignition to open it. Ridiculously enough, the compartment light went on. He took out a dust rag, New York and New Jersey road maps, a plastic bottle of seat-cleaning fluid, a screwdriver, a notebook which was blank, and a car registration made out to a Francis MacKay, 618 East 83rd St., New York, N.Y., for a 1957 Oldsmobile. "Stolen car," the chief said.

Wilks, who was hunting around in the back seat, said, "And look at this." He held up a sawed-off shotgun by the trigger guard.

Fellows nodded. "I guess this is one of them. Anything else back there?"

"There's some other stuff under a blanket."

Fellows leaned over the back seat as Wilks pulled the blanket away. Underneath was a cache of three revolvers and two boxes of ammunition.

Halas came over and looked in Fellows' door. "The wrecker's here, Chief. All right to move things?"

"Show him the arsenal, Sid."

Wilks got out of the car and let the trooper have a look. Fellows said, "I guess you'll be wanting those. I don't suppose there'll be any prints but there's been at least one case where a print was gotten from a gun."

"I'll take care of them," the trooper said and Fellows went around to the trunk. That, except for a spare tire and jack, was empty. He slammed down the lid and stepped aside to let one of the bottlenecked cars creep by. "You seen everything you want, Sid?"

"I guess so. I hope they fingerprint that car."

The trooper, coming up beside them, said, "We will. I won't let anybody touch the inside."

Fellows said, "You can radio in that this is the getaway car. You can say we're going to talk to the driver."

Halas nodded and looked over at the black Olds again. "The lousy punk. I wonder what kept him for eight hours."

"He was probably hiding out in terror," Fellows said. "Probably thought it was safe to come out now and when he hit the road block, he panicked."

"And killed three people."

"And killed three people," Fellows echoed sadly. He and Wilks thanked the man and crossed to the esplanade again, this time detouring around the yellow wrecking car which had come across the grass and was trying to back into place. The twin line of cars stretching out of sight looked like a snake with a thousand eyes. There was no honking back up the line, only patience.

The two policemen climbed back into Fellows' car and swung it around onto the highway ahead of the wreck. Wilks said, "Well, there're three people who aren't going to celebrate Columbus Day. I only hope he dies too."

"I only hope he can stay alive long enough to tell us something."

It was a hope that wasn't realized. Fellows drove directly to the hospital Ed Trojan had been taken to only to learn the man had died en route. The highway toll was up to four.

When they started home again, Wilks said, "Well, we're cursed with bad luck. We catch one of the guys and we lose him. He could have told us a lot and we get nothing."

"Not quite nothing, Sid. I learned our fish are still in the net."

"Yeah? You did?"

"That's right, and the road blocks stay up. Logan and his gang are somewhere in the Stockford area."

"Is this some of your stratosphere stuff?"

"You might call it that. The main point, though, is where."

"The main point is, you'd better tell me how you reach that dynamic conclusion, Fred."

Fellows laughed a little. "It's easy. We were wondering how they planned to get through road blocks, right? Well, they obviously weren't even planning to try. In the first place, there's no short-wave in that car. That means they couldn't keep track of where the road blocks were if they wanted to. Secondly, it's a stolen car. The only way they could get through in a stolen car is to shoot their way through. That's risky business and doesn't fit in with our boy. This smells more like the Bergen bank and Pittsfield jewelry jobs where the robbers did a disappearing act. They've got a hideout, Sid, and we've got to find it."

"You're overlooking something, Fred. That was when they were going to escape in that car. You forget they've got a woman and a child with them now and she could get them through."

"We're going to have to hope they stuck to their original plan. If they did get through and the hostages haven't come back, it probably means they're dead. If, however, they're staying with the idea of hiding out until the money is split and the road blocks are down, then the hostages are probably still alive. We have to look where they'd be alive, Sid, not where they'd be dead."

CHAPTER TWENTY

ED LEWIS was at headquarters when they got back at twenty minutes of eight. Fellows said, "I forgot about you, Ed. You learn anything?"

"Plenty. That guy Krulevich was in with them all right. Everything points to it."

"Everything, such as what?"

"In the first place, Chief, he went out to see the crooks last night."

"Who says so?"

"His son for one. The oldest boy is about twelve. He's taking it pretty hard but he tried to help."

"The son knows about it?"

"Everybody in town knows about it, Chief. The son found out when one of the workers drove Krulevich's car home for him at five o'clock. I hadn't got to him because I was canvassing the rest of the neighborhood, but I talked to him after and told him we wanted to find the men who did it and he answered a few questions. One of the answers was that his father went to the hospital to see his mother last night. He went out somewhere between seven and eight and didn't get back home until after eleven."

"Visiting hours at the hospital aren't that late."

"That's what made me check. The guy at the gas station said he filled Krulevich's tank up in the evening and Krulevich told him—made a point of telling him, in fact—that he was going to see his sick wife. I called the hospital and got the information that Krulevich was nowhere near the place last night."

Fellows nodded. "What else did you find out?"

"Well, he went out other nights too, before his wife went back to this hospital. There were mysterious visits to friends. I mean he usually sat around home after dinner in front of the TV until he fell asleep but he got socially inclined in the last month or two and was going out to see some 'friends'. That's the word the boy used. 'Friends.' He didn't know anything more about them than that."

"What about the other neighbors? Krulevich have any special buddy?"

"Nobody he'd confide anything to. I tried that angle but it didn't pan any gold."

Fellows laughed. "That's quite a metaphor, Ed. So what it boils down to is that nobody knows where these 'friends' lived or who they were?"

"That's right, I'm afraid. I got a pretty good picture of the guy's life from the neighbors but I couldn't find out anything that helps much."

"What about the guy who brought his car home?"

"He rides to and from work with him and they sometimes have a drink together but, like I say, Krulevich didn't do much with people. Other people, on week-ends, would get together and do things, but he'd rather stay home and spit and polish his new car."

Fellows scowled suddenly. "You say he's got a new car?"

"Three months old. He must be breaking his back on the payments but he pampers it like a baby."

"What condition is it in? Clean?"

"Dusty. He didn't get a chance to polish it today."

Fellows snapped his fingers. "There's just a bare possibility. Come on, Ed, Sid. I want to see that car!"

The car sat proudly in front of the Krulevich home, gleaming through its coating of dust, the symbol of a man who had stretched himself too thin. Fellows tried the doors and they were locked so he sent Lewis in for the keys. Wilks said, "I don't know what the hell you think the car can tell us."

"He got gas last night, didn't he? I'm playing a long shot, Sid. Or maybe it's not so long. Here comes Ed. We'll soon see."

Lewis came down the steps of the house and a young, sad-faced boy came out and stood on the porch, his arms around two smaller girls who were in tears, and a little boy of five who called out possessively, "That's my daddy's car."

"We won't hurt it," Wilks said reassuringly as Fellows fitted the key in the dark and opened the door. The older boy gently deposited his weeping sisters on the top step in the glow of the porch light, and came down to the car. His face was tear-stained and he had a bad cold but he struggled to be manly. "What are they going to do?" he asked Lewis.

"We're trying to find out where your father went last night."

"You're going to catch the men who shot him?"

"We hope so."

Fellows, sliding into the front seat, opened and sought through the glove compartment. He found a notebook, flipped the pages and said, "By God, it worked."

"What worked?" Wilks wanted to know.

The chief climbed out eagerly. "A new car. A man with a pet new car. He's not only going to spit and polish it, he's going to want to know what the gas consumption is. Look here. October eighth. Seven-point-six gallons at twenty-nine-point-nine a gallon. Mileage: three thousand four hundred and sixty and five-tenths miles. I hoped he might keep a record!"

"What's the reading now?"

Fellows leaned into the car. "Three thousand, four hundred and seventy-six and no tenths." He tore a page from the notebook, scribbled some figures, and said, "All right, this car has been driven fifteen and five-tenths miles since gas was put into it last night. Ed, where did Mr. Krulevich get his gas?"

"Down at the corner and over a block, at Grafton and Dennis."

Fellows looked down the small block. "That's only a hundred yards. We don't even have to consider it. Son," he said to the boy, "when your father went to work, which way did he go, do you know?"

"That way," the lad said, pointing toward Grafton. "He picked up Mr. Hardy every morning and he lives on Veegal Street. My father would meet him on the corner."

"And somebody this afternoon brought the car home here directly?"

"Mr. Hardy. Yes, sir."

The chief put a hand on the boy's shoulder. "By the way, son, who's looking out for you and your brother and sisters?"

"My aunt is coming over. Mr. Hardy called her. And the people upstairs brought us down some supper. We're all right."

Fellows said, "I guess you are. I guess you can manage yourself. Now we'll see what we can do for you. We're going to take the car now. We'll bring it back after a while." He turned to Lewis. "Get my flashlight, will you, Ed? I want to see what kind of dust is on this car before we get it dustier."

Lewis got the light and Fellows asked the boy when the car had last been wiped down. Yesterday evening after supper, the boy said, before his father went to see his mother in the hospital. Fellows almost beamed. "For once the luck is running our way. Take a look at this car, Sid." He rubbed a finger hard along the base of a fender. "That's dirt. See? It's thicker at the bottom and thins out as you go up."

"He drove on a dirt road."

"That's right. That isn't dust the car picked up out at that windy parking lot at Grafton. He drove somewhere on a dirt road and I know what road it was."

"Cloverdale Road?"

"It has to be."

Lewis said, "Where's that?"

"Off County," the chief said. "Not far beyond where they abandoned the Pontiac."

"There are other dirt roads, Chief."

"Not in that direction, Ed. And it's got to be that direction because that's the way they headed after the robbery. Come on, get in. We're going to take a little ride."

CHAPTER TWENTY-ONE

THE trip to the Grafton Tool and Die Company measured one mile, one and a half tenths. Fellows drew up at the gate and looked in at the black silhouettes of buildings against the dark of the night. "Call it another tenth of a mile to get the car in the lot. That makes it a mile and a quarter to and a mile and a quarter back. Two and a half miles from fifteen point five leaves us with thirteen even. That means the distance from Krulevich's place to the hideout is about six and a half miles. We've gone a mile and a quarter already. Let's follow their escape route and see where we come out."

The speedometer reading was a little past 3,477.1 when they started on. It read 3,478.3 when they reached Edgewood Farm Road, and 3,479.5 when they came out on County. The reading they were after was 3,482.4 and they still had a mile to go when they turned onto Cloverdale.

A quarter of the way in they passed the lights of a modern ranch house, expensive and populated. A couple of people were holding drinks out on the terrace and three cars were in the drive.

"That's not it," Wilks said.

"Not yet, but from now on keep your eyes peeled."

They drove slowly, through dark looming woods, unable to make out any details. "I hope they've got a lamp in the window," Wilks muttered. "I can't see a thing."

Four minutes went by and then Fellows stopped and turned off the lights. "This is it," he said quietly. "What do you see?"

"I can't make out a damned thing."

"No lights?"

"Not a glimmer."

Fellows opened the door. "Let's get out and look around. Sid, you and Ed go on up ahead a couple of hundred yards. I'll go back. There ought to be some kind of a driveway at least, or some kind of turnoff."

He got out and the others followed suit. "Don't be gone more than five minutes. It shouldn't be more than a tenth of a mile either way."

The men separated and disappeared in the darkness. Fellows, working his way back up the road, accustoming his eyes to the night, searched diligently and in vain for a distance of three hundred yards. When he returned to the car, the other two were waiting.

"Any luck?" Wilks whispered.

"Nothing."

"Same here. Nothing but woods. There isn't a house anywhere around."

Fellows leaned against the car and squeezed his hand over his eyes. "Damnation!" he said. "It must be a dirt road and it's got to be this one. What the hell is wrong?"

Lewis said, "Is your arithmetic right?"

"Yes, it's right, damn it."

"Maybe we passed the place. Maybe Krulevich drove around a couple of extra blocks somewhere."

"We should have seen it. We were going slow enough."

"Then maybe you misread the evidence. Maybe it's not a dirt road. Or maybe it's a dirt road on the other side of town."

"You're no help at all. Damn! I've got to be right about this or we're lost. Sid, am I crazy?"

All of a sudden, Wilks laughed. He clapped Fellows on the shoulder. "No. You're not crazy, Fred. Just dumb."

"What are you laughing at? I don't get it."

"Krulevich started from his house. He wouldn't go all the way out past the plant. The quickest way would be to pick up County Road three blocks from the gas station."

"That's it. Why didn't you say something?"

"It only just came to me."

They climbed quickly into the car and backed around. "I'm not going to guess," Fellows said. "We'll do it all over again. No telling how much distance that might save."

They raced back to County Road, swung left and opened up, speeding past Edgewood Farm Road, past Massasoit Road, past the turnoff to Webber's Lake and Long Mountain Road, past Lee Street and up to Grafton Boulevard in the middle of the factory district. They turned around again at the gas station and took a new reading. "Three-four-eight-eight and not quite two-tenths," said Fellows. "Six and a half miles would make the magic number three-four-nine-four point seven. Right?"

"Right," the other two chorused.

They started back again, driving rapidly to the entrance of the dirt road. "A mile and seven-tenths to go," Fellows announced, "That's seven-tenths more than before."

They wasted no time covering the familiar part of the road but beyond the spot where they had got out they slowed and went carefully.

Fellows called the tenths as they passed and the men strained for a sign. "One to go," the chief said. "We're coming close."

"Up there," Wilks said suddenly. "Drive on, Fred. Quick."

They went another hundred yards until they were hidden from view and the chief stopped. "Where was it?"

"That clearing back there. A dirt drive up the side. I could just make out the house. It's blacked out."

"That's got to be it." The chief switched off the lights but left the motor running. "I'm going to look around. If I'm not back in ten minutes, you know what to do. Or if you hear shots or something." He opened the door.

Wilks seized his arm. "You aren't going alone, Fred."

"I'm not going to let anybody else go."

"I'm going with you. I don't care if you are the chief. We don't have to have two people to radio an alarm."

"All right, Sid."

Lewis said, "How about me? I'm not going to sit here. Three heads are better than two."

"Somebody's got to mind the store, Ed," Fellows told him. "You're outranked, boy. You get the lousy job." He shoved himself into the road and half latched the door quietly. Wilks did the same.

They walked back together in the stillness, their footsteps harsh on the road. Fellows carried a flashlight but he didn't use it and they felt their way gingerly. Overhead the sky was still clouded. A warm breeze rustled dry leaves and fanned their faces.

They found the drive and walked up on the grass beside it toward the black, looming house and barnlike garage to its right. There was no sign of life and no sound, though the breeze was blowing their way.

Fellows peered in a living-room window at the side. The shades were down but no light was on behind them. "Looks empty," he whispered. "See any cars?"

Wilks went off to the back while Fellows proceeded from window to window. "No cars," Wilks whispered, returning. "Nothing."

"It's a pretty run-down house. Doesn't look cared for."

"I think we're down a blind alley."

"Cover me. I'm going to try to get in this side door."

Wilks backed off and got out his gun. Fellows gently turned the knob and the door opened readily. He stepped inside and threw a switch and lights came on. He was in a narrow hall, door to the living room on his left, door to back stairs on the right, kitchen entrance ahead. He threw another switch in the living room and looked around. Wilks came in behind him. "Anything?"

Fellows pointed to a card table with a chair behind it standing in the center of the tiny room. "This place has been lived in, Sid. The question is by who."

"Maybe an old couple off at the movies. I don't guess they lock their houses out here."

"Maybe. You'd better go down and tell Ed it's all right."

Wilks went out, using the front door in the narrow hall between living and dining room. Fellows turned on the hall light and then went through to the dining room, repeating the process. He observed the layer of dust on the table, the drawn shades, and then his attention was caught by the ashes in the fireplace. He stooped and studied them at length and without touching them.

When Wilks came in the front door with Ed Lewis, Fellows was digging in the hall closet under the front stairway. "Take a look in the fireplace. See if those don't look like envelope ashes to you."

The two men did and came back just as Fellows stepped out saying, "Look what I found tucked way back under the stairs!" He was holding two scorched canvas bags with locks on them. One had the lock open but the contents of the second bag had been reached through knife slits in the bag itself and the lock was intact. On the face of the bags was stenciled THE FIRST NATIONAL BANK OF STOCKFORD.

"Fireproofed," Lewis said. "How did you think to look there?"

"No bag ashes in the fireplace. I figured they'd hide them in a nearby closet way at the back."

"This is the house," Wilks said, "but where are the people?"

"That's the question, but one thing we know. They did come back here to divvy up the money. They haven't crashed any road blocks, Sid. I hope that means Mrs. Lary and her daughter are still alive."

"But if they came back here, why did they leave again, and when?"

"I can't answer that but if it was in a hurry, they might have left something behind. Let's take a look upstairs in the bedrooms."

The three climbed the narrow front staircase and separated. There were four bedrooms and a bath up there. The beds were unmade and the rooms undusted, but they had been stripped of belongings. Only Lewis had any luck. "They held Mrs. Lary in here," he called and showed Wilks and Fellows a pink-stained tissue from a wastebasket.

"Lipstick," Wilks said. "That can't be Mrs. Lary's. She wouldn't be wiping off lipstick in this place. There's another woman."

Fellows said, "A blonde, judging by the shade."

"A glamour blonde," Wilks said. "That's one of those off-shades they make a fuss about down in New York."

"I guess Logan couldn't stay here five or six weeks without a girl. Let's keep looking."

There was nothing more on the second floor and they came down the back stairs and turned on the lights in the kitchen. The table was clean but there were five soiled dinner plates in the sink and half a dozen glasses, two of which had contained milk. A cold pot of coffee was on the stove and the cans from which the meal had been prepared were in the garbage pail along with two containers of milk. The refrigerator contained two quarts of vanilla ice cream, three quarts of milk, a half-dozen oranges, cream, and half a bowl of sugar.

"Six glasses and only five plates," Lewis said. "Somebody didn't eat."

Wilks said, "What they did eat came out of cans. I guess blondie wasn't much of a cook."

"Maybe," said the chief, "but that's not important. What is important is why they left."

"Not why they left," Wilks corrected. "Where they went."

"Why they left might tell us where. I think something scared them. They ate dinner but no dessert and no coffee. If so, they had to decide on their move in a hurry. It's going to be makeshift."

"They might have seen some cops driving by."

"That wouldn't scare them, Ed."

"Maybe someone came to investigate."

"If someone did, they'd just have another hostage. It's not that. None of our men is missing. It's got to be something else."

"But what?"

"I don't know yet. Anyway, they can't get through those road blocks and they're not coming down until we catch them." Fellows turned and looked wistfully at the enameled coffeepot with its brimming, untouched contents. "I don't know," he said. "I wish I had time for a cup but I guess we'd better get moving. It's after eight o'clock."

CHAPTER TWENTY-TWO

BACK in the car, Fellows sat for a moment before starting the motor. "All right," he said. "They left in a hurry and the only car they had was Lary's Buick. They didn't get through any road block in that."

"Therefore," Wilks said, "they're still around."

"That's right. Now where would they go?"

"Maybe they have another hideout."

"That's a nice, uncheerful thought."

"You say Logan plans carefully."

"I hope he didn't plan that carefully. I hope he didn't figure on having to move. If that should be the case and he's unexpectedly dispossessed, what does he do?"

"Take possession elsewhere."

Fellows nodded and started the car. "And not too far away. That's my guess. Everybody in the area is looking for a blue Buick. I think they're going to be somewhere along this road."

Wilks said, "I think it's a good first place to look."

They drove on slowly for over a mile, straining their eyes for signs of habitation, a driveway to a blacked-out house, a silhouette among the trees, a glint of light under a black window shade. There were none of those things and the first sign of life was a well-lighted house on the right, its bright rectangles of shaded windows gleaming warmly in the darkness.

Fellows continued past the house and out of sight before he stopped at the roadside and killed the lights. "It doesn't look promising," he said. "Not a Christmas-tree setup like that. But we've got to make sure."

Wilks said, "Same deal as last time, Fred. I'm going with you."

"All right, Sid. Mind the radio, Ed."

The two men got out and latched the doors quietly. "There might be a lookout," Fellows warned, "so keep twenty feet behind me. If somebody opens fire, I don't want us both getting it at once."

They went back single file, hugging the far side of the road until they found the drive. As far as they could make out, the inhabitants were unsuspecting. No one peeked through the curtains, no one opened the door, and as they approached silently up the drive, no one called out through the darkness.

There was a car in front of closed garage doors and Fellows was groping his way around it when Wilks caught up to him. "It's not it," Fellows whispered. "It's a '53 Chrysler."

"How the hell do you know that?"

"I know all makes for all years. Part of my hobby."

"Let's go."

"Keep it quiet, Sid. Whisper."

"Why? They didn't steal a Chrysler."

"They wouldn't leave the Buick out, would they? I'm going to look in the garage."

There were windowpanes in the doors but the interior was so black it was impossible to see anything. Both men strained with their noses against the glass but neither could make out whether the garage was empty or occupied.

"We've got to try to open the door," Wilks whispered.

"Too noisy. We'd be dead ducks." Fellows put his flashlight

up, clicking it accidentally against the glass. "I'll risk this," he said. "I think it's safer."

"You're the boss."

"Cup your hands around it."

Wilks did so and Fellows aimed the flash at a downward angle. They both pressed their faces against the panes again and the chief turned the light on, moved the beam in a small arc for two seconds and snapped it off. "Did you see it?"

"There's a car in there. I couldn't tell what it was."

"The license, Sid. The license."

"No."

"It's AM9687. It's the Larys' car."

Wilks whispered, "C'mon. Get behind the Chrysler," and he took out his gun.

The two slipped back quickly to the big car's protection and waited for thirty seconds. Nothing changed. There was no sound. No one apparently had seen the brief, sheltered gleam of the flash.

Fellows nudged Wilks. "Let's get back. We've got business."

They drifted quietly down the drive and into the road where they walked with half-running strides back to Lewis. "It's it," Fellows told him, sliding into the car. "It's the jack pot."

Wilks said, "It smells funny to me. No guard, no nothing."

"I saw that license, Sid. I'm not wrong about that." He picked up the mike and depressed the button. "Doris, this is Fellows. Over."

"Yes, Chief."

"We've found them, Doris. We've spotted their hideout. Now here's what I want you to do. First, notify the State Police. Tell them——" He stopped and let go of the button and stared musingly out of the window. Doris said, "You're loud and clear, Chief. What's the matter?"

"Nothing, nothing," Fellows said, recovering. "Tell the State Police to send every available man they've got to headquarters. Every man except the road blocks. Keep those road blocks up in case they make a run for it. Everybody else I want at my headquarters. And listen, Doris. Call in every available man I've got; regulars, supernumeraries, and as many of the auxiliaries as you can. They're in a house up here on Highland Road, a saltbox with a blue Buick in the garage, and they're probably crawling with hostages. I don't know how many they may have. Get everybody you can as fast as you can. I want them armed and ready for a siege. I want tear gas and searchlights. You got all that?"

Doris came in. "Yes, Chief." She sounded breathless. "Highland Road, but you want everybody to meet you here. Right?"

"That's right. I'm coming in right away. Out." He hung up the mike.

Wilks said, "What the hell is all this? What do you want to meet them there for? And what's——"

"Sid, it just came to me why Logan and his crew fled from their hideout and it's a complicated mess. I guess I'm all loused up too. I don't know how to work this out. Listen, I think the only thing to do is leave you and Ed here. Sid, you watch the house. I don't know what you can do if they try to leave, but you'll have to work it out. Ed——"

Wilks said, "You're absolutely off your nut, Fred. You ought to get every man here as fast as possible, not run back to head-quarters."

"I wish I could but there are hostages in that house. I'm trying to think about them and we've got to play it this way if they're to have any kind of a chance. Ed, you stay in the road right here and stop every car that comes up this way from route seven. Don't let them through and that means us. I'll lead the way back and I want you here so I'll know where to stop. And for God's sake, don't either of you tip them off we're here."

Wilks got out of the car again. "You're running it, Fred." He let Lewis climb out beside him, then leaned through the window as he quietly latched the door. "I only hope you know what you're doing."

"You don't hope half as hard as I do." Fellows started the engine and eased off down the road.

CHAPTER TWENTY-THREE

Lt. Carl Biloxi was the first of the State Troopers to arrive and he found Fred Fellows pacing the headquarters room anxiously. The chief was not alone, however. In addition to Sergeant T. C. Unger, there was Sergeant Gorman and every other man in the Stockford Police Department except Wilks and Lewis and one man in a squad car whose temporary beat was the whole town. The fourteen men were standing around, dressed and armed, smoking cigarettes and discussing the situation in low tones.

Fellows' first words to Biloxi were, "How many men've you got, Carl?"

"I should have five in five cars inside of ten minutes. I called the neighboring barracks for additional men but it'll take a while."

"Five and my gang and you and I and two men already there makes it twenty-three. I'd rather have fifty-three, but I can't wait. I'm turning gray as it is."

"They'll be here with tear gas and searchlights and one of the cars has loud-speaker equipment. You say there are hostages?"

"I count Mrs. Lary and her daughter and whoever's in the house they've taken over." Fellows spread his road map on the large table. "Here's the setup. They're holed up right about here."

"You're sure?"

"Of course I'm sure. I'm not chasing wild geese." He forced a wry smile. "I guess you'll have to pardon me, Carl. My temper's kind of short about now."

"To hell with your temper. What's the story. What do you want us to do?"

"First, block off the road at this end here, and I mean barricade it. Put two cars across it so nothing can get through. I don't want anybody going in and out, including police. We're coming in at this end, in Wilton, off route seven. Ed Lewis is there to stop us a hundred yards before we get to the house. We're going in there, as many men as we have, and surround the place. There's a front door and there's one at the side. There may be others but I don't know about them."

Biloxi said, "We can surround it, but it's not going to be easy taking it if they hold hostages."

"That's the thing that's bothering me. We can turn search-lights on the place and we can threaten them through the loud-speakers and we can even lob tear gas at them, but I don't like it. It's a rough, murdering gang, and they know what's coming to them if they get caught. They're going to fight, Carl, and it's my hunch we're going to have to kill every last one of them right there in that house and God help the women and children. They'll make damned good and sure every last hostage dies before they do."

Biloxi nodded. "That fellow Lary know about this yet?"

Fellows shook his head. "He went home an hour ago, Unger

says, on Unger's word he'd let him know as soon as anything developed. Unger's holding up on that."

"That's good."

"But it doesn't help solve our problem of what to do. They're obviously planning to stay the night in that house but I don't see that it's any use waiting till daylight. I don't hold any hopes of keeping twenty or thirty men around there in the daytime without their finding it out."

Two troopers came in, big men and husky and very capable. Fellows showed them the map and sent his own men out to get in their cars. "Remember," he said. "There's to be absolutely no radio and no sirens. It's got to be complete silence. You all understand that?"

The men nodded and disappeared. Biloxi said, "What kind of a watch do they have at that house? Any idea?"

"None," Fellows said. "At least as far as I could make out. We crept right up to the garage and shone a flashlight through the glass and there wasn't a whisper of an alarm."

"That sounds crazy but, if so, we're in luck. If they don't have a watch on the place, we can get men in close, especially on a dark night like this. If we can do that, we've got a chance."

"What's the chance?"

"If we can get close enough to rush the place, we can fire the tear gas without warning and then jump in on them."

Fellows said, "Hell, we don't have gas masks."

"My men do. They'll do the rushing."

"Five men?"

"Five *good* men, Fred."

Fellows shook his head dolefully. "It's not the best bet in the world but unless I or somebody could come up with a brainstorm, I guess it's the only chance we've got."

"It'll work, Fred. If they don't have a guard out, it means they're relaxing. The moment that gas comes through the window the men will charge. If those guys do any shooting, rest assured it'll be at my troopers, not at the hostages."

"If we do it that way, I'm going to back you up with my men, masks or no masks."

"Any way you want, Fred. It's your territory."

By the time the fifth trooper drove up, the numbers had been swelled by the addition of eight supernumeraries, and all of the policemen were packed into six cars, ready to roll.

Fellows gave the story to the trooper and climbed into his own car to lead the way. The caravan took off with a rush and roar and the chief led it south on Lake Avenue down to Cannondale where he picked up route seven to Wilton and the lonely dirt road.

Ed Lewis flagged the chief's car two and a half miles up the road and Fellows pulled in at the side, the cars behind following suit.

"Nothing's happened," Lewis said in a low voice. "Wilks is still up watching the house."

The chief got out, leaving his door hanging open, and walked back to the other cars. "Everybody out, but don't slam any doors." He went to Biloxi in the dark. "I'd like two men to take two cars up to the other end for the barricade. And turn a couple of cars broadside here so nobody can get through. And no talking, you men. Let the lieutenant and me do the talking. We've got to get thirty men around that house without the people inside knowing it."

Biloxi gave his orders and two of the cars went off at one-minute intervals. Wilks appeared out of the darkness. "Where's Fred? Fred, they're still there and they don't suspect anything yet, but these cars coming in are making noise. I could hear it up the road."

"It's the damned wind blowing the wrong way," Fellows said. "All right, Sid. Do you think you could take six men and work your way around back of the garage and cover the rear of the house?"

"Sure thing."

"O.K. You pick 'em and get ready. Gorman. Where's Gorman?"

"Right here, Chief."

"I want you to take six men up in the woods on the left side of the house. Keep well away from the place and be as quiet as you can. Don't go rustling any more bushes than you can help or bump into a lot of trees. And remember. No lights and no conversation. The wind's blowing from there and any sound will carry." He clapped him on the shoulder. "Go to it."

"What kind of a signal do we get?"

"I don't know yet. But that's not your job. Yours is to hold fast and catch anyone making a break in your direction. However we do it, you'll know it when we start. Can you pick your men and get stationed in twenty minutes?"

"Yes, sir."

Biloxi came up and said, "I sent two of your men for the barricade. I need all of mine to rush the house."

"You're taking all the risks."

"That's what we're here for."

"There's been a damned lot of lives lost already today," Fellows growled. "I don't want any more killed."

"My men are better equipped to come through than yours, Fred."

"I guess I have to go along with you there, but I don't like it. All right. I'll take four men and cover the side door. You and your men watch the front and the rest of the men will back you up. Gorman, you got your men? Sid, you got yours picked out?"

They replied in the affirmative and Biloxi said, "We've got the masks and tear gas. We're set."

"All right. Let's move up the road and take a look at the house."

CHAPTER TWENTY-FOUR

LLOYD RAGAN sat slumped in an easy chair in the corner of the room, his left foot tucked behind his right in his characteristic pose. His face was heavy and lined and looked older than it had that morning. He was in shirt sleeves and his tie was loosened. Strapped to his left shoulder was a holster containing the gun that had killed two men twelve hours before. Beside his chair was the bright new briefcase he had carried to the Grafton Tool and Die Company, only now it didn't house a gun. Instead, it was bulky with $46,774, his share of the payroll. His left arm hung over the side of the chair where his fingers could frequently re-assure him of its presence and his right hand lay limply on his lap, but never more than inches from the gun.

The living room of the rambling old house was pleasant and simply furnished, with flowery covers on well-used chairs and sofa. The newest item in the room was a television set and on the set the Friday night fight was in progress. It was a listless battle and one that Pete Gudge alone paid attention to. He stood in the doorway across from the set and was wrapt in the pawings and jabbings to the point where he almost forgot where he was.

The others in the room did not forget. Lela Trojan sat on the sofa across from Lloyd and, beside her, sat Helen Lary. Helen was a moderately pretty, very wide-eyed brunette in a blue polka dot maternity blouse. She sat straight and tense, holding a dead-tired, but still awake little girl against her. The child, a thumb in her mouth, was too exhausted to stir but something of the nervousness of her mother had seeped into her and she could not sleep.

On the other side of Mrs. Lary was an elderly woman, plump and impudent. Her dark eyes flashed behind rimless glasses and she was more outraged than frightened. She had not seen her unwelcome visitors in action and she did not know her own danger.

Her husband, a man named Merton Hicks, was white-haired and bent with years, though still muscular and slender. He sat in a neighboring chair staring at Lloyd but he had no desire to antagonize his captors. He had been knocked down by Lloyd in the beginning and whatever fight was in him had been drained by the blow. There was a blue bruise on his left cheekbone, tender to the touch, and his stomach still felt queasy.

Deacon rounded out the complement of players. He stood by the window and at intervals pulled a gap in the drawn shade for a look outside. No one spoke much and the stamping of the crowd on television and the between rounds commercials acted with mesmerizing effect. Everyone appeared to be waiting but only Ragan seemed to know what for. Only he had not lost his alertness, for even Deacon seemed to be doing his job with more mechanical than conscious motivation. As for Pete, he had forgotten they were waiting for anything.

Lloyd looked over at the little man calculatingly. At length he snapped, "You're supposed to be minding the radio."

"Yeah," said Pete, only half hearing. "There ain't been nothing on it since the Highland Road call. It's dead air."

"How the hell do you know? You ain't at it."

Pete said distractedly, "Aah, Lloyd. It's O.K. I wanna watch the fight."

"You wantta watch the fight!"

"Yeah. I used to be in the amateurs. No kidding. I'm nuts about fights. I even thought about turning pro. I couldda gone places as a lightweight."

"Get your brains scrambled for peanuts? You're just about that dumb. Get back in the other room and watch that set."

Pete grumbled and Lloyd said sharply, "I make you enough money to buy a hundred sets. What are you trying to do, throw it away?"

Pete returned reluctantly to the other room and Ragan turned next on Deacon. "What the hell kind of a lookout do you call that?"

"I'm looking, ain't I?"

"What can you see? Nothing but darkness. An army could crawl in on us and you'd never tumble. Don't be so goddam lazy. Go out and walk around the house."

"And leave you alone with——?" Deacon gestured toward the guests.

"I ain't alone," Lloyd said. He pulled out his gun. "I got this and if they start anything, the kid gets it first." He waved. "Go on. Take a look outside."

Deacon shrugged and went to the front door, opening it a crack for a lookaround while Ragan kept him covered from his chair. Deacon slipped through and closed the door behind.

On the television set, the announcer tolled out the round score of a split decision. Pete came in and said, "Who was it? Who got it?"

"How do I know?"

Pete watched long enough to see which man jumped around, then went off again. Deacon came back in and Ragan said, "Well?"

"Well what? There's nobody around. You ought to know nobody could find us here."

"I don't know nobody could find us here. How do I know this old bird ain't got some poker-playing pals coming around here for a late game? How do I know some pal of theirs ain't found out the phone ain't working and the phone company's got a man coming around?"

"So they come to the door and we let 'em in. So what?"

"So I'm running this show. I got you the dough, didn't I? You do what I tell you, how I tell you, when I tell you!"

Deacon growled, "Oh, for Christ's sake. You act like this is the invasion of Europe and you're Eisenhower."

"It pays off, don't it? I got you the dough, didn't I?"

"We got the dough thirteen hours ago. Why don't you relax a little?"

Ragan sat up straighter in the chair. "Because the cops ain't relaxing, lame brain. The cops still got road blocks up. You know what that means? It means they think we're still inside the net. I don't know why they think so, but they happen to be right."

At the angry voices, the little girl suddenly burst into tears and sat up on her mother's lap. Ragan said, "Shut up that kid!"

Mrs. Lary rocked and tried to soothe her but the screams got louder. Mrs. Hicks tried to pat the blonde head and muttered something. Ragan said, "What's that, Grandma?"

"I said 'uncouth'," the old lady retorted. "I said you're uncouth."

"How'd you like your teeth down your throat?"

Lela spoke for the first time. "I'll bet you're good at shoving old women's teeth down their throats. That's about your speed."

"Little Miss Acid. Your turn's coming, sister."

"Like Chick's turn? You're going to do to me what you did to Chick?"

"What are you talking about?"

She said bitterly, tears glistening in her eyes, "You know goddamned well what I'm talking about. You had a fight with Chick. So you go out and when you come back, Chick's dead. Nobody else has a scratch but Chick is dead. You sandbagged him, you bastard. You set him up."

"Me?" Lloyd was startled and outraged. "*I* killed the guy who plugged him! What do you take me for?"

"I take you for a guy who'd double-cross his mother. That's what I take you for. You know what I want to hear on the radio? I want to hear how Chick died. I want to hear if he got it in the back."

Ragan leaped to his feet, his face an unholy white. The little girl screamed louder. Deacon shouted and ran to grab him.

"I'll kill her," Ragan said between his teeth.

Deacon shook him. "For Christ's sake. For Christ's sake!"

Behind them, Mrs. Hicks gestured wildly. "Mert! Do something." When he didn't move, she glared at him in desperation, then seized a glass table ornament beside the couch and hurled it with feminine force at the struggling men.

It hit Deacon behind the ear and he sagged, half-stunned, into Lloyd's arms. It was a good effort and it caught the men off balance but there was no one to follow it up. Helen Lary was burdened with a howling child and Lela had been around such men too long to take liberties. She had her place and she knew where it was.

Ragan half supported Deacon while the staggered man recovered his legs but that was only with one hand. The gun was in the other, steady and ready. Lela and the old man had played it right. They'd known from the beginning they weren't going to get any jump on Lloyd.

"Foxy Grandma," Ragan said, showing his teeth. "Quite a cutup." He let go of Deacon who turned and leaned against a table, rubbing the bleeding spot on the back of his head.

Mrs. Hicks wasn't quite so sure of herself now but she brazened it out. "I'm only sorry I didn't hit you," she said smartly.

"Is that so? Well, we'll see how you like getting hit," Lloyd said, advancing on her.

The child wailed and looked away. The old man leaned forward. "Please," he pleaded. "She didn't mean it."

"Shut up, Grandpa, or you'll get it too."

Lela said, "Why don't you pick on someone who can take it, you goddam coward. If you're going to hit women, hit me."

Lloyd stopped. "Yeah," he snapped. "I've been saving it for you for a long time." He switched his gun to the left hand and lashed her across the face so hard she screamed. Lloyd wasn't big but he was sinewy and when he slashed it was like the crack of a whip.

The little girl started to shriek with terror and Lela, cowering against Helen Lary's shoulder, whimpered. Deacon said, "Lloyd! Cut it out, will you?"

"What's the matter?" Ragan said, whirling on him. "You getting chicken, Deacon?"

"I don't feel good. It's that clunk on the head."

"Well, I'll tell you what you do. You take yourself a nice walk in the outside air. You're gonna take your gun and you're going out and look over the whole area. You're going to check the car out back and make sure nobody's been snooping around, and you're going to check everything else in the neighborhood, and it's gonna take you half an hour. Get me?"

"Lloyd, listen——"

"You listen. Get your cracked skull outta here. I'm sick and tired of getting an argument every time I say something. Get out."

Deacon said, "Oh, hell, Lloyd," but he started to shamble toward the door.

"What am I running around here, anyway?" Ragan called after him, "a kindergarten picnic? What a goddamned gutless bastard you are."

Just then, from the other room, Pete started yelling, "Lloyd! Hey, Lloyd! C'mere quick."

"Stay here," Ragan ordered Deacon and left quickly.

Pete was in a first-floor bedroom at the radio. A voice was crackling in the receiver, "—They're bringing them in now," it said. "They were captured in a house on Highland Road. The money hasn't been recovered yet but they're being brought in for questioning. Remove all road blocks. Repeat. Remove all road blocks. We got them. Acknowledge. Over."

Other voices started coming in in acknowledgement and Pete said, "That's us they caught." He was grinning widely. "They caught us holed up in a house on Highland Road. How's that for a laugh?"

Ragan wasn't amused. "O.K.," he said. "We can't lose any time. Let me hear this." He listened as trooper after trooper called in. Then he said, "That clears the Merritt and the Turnpike. Let's move."

"You're going now?"

"Goddam it, of course we're going now. Those dumb cops are going to discover pretty fast they grabbed the wrong people and it's six to one they'll put the road blocks back up again. This is our chance."

"I thought the original plan was to stay overnight."

"That was when we had our own place, you dummy. We're on a hot stove here. We don't know who might come snooping around. We're fading while we can still fade. Grab that radio and your coin and get out the back into the car."

"Which car? The Buick or the one this guy's got?"

"I don't give a damn which one you take. I'm taking the old man's. The Buick's hot."

"I'm going with you."

"Suit yourself." Ragan turned back to the living room. "C'mon Deacon. We're gonna shove. The roads are clear."

Deacon said fervently, "Thank God."

Ragan went for his briefcase, tested the lock to assure himself it hadn't been tampered with. "Pete," he called. "You put that radio set in the trunk!"

The wailing of the dead-tired child caught his attention and he glowered, "Shut up that kid!"

The white-faced mother began to croon desperately and rock the child. Lela leaned over her maternally and tried to soothe her. The little girl kept sobbing. Pete came through the room lugging the radio and departed through a hall and out a side door. Ragan said to the old man, "Give me your car keys, Pop."

Mr. Hicks dug in his pocket without a word. Lloyd jingled the keys in his hand. "O.K., Deacon. You ready?"

Deacon said dryly, "I've been ready for the past twelve hours."

"Take my briefcase and wait in the car for me." Ragan took out his gun as Deacon put his away.

Deacon said, "Wait for you? What for?"

"I got some unfinished business with little mother here." He turned to Lela. "You're quite the maternal bitch, aren't you, nosing the kid. You think maybe I forgot about you."

Deacon picked up Ragan's briefcase and came back. "Leave her alone, Lloyd. She ain't done nothing."

"That's your opinion."

Lela had straightened. She stared at Ragan impassively but her face was ashen. Deacon said, "Lloyd cut it out. We got the dough. We got it made. Let's lam out before they get the road blocks back up."

"Don't you worry about road blocks none, Deacon. We're going to take the kid with us."

"Don't for Christ's sake!" Deacon pleaded. "Don't saddle us with a bawling kid."

On the couch Mrs. Lary hugged her child closer. Her eyes were dark and ominous. Ragan whirled on Joe Deacon. "I'm fed up with your yellow belly. I'm sick of your whining and bitching." His voice flattened out hard. "Maybe you ain't got it through your thick skull that I run the show, that I'm the one who says what to do and how we do it. You forget that, Deacon?"

"No, Lloyd."

"Then don't try to countermand my orders."

Deacon said, "O.K., Lloyd, but I ain't gonna stay around and watch."

"Get out to the car then and wait for me."

Deacon turned and Lela said, "Help us, Deacon. Don't leave. The guy's crazy. Can't you see he's crazy?"

For a moment Deacon's steps slowed. Then he went out, head down, without speaking. The door bumped against the frame behind him and she and the others were alone with Ragan.

He looked at her pitilessly. "You try everything, don't you, sister?"

"You're a coward," she said bitterly. "You're a sneaking, murdering, crippled, no-good, son-of-a-bitch coward."

He turned from her. "Gimme the kid," he said to Mrs. Lary. "C'mon, kid. Go over to the door."

The child shrank and sobbed louder. Ragan seized the child by the arm and yanked but Mrs. Lary clutched her tightly. "Leave her alone," she shrieked with the anger and ferocity of a cornered puma.

Mrs. Hicks, beside her, half rose, striking at Ragan. "You cad."

He backhanded her across the mouth, dislodging her false teeth and knocking her half over the couch arm. Her husband, tense in his chair, said helplessly, "Don't, Martha. Do you want him to kill us all?"

"You got the right idea, Pop!" Ragan turned again to the woman. "All right. Do you gimme the kid or do you want a bullet right through your other baby?"

He was close to her, his gun tight against his waist. Lela made a dive for it. The collision of body with body knocked him off balance. She got the gun hand in both of hers, trying to twist the weapon loose. Ragan clubbed her with his free hand, then seized her arm. Mrs. Lary didn't wait for him to break Lela's grip. She pushed her daughter aside and threw herself at the struggling pair. Under her impact, they all went down but Ragan held the gun in a death grip. "Pop! Help!" Lela cried out above the scramble.

Mr. Hicks didn't help. He sat staring dully, remembering, perhaps, the blow he'd earlier received and, perhaps, the fact that two armed men outside could upset the balance of power by the mere act of walking back through the door.

The women fought fiercely but Mrs. Lary was a frail creature to begin with and handicapped in addition while Lela, big as she was, was no match for a strong and wiry man as experienced in handling himself as Ragan. He lashed out with his feet, kicking Mrs. Lary clear, and grabbed Lela by the throat. She still struggled for the gun but his strong fingers cut off her wind.

Mrs. Lary looked desperately for a weapon, but there was nothing at the base of the couch. In front of her, Ragan was slowly getting his feet under him. Lela had ceased struggling for the gun and was tearing at the fingers around her throat.

Mrs. Lary came forward again but now she was looking into the mouth of Ragan's revolver. He got to his knees and then to his feet, his violent fingers still clutching Lela about the neck. Her face was red and her eyes were beginning to bulge but she had got one hand around his thumb and was bending it back.

He let go, but as he did, he yanked her forward and brought his knee up in a vicious blow under the heart. Lela went backwards and groaned, gasping for breath.

"All right," he said panting. "Say good-bye."

He brought his gun up but as he did, a voice from the doorway said, "Drop it!"

He turned with a start as Fred Fellows walked in with a .38 police special in his hand and four State Troopers behind.

CHAPTER TWENTY-FIVE

THEY brought Lloyd Ragan, manacled and disarmed, outside to where Deacon and Pete, similarly restrained, were guarded by three other men. There were shouts going out to men in the woods and more and more appeared out of the darkness, all armed, all hard-faced, as they gathered around.

Fellows sent two of them inside to look after the hostages and he turned to Biloxi. "All the money here?"

"So far as we know. We'll count it when we get back to town."

"All the weapons picked up?"

"These two men are clean." He looked at Ragan who stood numbly, as if in a trance. "I don't know about him."

"I looked him over."

"That's the job, then."

Fellows sighed. "Thank God." Then he said, "Where's Ed Lewis? Ed, listen. I want you to radio headquarters. Mr. Lary would like to know his wife and child are safe. And you better tell Doris to call my home. See if there's any supper left." He turned to Biloxi. "You know something, Carl? Now that the pressure's off, I suddenly remember I haven't had anything to eat all day except a sandwich. My stomach's starting to claw like a wounded lion."

"Relax. The Grafton Tool and Die Company will probably throw you a banquet."

Lela came out the side door of the house and made her way in the gleam of the flashlights up to Fellows. She said, "I want to shake your hand, mister. What you did is known in the vernacular as 'arriving in the nick of time'."

Fellows took her hand and stared closely. "I guess you're the girl who was with them, right?"

"My mistake, mister, but they'll find out it was their mistake when they come to trial."

Wilks pushed through the surrounding people, looked at the girl, and said to Fellows, "What's the idea of capturing the whole gang without letting me in on it? I was stuck in the woods waiting for the tear gas and the fireworks and I come to find the whole thing's over. What the hell did you do?"

Fellows rubbed the back of his neck. "You know when I said I figured out why the gang quit the hideout? Right while I was starting to call Doris it came to me that the only thing that could've made them think we were going to find them was the report that you and I were going to quiz that boy Trojan. He had his accident right about supper time. So the only way they could know that was for them to have a short-wave tuned in to our calls. That's why I said they were hiding on Highland Road instead of here on Cloverdale—to keep them from getting suspicious. That's why I had to go back to headquarters to set the thing up."

"That doesn't tell me how you got them out of the house without firing a shot."

"I fed them a phony broadcast. I didn't know if it'd work or not but it seemed worth trying before we let go with the tear gas."

Lela started to ask about her brother but before she had a chance, Lloyd Ragan suddenly started screaming. He tore loose from his captors and leaped on Fellows, lashing at him with his manacled hands.

Fellows, caught unaware, took two blows around the face before he could grab the man in a bearhug and give him a short, hard jolt with his right fist under the heart. Then three men were on Ragan, dragging him to the ground where he kicked and screamed and writhed.

Fellows brushed a smear of blood from his nose. "What's got into him?" he said in wonder rather than anger.

Lela, looking down at the struggling figure, ground into the dirt under the weight of his captors, said, "I'll tell you, mister. He just found out he didn't think of everything."

FAITH HAS
NO COUNTRY

R. Vernon Beste

*"Faith Has No Country" is published by
Hodder and Stoughton Ltd.*

The Author

Born in London in 1910, Vernon Beste was the son of an African explorer father, and his mother was a Bond Street jeweller's daughter. In his time he has been variously a teacher, tutor, law coach, speech therapist, salesman, journalist, playwright and actor. From 1948 to 1958 he was Associate Editor of "The Daily Cinema", and has also written and adapted several plays for television. Now living in Brighton with his wife and two daughters, he is justifiably encouraged by the success of his first novel, *Faith Has No Country*.

CHAPTER ONE

HE knew he shouldn't.

As usual he felt the tightening in the centre of his chest. That was the sign. Even as a small boy it had been there when he had reacted to a scolding by refusing to eat his dinner. Since then whenever he turned his back on self-interest, determined to punish himself because of his anger with someone or just the world in general, it was there. And as long as he went on obstinately beating himself, the feeling that he had a piece of rock for a breast bone remained.

His torment showed in the way the corners of his soft, well-shaped mouth were drawn downwards as he smiled at the woman behind the bar. But Maltby did not know this.

"Whisky."

The woman was fat, sluggish and middle-aged. She looked at Maltby carefully. Behind her disinterested, impersonal gaze, she calculated. He wasn't a regular and she was inclined to tell him that there was no more whisky. In the end the captain's pips on his battle-dress decided her. He might be a new one come to work at the offices across the street. Reluctantly, she poured out the drink.

Maltby took his glass over to a tile-topped table beside a palm. The glazed surface and brass corners of the table gleamed from much polishing, but the leaves of the palm were thick with dust. Evidently whoever did the cleaning had eyes only for the useful.

The first mouthful Maltby swilled over his tongue a couple of times before swallowing it. He did this not to savour the spirit but because until it actually slid down his throat, he could still turn back. While he held the liquid between his cheeks, he thought of the way the doctor had looked at him as he said, "And no alcohol." The vice round his chest closed in another notch. With a defiant gulp he shot the whisky down his gullet. There was no immediate reaction. That will come later, I suppose, he thought. He took another pull at his glass.

He could not make up his mind whether the whisky was good

137

or bad. In any case he had never liked the stuff. Only what it could do for you. And for that his glass seemed to be correctly loaded. The first pale feelers of warmth were welling up from his innards.

The bar was fairly full and Maltby looked about him with sardonic interest. A number of the men were in uniform. Although prepared to allow the younger ones a share of his self-pity because their pink freshness would be so short-lived, their eager-beaver urgency and shrill bonhomie disgusted him. The death of youth was too sombre to be accompanied by a heedless rattle. But, he told himself, only those already across the Styx could know that. Maltby, twenty-six, looked back at them with satirical affection, cheered by the felicity of his image.

For the older officers, with their swelling bellies and tracery of burst blood vessels on their cheeks, sucking absently at their pints, he had nothing but contempt. Has-beens. Chair-borne heroes. One day some such dodderer would do a sum wrong or put an inaccurate construction on a report and Maltby would end up in the next world. If there was a next world.

Maltby felt better, much better. He was beginning to enjoy the vicious hatred he felt for the world in general and himself in particular. But for his appointment with B.6., two drinks from now he would be picking quarrels and really letting rip. Once it would have taken a lot more Scotch than that to get him there. Nearly three years of enforced abstinence and six weeks in hospital had taken away his resistance.

But one more would be all right. It would set him up to deal with Mr. B. bloody 6., whoever he might be. He went over to the bar. This time the fat woman snapped at him.

"We only get a quota, you know. 'Tisn't fair to the regulars if crawlers come and mop it all up."

She swabbed the counter vigorously. Maltby thought he recognized the hand that kept the furniture so burnished. He guessed her indifference to plants probably extended to anything that breathed, but he refused to go down without a struggle.

"Wouldn't you like me for a regular?"

He bent towards her deferentially. She took in his pear-shaped face, the even teeth disclosed by the smiling lips, the slight patrician hook to the nose, warm, mud-brown eyes above high, pointed cheek bones over which the skin, yellowish after the fading of a heavy tan, was drawn thin and taut. A good-looking feller.

Without comment she poured him his drink. Maltby did not pick up his change. If the interview with B.6. lasted some time and didn't go too well, he might need a drink when it was over.

Maltby thought the civilians in the bar were looking very well on the war. An average lot, he supposed, but the men were much better turned out than the French after three years of war. Perhaps British cloth was better. Or the black market more efficient. The neatly pressed, dark business suits and trim black Anthony Edens that they all seemed to affect made him want to laugh. His countrymen's anxiety to be always properly dressed on parade was irresistibly comic. Like dressing for dinner in the jungle while the war drums crashed all round, these men faced a nastier war by getting themselves up as though it had never happened. In a way it was magnificent—as an idea. But when you saw the British doing it in practice it was just absurd.

Letting his eyes wander around, he noticed a party of four girls, two in ATS uniform, clustered in a corner round a bald, heavily-built man. Three parts through his second whisky, next to hating himself, Maltby was about ready to notice girls. The only one of them who was facing towards him was decidedly pretty. They were chattering together in low tones, bending towards their gross companion intently. Every now and then they drew back to gurgle amusedly at something he said, but a moment later all their heads were stretched attentively towards him again. The man seemed to be talking continuously but hardly moving his thin, smiling lips.

Despite the humorous crinkles round his small eyes, there was something definitely pig-like about the man, a likeness accentuated by his hairlessness. He wore a well-cut greenish sports jacket, patched with leather at the cuffs and elbows, over a grey woollen pullover. His neck was so short that the points of his white soft collar curled upwards round his jowls. In those clothes he looked like a Rugby forward gone to seed. What could the girls see in that pig face, he wondered irritably. Unless he was their "contact" for black market stockings. That could be it—except that black marketeers did not usually wear patched jackets. If he were still in Pontrecy instead of in London he would have had no hesitation in placing that polished bullet head, short neck and barrel chest. Gestapo.

This manifestation of the universality of the human form tickled Maltby. He reflected moodily that human vileness was probably equally universal. It was in all of us. Given the right circumstances it came out, too.

Maltby finished his drink and got up. His appointment was in ten minutes and he wanted to take a turn round the block first to get some air. As he reached the door the quintet in the corner burst into laughter so sharply that he turned self-consciously towards them. They were not interested in him, however. A dark girl with thick lensed glasses was looking straight at him, but from the rapt expression on her face he was sure she wasn't seeing him. He stalked out into the dusty September afternoon.

Looking around him he wondered how long it was going to take him to get used to the sight of wartime London. It was strange how ideas fixed. He felt a stab of surprise whenever he saw a petrol-driven taxi instead of the charcoal-fuelled *gazogenes* that were the norm in France. He had expected to see bombed buildings. But in the West End these, instead of being heaps of untidy rubble, were neatly swept spaces protected from trespassers by carefully carpentered palings. Or else they had been turned into emergency water reservoirs by surrounding them with well-kept walls. Children sailed boats on these artificial ponds, and old men peered into them pensively as though they were endeavouring to weigh up the fishing prospects. These placid pastimes made it hard to think of the tanks as part of the paraphernalia of war.

He began to walk, still feeling uncomfortable in his battle-dress, unworn for so many years. Three Americans slouched along the pavement towards him. He observed their sloppy, crumpled uniforms, critically comparing their appearance with the Wehrmacht soldiery. At any rate he could not possibly look as ghastly as they did, he consoled himself.

As he walked, it nagged at him. What was this bloody B.6. business about? He hated tackling the unknown as he hated the dark. If you went into things blind you generally ended up by being stuck with something you didn't like.

There was nothing for him to go on. The letter had been laconic to the point of brusqueness.

"You will report to B.6. at 27 Fairholt Street W.1 on the 8th inst. punctually at 2.30 p.m.

"This letter is to be destroyed as soon as you have memorized these instructions."

He sneered at the memory of that last paragraph as he had

sneered when he had first read it. The earnest deviousness of Intelligence *führers* leading a life of make-believe danger from the comfort of Whitehall was comic. But he had burnt the letter. He would have anyway, without being asked. Where he had been, you and your best friends were liable to wind up in the ovens of Buchenwald if you made a habit of keeping notes of assignation.

It could be, of course, that he was in for nothing more than a final interrogation before they booted him out of the Army. The doc. had more than hinted that he wasn't in any sort of state for active service. If that was what was coming, B.6. was not going to have a very fruitful afternoon. The Intelligence chaps had squeezed him dry in the first two weeks he was in hospital.

What would he do if the Army slung him out? He didn't know. Should he try to stay in it? Did he really want a desk job? They might want to use his experience for the instruction of potential secret agents at one of the special training schools. He remembered how Pinto, their last W/T operator, had described those schools to him the night before the chump got himself arrested. Maltby could not see himself fitting into the atmosphere of Old School Tie boy scoutery which apparently pervaded them. In a couple of weeks he'd be out on his ear for conduct unbecoming to a saboteur. He decided that if they wanted him to become an instructor, he would ask to be excused but offer to pass on his first-hand experiences in odd lectures if that would be any practical use. But as a free-lance, not as a member of the staff.

Try as he would, that was the only decision he was able to make. If he was off the beam and that was not what was going to be put up to him, he'd have to sort it out as it came up.

Standing in front of 27 Fairholt Street, Maltby became conscious of his stomach. The same dull ache he had noticed for the first time over a year before as he waited in the dark straining to catch the hum of the aeroplane carrying out the night's parachutage. He hadn't known then to what excruciating agony that ache was to grow during the months that followed. He didn't want to face that again. And he wasn't going to, if he could help it. He cursed his belly for being weak and always reacting to uncertainty like this. Characteristically, he did not blame the whiskies.

The house was old. Maltby judged it to be Queen Anne. Its faded elegance had the uncared-for look that comes over houses when they are in the hands of people who, conscious perhaps of their own impermanence, have no personal interest in them. The windows were dirty and uncurtained, partially obscured by soot-stained creeper which had not been cut back for years.

Looking at his watch and seeing that it was 2.29, Maltby went in. Leading off the hall were two doors marked A.1. and A.2. From behind A.2. came the click of a typewriter being tapped desultorily. Maltby went up the staircase. On the first floor, facing him across the landing, was a door inscribed B.6. Like the others, it carried no other information beyond the bare number.

He knocked and without waiting for a response entered.

CHAPTER TWO

THE man facing Maltby across a plain table had the palest and brightest blue eyes he had ever seen. The lids had a faint pink edge, while the fringing lashes and eyebrows were so fine and fair as to be almost invisible. Not an albino, Maltby concluded, but how much nearer could you get and still miss?

Besides the table, the furnishings consisted of two chairs and a green filing cabinet. No carpet or linoleum. Just bare boards. The uncurtained windows looked out on to a square of public gardens which had once been a graveyard, Maltby judged, from the church that took up one side of the square.

"Not being very clever, are you?" said Pig-Face, taking off his wristwatch and laying it on the table in front of him. He nodded Maltby into the other chair.

Maltby knew the watch trick. He sat down feeling he was one up. In Intelligence, punctuality was more than godliness.

"Those whiskies will make Harriet curl at the edges."

How the devil could he know about Harriet? It was part of the buffoonery of the medical ward at Wilberforce that the officers gave their ailments women's names. Harriet was Maltby's ulcer.

"I should have thought you were too busy with your harem to count them."

The blue eyes glinted approvingly and the wrinkles round them deepened in private amusement. Not betraying surprise at Pig-Face's unexpected revelation was obviously going to be entered to his credit. Two up.

"I'm Tonkin. Major Tonkin. The major is for your benefit. If you had been a major, I'd have been a colonel. For lieutenants I usually make do with captain. It's not important. Only you may

see me again and there's no need to be surprised if I jump about
a bit in rank. See?"

"Perfectly."

"Now, Captain Maltby, what are your plans?"

"Isn't it rather, what plans have you for me?"

"Well, what would you like to do then?"

"Be promoted Major-General and retire to Bali on my pension."

Tonkin seemed to give this careful consideration as he leafed
through a green-coloured file in front of him. He had taken off his
jacket and hung it on a nail hammered into the window frame
behind him. In his grey pullover and with that obstinately curling collar, he did not look like a major. Or anything military at
all. He could be policeman, though, Maltby decided. A bright
detective-inspector, perhaps.

"Ever thought of being dropped back in Pontrecy?"

"No."

"How does the idea strike you now?"

"It doesn't make me want to jump to attention and volunteer,
if that's what you mean."

Tonkin sat very still, his pale blue eyes like chips of ice.

"For me, you can stuff my cloak and dagger where the monkey
put the nut," Maltby added sullenly and then smiled. "Sorry,
major, but it's not the fun and games I enjoy."

Tonkin made no comment but dropped his eyes to the dossier
and apparently became absorbed in studying it.

Maltby felt clammy about the neck. He rolled his buttocks
uncomfortably on the wooden seat of his chair. This was one
right out of the bag. The problem had seemed simple. Just whether
he should claw on to a job or not. That they might want to dump
him back in Occupied France, he had never even considered.
After what the M.O. had said, it could hardly have been dreamt of
as a possibility. In which case the only feasible explanation was
that Pig-Face had not seen the M.O.'s report. If this were so, then
he might get a good mark for keenness at no expense whatever by
volunteering. The Section would certainly not allow him to go
once they got that report in their hands. Partly because he disliked appearing keen, partly because he wanted to see what Pig-
Face's next gambit would be, and partly because mixed in with
the fright there was excitement in the prospect that he might go
back, he decided to say nothing. If he wasn't careful, in no time at
all, he'd be genuinely trying to do what Pig-Face wanted. He'd

seen the bad times and it was only natural to want to be around now that the good were coming. It was also damn silly. Far better to remember the screams coming from the second floor of the Gestapo headquarters in Caude.

"You never had any training as an agent, did you?" Tonkin mumbled ruminatively, his eyes still on the dossier. "You were just left behind at Dunkirk?"

"Yes."

"How come?"

"It was 'Bunty' Posford's idea. Intelligence wanted to leave some chaps behind so that they could get the gen on what went on after we bunked out." Maltby grinned cynically. "I believe some of 'em even thought that we might be back sometime. Though how they imagined we were going to do it then, I wouldn't know. 'Bunty' knew I spoke French so suggested I should stay. He didn't have to twist my arm."

"Why not?"

Maltby shot a sideways glance full of amusement at the big man. Tonkin would have liked to kick him in the crutch. Why the hell did he always have to cope with nuts, he wondered, not for the first time. They were all awkward bastards. Or fools. This one wasn't a fool but would be awkward all right. For the hell of it.

"Well, what would you do, chum? There was an old tramp a couple of miles off the beach blazing like a ruddy torch. Little boats loaded down to their gunwales with men were capsizing all over the place. And a lot of nasty stuff was falling out of the sky, too. A right party. It looked a darned sight safer inland."

"And that was the only reason . . . that you thought it safer?"

"Yes. Not the right answer, is it?" said Maltby, feeling pleased with himself. "It just happens to be the truth."

"I see."

Tonkin closed Maltby's dossier and pushed it to one side.

"You're going back to Pontrecy."

"You mean you're asking me to volunteer?"

"No, I'm telling you."

This direct approach caught Maltby completely by surprise and he chewed on it unhappily.

"You're about the last man in the British Army I'd have chosen if I had a choice. Which I haven't."

"Thanks."

Tonkin smiled, apparently genuinely amused. For the first time Maltby saw that there might be something besides the man's obvious animal vitality which would be attractive to women. Pig-Face had charm.

"The truth is you're unfit, untrained and unsuited temperamentally for the job."

"Flatterer."

"Just as it was for you at Dunkirk, self-interest is my only guide. It happens that you are the only one who can do this job. And you're going to do it."

"I do what the man says, eh? And you're the man that says it?"

"Right."

"And it's not the sort of sabotage I was doing before but something special?"

"Also it won't take long. As soon as it's completed you will be pulled out. The quicker we can get you out of it the better we shall be pleased."

"Who shall I be fighting on this trip, the Maquis, the Free French, the Communists . . . or could it be the Germans?"

Tonkin rested his hands on the table and laced his stubby fingers. Maltby saw that his hands were heavily muscled and covered with very fine fair hairs that glinted in the sun.

"Politics much of a bother in Pontrecy?" he asked.

Maltby shrugged.

"'Love is for the birds. You know how it is with these Resistance groups. Or with us for that matter. I had a regular monthly warning to give nothing away to the de Gaulle boys."

"What about the Communists?"

"Bloody nuisances. They never keep us in touch with what they're doing and complain all the time that we're not giving them any weapons, which we aren't. But they carry out more operations and lose more men than all the other groups put together. This job you've dreamed up for me, is it political?"

"Yes and no." Tonkin leaned back in his chair and added casually, "The Gestapo have a man among the Pontrecy group."

"They could hardly——" Maltby began and broke off suddenly. "Do you mean among the agents or the group?"

"The agents."

"But that's impossible. Unless he got in after I left."

"He was there when you were."

Maltby felt himself go very cold.

"But there were only six of us in Pontrecy . . . seven including Pinto."

"It wasn't Pinto and it isn't you. That leaves five."

Maltby ran over the group in his mind. Buchan, Harrison, Lestocq, Gringoire and Hélène Dunois.

Hélène! If he went back, there would be Hélène! He had forgotten that.

"You mean it's one of them?"

Tonkin nodded.

"Which?"

Very deliberately Tonkin ran his fingers forward over the table and then said quietly, "We don't know."

Maltby felt relief surge up in him, though he didn't know what answer he had been fearing.

"I don't believe it," he said decisively, "I don't believe any of them is a Gestapo stooge."

Maltby looked hard at the big man. He was sitting back comfortably in his chair, quietly observing him. The bastard knows he's hooked me, he thought, and he's going to leave me to thresh about.

Maltby cracked his fingers. If one of the bunch had been a Gestapo stooge while he was there—— He felt sick and his stomach griped.

"All right, tell me what you know."

"I thought that, given this lead," said Tonkin, "you might come up with something yourself."

Maltby said nothing. He'd shifted the pitch and Pig-Face could play on it or not as he chose. He chose.

"You did a pretty good job at Pontrecy. Particularly on the railway. That's why we built up your group so that it became the largest that we had outside Paris. I mean of agents. There are of course much bigger groups in the Maquis, but they are locals and their operations are not under the control of the British. You were reinforced because we needed to be sure that the organization you had built up would not go for a Burton if you were blown. Clear?"

If Maltby made any move at all it was only to droop an eyebrow but it seemed to satisfy Tonkin, for he went on:

"Didn't you ever wonder why it was that things began to go wrong about six months ago? Nothing that could be called a total disaster, but a series of accidents that spiked your efforts. They began with one of the most serious when the Wehrmacht surrounded the only fully operational platoon of the Maquis in your district while they were still asleep. How did the Germans know that they were in camp in the woods above Addor?"

The question was snapped out sharply, demanding an answer.

"Christ, the real question is how they thought it possible that the Jerries didn't know they were there," Maltby said irritably. "You don't know what blasted fools the French are. They haven't the first idea of security. Everyone in the province must have known about that camp. Of course, they were copped. It's a marvel we all haven't been." Maltby looked down at his feet and moodily cracked a finger. "Why, when I first used to go into Pontrecy or Quoix I had kittens because all the old crones I passed would nudge each other and cackle, '*l'Anglais*.' They only stopped doing it because I was around so long it ceased to be news. And you ask how the Germans knew!"

"If that were the only occasion, you might be right to blame the ham-fisted French," said Tonkin unperturbed. "But there were plenty of others. Didn't you ever consider that you were getting more than your share of bad luck when patrols always turned up on the railway stretches you planned to blast? And the bridge at Camaret-Rouge. Wasn't it queer that the whole area should be bristling with Huns the night you were going to blow it up, when it had never had a guard on it previously? And then the charges at Beauvac . . . the charges that didn't work. Why?"

"Search me."

"Who planned the Beauvac job?"

"I did."

"Can you remember it . . . in detail?"

Of course he could. Beauvac was an important objective. A half-mile beyond the station, two branch lines, one from the north-west and one from the south, connected with the main east-west line to Paris. If the points could be thoroughly wrecked, the line would be out for at least a week, as there were no replacements nearer than Dijon. He remembered how carefully he had worked on the plan of attack, because its success would have more than set off the frustrations that had been dogging their recent attempts at sabotage around Pontrecy.

"Tell me particularly about the charges. Who made them?"

"Buchan."

"Was that normal?"

"Yes. He was the explosives expert."

"Where was the stuff kept?"

"In a cache we had made when we took it from the parachuting field."

"And Buchan went there to prepare the charges?"

"No. Harrison got the stuff from the cache and brought it to Buchan and me. He then went off and I stayed, giving Buchan a hand whenever he needed it."

"You were with Buchan the whole time? He was never alone with the explosives?"

"No . . . except for about a quarter of an hour when Harrison left. I walked down the road with him."

"Why?"

"I think I wanted to talk to him about a radio message to London. Harrison was on his way to see Pinto, I know that."

"And then?"

"I hid the charges in two sacks of firewood and took them to Hélène's the next morning."

"Why was that?"

"Hélène's place was on the other side of the village, four miles nearer Beauvac than Buchan's 'safe' house. As a peasant it was quite all right for me to deliver firewood to her house in a truck."

"I see."

"Lestocq picked it up from there. He has a workman's permit which enables him to travel about and makes it unlikely for him to be searched even if he runs into a road block. His cycle has a genuine licence, too. He hid the charges in some bushes near the Beauvac points on the south side of the line. He then crossed over the railway and went to a Maquis camp to get some rest before the attack."

"Leaving the explosives unguarded?"

"That was nothing unusual. They seemed all right when I collected them and handed them over to Gringoire. The clump of bushes was our rendezvous. He met me there a little after midnight, bringing four Pontrecy maquisards with him."

"Then you and Gringoire put them on the lines?"

"No, Gringoire did that on his own. I covered him with the maquisards from the south side of the embankment. The north was taken care of by Lestocq and some men he had brought with him from the camp."

As he spoke, that night, so silent yet so full of sound, welled up round Maltby. He saw again the pencilled parallel lines of the track looking like silver in the moonlight, curving away to his left and disappearing into the tomb of Beauvac station on his right. From the station came snuffles and grunts of engines in travail, voices and the clank of metal against metal. Plumes of smoke hung languidly in the air and once there had been a long sad whistle. The sounds, even the rattle of a stone, disturbed by some rabbit or possibly a rat, rolling down the embankment on to the permanent way, were so distinct, so utterly separate and unconnected, that each seemed to exist in a private limbo of its own. The only real things were his pumping heart and the humped figure of Gringoire methodically placing the explosives in the intersections of the points.

"Well?"

"There was nothing more," said Maltby. "When he'd finished laying the charges Gringoire went into Beauvac to warn the *cheminots* not to go near the points as they were going up in an hour. The rest of us beat it. Gringoire joined Lestocq and they made their way back to Pontrecy together."

Maltby remembered the panic he'd been in when an hour and half later there had still been no explosions. He had thought of going back to see what had happened, but it would have been light before he could reach Beauvac. Besides, the excitement had made his ulcer flare up and he was in agony. It would have made no difference anyway. When the points did not blow up, the railwaymen, fearing that the early morning workmen's train would be wrecked, reported to the Germans that the line had been tampered with.

"There was one other thing. The stuff might have been dud or deteriorated in the dump. I couldn't test it because there was no more left in the box Harrison had taken it from. But the other stuff in the dump was O.K."

Tonkin swore.

"That gets us no place."

"Where did you expect it to get us?" Maltby snarled.

Tonkin shot him an exasperated glance.

"Don't you see? Every one of them had the damn stuff in their hands at some time. Any of them could have made it useless. If there had been just one who had not touched those charges, we could at least have eliminated him. As it is they're all still in it. Just as deep."

"That goes for me, too."

"You're in the clear."

"I'm touched by your faith in me."

Tonkin looked at him with unconcealed disfavour.

"You'd be top of my list." He spoke gripping the table with his fists, his round head thrust as far forward as it would go on his short neck. "First, because that chip on your shoulder is going to get so heavy one day that there's no ditch it couldn't land you in. Second, because I think you're crackable material. If not by the Gestapo, certainly by me. Only," he dropped his eyes to the table, "you don't happen to be a starter. The 'accidents' have still been going on since you left."

"Pity." The big man cocked an eyebrow. "I should have liked to see your cracking machinery in operation."

Tonkin chuckled.

"Don't take that too seriously."

"You could still be way off, you know. They could be accidents."

" 'Fraid not." Gently he polished his bald head as he weighed his next words. "You see, it's not just guesswork. The French have tipped us off that one of our people is in touch with Caude Gestapo. Apparently they have an inside contact."

"Who do they say it is?"

"They don't. They claim they don't know."

"But you think they're lying?"

The big man held Maltby steadily with his eyes. Since his outburst the atmosphere between them had improved appreciatively. Maltby marvelled that such a gross body could contain so much power. Not merely physical power, but a quick and nimble brain that probed out, made contact and held on to it. Yet, with his bald head and frayed pullover, he looked a plain oaf, completely *déclassé*. He could have been a shabby warehouse clerk or an all-in wrestler gone flabby and turned pub bouncer. How on earth did he manage to fit in with the needle-bright Public School sprigs who had grilled him when he got back to England, Maltby wondered. He squared no better with them than the sparse, utilitarian furniture did with the well-proportioned windows and beautifully carved but dust-laden cornices of the elegant room.

"I just don't know," Pig-Face said judicially. "But I think they've known that we were wide open for quite a time."

"Charming!"

"Just human, I'd say. The French boys are pretty sore at us, you know. They have a good idea of what we think about them. And they resent our running a separate Intelligence show of our own. I think they enjoyed watching us being twisted. It's understandable."

"Not if you were in Pontrecy."

"It's a bloody silly way to run a war, I agree," said Tonkin amiably. "But from now on it's going to be different. All Resistance activity is to be co-ordinated. Naturally, knowing what they do, the French have refused to go along with the new policy in the Caude region until we've pulled out our blown Pontrecy group. Only we can't do it just like that."

Maltby nodded. Obviously, as soon as the orders to return home were received, the rat would spill it to the Gestapo and all of them would be picked up.

"But if we'd been blown for months, why did they just nab Pinto? They could have had the lot of us."

As Tonkin explained it, it seemed simple enough. The Gestapo had everything to gain and nothing to lose by leaving the group undisturbed. Through their spy they would learn all about the sabotage operations planned and frustrate them. They also knew that the Resistance throughout the whole region would soon be linking up. The chances were the British group at Pontrecy, because of its strength in trained officers, would be picked to lead it. This would mean details of the whole organization would come into their hands and they could crush all the Resistance in the province. A much bigger prize than the capture of half a dozen British agents who could tell them nothing they did not already know. In the meantime they could keep their hand in, so to speak, by arresting a fair proportion of the Frenchmen who were co-operating with the Pontrecy group. This they had done and were still doing.

"There's still Pinto," Maltby objected. "Dropping on him doesn't fit into that picture at all."

Tonkin considered this for a moment before speaking.

"Just tell me exactly how Pinto was taken," he said.

Maltby described what had happened. Pinto had been a damn fool. He was holed up in an isolated farmhouse to the west of Cerigny. As a transmitting post it had both advantages and disadvantages. Being so isolated, there was little chance of anyone hearing the noise made by Pinto's transmitter, a desirable feature even though the Cerigny villagers were better than most at concealing their curiosity about the saboteur's activities. The dis-

advantage was that if the Germans got bearings on the transmitter
from their direction-finding wireless cars, they would immediately
be certain that it was sited in the farmhouse, as there were no
other houses within a quarter of a mile. For Pinto, though, the
farmhouse had special attractions.

"These W/T operators have it rawer than any of us," Maltby
said. "On duty all hours of the day and night. Always on the
move, through the back door at the double as often as not. Pinto,
like most of the ones I've known, couldn't speak a word of French
and so couldn't take any exercise."

Maltby was silent for a moment.

"No exercise . . . it's unhealthy. Not that I've got anything
against a chap for wanting a woman once in a way. But being
cooped up made Pinto as randy as a rabbit. Come to think of it,"
he grinned, "the poor devil looked like one. And he had a whining, adenoidal voice that grated on your ears. But the women
never seemed to mind. Pinto liked the Cerigny farmhouse. He
had a large room to work in, bags of first-rate grub, and the
farmer's daughter, willing and more than ready, always on tap in
the next room to his."

After he'd been there a couple of days, he had been ordered to
move on. Pinto, naturally loath to be parted from such a cushy
billet, decided to ignore the order and stay on for a while.

Two days later, while he was busily tapping out a despatch, the
D/F vans closed in. Before he had finished it, a truckload of
soldiers came dashing up to the farm, debouched and surrounded
it. And that was that.

"That about ties it up," said Tonkin. "Nothing to do with the
Gestapo. Just soldier boys playing. They wouldn't know about
the Gestapo's larks. Must've made their stomachs flip to find the
military blundering about among their tame pheasants."

Maltby was moodily picking at his memories. He could shrug
off what had happened to Pinto. He'd stuck his neck out and had
no kick if the chopper had fallen on it. It was the farm people
that troubled him. They had so much to lose. The farm and its
solid comfort, their pride in their daughter, their shared happiness and their lives. Yet they willingly put all in jeopardy to
help *les Anglais.*

These people had been destroyed by Pinto's stupidity, but it
was his own hand that had spun the wheel. He was the one who
had introduced Pinto to their house. That was the worst part of

his sort of war. You could not fight your battles alone. You depended on involving other people, people who were not soldiers. When they paid the penalty for involvement there was nothing you could do except turn your back on them. Care for his own skin had taught him how to turn his back. But he could not forget them however quick he was to look the other way.

Looking up he saw that Tonkin was quietly watching him.

"Hell, isn't it?" the big man said gently, as though he had read his thoughts.

Maltby ignored this. There might be a friendlier feeling between them but it wasn't that friendly.

"The worst part of this job is that we're boxed in by time every inch of the way. You're to be dropped back in a fortnight from today. You'll need every moment of that to mug up the details of what you have to do. There'll be no time to put you through a proper course."

"Look," said Maltby, "I'm not the heroic type. I'm not volunteering to go back to Pontrecy. Knowing that I'd already been blown and that there'll be a Gestapo stooge waiting to welcome me, I'd be crazy. Besides, what use can I be? It's a job for one of you detective blokes. I wouldn't know where to start on it."

Tonkin decided that there were no more bushes for him to beat about. It had always been a forlorn hope that this narky devil would show willing and play it for its own sake. Nevertheless he'd tried. If he'd failed he didn't blame Maltby. He preferred that after seeing so much he should want to get out of the racket to the unpleasant eagerness to get back to knifing and garrotting that obsessed the keen types. Only the corrupt could find killing anything but degrading and unclean. Now he'd hit him. Hard. Would the pieces come down the right way up? He thought so. But the only way to know was to do it.

"We've agreed with the French that in six weeks precisely the Pontrecy group will be cleaned up. One way or the other. You're one way."

"And the other?"

Tonkin left him to work it out for himself.

"All five?"

"All five."

Maltby was with them, seeing them as they had looked during his last week at Pontrecy. Possibly being so ill and in such pain then had made his senses extra perceptive and that was why he remembered them so clearly at that time. Or it may have been only that he'd seen more of them in that week. For Hélène and the four men had fussed about him endlessly, reassuring him that the work was going forward well—as if he cared!—so that he would not worry, and flapping about quite unnecessarily in their anxiety that his departure should be managed without a hitch. He had been amazed at their concern for him. And because he was what he was could not pretend to like it and bitched viciously.

His thigh muscles were twitching violently. Rolling on his behind, Maltby crossed his legs in an effort to stop the quivering. If he didn't get hold of it, it would run right up his body.

"I haven't much option, have I?"

But Tonkin was not going to be satisfied with that.

"I don't know," he said dispassionately. "Look at it this way. Four of them are dead ducks anyhow. They're blown and living on time borrowed from the Gestapo. It hardly makes any odds to them whether they're executed by the French or the Huns. Either way they'd be stiff and cold. But to the fifth it would make plenty of difference. And that's the one we're after. But the French will deal with him whether you go back or not. Yes," he said almost enthusiastically, "you could see it that way."

Maltby fumbled in his pockets for his cigarettes. Taking one from the packet Tonkin pushed towards him, his hand shook so much that he tipped half a dozen out on to the desk. But the tremble was only momentary. He got hold of himself at once. After he had lit his cigarette he held the match up for a full minute so that Tonkin should see it. It was rock steady.

"I'll go," he said. "But there are a lot of things I'd rather do."

"When you come back, you can take your pick."

"I'll hold you to that."

"If you can find me," grinned the big man.

Now that the decision had been taken, Maltby felt crisp and businesslike. The reaction would come later. For the moment he was only conscious of the ball at his feet and a desire to kick it.

"Well, what now, major? Where do I collect my 'Make-do and Mend Sherlock Holmes Outfit'?"

"You'll be lucky if you get issued with as much as a magnifying-glass! Mostly you'll just have to use your loaf. But there's a secondary job we'd like you to do if you can. It is secondary, though, and if you can't get around to it . . . well, just set as much of it up as you can for whoever takes over from you to finish."

Casually he took up a cigarette, lit it and blew smoke before going on. "We'd like the ball-bearing foundry at Evine put out of action."

"Cripes! What would you like me to do in my spare time? Bring Hitler back alive?"

"Another time, perhaps. I know it sounds a bit tough——"

"This English under-statement kills me."

"——but we can give you quite a lot of helpful dope."

By a stroke of luck, Tonkin explained, they had just discovered that the key machinery in the finishing shop of the works at Evine had been put in by a Birmingham firm. If this could be smashed, the works would probably be out of action for the rest of the war. Their information was there were no replacement parts on the Continent and improvisation would be extremely difficult, if not impossible. Better still, among the British firm's records were not only full details of the machines supplied by them but complete plans of the Evine factory showing clearly where their plant was sited. That didn't exactly mean that its sabotage was a piece of cake, but it was a short cut in laying it on.

Maltby listened bristling with contempt, the contempt of the man of action for the "planner", of the man in the "field" for the home staff, of the worker for the front office.

"With the help of one or two workers inside the factory, it should be possible to do it without sticking your neck out too far. If you've already got inside contacts, that'll be fine. If not, we'll let you have at least one name before you leave. The French are working on that now. What do you say?"

"I wish 'em the best of luck. The French, I mean."

"Is that all?"

"Oh, it's a luvverly idea!"

"If you could bring it off, you'd be certain of doing more damage to the German war effort than we could be sure of even if we raided the factory with a hundred planes."

Feeling cramped, Maltby got up and walked across to the fireplace. The mantel-shelf was bare except for a cut-glass pin-tray and a wooden pen with a broken nib.

"What does it amount to, anyway?" he asked.

"Two or three per cent of the German ball-bearing production. Maybe more. We've been slugging their other plants pretty hard lately, so it's difficult to tell how much is still operating."

For so much, thought Maltby, a big price would be paid.

Especially if it didn't come out of your pocket. Why the hell should he care, anyway? If Evine were to be bombed, there would be plenty who would get theirs because someone's aim was off or aircrews so windy that they laid their eggs regardless. Nobody would lose any sleep over that.

"No can do?"

Maltby shrugged.

"Why not? With a bit of luck, a plan of the Tower and a couple of Beefeaters to give a hand, I reckon the Crown jewels could be knocked off. So why not Evine ball-bearing works?"

Tonkin was puzzled. Maltby's yellowish skin had changed to a kind of dun grey. The man looked damned ill. It was bloody awkward having to use a crock for a job like this. Well, somehow he'd got to be kept in one piece till it was completed.

Was he just scared? Not in the accepted sense, Tonkin felt sure of that, though he could not tell why. Nor why the mention of the Evine works plan had been a boner. Somehow he'd gone wrong there.

"Well, have a crack at it, if you can. But it's not the vital part of the mission. Smelling out traitors is nasty, negative work. We thought you'd like to give the Huns a real kick in the pants as a sort of relief."

"Fairy Godmother stuff, eh? Not the role I'd have cast you for!"

"An Ugly Sister, perhaps?"

Maltby grinned cheerfully, showing his even white teeth and his eyes dancing with amusement. Pig-Face was all right.

"Thanks all the same," he said. "You weren't to know that I'd prefer the pumpkin to the coach."

Uncertain what had caused Maltby's change of mood, Tonkin let that go.

They discussed details. There was a hell of a lot to be done. Worst still, it could not be done in one place. He would have much of his precious time wasted in travelling about to the various "schools". Despite that, Maltby insisted that he should have the next twenty-four hours free. To this Tonkin finally agreed. The day after, Thursday, he was to go to Birmingham. It was better to get the Evine malarky out of the way first, said the big man, then they could concentrate on the real business.

"Now, let's see, what's the time? If you'll report to your Section at 5 o'clock, that'll give me time to get your file back to them. Anything else you'd like to ask?"

Maltby stretched out his legs and looked down at his shoes. "Suppose I don't find the stooge?"

"Then we'll be where we are now."

"There's no chance of more time . . . say, an extra week?"

"'Fraid not, boy. We'd lose the moon for getting you out. The moon wouldn't be right for landing a plane again for three weeks after our deadline. Anyway, it's something that's got to be done fast."

If it were done when 'tis done, 'twere well done quickly. Because of the moon. Because of his ulcer. Because of the French. Because of the Gestapo. Because——

"If I don't dig him up, what do I do? Just light out . . . or wait till the job's finished?"

"You get. The French will finish it. They will, too, if you like if you get your finger on him. But I expect you'd rather take care of that one yourself."

Would he? It would depend who it was, wouldn't it? Or would it? Much as he loathed Buchan and Lestocq, would he like "taking care" of one of them in cold blood if he turned out to be the spy? And it might be one of the others. Well, why not? He had killed before. Three times. Two soldiers during the 1940 retreat and the Feldgendarme at Airvout. The last messily with a knife. The Germans had picked out five citizens of Airvout at random and shot them in reprisal for his death. Perhaps he ought to count those five among his "bag", too.

Maltby stood up.

"Shall I be seeing you again before I go?"

"I shouldn't be surprised. I get around."

With a nod, Maltby went out and down into Fairholt Street. At the chemist's on the corner he made haphazard choice of some indigestion tablets. He also got himself a pound's-worth of silver. If Judy was difficult, he didn't want to be cut off in the middle of his argument because he had no more small change to put in the coin-box.

He found a telephone kiosk and got through to the hospital. After some argument and much swearing that it was a matter of life and death, he persuaded the operator to find Judy and put her on.

"Hullo . . . who is it?"

"Miss Horton, it's your great-uncle, Wilbur Schittlemeister——"

"Who?"

"—who I regret to inform you has fractured his truss——"

"What?"

"—trying to jump from his box on to the stage at the Windmill."

"Harry! You idiot!"

"Darling!"

"Darling."

"You're coming out with me tomorrow."

"I can't. I'm on duty."

"Then get off duty."

"Whatever for?"

Maltby told her.

"Harry! You're a coarse beast!"

"I promise I'll stay that way. You'll come?"

"I can't, really I can't. But I'm off on Friday."

"Friday's no good. Judy, you've got to come. I'm going back and tomorrow's the only day I've got."

There was a long pause while the line clicked and whirred. Maltby wondered if it had gone dead on him.

"All right." Her voice was soft and low. "I'll manage it somehow."

"Good. Be on the 9.20 and I'll meet you at Euston."

"All right."

"I love you, Judy."

"I love you, too."

"Just for tomorrow, of course."

"Of course," she giggled.

The pips went and they hung up.

At H.Q. Maltby was breezily welcomed by a young lieutenant who looked like a whippet. His fair hair was cut very short and he carried his head thrust forward as though on a leash. He chattered incessantly and some part of his stringy body was always on the move.

"Jolly good show," he said, "your being able to get round B.6. How did you find the old boy?"

"Pleasant enough."

"N.Q.O.C., of course, but decent. Too soft-hearted to understand us types."

N.Q.O.C. Not Quite Our Class. Maltby was amused at this airy assumption that he belonged to the same Public School bandit *élite* as the lieutenant. Must be the uniform, he decided.

"When we got your letter, old B.6. got into quite a tizzy. Said you'd only volunteered because that was what we'd expected you to do. Insisted on seeing you himself so that he could talk you out of it. Of course, we knew you really wanted to go back. To be in at the kill now that we're going to hit the Hun for six."

Maltby was intrigued.

"Could I see that letter?"

"Eh?"

"Something B.6. came out with made me wonder what exactly I'd said in it."

"Of course, old boy." He pushed the folder across the desk to Maltby.

It was written on Wilberforce hospital paper and dated a fortnight earlier. Very simply it asked that now he was fit again he should be re-employed on operations in Occupied France. No hanky-panky with a typewriter, either, but in his handwriting throughout. It was a first-rate forgery despite the content being so far out of character. Maltby felt a new respect for Pig-Face.

"There's no limit to human lunacy, is there?" he said, handing back the file.

"No . . . er . . . no," the whippet replied vaguely, looking at the letter trying to make out what Maltby thought was so funny about it.

CHAPTER THREE

THERE was one thing about being back on the job, it would get him away from Southgate. As he walked towards his mother's house, he was full of hate for its trim suburbanism. He loathed the lack of individuality of the houses, each one identical right up to the ridiculous fretwork frippery decorating their single gables. And on either side were other exactly similar streets. Only this one had been built by his grandfather, and he'd built it without allowing a single mark of his personality to appear on it. Naturally these Southgate streets were not called streets but roads. Street was urban and therefore "common".

Even dimly perceptible in the black-out, the houses bore down on him, depressing him with the thought that his escape was only temporary. In a couple of months the Army would have had him.

By then he'd either be occupying sixty cubic feet of earth or have his ticket. Supposing he did survive, what would he do? If he were to go back to schoolmastering, Southgate would get him for sure. He did not dislike teaching but shied from what it did to those who pursued it. But if he didn't go back to teaching, what else could he do? Or want to do? He didn't know. Just to be discontented was weak and gutless. Well, I'm gutless all right, an inefficient metabolism on two legs.

The metaphor amused him by its aptness so that he was feeling quite cheerful as he let himself in with his latch-key.

"How nice that you're back so early, Harry," his mother called. "Your chocolate's all ready. I've only to put it on the gas."

Maltby grinned to himself. In twenty years the only French thing his mother had acquired was the habit of referring to cocoa as chocolate. Not even that, really, because he remembered that she always pronounced *chocolat* as chocolate even when they lived in Grenoble.

He marvelled that people should be so different, that his mother should have left Grenoble after his father died, willingly and without regrets, to settle in this characterless suburban box with such obvious pleasure. He had been amazed when she had told him that she had always disliked their large but rather stuffy Empire apartment at Grenoble, for it was the only place for which he had ever felt an affection.

The house had been a wedding present to his mother. Though its value trebled as the years passed she never considered selling it; her plan was always to make it their home when her husband retired from his post at Grenoble University. Providentially, in Maltby's opinion, death and not retirement had ended his father's career, for he could not imagine how the poor man could have borne Southgate's smugness after the intellectual circle in which he had moved in Grenoble.

For Maltby, his father's death had been a tragedy since it put paid to the plan for him to take a degree at Grenoble. Instead he had taken a course in a teachers' training college and from there straight into the Army to do his military service.

His mother brought him his cocoa on a tray covered with a cloth of her own crochet work. The cup and the matching plate on which she had set out a few biscuits were elegant Sèvres, and Maltby was amused by the contrast they made with the plebeian liquid. But he made no comment because he knew she had brought out the best in his honour and would be unable to comprehend the incongruity.

"Well, dear, tell me how you got on."

"I'm off again in a couple of weeks."

"Oh, dear, do you really think you're well enough?"

"They can't do without me, *maman*."

"Well, I hope it's not to some nasty hot place again, where you can't get the proper food." She had no idea where Maltby had been serving but had assumed that it had been in Africa. The nurses at the Wilberforce had jumped to the same conclusion. It was a lot easier to leave it that way.

While he drank his cocoa, his mother chattered about her friends and the afternoons she spent at the W.V.S. Years ago, Maltby had stopped listening when his mother talked about herself, developing a sort of sixth sense that enabled him to interject the monosyllable here and there that was sufficient to keep her recounting the small happenings that made up the absorbing interests of her life.

How strange that he should once have been part of this perky, self-centred, plump woman who, happily and uncritically, explored each humdrum day so energetically. Except perhaps about the mouth, they had not a feature in common. Blonde and blue-eyed and with the remains of a chocolate-box prettiness still discernible, her skin was soft and unlined for she was unharassed by guilt for the past or concern for the future.

Did she think of him as a son, he wondered? Or simply as a man to fetch and carry for and feed when he happened to be around, a duty founded somewhere in the remote past, its reason long forgotten but accepted as part of the immutability of life, as unquestioningly as she accepted her annual visit to her sister in Weston-super-Mare? Did she, or could she, love him? Did he, could he, love her? He didn't know. He thought he had a greater affection for her now than he had had when he was in her power and she could grant or refuse him permission to do as he wished. That might simply be a personal character trait, that he could give freely what he was unwilling to pay on demand. Or was that feeling of affection all there was; what, for a grown man and his mother, was given the name of love? He didn't know. All he knew was he had never felt so separate, so much apart. It was good to be going away. If he stayed in Southgate long he knew this idea would begin to oppress him.

"Will it be very dangerous?"

His mother's question came unexpectedly, startling him into thinking that, perhaps, beneath the rattle of trivialities her thoughts had not been very far from his. Her eyes had a misty tenderness.

"Dreadfully," he bantered. "They want me to steal a pair of Eva Braun's panties. I volunteered to do it. She's just my type."

She looked at him doubtfully, uncomfortable as always when he spoke of anything to do with sex.

"Don't worry, you silly old woman. Don't you know even now that it's much safer in the Army than here in Southgate among the bombs?"

"The bombing hasn't been bad lately. When it is I get into my little cubby-hole under the stairs. I feel safe there . . . and very comfortable."

Her absurd faith was touching.

"It'll be the same sort of job as I've been doing. If I've been all right for three years I should be O.K. for another two months."

Undressing, Maltby was in an unusually cheerful mood. Generally this was the time when past failures came to niggle him and future problems blew themselves up to gargantuan proportions in his imagination. But tonight nothing came to disturb him. The memories and disquiet stirred up by Southgate had receded into the background of his mind. They were still there but they no longer bothered him.

Not once during the evening had he thought of Pontrecy and the job he had to do there. He thought of it now and found that he could quite easily put it out of his mind. He told himself that there was nothing to be gained by bashing his brains out on it until he really got to grips with the problem at the end of the week.

More important, between him and his having to face the problem was tomorrow. And Judy.

*　　　*　　　*

At Euston that morning he had had to look at her twice before he recognized her, because he had expected her to be wearing her nurse's uniform. In a neat suit and with a scarf wound into a turban round her head, she contrived to look so radiantly elegant that he had been momentarily abashed. But she greeted him easily, squeezing his arm and holding up her face to be kissed.

In the taxi driving to the Paddington hotel where he had booked a room, she was intrigued with the large brown paper carrier bag he had brought with him.

"Provisions, my sweet, to repair our strength when it flags. And wine. Wine is for love."

"You seem very practised."

"No. Inspired," he had replied, and she had smiled and pressed his hand.

He had been ill at ease going through the formalities of signing the register. He had never been to a crumby hotel like this before. That it was the middle of the morning and Judy so beautifully turned out made it worse, too. He felt shifty, criminal. But the bedraggled old woman who took them up to a room on the second floor showed no interest in them whatever.

"What a ghastly dump you've brought me to, darling," Judy said lightly.

Because it was true, he was angry. Angry, too, with himself for being too shy to risk going to one of the richer, sleek hotels. But in their passion he had forgotten his anger, forgotten the shabby room and the seedy hotel. It had all been all right.

No day-dream he had ever had had achieved the completeness of this reality. Never before had he been able to be with a woman, hour after hour, without something entering between them to turn the pleasure sour, soil it with bitterness and reproaches. It was incredible that it should have been so simple as this. It could only be Judy who had made the day so perfect, for he had made no conscious effort to be other than himself.

She was lovely. Even tousled and with every scrap of make-up long since gone, she was lovely. Her colours were the tints of night. Her hair midnight, her eyes the sky immediately after the sun had disappeared, her silky skin moonlight and the bluish tinge within its translucency the air in the moment before dawn. He would explain to her how she was the night. Not now, for he wanted to keep the image to himself a little longer, but one day.

And at that, suddenly, as he lay with his head resting lightly against her breast, tomorrow was upon him. Pontrecy where each hour would be boxed in danger, where he would be forever looking over his shoulder for stolid, mutton-faced, grey soldiers, for the raincoats and pulled-down trilbies of the Gestapo and, worst terror of all because it was invisible, the stupidity of ordinary, decent people who could not understand the peril they could wish on others with their tongues. And this time there would be treachery as well. The knowledge that one of those at his elbow who smiled and seemed to help belonged on the other side.

He shivered slightly, and as though to catch him Judy's arms tautened about his shoulders. For the first time he realized fully what going back to Pontrecy meant. His muscles knotted, and the dull ache came again, deep in his stomach. He was afraid. But he was damned if he was going to let it beat him. Even if there was no hope for him in Pontrecy, it was not going to spoil his day.

"Judy . . . will you marry me?"

The fingers caressing his hair were still for a moment.

"Will you?"

She drew his head on to her shoulder and rubbed her cheek against his hair.

"Of course, darling."

He pulled away and looked down at her.

"Now, I mean."

Her eyes danced roguishly.

"Shouldn't I put a hat on first?"

"Next week . . . before I go overseas."

When she answered she was no longer looking at him and her voice was very soft.

"Darling, I'm yours for whatever and whenever you please . . . for ever and ever."

He caught her to him and she held him against her so hard that the muscles in her arms began to tremble.

For some time they did not speak. And then they began to talk about themselves, something they had never done before. It was as though they had passed a barrier and entered a new country quite unlike where they'd been before.

Judy told him of her home in Ireland and how strict her mother had always been with her.

"Will she approve of me, do you think?" Maltby asked.

"I shouldn't think so. She always warned me to beware of dark men, and look how black you are!"

Now she had started she babbled on without pause, telling him of the convent where she went to school, of her erratic father, whom she adored, of the farm and the people they knew, the houses she visited and the horses she rode. As she spoke Maltby felt himself growing chill. Judy the nurse, Judy the lover, he was equal to, but Judy of convents and huntin', shootin' and fishin' gave him the same feeling of insecurity and inadequacy as had shot through him when she came past the barrier at Euston looking so elegantly unfamiliar.

"It all sounds frightfully grand," he said miserably.

"It's not a bit grand really. Everyone is dreadfully poor in Ireland. But everything is higgledy-piggledy there. Being poor in Ireland is not the same as being poor in England."

"If you marry me, that's what you'll be. Poor in England."

"*When* I marry you, I shall be rich wherever I am."

"Judy, you're just a baby——"

"I'm nearly twenty-two!"

"—and I don't know what future I've got, what I'll ever have to offer you. I may only be a teacher. You ought to think what you're letting yourself in for. It's not much fun being a teacher's wife."

"If that's what you want to do, I'll be a teacher's wife and like it."

"That's just it. I don't know whether it is what I want to do."

"Then you do whatever it is you want and I'll like that, too."

"You don't know me."

She pulled him towards her and cradled him in her arms. The touch of her skin soothed and delighted him. Snuggling closer to her, he relaxed.

"You're the silliest thing, but I love you," she whispered. "I don't believe there's anything you couldn't do if you'd only let yourself try, but you're so scared of missing that you won't even aim at a target."

God, he must be as transparent as glass for her to see through him like that. Would he ever be able to hold the essence of her mystery in his hand as she held his?

"You're worrying now because you see me as a responsibility. But you've had them before and done pretty well. Some people must have thought so or they wouldn't have made you a captain. You'll spoil everything if you make me a responsibility. You see, to me, it means much more that you should need me than that I should need you. Much more."

This feeling of being shared was something he had never experienced before. He was amazed that he should ever have had the sense (for that was how he thought of it) to fall in love with anyone so wonderful, and awed that she should love him.

He wanted desperately to tell her how he felt but could find no words. Holding her face cupped in his hands he bent towards her, meaning to touch her lips so tenderly that she would guess what he was unable to say.

But at that moment the air-raid sirens wailed out, jangling his nerves so that he drew back.

"The gipsy's warning," he grinned, his teeth showing white in the dusk gathering in the room. "Better take heed!"

There was gunfire, not heavy, but two of the reports were close enough to rattle the windows of the hotel. Judy shifted uneasily.

"Ought we to do something about that?" she asked.

"You've promised to live with me forever. Do you object to dying with me?"

He said this casually, fondling her hand and lightly kissing her finger-tips.

"It's my mother. It's silly, but I shouldn't like her to know I'd been found in a hotel bedroom nude with a man she'd never heard of. It would upset her . . . and I shouldn't be there to tell her how it really was."

To her surprise, for she had not expected him to react so seriously, he nodded and suggested they should make for the nearest Tube as soon as they were ready. He was thinking as he spoke that a bomb now could kill not only him but four people in Pontrecy. And with the thought he took a foothold in tomorrow, not fearful of it but conscious and approving of its purpose. The perfect day was nearly over.

They began to collect up their clothes. To see her moving about the room with such unconcerned intimacy thrilled him so that he stood stock still watching her.

"Do you think I'm nice?"

He caught her round the waist.

"I love you," he said hoarsely. "God, how I love you!"

"For ever and ever, Harry."

There was no more gunfire and before they went they finished the last of the wine, leaving the empty bottles and the remains of the food in the brown paper carrier on the hideous marble-topped washstand. As they went out Judy turned to blow a kiss. "Dear, horrid, sordid room, I will remember you always!"

Settling the bill, Maltby found he no longer felt in the least embarrassed that the hotel people should know that he and Judy had spent the day making love. He felt fulfilled, complete, incapable of being touched by meanness or soiled by the sordid.

As they had time, they went to Euston by bus. Nearing the station, Maltby was overwhelmed with melancholy that she was leaving him and pressed her to stay the night and go back to the hospital first thing in the morning.

Judy would not hear of this. If she were to stay, she said, she would only be unhappy knowing that she would be hours late on duty in the morning. That would spoil everything. When all had been so perfect they should not risk losing their luck by pushing it. She was so earnest that he said no more.

There was almost half an hour before her train left, and they spent it in the shadows beyond the booking office among a dozen other forlorn couples kissing and clinging to each other tightly. In the end she only caught it by the skin of her teeth, scurrying along the darkened platform in a flurry of silk stockings to leap on to the already moving train.

CHAPTER FOUR

His expedition to Birmingham was nothing like the bore it had appeared to Maltby as he clawed over his bedside table to switch off the alarm clock. The thought of his journey blanketed out the joyous memories of Judy with which he had woken.

Kicking off the bed-clothes and sitting up brought him other reminders of the previous day. His head ached slightly, his eyes were sticky with rheum and he had a pain across the base of his spine. Harriet was also playing up a bit. That was not good.

By the time he had washed and shaved, however, he felt fine again except for the suspicion of an ache in the pit of his stomach. Nothing serious, but enough to make him cautious so that he refused all his mother's efforts to get him to eat what she called a "proper" breakfast. He would have nothing but milk and a couple of slices of toast.

Not knowing how much time he was going to have for writing before he left for France, Maltby wrote a long letter to Judy on the train. Never a good correspondent, there had been nothing during the previous three years to encourage him to commit his thoughts to paper. But with Judy he found an urge to write the things that he had wanted to say to her but either had been badly expressed or just had not achieved a place among all that they had talked about. He posted the letter in Birmingham before taking a taxi out to the factory.

The Birmingham people had really laid it on for him. They had found a plant almost identical with that at Evine and he spent the morning, under the direction of the engineers, practising placing charges in the most vulnerable spots. There were eight of these and his best time for laying them was eleven minutes. That meant, to give himself a comfortable margin, he ought to allow twenty minutes for the actual job.

If he could get into the factory it should be a piece of cake, he reluctantly admitted to himself. He had come to Birmingham hoping that he would find a practical snag in B.6.'s plan.

In the afternoon he studied and copied the plans of the Evine factory and annotated a set of blue-prints of the machinery. He finished in time to go to the Town Hall before his train left and ask how he applied for a special marriage licence.

The London express was very full. In the third class it was more than full, the passengers overflowing into the corridors to sit disconsolately among the kit-bags, small arms and assorted excess baggage inseparable from travel in a country at war. Maltby, arriving early, got himself a first-class seat without difficulty.

As the train pulled out of Snow Hill, Maltby looked up and saw Pig-Face standing in the corridor looking at him. He gave no sign of recognition, but with a scarcely perceptible flick of his head moved on down the corridor. Maltby got his brief-case down from the rack and followed him.

Pig-Face was waiting for him standing in the doorway of an empty first-class compartment in the next carriage. He stepped aside to let Maltby enter, and, after a quick look up and down the corridor, drew the door to and pulled down the blinds. Then he sat down opposite Maltby.

He was wearing the same patched sports jacket and grey pullover, but his bald head was covered with a flat blue-black cloth cap such as French artisans wore. It looked so utterly ridiculous that Maltby whistled derisively, "Where did you get that hat?"

"*Printemps*," said the big man, throwing the cap on to the seat beside him.

"When were you in Paris?"

"January."

The reply was unexpected. Maltby had not imagined that Tonkin ever did anything in the "field" himself.

"How did you know I'd be on this train?"

"That I did know is enough," he shrugged.

What a baby the man was with his perpetual game of Cowboys and Injuns! As this was the best evening train it was ten to one on that it would be the one he'd catch.

"But what's the idea?"

"I thought it would be pleasant to have a chat about this and that."

Maltby took a pound note out of his wallet and smoothed it out over his knee.

"What shall it be?" he asked, "this or that?"

"Eh?"

"Schopenhauer used to dine at an inn where a lot of English officers ate. Each day he would put a gold twenty-mark piece on the table in front of him. If the officers' talk did not turn on either horses or women he said he would put the coin in the poor box. I don't think he ever lost."

"I know nothing of horses."

"But women?"

"Less. Though"—the grin was sly, self-satisfied—"I've nothing to complain of."

"Huh! What about your harem?"

Tonkin looked at him coldly.

"By tomorrow all of them will be in France."

"What a bastard you are! They're only kids!"

"Yeah, what a bastard I am," Pig-Face said quietly, looking down at his fingers which he laced together and bent backwards. "There's no one too young to be expendable. That's what this war is. And there's no one so old or so maimed that they should not be cherished. That's what it's about."

Momentarily, the lift and sparkle had gone out of the big man and he slumped dejectedly in his seat. What he's done to those kids hurts him all right, thought Maltby, but I bet it never occurred to him not to do it. He envied Pig-Face his ruthlessness and fixity of purpose.

Pig-Face's "this and that" turned out to be the Evine factory, of course. He made Maltby tell him what he had learnt in Birmingham and went through the blue-prints and drawings with him. Nothing was allowed to be glossed. That was for his benefit, Maltby quickly saw, for the big man absorbed the details incredibly rapidly.

While they worked they ate. Once again, Maltby was impressed by Tonkin's staff work, for the food he took from his suitcase had obviously been chosen with Harriet in mind. There was cream cheese, rusks, lettuce, apples and a quart of milk. For someone who looked as much like a steak-and-chips man as Pig-Face it was an unlikely menu, but he dug into it with every appearance of relish.

"Hm, you've done a good job, boy," the big man said at last as Maltby folded the plans away. "It all depends now on your being able to get inside the works. Any ideas on that?"

"Several. It shouldn't be too hard. There aren't many troops guarding it and they're a poor lot, mostly old men. I've been inside once, not in the factory itself but in the yard."

"You didn't tell me that?" The question came sharp as a whip-crack.

"You didn't ask me."

"What were you doing there?"

"Having a look-see. I thought once the factory would make a good target."

Tonkin looked at him quizzically, puzzled. He couldn't sort this one out at all. The boy's work so far could hardly have been better. Any of his other "moonbeams" would have been alight with excitement at the prospect of going on a job that had been teed up so beautifully. Yet, far from being excited, this bloke was shy of it. It didn't make sense, didn't add up. He didn't like things that didn't add up.

"What's scaring you?" he snapped. "What don't you like about this job?"

"Oh, Major Tonkin, I never knew you cared!"

But Tonkin was not to be drawn by fooling. His eyes remained cold and hard as glass and sharp as needles.

"You blokes sitting on your backsides in England," said Maltby savagely, "think we go pansying about like pantomime fairies planting explosives here and there while merry peasants applaud us happily. Do we, hell! If that factory is blasted the Germans will lose some of their ball-bearings, but do you know what else it will mean? Do you?"

Tonkin frowned but said nothing, and Maltby went on speaking more quietly.

"Gibault's at Evine is where everyone in Pontrecy and four other villages works. Three thousand men and women. Maybe you haven't thought what will happen to those people if that factory is wrecked? Or what the Germans will do?"

Relaxed now, Tonkin was lying back in his seat. In the long silence that followed, the rhythmic drum of the wheels on the metal road filled the compartment. Now he had begun to talk, Maltby took no notice of Tonkin but gazed moodily at the floor between his feet.

"They'll take hostages and shoot them. Maybe twenty, thirty, fifty or even a hundred picked at random. Then all the able-bodied will be packed off to labour camps in Germany. The rest will be left to starve. Quite a price, isn't it, the ruin of two thousand families unlucky enough to be caught on the sidelines, for a few ball-bearings!"

"Nobody's on the sidelines."

"An easy get-out. A Buchan view. He said that of the Airvout hostages."

"What's this about Airvout?"

Maltby told him of the Feldgendarme he'd killed and the reprisals the Germans took on the village.

"Buchan shrugs that sort of thing off. To him there's just the British and wogs. The French are wogs, just tolerable if they're bomb throwing alongside us. Otherwise not worth a thought. He didn't actually say that it served those poor devils in Airvout right for not co-operating more fully with us but he dam' well thought it!"

"People just as innocent get killed here in air-raids, you know."

"Sure. But we don't light signal fires in the middle of Coventry to guide the bloody bombers!"

"It's not our fault if the Germans behave like heathens."

Maltby dragged on his fingers till they cracked.

"No . . . no . . . but knowing how they will behave . . . shouldn't that alter what we do? If we don't, doesn't that mean that we become—actively—part of the total barbarism?"

"That's too clever for me."

"If you put arsenic in the baby's bottle knowing its mother will put it in the baby's mouth, is the baby poisoned by the arsenic, you or its mother?"

"Ingenious," Pig-Face said alarmingly. "Only it's difficult for me to think of the Nazis as loving mothers!"

Carefully he gathered up the rubbish from their meal and stowed it conspicuously in a corner where a cleaner would be sure

to see it. In ten minutes they would be running into Paddington.

"I'm glad that we had this talk, Maltby," he said seriously. "As
our operations get bigger the sort of considerations you raise will
have to be taken more and more into account. Do you want me,"
he added casually, "to have you taken off this job?"

Pushed up against this decision, Maltby struggled with it while
the big man watched him, careful not to betray his concern for
its outcome.

"No," he said at last, "I'll do it, if I can. If I don't, you'll send
somebody else, so it doesn't make any odds, does it? It's the whole
damn thing that's wrong and that's not my decision. You just
can't see anything but bloody ball-bearings. Bloody military," he
exploded disgustedly.

The boy's all right, thought Tonkin. He'll cling to that chip
on his shoulder but push on however big it grows. Until it kills
him or someone knocks it off.

"That's how it is, boy. There's a lot of dirt to be eaten. Sometimes more than we think we can swallow. But we do."

Maltby guessed he was not thinking of him and the factory at
Evine but of the girls he'd dropped into France.

"If some of the parts are rotten, the whole's all right," he went
on. "You got to hang on to that or go crazy."

"Is that your private fear—that you'll let go?" Maltby asked
curiously, for the big man had spoken earnestly.

For a moment Tonkin thought of telling him the truth. Of the
screams that came between him and sleep or woke him, sweating,
in the small hours. Screams coming from someone—they were
never identified with anyone in particular, nor was he sure
whether it was a man or a woman—having their finger-nails
pulled out and their teeth broken by the Gestapo. The horror for
him was that he knew they were in the torture chamber because
of him, because his staff work had failed them.

Maltby, he guessed, would be astonished to find that lack of
self-confidence was his Achilles heel but would understand his
terror. It might even help the boy to know that even the unlike-
liest people suffered as he did. Also to tell someone would be a
relief, might even help him to get to sleep quicker when he went
to bed, for he was feeling very low after the strain of appearing gay
and light-hearted while saying goodbye to the girls.

But he hung back from putting into words something so

private, a secret that he strove to bury deeper and deeper in his innermost being. Not even to help Maltby, not even to help himself, could he break down his protective reticence. Rationalizing his reserve, he told himself it was poor tactics in a commander to expose his weaknesses to subordinates. He knew, too, that he could not have borne it if the boy were to betray the slightest suspicion that he thought he was being sold a line.

"Fear's a big word for someone like me," he said lightly. "It's you blokes in the field that have to face up to it, not us at home. What particularly gives you the willies?"

"That I'll wake up in the morning and find I'm alive."

For the big man that added up. By God, it added up, analysing the kernel of the chip precisely, perfectly.

But Maltby was thinking that it wasn't true any more. Not since yesterday.

CHAPTER FIVE

THE next two days were the most gruelling Maltby had ever known. Tonkin gave him the full treatment, squeezing him dry and then putting him through the mincer. Or that was what it felt like.

The big man's drive, concentration and powers of endurance awed him. He seemed to have inexhaustible reservoirs of energy to call on. And apparently he needed no rest, for when Maltby, utterly worn out, staggered home to bed at 11 o'clock on Friday night, B.6. went off to some benighted place halfway to Bristol to give final instructions to one of his men who was going to be dropped the following night. Yet he was waiting for Maltby when he arrived at 9 o'clock the next day, sitting at his desk and looking as though he had been absorbed in work for at least an hour. What breaks they had for food, or simply to get the cramp out of their limbs by walking about the room in Fairholt Street, were chosen by Tonkin when he judged that they had become absolutely necessary for Maltby if he were to get anything further out of him.

At first it had been fascinating. Tonkin led him into a world in which everything could be exactly as it seemed or equally its opposite or something quite different. He had had a glimpse of this when B.6. had told him there was a Gestapo man in the

Pontrecy group. Now he was shown it as a place where there was no sure foothold but uncertainty, where all virtue was suspect and most of all loyalty, friendship and trust, where truth had no more shape than water.

For the next six weeks this was to be his world. B.6. in the two days that he had did what he could to equip him for it.

Together they dissected the dossiers of each of his fellow agents. The first one Tonkin pushed across his desk was Buchan's.

Maltby found it scarcely worth studying, for he either knew or had guessed what it contained. Origins Scottish but the family had been settled in England for over a century, a good but not a top public school, a prosperous career stock-broking, commission in the county yeomanry—he would call it that, thought Maltby—hobbies, hunting and soldiering. He had apparently handled a rearguard action on the retreat to Dunkirk rather well and immediately after the evacuation volunteered for special service in France. There was a glowing report from Security on his fitness for this role. And they should know, Maltby commented cynically. The one thing that surprised him was to learn that he was only thirty-six. He would have put him ten years older.

"Sterling type," Maltby said, wrinkling his nose in distaste. "Nothing sinister there. Does that mean we wash him out of the list of suspects?"

"It's not the whole story, boy. We've dug a bit more since then. He belonged to the Friends of Franco. He even went to Burgos to see if he could join in the fighting. As far as we can judge, he got a flea in his ear from El Caudillo, who naturally didn't want an Englishman poking around while his German and Italian pals were performing."

"Fascist lover, eh? I'm not surprised. But if Franco brushed him off——"

"He's also a Catholic convert."

"What the hell's that got to do with it? Or are we fighting the Catholics now?"

"It might mean nothing, of course. But you could look at it this way." Tonkin held out his hand and ticked the points off one by one of his fingers. "He becomes a Catholic. Then he tries to join Franco because Franco is fighting Communism, which he sees as the greatest enemy of his Church. Then the Russians come into the war on our side. It's the Germans who are fighting Communism now while we are aiding it. So he switches to their

side. It could be, you know. Have you thought of something?"
Maltby had.

He remembered how Larisse, who commanded the Communist
Francs Tireurs group in the adjoining Dinville district, had come
to see him in a furious passion, accusing the English in the
Pontrecy group of having murdered two of his men. They had
both been killed in the same way, their Adam's apples smashed
with a single blow. Larisse said he knew that this was a favourite
trick of the British. Maltby swore that he was out of his mind,
that it could not have been any of his bunch, but Larisse was
anything but convinced and he departed threatening that if he
lost any more men that way, he'd take reprisals on the Pontrecy
group. As he didn't hear from Larisse again, he presumed there
were no more commando attacks on his men. Buchan, he remembered, was in each case the agent nearest the spot where the men
were killed. And like the rest of the group he was told of the
reprisal threat.

"Hm," said Tonkin. "I don't think we'll cross him off the list
yet."

The next one was Harrison. Was it accident, Maltby wondered,
or the indestructible mystique of the pre-eminence of all things
British that the Englishmen were given precedence even in investigation? Harrison's class background was the same as Buchan's,
but after leaving school he had gone into the Army, serving first
with a crack ceremonial regiment and then in 1930 transferring
to a nondescript infantry unit. Retiring six years later, he took up
a directorship with a wine importer's. Hobbies, bird watching and
lepidoptera. He, too, had been through Dunkirk. Security, while
approving, were less eulogistic than they had been over Buchan.
Thinking of the man as he knew him, seeing him standing, his
tall, lean, almost stringy body absolutely motionless, his long
head with its beautifully modelled but strangely unexpressive
features thrust forward on his graceful neck, watching birds
take their evening drink at a pool, Maltby could not understand
why. He was three years older than Buchan.

"Looks kosher, doesn't he?" said Tonkin.

"Isn't he?"

The big man rolled his shoulders irritably.

"None of the bastards are. With Harrison it's not much. He
was in Germany in 1938 and again in August 1939. Nothing
underhand about it. He was over there on business. Buying wine."

B.6. looked hard at Maltby. "It happens that Ribbentrop was also in the wine business. It also happens that one of his visits coincided with the Nazis' Nuremberg Rally. Straws like that are what we have to build on in this business. Not that they make much of a brick here." He drummed on the desk with his short stubby fingers. "You know what bothers me most? Why did he transfer to that crumby crowd of foot sloggers?"

"Maybe because they were cheaper and he couldn't afford the Guards any longer."

"Could be, but eight years seems a hell of a long time to find that out. All the officers who would have known the reason are either dead or in P.O.W. camps, so we're stymied."

"Is it important? If he were a spy, would he have left the Army?"

"Everything we don't know, that doesn't add up, is important. But it's a point. It's more likely he turned Nazi after he became a wine merchant."

"On the list but not very high up, then?"

Tonkin frowned.

"We don't know enough yet to judge priorities," he snapped, "so don't try it. Think of them all as lining up on level terms."

He tossed another folder across the desk. It was Hélène's and much thinner than the other two.

Hélène Dunois, schoolteacher, recruited at Suresnes for work with the British Secret Service. Served as courier in the Paris area until the Gestapo rounded up her circuit. It was then considered too hot for her to remain in Paris so she was transferred to do the same work at Pontrecy. Maltby smiled at seeing she was thirty-three. In April she had given them a little party on her birthday. "Twenty-five!" she had said, "isn't it old!"

"On that, we recommend her for the *Croix de Guerre*."

"Now let's see how she measures up for an Iron Cross . . . with Oak Leaves," Pig-Face retorted sourly.

First of all, the source of her recruitment was tainted. The old clergyman who had acted as their recruiting officer was known to the Gestapo. Exactly when the Nazis had got on to him Intelligence was not sure. The Germans did not arrest him at once but used him to infiltrate their agents into the British network.

"Of course, even after he was known he must have signed on some genuine agents," Tonkin said, "so that is not conclusive even if we knew for certain that the Gestapo were alive to him at the time he recommended Hélène to us. But it's enough to make us nervous."

Then it was strange that when her circuit was wiped out, she was the only one that got away. Was it luck, mismanagement or design that caused them to miss her?

"But," Maltby objected, "Hélène arrived in January. Things didn't start going wrong as far as I can remember until March."

Tonkin had a counter for that. Hélène would have been given a couple of months to ferret out all the group's contacts so that when they swooped the Gestapo could be sure of making a complete haul of all the Resistance centres in the area. But by that time they would have known that the fusion of all the anti-Nazi factions was imminent. They would have guessed, too, that for the British to have concentrated so many agents in Pontrecy could only mean that the group was to be assigned an important role in the combined forces throughout the whole North Western area. So they held their hand but protected themselves from the group's activities by "fortuitous" accidents.

"It adds up that way." He grinned maliciously. "I wonder if you'll ever know how near you were to being in Buchenwald instead of here!"

Maltby was troubled.

"It's all balls, you know," he said surlily. "You just take the facts and squint at them from right to left instead of normally from left to right and then say 'Ha, ha, see, they're different!' But the only different thing could be the way you were looking at them."

Tonkin nodded.

"That's right. And both ways may be wrong, don't forget that, and the proper way of seeing them turn out to be from below or above or even askew. If you've grasped that we're getting on!"

They took Lestocq next. He had been a cook in Saarbruecken but had come to England after the Saar had been incorporated into the Reich because he did not like the Nazis (so he said). In 1939 he had opened a café in Hampstead Road. After it had been bombed two years later, he joined the Army, being used first as an interpreter and then transferred at his own request to Special Duties. Security had given him a clean bill, but the interrogator's report lacked enthusiasm. He was thirty-nine.

"It says nothing about his hobbies," said Maltby. "I could guess at a few. Peeping through the key-holes of ladies' lavatories would be among them."

"Unpleasant?"

"A sewer rat. A *graffito,* a scribbler on walls. Talks about sex incessantly in the nastiest way. The sort that ends up in court for assaulting five-year-old girls."

"My! Quite a pal of yours! What's he like as a 'moonbeam'?"

Maltby considered this. He could not think of anything to hang on him.

"All right," he said reluctantly.

"So?"

"So blow him up. I suppose you can?"

Tonkin obliged. It was all very fine for Lestocq to say he had emigrated from the Saar because he didn't like the Nazis, it could equally well be that they'd planted him in England to work for them. It was curious that, pretending to be so patriotic, he had failed to report to his unit in France when it was mobilized at the outbreak of war. On the other hand it had to be remembered that he had only just opened his café and with Frenchmen loyalty to *la patrie* rather tended to take second place to one's private business interests. There was one thing about himself which he had not revealed but which had since been discovered and might be significant. From the time he came to England until he started in business for himself, Lestocq had been employed as a cook at Heinrich's Restaurant in Percy Street.

"You mean that place that was always full of Mosley's fascists and Nazis from the German Embassy?"

"Yup."

"Then that's it, isn't it?" said Maltby excitedly, "he's our man!"

Tonkin laughed.

"Have you forgotten the others? Look at it this way. Suppose Lestocq did clear out of the Saar because he hated the Nazis. Suppose, too, that the only introduction he could get was to the chef at Heinrich's—as it happens, he was also a Saarlander. He goes there until he has saved enough to open his hole-in-the-wall in Hampstead Road. Just as he does so, along comes the war. He decides the war can get along without him but his café can't. So he stays where he is until he's blasted out by those damnable Huns. He'll have their guts for that, he will! So he volunteers for Special Duties. Reckoning that if he says anything about Heinrich's we'll think—just as you're thinking now!—that he's probably a spy, he forgets to mention it. That adds up, too."

Maltby had to admit that it did, though he would have liked to hack Pig-Face on the shins for looking so smug about it.

With Gringoire Maltby needed no help from B.6. to spot his eligibility to the role of suspects. It would have been transparently obvious to a child of ten. Gringoire, real name Armand Rules (this was news to Maltby, for at Pontrecy, Gringoire was the only one of the group who adhered strictly to the rule that only code and cover names were to be used when in the field), railwayman from Alsace (the dossier was so incomplete that it did not record either his place of birth or where he had worked). In the phoney war period he had turned up at an advanced Intelligence HQ with the suggestion that as he spoke German he might do a bit of free-lance spying. He offered his services to the British rather than the French because he thought the British would be likely to pay better than his countrymen. Apparently Intelligence had been disarmed by this honest cupidity, for with hardly any questions asked he had been despatched into Germany via Belgium. He came back with some useful but not vital information which caused great joy to his sponsors. (The sort of stuff he had brought back, Tonkin observed, was what any power would be willing to give away to get an agent in well with another's Secret Service. Equally, it was about as complete as a simple railwayman without special training could be expected to collect.) Before he could be employed on further missions, the Germans were through the Low Countries and into France. Gringoire claimed that he had then gone to Spain—which Tonkin pointed out might be true, since after his bit of spying he was not likely to seek German company—later returning to carry out sabotage. He had linked up with a British group and had taken part with them in a number of raids on marshalling yards round Clermont-Ferrand. From there he had been transferred to Pontrecy. He was forty-three.

"Hm," said Maltby. "Not to say, Hm and Hm."

"Yes, but there's this to be said in his favour. So far as we know, none of the groups he was with suffered mass arrests while he was with them. The Clermont-Ferrand group did lose twenty-three of their men, though, less than a month after he had left it."

"You know, he could be a German," said Maltby thoughtfully. "If he were, it would be natural for him to claim to be an Alsatian to explain the thickness of his accent—although as a matter of fact he has very little and uses a lot of *cheminot* argot. How the hell," he grumbled angrily, "did you people come to wish on us such an uncertain character?"

"It's easy to look back. But things are moving so fast now that risks have to be taken. We have to work with what we've got. If we stopped to screen everybody from the cradle, the war would be over before we'd got a single 'moonbeam' in the field. Not even you."

"Me?"

"Yes, you. Do you think you wouldn't have a place on the starting line if you hadn't been in England when some of those 'accidents' occurred? Like hell!" The big man thrust his head forward pugnaciously. "Remember Huggins?"

"Huggins?" said Maltby blankly.

"Yes, Huggins. You worked alongside him for nearly a year. He was science master at——"

It came back to Maltby in a rush. The little red-faced, arrogant man whose black hair was so coarse that it stood out from his head like wires, who was always arguing angrily the most utter tosh in the common room.

"I remember," he interrupted. "A complete nut."

"M.I.5. don't think so. His real name's Huegenberg and he's on the Isle of Man, detained under 18b. One of Mosley's backroom boys, and, according to M.I.5., one of the principals, perhaps even the top man, in Hitler's pre-war network in this country."

"Cripes! Of course, all the cock he used to spout about Blood and Soil, race purity and superiority was Nazism!" Maltby grinned ruefully. "Do you know, I thought it was just that he had swallowed too much D. H. Lawrence for his poor scientific brain and got it all mixed up with Rosicrucianism or some such tripe. So you think he recruited me to work for the glory of the Fourth Reich?"

Tonkin was beaming delightedly.

"Could be. Temperamentally you'd have been the type I would have picked as likely to be receptive."

"Thanks!"

"Still, significant though this contamination undoubtedly is," he added with mock solemnity, "we'd have to weigh against it your record in the field, which hasn't been too bad."

"But the fellow was a complete nitwit!"

"I expect, like us, Adolf has to work with what he's got. Unless," he added slyly, "M.I.5. have got him all wrong and he's not Huegenberg at all but I am."

"Now *that* I could believe," said Maltby, getting up and stretching, for Harriet was beginning to prod him. "All this makes me feel as though I were standing in the middle of *Concorde* without my pants."

"Draughty about the middle?"

"And how! It's going to make me look more carefully under my bed in future."

"About time," Pig-Face said nastily.

Leaning against the mantel-shelf Maltby fished in his pocket for his cigarettes. The packet was empty and he slung it in the fireplace. Tonkin picked up his intercom. and asked a messenger to go out and buy some.

"You smoke too much," said the big man, gathering up the dossiers, "Harriet will bite you."

The bloody man was infuriating. He was right, of course. Well, he'd given it up in hospital, he could give it up again when he got back to Pontrecy. He'd have to or he wouldn't stay the course.

"Those dossiers are incomplete," he said, trying to get some of his own back. "They don't give code names, cover names or any details of operations in which they had a hand."

In the look Tonkin flashed at him, amusement was blended with approval.

"So you spotted that? We have them, but it would have been a waste of time to show them to you because you know all that stuff first-hand."

Maddening he might be, but you couldn't help admiring his comprehensive passion for detail. Fancy the blighter going through those files rooting out whatever he considered irrelevant!

An hour later Maltby was finding no pleasure in B.6.'s besetting passion, for he was being borne down by its weight. The big man had produced copies of all the reports Pinto had radioed back and a set of charts.

These charts were on sheets a little larger than foolscap ruled into six vertical columns. The first column was headed "Operation", the other five each bore the name of one of the Pontrecy agents. Under "Operations" was listed the data of the group's actions taken from Pinto's messages. There was a set of charts for the ones that had succeeded and another for those which had been frustrated.

The idea was, Tonkin explained, to try to find a common factor. He proposed that they should examine each action and set down how it was conceived, who was involved in it, who knew about it and when.

"We'll be looking for a pattern. Suppose we found that all the frustrated attacks had been suggested by one of them. That would be significant. So it would be if one of the team had never taken part in any of these actions. The time when each of them knew of a projected attack is also most important. Some may have been successful because the stooge did not know of it early enough to warn the Nazis."

It was too much to hope that they would uncover so concrete a pattern as that, but it was just possible that there would be enough of it to give a positive pointer. With any luck it should enable them to eliminate some of the suspects.

Maltby was intrigued and went at the charts enthusiastically. Soon, however, he was discouraged by the sheer drudgery of the work. Tonkin plagued him, insisting on absolute precision, forcing him to go over in memory every detail of the group's preparation for action, questioning each statement and demanding corroborative evidence for it.

There was one thing which quickly convinced Maltby that they were not likely to get much joy from their efforts. The group's normal method of work was for them to evolve their plans in joint discussions. They met together at least once a week and usually more often.

"Not all of you?" Tonkin queried, aghast.

"Yes."

"I never heard anything so crazy! What did you think you were running, a Band of Hope or something? If the Milice had stumbled across you accidentally—Bingo! We'd have lost the whole shooting match!"

It was quite true. What's more, he had always been aware of the hazard. But there were plenty of "safe" houses and they were careful to choose only those where there were no signs of Gestapo or Milice activity.

Besides, those meetings were valuable. They enabled the group to work out things in an hour which would have taken a week if contact had had to be made with each member individually. It also saved Hélène a lot of running about, ensuring that she would be on hand if she were to be wanted in an emergency. (Only in an emergency? his sub-conscious shot at him obliquely.) The disadvantage of those meetings to them now was that all the group knew about what was being planned at the same time.

Tonkin, though clearly dashed by what he had learned, insisted they continue. They had chosen the shorter list, that covering the group's successful sabotage attacks from the middle of February to the middle of July when Maltby had been brought home, to begin on. When they had completed them, they saw that they did not show a vestige of a pattern.

The results were not without interest, though. Gringoire had been on every one. Lestocq had missed three but had known all about them. Hélène had definitely not known about two and possibly a third. Buchan had not been used on two and had almost certainly not known that one of them was taking place. Harrison had the same score as Buchan, but the two actions he had been absent from were different.

It wasn't much to show for six hours' work. Nevertheless, Tonkin made Maltby memorize the results. You never knew, he said, something might come up when he got back to Pontrecy which would give them a meaning.

Maltby wanted to go home then, but Pig-Face kept him at it for another four hours. By then his eyes were red and sore and he was almost asleep on his feet.

"Not bad," Tonkin said, putting all the charts together tidily, "we'll be able to finish them tomorrow."

Maltby groaned.

"What's the use?"

"Probably none." The big man was quite cheerful, almost chirpy. "You have to pan a lot of grit to find a grain of gold. Some never find any. But if they're good they go on panning."

"If they're bonkers, you mean!"

"Get some sleep. You'll feel better about it in the morning."

Maltby was feeling better when he arrived the next morning. But it had nothing to do with the charts and was only partially due to sleep. Judy had written to him, a breathless little note, apparently dashed off in her lunch hour so that it would catch the afternoon post.

Darling, darling, darling,

Your wonderful letter makes me all ashamed because I don't know how to answer it. I never write letters—except to daddy

and mummy and they don't count because I don't want to say
to you what I say to them. I love you, darling. I long to see you
again. Come and fetch me soon. Of course I know you can't
write every day but if not for many days please phone me.
Hancock 23 is the hostel's number. Only not after 11 o'clock
because then it rings in the Warden's room and she gets shirty.
What a horrid letter this is. I don't want to write about all the
silly things I do here every day (they just don't matter to me
any more) and I'm sure you wouldn't want to read about
them. And really I can't find words like you can to put down
what I feel. Something else you'll have to teach me, darling.
All I want is to write I love you over and over again. I do,
too.

    All my love from toe to tip.

                                                  Judy

P.S. Come quick, quick, quick.

It was like having her with him, in his hand, as it were, the letter
was so like her. So like one side of her at any rate. Even during
their perfect day he had been aware of sides other than this yielding self, of a tough, resolute self-confidence that did not despise
his own instability of purpose but buckled and strengthened it as
tenderly and with the same determination as she dealt with her
patients at the Wilberforce. But she had put none of that side of
herself in the letter. He felt that it had made his day.

"Now let's get on with these," said Tonkin, laying out the charts
on the desk.

They worked right through the day and well into the evening
before the charts were complete and they could set about corre-
lating the data. There was even less profit to be found from this
longer list of frustrated actions than from the first.

Gringoire had missed five actions but knew all about them. So
far as Maltby could remember, Hélène, either through her work
as a courier or from being present at a meeting when an action
was under discussion, probably knew of all of them, but he could
not be absolutely certain about three incidents. Buchan had not
been on one and might not have known anything about it. Maltby
thought he hadn't. Harrison had not gone on two forays but had
certainly known all about one of these. Lestocq had not been with
them on three occasions, certainly knew about two of them and
very probably of the other as well.

That got them exactly nowhere. Most disappointing was that the time when group members learnt about an action gave no help at all. Because of the group's way of working it was rare for any-one to have less than twenty-four hours' notice of what was planned.

"You know this is all hooey, anyway," said Maltby, who was tired and irritable from Pig-Face's bull-dozing. "It's only what I knew, even if I've remembered it right. I might think one of them did not know of a job but one of the others may have told him. There was no reason why he shouldn't if they met casually. We never treated these things as secret amongst ourselves. Why should we?"

Tonkin nodded.

"True," he said. "And we ought not to forget that some of these 'accidents' could actually have been accidents. It can't be ruled out anyway. And then some of the successful incidents may have come off because of a failure in the line of contact between the stooge and the Gestapo. Because of all the unknowns, we need at least three pointers in one direction to give us a scent. Four to be reasonably certain that it's the right one."

"We haven't got anything like that," said Maltby looking at his list.

"No. A pity, because I'd hoped we'd at least be able to eliminate one so that you'd have someone you could rely on out there. But you'll have to do it on your jack."

That was the limit of the big man's regrets for the empty results of their two days' grind at the charts. He now simply pushed them to one side and began to discuss how Maltby should go at testing the agents one by one.

The best way would be to take each on a job that none of the others knew about, Maltby said, briefing them at least a day before, so that they would have plenty of time to tip off the Boche if they wanted to. If everything went all right, that one could be reckoned in the clear.

Tonkin was not happy with this. A single test of that kind could easily—too easily—give the wrong result. Not being able to think of anything better that Maltby could carry out in the time he would have to do the job, he said nothing of his misgivings. If he were able to dream something up when he was feeling less tired, he'd put it up to the boy before he was parachuted. He did warn him, however, that these test actions should not be relied on

entirely but that Maltby should strive to corroborate their
evidence by careful questioning and being watchful for details
that previously he would not have considered to be of the least
importance.

The ball-bearing factory, if he got round to that, had to be
wrecked on his last day in Pontrecy.

"It just cannot be done at any other time," Tonkin explained.
"Because you'll have to use the whole gang on the job, it can't be
done until you've uncovered the traitor. Also the lot of you must
be out of Pontrecy in a matter of hours after you have dealt with
him, otherwise the Gestapo will pick up all of you as soon as they
know that we've swatted their man. If you get on to whoever it
is quickly you'll just have to leave him alone until you're ready
to go."

"Yes, I see that."

"We plan to have you back here that night. It may be some
days, even a week or so, before we can get all the others out. But
you will lay on their escape routes. These will be given to you
before you leave but they are not"—the pale blue eyes were very
cold—"repeat, *not*, to be passed on until the very last moment. Is
that clear?"

"Of course. But what about the new boys? How shall we hand
over to them?"

"You won't. As we see it, the Pontrecy group is finished. There's
nothing we can salvage from it safely. We don't know whether it
has a single contact or 'safe' house that the Gestapo does not know
about. The odds are that there are none. So the only thing is to
let them all go."

Of course that was true. Maltby was appalled.

"Can't they be warned?"

Tonkin frowned.

"How can they, boy?" he said gently. "You won't have time
to do it when you're ready to leave. And you can't do it before in
case one of them blabs."

"Not even old Gallot?" Maltby pleaded. "He's been so damn
good to me, I'd hate to leave him in the lurch."

The big man pondered this. If he said "yes" it would mean a
loose end that could become a whole bagful of loose ends. In his
book it was better to have clean-cut, irrevocable orders that left
no leeway for individual interpretation. But if he were to seem
to want to stick to the letter callously for the sake of doing so, he

was not sure how Maltby would take it. Probably he would revolt and take a delight in acting contrarily.

"Look, there's no reason why anyone who can be saved should be thrown to the wolves," he said very slowly. "If you can warn the Gallots without any risk, I don't see why you shouldn't."

"Thanks," said Maltby, surprised, thinking you could never tell with these chair-borne oafs, sometimes they were almost human. He remembered then that Pig-Face was not always chair-borne but had bought the ghastly cap he now put on in Paris.

They left the office and got into a staff car that was waiting for them. For five minutes they drove in silence. Maltby, who was limp with weariness, settled himself back and let his eyes close. Tonkin's mind, however, was still on what Maltby had said.

"How many of those contacts' names and addresses can you remember?" he asked suddenly, causing Maltby to jerk himself upright. "To write down, I mean."

"I don't know. I knew all of them, of course, but there must be between fifty and a hundred of them. I could easily forget one or two. Why?"

"Make a list of those you can remember."

The bloody man was bumf crazy!

"Whatever for?"

"So that you can take a copy with you to give to your reception party. When the time comes we'll tell them to send couriers into the Pontrecy district to warn everyone on the list." He chuckled, for although he could not see Maltby's expression in the darkness he knew he must be staring at him with the supercilious contempt that overcame him too often and too easily. In the saboteur's world anyone who wrote down lists of contacts and carried them about with him was too dangerous to leave alive. "Don't you see," he went on, "it doesn't matter a curse if the Gestapo get the list? They know everybody on it already. There's no risk and it may allow some of them to get away."

Maltby thumped him on the knee delightedly.

"Now, why didn't I think of that?"

Tonkin felt rather pleased with himself. He reckoned he was collaring this narky soldier boy. Chip on the shoulder and all. It was true, too, that he hadn't given enough thought to these contacts. Though French, they had worked with the British group, and so, to a certain extent, he had a responsibility for them. It wasn't good enough to shrug them off as expendable, even though everyone was in the end. Would any of his other "moonbeams" have been as concerned for them as Maltby? He doubted it. None of them had ever lived for three years in one place for one thing. Nor were any of them such awkward war-hating cusses. It only showed you could learn something from the most unlikely tykes.

CHAPTER SIX

DERISIVELY, Maltby named his agent's course, "Bomb Throwing for Ulcerated Officers in Six Easy Lessons, or, How to Suspect Your Friends and Not Influence Your Enemies".

It was crammed and comprehensive, though much of the regular training "moonbeams" underwent was omitted.

For instance, as he already had genuine identity and ration cards wangled for him by the Pontrecy Prefect of Police three years before in the name of Gaston Minaud, farm labourer, he had no need of a "cover" story and forged papers. This gain was partially offset by his having to spend a gruelling day with two quietly efficient Special Branch officers learning the principles of counter-espionage.

HQ decided that, while he could go on using his code name of "Oignon" with the group, he must have another for his special mission. He plumped for "Punch", certain that no one would guess the sentiment prompting his choice.

A lanky, donnish type with buck teeth and an ink-stained battle-dress, named Chivers, briefed him. His base was to be Larisse's Maquis at Dinville. This group and that led by Paturin to the north of Pontrecy were the best in the area. Both were Communist. Larisse had been preferred to Paturin because there were more east-west roads than north-south.

"Larisse is making us pay a hell of a price for playing ball our way," Chivers told him. "Two hundred thousand francs and eight containers of weapons and explosives to be dropped with you."

To Maltby, it seemed a lot to fork out for four "blown" agents.

It was not until 8 o'clock on Monday night that he was free and he could put a call through to Judy. To Maltby, the lover, it was a profoundly unsatisfactory contact. Judy was tired and inclined to be peevish because he hadn't phoned before. Maltby, holding in his mind the image of the gay, bewitching Judy of their last meeting, was disconcerted and retorted angrily that he had not had the time and she damn well ought to know that was why.

They did not actually quarrel but it came close to it. Gradually as they talked the warmth came back to them but neither became completely relaxed before they hung up. Even when he told her of the plans he had made for them to be married, he thought he detected a lack of enthusiasm in her agreement. When he threw this at her, however, she denied it.

"Darling," she said desperately just before the pips went for the fourth time, "I don't know what's the matter with me. I've been so looking forward to having you phone and now it's all gone wrong."

"One of those things." His voice was stiff and awkward.

"I do love you so."

He wanted to say something bright and lively, something that would sail them out of the heavy weather they were making, something that would enable them to go on talking in their old, flippant, inconsequential way. But he could think of nothing. He was too far down.

"I love you, too."

And that was all. They were both relieved when their silence was broken by the pips and they could hang up.

Travelling home to Southgate he let his disappointment turn to anger against Judy, blaming her for spoiling their talk. After a while, however, he softened towards her, telling himself that it was nearly a week since he had seen her and naturally she would be sore that he had not spared a moment to talk to her. She couldn't know that it had been impossible and was justified in thinking he was treating her lightly.

He considered ringing her again but decided against it for fear the inhibiting mood would persist and make things worse between them. If he left it to the following night they would have had time to forget about the debacle.

And that was how it worked out. Judy was bubbling over when he rang and properly contemptuous of the way they had behaved the night before. Like a couple of mean old misers squabbling over twopence, she said, and gave an imitation of the grumpy way he'd flown at her. Maltby laughed and told her that she deserved a spanking because she had gone for him like a shrew. He would not be hen-pecked.

"I don't peck," she said aggrieved, "I bite. I'd like to now, every bit of you!"

Nevertheless there was a nettle or two among the roses.

"Must we go to some old registry office?" she asked suddenly. "Couldn't we be married in church?"

"Where would you like? St. Margaret's with twelve bridesmaids and six pages to hold your train and a guard of honour from the Intelligence Corps making an arch for us with crossed dossiers when we leave?"

"Seriously, Harry."

"Darling, I've not given it a thought," he said, shaken. "We've less than a week left till Tuesday. I don't know how long it would take to fix."

"It doesn't matter." But her voice was wan although in a moment or two she was chattering gaily enough.

Still disturbed by what she had said, Maltby returned to it five minutes later.

"Judy, I ought to have asked you about the wedding before I made any arrangements."

"But you couldn't, darling, could you?"

"You're not upset?"

"Of course not. I would have been though if you hadn't done anything about it at all. What does it matter where we get married?" she added. "It's getting married that counts, isn't it?"

"As the bishop said to the actress."

In all their phone talks during the remaining days he was in London the wedding loomed large. Maltby had worked it out that he would be back and free to spend Monday night with her. Judy would have to catch an afternoon train after the ceremony as she was due to go on night duty at the Wilberforce. Maltby was relieved that she would be going before him. He disliked good-byes and it would have only added to their pain if they had dragged out their leave-taking until he had set off for the aerodrome in the evening.

They also decided that they would invite no one at all to the wedding. For Judy's mother to have come over from Ireland would have been difficult and for her to come just to stand for five minutes or so in a bare room in St. Pancras Town Hall seemed pointless. As Judy would not have a relative with her, he decided not to ask his mother, although Judy wanted him to, preferring for no reason that he could name to have no one present that they knew. In any case, Judy had no friends in London and Maltby in the three years that he'd been in France had lost touch with his.

After sessions with a stomach boffin learning how to take care of Harriet with all the medicines, dehydrated eggs and milk he was to take with him, he went off to assault and explosive schools.

This was a trying time for Maltby, for now he came into direct contact with regular saboteur instructors. He hated their upper-class voices and their Public School jargon made his hackles rise. It consoled him that by the end of the courses he had made them return his dislike. With interest.

His contempt for the atmosphere of hysterical *esprit de corps* which surrounded the schools did not prevent him from absorbing what they had to teach. He acquired proficiency in half a dozen ways of committing murder quietly and quickly, mastered the techniques of the new sabotage weapons and explosives which were being evolved in increasing numbers, and learnt something of the basic tactics of guerrilla warfare.

It was at the explosives school that he saw B.6. again. He was shaken out of a deep sleep on his first night there to hear Tonkin saying sharply:

"Do you know Larisse's second-in-command?"

"No," Maltby answered, wondering how this great bull had got into his room without waking him. It was his conviction that he woke up the instant anyone entered his bedroom.

"Hm. Pity. I'd hoped you would."

Pig-Face was looking uncommonly spruce. Maltby had not seen him in uniform before. There were three pips on his shoulder tabs.

"Why?"

"Larisse has been taken by the Gestapo," he said and walked quickly out of the room.

Maltby looked at the clock. It was 2.25. You'd think the telephone had never been invented the way Pig-Face rushed around the country at all hours. An overgrown schoolboy still getting a kick out of jumping up unexpectedly from behind the sofa. If the damn fool thought he would be impressed by his jack-in-the-box act he couldn't be more wrong. Maltby turned over and went back to sleep.

His last assignment was with the parachute school. It ended with his making an unspectacularly correct drop from a moving aircraft on the afternoon of the day he was to meet Judy. Without waiting to hear his instructor's comments he dashed straight from the airfield to the railway station.

His train was only a little late, so that he reached the hotel in Woburn Place where he had booked a room for them a few minutes after nine.

CHAPTER SEVEN

JUDY saw him as he pushed his way through the black-out curtains round the door, and by the time he had freed himself from their folds she had crossed the entrance hall and was standing before him. She did not speak but took his hand and pressed it gently, holding her face towards him. He kissed her quickly and tenderly.

"I thought I'd never get here," he said.

"Have you eaten? I thought you wouldn't have done," she went on when he shook his head, "so I had something taken up-stairs for you. I had dinner here. You didn't miss anything by coming too late for it."

He registered and she led him up to their room.

"Darling," she said as soon as the door was closed, "I had to register before they would let me come up here. What do you think I put?"

"Mata Hari."

"Judith Maltby! For the very first time. It made me go all gooey."

He caught her in his arms and she clung to him drawing his lips into hers. But when he tried to go on she pulled away insisting that he must eat the spam and rather limp salad that she had saved for him as he must be famished.

"I'll just sit and look at you while you eat. I want to take you all in."

Because she had been the first to arrive, she adopted a pro-prietorial air about their apartment. When he criticized the hotel's stuffy commercial atmosphere, apologizing that it was the only place he could find which could let them have a room with a private bath, she cut him short.

"Don't be nasty about it, Harry. And please don't hate it. It's our first home."

"First? What about Paddington?"

She did rise to this, giggling and sticking her tongue out at him.

"That wasn't a home. That was sin."

"Can't we sin here?"

"You can do whatever you like with me, Harry," she said with unexpected seriousness, "but it won't be the same."

She was right. Because they meant so much more to each other now, because imperceptibly while they had been apart the demands of each had grown, they would never again be able to recapture the trivial inconsequence of that day. Each now knew they could be hurt and could inflict hurt.

It was not that the night was spoiled or a disappointment. It held moments that Maltby was to remember with greater longing in France than any of the Paddington excitements. In it were chills as well as warmth, fear that was not lessened by being shared, desolation and rejection balanced with the fusion and ecstasy. Their Paddington orgy had been a point without ties to past or future, but on this night before he left for France, Maltby and Judy were aware that they were setting off in time and their lives were being plaited together. This did not inhibit the pleasure, the simple animal pleasure, they took in each other. It did pose questions that had to be answered and in answering they had to probe ever deeper into regions of themselves that they had not touched before.

"Do you really have to go tomorrow, Harry?"

Judy spoke very softly. They were lying, holding each other gently, relaxing after the first tension of their desire had been loosed.

"No, you don't. I've talked to Doctor Cardin. He says you're absolutely unfit for service. And he'll say that to any Medical Board."

"He's an old woman."

"Go sick, Harry. Then they can't send you."

"I'm not sick."

"Yes, you are. That's what Doctor Cardin says. He just wouldn't believe it at first when I told him you were going back. He said there isn't a doctor in his senses who would accept you."

"Well, he's wrong, isn't he?"

"You're making them take you back, aren't you?"

"Not me, darling," he laughed. "I'm the original lead-swinger."

"For my sake, don't go."

He held up her face and looked into her eyes.

"You're not serious?"

"Of course I am. You owe it to me. Oh, don't you see, I wouldn't say anything if you weren't ill. But why should you go away from me when you needn't? It's not fair."

"Darling, it's only for a month at the most."

"So you say."

"No, I've been promised."

"Then they must know you're ill or they wouldn't tell you it was only for a month," she said shrewdly.

He must be careful. To cover up he yawned and stretched.

"I meant this tour abroad is only for a month."

"But if it's only for a month it can't be very important. Why can't someone else go? You can't be indispensable."

"Look, darling"—he had got to kill this—"I'm being sent back to finish something that I'd begun before they brought me home."

"No one else can do it?"

"That's what I'm told."

"And you wouldn't go if you didn't have to?"

"No." That at least was true. "If I could get out of it I would."

Judy traced a pattern on his chest with her finger.

"It's wicked of them to send you back to Africa after what it did to you before, even for a month." She stuck her nail into him so hard that he yelped with the pain. "If I thought you were just being heroic or silly enough to think it wrong to go sick because you can stand up, I'd . . . I'd skin you! I want you alive, Harry. I want all of you. And I want you now."

"Ulcer and all?"

"I'll cure the ulcer."

To quiet her, he told her of the care the Army was taking of him so that Harriet would not go on the rampage again, of all the pre-digested pap he was taking on his trip. Judy, listening to him carefully, grew withdrawn and preoccupied. She was thinking that it must be something very important that he was doing for so much trouble to be taken over him. In her mind, important meant dangerous and it frightened her. Without saying anything of what she felt, she sought his hand and pressed it between hers for comfort.

Maltby, too, was thinking of his mission. Once he had accepted that he would go back to Pontrecy in B.6.'s office, it had not occurred to him that he could still pull out. But he had accepted before he had asked Judy to marry him.

If he wanted to, he could go to HQ in the morning and tell them that he was not fit enough to go. If he did, there was nothing they could do but give him his ticket. He wouldn't be duck-shoving either, just stating the plain truth.

Then why the hell shouldn't he? The whole thing was crazy anyway, going back on a job when you knew you were already blown. It was all very well for Pig-Face to say Schwartzkopf would not move until the Resistance forces linked up, but he was only guessing about that. Schwartzkopf might get tired of waiting and collect the lot of them. Including him. The odds were that he would not be able to spot the Gestapo stooge, anyway, and so would have stuck his neck out to no purpose.

In any case, what was the group to him? They'd taken on the job themselves, knowing its dangers. He was not responsible for the mess they were in, so why should he risk his life to pull them out? Personally they meant nothing to him. He even disliked two of them thoroughly and had no feelings one way or the other about the rest. He shifted uncomfortably, realizing that he had included Hélène among these. It was true, but he felt that it couldn't or shouldn't be possible to forget so quickly or easily as that.

So they died, four innocent and one guilty. So what? People went out that way every day because someone refused to take the risk or pay the price needed to save them. You calculated these things and made your choice.

Then why was he going back, for he knew he was? Because he had no guts, no guts at all. It was the weak and the cowardly who always chose self-sacrifice. The strong would have no truck with it.

Lying quietly, holding Judy close to him and lightly fondling the soft hair at the base of her neck, he probed into the implications of his mission. What price would B.6. be prepared to go to to save his four Pontrecy agents? Would he have risked four others? Maltby doubted it. Even one? Would he have even sent Maltby if he were not already a dead duck as an agent and to lose him would be to lose nothing at all? To give him his due, Maltby thought he might but ought not to if he went strictly by the book. Stripped to its realities his task, no matter what he endured, no matter what success he achieved, was nothing offered for nothing. There was no currency insignificant enough to express the value of a blown saboteur. Four people who might have died would live on to become inconsiderable specks in the clutter of humanity. But this was not something B.6. could include in his accounts.

Only if the Gibault factory was wrecked as well could he make an entry on the credit side.

For the rest of the night, the menace that lay on the other side of their parting obtruded intermittently. When they made love it was as much anxiety to escape its shadow as desire that whipped them on.

There were also mundane things to discuss. Judy told him that she planned to get a transfer to London so that she could look out for a furnished flat where they could live when he got back. For his part Maltby realized that he must arrange for her to get a marriage allowance. This would mean stopping the one he now gave to his mother, but he knew she would not mind this as she never touched it herself but paid it straight into his bank.

It was almost dawn when he dropped off to sleep, only to awake with a start a few minutes later to find Judy sobbing violently. He tried to comfort her but she pushed him away roughly. Every time he touched her she wriggled away from him, burrowing her head deeper into her pillow. He watched her painfully, feeling inadequate.

Presently her shoulders ceased to heave and the sobs that tore her less frequent. Diffidently she stretched out a hand towards him and when he took it in his, clutched on to him so hard that her fore-arm trembled.

"I'm sorry, darling," she said tearfully, "but I can't bear anything to end. It's that you're going away."

"Or getting married?"

"That's a beginning, not an end."

He kissed her.

"Hold me tight, Harry. I'm all right now."

She lay quite still for a while and then began to snuggle against him. Impishly, she smiled and nipped the muscles below his shoulder with her teeth, seeming to have forgotten completely that a quarter of an hour before she had been weeping.

But his utter helplessness in the face of her grief disturbed Maltby. He felt that he had been shut out, that there were private places in her which she would never let him enter, private experiences which she neither needed nor wanted him to share. Were there things, too, from which he would exclude her, he wondered. Not consciously, he thought, but perhaps with love it was always the excluded and not the excluder who was aware of the rejection.

Finding that he did not respond to her play, she stopped teasing him and gently caressed his body.

"Would you mind if we got married all over again in church when you come back?" she asked.

"In all the churches in the world if you want to," he answered lazily and quoted,

> " 'For, lady, you deserve this state
> Nor would I love at lower rate
> But at my back I always hear
> Time's wingèd chariot hurrying near.'

But why?"

"It's mummy. If I wasn't married in church she'd think I was living in sin."

"And you?"

"Oh, I don't care. I know what a lovely sinner you are to sin with, but she doesn't." She smoothed his hair back from his forehead. "I thought if you could get leave soon after you come home we could go to Ireland to stay with mummy and daddy. We could be married there. Just quietly in the village church."

"Are you a Catholic?" This was something that had not occurred to him, religion playing no part in his life.

"Not seriously. But mummy and daddy are. You're not, are you?"

She asked the question solemnly, a small cloud of fear shadowing her eyes. Good God, thought Maltby, her religion has upped and bit her and she's wondering if I'm not the Devil who has taken my shape to damn her. He only just stopped himself from laughing aloud.

"I'm nothing at all."

"Don't you believe in God at all?"

"No."

She frowned.

"I don't think I could be like that. It seems so conceited."

"If we were to get married in a Catholic church," Maltby said slowly, "would I have to sign that we'd make our children Catholics?"

"I expect so. Would you mind that so very much?"

"I don't know. . . . This is the first time I've even thought of us having children at all, let alone whether I wanted them to grow up full of pi in the sky."

"I'd like to have babies."

"So that's your idea," he grinned, "planning to have me father a brood of Papist whelps, eh?"

"Please, Harry, don't be nasty. Not now we've got so little time."

That was a plea which could not be rejected. He flung his arms round her and at once she began to kiss him passionately. In that moment he decided that he would do whatever she wished. If some silly superstition attracted her, why should he mind if she believed in it whatever it was? Provided she allowed him not to believe if he didn't want to.

By the time their breakfast was brought up to them they were ravenously hungry and unappetizing though it was they attacked it wolfishly. Judy had persuaded the hotel to give them boiled fish instead of the sliver of fat bacon and mess of dried egg which was normally served.

"Very clever of you, my sweet," said Maltby looking disgustedly at the whitely transparent blob on his plate, "but how did you get them to cook it as ruinously as they do at the Wilberforce?"

"I have hidden depths."

"Like an iceberg."

"Frigid, that's me."

"Well, the toast will help push it down. By the way, can you cook?"

"I can boil an egg."

"*Formidable! Un Cordon Bleu!*"

Though they did not feel tired, their lack of rest was beginning to show. There was a hysterical edge to their repartee, a forced, unnatural brightness in the way each reacted to the other's fooling. When Judy asked him if he took sugar in his tea, they laughed till the tears came, thinking how that question would have blown sky-high her masquerade as a respectable married woman had they taken their breakfast in the dining-room.

Such nervous high tension usually ends in quarrelling, but they were saved from this by Maltby having to get dressed to report to HQ before the breaking point was reached. Judy was still soaking herself in the bath when he was ready to leave. Taking her face in his hands he kissed her, thrilled by her loveliness and intimacy.

"Don't you dare be late," she said. "I couldn't bear that."

He went off with the gay over-wrought mood still upon him.

At HQ he learned that the man who had taken over from Larisse had the improbable name of Le Feu.

"I expect it's Dupont or something like that really," Chivers commented, "but you know what these Reds are. Anyway, he seems efficient. Our W/T bod is with him and transmitting regularly."

He gave Maltby the escape routes for the agents who were to be brought home after the spy had been caught. A Lysander had been earmarked to pick him up in just twenty-eight days. It could not come later, but if he signalled for it, it could be laid on earlier.

"What a hope!" said Maltby.

"You never know your luck."

"I know mine."

After he had checked his personal gear and been told to report back promptly at 6 o'clock there was nothing more for him to do. He phoned the hotel thinking that as he was free earlier than he had expected he would collect Judy, but she had already left. The ceremony was timed for 1.30. Without hurrying, he arrived at St. Pancras Town Hall only a little after one.

He had smoked one cigarette and was making up his mind whether to light another, when Judy arrived. The night before, she had worn a summer cotton frock with a gay print pattern, and he had looked out for this slash of colour among the passing crowd. But she had put on the elegant suit she had worn when they had gone to Paddington. Instead of the scarf tied round her head like a turban that she had worn then, she had put on a perky little hat. She looked so *soignée* in the drabness of Euston Road that Maltby wished he had done something to match her dash, added some *panache* to mark his happiness and draw all eyes to see her as he did. As it was he had not even thought to have his hair cut. Nevertheless her smartness no longer abashed him and he took her arm easily and with pride.

"I've been waiting," he said idiotically.

"If you hadn't been I should have gone to hide round the corner. I would not wait for any man on my wedding day. Not even you, darling. Do you like my hat? You'd better. I went absolutely everywhere this morning trying to get it. I'm exhausted!"

He squeezed her elbow and they went inside. The previous ceremony had just been completed and they were immediately shown in to the registrar. Discovering from a clerk that they needed two witnesses, Maltby went into the waiting-room and brought back a young sailor and a very pregnant pasty-faced girl in a coat of muddy blue who were the next couple due to be married. Maltby thought the girl one of the least appetizing females he had ever seen and wondered that her husband-to-be, his face flushed and shiny with sweat, should look at her so adoringly. The girl was nervous in the presence of officialdom and clutched a drooping bunch of chrysanthemums so tightly that the knuckles showed white on her work-ruined hand.

The ceremony itself was more than a disappointment to Maltby. It shocked him. Two or three questions, a couple of formal responses, the ring jammed clumsily on Judy's finger, signatures and the registrar was shaking Judy's hand and saying archly, "May I be the first to wish you every happiness for the future, MRS. MALTBY!" They were out in the Euston Road again as the clocks were striking the half-hour.

He felt outraged. There had been as little dignity about it as being pushed down a helter-skelter. It seemed to him that he had been inexcusably insensitive in not arranging for them to be married in church as Judy had wanted. He was on the point of asking her forgiveness when he saw that she had apparently not found anything to disturb her in the ceremony, having invested it with a solemnity of her own. Her eyes were bright with happiness as they came out of the Town Hall and, characteristically, she pressed his hand. Seeing her look so pleased dispelled his depression.

"I thought he was such a nice little man."

"Mrs. Maltby!" he said derisively.

"It'll be true when I write it now," she answered smugly, holding up her hand to show the ring on it.

In front of the underground station he bought her a button-hole of red and white carnations. It had not occurred to him to buy her flowers before, and it had shamed him that the sweaty sailor had done this simple courtesy for his repellent bride while he, with so much more reason to pay tribute, had not.

They lunched among the hideous heavy Edwardian mahogany and plush at Reggiori's. The food was indifferent even by wartime standards and, since they were not regulars, the aged, snuffling waiters paid them little attention until Maltby called for the wine list. The burgundy that he ordered turned out to be tolerable and made the tasteless messes on the menu somewhat more palatable.

To prevent themselves from thinking of their imminent parting they fell back to their silly mood of breakfast, making fun of the waiters who quarrelled apparently bad-temperedly among themselves and with the staff in the kitchen.

Maltby had had no time to find a present for her and had not been able to think of anything that he particularly wanted to give her. It was not only that there was little enough in the shops but he simply did not know her well enough to be certain of her tastes or familiar with her possessions. As his pay for the past three years had been put to his account while he had had no opportunity of drawing on it, he was better off than he had ever been. So his wedding present to Judy was a cheque for a hundred pounds. After what he had said about the poverty-stricken existence schoolteachers faced, she was surprised, almost overwhelmed, by it.

"It's for you. Your own, I mean," he said. "Don't you go blowing it on flats or things for us. I'll pay for all that."

"This place is horrid. I want to kiss you."

She fumbled with her bag.

"I've got something for you, too."

It was a gold watch.

"You're to promise me you'll wear it always. I got it specially so that you would have something of mine touching you always."

He took off the service one he was wearing and she strapped it on his wrist. She insisted that he promise not to use his old one again and he did so without argument, though he knew that it would be impossible for him to take such a piece of jewellery with him. For it to be seen on the wrist of a supposed farmhand would be an invitation to arrest.

Leaving Reggiori's and not knowing what to do with themselves until Judy's train left, they wandered aimlessly up Pancras Road. They walked in silence, Judy cuddling his arm tightly to her. Maltby wished that they could part then, that they could suddenly find that they had made a mistake in the time and had to run to the station. There was so much that they had to say to each other if they had the time. Without it there was nothing, but the magnitude of all that was being left unsaid oppressed them harshly.

They came upon some gardens and went in. Once the gardens had been a graveyard but it had been paved and children, watched over by slatternly women, played in the grimy dust. Maltby, ignoring the women's curious looks, put his arm round Judy's waist. Like that they sauntered round the small playground. In a corner he stopped and they kissed deeply and passionately. It was too public for them to continue like that, absorbed in each other though they were, and they mooched round again, this time reading the inscriptions on the gravestones and conjecturing what these men and women were like who had known King's Cross when it had been a village and only green fields stretched where there was now a tangle of railway lines.

Suddenly Maltby found a name he recognized.

"Look," he cried, "old William Godwin's buried here!"

Judy had never heard of William Godwin, but the old anarchist was a favourite of Maltby's and he spoke enthusiastically about him.

"You know, he believed that men being capable of reason must act reasonably. I wonder if he would have liked to come back to amend his theories when Adolf's bombs came bouncing about around his grave. Probably not. I expect that he would have gone off to explain to Hitler that he was not behaving rationally. In the face of all the evidence of man's incurable stupidity he obstinately believed that rational persuasion could solve everything. Which, come to think of it, wasn't very rational in itself!"

"He sounds dreadfully stuffy. I hope the poor dear did some nice ordinary things, too."

"He had his moments. Do you know he called for equal rights for women a hundred years before Mrs. Pankhurst and her suffragettes?"

"Good for William!"

"His daughter married Shelley. She wrote *Frankenstein*."

"You mean that creepy film?"

"It was taken from her book. His women seemed to go for poets for his stepdaughter lived with Byron. They had a daughter whom, believe it or not, they called Allegra."

"How dreadful for her!"

"She died before it could have bothered her."

Maltby stood for a while in silence, leaning on his hands and looking down at the tomb.

"I don't think he had a happy life," he said at last. "At any rate, there was a lot of sadness in it. If he were alive today and I knew him, I should think him a damned fool and be rude to him. Yet looking back and seeing him whole, as it were, I've an affection for the tough old atheist who never gave in. His faith in human beings, in their reason and dignity, and his personal struggle to live by that faith, may have been cock-eyed but it certainly wasn't despicable. And it's something that he should have two lovers to talk about him a hundred years after his body has mouldered away."

He turned towards Judy and saw she was looking at him intently, setting the picture of him in her mind as he talked so that she could recall it when he was gone. He took her hands in his and fondled them.

They recommenced their circling of the playground in silence. When they reached the quietest corner of the gardens where they had kissed before, she stopped, pulling him round in front of her.

"In a minute you will be saying we've got to go, so kiss me, Harry. Only about twenty people can see us here, but please kiss me properly!"

He took her in his arms. Almost immediately she began to tremble, and he drew his arms tighter about her, trying to still her.

"I'm all right, darling," she whispered, running her lips along the line of his jaw. "Really I am. Just hold me, that's all."

Maltby was uncomfortable. He did not care that the slatternly mothers were watching him and Judy with a lively interest. All he wanted was to end this leave-taking which they had masochistically inflicted upon themselves. He cursed himself for not having pretended that he had to be back at HQ immediately after lunch. To go through this drawn-out agony was not only painful but utterly pointless.

They clung to each other for so long, Judy desperately, Maltby with rising impatience, that they had to hurry to reach the station in time for Judy to catch her train.

"I'd like to go to see your mother," said Judy as they came out into Pancras Road. "Would you mind if I did?"

"Of course not," he replied, wondering what on earth they would find in common. "You'll find she chatters a lot."

"I'll like that."

Judy laced and unlaced her fingers through his as they walked rapidly along. About a hundred yards from the station, she began to shiver violently, but when he made to put his arm about her she pushed him away roughly.

"I'm all right, really I am. Just leave me alone. And I won't cry," she added savagely, "I won't, I won't!"

By the time they had retrieved her case from the Left Luggage office there were only two minutes remaining before the train started. At the barrier she hung on to him, burrowing her lips into his.

"Come on, miss, if you're going on this one," the ticket collector called out when the guard's whistle shrilled, "leave a bit of him for the Army."

"Come back to me, Harry!" she whispered and flung herself through the barrier.

Watching her back as she dashed down the platform, he knew that she had let go at last and was sobbing as uncontrollably as she had in the night.

The ticket collector looked after her admiringly.

"Coo," he remarked, "how nice to be young and have three pips on yer shoulder!"

"How nice to be in a reserved occupation and stay at home," Maltby snarled, turning on his heel.

At the moment his feeling was simply of relief that the stifling oppression of the last hour had been lifted and he was free. He had been so mauled emotionally that he was only conscious of the cessation of the pain. That Judy had actually gone did not cause him a pang, for his senses would have to re-adjust themselves before they could digest its meaning.

Taking a bus to the West End, he thought over all the things he still had to do. There were quite a few. He bought some writing paper and envelopes and settled himself down at a marble-topped table in a teashop off Whitehall that was both reasonably quiet and handy for HQ.

He had collected a marriage allowance form from the whippet-like lieutenant that morning and he dealt with that first. Then he wrote to his mother telling her of his marriage and that she could expect a visit from Judy.

"I hope you will like her," he wrote, "it would be nice if you did. I know that Judy wants you to. Her people, whom I have not met, seem to set more store by this family feeling than we have ever done."

Then he tackled his will. He wasn't at all sure of the exact way in which such a document should be worded, but he remembered hearing somewhere that it did not matter so long as the intention was perfectly clear.

Last Will and Testament

"I, Harold Stanley Maltby, Capt., Intelligence Corps, of 38, Dingle Road, Southgate, London, do hereby will and bequeath all the moneys and securities that I die possessed of to my wife Judith (née Holton).

After my mother, Freda Maltby, has selected such of my personal effects as she may wish to have, the remainder to go to my wife Judith."

That looked all right, he decided, but why on earth was it called a will and testament instead of simply a will? He hadn't any securities for that matter but had included them because he was not sure whether the nine pounds-odd he had in the Post Office was money or a security. After a moment's thought, he added:

"It is my hope that my wife will not grieve too long for me nor delay re-marrying on my account."

While he had been writing someone had set a cup of tea down on the marble and settled in the seat on the other side of the table. As he was reading this last paragraph over, he saw out of the corner of his eye a sleeve with a leather patch on the elbow that seemed familiar. He looked up.

Pig-Face was sitting there placidly waiting for him to finish writing.

"Good," said Maltby, refusing to give the big man satisfaction by showing surprise, "I've just been making my will. You can witness it."

"Depends whether I figure in it. I shouldn't like to do myself out of a legacy."

Maltby was thinking that the last paragraph was idiotic. But he had been thrown by Judy turning out to be a Catholic. He didn't know whether they had daft ideas about re-marriage. He signed and Tonkin scribbled his name as witness.

When Pig-Face had handed the will back to him, Maltby said, "I got married. Today."

That'll shake you, he thought. It did.

"I ought to have guessed it, of course, and sent you a present," the big man said equably after a pause. "Being single was the only desirable quality you had as an agent, so naturally you had to get rid of it. Congratulations."

"Thanks. I deserve them, for she's a corker."

"She would be! There's no justice in the world!"

"What did you want to see me about?"

He said this casually as though Tonkin's appearance in the teashop was the most natural thing in the world. But he was not allowed to get away with it.

"It was quite simple, really. As the pubs were shut this was the most likely place to find you."

It was uncanny the way the bastard could read your thoughts!
Even while listening to you he must be analysing not only what
was behind your words but how it had got into your mind and
where it would lead you next.

"I wanted to have a chat with you."

"About this and that?"

Tonkin nodded, putting his hands face downwards on the table
and looking at them. Each nail on the stubby, muscular fingers
was neatly pared and polished.

"Uh-huh. That was quite a point you made about the reprisals
that would follow the blasting of the Gibault factory. As I see it,
there's nothing we can do to help any hostages they take. But the
rest can be warned that, as soon as they get wind that they are
going to be transferred to forced labour in Germany, they can, if
they wish, take to the Maquis. If they do, we'll pay their families
an allowance. We'll also look after the families of any hostages
who are shot."

"How will you warn them?"

"Le Feu can do it as soon as we give him the wire." The pale
blue eyes levelled with his. "It's not much, boy, but I don't see
what else we can do."

Wasn't it, Maltby wondered. True, it wouldn't prevent a lot of
suffering. That was war, anyway. On the other hand, it meant that
people who were shoved off the sidelines into the battle through
him would be treated as soldiers and not just ignored. That
was something, more than he had expected from the chairborne
brigade. He would have liked to have thanked Tonkin but could
not find the words.

"It's something," he said lamely.

Tonkin understood what he was trying to say and sat back in
his chair looking pleased.

"And here's something for you, boy. You're a major."

That will mean a bigger pension for Judy if I'm knocked out
was the first thought that went through Maltby's head.

"I suppose that makes you a colonel?" he said.

"Right," the big man chuckled. "Just you hurry up and become
a general. I've always wanted to be a field marshal!"

"Was the crowning your idea?"

"Yep. I thought you might find it useful to out-rank the others.
We've already let them know you've been promoted."

This had never occurred to him but he saw that Pig-Face was

right. Both Buchan and Harrison were senior to him but he had been able to assume leadership over them because he had been in Pontrecy so long before they arrived. Both had tacitly accepted this set-up, but in whose hands authority lay in the event of a serious disagreement had never been tested. But now things would be different. He had been away three months and in that time a new pattern of command would have been established, a pattern which they would resist having broken simply because he had returned. His promotion put all arguments about command responsibility out of court.

"You think of everything, don't you?"

The big man preened himself like a cat that had been stroked.

"We try to do our small best," he said, producing an oblong box from beneath the table and pushing it across to Maltby. "For you."

"What the hell is it?" Maltby asked when he had lifted the lid, "a monkey's breast-plate?"

Tonkin grinned. "It's a stomach shield developed from the sort of thing cricketers wear sometimes. No one likes a boot in the belly but you could do without one more than most."

It was quite a contraption, constructed from a shaped and curved sheet of some very light tough metal and lined with a kind of flannel while its face was covered with ribs of rubberlike material. Maltby judged that it would cover the area between the waist and the groin completely.

"Neat and very gaudy," he commented. "How the hell do you sit down in it?"

"Uncomfortably on the edge of your chair. It's not designed for social calls."

Maltby folded it in its straps and put it back in the box.

"Wear it, boy. Don't take chances. Jump in it tonight."

"O.K. Time I was pushing off."

Tonkin hauled a book out of his pocket and pitched it across to him. It was an early nineteenth-century edition of Voltaire's *La Pucelle*, beautifully bound in green calf with the Napoleonic emblem, an encircled "N", stamped on the spine. Evidently it had been among the loot from the Tuileries auctioned to the mob on the fall of the Empire.

"A memento from me. Something for you to read in the long winter evenings after you get back. It should appeal to your narky view of humanity."

Maltby was touched. Usually agents were given cuff-links or silver pencils or something equally useless and dangerous by the officer speeding their departure. By refusing to draw on this official bijouterie, Pig-Face had put himself to the trouble of finding something special for him. It was damned decent of him. Another thing that pleased him was that he had not said, *"Merde!"*, the traditional valediction, because to wish a saboteur good luck was supposed to bring bad luck. The old blighter knows that's the sort of tosh about this racket that I hate, he thought. It flattered him that he should be recognized as one apart.

"Let me have your wife's address," said Tonkin, when Maltby gave him his will to look after, "I'll keep her informed about you."

"All right. Only stick to the official forms. I like to write my own love letters. I'm not fussy about the other sort."

B.6. shot him a shrewd glance which Maltby held. He said nothing, but the wrinkles in his heavy face deepened and the blue eyes gleamed with amusement.

CHAPTER EIGHT

"COME on, chum," the despatcher was shaking him by the shoulder and shouting in his ear, "you'll want to rub the sleep out of your eyes!"

"Are we there?"

"Will be in half an hour. I've got you some cawfee."

Maltby took the cup and sipped at it. The noise of the engines in the belly of the Halifax made conversation impossible. Their rhythmic beat had helped rather than hindered his sleeping.

He felt terrible. Morning after the night before. Or rather the night after the night before. He had dozed in the car on the way to the aerodrome and must have been out, dead out, for—he looked at his watch—an hour and a half in the plane.

What a bloody fool he was! He always felt like this if he dropped off and didn't get his full whack of sleep. Much better to have kept awake however tired he'd felt. He ached all over for, encumbered with his parachute and his belly shield, he had lain awkwardly.

He was cold and wondered whether this was due to jitters until he saw that the hatch had been opened and cold night air was streaming into the compartment. He looked down but could see nothing but blackness.

A hand gripped his shoulder. The despatcher took his cup.

"Moon's showing up real nice," he bellowed in his cheerful Cockney. "More cawfee?"

Maltby shook his head.

Steadying himself against the aircraft's curving side, he clambered to his feet and stretched. He tried a few exercises but the gentle bucking of the plane made it difficult for him to get a purchase with his feet. Twice he reeled over on his back before he gave up the effort and settled for leaning against the wall using his parachute as a cushion.

None of the sensations that he had expected came to him. He had seen himself as so scared that he screamed and refused to jump. But he wasn't frightened now that the jump was imminent. Nor was he gnawed by impatience. He had no feelings about it one way or the other. His head was too full of cotton-wool to register anything at all.

Presently the despatcher listening on his intercom. waved excitedly and shouted something. Maltby crawled over to him.

"They've picked up the lights!"

Lying on his stomach he looked forward through the hatch. Soon he could see them, too, five stars set in the shape of a Y. This caused him a moment's panic because they had always used an "L" at Pontrecy. Then he thought, what the hell, it's not my business to read the bloody signal. I suppose the pilot knows what he's looking for.

They swept over the field and he saw the lights directly below as though in a void. The Halifax began a wide sweep.

As it completed the turn he seated himself on the edge of the hatch, his legs dangling into space and his back to the pilot's cabin. Looking down, he thought how amazingly peaceful it all was. It was hard to imagine that they had been over enemy territory for over an hour and as far as he knew had not been fired on by so much as a rifle. He had to sit up very straight or B.6.'s boot repeller rammed up under his rib-cage.

The despatcher hooked to its wire the static line which would open his parachute automatically.

"Blast the daylights out of 'em, mate," he yelled, patting him on the arm.

Then he took up a position with his arm raised and his eyes fixed on the red and green signal lights.

Maltby waited. It seemed that he was going to wait there for all time when the despatcher's arm suddenly dropped.

"Go!" he roared, at the same time heaving him forward with his foot.

As soon as his parachute opened two things hit Maltby. First, he had been dropped too late and would over-shoot the lights. Second, that moon or no moon he couldn't see the ground. He now saw the reason why they had insisted at the parachute school that you counted your descent. He had rejected this as daft because no one in his opinion could count forty-five seconds accurately nor could the plane's height be depended upon within ten feet either way.

Hastily he doubled himself up into the landing posture. The next moment he seemed to pass something that was apparently in the air alongside him. As his boots touched the ground his parachute stopped dead, knocking the wind out of him.

Undoing his harness, he scrambled to his feet. He had jarred his elbow and it hurt damnably. But he forgot this as he saw his parachute. It had been caught on a sapling and lay festooned over a hedge, gleaming with such a bright whiteness in the darkness that he thought it must be visible for miles.

Hurriedly he got it down and bunched it up. He was holding it in front of him like a bundle of washing when he had his second panic. He could see the lights of the dropping field on the other side of the hedge but nothing else. And there was not a sound, not a solitary sound except the distant hum of the Halifax completing its sweep before coming in to drop the weapon containers!

The Germans! It must be the Germans had taken over the parachutage! Christ, and why not? They had Larisse. If he had talked they would know all about the fields he had prepared!

Cautiously he moved along in the shadow of the hedge. He had gone about thirty yards making what seemed to him a tremendous din because carrying his parachute and still wearing his flying suit made his movements clumsy. He had just decided that he must bury all this surplus junk before he reconnoitred further when a branch snapped loudly almost next to him. In his fright he nearly put a burst from his Sten through the hedge.

"Who are you?" someone hissed in French. "Londres."

"Berlin." So great was his relief that the breath rushing out of his body almost drowned the password and he repeated it, "Berlin."

"There's a gap in the hedge along here to the right," the voice continued.

Maltby found the gap and went through it into the parachute field.

"I'm Le Feu," said the man waiting for him, still in the same low voice.

"I'm Punch. Germans about?"

"No, but keep your voice down. Come on."

Le Feu was a lightweight and he moved as surely and silently as a cat on his rope-soled espadrilles. Over his overalls he wore a Sam Browne from which a large upholstered revolver protruded, and an assortment of grenades and knives hung down about his thighs and buttocks. In the crook of his arm he carried a Sten and on his head a forage cap was set at a jaunty angle. It was too dark for Maltby to make out his features, but as he stumbled after him, his silhouette struck him as familiar. Why it should he could not determine, for nothing could be more dissimilar from the homely figures of the Pontrecy Resistance men and women than this over-weaponed brigand.

"They are mad, your English flyers," Le Feu threw back over his shoulder, his thin rasping voice full of arrogant contempt, "they dropped you too late. They are mad."

His tone angered Maltby. He felt, too, that he must look ridiculous clinging to his bundled parachute and staggering about like a decrepit washerwoman as he strove to keep pace with Le Feu's light, triggered lope. He grunted non-committally.

"The English do not understand parachutages as the Soviet airmen do. They have no technique. They won't learn. They are mad. The Russians invented the parachutage."

"They also invented radio and wrote Shakespeare," snarled Maltby.

He might have saved his breath, for Le Feu simply nodded sagely, evidently agreeably surprised to find a British officer so well informed. Why am I such a bloody fool, Maltby groaned. Why must I always rise to every damn idiot who yaps?

Except for the fires burning out on the field there was no sign of activity. Maltby asked Le Feu how many men he had on the parachutage.

"Nine."

"They keep in cover well."

"What else would you expect? They are disciplined. They are Francs Tireurs!"

He had asked for that and he had got it!

Le Feu whistled softly and two figures moved out of the hedge and came quickly towards them. He spoke to one and he ran off. These two, Maltby noted, were not got up in the same picturesque way as Le Feu but looked like ordinary workmen.

The Halifax was coming in on its second run. This time the drop was handled perfectly and the containers came swinging down on their parachutes in a line through the centre of the field. As they fell, men broke from the shadows and immediately began to manhandle them towards the hedge. Le Feu counted the parachutes as they opened up and then nodded to the man beside him, who at once began to extinguish the signal lights. In ten minutes the centre of the field had been cleared of all evidence of the drop and Le Feu's men had begun to load the containers on to a cart. An impressive performance by any standards.

"There were nine parachutes. I was expecting only eight."

"The other one had my gear." Maltby told him.

The Communist chewed on this.

"We shall see," he said.

Maltby got out his spade and made ready to dig a hole for his flying kit and parachute which he must now jettison.

"That's not necessary. Come."

He led Maltby over to the cart. Beyond it, in a copse, a pit had been dug and the men had already thrown into it ropes and other odds and ends that had to be got rid of. He threw his parachute into this, but Le Feu had it taken out again. The nights were getting cold and the material could help to keep them warm. He also took Maltby's flying suit, saying that they were short of clothes and it could be adapted to wear in camp if nowhere else.

Maltby saw that his two suitcases had been loaded on to the cart. He took them off.

"These are mine."

"It was agreed that I should have all the weapons dropped."

"There's no weapons in these."

"No? Radios, perhaps?"

"No. Only personal things."

"So much?" Le Feu sneered. "Surely you should have brought

your valet with you, too? British officers take their valets to war with them, don't they?"

His men sniggered.

"You've got your eight containers of weapons, Le Feu," Maltby rapped out sharply, "these bags are mine. Now let's see how you carry out your part of the bargain. Get going!"

Le Feu hesitated.

"I must examine your cases first."

"All right."

"There is not enough light here. You must bring them to the farmhouse."

The bags were so heavy that it was as much as Maltby could do to lift them.

"How far is the farmhouse?"

"About half a kilometre by the path through the woods here."

"Then your men will have to carry them."

"The cart can bring them round by the road."

"In that case, I'll go with the cart."

The Communist laughed pleasantly.

"Come, we are allies. Do whatever you wish but it is at least two kilometres by the road and you must be tired. Do personal things mean so much to you? You have to go to the farmhouse, anyway, because that is where we have hidden the car."

"O.K. I'll come with you."

What the hell did it matter, anyway, if this gang of pirates pinched his dried eggs? He'd probably dump them, anyhow.

At the farmhouse, which turned out to be little more than an enlarged pig-sty, smelling evilly of decay and utterly filthy, they gave him a cup of ersatz coffee made from roasted corn. It almost made him retch.

It came to him why he had thought there was something familiar about Le Feu. The man was got up exactly like a militia-man in the posters put out by the Spanish Government during the civil war. He even had a red scarf round his neck. He looked every bit as unreal as the poster from which he had copied his uniform.

"Were you in the International Brigade?"

"Of course," Le Feu answered, throwing out his chest.

Looking at his close-set eyes and long thin acquisitive nose, Maltby did not know whether to believe him or not. On the whole he thought not.

Maltby's question had the effect of thawing Le Feu. They discussed the details of their future liaison and he found that the Communist had thought them out with a thoroughness which would have pleased B.6. Liar he might be, but he was certainly efficient. On the other hand his obvious theatricality and idiotic fanaticism were worrying. It appalled Maltby that the man should consider that his having lost more men than any other group in the province was something to boast about.

When he turned out his cases and explained what all the tins contained and why, Le Feu was amazed, bewildered that the British should have sent over a saboteur who was physically unfit. "They are mad," he kept repeating, "they are mad." It was an expression which he used in every other sentence. The Gestapo were mad, the de Gaulle men were mad, the British and Americans were mad, everyone, in fact, except the Russians were mad. Maltby nicknamed him *"Ils sont fou!"* and never afterwards thought of him by any other name.

Maltby had with him two thousand cigarettes for the group and seven pounds of coffee. He thought the Communists would be certain to loot these. Le Feu ran his fingers lovingly over the packets while his men's eyes popped wolfishly but he left them untouched.

Maltby gave him a box of a hundred and, before they left, his parachutist's knife. This he had overlooked when he had thrown away the rest of his things but *"Ils sont fou"* was delighted with it. It did not seem to bother him in the least that it was equal to a ticket to a concentration camp to be caught carrying one. And *"Ils sont fou"* would never go anywhere without it, he was pretty sure of that. He felt that he should have thrown it away instead of giving it to such a baby.

They bundled him into an ancient *gazogene* which smelt powerfully of charcoal fumes. He used his cases to wedge himself more securely on the back seat, for as they travelled by rutty, little-used roads, he was constantly being thrown from side to side. A pleasant-faced youth of about nineteen drove without lights and his foot hard down on the accelerator, swaying grandiosely as they cornered and most of the time gustily singing bawdy songs, of which he had a remarkably extensive repertoire. The Reds were supposed to take him to the edge of the Pontrecy area and leave him to find his own way from there. But *"Ils sont fou"*, who seemed to have forgotten that he was dealing with one of the hated bourgeoisie, announced that they would take him all the way to Gallot's farm.

Maltby was all in. Even in the jolting car he dropped off intermittently, his head bobbing and weaving drunkenly with the bumps. Once he noticed that his stomach was griping painfully but for the most part he was conscious only of the agony of fatigue that racked his whole body and made his eyes smart if he tried to keep them open.

The car stopped and he got down. His cases were shoved out into the road by the singing driver.

"Fight well, comrade. Remember we are behind you," said *"Ils sont fou"*, sententiously. "Victory is sure!"

In a cloud of smoke and sparks, the *gazogene* spun round and set off down the road the way it had come, Le Feu, clinging to its side, waving his Sten in a heroic salute and singing, Maltby thought, the "Internationale" but it could have been the "Marseillaise".

He half slid, half carried his bags a little way beyond the farm gates and covered them with straw and sacking. Either from tiredness or the sharpness of the pre-dawn air, he shivered. Not even the effort it had cost him to move his cases off the road had relieved the chill which seemed to run right down to his bones.

To his surprise, the Gallots were waiting for him.

"How did you know I was coming tonight?" he asked as he let Madame Gallot fold him in her arms and plant smacking kisses on his cheeks.

"Le Soleil told us, of course. She said if you were coming back on this moon it would be tonight." She pushed him from her. "You're cold. Go and warm yourself by the fire while I get you some soup."

Le Soleil was Hélène's code name. She would have known that he was returning, but it was clever of her—and thoughtful, too —to alert the Gallots. Had the others known of her intention? Or hadn't they cared, or not thought it their business as they had been given no date for his arrival? Or were miffed about his coming back anyway? He was too tired to think. What did it matter, anyhow? It was nice of Hélène, though. Too nice, he thought wryly, much too nice. The worst part of the whole business, why he should never have been sent back to Pontrecy at all, he had not mentioned to B.6.

Papa Gallot had not got up when Maltby entered. With his grizzled hair curling up round the edges of the cap which, except when in church, he always wore when awake, he sat in his wooden armchair his eyes reflecting the fire's sparkle. Maltby, feeling the warmth from the flames pressing through his trousers, bent down toward's Papa's sun-blackened face, resting a hand on each of the arms of his chair.

"And how's this rascally midwife of the soil been doing?" he said loudly, for the farmer was deaf.

"Working too hard, of course. What do you expect when my farmhand, when he doesn't go away altogether because he's sick, is always too busy making explosions to help me."

Madame Gallot came back with the soup. Maltby would have liked to refuse it but knew she would be offended if he did.

"Papa, I've left my bags just inside the gate under some straw."

"Don't worry. When it's light I'll bring them up on the barrow."

"I didn't mean that. I just didn't want you to think that the Lord had sent you a present if you found them. They'll be quite safe where they are until I can get them."

"Any present that he had he would know hadn't come from the Lord," said Madame darkly.

Maltby yawned. He'd got to go to bed.

"Any news?" he asked, putting down his plate.

"Your Captain Buchan had a fight with Louis at the smithy."

Louis was Pontrecy's roughneck, the acknowledged leader of the local toughs.

"What happened, Papa?"

"He got a black eye, your Captain Buchan did."

Maltby grinned. So Buchan got a black eye. Serve the little cocksparrow right for not having the sense to leave someone twice his size alone!

"It could have been serious," said Papa, "Louis is a bad lot. He could have been dangerous if your Captain Buchan had hurt him."

"Well, he didn't. I'm dog tired, Madame. I must get to bed. I'm not getting up again until tomorrow morning."

CHAPTER NINE

HE slept for more than twelve hours. When he woke he was still
woolly headed, but except for a slight stiffness his body worked
reasonably well. Feeling off-colour, he examined himself morbidly.
He had taken the skin off his elbow in landing and his lower ribs
were sore from the stomach shield's chafing. Deep down, Harriet
gnawed—not viciously, just letting him know she was there. An
oval blue-black bruise below his left shoulder puzzled him for a
while. Then he remembered that it was where Judy had bitten
him. It seemed a very long time ago and he was astonished when he
calculated that it was only a little more than thirty-six hours away.

Downstairs he washed and shaved. Immediately his head began
to clear.

Hélène had called at the farm. There was a meeting of the
group the following afternoon at 3 o'clock.

"She wanted to wake you, Oignon, but I wouldn't let her," said
Madame Gallot, using his code name, as always, as though it were
a term of affection, "you looked so tired this morning. And so
pale!"

He did. It worried him. A genuine farmhand could not possibly
have such a white face at the end of summer. They had wanted
to stain his skin before he left but he had refused to let them,
saying that it was not important. Actually he had stopped them
because he could think of no possible explanation he could have
given Judy if he had turned up at St. Pancras Town Hall looking
like an Indian.

Though hungry, he ate sparingly despite Madame Gallot's
protests. Like most women of her generation she believed that the
cure for any ill was simply to stuff the patient with food.

Afterwards he pottered about for an hour, demonstrating to
the farmer's wife the way in which the various concentrated foods
he had brought with him had to be prepared. Mutinously she
declared that there could be no goodness in any of the messes. But
when he gave her the bulk of the coffee he had packed in his
cases, she flung her arms round him and wept.

Although by this time he was feeling quite lively, he went back
to bed to rest and doze away the night. As soon as the sun came
up he dressed and went out.

An unlovely dump, he thought, seeing Pontrecy once again, but I like it. He supposed he felt this way because the landscape was so familiar to him, the people identified with it and he with them. Not that they were much as people go. Most of them would see their grandmothers burnt alive if it would add a hectare to their miserable holdings. And some of them would allow themselves to be burnt alive rather than betray a stranger. Patriotism which seemed incapable of going beyond the limits of the family farm in one, would reach out beyond the sky in the next. Easy enough to call these little grubbers mean, but peasant materialism was hard sense. Their faith had nothing to do with their religion. Their faith was in what they could own and touch and change according to their will, in their land and the hoard of gold under the kitchen floor. Only idealistic fools thought the question, "What's in it for me?", a despicable test to apply to an act. Empires collapsed when they gave up using it as a precept, and the human race itself would be for the high jump if it didn't start asking the question pretty damn quick. Give me these crude solid bastards any day, he thought, it's the prissy do-gooders that stick in my gullet.

Crossing the road he climbed upwards towards a patch of scrubby woodland. Gallot's farm lay to the west of Pontrecy on rising ground. Like the others surrounding it, it had the despoiled air of autumn, the unplanted ploughland crumbling in ochreish dust and the pastures shorn down to a coarse stubble.

From where he was Maltby could look over the clustered village to where on more rising ground to the east, the smoking chimney of the Gibault factory at Evine poked towards the sky. A train, a local with just two carriages and a few goods wagons, pulled out of Pontrecy going north-west towards Airvout junction and the main line to Cherbourg.

Reaching the trees beyond the field, Maltby found a spot facing south where he would not be seen by anyone until they were almost treading on him and settled himself down. After this morning he would stir himself and beat about crying, "Activity, activity!" like Nelson. The idea that there was or could be any comparison between himself and the little bustling passionate patriot amused him—but for the moment he was just going to let the sun, the sun of France, fall on his face. In six or seven hours you might get quite a tan, though that way you also risked a burn.

He did not even try to deceive himself by pretending that he was thinking about his problems. He did think of them but in a desultory way. More often he daydreamed about Judy.

When he got up to go to the meeting, he had made only one positive resolution. If he were going to last the month, he must look after Harriet. If he were to have even a chance of success, his ulcer must be prevented from breaking out again. That meant taking sops every two hours or so and lining his guts with bismuth before tackling solid food. He had already given up smoking.

Hélène had two rooms over a bicycle shop facing the village square. Their special advantage was that they could be reached in two ways, either through the shop or by a side door that led directly to the living quarters above.

He saw her leaning out of the window smiling and waving to him as he sauntered across the square. The church clock beat out the hour. Because he had not wanted to risk being alone with her he had timed his arrival carefully. With a little flip of alarm it occurred to him as he returned her greeting that she might have given the Gallots the wrong time just to get him there before the others. What the hell, he shrugged, it's got to be faced sometime.

But the others were already there. They welcomed him variously.

"It's nice to have you back, Oignon," Hèléne said primly.

Lestocq pumped his arm and exclaimed oilily, "Now we are whole again!"

Gringoire smiled and nodded but said nothing.

"How's the Old Country? The spivs still finding plenty of openings, I trust?" Harrison enquired with aloof distaste.

Buchan, his battle with Louis of the smithy still evidenced by a yellowish swelling below his left eye, did not attempt to be pleasant.

"New thing, isn't it? Being promoted because you get a belly ache."

"Get cancer, Lulu, dear," Maltby drawled. "That'd make you a colonel, at least!"

The little man's eyes blazed and his fists clenched. Christ, thought Maltby, it really has caught him on the raw.

"Now, now, I'm not one of the village roustabouts," he said. "Superior officer, you know. Your eye is healing well, I'm happy to see."

"Why did they send you back, Maltby?"

The question came from Harrison and Maltby carefully stored it away in his mind. Somewhere in these first minutes of his re-union with the group there should be a clue, if he were only sharp enough to recognize it when it was dropped.

"They thought you'd be lonely without me."

"No, seriously?"

Harrison again.

"What else would they do with me now I'm patched up? I've had three years' experience in Pontrecy, hold a genuine identity card, have a bicycle licence . . . was all that to be wasted?"

This time Harrison nodded, apparently satisfied.

"You looked so ill when you left that we thought you would never come back," Hélène said, "that's why Lulu thought it must be something special for them to send you here again."

So that was what Buchan thought.

"Surely you didn't think the Great White Chief would trust me with anything special, Buchan?"

"Are you saying that you haven't been?"

Maltby waited to see if anyone else would talk. After a moment Lestocq began to rub his hands theatrically.

"It's a big job, isn't it?" he said. "A big job that they have found for you to do, yes?"

He still did not answer. But not one else spoke.

"It's not that I have something special to do, but the group is special."

He explained to them about the link-up of all Resistance forces. Tell them that, B.6. had said, it can do no harm. It won't be news to the Gestapo if it is the reason why they have left the group alone so far, and if it isn't, then the knowledge that a lot more big fish are about to swim into their net will give them an incentive to go on waiting.

To his disappointment it was Hélène who asked the first question. She spoilt everything with her blasted adoring eagerness.

"And will you be in command?"

Before replying he glanced quickly round the men. Each was looking at him interestedly. He could make no more out of their faces than that.

"It's not likely because I should say the French would insist on one of their own people being at the top. Besides, the Maquis is growing fast. There'll be several thousand in the combined force and that will mean at least a colonel as boss."

"But us? What do we do?" Lestocq shot at him.

"I haven't been told, but I suppose we will form the command staff. We're the biggest British group in this part of the country and they want to keep us that way. That's one reason for sending me back. To keep up the strength."

"When's all this to be?"

This came from Harrison.

"No precise date fixed but very soon."

Buchan moved jerkily in his chair.

"What do you mean by all the Resistance forces?" he demanded. "Does that include the F.T.P.?"

"Of course."

"God Almighty!" The little man was so angry that he could hardly get his words out and a purplish flush covered his face. "Have they gone quite berserk in London? We can't work with traitors! Gutter savages . . . must be wiped out! Worse than Nazis! Nun rapers!"

"At the moment the Reds seem to be killing Germans rather than raping nuns," Maltby said mildly. "Stalingrad wasn't a bad effort."

"You don't understand Reds, Maltby, because you're a fool. They're evil. Not just uncivilized, the scum of the earth—though they are that, too!—but evil. Doing the Devil's work on earth! If these swine are with us then we're fighting the wrong war, that's what I say! The wrong war!"

I've got to be careful here, Maltby told himself, biting back the jibe that had leapt into his mind. He mustn't feel he's gone too far and given himself away, if he's the one. Buchan's eyes were flicking round the room at the other men who were regarding him curiously. Hélène was looking at Maltby, smiling in her irritatingly superior way, evidently waiting for him to smack the little pipsqueak down. She was going to be disappointed.

"The idea is that at the moment all that counts is that they are killing Germans," he repeated mildly.

Buchan snorted but said no more. Obviously still fuming, he sat bolt upright in his chair, jaw clenched and his nerves jerking him spasmodically.

Maltby decided that it was time to get the meeting going, but before he could call them to order, Lestocq was at him again.

"What about the Second Front? When is it to be?"

"I wasn't told."

"The BBC says it will be any day, now," he wheedled ingratiatingly, with a smile that made him look more rat-like than usual. "Is that true?"

"You know as much as I do."

"But you heard things?" the man insisted. "People talked, yes?"

"People talked as they do here. And they know about as much."

"And they said it would be soon, yes?"

"They listen to the BBC, too."

Lestocq sat back nodding with self-satisfaction. And the best of British luck for you with that, thought Maltby.

They got down to business. Maltby found that the group's meetings had not changed. Reports were made, people threw out odd suggestions and plans were laid for a sabotage operation the following week when Lestocq's assessment of the project had been checked.

After the meeting, Maltby gave each of them fifty cigarettes while Hélène made coffee.

"Stay till the others have gone," she whispered as she handed him his cup and, when he shook his head, pleaded, "Please!"

As usual they would leave singly and Maltby settled the order. Buchan would go first, then himself, followed by Gringoire, Lestocq and Harrison. Hélène glared at him angrily. He noticed that she had done her best to make herself attractive, having put on a clean cotton dress and made up carefully, giving her sallow cheeks a touch of rouge. All done, he knew, for his benefit.

When he left the meeting he went into a café a few doors from the bicycle shop and ordered a beer. He took his drink to a table near the window. If Gringoire did not come in, he would see him pass and could catch him up. But as he had expected he appeared in about five minutes and at Maltby's smile of recognition came over to his table.

"So, Gaston," he said, but not sitting down, "you are well again, eh?"

He spoke in a loud voice, evidently for the benefit of the man behind the bar. The Gestapo counted on bar-keepers for much of their information and for this reason cafés were in general regarded as "unsafe".

Maltby made an assignation with the Alsatian at the farm for the following day. Gringoire nodded and drifted over to a table where some *cheminots* were playing *belote*. They greeted him as

an old crony. Maltby knew he must wonder why he had not fixed
up the rendezvous at the group meeting but he had shown no
curiosity.

The square had come alive with a scurry of bicycles and the
café was filling up. Outside, open trucks in which stood tightly
packed men and women, mostly of an older generation than the
cyclists, pulled up for their cargo to jump down and drift away
among the side streets. The workers were home again from their
day's work at Evine.

Maltby finished his beer and went out into the square. Crossing
it, he turned up a mean alleyway that led off it to the north. After
checking that he was not being followed by turning off first to
the left, then to the right and to the right again, he knocked on
a door in the middle of a terrace of workmen's houses. Inside a
woman's voice called out something he could not distinguish and
then the door was opened by a muscular man about his own age
with a handsome, open face. He was stripped to the waist and held
a trowel in his hand.

"Are you Henri Scoutier?" he asked, and when the man
nodded, added, "I am Punch."

Scoutier glanced quickly up and down the street.

"Come in."

Maltby followed him into the front room, which was over-full
of furniture and untidy. A woman was standing by the window
and from her attitude he guessed she had had her ears cocked for
what had been going on between the two men. He judged her to
be some years older than Scoutier, for her flashy good looks were
fading, though her eyes, as hard and black as coal, were sharp
and bright.

"This is Punch," Scoutier said, unnecessarily since the woman
had clearly heard Maltby announce himself.

The woman moved her head slightly but there was no friendli-
ness in her look.

"They told me you would be coming," Scoutier explained, "but
I did not know when."

"I didn't know myself."

"Le Feu's a great chap, isn't he? A real bolshevik!"

In Maltby's world "bolshevik" was a term of abuse but Scoutier
used it as a mark of high praise.

"I would like to join his Maquis but the Party won't let me.
They say I must stay at the factory."

"You're a fool!" the woman snapped venomously. "All your life, a fool!"

"My wife does not understand what it is to be a man. It is because I am civilized and do not hit her. It is unbolshevik to hit your wife. So! She has her opinion!"

"You do not hit me because you know that I should scratch your eyes out if you did!"

Scoutier accepted this with a cheerful grin.

"You want my help, yes? If it's to do something with the workers at the factory, you'd better forget it. They're a useless lot of lickspittles, no fight in them at all. And the Party group is very small."

Maltby evaded saying anything about sabotaging the Gibault works, claiming that he was only there to establish contact and that they would have to have further discussions before it could be decided whether they could undertake any actions together. The woman's hostility made him nervous, and he arranged to meet her husband the next day at the farm where they would be out of range of her ears.

"You speak French well for an Englishman, Punch" (he pronounced it Poonch), Scoutier said as Maltby was leaving, "but you speak it like a Paris gent, not one of us."

That's a warning, thought Maltby. In the three years he had been in Pontrecy he had picked up the local twang. It had taken just three months in England for him to grow careless about using it. He must watch himself.

He spent the evening setting down what each member of the group had said to him and what questions they had asked. B.6. had told him to do this immediately after he met them, and having this in mind had enabled him to get so clear a picture of each of them that he could conjure them up at will, seeing the movement of their features and hearing the inflections of their voices as precisely as though it were happening then and not six hours earlier.

Though he read over what he had written several times and analysed what each had said in relation to what he had learnt from their dossiers, it got him nowhere. Or rather it got him too far. Applying B.6.'s method of reading everything forwards and backwards and upside down, all the suspects could be said to have acted suspiciously. Equally they all could be said to have acted naturally. So far as he could see he had wasted his time.

On the face of it, it seemed to confirm his prejudice that his man was either Lestocq or Buchan. But he was guiltily aware that any-one with different prejudices might find just as good pointers to the others. Christ, he thought, if I'm not careful I shall get so lairy of making a mistake that I'll refuse to believe my own eyes!

He didn't like keeping all this stuff that he'd written down. He'd disguised the names, but if the local Gestapo were to get hold of it they'd rumble that he was wise to there being one of their stooges in the group. B.6. had asked for this piece of analysis to be sent to him. He decided to get Madame Gallot's niece, Celestine, to cycle over to Dinville with it the next day and drop it in one of Le Feu's "letter-boxes".

The following morning he went over to see Harrison at the farmhouse on the edge of the woods to the south of Pontrecy, near a small hamlet called Aigunes. Because his "cover" story was a good one he, like Maltby and Hélène, had been able to give him-self a semi-permanent residence, only moving out when there appeared to be any unusual German activity in the Aigunes dis-trict. He was supposed to be a traveller in agricultural equipment, and once upon a time there had been a genuine salesman who had used the farmhouse as his headquarters and his office para-phernalia was still there to substantiate Harrison's story.

Harrison was the group's quartermaster, the woods about the farm being an obvious place for them to store their weapons.

"I'm going to shift some of the arms away from here," Maltby told him.

"Oh, where to?"

"I'm not telling you."

The tall man's handsome, almost beautiful features remained as expressionless as always.

"It's London's bright idea, not mine," Maltby lied. "They gave me a terrible bollocking when I told them we kept all our fire-works in one cache and every one of us knew where that was."

"What do they suggest as an alternative?"

"That each of us should be responsible for a small dump and not tell the others where it is hidden. That way if one of us is caught and the Gestapo cracks him he can only tell them about his own dump."

"It sounds all right in theory, but I should say that it's going to be damned inconvenient in practice having to pick the stuff up from all over the place whenever we want to use it."

"As quartermaster you will, of course, know exactly which of us has what. But you won't know where. When we plan an operation, you will just instruct one of us to produce whatever weapons are necessary."

"I hope you're right. I think we're more likely to find that that little runt Lestocq has flogged his lot to the F.T.P."

Maltby grinned.

"We're getting bigger, Harrison. That means that our organization will inevitably become more complicated. And also——"

At that moment he was interrupted. They were sitting in Harrison's "office", a lean-to wooden hut which had a high desk fixed to one wall and decorated with pre-war posters of ploughs and harvesters and an assortment of broken spare parts and bits of wire. A door led into the barn to which the hut was attached and another opened directly on to the farmyard. It was this door that was opened suddenly by a weedy youth of about seventeen.

The youth entered with insolent assurance, but seeing Maltby fright showed on his pimply unhealthy face and he immediately began to back.

"Oh, excuse me, Monsieur Loubet," he stammered shiftily (Loubet was Harrison's "cover" name), "excuse me, please."

He got out and quickly closed the door.

"Who was that?"

Harrison shrugged his shoulders.

"He hangs about the farm doing odd jobs."

"He's lucky the Germans haven't picked him up for work over at Evine."

"Yes."

Maltby hadn't liked the look of the boy. He had the appearance of a city gutter rat rather than a farm boy. There was a slick precosity of manner about him that was fungoid. He stank of corruption.

"Can he be trusted?" he asked.

"Can any of them?"

That was true. You didn't know. Still, the fact was he had not been given away in three years. There was nothing else to do but go on trusting hopefully.

"We've got to be as careful as we can. Does he know where the arms dump is?"

"I doubt it."

They went out and began to walk towards the woods. Suddenly

Harrison froze. Turning to follow his gaze, Maltby thought he
saw a head pulled back behind a cart on the edge of the meadow
that lay beyond the yard. The boy? He looked at Harrison but
the tall man's eyes were following a bird which ducked and weaved
as it flew close to the ground towards the trees.

"Curious," he said as they moved on, "from its flight it looked
like some kind of lapwing. Couldn't be, of course, because we're
much too high for them here."

If he had seen the boy he obviously wasn't going to mention it.
Maltby kept a sharp look out but he saw no more movement near
the cart. Either he had imagined that he'd seen a head, or whoever
it was was being exceptionally cautious not to show himself again.

"What do you make of Buchan?"

Harrison asked the question abruptly.

"In what way?" Maltby stalled.

"Acting queerly, don't you think?"

"More queerly than usual?"

"All that stuff about evil and fighting the wrong war doesn't
bother you?"

"Just Buchan being Buchan, wasn't it?"

"You don't think he's cracking up and going round the bend?"

"Could happen, of course," Maltby said thoughtfully, feeling
that if he were to keep Harrison on this tack he'd have to throw
something in himself. "We're all under a pretty heavy strain.
But why Buchan particularly?"

"You know he picked that fight with Louis quite deliberately
and for no reason at all?"

"Did he?"

They had entered the wood. The tall man put his hands in his
pockets and looked down at his feet pressing through the weeds
that overgrew the path. Even in his shabby clothes there was an
air of elegance about him. They had been talking in French as
they always did, but when he spoke again it was in English.

"He came up here that afternoon and said he wanted to fight
me."

"Why?"

"That's what I asked him. He said for no reason except that it
was a lovely afternoon for a fight. I told him to go to hell and
he took a slug at me. But I saw it coming and caught him in a
judo hold. He wasn't expecting that and raved like a lunatic. That
I was cheating, that it was un-English, not the kind of thing you

expected from a sahib, and a lot more of the same sort of balls. All pure Kipling."

"And then?"

"I told him I'd break his arm if he didn't clear off. And at that he went. Apparently he walked straight up to Louis in the smithy, just said he'd never liked his face and tweaked his nose."

"Just like that?"

"Just like that."

"What damned idiocy! It must have been the talk of the village. Is he trying to draw the Germans' attention to him?"

They had reached the arms cache but Harrison made no attempt to uncover it.

"You think it more dangerous than his ravings about evil?"

"Don't you?"

Harrison reached up and took hold of a branch. Resting his cheek against his outstretched arm he looked down at Maltby.

"You know, Maltby, this war is different. Once men fought for what they could get. For the loot. Then they fought not for themselves but for their countries. Out of patriotism. Now we are told that our country is not important because we are fighting for ideas, ideals, a way of life, the things we believe in. Faith has no country." He paused for a moment or two. "You and I are here because by and large we are willing to accept this and act on it. But it is also exactly what Lord Haw-haw in Berlin and the Germans in the BBC are doing—fighting for what they believe in irrespective of their countries. What does a man do who suddenly realizes that his ideas and his faith are being fought for by the enemy and betrayed by his own side?"

Maltby scuffed his foot through the thick moss beneath the tree.

"Depends on the man, doesn't it? Somehow I can't visualize Buchan marching down to Caude and saying to Schwartzkopf, 'I'm on your side now.' "

"Is it any less likely than that he'll co-operate with the Reds?"

"Makes Security hell, doesn't it? Once you start this sort of thinking."

"That's your pigeon. Only please remember it's my neck as well as yours that you're playing with when you do nothing about types who may turn out to be unreliable. Or worse."

"What is it you think I should do, then?"

"If I were in your place, I'd pack him off home."

"It's one solution," Maltby agreed. "I'll think about it."

They uncovered the dump and Maltby took enough explosive, fuses and plastic wrapping to make up a dozen standard charges.

"I shall want some more," he told Harrison, "but this is about as much as I can carry on my bike without looking over-loaded."

"Want me to come with you, with another load?"

Maltby didn't. Neither Harrison nor anyone else was going to see where he hid the stuff.

"I'll pop up here whenever I can and take a little each time. If you're not around, I'll leave a chit in the dump saying what I've pinched."

"For you it'll always be open house," said Harrison and almost smiled.

If only men did act according to reason, as William Godwin insisted they must, Maltby moaned to himself as he cycled home from Aigunes. From what Harrison had told him, if judged in the light of pure reason, Buchan could not possibly be the spy. No one who was could act as he had done. Not reasonably, anyway.

The trouble was that Nazism wasn't reasonable. It made its adherents feel larger than life. If someone like Buchan were to be bitten with it, he would be so blown up with his own superiority and have such contempt for the rest of them that he would be capable of any folly.

But why was he only showing how he felt now? It might be, of course, that he was cracking under the strain as Harrison had suggested, though not in the way Harrison had meant. It might be concealing that he was a Nazi which was becoming too much of a burden. It certainly could be that. If so, it should simplify his job considerably.

It could be, however, that Buchan, though cracking, had not yet cracked and was not the spy. He might be just in the process of realizing that much that he believed in was being fought for by the Nazis but had not yet decided that his actions should be brought into line with these ideas. If that were so, then he presented a different kind of problem.

Then it could be simply that Buchan was an anti-Red and there was nothing more to it than that. He needn't be the less anti-Nazi for being anti-Red. There were plenty of people who regarded the Russian alliance as a dangerous expedient. Buchan was a soldier and as such was used to having political decisions made for him. He might grumble about them but his instincts must surely be to accept them. Provided he didn't let his Red phobia get hold of him completely, there was no reason why he should be disloyal.

Always providing that he was not the spy.

Back at the farm, Maltby hid the explosives in a disused well where they would be safe from any cursory inspection. Then he went off to meet Gringoire.

He liked the stocky railwayman. There was an absence of nerves in all he did and he never "flannelled". He was anything but talkative, but when he spoke it was usually sense. Despite the paucity of facts in his dossier, Maltby felt he was one of the five he would have been prepared to bet was all right.

He explained to the railwayman that he proposed they should blast the points beyond Airvout where the line branched north, fixing a rendezvous for the following evening.

Gringoire nodded appreciatively. It was a job that ought to be done, he said. Because the R.A.F. had peppered the railway to the north, the Germans were diverting three more trains a day through Airvout. These trains used the branch line and carried building material, for the Atlantic Wall mostly. There were still spare sets of points at Airvout, however, and they might have to do the job again.

"It's always like that with points," said Maltby. "The idea is to keep the Boches' production stretched to the limit as well as putting the line out of action for half a day or so."

"Bicycles?"

"No, we're walking across the fields. There's less chance of running into a patrol afterwards if we keep off the roads."

Gringoire made a face. He hated walking.

Maltby did not tell him that they were going to do the job alone nor warn him to say nothing about it to the others. It was most unlikely that he would run across any of them in the next twenty-four hours or would speak to them about the points if he did.

But when they met the following evening, Gringoire was obviously surprised at the absence of the others. Characteristically, he asked no questions but Maltby thought it wiser to explain. He had decided, he said, that as there were only three charges to be laid, it was not necessary to involve the whole group. In the past too many of them had been going on operations. For the future he was planning that they should undertake many more jobs which could be done by units of two or three. In that way, they could carry out several pieces of sabotage in a single night. Such constant harrying of the Germans could be as effective, even more effective, than the odd spectacular coup, though of course they would not drop those altogether and for them the group would use all its forces.

Gringoire, plodding steadily up the side of the valley on his short sturdy legs, nodded approvingly. They were walking in a straight north-westerly line which would bring them out, after they had crossed the wide plateau at the top of the ridge, about a mile to the east of Airvout junction. Both the road and the railway followed the valley away to their right through a cleft in the hills which ran west to east. They had all of five miles to cover and the going was rough, but this way they saved three miles on the distance by road.

"It's good you are back, Oignon," the railwayman grunted, "you're needed here."

Maltby did his best to pump him about what the group had been doing while he was away. Before leaving London he had read all the despatches sent back to HQ by the group so that he was primed with the official information about their activities. But this gave him no idea of the feeling within the group, and that was what he sought to get out of Gringoire.

Clearly, Gringoire had no very high opinion of the way they had gone on. Meetings had been largely wrangles between Buchan and Harrison. Since both Lestocq and Gringoire were only nominally soldiers, they normally took orders rather than formulated them, though they did make suggestions.

The main cause of dissension was a pet plan of Buchan's for raiding the Caude headquarters of the Gestapo and destroying the files and dossiers. This was an old idea of Buchan's, one that he had been putting forward ever since he had arrived in Pontrecy. Twice he had set it up, said Gringoire, and both times it had been cancelled at the last minute. Maltby knew why. A peremptory veto had been sent from London.

If Buchan were the spy, would he try to make the group undertake an operation which, if it were to be successful, would be a shattering blow to the Gestapo? Or was it simply a piece of provocation intended to destroy the group by leading it into a carefully set trap? Would he persist in putting the idea forward after it had been repeatedly turned down? He might, Maltby had to concede. Spy or not, a clot Buchan would always be.

He asked Gringoire why he didn't like the plan. Didn't he

think it feasible? The railwayman thought it could be pulled off. In his opinion, though, there would be a lot of casualties either among the group or Sarrut's Caude Maquis. Sarrut's men were mostly shop-keepers, clerks and lawyers, respectable citizens most useful for providing funds and hiding places but quite inexperienced in fighting. They were essential to Buchan's plan, but if they were to be badly mauled, recruiting to the Resistance would stop throughout the whole province. These sort of people, said Gringoire with class-conscious pride, not being workers, scared easily. Besides, they would be certain to kill a lot of Boches and that would mean there would be heavy reprisals taken against Caude. So even though it could be done he did not think it was worth the price at the moment. If there was already a Second Front it might be different.

The shrewd way Gringoire saw all the facets of the operation impressed Maltby.

He also learnt that the group's one handsome success in the last three months had been carried out by Gringoire acting on the spur of the moment. It had been one of those miraculous strokes of luck that occasionally come the way of secret agents and pay off better than coups which have taken weeks of preparation.

Taking advantage of a couple of his card-playing pals being on night duty maintenance work there, Gringoire had gone down to inspect the small shunting yard at Orlivaux on the edge of Le Feu's territory. He was interested in this spot because the line which came down from Airvout was single until it reached Orlivaux, where it again became double beyond the goods yard. He was looking for a way of cutting the single line so that the whole branch would be made totally unusable.

While he had been memorizing the lay-out and pumping his friends about the patrols, a goods train had limped into the station from Airvout in an obviously defective condition. Gringoire saw his chance and seized it. The shunting yard was practically deserted, most of the *cheminots* having gone to a small hut near the station for their meal break. With the help of his pals he had fired two engines, one after the other, and an assortment of trucks, head-on into the train waiting in the station. There had been a simply magnificent pile-up which had put the line out of action for over a week. Hardly less important was the quantity of wrecked rolling-stock.

It amused Maltby that in the report of the action radioed to

London there had been no mention of Gringoire or that it had been a piece of sheer luck.

After they had crossed the plateau and descended halfway down the other side of the ridge, they stopped to rest. Their plan was to go on down to the railway and then walk along beside it, skirting the village, until they came to the points on the other side. The night was very black but Gringoire was at home in the dark. He had the facility of a bat in avoiding obstructions, and when their path had lain through a plantation, Maltby had let him go first. He himself had felt totally blind, but the railwayman had hardly slowed his heavy tread at all.

Maltby stretched himself out full-length on the turf. He had not yet mastered a way of adjusting his belly-shield so that it would not stick into him when he was climbing a hill. Still out of condition, he felt tired and the rough going had made his feet sore in their espadrilles. Gringoire wore boots as always when not on a job where silence was essential. Probably, thought Maltby, because he has had so few pairs of boots in his life he is afraid of dying before they are worn out. Or if they are not on his feet, someone may steal them and he will have to take to espadrilles again. Perhaps it was a French prejudice, for it was the devil's own job to get Lestocq to leave off his boots. The British invariably wore espadrilles, preferring the silence of their rope soles to the clatter leather made on cobbles.

After resting for ten minutes they set off again. They had gone along the railway to within about half a mile of the station when the Alsatian held up his hand for Maltby to keep still. Cautiously he went forward on his own exploring the embankment. Presently he came back.

"There's no one there," he said, "no one at all."

"So?" Maltby answered impatiently, for he had not expected a patrol on that part of the line at that hour.

"The water tower. There's no Milice on guard."

This excited Maltby so much that he let out his breath in a long hiss.

The water tower had been the scene of two of the group's frustrated actions. Each time they had found it strongly guarded by Milice when they had arrived to destroy it. It was an important objective, much more important than the points. Maltby knew that this was the first water tower still in working order between Airvout and Dijon. Maquis groups further up the line had wrecked the others. Without towers it took many times as long to fill the railway engine boilers and thus the whole system was thrown out.

"We'll blast it," he said.

They scrambled down the embankment and examined the tower. It was all metal, even the hollow legs on which it was supported. If they could pack a good charge against its underbelly the whole lot would be torn apart. It was important that it should be wrecked so completely that it could not be repaired.

"Yes?" Gringoire queried.

"I think so. Where do you suppose the Milice are?"

The railwayman shrugged. He had no idea.

Maltby was worried in case the tower was not really unguarded but had been temporarily left like that while the sentries were having a snooze or gone on a short patrol. They would have to work quickly.

He had prepared three standard charges for the points and he now decided to use all three banked together to make a single charge. While he worked on this, Gringoire found an iron bar which he used to prise back a piece of loose metal on the base of the tower to form a pocket for the charge.

Together they rammed the explosive home. From the station came the voices of workmen shouting to each other, and beyond a small engine puffed and banged trucks about. But no one came near their part of the line.

When the charge was in place, Gringoire set off towards the station to stop any *cheminots* who might come along the line and get hurt when the tower went up. No one would come from the other way, he said, or if they did, they would be patrolling Germans or Milice and they didn't matter.

Maltby set going the fuse, which he had shortened to go up in about five minutes, and ran as hard as he could along the line away from Airvout. After about three minutes he was blowing hard and he scrambled up the embankment. He stumbled on for another minute, putting distance between himself and the tower. Then he lay down on his stomach to watch.

From where he was he could see the tower outlined against the sky above the station, a hard black shape set against the luminous night.

When he saw from his watch that six minutes had gone by and nothing had happened he began to worry. At six and a half he was cursing himself for a fool for allowing Gringoire out of his sight. If he was the one, he could have come back and pulled the fuse. Or tipped off the Milice guards to do it.

It was a minute later and he had decided that he must go back to see what had happened when there was a tremendous flash and a second afterwards a thunderous roar. For what seemed an age bits of metal went on crashing among the trees above the embankment and dropping on the track to clank against the rails.

Faint smoke hung where the tower had been but there was no hard outline against the sky. Neither Gringoire nor anyone else had pulled the fuse. He had miscalculated its setting.

Gringoire was all right.

CHAPTER TEN

THOUGH he had been back at Pontrecy only a few days, Maltby found the amount of work he had to do prodigious. He punted about for a way of testing the others which did not force him to go out on individual sabotage sallies but could think of nothing.

One thing he had not realized was that with his promotion to major everyone in the group not only accepted that he outranked them but insisted he lead them. They did nothing unless he gave the order which meant that he had to think of ways to keep them all employed. However he delegated, this ate into his time, as did the formal planning of the group's next project. It was the bridge at Camaret-Rouge which they had previously tried to demolish but had found it too strongly held.

He got out of the irksome business of transcribing reports to London by giving them to Buchan to write, just initialling them before they were sent. But he still had to send his own personal reports via "*Ils sont fou's*" radio. Madame Gallot's niece Celestine went into Dinville almost every day for him. If he were to drop these, he knew he would soon have B.6. screaming.

Then the blowing up of the Gibault factory at Evine, he found, could easily be a full-time job. There was so much to be done in laying it on and no one to do anything about it except himself, not even to run messages.

Scoutier had come to see him. He had come in his best suit with a clean shirt and tie, his face carefully shaved and his hair slicked down with what to Maltby looked like engine oil. It was, he said, uncultured and unbolshevik not to make yourself smart. Maltby, with two days' growth of beard and a dirty pair of overalls, felt he was definitely unbolshevik.

Henri was as co-operative as Le Feu had been shifty and suspicious. The Party had instructed him to aid Maltby and that was enough. His naive, unquestioning loyalty and his puppy-like anxiety to please were disarming. Unable to resist the pun, Maltby nicknamed him "Boy Scoutier", for he had the earnest, serious eagerness of a twelve-year-old boy scout who had just realized the implications of his code of honour and was trying to rise to them.

"You'll have to have a code name," he said, intuitively divining that this would please him, "what do you say to 'Boy'?"

Scoutier beamed with pathetic gratitude and Maltby knew that this man was his forever. At the same time the success of this psychological stroke gave him a queasy feeling. It had been too easy. Men ought not to be able to dominate—or to surrender themselves—as easily as that.

Maltby did not tell Henri what was planned for the Gibault works, pretending that all he wanted was information about the way the factory was run and guarded. When they had got all that together they could decide on what they could do.

"We'll get the information. We'll make a plan." Henri was despondent. "So! The workers go on sitting on their backsides as always. What good is the plan?"

"We'll see."

Shrewdly, Maltby considered that one of the reasons why the Gibault workers showed so little fight was that Scoutier had no leadership ability. He was a born follower, a trusted henchman, not a commander.

In one respect this situation was pleasing. Because of the docility of the workers the Germans had only a small force guarding the factory. As acts of sabotage by the workers had never been attempted, security checks, never very stringent, were now carried out laxly when they were carried out at all.

Maltby told "Boy" how he had managed to get into the yard before. He assured him that he could do the same thing again, only it would be more certain if he were to enter at the same time as the workers clocked on.

The next day they did just that. Maltby did not pretend to be a workman but an engineering draughtsman. He carried a roll of blue-prints under his arm, a set of pencils in his breast pocket, and had a soft felt hat pulled over one eye.

The gate was kept open wide enough to admit four people walking abreast. On either side was a steel-helmeted soldier, neither of whom showed more than cursory interest in the passes waved at them. As he and Scoutier pushed up to the gate, the two guards began to chat together across the heads of the incoming mob. Henri nodded to one of them as he passed, but the man was too engrossed to notice.

It had been ridiculously simple, but as soon as he was inside the yard, Maltby noticed that his heart was pounding painfully.

It was always as easy as that, Henri told him, except about once a month when the lieutenant appeared at the gate and every pass was checked. This was not done more often because it took over an hour and delayed the work.

Henri went off to the polishing shop where he worked, leaving Maltby to explore on his own. In fact, all he did was to walk round noting any changes in the layout from that shown in the plans he had got from Birmingham. There were remarkably few.

About an hour after the day's work had begun, a motor coach drove in through the gates and a detachment of soldiers got out. Maltby counted thirty men with a sergeant and a lieutenant in charge. Like the two he had seen on the gate, they were all oldish and rather shabby. They looked like men who were having a quiet war and preferred it that way.

After forming up in two ranks they were brought slackly to attention. The sergeant then marched off the rear rank to the guard post at the far boundary of the factory while the lieutenant led the others to the one overlooking the gate. Presently the men they were relieving came out and got into the coach and drove away. Maltby reckoned that the size of the garrison had been determined by the size of the coach.

The factory lay to the west of Evine, on the Pontrecy side of the village. A ten-foot-high wall with a gate in it faced the road to the south and there was a similar wall to the north, but the Germans had blocked up the gate which led out into a smaller road running parallel to the main one until the two joined up a mile towards Pontrecy. These walls were U-shaped, each wing running back for about twenty yards on either side of the factory, leaving about a hundred yards open between the north and south extremities. The Germans had closed these gaps with two wire fences about three yards apart, filling the space between them with rolls of barbed wire.

The guard towers were high, covered, wooden platforms erected at diagonal corners so that each had a clear view along two sides of the factory yard. Two light machine-guns were mounted on each.

On the Evine side the land between the factory and the village was open. But on the other side a wood with thick undergrowth grew to within half a dozen yards of the wire. That the Germans had not thought it worth their while to clear this was a measure of how little they thought they had to fear. This was the side where the finishing shop lay. The two great sliding doors in its wall, through which lorries backed to be loaded, were open and Maltby was able to look inside. He recognized the British machines. They were still fixed in the same positions as they were shown on his plans.

"Taking it all in," said a gruff voice behind him.

His stomach went tight and his blood raced but he forced himself to turn round slowly. A broad-shouldered man in grease-stained overalls with a charge-hand's brassard was looking at him surlily.

"Just looking in as I passed," he said, furious because his voice quaked.

"Seeing where the real work's done, eh?" the charge-hand said contemptuously. "Nice to draw a fat pay packet for mucking about with a pencil and a bit of paper!"

With a little snort he walked on into the finishing shop.

Maltby's stomach relaxed. Time he was getting out. He'd seen all that he needed to and there was no bonus to be earned by going on chancing his arm just for the sake of it.

He still had to get out, though. Henri had said that there was nothing to this. All he had to do was to walk through the gates. The factory drawing offices were down in the village and draughts-men were always leaving the works to go to them.

The encounter with the charge-hand had scared him. He had to force himself to walk unhurriedly towards the guard on the gate. As he approached, the man looked towards him. Curiously, Maltby thought, and his legs grew so leaden that he nearly turned back into the yard. But the sentry looked away again and he went on towards the gate. Just as he reached it, however, the soldier lifted his head and eyed Maltby squarely, seeming about to speak.

Quickly, Maltby forced his lips into a smile and nodded his

head. The guard smiled back and he was past him. It may have been imagination but he felt the man's eyes following him. He dared not glance back to see.

He walked down into Evine, and then doubled back, making a wide detour to avoid passing the sentry, to where he had left his bicycle hidden in a clump of bushes. As he pulled on his labourer's overalls he became conscious that his stomach was throbbing painfully. To quieten it he drank half a pint of reconstituted dried milk and ate a couple of rusks. Christ, he thought, there must be an easier way to fight a war.

Cycling back to the farm, he took a by-road to avoid going through the square in Pontrecy. He did not want to run into Hélène. When he got back he found she had called at the farm to see him but finding that he was out had gone away again without leaving a message. She had also missed him when he had been seeing Harrison. Hélène was beginning to bother him. He could not put off meeting her much longer. He had just got to face it.

As he had expected, the group's attack on the bridge at Camaret-Rouge was aborted. They arrived to find it guarded and patrols strung out along the railway embankment on either side. Maltby estimated that the Germans had put at least fifty men on the job. He calculated that this large party had been chosen in case the agents should have risked attacking a small one.

Maltby noted that there was no attempt to set a trap for them. The soldiers did not try to conceal their presence, talking to each other in loud voices as though they were on a picnic. To make it even more like one, they had lit a fire and were cooking a meal over it. If he wanted confirmation that the Gestapo were, as B.6. had said, intent on leaving the group intact while preventing them from doing serious damage, he had it now.

The others were depressed by their failure.

"The bloody Huns are always one jump ahead of us," Buchan grumbled. In some devious way he seemed to imply that Maltby should have foreseen the appearance of the patrol since he was in command.

"But there has been no one there for a week," Lestocq wailed. "I have been up here myself every night to check. I swear it."

He was sweating, Maltby noticed. He ran from one to the other of them repeating that the bridge had been unguarded, apparently only concerned that they should believe he had checked it as he had been ordered. Maltby wondered whether his anxiety arose from guilty knowledge that he had not kept the bridge under such thorough observation as he claimed. Or whether the noise he made was to cover some other guilt.

Gringoire took the set-back phlegmatically.

"It's war," he shrugged.

Harrison made no comment whatsoever. He strode along beside Maltby apparently absorbed in his own thoughts.

When they were a safe distance away from the bridge, they stopped and had a desultory discussion.

Buchan was in favour of their going off to look for something to destroy now they were out and armed with explosives and weapons. In this way, the night might not be a complete loss. Maltby turned this down. To go roving about setting off blasts here and there without any planned objective was asking to run into trouble.

This suggestion by Buchan disturbed Maltby. Not because it was a strange one if he were not the spy, but because if he were he must have put it forward confident that Maltby would turn it down. Did Buchan think he could read him as he knew he could read Scoutier? He would have to deal with Buchan next.

On the spur of the moment before they broke up, Maltby changed the time and venue of the next group meeting. He said it would be better for them to meet at the farm instead of at Hélène's again, that they should not be seen going to Hélène's too often. Afterwards he wondered whether the real reason was not that it was less easy for him to avoid being left alone with Hélène if they met in her room. In the old days, it had been taken for granted that he would be the last to leave.

As it was, the meeting at the Gallots did not make it all that much easier to avoid her. She had arrived twenty minutes early and gone straight to the barn which they always used for their meetings at the farm because the Gallots could keep watch from the farmhouse and send them a warning if any strangers appeared. She had expected Maltby to be there waiting for them, but he did not go out to the barn until ten minutes later, by which time Lestocq had also arrived.

He saw at once that Hélène was seething, her sallow cheeks flushed. Pretending not to notice this he greeted her warmly, kissing her hand with a flourish. She melted immediately, rubbing the back of her hand against his cheek. She could never stop herself from pawing him.

"I've seen nothing of you since you came back," she complained.

"That makes seeing you now all the nicer," he lied.

"I am your courier, you know," she pressed, making it plain she disliked the way he used Buchan to carry his messages to her.

He smiled and let her hand fall with playful reluctance. Lestocq was watching them intently with his close-set little eyes, his damp lower lip hanging down. Bloody *voyeur*, Maltby thought disgustedly, does he expect me to put my hand up her skirts?

One by one the others arrived and they began the meeting. That it went unhappily was Maltby's fault. He had not made up his mind what they were to do next, nor really given any thought to the group at all, being preoccupied with his mission. It was a good thing that it would all be over in three weeks or they would become restive. At the moment they were willing to put his shortcomings as a leader down to his need to get himself completely in the picture again after his absence.

They discussed two or three possible actions without coming to any decision except that they should be explored. Off the cuff, Maltby invented a number of tasks which would keep each of them individually busy for several days. None of them was vital or likely to turn up anything of immediate practical interest.

As is the way of meetings held without a positive purpose, it rambled on with everyone growing irritable.

Looking round them, sitting on boxes, barrows and odd bits of farm lumber in the dim light of the barn, Maltby thought they looked much more like conspirators than they ever did at Hélène's. There they always reminded him of a tea-party at the vicarage discussing a sale of work. What was coming out of the meeting, though, he admitted, was nothing as useful as that.

When they finally broke up there was barely enough time for Hélène to get back to Pontrecy before curfew. Instead of hurrying away she hung about waiting for him to suggest that she should stay the night at the farm.

"When shall I see you?" she asked when it became obvious that he had no intention of asking her to stay.

"I'll try to get down to see you tomorrow or the day after," he hedged, "there's a lot to do, you know."

"Not as much as that," she had replied.

He had planned to keep Buchan until last so that he could arrange a joint action with him unknown to the others, but this proved impossible. Buchan was staying temporarily in a house where the people were frightened out of their wits because they were sheltering a terrorist and they probably would not let him in at all if he arrived back after curfew. It was a law of the service that the nerves of weaker members should be considered as far as possible so he dashed away immediately after Hélène.

The following morning when he again tried to contact him Maltby was also unsuccessful. Maltby had instructed him to make a survey of all likely ambush points on the main Dijon road and the little man had apparently made an early start. Or was losing no time in reporting last night's meeting to the Gestapo!

He spent the day catching up on group business and by the time he got back to the farm he reckoned that he had done enough to make a reasonable show of activity.

To his surprise, he found Gringoire waiting for him. Usually the railwayman waited to be contacted. He was not one to hang around the other agents, for he had, unlike the others, contrived a social life of his own in Pontrecy. Since this was almost entirely confined to the local *cheminots* it netted a great deal of information.

Gringoire made it plain that he was not going to say what had brought him to the farm in front of the Gallots so Maltby took him out into the yard.

"You could have spoken in there," Maltby said when they were outside. "They're fine people, absolutely trustworthy."

The Alsatian grunted non-committally. The damn fool hasn't got anything positive against them, Maltby thought irritably, it's just prejudice, the worker's distrust of the peasant. That they're risking their necks in the Resistance just like him doesn't count at all against that!

They propped themselves up against a fence, watched by two or three hens having a last scratch round the midden before settling down for the night. The evening was chilly and Maltby would have much preferred to be in the Gallots' kitchen. Gringoire seemed in no hurry to begin. It was only afterwards that Maltby realized the naturally taciturn man was having difficulty in launching on what seemed to him a vast quantity of talk.

"You know the north signal-box at Pontrecy," he said at last.

"Yes."

"It's manned by two signalmen at night. You knew this? Well, it is. This week Phillipe Morin and Lemaire have the duty. Know them?"

"No."

"They're all right. Lemaire is married, has two children. You know how it is then. You don't want to do anything risky. Morin's different. He wants to be a maquisard. He wants to blow up the box first."

"Is that possible?"

Gringoire nodded.

"It can be done."

"What about Lemaire? If the two of them are on duty he must co-operate. But you say he doesn't want to be involved."

"He could be ill and not go on duty. He'd do that if we can find him a doctor who would give him a certificate. We can, yes?"

"I think so."

This was exciting. A signal-box, even a small one like the two-man affair at Pontrecy, was quite an installation to wreck.

The plan that Gringoire and the two railwaymen had worked out had the virtue of simplicity. Lemaire would not come in to work, but Morin would not tell the station-master in case he were to send another man to the box. Though, said Gringoire, this would not be likely if it were a Saturday night, for Morin had operated the box single-handed on a Saturday before when Lemaire was sick. Saturday was the best night to choose, anyway, because there was often no traffic at all coming through Pontrecy after midnight on that day. Gringoire and Maltby would go out to the signal-box about 1 o'clock and with Morin's help lay the charges. Morin would then take to the woods with Serpier's maquis.

"Morin is not a Communist, then?" Maltby asked, for Serpier's maquis was F.F.I. not F.T.P. like Le Feu's and Paturin's.

"He's for de Gaulle."

"We'll get Serpier to pick him up at Calvine in a car. If we lay half-hour fuses he can be there about the same time as the box goes up and away before any road blocks can be thrown up. It's a good plan, Gringoire."

"I thought you'd like to handle this yourself," said the railway-man cryptically, "so I came to you direct."

Maltby gave him a sharp look but there was nothing in Gringoire's rugged face to indicate what he was thinking.

CHAPTER ELEVEN

He had intended to use the signal-box as Buchan's test. It had seemed an ideal project when Gringoire had told him of his plan. After sleeping on it, Maltby changed his mind.

To use it to test someone as high on his list of suspects as Buchan would be crazy. Quite apart from the value of the objective itself, there were the signalmen to be considered. If Buchan "blew" the plan to the Gestapo, not only would they not get the signal-box but both Morin and Lemaire would be whipped away to concentration camps or just executed out of hand.

But he had to use it to test someone. Time was getting so short, he could not pass it up. Already he was being forced to consider whether he should not give up all thought of sabotaging the Gibault factory.

It had to be Hélène. As she was the least likely so far as he could see, she would be the safest. There was another point. Hélène only had to be told. She would not come on the job. If he chose one of the others, he knew Gringoire and the railwaymen would be bothered by finding the bombing party increased.

As he walked down to the village, Maltby tried to think how he should handle Hélène. He told himself that he was a fool to feel guilty about her. But he did. He felt so guilty that he loathed being with her. His guilt was not for the past but for what she would have built out of it for the future.

He had toyed with the idea of telling her about Judy. But he did not know how she would take it. It was not that she had any claim on him. He had made no promises. But she had assumed what she had wanted to believe and turned aside his protests with her superior smile. She knew why he spoke like that, she told him, it was the war. He was being noble. Because of the dangerous life he was living he would not enter into personal commitments. She just refused to admit the possibility that he did not love her as she loved him. He could pretend what he liked but she knew better. Her illusion was proof against any slights or indifference that he showed towards her.

The crux was, of course, that he did owe her something. In the last month before he had gone back to England, he had been so ill and in such pain that he had clung to her for comfort. Night after night she had soothed his tortured belly with her fingers and hot fomentations. From the surrounding farms she had scrounged milk for him, though in all France there was not enough even for babies. His dependence on her had been complete.

But it was not the thought that he was in her debt that held Maltby back from telling her that he had married while in England. It was fear of the consequences. The depth and ferocity of her passion frightened him. Even if he told her she might not believe it. If she did, he was certain she would not accept it. He simply could not face the emotional crisis that she would be certain to create. Not on top of everything else.

But there was a price to pay for not facing it. He would make it as small as he could. But there would be something. The thought of it nauseated him. He did not feel that he would be being disloyal to Judy. Once at Rigue, he and Pinto had escaped when the D/F vans had picked up the radio they were operating by crawling through a sewer. The stench and the touch of the slimy fæces over which they slithered had made him retch. But he had not turned back, for it was something he had to do, even though it was days before he felt free of the smell and the dirt. With Hélène he might have to endure another form of defilement just as necessary as the sewer at Rigue. But he could cleanse himself of that, too. It would not touch Judy.

The side-door to the bicycle shop was shut but he had a key. As he let himself in he wondered whether, if he had told B.6. about himself and Hélène, this would have been the final straw of his unfitness for the job and the whole idea of sending him back to Pontrecy dropped. Probably not. However bad he was, there was no one else and whatever mess he made of it nothing would be lost.

Before entering her room he gave the group signal, three short raps and a long. As he came through the door she appeared through the curtain that separated the living-room from her bedroom.

"So you've come at last!"

She put her arms round him and pressed hard against him. She was so small his chin was above her thin mouse-blonde hair. They remained like that for a long time. Or so it seemed to Maltby. Then she reached up and, drawing his face down to hers, kissed him. Her breath had a faint odour. He remembered that it often had when she was off-colour or over-tired.

"Harry, oh, Harry," she whispered, caressing his cheek with hers.

He was uncomfortable and off-balance with her arms dragging his head downwards, but he did not draw away.

"It's wonderful to have you here, my darling. When they took you away I thought I shouldn't see you again until after the war."

When he still stayed motionless, his arms slackly about her, saying nothing, she let out a gay little murmur and, pulling up her sweater, placed his hand on her small round breast.

"Mmm! Nice!"

This, he realized, was something done by him more than by her. She behaved the way she did believing it was what he wanted of her.

He could go on from here. It would not be impossible for him to sweep her up and make love to her. There was a part of him that even wanted to, a part that sent images of her familiar body and past satisfactions floating up into his brain. It would be simple enough to act just as he would have acted three months before. Or it would have been if he were still the same, or actions could be forgotten like desire in the moment of fulfilment.

He stepped back, drawing his hand away from her breast in a caressing movement that was entirely instinctive.

"I'm sorry, my dear, it's no use."

"What is it?"

"Or rather, I should have said that I'm no use."

"Why, what's the matter?"

She was all concern for him and he felt that he must make some gesture to her. He had sat down so now he took her hand and drew her down beside him.

"It's ghastly, my sweet. I'm no use in bed. The doctors say I'll be all right in a month or two but at the moment I can't do a thing."

"Is that all!"

"Isn't it enough? Now you know why I haven't been to see you."

"As if that mattered!"

"You know damn well it does."

She stroked his hair and kissed his eye-lids. Suddenly she began to laugh.

"Poor Harry! How angry it must make you to be impotent!" She rocked herself against him roaring with merriment.

"Stop it or I'll spank you!"

"Please do!"

"What's the use? It won't give me any pleasure!"

And at that they both laughed.

It was easier than he had thought.

She made coffee and, while she did, questioned him about himself. She's like an old hen re-discovering a lost chick, he thought. He was fascinated to see the way she had thrown off her sexiness as easily as if it had been a slip. Was it ever truly a part of her, he wondered, or was that his creation too, as he knew the way she expressed it was? No, he decided, it was there all right and it would not always allow itself to be relegated so casually.

"I ought to come to live at the farm so that I can look after you," she said when he explained about the care that he had to take of his diet. "You can't expect Madame Gallot to do it. But I'd like to."

"I look after myself very well. Besides, you're my courier not my nurse."

She handed him his coffee.

"Well, they didn't take your beautiful eyes away from you."

For once she did not try to kiss him or even take his hand but settled herself down opposite him, looking up into his face.

When he told her that he was going to blow up the signal-box, Hélène was troubled.

"Alone? You mean you are going to do it alone?"

"Yes."

He lied because he had decided if he were to test Hélène he must act exactly as though he suspected her. That meant that he could not tell her of the railwaymen's complicity in the raid, for they had to be protected.

"But isn't that too dangerous?"

"I don't think so. There's only two men in the box and they won't resist as soon as I show them my gun. You know that we can always rely on the *cheminots* looking the other way when we are on the job."

"But supposing there are soldiers. Like it was at Camaret-Rouge?"

"It's a signal-box not a bridge."

"All the same, there might be guards."

"Only one or two and I could shoot my way past them, do the job and be away before any more could arrive from the village."

"There might be more."

"Is it likely that the Germans will surround that particular

signal-box on Saturday night when they have never done it before?
What could make them? It's a piece of cake, my dear."

But Hélène was still uneasy.

"Why not take the others?"

"Because they're not necessary. It's a simple job and a lot of us
might mess it up. So don't say anything about it to any of them.
I don't want them horning in. Or thinking I've left them out
of something."

Hélène frowned and picked at her skirt.

"Did you mean what you said . . . about shooting your way in?"

"Yes."

"But you've never done that before. If there have been soldiers
about they've been left alone."

"Time marches on, my girl. Because we're getting stronger
we've got to be tougher. We've even got to be prepared to fight
pitched battles with the Wehrmacht. When the Second Front
opens the value of the maquis will depend on how many Boche
troops it can pin down."

"But you'll be alone, Harry."

"Because it's better that way."

"I'm frightened. I couldn't bear to lose you now you've come
back again."

"Don't worry. It's not as dicey as it sounds."

She held her face up to him, her grey eyes deeply troubled.

"I don't like it. The group's been so unlucky. Promise me you
won't do anything silly?"

He laughed and kissed her gently.

"I promise that I won't do anything else but blow up the signal-
box."

Maltby wanted to go then but Hélène kept him back, asking
him to tell her how London looked, had the bombing been bad
while he was in England, what he had done, who he had seen,
where he had done his training and a dozen other things about
people at HQ that he could not imagine really interested her.
But he answered her good-naturedly, even giving imitations of
Chivers and the whippet-like lieutenant that made her smile. She
had accepted his lies so easily that he was feeling almost gay.

"Were your nurses pretty?"

The question came quite unexpectedly.

"Exquisitely."

"You fell in love with one of them?"

"Head over heels. Are you madly jealous? There are pretty girls in Pontrecy, too, you know."

"Here you are under my eye!"

"That's what you think! There's quite a piece in old Bibot's café. The way she rubs her tits across my nose when she leans over to wipe the table is an invitation to rape."

"That's Françoise Vassen," Hélène said in a serious tone, "I don't think you'll see her at the café any more."

"Don't tell me such a luscious push-over is going to waste herself in marriage!"

"Old Bibot will get rid of her because of her brother."

"What brother?"

"Polidor. You knew he'd joined the Milice?"

"No. But why should that upset Bibot? He's never had patriotic feelings for anything except his cash register."

"It's his customers. There's a boycott on the Vassens. Their house was chalked with slogans yesterday."

"Because Polidor has joined the Milice?"

"Yes."

"Who did it?"

"I don't know. Some of the *cheminots,* I expect. But it could have been anyone."

Maltby was excited.

"This is important. Why didn't you tell me about it?"

"I thought you would know. Why is it important? It's happened before."

"Not in Pontrecy. Don't you see, if the villagers have done this on their own it means that from now on instead of just being tolerated we can rely on their active help. After what has happened to the Vassens none of them would dare to refuse."

"It may be they just didn't like the Vassens."

"I doubt it."

"Why? Other men from the village have joined the Milice and their families were left alone."

"Then the Germans were winning. It's not the same now, after Africa and Stalingrad. They've had it. Even here in Pontrecy it can be seen. That's what makes it difficult to understand why this fool should want to be a milicien now. Any ideas?"

"Perhaps he thought it might be best for France if the Germans win." Maltby blew a raspberry. "Or perhaps he just wanted the extra rations. He's a bad lot, anyway."

"Or perhaps the whole family are informers and that's why his sister has been flopping herself all over me."

Hélène looked at him quickly.

"Do you think that possible?"

"It could be but I hope not. I like to be seduced for myself alone."

But to Hélène this was serious.

"But it's dangerous. She could denounce you."

"So could the rest of the village," Maltby shrugged. "They haven't yet. . . . And in any case my papers are genuine."

"As if that mattered!"

"You've very down today, darling."

Before replying she turned her head away, looking down at the floor.

"I'm afraid," she whispered.

"Afraid?"

"You wouldn't understand. You're not French. You haven't seen your country fought over twice. And now it's going to happen again . . . and I'm afraid."

"But it's what we've been working for! You can't let it get you down now."

"It could mean that I'd lose you," she said in a piteously bleak voice.

Was she cracking? She'd been in the underground for a hell of a long time and it had been no picnic for her in Paris.

"You need a break. I'll fix for you to go down to the south for a rest. We can get someone else to work as courier while you're away."

"No, Harry, you mustn't send me away!" Her eyes were full of fear and Maltby looked at her curiously, wondering why she should be so frightened, until she added in a quieter tone, "Not now you've just come back."

He took her hand. This blasted war was hell for all of them.

"All right, but only if you keep bouncing. Any flopping about with the wind-up and off you go."

He asked her to call a group meeting for Sunday and then got up to go.

"And you will take care?"

"Of course."

"You know it's not for myself I'm afraid, Harry." She took his hands and pressed them between hers. "There's no risk I wouldn't take to save you."

Her solemnity embarrassed him.

"The only risks you'll ever take for me are in bed. And you can't even have those now!"

She smiled.

"I don't mind not having them again ever so long as you're like this. You've never been so nice to me, Harry, as you have been today."

It was true, he thought, as he went down the stairs to the alley, I've behaved like a little gentleman. Most unnatural. He knew that it was only because he had been so tensed up about meeting her again and then relieved that it all should have been so easy. It wasn't an attitude that was likely to last.

He got out his bicycle and rode over to see Serpier. The maquis leader had his camp deep in the Dorac forest. As far as Calvine the road was good and the soft autumn day made cycling pleasant. As he was carrying no weapons or anything else incriminating and had thought up a good reason why the Gallots' hired hand should be going to Calvine he was completely carefree. After Calvine, however, he had nearly five miles of rutted forest track to cover. The going was so bad and in places so steep that he had to push his bicycle as often as ride it.

He was just beginning to wonder if he hadn't got the directions wrong, when a tramplike figure got up from behind a bush and challenged him suspiciously. When Maltby did not immediately answer, he found himself looking down a Sten gun and knew he had arrived, and this must be one of the camp guards.

Serpier was a round-faced, complaining men who had taken to the maquis rather than be conscripted for forced labour. Maltby suspected he had regretted his choice ever since.

The camp was filthy and had obviously been occupied for far too long, and Serpier's half-dozen companions were listless and demoralized from boredom. His transport consisted of a *gazogene* and an old Citroën. The *gazogene* had been dismantled for servicing, but so far as Maltby could see no one was bothering to put it together again. The Citroën was unusable because, having stolen it from a collaborator, they had made no attempt to get any petrol for it.

Serpier admitted that the group had not explored any reserve camp sites but said that it was something they would be doing.

They had not enough weapons, though, nor equipment nor cigarettes. Supplies did not reach them as they did other maquis groups, so what did Maltby expect? "What do you expect" was a favourite expression of Serpier's. Tactfully, Maltby refrained from saying what he did expect. Nor did he ask what Serpier wanted more weapons for, since he apparently had no plans.

He stayed at the camp till the evening making suggestions for its improvement as unobtrusively as he could. Before he left he also saw the *gazogene* almost complete again. Near enough, anyway, to expect that it would be in working order to collect Morin the following night. He promised to arrange for Serpier to have some more supplies and if possible to send him a military instructor.

It was dusk when he got back to Pontrecy. As soon as he rode into the square he knew something was up and he got off his bike. It was strangely quiet and there were none of the usual loafers sitting round the pump. A burst of confused shouting broke the silence. It seemed to come from a street that ran off the lower end of the square. A moment later a gendarme crossed the square in the opposite direction from the noise, moving as fast as he could without actually running. Whatever was going on, the police apparently did not want to know of it.

Curious to know what had sent the policeman scuttering off, Maltby left his bicycle and went in the direction of the noise. It did not sound like a fight, for the shouting had no continuity about it. Every now and then there would be silence except for a single voice. He was too far away to distinguish what the words were, but when the voice stopped there was a cheer and shouts and then another voice began to speak.

Turning a corner he saw a crowd which seemed to be composed of all the village layabouts ringing a small workman's house. When he got nearer, however, he saw that the layabouts were not taking much part but were standing round propping up walls and watching. The people they were watching were ordinary villagers, railwaymen and Gibault workers. More than half were women. The women were shouting insults at the people in the house. Maltby heard someone yell, "Traitor!" and then he noticed that the walls of the house were covered with chalk writing.

It must be the Vassens' house. When he was about thirty yards away from the crowd, Maltby stopped at the corner of a cross-road that ran away up towards Evine. He was elated but he did not want to get mixed up in the rumpus. Pontrecy was waking up all right if it was willing to demonstrate as openly as this against Frenchmen joining the Milice.

A big workman was shouting to Vassen to come out and be thrashed. The father of a son who had died for France had the right to punish the father of a traitor. A man's voice in the house shouted something that Maltby could not distinguish and the crowd jeered. A woman now began to scream abuse and threats with a shrill venom. The women should be marked, she shrieked, so that decent people would know them for what they were, the mother a breeder of traitors and whores, the daughter for the whore that she was.

"Mark them! Mark them!" she yelled hysterically. Her hair had come loose and flopped untidily about her shoulders. Though he was too far away to see, Maltby knew that her face was shiny with sweat and her eyes wild. She jerked and flung herself about as though possessed. "Cut off their hair! Shave their heads!"

"What, only their heads!" bawled one of the loafers.

The guffaw that followed momentarily lowered the tension. But the woman swung round on the crowd and began to harangue them with her back to the house.

"Call yourselves men and allow this scum to defy you! Get them out! Smash down the door! Burn them! What are you afraid of? The Germans? I spit on them! I spit on them for my husband who lost his legs in the trenches! But you! You have legs, why do you wait? Cowards! Do you want traitors to lie on your daughters?"

The crowd growled and surged unsteadily forward. Someone on its edge threw a stone which shattered a window. At the sound of the glass tinkling down, the men stopped. For all its hysteria and desire for violence, the mob was purposeless. It could be cruel, it was capable of wreaking a vengeance on flesh, blow feeding blow, to which frenzy would set no limit, but without a leader able to act with more than words it was powerless to make the decisive move which would set the orgy going. Any trifling distraction, a foolish remark, an unexpected sound, dowsed its uncertain urge to riot.

Three youths, scarcely more than boys, ran past Maltby carrying buckets of farmyard filth. Their flushed faces, twisted by grins of imbecilic mischief, were unpleasantly demonic. Their lips slavered and, as they flung themselves headlong, they let out little maniac giggles at the obscenities they threw at each other.

The crowd welcomed their arrival with joyous shouts. They fell on the buckets and began to pelt the house with muck.

Maltby lost his feeling of elation. The jerky, involuntary movements of the people in the crowd nauseated him. They weren't ordinary human beings but puppets jumping to the pull of emotional reflexes so indecent that normally they were kept buried deep within themselves. A bestiality from the roots of being had taken hold of them.

There was no courage in what they were doing. They were not even demonstrating against the Germans in hounding this one family, though they may have thought so. Nearly everyone in the crowd Maltby knew by sight and many of them by name. Among them there was not one Resistance supporter. These people shouting and screaming in the name of patriotism for the Vassens to be degraded were the same as the Vassens in all but the act of betrayal. They had waited for the right moment to lick the conqueror's boot and been saved by the bell. Now they wanted to purge their guilt in the blood of others too stupid to recognize its sound. He and whoever came after him would have to use this new-found patriotism. It didn't mean that he couldn't see it for what it was.

The crowd's delight in muck-throwing was shortlived. Maltby guessed that the difficulty of doing it without soiling yourself deterred all but the most ardent. The woman who had egged the men on so vigorously seized a bucket and running up to the house tipped its contents through the broken window with a new stream of abuse that made the mob laugh and jeer again.

That cow will fire the place if some bastard gives her a torch, thought Maltby, turning his head away feeling he had had his bellyful of the scene.

It was at that moment that he saw the girl.

Apparently quite unaware of what was going on, Françoise Vassen, a bright scarf tied coquettishly round her head, hips swinging in proud provocation, was sauntering down the road that inclined upwards towards Evine. She looked as though she were humming to herself. He saw her quite plainly outlined against the now rapidly darkening sky, but did not at first recognize her. When he did he felt a sharp stab of fear and made a movement to warn her of her danger.

She did not see him, for just as he moved she swung right down an intersecting street. Maltby calculated that this street must run diagonally and come out opposite the Vassens' house. If he were right, the mob would see her in a minute.

He waited for what seemed a long minute but could not have been even half as long. Then there was a shout. He saw heads turn. For a moment nothing happened. Then there was another shout and the crowd swept forward in a wave and disappeared.

Maltby began to run, too. He ran up the hill towards the intersecting street, guessing that that would be the only way for Françoise to bolt and that he was closer to her than the mob. He had no idea what he meant to do or what help he could be to her. It was simply blind instinct that set him going.

He was still fifteen yards from the side road when she appeared. She was running fast, close to the ground, head thrown forward in panic. Searching for an escape, she flitted rapidly from side to side of the street. Her crouching, ground-hugging flight resembled that of the bird which had flown across the meadow at Aigunes and puzzled Harrison. Suddenly she saw what she was looking for and darted out of sight through a gap on his left. A second later he saw her figure outlined as she leapt on to a wall. It was only there a moment before she disappeared beyond it.

Maltby had stopped at the side road and he slid into the shadows as the mob, yelling and cursing, stampeded out of it, rushing heedlessly in the same direction as the girl. But already the chase was thinning out. When they saw their quarry had disappeared, all but the youngest dropped to a walk and almost at once stopped altogether. They gathered in knots, talking and uttering loud threats. The youths and girls ran on up the hill until they were lost in the darkness which was now almost complete. It did not seem to occur to them that if Françoise had run straight on they must have still been able to see her after they turned the corner.

After a while, even the sounds of the chase subsided as the youngsters ran themselves out. The older people began to drift back towards the Vassens' house, and when the booing and shouting broke out again even the few who had remained looking hopefully up the road towards Evine hurried away to see what this new excitement was.

Treading softly, Maltby crossed the side road and made his way along to the gap where Françoise had disappeared. It was a short blind passage between two enclosed gardens. It would have been natural for her to have chosen the far wall to go over and he pressed himself against it listening. After a moment he heard a rustle and a stifled sob and knew he was right.

Not wishing to scare the girl by climbing on to the wall in case she rushed off in a panic that would draw the mob after her again, he felt cautiously along the wall. As he suspected, at the far end of the passage nearest to the house there was a door. It was open and he slipped inside, closing the door behind him.

The garden belonged to one of the better Pontrecy houses and was quite large and so heavily stocked with fruit bushes and trees that in the dark it appeared overgrown. Taking a path that skirted the wall and crouching low so that he would be in the thickest shadow, he crept towards the spot where he had heard the noise.

The gloom in the garden was so thick that he did not see her until she started back when he was almost beside her.

She opened her mouth and he rammed his hand over it hard before she could utter a sound. At the same time he grabbed hold of her hair roughly, wrenching her head back.

"Don't make a sound! I'm a friend."

When she didn't move he let her go. He found she had bitten him and he rubbed his finger painfully.

"Where are they?" she whispered.

"They've gone. But they'll be back. They'll catch you if you stay here."

As he spoke his ears caught the noise of the yobbos coming back down the hill.

"They'll see you if you stay near the wall and they've got a light. Get into the middle of the garden."

He lugged her to her feet and pushing her in front of him made his way to a clump of bushes well away from the wall. Unless they came into the garden she would be out of sight there even if they had a light.

"Lie here. Don't move and don't make a sound. I'll try to keep them from coming in here."

The noises were much nearer now. He went back to the wall. He didn't have time to go out by the door. There were two strands of barbed wire running the length of the wall held by iron supports to form a cradle to catch scrumpers. As he ripped away the end section he wondered how Françoise had managed to avoid it.

He pulled himself up on to the wall and sat on it. The youngsters were quite close now. They were running from side to side of the road, poking in any likely hiding place. Some of them had given up bothering about the chase and were chi-iking with the girls.

The leader came whooping along banging the wall with a fallen branch he had made into a club. He stopped abruptly when he saw Maltby sitting on the wall.

"She's not here," Maltby said quietly, "I've looked."

The others had come up now and they looked at him with curiosity and suspicion. "The Englishman", he heard one of the girls whisper. Uncertainly they clung together until one of the braver ones walked past Maltby's dangling feet to explore the passage.

"She must be hiding here somewhere," said the youth with the club, scrambling up beside Maltby and peering into the garden.

He took a tentative swipe into the undergrowth below. His stick caught the barbed wire and he swore.

"She's not up there," announced the boy who had gone up the passage.

"It's too dark to see." The youth dropped off the wall and looked up at Maltby. "We're going to the station to get some lights. Then we'll find her."

"Yes, we'll get her," the others chorused.

They moved off, the girls giggling in shocked delight as the boys invented lewder and lewder things they would do to Françoise when they caught her. But they were calmer now. They had lost their maniac exultation and were talking bigger and bigger in an effort to recapture their frenzy.

Maltby waited until they were well away and then slipped over the wall. The girl was lying exactly as he had left her.

"Come."

He led the way to the door. She stumbled behind him clutching his overalls.

"Wait here," he said when they were in the passage. "If I signal you to do so, nip back into the garden and close the door."

He went out into the road. It was clear. The girl came towards him quickly. The loud clop of her shoes on the paving made him wince.

"Take off your shoes," he snapped.

She started back at his sharp tone as though she expected a blow to follow. Seeing that he meant nothing more than that she should obey, she bent down and slipped her shoes off.

They set off up the hill without speaking, keeping closely to the shadows. After a hundred yards they were past the last house and in open country.

"You can put your shoes on now. But walk on the grass. If someone comes along, don't run. Do whatever I tell you."

For about another quarter of a mile they walked in silence. Then he turned into a meadow beyond the entrance to a farm.

"Sit down. You should be safe here. It's not likely they will come as far as this to look for you."

In the country, away from the shadows of houses and trees, it was lighter and he could see her plainly. She was in a mess. Obviously she had not avoided the wire when she jumped over the wall. Her clothes had jagged rents where the points had caught them. Through a hole in her sleeve he could see a gash in her arm and there was a long trickle of blood running down one leg into her shoe. Her face was dirty and scratched from the brambles through which she had crawled in her panic flight.

"It's my brother," she said, "I've done nothing."

There was a cattle-trough fed by a small spring in the meadow, and Maltby soaked his handkerchief in the water and began to clean her up. She accepted these attentions passively, making no attempt to do anything for herself but watching him interestedly.

He wiped her face and cleaned the blood away from the gash in her arm. When he had done this she pulled her skirt up to her waist and rolled on her side for him to do the same for the wound in her thigh. She did this quite naturally without a trace of hesitation or embarrassment.

She was heavily built but beautifully proportioned. Her thighs were not thick but tapered smoothly upwards above the knees. In the starlight her flesh had a white incandescent sheen. He rubbed away the blood round her ankle and worked up her leg. When his fingers touched the skin above her knee he felt himself tremble slightly. He finished cleaning the wound as quickly as he could. The wire had only just nicked her buttocks but walking had kept it bleeding. The gash on her arm was much deeper.

Maltby stood up, wiping his hands on his overalls. He would have liked to cover the cuts but he had nothing to put over them. As scabs were already forming he judged they would be all right.

He looked towards the village. He could hear nothing and there was no sign of lanterns. The search, if it were thorough, might not have reached the top of the hill. It might go on for another hour, and it was possible that some of the mob would hang about the Vassen house for another half-hour after that in the hopes of catching Françoise sneaking back. By now he reckoned the riot would have spent itself and would not be continued much beyond curfew. Without something fresh to stir it up it would simply peter out.

"Stay here for a couple of hours before trying to go home again. It should be all right by then. But watch out."

She had pulled her skirt down over her knees and was sitting holding her injured arm. Maltby, his eyes now thoroughly accustomed to the dark, looked round for somewhere more comfortable to leave her than on the broken ground near the cattle-trough. She had shown such a lack of initiative so far that he believed if he left her there she would not look for somewhere better herself.

There was a hayrick in the meadow and he pulled out some of the hay for her to sit on. Docilely she dropped on it, leaning her back against the rick. Feeling that he had done all he could for her he stepped back but she stopped him.

"Don't go."

Thinking that she was still frightened and did not want to be left alone yet, he sat down beside her. But her face was quite placid, without a sign of the terrifying experience she had gone through. In the same way as animals forget their fear the moment the object of it is no longer in front of them, she had forgotten hers.

She was like an animal in lots of ways, he reflected. He had thought so when he had found her cowering in the bushes too stricken to run from him. Her acceptance of his authority was animal rather than human. As was her femaleness which could affect him even while he attended to her hurts. He had told Hélène that she was pretty. This was true, but it was an unintelligent village prettiness he would not have noticed but for the way consciousness of her sex exuded from her.

"You are——"

"Gaston Minaud," he said quickly. "I work for the Gallots."

"I've seen you at the café."

"I go there sometimes. Do you like working there?"

"Bibot won't have me there any more because of my brother. Bibot's a pig."

"What will you do now?"

"Go to the factory."

"Do you mind that?"

"No. The foreman's good-looking. Not a pig like Bibot. I saw him today."

She gave a little laugh at her thoughts and let her head fall on his shoulder. He stayed as he was, hands clasped round his hunched knees plaiting a strand of hay.

"They say you're an Englishman."

"Who do?"

"Everyone does."

"You too?"

"It's what they say."

"You shouldn't believe fools' talk. Would an English milord work like a dog for the Gallots as I do?"

That's a bit hard on poor old Gallot, Maltby chuckled to himself, but in a good cause. Her head was slipping lower and lower so that her hair brushed his cheek and nostrils. It was soft and quite fine and, to his surprise, smelt clean.

She said no more for quite a long time as she digested what he had said.

"I don't think you're an Englishman."

"You're right."

"You'd kill me if you were."

"Why?"

"Because of my brother."

He nodded.

"I expect so. Shall I kill you?"

He turned his head towards her and she lifted her face, lips open in a smile of anticipation. He kissed her and with little wriggling motions of her buttocks she snuggled into him, pulling his arm about her.

Maltby's pulses were racing and he was at the same time trying to think. He had never meant to get himself involved like this. If he'd wanted an affair with a village girl—which he didn't— Françoise Vassen was scarcely the most suitable. But the touch of her was making him feel more ruttish each minute. Would he be able to get rid of her afterwards if he had her? Or would she hang around him? He ought to beat it back to Pontrecy.

What was also bothering him quite as much as what he ought to do as an agent was what he ought to do as a man. He'd had no experience with girls like Françoise. He might be imagining far too much. She was only a kid—not more than eighteen. It could be that she was quite unaware of the sexy feelings she aroused in him and was just hugging him for comfort. Wouldn't he be behaving like an old maid who is always imagining that any man who happens to be in the same street is following her if he were to run off?

His immobility made Françoise restless and she began to nudge him impatiently with her shoulder. When he still did not move, she swung round so that she faced him, fixed her eyes on his and then dropped them to the top of her dress.

The invitation was unmistakable. He slid his hand down her throat to her breasts, which were large and soft but not flabby. He took her roughly but she did not seem to mind. Or perhaps it was the only way she knew, for her own love-making was without finesse, tenderness or thought for anything but her own satisfaction.

Later he laughed at himself for ever having scruples, for nothing could have been more impersonal. To her the whole thing was of no more significance than brushing one's teeth. Because he had shown concern for her, she took it as natural that that was what he expected and it was enough for her that he was a man. It was as simple as that. Equally laughable was his nervousness that she might think being tumbled would give her a hold over him. It was evident that if she didn't see him again she would never give him a thought. He could understand why the women in the mob yelled for her blood so easily and the youths could make up such exquisite tortures for her. They knew her very well already.

He tried to pump her about people in the village, about Bibot and whether, as the group suspected, he was not above passing on to the Gestapo gossip he heard in his café. But he got little out of her. She was so unintelligent, so little interested in anything that was not under her nose at the moment, that he became bored with the effort. Now that she had had her sex she was dreamily lethargic. She did not paw him and apparently did not look to him for caresses. It would have been distasteful if she had not been so obviously happy and content in her self-absorption. But she was not without her surprises. One of them was a sudden question that came after a long period of silence.

"You go with that Marie Ducommon, don't you?"

Marie Ducommon was Hélène's "cover" name in Pontrecy. There was an edge to her voice that was unusual. When she had answered his questions it had always been indifferent, quite uncoloured by emotion even when speaking of someone like Bibot whom she said she disliked.

"I see her sometimes."

She smiled at this and told him vulgarly what he did with Hélène. But this was said without an edge, just warning him not to try to pull the wool over her eyes.

"She goes with Germans, too."

The "too" told him a lot. Not only of her venom against Hélène but about herself. He must remember to tell Harrison that ideas and beliefs recognizing no frontiers was not new but a return on a different plane to the most uncomplicated of primeval urges. Sex, as a way of life, also had no country.

"Why don't they shave her head? I've seen her in Caude with her fat Boche."

"Who?"

"A Gestapo man."

It amused him that she should mistake Sarrut, a respectable grocer struggling manfully to overcome his natural timidity and do his duty by the Resistance, for a Gestapo thug. He wondered whether Sarrut would be flattered or angered if he knew.

"I have never taken money from the Boches," she said loftily. "But she lets hers keep her."

"Does she?"

"Of course. You don't keep her, do you? How else could she live here without working?"

"She may have money of her own."

Françoise snorted, pained that men could be so foolishly gullible. In her world young women did not "have money of their own". If they had money and did not work, there was only one way they could be getting it.

Bored, Maltby lay on his back looking at the stars. They spoke little, for there was nothing that they wanted to say to each other. He could have left her to wait by herself until it was safe for her to go home. By staying he afforded her no special protection, and she certainly would have been neither surprised nor offended if he had gone off. But it did not occur to him to go. Without knowing it he was responding to his Southgate conventions which demanded that a gentleman should always escort his lady to her door. He would have been enraged if this had been put to him but it was true.

Half an hour after curfew, he got to his feet.

"You'd better get home."

He had been right in estimating that the mob would disperse at curfew. The village was quiet when they reached it, and they met no one. For this he was thankful, for he had no wish to be seen with her. That was why he left her at the corner of the street she had turned down when he had first seen her coming from Evine. He guessed that behind the curtains in the houses opposite hers, eyes might be watching.

Françoise did not kiss him when they parted. Either she was too preoccupied with covering the remaining yards between her and safety to remember to, or had no use for such courtesies except as inescapable preliminaries to more serious business.

He watched her run swiftly, silently, through the shadows, carrying her shoes. With a quick dart she was across the cobbles and fumbling at the garbage-fouled door. A window was banged open and a hoarse voice bawled imprecations. To the empty street, for by then she was inside.

Maltby went back to the square and retrieved his bicycle. He slipped off the chain and wrapped it round the handle-bars. If he ran into any Germans, the uselessness of his bike would be a sufficient excuse for his being out after curfew. But he only saw a gendarme and he looked the other way as soon as he recognized Maltby.

He pushed his bike with one hand, walking beside it lightly, feeling good. His stomach throbbed but not painfully. A meal was all that was needed to quieten Harriet for the night.

"Bear up, old girl," he said aloud. "You haven't got long to wait now."

He felt he was getting things under control. He might even be able to do the bloody job. He might. He might.

If it was Buchan he was after, he'd know in a week. That would even give him time for the ball-bearing factory. Hold your horses, boy, he cautioned himself, you're getting too fond of thinking that it is that cocky little bastard. You could be wrong.

Passing a familiar spot on the road he remembered the last time he had passed it late at night was on his way back from the abortive attack on the bridge at Camaret-Rouge. Then he had been wearing his stomach shield and it was chafing him painfully.

If he had been wearing it tonight, what would Françoise have thought if he'd had to take it off? He pictured himself struggling to free himself from it while she watched him, impatiently bouncing about on her buttocks, and laughed till the tears came.

Françoise had been an experience. Hitherto his affairs had had a pattern, which included a period when he got to know the girl. Often he had not been conscious at the beginning that his object had been to go to bed with her. It was something which had grown out of what might just as easily have been a passing acquaintance. But this! This was what the louts in the unit in which he had begun his military service had called "having a bash". He had thought they were lying braggarts when they came back with stories of what they'd done with local girls they had picked up. If Françoise was not unique he could have maligned them.

If he had, he marvelled that they should find such uncouth copulation satisfying. Perhaps they were just ignorant of any other. Or perhaps, like Françoise, they felt no need to search beyond simple release from a totally focused urge. Either way he was sorry they should miss so much.

But satisfying or not, he was honest enough to recognize that his unusual feeling of well-being was in part due to Françoise.

CHAPTER TWELVE

"Boy, you're a jewel."

"It was easy, comrade, nothing at all."

Henri Scoutier spoke deprecatingly, but on his frank open face was a smirk of pleasure.

"A jewel, I say," Maltby went on enthusiastically, deciding that he had nothing to lose by laying it on a bit, "a ruby, the Koh-i-nor, a pearl without price!"

"It was Boullanier on the night maintenance shift who really got it all," said Henri, now somewhat overwhelmed and feeling that he could afford to share the praise that was being showered upon him so abundantly. "He is a good practical comrade but does not understand the value of education."

"I'll have Oxford make him an honorary master of arts!"

"I meant Marxist education," explained Henri loftily, humour not being his strong point.

"Oh, well, we'll make it Moscow!"

What had pleased Maltby was that Scoutier had brought him details of the routine of the Gibault factory from the time the workers left at night to the time they arrived again the next morning. When he had asked for this information he had expected that if he received anything at all it would be in the most general form. Instead, Henri had produced a series of precise time-tables, setting out the numbers of men on duty at each of the guard towers, when they were changed, the routes of the night watchmen and the times they visited each shop, even a monthly schedule of regular maintenance work.

"Did Boullanier draw these up on his own?"

"No. He got the information and I wrote it out."

"You shall be a master of arts, too!"

Henri shuffled about uncomfortably, going very red before he finally plucked up courage to ask a question.

"But, comrade, what are you going to do? These times we have always known. Why are they important now?"

Maltby looked him hard in the eye.

"You tell your pal Le Feu to keep his nose out of my pot. If he wants to know anything, let him ask me himself, not set you on to pump me. For one thing, Boy, you're not up to it."

Scoutier looked crestfallen, utterly miserable with his failure.

"Do you want to work with me?" Maltby asked him.

"Of course."

"I can't work with you if you're spying on me for someone else. Even if that someone is Le Feu."

"But I have to do what the Party——"

"The Party nothing. Look, Boy, you tell Le Feu that either I have you and he leaves you alone until I say you can return to his group, or I don't want you. And don't think you can get away with it without telling Le Feu, for he'll spot what you're up to as quickly as I did. Understand?"

Henri nodded unhappily.

"Anyway, I don't know myself yet what I'm going to do. You can tell Le Feu that if you like." He shuffled through the time-tables. "You couldn't get anything on where the electricity cable enters?"

"There isn't one. It is generated in the station house."

"I ought to have guessed that. What about the telephones?"

"There's a line that the Germans always use which runs out

near the back watch tower. It's an Army line which the engineers laid about two years ago."

"Buried?"

"Yes."

That was awkward. He'd have to think about that.

"Any radios?"

"I've never seen any or heard any being used. Nor has Boullanier."

"Could I get in at night the same way as I did the other morning?"

"No. Draughtsmen are never there at night. They'd drop on you at once."

But Henri thought it would not be difficult to go in as part of the maintenance staff. So long as you had a pass to wave, there was apparently no certain check on the total number of workers or who the individuals were. Altogether, including watchmen, there were about forty workers in the shops at night, enough for one or two more not to be noticed.

"Well," said Maltby cheerfully, "that looks all right."

"You'd have to stay in until the day lot arrived."

"Why?"

"After the maintenance men come in, the gates are shut and no one can get out till the morning."

"You're sure?"

"Of course. Why should anyone need to go out? So! No one goes out!"

Oh, well, thought Maltby, it can't fall in your lap all the time. Not being able to get out might put the kibosh on some of the ideas he had been playing with for Evine. But he at least now had some dope to work on, thanks to Henri.

"Suppose I did want to get in, could you get me two or three passes?"

"Two or three? So many?" Henri queried doubtfully. "I could let you have mine and perhaps the other comrades would lend——" An idea struck Maltby and he interrupted.

"Do you know where the passes are printed?"

"No."

"Could you find out?"

Henri frowned.

"There's a girl in the office——"

"I don't want to hear the nasty details of your love-life, Boy, just stir her up. See if she can find out whether they're printed locally."

Henri still looked so abashed that Maltby gave him a pat of encouragement.

"You don't understand why I won't have you carrying tales to Le Feu, do you? It's not that I don't trust Le Feu. But if we do a job together I'd like it to be something big, wouldn't you?"

The young Communist nodded eagerly.

"That'll mean that a lot of lives will be in danger. So the fewer people who know what we're up to the better. Then I may not tell you the whole plan, but Le Feu might think I had and try to do something to help without telling me and wreck everything."

"I see, comrade."

And that should be that. Maltby saw that he would always have to give the boy explicit instructions. If he didn't understand what he was being asked to do, he became confused.

"Could you take something into the factory for me? Something about this size?"

Maltby drew the shape of a standard charge in the air.

"I think so. I could put it at the bottom of my lunch basket."

"Good. I may want you take in several, one each day, and hide them. You could do that?"

"If I can take in one, so, I can take in more."

"Right. I'll bring them to your house—which evenings will you be at home next week?"

Henri shuffled unhappily.

"Couldn't I collect them from you? You know my wife, comrade. She's backward. If she sees you, she'll make a fuss."

"All right. But it's you who should make a fuss about my seeing her. She's too pretty for you."

"When shall I come, comrade?"

"Tuesday, about 7.30. Is that all right? Then buzz off and do your duty by your wife."

Maltby watched him swing away down the road and then went into the farmhouse and up to his room. After reducing Henri's neatly inscribed time-tables to a couple of notes in code he destroyed them. As he had nearly four hours to wait until he went to meet Gringoire, he threw himself on the bed to rest.

The mood of elation which had affected him on and off all day had unaccountably evaporated. He felt worried and depressed without being able to put his finger on the reason. Except that things were going too well. Was it Harriet getting ready to play up? At the moment she was giving him no pain, not even a throb. Oh, hell, he groaned, looking at the ceiling and for the thousandth time trying to think of the single stroke which would reveal the Gestapo spy without a shadow of doubt. In his depressed state his methods of testing seemed ridiculously clumsy and uncertain.

That morning he had ridden over to see Paturin. There were thirty men in his group and the camp seemed to be very well run, clean, with well-planned escape routes and an efficient look-out system. Paturin himself, a thick-set man of medium height, with a short, round, French face, had subtly changed himself since Maltby had last seen him by clipping his moustache *à la Stalin*. The theatricality of these damned Reds was always making him smile.

The maquis commander received him in his "office", a folding card table set up under a tree a little way from the main living quarters of the men. He wore a black leather jacket and a cloth cap but, in contrast to his men who, even in camp, carried weapons in their belts, was apparently unarmed. His favourite posture was sitting with his clasped hands resting on the table in front of him, his grey eyes below their bushy brows fixed warily on his visitor. He was as laconic as *"Ils sont fou"* was voluble, but his taciturnity had not the relaxed naturalness of Gringoire's. His silence was too calculated, too obviously intended to give his pronouncements an importance they did not possess in themselves.

He was something of a bureaucrat, and on his desk beside a little pile of well-thumbed Communist pamphlets with titles like *Wages, profits and prices*, *The Problems of Leninism*, *Stalinism*, was his "filing cabinet", a battered suitcase crammed with folders. Paturin kept records of everything he could think of, the group's weapons, the men's pay, even the quantity of rations consumed at each meal. One folder marked "Unit Classification" was not without its funny side. In it was tabulated the fighting functions of the men under his command, worked out in accordance with their civilian occupations. To classify a couple of stone masons and an Asturian miner as sappers was sensible enough, and it was just possible to recognize the connection between a plumber and a mortar-man, but to name all his men able to drive a car "tankists" indicated that the guerrilla leader was not without his delusions of grandeur.

For all his pomposity, he was shrewd and tough. He knew all about the supplies the British had given Le Feu, and he didn't intend to sell his co-operation at a lower rate. This put Maltby in a difficulty. He did not know if he would want to use Paturin in blasting the Evine factory. He hoped that he would be able to do it with the help of the Pontrecy group alone. If that were to be impossible, then he would need Paturin. But by the time he had devised his plan it would be too late to get Paturin the supplies he demanded. In the end he agreed to the maquis commander's terms, feeling that he could not do without him in reserve and confident that weapons put into his hands would not in any case be wasted.

The bargain struck, he asked Paturin to watch the bridge at Camaret-Rouge. As soon as the Germans withdrew their guards, his stone masons were to cut four cavities in the brickwork to take explosive charges. When these were ready, and providing the Germans had not appeared for three consecutive nights, a message was to be sent to Maltby.

"Why not let us blow the bridge?"

"I've a particular reason for wanting to do it myself. Just send one of your men to Gallots' farm to tell me I can have the eggs on Wednesday. In case I'm not there he had better have it written down so that he can leave the note for me."

"Why Wednesday?"

"Why not? You can make it Friday if you like or any other day."

Paturin frowned.

"It's confusing. Why not just say 'You can have the eggs'? It's simpler."

"It's also obviously a code message."

"Eh?"

"Why should anyone deliver a message like that instead of bringing the eggs with them? *Ergo*, the message cannot mean what it says and eggs must be a code word for something else."

This was accepted with a reluctant grunt.

"All the same," Paturin said, "it's best to be simple. Even codes should include nothing without a meaning."

That may be another reason why French security is so bloody awful, thought Maltby. All the same it was reassuring to know that he could now count on Paturin. His men were disciplined, reliable and tough, many of them hardened by having been on the run for more than a year. Even the silly bastard's mania for paper work might have had its uses as an example of neatness to his men. In any case, it was not dangerous, for even if his "filing cabinet" were to be captured it contained nothing that was likely to be of any value to the Germans.

But lying on his bed now looking at the ceiling, he found small comfort in remembering his deal with Paturin. What the hell was the use of his galloping about laying plans for the Gibault factory which would be utterly pointless if he couldn't get the Gestapo's man by the nuts? And if he failed, how could he just walk out and leave Hélène and the others to be quietly murdered? It was all very well for B.6. to argue that this merely left things as they were before he came. It wasn't true. He'd seen them all again. Seen them, the ones he liked and the ones he disliked, looked into their faces knowing that four of them depended on him for their lives. It was no longer the same. If he had not come, four of them would have died blamelessly but necessarily, their deaths regretted but a hazard of their service. Now they would be the responsibility of his failure. That was the difference.

He groaned. The little boffin with his chemical foods had warned him that he would be depressed at times.

"There's an intimate relationship between the digestion and the mind," he had said. "As we don't understand it very well there's not much we can do to help it. If you begin to feel that everything is looking black, though, it'll be ten to one it's your tender stomach which is doing your thinking."

When you see a brick wall, take no notice, in fact. Just walk straight into it. Bloody fool.

He went over the details for the attack on the signal-box in case his discomfort arose from a sub-conscious hunch that it was a trap. But it seemed about as fool-proof as anything could be. Except that he wanted no part of it.

He wanted no part of the whole business. For the first time since he had arrived back in Pontrecy, it weighed on him remorselessly. He just wanted to run. Or better still, never to have heard of it. At that moment his burden was so heavy that he could have screamed out loud as he pummelled the quilt with his fist.

His self-pity took another turn and he longed for Judy. But he did not think of her in a reverie, reconstructing in his mind their hours together. Nor did he think of her in sexual fantasies. He needed her, he needed her smile, to see her deft, practical hands, her strength. He wanted her presence to reassure him that Pontrecy was not real but a nightmare. Thinking of her, of the poise of her head looking up at him, hearing the lilt of her soft voice that so easily bubbled with gaiety and yet could be so deeply solemn, made him physically ache.

This was no use at all. He'd got to snap out of it. He was feeling more tired after lying down for two hours than he had when he went up to his room. He mixed himself some of the medicine he'd been given to relieve the pain if it got bad. He didn't feel ill, but if it was Harriet who was making him feel so down a pick-me-up wouldn't do her any harm.

He fetched the explosives from the disused well and made up the charges they would need for the signal-box. Afterwards he wrote a report on his deal with Paturin and the map reference of ground where his supplies were to be dropped. This Celestine would take over to Dinville on the following morning after he had added the details of the signal-box job to it. By then he was feeling more cheerful, but whether it was because of the medicine or that in working he had forgotten to feel sorry for himself, he did not know.

When he arrived at their rendezvous Gringoire was waiting for him, watching the rail track for any unusual activity.

"Everything all right?"

"Looks like it," the railwayman grunted.

He had been on the job all the evening. He had seen the doctor go to Lemaire's house. After he had left, he had waited to see Lemaire's wife go to Morin's lodgings. She had not been told of the plan to ensure that she would act naturally in carrying the message that her husband was ill. Gringoire had then gone to check that there was nothing abnormal about the railway that night.

"And Morin?"

"I haven't seen him but he'll be all right."

"Let's start then."

It was very dark. Thick clouds were overhead and there was a light drizzle falling. And it was cold. If Gringoire had been out on the embankment for the last two hours, Maltby guessed he must be chilled through and soaking.

They were about half a mile up the line beyond the signal-box and they set out towards it. On their left was a deep cleft of blackness that was the railway. If he screwed up his eyes and concentrated, Maltby could just see the twin tracks of polished rails as faintly luminous parallel lines at the root of the blackness.

The silence was clotted, permanent, as though the world were dead. It quickly swallowed the swish of their feet through the grass of the embankment.

For ten minutes they moved along quite smartly. By then they could see the heavily shaded light in the signal-box quite clearly. From then on, they moved only a few steps at a time. For one thing they were early and they did not want to frighten Morin by being more than punctual. For another, Maltby wanted to be reassured by examining every scrap of cover that there were no Germans lying in wait for them. That he was sure there would be none made him doubly anxious in his checking.

Just as they reached the box there was a tremendous clatter from the station and they froze. It was only one of the night men leaving the office on one platform and scrambling across the line to the other. In the heavy silence the cutting acted as a funnel for the sound, so that it seemed to come from only a few yards away. Maltby was only able to focus where it came from when it ended as the man slammed a door behind him.

They moved on and, still being careful to make no noise, climbed the signal-box steps. Gringoire entered first. Maltby, his Sten at the ready, hesitated. If a trap was to be sprung it would be now.

"So you're here," said a surprised voice, "I was watching for you but did not see a thing!"

"Good."

Maltby felt himself relax. He tucked his Sten into the crook of his arm and went into the box.

Morin was in an acute state of excitement and he began to fire questions at them. But Maltby shut him up. He wanted to get to work. Ignoring the signalman, he made Gringoire tell him the functions of the various apparatus with which the box was filled. Together they assessed the placing of the charges where they would ensure that the whole installation would be irreparably smashed. It soon became obvious to Maltby that Gringoire had already worked this out in his mind.

In less than five minutes after they had arrived, Maltby was packing in the first charge. While they kept watch at either end of the box, Gringoire tried to quieten Morin by answering his questions. The young railwayman had been keyed-up for the most sensational moment in his life, and it upset him to have Gringoire and Maltby acting as quietly as though they had merely come to mend a fuse. He was restless and hungry for action.

Maltby laid the last charge and stood up. He looked at his watch and saw that he was ten minutes ahead of schedule.

"Now," he said to Morin, "you know what you have to do? Where's your bike?"

"Hidden on the other side of Poitier's farm."

"Good. You will tell Serpier that it was he who organized the blowing-up of the signal-box with you. You understand that? You and Serpier did it. Tell Serpier I don't mind how much he boasts about it. Is that clear?"

The young railwayman looked puzzled.

"But I've never seen Serpier."

"I can't go into that now. Just tell him what I say, that you and he did it. In the Resistance you'll have to learn not to ask so many questions."

"Yes, sir."

Crikey, I must be sounding formidable tonight, thought Maltby, to have dug that "sir" out of him.

"Watch out for Germans. It's more likely that you will run into a gendarme. Try to avoid him if you can. Should he stop you, tell him you're Resistance and you should be all right. Anything else?"

Morin shuffled boyishly.

"Can I have a gun?" he pleaded.

"No. You don't need one to get you to Calvine. You have to be there in half an hour. So get!"

They were on the steps leading down to the rails when the telegraph rang suddenly and loudly in the box. They froze.

"Answer it," Maltby hissed at Morin.

It was only the station-master making up his log, wanting to know if Morin had anything to report. The signalman told him that all was well in the box and, as there was nothing more due before the morning, he was going to put his head down for a couple of hours.

Maltby was furious that Morin had not told them that they could expect this routine call. If they had left as soon as the charges were in place, there would have been no one to answer the phone and the station-master might have sent someone along to find out why he could get no reply from the box. If the box had been saved in that way he would never have known that it was through a genuine accident—what that would have implied made him sweat to think of.

There was no time now for him to vent his anger on the signal-man. Hastily, they scrambled down on to the track. Maltby sent Morin off at the double with a hearty thump on the back, and then told Gringoire sharply what he thought about so elementary failure in their intelligence.

The jangling of the telegraph had so rattled his nerves that Maltby decided to stay and watch the box until it would be too late for the charges to be removed even if they were to be discovered. He was on edge in case Morin had not told them of a dozen possible visitors to the box in the same way as he had not thought it necessary to mention that the station-master always contacted the signalmen when making up his report.

So as to make it more difficult for the charges to be spotted should someone get into the box, Gringoire went back and smashed the lamp. They had left it burning in case someone should be made suspicious on seeing the box in darkness. This seemed less of a risk now than that some *cheminot* would decide to drop in on the signalmen for a chat to while away the slack night and get out of the chill air for a space.

"You meant that I should also say that Serpier did this job?" Gringoire enquired quietly.

"Yes, even to the rest of the group." The Alsatian accepted this impassively. As he was clearly not going to ask for an explanation, Maltby went on, "The morale of Serpier's maquis is shockingly low. A success would give it a boost. I thought it would be a good idea to give them this one."

Would that satisfy the shrewd old bastard, he wondered? He certainly wouldn't like to bet on it. It was something to be thankful for that whatever was going on in his head would not be blurted out to any of the others.

Maltby wanted Gringoire to go home but he pointed out that it would be better if he stayed and Maltby left. His lodgings were only five minutes away while it would take Maltby fifteen to reach the Gallots' farm.

"Besides, I see better in the dark than you."

That was unarguable. Reluctantly he agreed.

"All right. If any *cheminots* come near just warn them to keep away. But if it's Germans, you'll have to shoot."

"It will be all right."

Gringoire spoke with solid confidence.

He was right. Standing at his bedroom window, Maltby saw the flashes and counted the explosions. All the charges had blown, going off one after another to sound like some giant Chinese cracker.

Behind his relief, which was huge, lurked the realization of how close he had been to making the mistake he most feared. He could not shake it off.

He was stretching upwards putting away his belly shield when the pain hit him. It hit him hard, harder than he'd had it since the day they flew him back to England.

He lay on the bed writhing, as the knife twisted sharply this way and that in his guts. The pain drew up his thighs and covered his forehead with droplets of sweat.

When it eased slightly, he poured himself a draught of his medicine and took a sleeping pill. Slowly the pain ebbed and as it did he cursed, stringing obscenities to make a lullaby.

Oh, you bitch, you bloody bitch, you've got to hold up. You can't lie down on me now. Not now, not now, not now. . . .

Incoherent and inexplicit, the refrain ran through his mind as he grew drowsier. He fell asleep without noticing that it was not to save his body from the pain which racked it that caused him to cry out for release from his agony.

CHAPTER THIRTEEN

THE next morning, half an hour after his breakfast, he vomited. Despite this, though his stomach was tender, the violent pain had gone. And, helped by a dose of his medicine, he had no difficulty in keeping down a second meal of slops.

As the day wore on he felt better and some of his confidence returned. But the pain had given him a bad scare.

It's the tension and the way I work myself into states that does it, he told himself. I've got to take it easier. There'll always be tension when we're doing a job. It can't be helped. But I've bloody well got to stop worrying, got to stop going over things in my mind just for the hell of it, freezing my behind with the breeze. If I think of a problem it must be because I intend to come to a decision. Otherwise I've got to let it go.

He stroked his belly.

Harriet, old girl, you be nice to me and I'll be nice to you. I'll dose you regularly and feed you by the clock. Only no high kicks.

The drizzle which had begun the night before still persisted, effectively taking away any inclination he might have had to go out walking, even if he had not decided that he should rest as much as possible. He was sitting in front of the fire reading, enjoying an hour's solitude while the Gallots were at Mass, when Gringoire called.

The signal-box was a total wreck. Most of Pontrecy were taking in the sight of the devastation on their way home from saying their prayers. Already everybody was talking of Serpier having done it.

"Good," Maltby grinned.

"Lulu was there."

He's wondering why I wasn't, thought Maltby. Well, he could damn well go on wondering.

"Yes?"

"He was angry about Serpier. He thinks our group should have done it."

"He'll get over it. How do you feel about it?"

Gringoire shrugged indifference.

"The box is *kaputt*," he said.

It was a comfort to have one member of the group who wasn't neurotic! To have just one concerned only with the job and not with promotion, medals, emotion—or his guts!

That Buchan should be annoyed that the signal-box had been blown without his getting wind of the operation was another pointer. Not decisive, he was careful to point out to himself, but well worth noting. The afternoon's group meeting might give more.

In fact it did not. The others were on the whole inclined only to cheer.

"It's good, isn't it?" Lestocq said unexpectedly when Buchan made his complaint. "Serpier's maquis has always been a bit of a joke. It's good to know that it isn't, yes?"

"But that's my point," Buchan said irritably, "they're a lot of half-baked amateurs. We're professionals. That's why I say we should have done it."

"Well, it's been done, and done damn well," Harrison said aloofly. "Might I suggest we get on with our professional business?"

Hélène watched him during these exchanges, and Maltby realized she must be puzzled why he did not tell the others that he and not Serpier had done the job. He would have to think up a story for her that made sense. The one he had given her for not telling any of the others before the job didn't really hold for keeping it a secret afterwards. Luckily she had not blurted it out.

The operation Maltby had planned for the group to undertake the following day broke new ground. Up to then they had concentrated on the network of railways. He now proposed an attack on the Germans' road transport. Most of this traffic by-passed Pontrecy, travelling along the main trunk road four miles to the south of the village and roughly parallel to the Pontrecy-Dinville route.

An over-night transport park had been laid out for the through traffic at Belcrete, a small hamlet that had been little more than a pump station and a transport workers' café before the war. Usually there were a fair number of trucks in the park, and on Mondays it often happened they were lined up bumper to bumper for the night.

There were few guards, because most of the vehicles did not arrive in convoys but singly. There were in consequence no forces available to cover the whole park. If there were any sentries at all, they were posted along the side of the park which adjoined the road.

The lorries arrived between four and six o'clock, and the crews then went off to some huts on the other side of the filling station to eat and sleep. They did not go near their trucks again until they drove them out at about six in the morning.

Maltby's plan was to get into the park from the back, where it was simply an open field, and fix incendiaries on as many trucks as they could. They would choose vehicles on the east and south side and with any luck the wind would carry the fire to the rest. At the worst, their bag should be a dozen and it could be fifty or even more.

The group were enthusiastic. Even Buchan acknowledged that it was both simple and spectacular and did not require too many risks to be taken. Even if it hadn't been, he added nastily, he would have welcomed it as evidence that Maltby was not planning that they should all sit on their backsides for the duration.

It was decided that Lestocq should go over to Belcrete the following afternoon to observe the lorries as they arrived. He was to make a sketch of the park and take note of any lorries carrying oil or any other inflammable cargo. The rest would join him about 10 o'clock and the attack would be carried out as soon after that as they were ready.

They were cheerful, almost excited, as they drank the coffee Hélène made for them. Afterwards, they broke up, going off singly as usual. Maltby left after Buchan and Lestocq but took Hélène downstairs with him, letting her think he wanted to kiss her but in reality to be reassured that she would keep her mouth shut about his part in blowing up the signal-box.

The following night when they met Lestocq on the trunk road half a mile to the west of Belcrete, they lost their cheerfulness. Lestocq had seen the lorries pile into the park as usual. By six o'clock there were between a hundred and a hundred and twenty there, including fourteen tankers. Then just after seven he had seen the crews come running from the huts, get into the trucks and begin driving away. In half an hour there wasn't a single vehicle in the park. And none had arrived since.

Maltby was intrigued. He had wondered how Schwartzkopf would deal with this. Obviously the Gestapo chief was not hidebound. He probably recognized that the sudden appearance of large patrols in unusual places must sooner or later arouse suspicions. But besides that there was another danger. Sooner or later the group would try to shoot their way through the troops barring them from an objective. In this way the group might be destroyed, for he could not explain to Wehrmacht soldiers that he didn't want these resisters killed. Pulling the transport out was a neat solution to his problem.

For the others, this was the worst frustration yet, a complete disaster. It was a new type of raid, away from the areas of their previous failures, and had everything that was necessary to make them feel that their luck was about to change. They were appalled and unwilling to believe what Lestocq had told them and insisted on going along to the empty park to see for themselves.

"'He withers all in silence, and his hand
Unclothes the earth, and freezes up frail life',"

Harrison quoted, looking at the waste where they had hoped to find their quarry.

"Poetry's a fat lot of use," rasped Buchan. "Something's bloody wrong."

He stood with legs apart, neck stretched upwards, head slightly on one side, the monocle he always jammed in his eye when on a sabotage job glinting vaguely in the starlight. He's not a man, he's a bloody cartoon, Maltby said to himself.

"They just came out and went away," Lestocq kept repeating, running agitatedly about from one to the other. "They went away. All of them, you understand? What could I do? They just drove away."

He spoke smarmily as though he felt he had to placate the others' anger. It was as though he were afraid of being blamed for the disappearance of the Germans, and it drew Buchan's fire.

"If they were ever there," he said suspiciously.

"They were. they were. I swear it," Lestocq whined, waving his sketch. "Look, see for yourself. Look at it."

Buchan took the sketch and examined it by the carefully shaded light of his torch. Harrison peered over his shoulder. But Gringoire did not bother to get up from where he was sitting to look. He's no more surprised we've come unstuck than I am, thought Maltby, and the only thing bothering him is the five-mile hike back to Pontrecy.

Buchan handed the sketch back.

"Do you think they saw you making this?" he asked, "and that was what made them bunk?"

"Be your age!" Maltby said unpleasantly. "Lestocq routs three hundred Germans with a pencil and paper! Why, even you are not that good, Lulu!"

"Well, something's bloody wrong," the little man retorted belligerently.

"And it's my fault?"

"It was your plan, wasn't it?"

"What was wrong with it?"

Buchan flung out his hand theatrically towards the deserted transport park.

"That!" he snapped.

He's not half going it, thought Maltby, but it's too big to be real. It was reasonable to suppose that all this tiz was meant to hide something. But it could be equally true of the Uriah Heep performance Lestocq was putting up. He'd got to keep a balanced mind. Why couldn't one of the bastards give himself away properly?

They did not speak much on the way back to Pontrecy and they dispersed with only the briefest nods to each other. No one suggested that they should fix a time for the group to meet again. Discouragement made them silent. Only in one of them, thought Maltby, it was not discouragement but circumspection.

He had intended to see Buchan the next day, but Buchan made his journey unnecessary by turning up at the farm early in the morning. Ostensibly he brought a report of the previous night's foray for Maltby to initial so that it could be sent off to London. While Maltby read the message, the little man hopped about from one foot to the other.

"Said some damn silly things last night," he said jerkily as Maltby gave him back the message. "Cock-up wasn't your fault. Couldn't have been. I'm sorry, damn sorry."

The little bugger thinks he over-played and is trying to straighten it out with me, thought Maltby, but he accepted the apology affably.

"Wanted to see you, anyway," Buchan explained. "Wanted to talk to you."

"Yes."

"Something is bloody wrong here, you know."

"You're telling me!"

"First that water tower and now the signal-box."

"Why them particularly?"

Maltby had not expected him on this tack.

"Can't have Reds all over the place without us knowing what they're doing. It's dangerous. You should do something about it."

"Serpier is not a Red——"

"So he says!"

"—and Paturin denies he did the water tower."

"There you are!" Buchan exclaimed triumphantly. "Shows what slimy liars they are!"

"It's the bad luck that keeps buggering up our sorties that bothers me."

"Might be connected."

"But their jobs came off. How could they be connected with our failures?"

"Think it over. You'll see. Better than me, perhaps. You know more."

"Such as?"

"You meet the bastards. I don't, thank God!"

"So what do I do?"

"Get control so that we shall know what the scum are up to. You've got to get control."

"Hm. I'll have to think this over and come back to you. Look, the Huns are putting a lot of stuff through Airvout because the RAF are strafing the daylights out of them on the main line. I want to do the points beyond the goods yard. Do you know them? The ones that link in the branch line to the north. What do you say to us doing it together tomorrow?"

"Without the others?"

"Yes. Then we can talk. We won't let them know anything about it. That will make certain none of them will want to come."

"Right."

"I wanted to speak to you about your plan for wrecking the Gestapo HQ at Caude, anyway," Maltby added, laying it on.

"Good-o! Time we did some big stuff."

"And if we have our usual bad luck," Maltby said as they parted, "we won't exactly have wasted our time."

Maltby was exultant. This was it. It must be. Of course, Schwartzkopf must have been livid about the signal-box. The water tower was bad enough but the signal-box was ten times worse. Naturally he didn't want "accidents" like that continuing. It made leaving the Pontrecy group untouched too expensive. He would have belted his man good and proper for not warning him. And here was Buchan demanding that there should be no more of these accidents, no sabotage unless the group gave its consent! It added up, as B.6. would say, by God, it added up!

Buchan's visit had given him such a lift that he had difficulty in spending the whole day resting. He felt too excited. Nevertheless he put himself on a routine which followed exactly, as far as he could remember, the one he had been put on when he had first arrived at the Wilberforce.

He had no recurrence of the intense pain, and the operation against the transport had held so few surprises that he had been able to loosen himself up every time he had felt himself growing tense. Nevertheless, he had vomited when he got back to the farmhouse. By the time he met Buchan the following night, he felt that he was getting better rather than deteriorating. He would have even been willing to take a small bet that, if he kept his head, his guts would hold out for another fortnight. It may be that being convinced they would not have to made him reckless.

They followed the same route Maltby had taken with Gringoire the night they destroyed the water tower. The night was lighter than that one but Buchan was nothing like so adept at moving about in the dark as the Alsatian, and Maltby found that even though they went at a slower pace than the first time he had crossed the plateau, he had to concentrate all his attention to prevent himself barking against barely discernible objects in the general gloom of the plantation.

He picked the same spot to rest as Gringoire had chosen, looking down on to the railway line. Maltby noted with satisfaction that he was nothing like so winded and keen to flop down as he had been a fortnight before. True, they had not walked quite so steadily as then, but, even so, he was sure the last two weeks' activity had got his lungs working properly again if nothing else. No cigarettes probably helped as well.

Maltby had not spoken much. He had simply set Buchan off on his pet hobby-horse of the Gestapo HQ and kept him going with the odd question without bothering to attend to what he was saying. He was feeling the excitement of the moment, the knowledge that in a matter of minutes rather than hours he would have completed the first half of his mission. Against that, what Buchan had to say about his barmy scheme for raiding the Caude Gestapo could hardly be of interest.

After only five minutes breather, Maltby insisted on their pushing on. He wanted them to be in position opposite the points by 10 o'clock. From Gringoire he had learned that since the water tower had been blown up, Milice patrols were out on this section of the line. They passed at regular intervals of approximately two hours, going through Airvout at 10 o'clock or thereabouts and coming back at 12 o'clock. This gap would give him and Buchan plenty of time to pack the three charges into the points.

They skirted round the village, moving with great care as neither of them was very familiar with this part of the country. It was completely silent except for the noise from the station and the occasional howl of a dog. The sharp clang of the buffers on shunting trucks seemed to hang for a long time in the otherwise noiseless air.

They hid above the embankment opposite where the cutting branched off from the main track. From where they were they could see the station beyond the shunting yard. There was quite an amount of activity going on, as the last passenger train of the day was due. The Germans knew that the Resistance would not sabotage the line before it was clear of passenger traffic and so never sent out patrols until the last one had gone.

While they waited Maltby took out the charges and checked them. He was amused that, seeing him do this, Buchan ostentatiously reconnoitred the embankment. He was certainly putting on a good front. But what was Schwartzkopf going to do? Maltby had not expected to see posses of soldiers, but he had expected to see something. A gang of plate-layers at work or a track inspection in progress. But there was nothing unusual as far as he could see. How was it going to be done?

"Shouldn't take us more than ten minutes," Buchan whispered when he came back.

The last train puffed into the station, lay down for a while and puffed out again. They watched it pass them and disappear into the night. And still there was nothing, not a single sign of anything in the least abnormal. Maltby shifted about uneasily, peering hard along the track in both directions. Whatever was coming must come soon.

"Won't be coming yet," Buchan said, making Maltby start violently. "Won't leave the station for another five minutes."

It was a few moments before the penny dropped. Of course, he thinks I'm looking for the Milice patrol. He should know!

The deserted lines worried Maltby. He did not fear a trap, for it was in Schwartzkopf's interest that they should not be killed or captured. But he had to prevent them from wrecking the points. Even if he were willing to have the points destroyed—which really wasn't likely, because replacements were getting very short—he simply couldn't afford to have the railway out of service for half a day or more, with the main line already out of action.

He looked at Buchan. The little man had his chin stuck out arrogantly and was peering towards the station with a fierce intensity. Despite his ridiculous monocle he had about him the triggered eagerness of a coiled spring. This, however, told Maltby nothing, for it was how Buchan always held himself as they prepared for action.

A peculiar tension gripped Maltby, a tension of anticipation, not of danger. It was like looking at a print in a developing dish in a photographer's darkroom before the picture appeared. You were certain that it would appear but not what the picture would be.

"Here they come, the bastards," Buchan whispered.

They could hear their boots clattering on the platform but were too far away to see them. Maltby judged that there were about twenty men in the patrol. They listened to the crunch of their feet as they marched towards them along the permanent way. Once they stopped and Maltby stiffened. But a minute later the heavy tread of their feet was resumed.

Presently the column came in view. If they were expecting trouble it was not apparent, for they slouched along in a ragged double line without even the pretence of being on the alert. When they were exactly opposite the points and below Buchan and Maltby they stopped. After some shuffling about, they went on again, leaving one man behind.

This was it! Instead of patrolling, they were leaving sentries strung out all along the line at quarter-mile intervals! That was what they were doing when they had heard them stop before, posting the first man beyond the station.

As the column swung off into the darkness, the man they had left behind began to pace up and down a twenty-yard stretch in front of the points. Maltby squeezed Buchan's arm and very cautiously they pulled back from the top of the embankment.

"Well, that's that, I'm afraid," he said when he was sure they were out of earshot of the sentry, and hoped that the satisfaction he felt didn't show in his voice.

Buchan's reply caught him completely by surprise.

"I don't think so. I could take that bastard easily."

Is the little bugger trying to bluff me? Betting that I'll not let him because it's too risky? You try that, son, and I'll fry you!

"How?"

"There's a hollow just by where he turns. If I could work my way round to it, I could take him from behind."

"What about the noise?"

"There won't be any. Not the way I do it."

"O.K. I'll cover you from this side."

Now talk your way out of that, he thought.

But Buchan did not talk at all. He simply took out his monocle and put it carefully in his pocket.

"Here," he said, tossing Maltby his Sten, "look after that."

And he went off into the darkness.

Maltby slung the gun across his back where it would not get in his way and crawled back to the embankment. Picking his time to move when the sentry had his back to him, he found a spot about the centre of the milicien's beat and settled down to watch. Whatever hanky-panky Buchan thought he was going to pull, Maltby was determined to see it.

The sentry passed twice before Maltby saw Buchan slip quickly down the bank and disappear from view. The milicien had grown bored with his parading and was dribbling a pebble in front of him.

He had turned and taken two steps towards Maltby when Buchan landed on him. Maltby saw the two figures go down heavily but noiselessly, for Buchan had angled his attack so that the sentry fell on the grass. Limbs flailed about for a moment and he heard Buchan grunt twice. Then everything was still. He got to his feet, trying to see what had happened.

Buchan walked out on to the track and signalled to him to come down. Quickly he scrambled down the embankment to where the sentry was lying. When he lifted the man's head he saw that his neck had been very efficiently broken.

Maltby's mind was working furiously on two levels. On one he was thinking irrelevantly how ironical it would be if the dead man were to be Polidor Vassen. On the other he was struggling to get himself straight about Buchan.

If the Milice had posted sentries to stop them from blasting the points, then Buchan, knowing this, would never have murdered the man. *Then it was not Buchan.* The sentries were an accident! Because the miliciens did not like walking or because someone thought sentries were better than patrols. Or maybe just because. God, he thought, how far off the beam can I get!

"Come on," Buchan hissed, "no time to say the burial service over the swine!"

They went out on to the track and packed the charges in between the points as quickly as they could. Out there among the lines they were visible for a long way since there was no cover for them to take. They did the next best thing, made no attempt to act stealthily, in the hope that if anyone should see them they would be mistaken for *cheminots*.

As soon as they had finished they made their way back, taking the same route round the village as they had followed coming. Where their path entered the plantation that spread over the plateau they sat down to wait for the explosions.

"It was a nice job you did on the milicien."

"A sitting duck. Damn slack. Can't expect any better from traitors, I suppose."

You should know what I've been thinking about you!

"What exactly did you mean about the Reds having something to do with the group's jobs coming unstuck?"

"They're blowing our plans to the Gestapo."

"How can they be? They don't know what they are."

"Don't you tell them?"

"What? Oh, I see. But you're quite wrong. There's been no link up between the groups yet. Everyone's still working quite independently."

"Maybe. But they know, don't they?"

"Why do you think so?"

"Obvious. Their jobs come off. Ours are flops. They're flops because the Reds tip off the Gestapo."

"So that's how you work it out!"

"Been on to the bastards a long time. Thought once they had put a microphone in Hélène's place."

God, that was an idea he hadn't thought of. It could be that there wasn't a spy at all!

"But there isn't," Buchan went on, "I searched both rooms."

"When?"

"When you were in England. I got in one day when Hélène was out."

"Why did you do that? Why didn't you tell the group what you thought? Then you could have searched the rooms openly."

"Think I'm a damn fool," Buchan mumbled, uncomfortably, "all of them. Wanted to be sure I could show them proof."

It had cost the little swashbuckler something to make that admission. The question had caught him on the raw and it wasn't normal for him to let anyone inside his guard after that. Maltby sensed that Buchan was pleading to be believed, asking for his help. It flashed into his mind that he should tell him the truth. After all, Buchan was half right, he had guessed that it was the

Gestapo who were foiling their sabotage forays. Damn fool though he was in some ways, he could be useful. For one thing he could take over putting either Lestocq or Harrison through their tests. Or, even more important, Buchan could be left to finish off the job if his guts gave out on him.

"Look here, Buchan, you're wrong," he began, "if it were the Reds—and it's not possible that it is—why should they be content to spoil what we're doing? Why not just blow us to the Gestapo and finish us altogether? It——"

"You don't understand how that scum think," Buchan broke in with eager venom. "They're twisted. Fiends. They don't give us away because they don't want to help the Nazis. We're useful. We get information back to London. They're out to capture the world. Our souls. They don't want the Nazis to win. They hate 'em. Always have. They want the Nazis beaten but don't want us to win. They want to be the only winners. Winners will be decided when the shooting stops by who leads the peoples. That's what they're doing here in France. Posing as the leaders. So they bugger up our sabotage and pull off their own to show what fine fellows they are."

It was hopeless, and Maltby let him go ranting on without bothering to argue or having any further thoughts of enlisting his aid. He would never see anything but a Red at the bottom of the pot. And if he couldn't see the Red because there wasn't one, he still would not believe it but think his eyes were playing him up. Or that the Reds had added invisibility to their other devilish tricks! You couldn't argue with a maniac. And you certainly couldn't trust his judgment.

Buchan was still on his hobby-horse when they heard the explosions. They came loud and clear, tearing the silence of the night.

"And very nice, too," said Maltby. "I don't think we'll tell the group we did it, though."

"Why not?"

"Their morale is so low that they'll be even more deflated not to have been on an action that was successful. Better for them to think that it was done by one of the freelances."

"Don't see that. I——"

"Buchan, I'm sure I'm right. They want something big to set them up again. Like your plan to grab the files of the Caude Gestapo."

That'll shut you up, he thought.

It did. It even stopped Buchan maundering on about the Communists.

For a little while they observed, or rather listened to—for except for the swaying pinpoints of lanterns being carried by railwaymen setting out to assess the damage, there was little that they could see—the furore that the explosions had caused at the station, and then set off for Pontrecy.

Maltby had not been entirely bluffing when he had spoken of raiding the Caude HQ. For one thing, he had a conviction that the idea was nowhere near as crazy as he had thought. At any rate it could be dressed up to look feasible. And that was all he wanted. It could not possibly be set up before the group dispersed, but its planning would involve all of them in so much activity that it would relieve him of thinking up other actions to employ them on, actions which in any case were futile as they would be certain to be frustrated.

He was feeling tired by the time they got back. Though he had been careful to take milk and rusks with him, his stomach was queasy. When he parted with Buchan and stood watching him strut away into the night, weariness came down on him like a blow. The weakness that he felt was not only physical. There was disappointment, too. He had been so sure that Buchan was his man.

"And now there are two," he said to himself, adding with stupid facetiousness, "And if one green bottle should accidentally fall . . ."

But nothing fell for him accidentally. He always had to push it. All the same there *were* only two now. He was over the hump.

CHAPTER FOURTEEN

"THEY gave me this for you, too. They said it came last night."

Celestine held out a small package to him.

Maltby, who was sitting in front of the fire, a dog-eared Tauchnitz edition of *Old Goriot* which he had picked up for a few francs in the village open on his knees, took it curiously.

It was two days since he and Buchan had blasted the Airvout points, two days in which he had done nothing but rest and doctor himself. He did not count the leisurely ride over to Evine and back that evening to watch the night men going into the Gibault factory as doing anything.

In that time he had had no serious pain nor had he vomited. But he took as the surest sign that he was over the danger he feared most, a haemorrhage, that he was finding the smell of Madame Gallot's cooking inviting and beginning to look upon his diet of slops with disfavour.

"You're sure they're not love letters from you, Celestine?"

Celestine blushed scarlet. She always did when Maltby teased her, for the dumpy girl, whose thick powerful legs drove her bicycle quickly and devotedly up the gradients to Dinville for him, had no gift for repartee.

"I wouldn't write to you, M'sieur Minaud!"

"How sad you make me!"

The package was addressed on both sides simply with his code name "Punch". It could not be from Le Feu for, sending it by messenger, he would not have addressed it at all.

"When will you want me to go to Dinville again?"

"I don't know, my sweet dove. Not before Monday, anyway."

Celestine, still blushing painfully, managed to shuffle herself out and he was able to open the packet.

Letters! Five letters from Judy!

He whipped them open and rapidly read them through. The prohibitions of censorship and the responsibilities of being a married woman had somewhat inhibited her style, but he loved them. He was so lifted up and excited that he had to leave his chair and walk round the kitchen holding them in his hand.

That old bastard, B.6.! He loved the beautiful bald-headed old bastard! Only he could have thought of including letters from Judy in a parachutage to *"Ils sont fou"*.

Poor Judy, how difficult she must have found it to write these letters, which must not betray who she was or to whom they were written, and from which she had to repress her feelings out of fear that they would be read by others. He read the stilted phrases in which she told him of her small doings and felt himself tugged towards her, sensing her rebellion that she had to be so prosaic when she wanted so much to be passionate.

She had been to see his mother.

I think she is very nice, [she wrote primly] *much nicer than you deserve. I don't think she gossips. You may not be in-*

terested in the things which interest her, that's all. You probably
bore her, too, but she's too sweet to say so. But I think we upset
her very much by not having her at the wedding. I did what
I could to explain why. She says she understands but I'm sure
she's deeply hurt. We must do what we can to make her believe
we wanted her with us. I feel worse about her than I do about
mine, who, after all, was in Ireland.

Dear, dear Judy, what an awful kafuffle you make about our
families. As if they mattered. And she was wrong about his mother.
If she was hurt at all, it was not in her feelings but in her sense of
what was right and proper. It was a mother's duty to attend her
child's wedding.

But he didn't care really what Judy had said. It mattered so
little beside the fact that she had written it and here it was in his
hands. He had just finished reading the letters for the second
time when Hélène came in, and he hurriedly stuffed them into
his pocket.

He looked at her as she came towards him with her perky walk,
the love-light shining in her eyes, and he hated her. He hated her
for breaking in on him at this moment, hated that she should exist
and was part of his life. His chest tightened and he knew he was
going to lash out. Well, she bloody well asked for it!

"Gallot told me you were ill again," she said, kissing him lightly
on the forehead because he kept his head obstinately tucked
down so that she could not reach his lips, "so I came to see
you."

"Gallot should keep his mouth shut. And you should have more
sense than to come here," he snarled.

His tone made Hélène droop.

"Why shouldn't I come here to see the Gallots?"

"Because I happen to be here, too."

"But I often have to come here to see you."

"All the more reason why you shouldn't come here when you
don't."

She slipped off her coat and sat down on the floor beside his
chair, taking his hand in hers.

"How could I stay away knowing you were ill? Has the pain
been bad?"

"I haven't had any pain."

"Then what's the matter?"

"What else could be the matter except that you behave like a bloody fool?"

He pulled his hand away from her. She did not attempt to resist his withdrawal but remained quite still looking down at the floor. Maltby ignored her sullenly. He desperately wanted her to go.

"If you're hanging around hoping that I'll start mucking you about," he sneered, "you're wasting your time."

Her sallow skin reddened, but she kept her composure.

"I might be able to get you some milk," she said levelly, as though he had not spoken, and added softly, "like I did before."

She's telling herself that it's only because I'm ill that I'm behaving like this. She would never accept that she made him crawl.

"I told you they dropped everything I'd need with me," he growled impatiently, the burden of the gratitude he owed her jibeing him.

"Someone sabotaged some points at Airvout on Wednesday."

"Yes."

"Was it you?"

"No."

"Was it Paturin again?"

"I expect so."

She told him that Sarrut needed money and without a word he got up and fetched a packet of notes from his bedroom. When he came back she had put on her coat. She stuffed the money in her pocket.

After standing irresolute for a moment, she put her arms round his waist and pressed him close. As always when she touched him like this she began to tremble.

He put his arm around her shoulders, unable to resist the mute appeal of her shaken body. He hated her and hated himself for his weakness, for his lack of ruthlessness. He wanted to punish himself, to feel such pain that he would writhe, to punish himself for the meanness in him that could only bitch and whine and had not the strength to kill cleanly.

"Oh, Harry!"

When she looked up at him he dropped his head so that she could press her lips against his but remained entirely passive.

"They will send you home as soon as you've settled the groups' link-up, won't they?"

"How the hell should I know?"

Her fingers tightened on to his arms so that they dug into his flesh.

"But they must! Please, Harry, say you'll make them!" she pleaded, "you're not fit."

She was weeping. Roughly he pulled himself away from her.

"Stop talking like a fool," he said with his back to her.

She did not try to touch him again but went out. As the door closed, he heard her sob.

He knew he'd got to grow up. God, he couldn't go on being immature for ever. This loathing and contempt for himself would wreck him. He'd got to face it, lick it.

Re-reading Judy's letters warmed him, but it was some time before they got the unpleasant taste of Hélène out of his mouth. Slowly the stone in his chest softened. He even had a twinge of sympathy for Hélène's unwanted love which had nothing to do with the pain it caused him.

The letters were a problem. He wanted to keep them for their touch. The rustle of the sheets between his fingers made him feel Judy's presence. But he knew it would be madness. There was no safe place where he could hide them and at the same time be able to get at them when he needed their comfort. There was nothing for it but to destroy them. He burnt them, reading each page over before dropping it in the fire, watching it blacken and glow red before turning to the next. Curiously, this did not cloud the feeling of nearness to Judy which the letters had brought, but made him stronger, urgent for action.

This feeling was still on him the next day when he cycled over to see Paturin.

"You can have the eggs," the Communist greeted him, "I was sending a messenger to you today."

"On Wednesday?"

"On Wednesday," Paturin replied, a ghost of a smile hovering about his lips.

Maltby told him that he had arranged for a supply drop to be made to him and the code signal that would be sent out by the BBC on the day it was to arrive. He had also asked for some limpet incendiaries and large wire-cutters to be dropped at the same time, but Paturin was to understand that they were not for him.

He also explained the part he wanted Paturin's maquis to play if he adopted one of the plans he had worked out for wrecking the Gibault factory. It was an ambitious operation, bigger than anything that had been attempted in the area.

"I've not finally decided to use this plan," Maltby told him, "but act as though I had. Do a recce of the ground. Work out your approach routes and the way you will withdraw. Decide exactly where you are going to place your men and a system of command communication which will be effective during the battle. Whistles would probably be best. Have you got any?"

Paturin shook his head.

"Well, get some. And train your men until they can do what you want them to do in their sleep. Keep rehearsing it. But don't tell any of them what it is you are training them to attack. I don't want every man, woman and child in the district talking about it."

"My men are not like Serpier's," the Communist said haughtily.

"Maybe not, but don't give 'em the chance to be. In five days set up a courier in Pontrecy to keep in daily touch with me at the farm. If you strike any snags, let me know. I'll try to see you again before the action but it may not be possible. Timing is of the utmost importance. Set your watch by the BBC. Do you think you have got it all?"

"Yes," replied Paturin, who had been making notes. But he insisted on going over it all again point by point.

Maltby picked up his bike and the maquis leader fell in beside him as he walked through the trees towards the cart track.

"Nothing should go wrong, but if it does you're on your own. I shan't be able to get in touch with you and you must act on your own initiative. And one other thing—it won't last long, twenty minutes at the outside, and you should be away before the Boches have recovered from their surprise. But while it lasts there may be a lot of stuff flying about. You could have some casualties, though I hope not. If you do, get all the wounded away you can without delaying yourself disastrously but don't bother about the dead. That's a hell of a decision to take, to leave your dead and badly wounded behind, and it's usually better to let the men know it's what they must expect. You know yours and must decide how to treat them."

"I'll tell them," Paturin said simply. "Shall I see you again afterwards?"

"Probably not."

"Have luck."

Maltby had bumped a hundred yards down the track before he realized the reason for the look of admiration Paturin had given him in parting. The blithering idiot must have thought his casual reply implied that his part in bashing the Gibault factory was to be a suicide effort. He roared with laughter.

"*Ils sont magnifique, les Anglais,*" he chortled, sending his bike swerving from side to side of the track in an excess of high spirits, "*formidable!*"

His sense of well-being arising from the knowledge that he was in the straight and could see the winning post ahead lasted him all the way to Caude. Things were definitely under way and could be pushed along without any more prodding about. He would blow the bridge at Camaret-Rouge with Harrison and then decide whether or not to put Lestocq on a test. If he did, it would be just for the hell of it, for he would know then that it was the nasty little sewer rat. Always supposing, he added with a caution he did not feel was necessary, Harrison and I send the bridge up. Then Gibault's and home to Judy with nearly a week in hand. Whoops!

Caude was lively, though the people in the streets were mostly older women collecting the rations for their families or poking about the few remaining stalls in what had once been a flourishing market in search of some extra tidbit they could afford. It was the week-end, and the week-end everywhere, even in Occupied France, was a milestone for housewives.

Maltby parked his bicycle and went into a café in the main street, where he ordered a coffee. The café was almost opposite the Gestapo HQ and he settled himself in the window where he could study the building. He wanted to get its details into his mind so that he could answer any questions the group might throw at him when they met on Monday.

Though this was the reason which had brought him to Caude, it was not what made his pulse run faster as he sipped his ersatz coffee. He wanted to see Schwartzkopf. The chances were that the Gestapo leader was not in the building and, if he were, there was no reason why he should leave it while Maltby was at the café unless he took his lunch elsewhere. Even so, he hoped his luck would hold and he would. He had seen him three times before, but not since he had returned from England.

Maltby could not explain to himself precisely why he wanted to look into the face of the Gestapo chief. He certainly would have avoided the main street a week ago in case he should see him. Normally he shirked the disturbance he always endured in the presence of his opponents. He had hated and still hated meeting the group knowing that one of them was a traitor, and knew that it made him shifty-eyed. Yet now he wanted to see Schwartzkopf, to measure the man who thought that he had him at the end of a string. He wanted to see him, despite the uneasy feeling the prospect gave him. He felt the need—though it was not consciously expressed—to know he had the chin to look at Schwartzkopf knowing what he did, to blow on the small spark of courage that had nothing to do with the noisy bravery of open battle, which he had nurtured within himself since he had come back to Pontrecy.

Looking at the Gestapo HQ again, Buchan's idea for raiding it appeared far from ridiculous. The house the Gestapo had taken over was old, large and tall for Caude, being four storeys high. Maltby judged it had been built at least two hundred years ago as a nobleman's mansion. On one side it was attached to a smaller building, the ground floor of which had been converted into a shop. On the other, it was separated from its next-door neighbour by a narrow alley, which ran directly through to the next street and gave the HQ a second and less imposing entrance than the terrace which fronted the main street.

Two men with Stens, Maltby calculated, could hold the alleyway and be completely covered from attack from inside the building by anything except grenades. And grenades were unlikely to be among the Gestapo's armaments. On the terrace in front of the main entrance were two guards. Ten men with a modicum of luck and surprise on their side could get in and be sure of having ten minutes to wreck the building. Getting them away afterwards, though, presented a greater problem, as there were barracks of Feldgendarmerie and Milice in the street.

He was thinking how this could be done when he was startled to see Hélène appear out of the alley beside the building. Hastily he turned his back. It was an instinctive movement, for he thought she would not so far break group rules as to come over to him even if she saw him. In a mirror over the bar he watched her walk past the Gestapo HQ without giving the café a glance. She hurried along the street frowning fiercely at her thoughts. He guessed she was going to the station, for she purposely varied the ways she came to Caude, often using the train or bus instead of cycling.

The next moment he was even more startled to see Harrison

come out of the alley and begin to walk along the street in the
same direction as Hélène. The tall man strode along on his long
legs with the flat, even gait of a hyena, without a trace of sway or
bounce, his shoulders seeming to be always the same distance from
the ground. Not that Maltby had ever seen a hyena except in a
film, but the comparison had occurred to him while watching a
travelogue he had seen when he was in London and it came back
to him now.

Hélène turned into the forecourt of the station. For a few
more strides Harrison went on after her as though he, too, were
going to the station, but if this had been his intention he changed
his mind, for he turned back and joined a knot of people waiting
for buses.

What the hell was he doing in Caude? Hélène was here to bring
Sarrut his money. But Harrison? Harrison's job was looking
after their W/T operator, finding places where he could set up
his apparatus and superintending his frequent moves. In doing
that he often went fairly far afield, but he couldn't be so cracked as
to be thinking of setting up a transmitting station in Caude itself.

Then what?

On the face of it, it almost looked as if the two of them had had
an assignation. But the idea that Hélène was having an affaire with
Harrison was laughable. And even if it hadn't been, that they
should come to Caude to do their love-making was so unnecessary
as to be utterly absurd.

Harrison got on a bus that, after meandering around the
countryside, wound up at Evine. From there, Maltby realized, he
would be able to get another which would take him close to the
farm at Aigunes. But it was a long and tedious way round.

It could be that both of them had been unaware of the other's
presence in Caude. Harrison might only have seen Hélène just
before she turned into the station yard, and then decided for
caution's sake to take another route home. That was, at any rate,
a plausible explanation. But it did not explain the extraordinary
coincidence that they should both come through the alley beside
the Gestapo HQ within a few moments of each other. Nor what
Harrison was doing in Caude at all.

He was so absorbed in trying to fit an explanation to this that
he almost missed Schwartzkopf. The Gestapo chief came out on
the terrace with another man and the guards clicked to attention.
At the same moment, a front-wheel-drive Citroën which had been

parked a little way down the street moved in smartly and stopped before the gate, its engine running.

The man was talking rapidly, and Schwartzkopf listened to him with the air of a busy executive who knows that every second of his time is precious and must be turned to account, even the few required for him to leave his office and enter his car.

Maltby was able to study his face, for he was looking directly towards him. His bearing was arrogant, but not military despite his uniform. His figure and thin-featured face, with gold-rimmed glasses on his narrow nose, were those of an administrator or an accountant. There were hundreds, perhaps thousands, like him in Germany, men who were doctors of commerce, economics and God knows what else, who would have been content to spend their lives giving advice, re-organizing factory personnel, totting up other people's money. Only there weren't enough people wanting their advice or to have them cooking their books so they joined the Nazis. And one named Schwartzkopf became head of the Gestapo in Caude in Occupied France.

It was generally said that this man was cruel. Looking at him, Maltby doubted it, if cruelty meant taking pleasure in inflicting pain. Schwartzkopf's pleasures would be more abstract, he was the sort who signed death warrants untouched by emotion but wept when he listened to Schubert's melodies. He would take no pleasure in the pain but only in its efficient organization. His delight would always lie in the ordering of the design and the totality of its fulfilment. For the thing created, whether it were beautiful or ugly, had value or not, brought happiness or misery, men like him had no concern. They were not policy makers and their great worth was that they did not seek to be.

I'll bet he's got a better brain than I have, thought Maltby. But the thought did not scare him. This was not a man who acted on impulse. He believed he had him on a string, he would not pull it until it was necessary to complete the pattern he had devised for Maltby. Only he didn't know the pattern was flawed by Maltby's knowledge of the string.

With a couple of quick nods Schwartkopf dismissed the man who was talking to him, got into the car and was immediately driven away.

If Lestocq were the one who had to report the Pontrecy group's activities to Schwartzkopf, Maltby could easily imagine how the little rat would cringe before that unyielding iciness. When the bridge at Camaret-Rouge was destroyed, Schwartzkopf would give someone hell. If he did but know it, it would be his last chance. But also, having seen the man, Maltby knew that the game he was playing was nearly up. If Schwartzkopf was not likely to act on impulse, he was not above making a new assessment. Let him once believe that his intelligence of what was going on in the group was not fool-proof and he would not be held back by a mirage of future profit. Paturin would have to claim the Camaret-Rouge bridge and claim it loud and clear. It would be hell if Schwartzkopf were to scrub them all out just as the traitor was discovered.

He took the ride back to Pontrecy easily, even though when he had gone halfway it began to rain. From now on rain was to be expected and would have to be taken into consideration in his planning. Fortunately it was downhill almost all the way, and he coasted along only using his pedals when he felt the need to keep himself warm.

In Pontrecy he left a message for Scoutier to begin taking the charges into Gibault's. Not wishing to meet his virago of a wife, he had simply slipped a note under the door. He knew the boy scout would go into action at once.

He was wet through when he got back to the farm, but after rubbing himself down briskly felt relaxed and cosy. Getting wet had never bothered him, for it never seemed to leave any effect on him. Though he was ravenously hungry he stuck to his diet. It would be silly to knock himself out now through being greedy.

When he awoke the next morning, he was feeling uneasy. It was idiotic, but it was seeing Harrison in Caude yesterday that had put him on edge. He'd got to find out what he was doing there. In any case he ought to go over to see him about blowing the bridge.

As it was Sunday he could not wear his farm overalls but put on a suit which he had bought in the village. Over a fortnight spent largely in the open air had restored a good deal of his tan, and he looked very much a farm labourer dressed in his best for a visit.

The farmhouse at Aigunes was deserted when he arrived, the family, he assumed, being at Mass, and he strolled down to Harrison's "office" to see if he were there, intending to wait for him if he were not. The "office" was empty, but the door was open and he entered silently on his espadrilles. On the high desk a copy of the local paper lay open, and instead of settling himself in a chair at once he stood idly reading the headlines.

Suddenly he was aware that there was somebody in the barn to which the "office" was attached. Through the open connecting door came sounds of movement among the straw and the low murmur of laughing, secretive voices.

With no other thought in his mind than to declare his presence, Maltby went into the barn. He had gone just one pace inside when the voices went dead and he pulled himself up short, transfixed. Letting out a half-strangled hysterical cry, a figure rose from a heap of straw and ran swiftly but unsteadily out of the barn into the yard. It was the unhealthy, spotty youth who had interrupted them the last time he had come to Aigunes to see Harrison. As he ran, tripping and rolling from side to side, he struggled to haul his trousers up over his buttocks.

Maltby did not know how long he stood there. For a while he was utterly numb, but as feeling returned to him he found himself incapable of speech, incapable of looking again towards the pile of straw pitched against the opposite wall. Somehow he got himself out of the barn into the yard, into the air. The spotty youth had disappeared.

Christ, he'd got to get hold of himself. Stop behaving like a Cheltenham old maid. These things happen, are a part of life, you just have to accept them.

But he couldn't. He couldn't because it wasn't a theory he was having to swallow, a dispassionate discussion on under-developed glands and psychological damage in infancy, but a fact. And the fact was that sly, revolting, corrupt boy. That was what stuck in his craw.

He felt awful. He breathed deeply, but the air did not drive away the nausea that swirled in him, nausea as strong as that which had gripped him in the sewer at Rigue. He could not have felt more revolted if he had come upon Harrison with his stomach blasted, his entrails a putrescent rainbow festooning from rags of flesh.

Harrison came out of the barn and stood beside him. He did not speak but just stood there, aloof, withdrawn, waiting.

"I'm sorry," Maltby mumbled, feeling that he must say something but unable to dredge up out of his mind anything adequate, let alone worthwhile.

"Since we're at war I suppose I shan't be chucked out. The

so-called normal won't object to my dying for them, will they?"

So that was the reason why he had transferred to that crumby regiment!

Maltby forced himself to look at him. The tall man held himself, as always, proudly upright and a little outside the ordinary workaday world. His beautiful, even features were impassive as ever but the eyes were hurt.

It came to him strongly that Harrison wanted to say more, that he was only waiting to be given a lead. But Maltby could not bring himself to it. He wanted only to escape.

"I wanted to talk to you about Buchan's scheme for raiding the Caude Gestapo. I think we should go into it seriously."

"Yes?"

Harrison's tone was completely indifferent, the hurt in his eyes deepened by Maltby's scared rejection of his plea.

"Have you been in Caude lately?"

"I——" he began and stopped.

For a moment something else came into his eyes, an intensity which clearly had nothing to do with his present situation. Maltby still could not bear to look at him. He no longer gave a damn about Caude, he only wanted to get away. Harrison knew it, and whatever it was that had come into his mind remained unsaid.

"I've been there once or twice to see Sarrut's optician pal, Dupont. He's put a new lens in my spy-glass which I dropped and broke."

Spy-glass! What the hell did he think he was, the commander of one of Nelson's frigates! Or did antique expressions go with antique vices?

"You've never thought the scheme practical, have you?"

"Not with the men we have."

"We'll be discussing it tomorrow, so give it some thought, will you?"

"There'll be nothing else in my mind."

Bitterness lay on the irony like a thick rust.

He could go now. He had made a pretence that life could still go on unaltered by what he had seen in the barn. Though both of them knew that it couldn't, he had made it and he could go.

"See you tomorrow then."

Harrison did not answer and Maltby walked away, schooling his legs to a casualness he did not feel. He knew without looking round that the tall man had remained where he was, his eyes on

Maltby's back. He could still feel them on him at the farm gate as he swung his leg over the saddle of his bicycle.

As he rode, Maltby struggled to free himself from the shock which had jangled every nerve in his body. He told himself that he was a fool, that he wasn't a baby to be shattered by seeing something not quite nice in the wood-shed. He'd never been morally indignant about pansies. At the school he had taught at before the war he had thought tolerantly, even affectionately, of the French and Science masters, Balby and Hartman, who had been happily living together for more than twenty years. He remembered that he had nearly landed in trouble through adding a hearty kick in the pants to the telling off he had given to a nasty little beast called Phillips Minor for mimicking Balby's mincing walk.

It was no good. He could not feel the same about Harrison and that horrible boy as he had about Balby and Hartman. The spotty youth was obscene, a foulness. He tried to see it all through Harrison's eyes, asking himself whether Harrison would not have been equally nauseated coming upon him copulating with Françoise. He might have been, but Maltby refused to accept that it was the same. Françoise was not disgusting, maggot-ridden like Harrison's frightful love.

It's no damn use telling myself I'm twenty-six and have seen enough to make me cynical if not decently tolerant, this hasn't anything to do with cynicism or tolerance, it hasn't anything to do with the mind at all. It's no use telling someone who is frightened of snakes that grass snakes are harmless. They're not frightened of being poisoned but of snakes. It's in their guts and it can't be shifted by reason any more than a strangulated hernia can.

I'm no different from Phillips Minor, he brooded, scared of something that is different from what I think is normal. Only instead of sniggering and wanting to hurt and be cruel I look for a stone to shove my head under. I deserve to have a kick in the pants as much as he did. I'll beat it, I bloody well will, he fumed. But the thought of meeting Harrison again, of working closely with him, made him flinch. He decided that if he had not got himself in hand by the following day he would switch plans and take Lestocq to blow the bridge at Camaret-Rouge. If he disliked Lestocq and suspected him of all sorts of mean perversions, his sensibilities had had time to be blunted.

The shock he had received had gone deep. How deep he realized when ten minutes after he had got it down, his midday meal of slops came back at him. Unable to free his mind in any other way from dwelling on what he had seen, he doped himself and slept it off.

CHAPTER FIFTEEN

WHEN he awoke, Maltby was inclined to think he had taken the discovery of Harrison's weakness so hard because he was not fit. The trouble with having an ulcer was that even minor mental shocks kicked back at you physically. If there had been any future in the group, he would have had to have a serious session with Harrison. Homosexuals with fancies for degenerate youths could be bloody dangerous. As it was, it was hardly worth bothering about.

All the same, though he was able to look at it more dispassionately, he felt the tension in himself the moment the tall man came into the group meeting. He sensed that Harrison had a similar feeling on seeing him.

It was then that he finally decided that he must take Lestocq to blow the bridge. Neither he nor Harrison would be able to endure going on a mission alone together yet. This was confirmed to him later when, as they drank their coffee, Harrison came over and spoke to him, taking care that the others should not see what he was doing.

"I'd like to see you."

At once Maltby felt himself take fright.

"I can't now."

Harrison brought his expressionless face close to Maltby's.

"I wouldn't ask but it's important," he said urgently.

No, he couldn't do it, not on top of everything else. He couldn't face a cosy discussion about Harrison's love life. He'd got his plateful without that.

"I'm sorry, can't be done. I'll come and see you."

"It——" Harrison tried to go on, but Maltby had snatched himself away and was talking to Hélène.

To make sure that Harrison would not try to waylay him, Maltby left the meeting first.

As it happened, it was Wednesday when he went to collect the "eggs" Paturin said he could have. As he cycled to meet Lestocq, he had a pang of regret that he was not likely to bring them home. One of the reasons why he had wanted to use Harrison on the job was because he particularly wished to see the bridge go up. The group had tried so often to put it out of action and failed that to see it go down at last would have given him immense satisfaction and wiped out previous disappointments. Now he was betting on being disappointed again. He wondered what trick Schwartzkopf would play this time.

Usually when the group was on one of its expeditions Maltby saw little of Lestocq. This was because he avoided the Saarlander as much as he could. Now they rode together and he had to listen to his whining voice in his ear. Sycophantically, because Maltby was English and the boss, he spoke ingratiatingly about the tremendous damage the RAF was doing to Germany, of how he was sure that any day now British troops would be landing in France, of how easy it would be then for Maltby to take over command of the whole province.

"The Boches are beaten. Everyone knows it. Even they do, yes?"

As he said this, Lestocq wiggled his front wheel for emphasis. If you're trying to make a mug out of me, you'd do better not to lay it on too thick, was Maltby's reaction to this.

Tiring of the world situation, Lestocq turned to the village. He seemed to have acquired an enormous amount of unsavoury lore about what went on between the inhabitants of Pontrecy. Village life is notoriously peculiar, but Maltby thought it was unlikely that there could be quite as much incest and debauchery as Lestocq claimed he was privy to, and he did not disguise his disbelief in the little rat's fairy-tales. Discouraged by the poor response he was getting, Lestocq finally drifted into silence and like that they rode for several kilometres.

"We are strange ones in the group, aren't we, yes?" Lestocq said suddenly.

"I've not noticed that any of us have two heads."

"But inside, that is where we are strange. Nothing in common."

"What about the war?"

"Oh, no. We fight all for different things."

"I should have thought to fight at all was enough."

"For you, yes, but not for the rest of us."

This interested Maltby.

"What are you fighting for?"

"My café, of course."

"And Gringoire?"

"Hate of the railway. You knew that, yes?"

"No."

"The railway was his life, his love. Then in 1937 he led a Popular Front strike and he was sacked. Since he is not allowed to work for the railway, to cherish it, he now only wants to smash it. He is like a man who, having been discarded by his mistress, determines to kill her, unable to bear the thought of another possessing her if he cannot."

Could this be true? Certainly Gringoire was preoccupied with railways. Still, it was difficult to believe that underneath his stolid taciturnity his strength was kinked as it was in the rest of them.

"And Lulu?"

"He fights for his soul."

By God, it was clever of the little bastard to see that. Yet he wasn't really clever, though he had a certain shrewd cunning. What was it then? Intuition? Or the ability of the obsessed *voyeur* to recognize the repetitive shape within the total pattern?

"And Charlemagne—Harrison—why is he here?"

"I'm not sure," Lestocq said after a pause, "the birds, perhaps. Or to be left alone. Or revenge. In such a deep one, it could be many things."

Maltby had asked about Harrison to see if the little rat had any inkling of his awful boy friend. Evidently he had not.

They had gone half a kilometre further before Lestocq spoke again.

"We do have one thing in common, all the same."

"What's that?"

"Courage. We are not afraid to die."

He said this without a flourish, quietly as a plain statement of fact.

"I am. And I'm bloody well not going to!"

Lestocq laughed.

"With you it doesn't matter. You are so afraid of being afraid that you will always be the bravest of us all."

This made Maltby fume. He wished he had arranged to meet Lestocq close to the bridge, then he would not have learnt how well the Saarlander read them all.

They now faced so many gradients that they had no breath

to talk. Whenever the road dipped, they sat back in their saddles listening to the whirr of their wheels in the dust and letting the air into their lungs. The last rise before the bridge was so steep that Maltby, hampered by his stomach shield, got off and walked his cycle up.

A little below the top they hid their bicycles and crept cautiously forward. The moon was almost full but low down in the cloudless sky. It lit up the valley and the bridge below them.

As far as Maltby could see there wasn't a human being within half a mile of the bridge. Compared with the noise the soldiers had made when he had last been there at night, the silence which surrounded them was eerie.

Maltby looked at Lestocq. He was keeping carefully within cover while his eyes steadily raked over the valley. He could be looking for something he knows is there, thought Maltby, but equally he could simply be observing normal caution.

Slowly, moving from shadow to shadow, Maltby led the way down to the bridge. There were no hidden guards.

He found the loose bricks covering the pockets which Paturin's men had made for the charges. If they'd had to cut them themselves, he reckoned it would have taken him and Lestocq at least four hours of chiselling to go as deep, and he had a momentary flash of pleasure that he should have thought of asking Paturin to make the preparations.

As they rammed the charges home, Maltby's mind was alert, running on greased wheels. If there were no guards, how was Schwartzkopf planning to save the bridge? There was only one way. Somewhere in the hills on either side of them eyes were on them. Men were waiting quietly for them to finish and go so that they could remove the charges. Once before when they had tried for the bridge the fuses had been tampered with, but that could not be the method this time, for he had set them himself.

Pushing up from the back of his mind even as he probed the possibilities was an uncomfortable alternative. He had once again backed the wrong horse and it was not Lestocq but Harrison who was the traitor. The thought made him jumpy. He didn't want it to be Harrison, for he felt too guilty about him already.

He took out all the fuses on an impulse, intending to cut them down from half an hour to twenty minutes and then changed his mind and put them back as they were. If he shortened them he could wait at the top of the hill for the charges to blow and only lose about ten minutes of getaway time. It seemed a good idea until he realized that Lestocq, if he had told Schwartzkopf anything at all, would have certainly told him the fuses might be as long as an hour but would certainly not be less than thirty minutes. If there were Gestapo men waiting to draw them they would inevitably give him and Lestocq time to get clear before appearing. By setting them off earlier he would get the bridge but wreck his chance of proving Lestocq's guilt.

When Maltby was assured that everything was properly set they climbed back up the hill towards the place where they had left their cycles. Just before reaching the top, he stopped Lestocq.

"We'll wait here," he said.

"But——"

"I want to see the bridge go up."

Lestocq, who had been clearly puzzled by Maltby's fiddling with the fuses, turned his head towards him sharply. But what he was thinking, Maltby could only guess, as his face was in shadow obscuring his expression.

It might only have been surprise, for it was extremely unusual for saboteurs to stay near their objectives once they had laid their explosives in place. In this case, Maltby calculated that there was little danger. It was a deserted area, the nearest house being more than half a mile away and no troops or Feldgendarmerie stationed nearer than five miles. He positioned himself to wait a little behind Lestocq and on the moon side of him so that he could see his face. There was nothing to read in it now as he squatted on his haunches, his small beady, black eyes fixed on the bridge.

The man had much more to him than he had imagined. He'd learnt that tonight anyway. Christ, we are a crew, he thought, remembering what Lestocq had said to him. All of the group appeared quite different to him from his picture of them at the time he'd been flown back to England. Of course, in the past three weeks he had been probing into them with a purpose. Before, he had simply had his cursory impressions to rely on. What he had found had no meeting-point with the popular myths about Secret Service agents.

Then what meeting-point had their life? For him to be sitting in the moonlight with a man he believed to be a double agent waiting for a bridge to dissolve into rubble squared with the myth. But what about him sitting in front of a farmhouse fire holding a glass of bismuth and milk and reading newly delivered letters from his wife? Or Harrison lying in his hide watching birds? Or Buchan spouting Goebbels propaganda?

He chuckled out loud and Lestocq turned towards him.

"What is it?" he hissed nervously.

"Nothing. Just a thought I had. You keep your eyes open for anyone moving about."

"You expect someone, no?"

The tone was surprised.

"You never know your luck—as the bishop said to the actress."

"How much longer?"

"Ten minutes."

"What did this bishop do with the actress? He had her, yes?"

Lestocq's thin lips were parted and slightly damp, eager for pornographic details. Evidently he was unaware of the English joke. In that moment, Maltby was convinced that he was not the Gestapo man. However lasciviously obsessed Lestocq might be, he simply could not have asked that question if he had been on edge waiting for Schwartzkopf's men to appear.

They still waited for the bridge to blow, but Maltby now had no doubt that it would. As the minutes ticked by, he thought without exultation that he had the answer he had come back to Pontrecy to get. He could if he wished kill Harrison tomorrow and go home. But he wouldn't.

He told himself that it was necessary for him to wreck Gibault's factory first, that he had vowed to do this for B.6. as he had burnt Judy's letters, as some return to Pig-Face for sending them to him. But it was only part of the truth and perhaps only a small part. If Lestocq had been the man, that might have been the reason why he would have stayed behind to attack the works. "You'll want to take care of the rat yourself," they had said. They were wrong. He didn't want to kill Harrison. If he was occupied at Evine he could leave it to the French, pleading he had not the time. That would be true if not the truth.

Suddenly the charges blew, making sharp cracks like thunder flashes. A great rumbling ran down the sides of the hills as the bridge, its supports riven, tumbled in on itself. Where it had been, a cloud of white dust hung, a trail or two of darker coloured, more volatile, smoke from the explosives drifting above it. In the silence which followed, a dog barked from somewhere far down the valley.

"It's gone this time, yes?" Lestocq cried excitedly, jumping to his feet.

"Yes," Maltby said wearily, "it has. Let's go."

As they were about to mount their cycles they heard the plane. It was a four-engined bomber. A Halifax, Maltby guessed. It passed over them quite low and plainly visible in the moonlight. Lestocq waved an arm and cheered. The plane swung round and came back.

The bottom dropped out of Maltby's stomach as he realized that it must be Paturin's parachutage. Not having listened to the BBC that day, he hadn't known it was coming or he would have called off the bridge-blowing. He could have buggered it up. Either way. If Schwartzkopf's men had been running all over the countryside or the pilot had arrived in time to see the flashes from the explosions and sheered off! He was a bloody fool, a criminal idiot not to have checked on the BBC messages. He should have remembered no one else in the group knew that the drop was coming or its code signal. How much longer could he go on making mess-ups and getting away with them?

The thought made him nervous and his confidence oozed out of his boots. Casting about for other mistakes he had made, he decided not to go back by the way they had come, openly by the main road, but to take another route which would be longer and carry them rather far to the east but by smaller roads.

Now their way lay mostly downhill, but a good deal of the advantage of this was lost in the stretches which were so badly surfaced that their handlebars had to be gripped tight to prevent them being twisted out of their hands as their front wheels ran into potholes six inches deep. Besides this, the roads they took, being little more than lanes, were full of bends which were difficult to see as they travelled without lights.

As he pedalled along, Maltby tried to work out what he must do next. He decided that he would attack Gibault's on Friday. He had not intended to do it before Monday, but he was suddenly overcome with a sense of imminent danger and he was windy of hanging back longer. He wanted to get to hell out of here. He was sick of the difficulties he faced, sick of his responsibilities, sick of himself. Most of all sick of himself, of his rotten guts, of his bloody incompetence.

Bringing the date forward for the attack on the factory meant only that he would have to work fast during the next forty-eight hours. All the groundwork had been done. The previous day he had been into the factory yard again, using the same disguise as he had on his earlier visit, for Scoutier to show him where he was cache-ing the charges behind a sheet of rusting corrugated iron. At the same time he had arranged with Henri that he should obtain the help of another Red in the factory in taking in the explosives. By Friday all eight would be inside.

Henri's office contact had stolen three blank passes, and an instrument maker in his group was making replicas of the rubber stamps with which they were counter-signed. The problem of getting into the works was as completely solved as it could be by him. But the number of people who were now involved in the operation was another reason why Maltby was anxious to cut down the delay before the action.

He wished that he could have done without Paturin's maquis, for he would have liked them to raid the Gestapo at Caude at the same time as he was attacking the factory. It was an idea that had come to him only that day, and it was exciting to think what a night to remember they would give Schwartzkopf if it were possible. But he had no one to replace Paturin's men at Evine. Le Feu was holding his escape route, Serpier's band was too small and too demoralized, and Sarrut's untrained in fighting.

Buchan would have the most to lay on, and he decided he must see him first thing in the morning to put him in the picture. Then Lestocq—he could save time by briefing him now.

While he had been occupied with his thoughts he had dropped some way behind the Saarlander, and he shouted to him to wait for him to catch up. Lestocq stopped pedalling but did not brake.

Maltby had got to within five yards of him as they turned the next corner and went straight into the Feldgendarmes waiting for them. There were eight of them and they had been resting, waiting for their transport to pick them up, after a gruelling exercise which had lasted the whole day, devised for them by an officious under-officer to toughen them up and make them familiar with the terrain, though this Maltby only learnt later. If they had not heard Maltby call to Lestocq, the appearance of the two cyclists would have taken them by surprise and just possibly they might have been able to get away, as the Germans were dead-beat. As it was, however, they were waiting for them.

Lestocq had no chance. Two of them leapt upon him before he realized they were in an ambush, and he went down still tangled in his machine and in a moment three men were sitting on him pummelling him with their fists.

Maltby had time to get off his bike and poise himself before the first man lumbered at him. He held a rifle in his hands clumsily pointing it at Maltby's chest. Side-stepping, Maltby went in close. With his hands gripping his rifle the Feldgendarme was virtually unprotected against in-fighting, and Maltby drove his knee into his groin and hit him hard in the face. The man dropped with a howl.

Maltby tried to get his revolver from his pocket but a rifle butt was driven into his kidneys and the breath whistled through his teeth in a shrill squeal of pain. Then all became confusion and three of them were attacking him at once, slashing at him with their rifles, kicking him, trying to get a grip of his flailing body. One of them fired, the spark from the barrel of the gun standing out like a star in the darkness, but the others, fearful of being hit, shouted at the rifleman for a fool.

Raising his arms to protect his head, Maltby managed to ward off two blows from the swinging rifles, but their force numbed his arms. Then one that he did not see caught him at the base of the skull, not full on but a glancing swipe which all but opened his scalp to the bone and sent him crashing down unconscious of anything but the singing fireworks in his brain.

As he hit the ground his head cleared sufficiently to feel the weight of the three of them land on him. They clawed at him, hitting him and twisting his arms. When they had taken his gun and were tired they stood up.

He sensed rather than saw the boot coming and rolled with it. It was an instinctive movement, made to protect his stomach, but it saved his belly shield from being discovered. If he had lain still and the full force of that vicious kick had stubbed against its steel, it would have been obvious that he had suffered no injury from the boot. One of the men asked a question which Maltby thought was an enquiry as to whether he was dead, and the reply was not yet. This was accompanied by a half-hearted kick in the thigh. It must have been the third man who kicked him so hard on the side of the head that he passed out completely.

The next thing he knew he was bouncing along on the floor of a truck. Lestocq was lying next to him and four of the Feldgendarmes were sitting on either side. His whole body rang with pain and waves of faintness dragged away his consciousness. He willed his spinning head to settle, but when it did it made him more aware of the agony in his flesh.

He was careful not to move for fear of drawing attention to himself, for even as it was the Germans were unconcerned where they rested their feet. They had trussed Lestocq up but left Maltby's hands and feet free. Evidently they thought he was so near to being cold meat that it was not worth the trouble. As long as he didn't move they might go on thinking that. Then if he could gather enough strength together he might be able to make a break for it sometime.

There would not be much chance of that if they were being taken to Caude. That would be the end of the road.

In the fantasies he'd woven of how he would behave and what he would think about if he were to be taken, he had seen himself as only thinking of Judy, crying out to be able to touch her just once more. Now it had happened he did not think of her at all. Lying there among the snorts and grunts of the dozing Feldgendarmes he felt only cheated and desolate that he should have failed, been beaten in the final moment when success was his.

The truck stopped, the Germans jumped out and pulled their prisoners after them. Biting his lip against the shock, Maltby managed to keep his body limp as it hit the roadway. As though they were sacks, he and Lestocq were carried in and dumped on wooden bunks in a small room with a heavy door.

The only furniture in the room was a plain wooden table and one chair. The Feldgendarme who was left to guard them sat on this and immediately his head began to nod and his eye-lids, red-rimmed with fatigue, fell down. His eyes were only closed for a moment at a time, for as soon as they shut, his body swayed forward and he woke up with a jerk. Maltby, watching through his lashes, was convinced that the man would not be able to last much longer without sleep. If only he weren't relieved!

At least they hadn't been taken to Caude. This place was obviously a small post. But where? Was it the one at Cavet or Ridac? Cavet was the more likely. And that was twelve miles from Pontrecy!

Someone kicked the door. The guard opened it and took in a tray of food which he set down on the table and began to eat ravenously.

Maltby guessed that it was intended to keep them there all night. If visitors from headquarters were expected, there would be a great deal less casualness among the guards. That was good.

The Feldgendarme finished his meal. He had apparently come to some sort of decision because he picked up the tray and went to the door moving quietly. He opened the door and put the tray down on the floor outside. Then he stood up and listened. Snores and heavy breathing came faintly to Maltby's ears.

The guard seemed satisfied with what he heard. He locked the door and put the key on the table. Going over to where Lestocq lay with his face to the wall, he examined the ropes pinioning his hands and feet. Then he came and stood over Maltby. After looking at him for a moment he jabbed the barrel of his rifle so hard into his ribs that Maltby nearly stifled keeping back the shriek of pain which rose in his throat.

If he moved it was missed by the guard, for the man gave a pleased grunt. He took off his belt and, after unshipping his revolver, hung it over the chair. Turning down the lamp to a glimmer, he loosened his uniform.

His next move caught Maltby completely by surprise. Being quite unprepared for it, he came nearer to betraying himself than when the rifle went into his ribs. Casually, the Feldgendarme took a grip on his chair and flung him on the floor. For a second he thought the man had guessed that he was playing possum and was going to beat him up. Then he saw it was only that the guard had decided a bunk was wasted on a near corpse, for he stepped over Maltby's inert body and lay down on it himself, putting his rifle beside him and holding his revolver between his knees. In less than two minutes, he let out a snore and after that they came regularly and noisily.

Maltby did not move. Presently he heard Lestocq wriggling about as he turned over. The guard did not move. Maltby lay still for another five minutes and then got up. He rose slowly, as much from the pain the movement cost him as from caution.

He crawled across to Lestocq, ears cocked for any change in the guard's breathing. But the man was sleeping so deeply, thunder would not have roused him. Motioning Lestocq not to speak, he looked at his bonds. They were too tight to be undone and he cautiously withdrew the bayonet from the Feldgendarme's belt and hacked away the rope securing Lestocq's hands.

The effort made his head swim and he gave the bayonet to Lestocq so that he could free his feet. That done he signalled to Lestocq to take off his boots. This he did but, loath to part with them, strung them together by their laces and hung them round his neck.

Now that he had been standing upright Maltby's mind was becoming clearer, though his head ached and all his muscles were raw and tender. Lestocq rubbed his legs to free them from the cramp caused by the rope. Though he was anxious to get moving, Maltby waited while Lestocq got the blood flowing again in his veins. If they had to fight their way out, the main burden would fall on Lestocq.

Maltby took the key from the table and unlocked the door. Snores were coming from a room to his left at the end of the passage. Now he was in a quandary. He did not know which way they had come in. He looked at Lestocq, who nodded that he understood Maltby's unspoken question.

Lestocq went along the passage to the partly open door from behind which the snores were coming. Gently he pushed it wide, holding the guard's bayonet at the ready. Edging himself round the door he glanced into the room and then beckoned Maltby to follow him.

Maltby's heart was pounding painfully. His lips were dry and he wiped them with the back of his hand. He moved up to Lestocq's shoulder. There were three Germans in the room, which was equipped as an office, and all of them were fully dressed but sprawled about in sleep.

Cautiously Lestocq crept across the floor towards a door on the opposite side of the room. The air in the room was stale and stank of sweat. A lamp stood on the table, its wick turned down low, but giving enough light for them to weave between the chairs and the sleeping Germans.

They moved infinitely slowly. Contrary urges rose and fell in Maltby. One second he would have preferred to make a dash for the door so that the menace of the room would be behind them quickly. The next, to remain transfixed, for even the slightest movement seemed to hold too much danger to risk.

At last Lestocq reached the door and pulled it open. As he did so its edge caught the boots dangling round his neck. Maltby stopped breathing. The clatter of the leather on wood rang sharply through the room. The breathing of the Feldgendarme nearest the door hesitantly missed its rhythm. Lestocq raised the bayonet and poised himself above the fat figure sprawled on the floor. Maltby's eyes flicked round the room in search of a weapon.

But the man did not wake. A second later they were past the door and it was closed behind them.

They were in a short passage or porch which served as an entrance hall for the house. Now they were in total darkness, but after a moment they made out the night glow from a fanlight which could only be above an outside door.

The door was bolted but not locked. Half a minute later they were in the street.

It was Cavet.

Now Maltby took the lead, moving as swiftly as he could and pressing himself close to the wall. He had only gone a few paces, however, when Lestocq gripped his arm.

"Wait," he hissed, "I must go back!"

Maltby looked at him stupidly but before he could say anything Lestocq was off, having first thrust his boots into Maltby's hands. He ran fast in his stockinged feet and disappeared into the Feldgendarme post.

Had he gone mad? Or was Lestocq really the spy after all, and had gone to rouse the Germans? Or more probably there were no Germans and he hadn't been captured but was in the middle of a nightmare from which he would wake at any moment. He was utterly dazed by Lestocq's inexplicable behaviour.

But it wasn't a nightmare. Standing there in the darkness, too many parts of his body were hurting for that. He breathed deeply to see if that would clear his head, and at once wished he hadn't for an agonizing stab went through him where the Feldgendarme had jabbed him with his rifle.

He began to panic. He couldn't stay where he was. It was twelve miles to Pontrecy and already he saw by his watch it was half past one. Fit, he could not be back at the Gallots' farm before five and perhaps not much before six. In his present condition he did not know whether he would be able to make it at all.

Slowly he began to walk along the street away from the Feldgendarme post. As he approached the first corner he heard footsteps coming from the side road.

There was nowhere for him to hide. Swiftly he moved forward until he was within two yards of the corner. There he waited. He had nothing he could use as a weapon but Lestocq's boots and he took a firm grip of their laces.

Whoever it was coming towards him was making no effort to

conceal his presence. His feet racketed on the cobbles and the sound, funnelled by the houses on either side of him, issued into the street as though enlarged by a megaphone. There were few people who could be about legitimate business at that time of night. As the man turned the corner, Maltby lifted Lestocq's boots on to his shoulder.

It was a gendarme, small and cocky. The man stopped dead on seeing Maltby, and at the same time his fingers went hesitantly to his revolver holster. But he did not draw his gun.

For a moment they remained like that, in tableau. Maltby knew that he must look a horrifying sight, for above the swollen flesh of his cheeks he could feel the blood caked hard.

"Resistance!" he whispered sharply, "beat it!" adding when the gendarme opened his mouth to speak, "at the double!"

The man did not move at once, but his eyes went past Maltby and rounded in surprise. Maltby did not follow his gaze, guessing that he had seen Lestocq coming out of the Feldgendarme post. Suddenly the gendarme turned sharply on his heel and went back round the corner the way he had come.

Maltby glanced over his shoulder to confirm that Lestocq was following him and set off at a jog-trot. By the time they had cleared the last of the houses he was panting painfully from the pain in his side, and his head was singing from the jarring it was taking with every stride.

"My boots!" Lestocq wailed. "I must have my boots. I shall be crippled!"

Maltby threw himself down by the roadside and rolled to see if he could press his ribs into a more comfortable state. It was obvious that he would not be able to do any more trotting. While they could, they would have to keep to the road. He would not be able to stand the rough going if they struck across country.

When he sat up, Lestocq had put on his boots and was waiting for him patiently.

"Why did you go back?" he asked irritably, "are you mad?"

"I had to get my teeth."

"Your what?"

"Teeth. I spat them out when they threw me on the bunk because I was afraid that when they came to beat me up they would break in my mouth and choke me."

Maltby did not laugh, being too amazed that the little runt should have risked both their lives for a set of false teeth. He tore a strip off him sharply for being indisciplined, but Lestocq insisted angrily that he had only done what he'd had to do.

"Where could I have got another set?" he demanded stubbornly.

When he had cooled down, Maltby would have liked to laugh,
but the pain in his side made it impossible to do more than let out
little sobs of amusement as he thought of Lestocq braving the
horrors of that tip-toeing walk past the sleeping sentries twice for
the sake of some plastic molars which didn't fit him anyway.
Lestocq, however, could see nothing funny in it whatever. As he
slogged along through the dust at the edge of the road, Maltby
marvelled that the little bastard should have had the guts. He had
always thought that Lestocq would fight with ratlike ferocity if he
were trapped, but what he had done needed a cold-blooded
courage. Maltby wondered whether there was anything he could
have left behind in their prison which would have made him do
what Lestocq had done. He could think of nothing. But then he
had all his own teeth.

Soon the sheer effort of keeping going drove everything else
out of his mind. For an hour he kept up a reasonable pace but
towards the end of the second he was swaying drunkenly about,
with Lestocq trotting anxiously at his side ready to catch him if
he looked like falling.

They came to a stream and Maltby washed the blood from his
face. The water stung his bruised flesh but freshened his mind.
Soon they would have to leave the road or risk being seen by early
morning workers.

Lestocq squatted on the bank of the stream holding his right
hand spread out in front of him. It was deeply stained by what
in the starlight looked like a birthmark.

"Boche blood," he said, his false teeth showing between his
evil, lascivious lips. "I don't want to wash it off."

It was a moment or two before Maltby took this in.

"What Boche?"

"Our guard. When I went back."

"Did you wake him up then?"

"No. I wanted this."

He held up the Feldgendarme's Luger.

Maltby looked at his face and knew he was lying. He had killed
the guard for the pleasure of killing and now the blood on his
hand gave him an orgiastic delight. He was utterly disgusting.

A memory stirred in Maltby's mind, a memory of a man with

fine thin features and wispy white hair which blew in the wind, whom he had met watching sea-gulls wheeling over Poole Harbour during his summer holidays in the year war had been declared. There were people, the man had told him, who fed the gulls with carbide so that they could see them explode when they swallowed water afterwards.

"It's those sort of people," the man had said, "who come into their own in wartime."

Lestocq was one of them. There had been no need to kill the guard, certainly not for the Luger. But he could not resist the temptation to destroy something which lived and breathed and perhaps found a happiness in doing so he had never known.

"Clean the filth off you," he rasped.

As soon as Maltby lay down flat, his head began to be full of whirring noises. He passed out cold.

He came round to find Lestocq mopping his face. His wiry hands were extraordinarily gentle as he cleaned the cut on the back of Maltby's head with tender care.

Maltby looked at his watch. It was nearly four.

"It's no use," he said. "I can't make it."

He told Lestocq that he must go on without him. He would hide somewhere until evening and then try to cover the remaining seven miles to Pontrecy.

Lestocq looked at him doubtfully.

"We could try to go on," he said, "you could lean on me."

"No."

He closed his eyes and tried to steady the ground which heaved beneath him. When he opened them again Lestocq was no longer there.

Presently the little man came back and hauled Maltby to his feet. Half supporting, half carrying, he got him to a clump of bushes where he would be out of sight of the road but still close enough to the stream to get water if he should need it.

"You stay here," he said, "I'll come back with Gallot's cart and take you home."

"Don't come unless it's safe," Maltby insisted, "and don't tell anyone about the bridge. Paturin did it. Paturin. You understand?"

"Yes," Lestocq answered, but plainly did not.

"Invent some reason for our being out tonight. Making a recce for a sabotage or something . . . what you like."

"I'll be back as quick as I can. You need a doctor, yes?"

"For Christ's sake, buzz off."

He went.

Maltby remembered little of the next seven hours. Some of the time he slept and sometimes he lay moaning to himself. Except once when the knife turned in his belly, the pain in his head was the worst.

When old Gallot and Lestocq came for him, he was mumbling lightheadedly. But he recognized them and was able to get to his feet with their help. His legs were stiff, and he was so cold that he was unable to stop his teeth from rattling.

It was not easy to get him to the cart drawn up on the road, for it was in full view of a house standing only a hundred yards away. To fool anyone watching, Lestocq had pretended to be crippled so that Gallot had helped him to the clump of bushes as though he needed to relieve himself.

Now Gallot supported Maltby back to the cart while Lestocq slipped down the bank of the stream and worked his way along out of sight of the house. He was able to move quicker than the other two and he was already in the cart lying flat on the floor when they got to it. The farmer pushed Maltby into the back of the cart, and as he did so Lestocq, as though he were the man Gallot were helping up, stood up and sat on the seat next to the driver. From the house it would have looked as if two men had come in a cart and the same two men drove off in it. Maltby, covered with sacks and surrounded by farm machinery, was completely concealed.

The doctor was waiting for them when they reached the farm. He went over Maltby's injuries, tut-tutting most about the gash on his head but also spending a lot of time on the blackening skin on the left side of his ribs.

"What's the verdict?" Maltby asked.

Dr. Clozot was middle-aged and cynical. He endured the tedium of a small country practice because of his garden and the time it allowed him to spend in his study reading. His reason for being in the Resistance, or at any rate the one he always gave, was that he could not bear the Germans' table manners.

"It's lucky your head's made of concrete," he said, his tone serious but his grey eyes bright with the amused tolerance with which he regarded the sick. "But then if it wasn't I suppose you wouldn't be here, would you? It is possible you will live."

"How long before I'm right?"

"Depends on how quickly the effects of the concussion subside. If you had a good doctor, he might have you on your feet in about a fortnight. With me, if I don't manage to kill you, it will probably take a month."

"Stop fooling. You've four days to get me fit."

"Really!"

"I must be able to get about by Monday. It's a matter of life and death, Maurice."

Clozot was no longer looking amused. Maltby knew he was trying to make up his mind whether he was delirious.

"It's not only your head, you know. You're terribly bruised and if your rib's not broken it's certainly cracked."

"That can be strapped up, can't it?"

"If you exert yourself before you're well again the consequences could be serious."

"That's a risk I must take. Can you have me walking about in four days?"

"No. But if you ordered me to, I could try."

"It's an order."

The doctor shrugged his shoulders.

"If you want to kill yourself I——"

"No, Maurice," Maltby said quietly, with his eyes closed and the throbbing in his head almost more than he could take, "it is someone else I have to kill."

Clozot said no more but began to fiddle in his medicine bag.

"Can you give me something to stop my head aching?"

The effort of talking to the doctor had set every cell in his head jangling. He felt like screaming and would have if every sound he uttered had not increased the pain.

"I'm going to do better than that. I'm going to put you to sleep for twenty-four hours."

And that was how Maltby lost one of his twenty-eight days.

CHAPTER SIXTEEN

MALTBY had very little to show for the next two days either, but what he had, he reckoned important as it was time gained, time he would not have had if he had been able to stick to his plan to blow Gibault's on Friday.

When he awoke late on Friday afternoon his headache was not too bad if he did not try to move. Clozot was with him sitting patiently waiting for him to open his eyes.

The doctor examined him. Maltby had quick healing flesh and the stitches in his head looked healthy. He complained that his side hurt him whenever he tried to take a deep breath.

"You're lucky to be able to breathe at all," Clozot said acidly but did not remove the strapping to look at the bruised rib.

"What now, doctor?"

"More sleep. But first a meal."

Maltby explained to him about Harriet and the medicines and messes he had brought with him.

"So you're not only a battered wreck but a chronic invalid as well! And you still think you will be able to gallop about the countryside on Monday?"

"Must."

"Well, keep dosing yourself with your medicine and add a little chicken meat to your three main meals. You'll probably get some pain after you've eaten your first meal, but I'm leaving you a draught which should put you to sleep before it gets too bad."

"Thanks."

"There are two men waiting to see you. My advice is that you tell them to come back tomorrow."

It was Buchan and Paturin's courier who were sitting in the farmhouse kitchen and Maltby told Clozot what he could do with his advice.

He dealt with the courier in less than a minute and waved aside Buchan's attempt to give him a group report. He had to conserve what strength he had, and the group as a group now had no importance whatever.

In a few words he explained to Buchan the preparations he had to make for his part in the assault on Gibault's without, however, telling him what the objective was. He also impressed on him that he should tell no one what he was doing.

"And that goes for the group, too, understand?"

Buchan nodded.

"Good security," he said. "Should have been adopted long ago."

"And send Lestocq to me tomorrow."

Buchan looked at him curiously.

"How was it you got smashed up and he didn't?" he asked.

"He ducked out, I suppose. Just what you'd expect from a Frog."

"He ducked out of nothing. Luck of the draw, that's all."

Buchan said no more but left smiling his superior smile.

In spite of his weakness Maltby was hungry, so hungry that he had the greatest difficulty in schooling himself to eat slowly the food Madame Gallot brought to him.

"My poor Oignon, how you *are* hurt!" she exclaimed at the sight of his puffed and bruised face.

"It is as nothing compared with the wound torn in my heart by your indifference."

"You're so brave. Those terrible Boches!"

"They're not so terrible as unrequited love."

"You! You will talk of love on your death bed!"

"I hope so."

The pain came half an hour after he had set the tray on the floor beside his bed. Long hot needles drove deep into his belly. But he only sensed them hazily because the sleeping draught was already dulling his brain. They were with him only for the five minutes he hung on the lip of consciousness before falling fast asleep.

The next morning he felt better although the drug had left his mouth dry and furry. He was able to eat without causing himself to vomit or feeling more than a slight discomfort as his digestion got to work.

Yet in some ways this was his worst day, for it was the one on which the self-pity to which he was always a prey closed in upon him. Previously he had been too ill to think of anything but what he had to do. Now he was sufficiently recovered to be aware of his weakness and the trials it had to face and he wept inwardly that he should be separated from Judy. In a panic he reviewed the obstacles which stood between them and decided that they were beyond him. He'd have to give up any idea of wrecking the ball-bearing factory if he were ever to see her again.

Why the hell shouldn't he, he asked himself. He'd done what he came to do. That was more than could have been reasonably expected of him. Besides, even if he were able to stand on Monday, he couldn't be in a fit state for the attack on Tuesday. He would be mad to kill himself for a bloody medal.

He thought he had finally made up his mind, but when Lestocq came in he instructed him to trace the telephone line from Gibault's and open it up where it entered the woods beyond the open ground to the north of the factory.

For a while he pretended to himself that he was only taking the necessary precaution against the possibility that a miracle would happen and he would be completely recovered in time. It was not long, however, before the self-doubt which fed upon his motives had gnawed away the roots of this consolation. He hadn't the guts to pack it in. Timidity prevented him from taking the "out" his fight with the Feldgendarmes had given him. Lacking confidence in himself, he was afraid of doing the sensible thing because it was also the easiest and what he wanted to do.

He was feeling at his lowest when Hélène came. She was all concern for him but disguised the shock his battered features caused her. He didn't want to see her. In particular, he didn't want her around in case she should see Paturin's courier or the one whom he had asked Le Feu to attach to him and was about due to arrive. If Hélène were to see them she would guess he was planning a new action and would certainly try to stop him. She might even radio a request to London for his immediate withdrawal.

He didn't bitch at her but played the wan invalid, letting her fuss about his pillows and make him a drink.

"You'll have to go home now, Harry, won't you?" she said. "You must see that."

"Clozot says I'll be all right in a couple of days."

"You don't look as if you would."

"All I need is rest. Don't come to see me again."

"But I want to, Harry." She picked at the fringe of the coverlet on his bed. "You've been avoiding me ever since you came back."

"Don't come here again. I'll come to you on Tuesday, late, after curfew."

Her eyes lit up and a pink glow of delight spread across her sallow skin. Because he was so down himself, Maltby felt a pang of pity for her.

"That means you'll stay! Oh, my darling!"

She kissed him and he noticed the faint taint in her breath again. Revulsion ran over him in a wave quenching the pity he had had for her, revulsion against her for existing, for her love and its demands. But before it made him lash out she was gone, running lightly down the stairs calling gaily to Madame Gallot.

After she had gone Maltby decided he had done rather well. He had not only ensured that she would not come to the farm but made it unnecessary for him to see her until after the attack on Gibault's. Otherwise he would have had to see her before he went to Evine, to give her new papers and escape route. This way there would be no time for tearful goodbyes. The thought made him feel better.

In the evening he got up and sat in a chair in front of the fire for an hour, wrapped in a blanket. He felt groggy going downstairs but decided that he could not risk staying in bed longer. By the time he went back to bed, his head was aching again but he had managed the stairs without difficulty, though not without some pain from his bruised limbs.

When Clozot came in the next morning he found Maltby sitting up in bed reading.

"The body is a remarkable thing," the doctor said cynically after examining him. "Yours ought to have expired from the rifle butts and now it looks as though it may recover from my treatment. Such things discourage one's faith in science."

"My side still hurts damnably."

"What else would you expect?"

"Could you strap me up more comfortably next Tuesday or do it in a way which lets me breathe less painfully? Or will it be better by then?"

"It's not likely to be right by then. I could deaden the pain for a short time with a local anaesthetic. For how long do you want the pain killed?"

"Seven or eight hours."

"That's impossible. Nor will you be able to keep going for as long as that by Tuesday."

"I meant it would be seven or eight hours after I saw you that I would want to be free to move. The action will take less than half an hour."

"All I can do is to strap you up in a way that gives you as much freedom as possible."

"Will it be all right for me to come to you about 3 o'clock on Tuesday?"

"I'll come to you. Though I'm a fool to pamper you. You refuse all my advice."

"But I get better!"

"Yes. If all my patients had the sense to do the same perhaps more of them would recover!"

Maltby got dressed and went downstairs for lunch. He found

that any quick movement still brought a sharp stabbing sensation to the base of his skull. Bending down to put his socks on had caused his head to swim, but he had managed to get them on by lying on his back and lifting his feet in the air.

As the day wore away he became less liable to attacks of dizziness. His mind, too, ceased to run on self-pity but turned to consideration of the task before him. He did not worry about it but reviewed it with excitement and a gathering keenness.

Harrison and his nasty little boy friend no longer bothered him. He had ridden it out, become adjusted to it. It disgusted him but he could live with it, as he could live with Lestocq's lasciviousness or Buchan's "Blood and Iron" poppycock or Hélène's sour breath. He could have worked with Harrison again if that had been necessary. He could have killed him, too. But there was no time for him to do that.

Paturin came to see him late in the afternoon. Maltby had asked him to come and, despite the danger of making so open a journey in daylight, the maquis leader had come. Tersely he reported what he had done.

"The heavy wire-cutters and limpet incendiaries? Did they arrive?" Maltby asked him when he had finished.

Everything asked for had been sent by London. Paturin's force was now completely equipped with small arms.

"If all goes right at Evine, could you carry through another major action the following night? Only you would have to do it entirely on your own, as there will be none of my group available to help you."

"It would depend on what it was."

"A raid on the Gestapo HQ at Caude."

Paturin cocked an eyebrow but said nothing.

Realizing that the Communist would not take anything on trust, Maltby gave him the background. The only thing he suppressed was that it was a member of the British group who had enabled the Gestapo to fill their files with the names of most if not all the Resistance men in the district. If the files remained intact, the choice which faced every one of them was between going on the run or staying and facing almost certain deportation to a concentration camp, for the Gestapo would begin to round them up immediately after Gibault's was blasted.

"And you believe such a raid to be possible."

Eagerly Maltby explained how he thought such an attack

should be planned. Paturin said nothing nor even so much as nodded his head.

"How many men should I lose?"

"With luck, none. But it could be as many as ten."

"That's a third of all I have," said the Communist, his face as impassive as ever.

"It will not be a twentieth of those who will join you after Tuesday. And ten times as many will be lost if the files are not destroyed."

Paturin breathed in deeply through his large flat nostrils. Maltby knew that he was thinking that the "blown" men were Maltby's problem, not his.

God, thought Maltby, what debased bastards war makes of all of us. In peace time, if just one man is placed in jeopardy at sea or in a mine accident, no danger would deter our efforts to save his life. Without a second thought a hundred, a thousand men would throw themselves into the rescue work. Yet here not only the cost but the dividend is carefully calculated when it is not one but a hundred or more who were in danger. Not that Maltby blamed Paturin for his ruthless detachment. He was too uncomfortably aware that the Communist was right and these people were his problem and he was running out on them, leaving them in the lurch. That was true, even though he could do nothing for them if he stayed.

Carefully, as he did everything, Paturin filled his pipe, pressing the tobacco down firmly with his stubby fingers.

"Success would make you the outstanding military leader in the area," said Maltby, seeing if an appeal to the stolid man's vanity would help him to make up his mind.

Paturin lit his pipe, blew out the match and put the burnt stick tidily back in the box.

"My group"—he emphasized "group"—"is the best maquis in the north-west, perhaps in all France."

He said this without a trace of the boastful flourish which *"Ils sont fou!"* would certainly have used, making it a statement of plain fact. Such solid confidence was proof against vanity's obvious snares.

"It's not only the military importance. It would put you on top politically as well."

The ghost of a smile hovered in the shadow of Paturin's Stalin moustache. Maltby knew he was thinking this Englishman neither

knew nor cared anything of politics and of the shocked fright of
the de Gaullists if they were to know he had made this suggestion.
Maltby knew all that. And he didn't care.

"These people matter to you?"

There was an unusual softness in Paturin's voice, almost sentimental.

"Yes."

The Communist nodded. With his hands folded on his paunch
he looked like a Buddha.

"Before the spring we shall be fighting open battles with the
Boches," he said briskly. "For that I shall need mortars and
bazookas. If I carry through this raid, will you send them to
me?"

"I can ask for them but I cannot promise they will be sent. I
haven't the authority."

"Can I rely on you to ask?"

"Yes."

"Then I will think about the raid."

It was not a promise of action but it was more than Maltby
had expected. There was so little in it for the Maquis leader it
had never been more than a forlorn hope that he would take it
up. There was precious little chance of him getting his mortars
and bazookas but this didn't trouble Maltby, for he guessed
Paturin understood that. He had simply wanted to appear to be
making a hard-headed bargain.

Maltby walked beside the Communist to the farm gate.

"Are you a Christian?"

Paturin asked this in the same tone as he had earlier asked
Maltby if he played chess.

"No."

"It's a superstition like the rest. But it was clever of Christians
to put all the sins of the world on one Man's shoulders. They
knew no ordinary man was capable of carrying all his own sins,
so the Christian is only asked to do what he can. The Son of God
takes care of what he can't."

"And that's how it is with you?"

"I'm no Christian, but, yes, I, too, do only what I can."

"And who looks after what you can't?"

"The Party."

"I see."

They were at the gate now and Paturin puffing at his pipe,

speaking casually, his eyes on the middle distance, looked the picture of a small farmer on a visit.

"It's atheists that conscience ruins. Doing what they can is never enough for them. They try to be their own Jesus Christs."

"Without a faith outside themselves, don't they have to?"

"No, they don't have to," Paturin said with a nod and walked off towards Pontrecy.

Maltby had thought Paturin had been trying to tell him obliquely not to count too much on his attacking the Caude Gestapo HQ. It was only after he had gone back to the house that he realized that Paturin had been talking about him.

The next day he took it easily but kept going. There was still a hell of a lot to do. He went to see Gringoire and the W/T operator.

With Gringoire he simply fixed their rendezvous for the following night. The radio-man, a pale nervy boy called Duggan, he hardly knew, not having seen him more than twice since he had come back to Pontrecy. And he presented a problem. He was closest to Harrison, who was the group member responsible for finding him places where he could set up his apparatus and moving him every two or three days. Therefore he could not be told in advance that the group was about to disperse in case he should blurt it out to Harrison. And there was no time for Maltby to see him on Tuesday evening. Maltby solved it by giving the boy a sealed packet containing his papers, money and escape instructions. These last were very simple, for Serpier was to meet him at the next village and from then on he would be in the Maquis leader's charge. Maltby did his best to put the fear of hell into the boy, instructing him to open the packet at 10 o'clock the following night, not a minute sooner and not a minute later, and act immediately on the orders he would find in it.

Then he went back to the farmhouse to write the last of his despatches and clear up such details as remained.

He made up an envelope containing twenty thousand francs and an affectionate farewell letter ready for him to put on his pillow when he left the farmhouse for the last time the following afternoon. It was as much as he could do for the Gallots. He felt a pang that he should be sneaking away without a word but he brushed it aside. There was so much milk going to be spilt it was ridiculous to weep over that particular drop.

He lay in bed with his nerves bright and his mind racing ex-

citedly in anticipation of the next night's action. Because it was
the biggest he had ever undertaken might have been enough to
key him up in this way, but that it was the last made it even more
important to him. He was oppressed by the finality of all that he
was to do and the knowledge that anything he did not do he
never would.

Blasting the ball-bearing works was a hell of a far cry from the
amateurish attempt to set fire to a railway wagon which had been
his first essay at sabotage three years ago. Then he had been alone.
Now, counting those on the first stage of the escape routes, more
than sixty people, spread over an area of four hundred square
miles, were involved.

Momentarily this thought made him shudder because his
dependence on so many opened the way for a thousand slip-ups.
But he also felt pride that the whole show was his. No one but he
knew what the whole plan was. And it had bloody well got to
succeed.

Though his body was tired his excitement would not let him
sleep. Worse, his head was beginning to throb and Harriet was
moving about uneasily. He put himself out with a stiff dose of his
sleeping draught.

CHAPTER SEVENTEEN

MALTBY glanced at his watch. In another twenty minutes the
others would be arriving.

He was lying on his back in the undergrowth which ran along
the side of the Gibault factory. The attack would not begin for
another five hours, but he and Gringoire had to go into the works
with the night men so the rendezvous had had to be an uncomfortable time before it was to start.

Looking again at the hazards which they were to face had given
him a queasy feeling. In theory, his plan would work, but in
practice there was a hell of a lot which could go wrong. If Buchan
got put out of action by a lucky shot, for instance, and failed to
get the wire down. Then he and Gringoire would be goners. If
there'd only been a way of getting out of the works without laying
on a pitched battle! He could have done the job quietly on his
own then. The watch towers with its steel-helmeted soldiers,
searchlight and machine guns looked a formidable hornets' nest
to disturb deliberately.

Another thing which bothered him and made him nervously on edge to get the night behind him, was that he had seen a Gestapo man in Pontrecy. Gestapo were rarely around in the village unless on a specific mission. It probably had nothing to do with the group, but the unusual appearance of the Gestapo today of all days set his teeth on edge. He had only seen the man from the back, but the thick, powerful-shouldered figure and short neck had seemed familiar to him in a way that could not be entirely accounted for by the supposedly inconspicuous raincoat and felt hat, which was in fact anything but inconspicuous in a French village. Before the man had disappeared round a corner he had seemed on the verge of discovering who he reminded him of, but once he was out of sight he could think of none of the Gestapo types he knew well enough to recognize who had precisely the same bull-like quality. Now, when he was not thinking about it at all, it came to him suddenly. The bloke had exactly the same back view as B.6.! He remembered how he had chaffed Pig-Face about his likeness to a Gestapo man and it amused him to have seen one whom he could have mistaken for him.

The amusement relieved his tension but did not entirely allay his misgivings. He hoped that whatever it was the man had come to the village for was not going to keep him there all night. Pontrecy was on Maltby's own escape route.

The first to arrive was Buchan. He showed Maltby where he had hidden the wide duck boards which he proposed to throw over the barbed wire between the electrified fences.

"More efficient than blankets."

"And a damn sight heavier," Maltby said crossly, put out that Buchan should have taken it upon himself to improve on his scheme. "This is not the bloody Military Tournament, you know. Will you be able to move them fast enough on your own?"

"Shan't be on my own. Got those bloody Reds with me, haven't I?"

Maltby was not inclined to be gracious.

"All right. But remember it's my neck you're playing with as well as your own. If you had any other brilliant ideas, I'd like to know of them."

Buchan glared at him, his brow beetling over his monocle. But before he exploded Gringoire joined them. Quickly Maltby explained to them that the group was dispersing after the action and gave them their money and forged identity papers.

The two men looked at him queerly, obviously wanting to ask him questions. But he told them that there was no time for anything but to get them straight on the routes they were to take as soon as he and Gringoire were clear of the factory.

The next figure to stumble cautiously through the undergrowth was Paturin's messenger. He brought the limpet incendiaries. The remaining Maquisards would not move into position for another three hours.

Lestocq was the last to arrive. His job was both the simplest and the safest. At 10.5 precisely he was to cut the telephone cable. He would then retire with Paturin's men. The little man was so surprised to learn he was being recalled to England that he went off to his post mumbling amazed epithets.

"And what is my fate?"

Maltby's stomach fell with a crash. Slowly he turned. Harrison was standing three feet away from him, his tall figure only just discernible in the gloom of the wood.

"How did you get here?"

"I met Lestocq by chance at the cross-roads. It seemed you were having the sort of party I don't like to miss."

If that were true, Lestocq meeting him so near the rendezvous would have naturally thought that Harrison was on his way to it. In any case Maltby could not remember whether he had told Lestocq not to talk to other members of the group about the action. Christ, what was he to do?

"I'm sorry you didn't send me an invitation."

Maltby had taken Lestocq aside to give him his instructions so the two of them were standing a little apart from the others. As they spoke in whispers it was unlikely any of them could hear what they were saying.

"Nothing for you to do, I'm afraid," Maltby said lamely.

"Now I'm here, you won't mind, I suppose, if I make myself generally useful?"

Maltby sensed the tall man's tension. It was as though he were poised on the balls of his feet waiting for the starter's pistol.

"We're all here, I see. Except Hélène. But then she wouldn't be. Though I suppose she knows all about it?"

"As it happens, she doesn't," Maltby answered automatically, his pulses racing and pounding in his brain.

"Well, it's nice to know I'm not the only one to be excluded."

He'd got to kill the bastard. Turn him round and stick a knife in him. In five minutes he and Gringoire had to be going through the factory gates. It had to be now, this minute.

But if he did, what about the others? With no time to explain to them why he had done it they would be on edge, knowing that they had been working with a traitor and wondering whether they were not in a trap which Harrison had set for them before he died.

But if he didn't kill him he couldn't let him out of his sight. Now he knew what they were going to do, that was impossible.

He must be thinking how he can warn Schwartzkopf or if he can't do that, how he can box up the action.

Oh, God, God, God, what the hell am I to do? His stomach was heaving under its shield and the tips of his fingers tingled. He had got to kill the bastard even if it buggered up the attack. Putting his hand in his pocket he took a grip on his knife, half withdrew it and pressed the spring which shot the blade out of the haft.

"Let's get going," he said.

Apparently suspecting nothing, Harrison turned. Maltby already had the knife clear of his pocket when his brain suddenly cleared.

He'd take Harrison into the works and kill him there!

"Wait a bit. I could use you, Harrison. We could do with one more in the raiding party."

"Good."

For of course Harrison couldn't just give the alarm. If he did they would be caught and Schwartzkopf's hopes of smashing all the Resistance throughout the north-west when the groups linked up would go up the spout! So he would only be looking to hamstring the job. And that, my boy-loving beauty, you won't do, Maltby thought. While he had his eyes on the bastard he couldn't do a thing.

Now there was no time to lose. Maltby gave Gringoire and Harrison a limpet incendiary each and took one himself. He also gave Harrison the spare pass which he had intended to throw away before entering the factory.

"I haven't got a gun," said Harrison.

"You won't need one," Maltby answered shortly.

Maltby and Gringoire had Stens concealed beneath their overalls. In his hip pocket Maltby also carried a revolver. It suited him that Harrison should be unarmed.

"Going to put one of my fellows up a tree," Buchan said to him hurriedly. "Better angle from there to shoot out that searchlight. Don't like searchlights."

"Don't worry. The Boches will come off their perch fast enough when the incendiaries go up."

Buchan nodded.

"*Merde!*" he said.

Maltby smiled to himself. Always the traditionalist, Buchan couldn't see one of the group off without using the accepted good-luck word.

Out on the road approaching the gate, Maltby gave more of his attention to Harrison than the guards. He made the tall man go first.

At the gate it was as Scoutier had said. The guards scarcely looked at them. Maltby felt his muscles tighten as Harrison walked forward holding his pass. But one after another all three of them were let through without question. One of the guards stopped the man behind Gringoire and demanded his pass. The workman swore and after much digging in his pockets produced it. Maltby realized that it had been a mistake for them to hold out their passes. Apparently it was not usual for the night men to do this. Fortunately, instead of making the guards suspicious, it had given them ideas. Everyone who presented himself at the gate after them was made to show his pass.

Once in the yard, Maltby led the way to where there was a shallow recess in the wall of the main building. There they waited for ten minutes, giving the factory time to settle into its night routine. They had four hours to kill, and Maltby was beginning to worry where they could hide for as long as that. Three of them together were much more conspicuous than two.

The last of the night men came in and they saw the guards close the gates and go into the enquiry office. An eerie silence hung over the huge works, broken occasionally by the clash of metal on metal or a snatch of song echoing lonelily in the emptiness.

Still keeping Harrison in front of him, Maltby slid along the wall. He counted the buttresses they passed. The sheet of corrugated iron covering the charges lay against the third one. Or should have done, for when they reached the third it wasn't there. Thinking he must have miscalculated, he pushed on to the next. There was no piece of corrugated iron there either.

In panic, Maltby went as swiftly as he could back to the corner of the building in the direction they had come, leaving Gringoire and Harrison to wait where they were. But it wasn't anywhere along there. Coming back to the others, who had no idea what he was searching for, he ran forward in desperation from buttress to buttress right to the northernmost end of the building by the watch tower. There was no sign of the iron sheet. All the factory jetsam, the shorn bolts, twists of rusting wire, broken bottles and scraps of paper which had come to rest at the foot of the wall had disappeared. So had the dust. And the charges.

THE CHARGES HAD GONE!

Maltby's tongue was dry and his eyes stared wildly. He went completely to pieces, whimpering softly to himself, as he ran unsteadily back to the others.

The charges couldn't have gone! It was impossible! Things like that simply couldn't happen! Oh, Christ, what could they do? Not a damn thing without explosives! God, he couldn't even stop the action!

The whole bloody firework display would go up for nothing! Nothing at all!

But what the hell had happened? Why had the yard been tidied, swept so unreasonably clean? Who could have blown where the charges were? Not Harrison. Not anyone in the group. He was the only one who knew where they were. He and Scoutier.

Scoutier!

No, it couldn't be Scoutier. Unless he'd been taken! No, not even then. Scoutier wouldn't talk.

But had Scoutier been spotted hiding the charges? Had they played him along, just watching and waiting?

Had they walked into a trap which had been quietly set for them?

He crumpled and hit bottom. He couldn't take it. The Gestapo in Pontrecy, Harrison, and now this. He'd had it.

Gringoire gripped his arm. Hard.

From the direction of the gate a figure was stealthily sliding along the factory wall. The movement was slight but just perceptible in the thick darkness.

The trap closing in?

Maltby looked the other way, past Harrison. He could see nothing moving on that side. And all was still in the yard in front of them.

He wiped his dry lips with the back of his hand. It was trembling slightly but the tangible presence of danger had steadied him.

"I'll take him," he whispered, and added as he slipped past Gringoire, "watch Harrison."

If this was a trap, Harrison could be the other half of the nut-crackers! If Schwartzkopf had learned of their plan through discovering Scoutier was making a cache of explosives in the factory, that could be the reason for Harrison being at Evine.

This time he did not run but inched his way along. The other man had come to a stop by the third buttress. Only a raggedness in the sharp perpendicular line of the brick outcrop revealed his presence.

As he began to move, Maltby took out his knife. Going sideways like a crab and keeping an inch or two from the wall to prevent his overalls dragging against the brickwork, he closed the gap separating them. He made no noise, but he knew that if the man looked along the wall he must see him. What he would do if the man shouted or broke and ran before he got near enough to close with him, he didn't know. Nor what Gringoire could do if Harrison had been lying and had a gun.

Maltby was still more than half a dozen yards away when he knew that he'd been seen. The man did not move from behind his cover of jutting bricks, but his face was towards him, a faintly luminous white blob in the darkness.

For a full minute they looked at each other while remaining absolutely motionless.

Maltby was puzzled. The bastard could see him but he didn't shout or come at him. He seemed to be waiting for him. Or was it for a signal for some general action? He would have liked to have seen what Harrison was up to, but he dared not take his eyes from the face in front of him.

"Comrade?"

It was a whisper, half-strangled, that barely carried the space between them.

Something like an electric shock ran through Maltby.

"Boy!" he hissed, striding forward, "where are the charges?"

"I had to hide them. They cleared the yard. There's an inspection tomorrow."

"Can you get them? Now?"

"Yes."

Maltby felt a great weight lift off him. For the sheer unspeakable joy and relief that rose in him, he hammered the wall with his fist.

Scoutier was beaming, too. For Henri had had his tribulations. First when the comrade who had helped bring in the explosives had told him the yard was being cleared of rubbish. Together they had joined the gang of sweepers and got the charges away. Not knowing where else to put them, he had stowed them under his work bench. He sent a messenger to Maltby, but knowing that he could not reach him in time if the raid were planned for that night, he had stayed behind.

Then he had been scared out of his wits when he had seen three men creeping along the wall. He had only expected Maltby. Deciding if one of them was Maltby, he would be certain to come back to the third buttress, he had gone there to wait, not knowing that Gringoire's keen eyes had picked him up as soon as he started along the wall.

"I love you, Boy, you don't know how I love you! Go and get the stuff."

Scoutier slipped away soundlessly and Maltby made his way back to the others. They were standing just as he'd left them.

"One of us," he said tersely.

He watched Harrison carefully as he said this, but it met with no reaction.

In five minutes Scoutier joined them. He had the charges in a small rubbish sack.

Four of them made quite a crowd. They had to find somewhere to hide. For Henri this was easy, for he knew every nook and cranny of the works and most of the workers as well.

Scoutier took them to a lavatory that was not much used by the night men. It had the disadvantage of being uncomfortably close to the gate with its guards, but was safer than hanging about the yard.

The three of them locked themselves in a W.C. and Henri went off into the works after arranging to meet them in the finishing shop at 10 o'clock. He would have to leave the factory with them, as the Germans would be certain to round up the night staff after the explosions and he would not be able to explain what he was doing there.

There was very little room in the W.C. and they had to be continually alert, ready to freeze into immobility whenever they heard someone come in to use the lavatory. There were few of these, though Scoutier had warned them that there would be quite a number about 10 o'clock when the men took their break

Despite their cramped position, Maltby managed to fix the fuses to the charges. The pitch darkness made this difficult, but he gave each one as he finished a quick check in the light of his torch, shielding its beam as thoroughly as he could.

They did not speak more than two or three times during the hours they crouched together in the evil-smelling cubicle. Maltby was concentrating on what he was doing and silence with Gringoire was natural.

When he had finished with the fuses, Maltby leant his head back against the wall. He was terribly tired but he reckoned he could about last out. He'd be all in by the time he reached Dinville, though.

Harrison no longer bothered him. That he did not kill him then was simply because he could think of nowhere to leave his body where it would be certain not to be found. The W.C. bolted on the inside, and any one of a dozen men might stumble on it and set the yard buzzing with Wehrmacht before the action started.

The best place for his execution was the finishing shop. When they left that, there would be nothing more to be concealed. He would get him the first move he made to sabotage the explosions. And if he didn't try to interfere, it would be time enough when the shooting started outside.

Looking at his watch, Maltby saw that it was 9.7. Paturin's men should be in position by now. The night watchman should be about leaving the finishing shop. He would not be back there again for another two hours. Between 10 and 11 o'clock was the only hour when he made no round of the workshops.

At 9.30 they heard the guard squad set out for its patrol of the yard. Maltby did a mental salaam to Scoutier for his precise time-table which had enabled him to listen expectantly for this. The squad halted at the lavatory. Heavy boots scraped at the entrance and a slit of light showed under the W.C. door as a torch was played along the passage-way outside. But that was all. The light went out and the squad moved off.

Maltby gave them a quarter of an hour to get clear. Before they left the lavatory, he took the limpet incendiaries from the others. The rest of the explosives and fused incendiaries he gave Gringoire to carry.

He left Gringoire and Harrison close by the wide double doors of the finishing shop. Like Gringoire, he had unshipped his Sten and carried it slung in front of him at the ready.

The action had started.

He slithered quickly along to the end of the wall. The two soldiers on top of the watch tower were talking idly together. He could make out enough of their heads to see that they were turned away from him.

Bending low he flitted swiftly over the twenty yards of open ground. He was panting and his side was nipping him painfully under Dr. Clozot's strapping when he arrived below the tower.

It took no more than a couple of minutes to fix the limpets to three of the supports. A piece of cake, though he would have preferred to set them higher, closer to the floor of the guardroom below the platform, but he had nothing he could stand on.

As he ran back the first drops of rain began to fall. He saw that the clouds had thickened overhead blotting out the sky completely. It flashed across his mind that if this were to keep on, the Lysander might not be able to get through to pick him up. He gritted his teeth. It'd bloody well got to.

For another five minutes, until it was exactly 10 o'clock, they waited while the rain grew into a steady downpour. Then Maltby eased open the double doors and they slipped inside. Together they pushed the heavy doors to and turned round.

Facing them sitting on an upturned box was a wizened little jockey of a man, apparently transfixed. His mouth was open and he was holding upright in front of him a sandwich, the edge of which had been scalloped by a large bite.

In the dim light of a single bulb which threw eerie shadows among the squat, silent machinery, the three of them stood stock still, looking at him. Maltby was the first to recover.

"What are you doing here" he snapped.

The little man's Adam's apple jerked convulsively.

"Electrician. I'm——"

"We're Resistance. Keep quiet and don't move and you'll be safe."

Footsteps sounded in the next shop coming towards them and they ducked behind the bulk of the machinery with their Stens in their hands.

But it was only Scoutier come to join them.

"Watch him, Boy," Maltby said, flicking his thumb towards the electrician.

He gave Gringoire the incendiaries to put in the roof of the next shop. It would be extremely lucky if they managed to get the roof to catch fire, but it was the only possibly inflammable part of the factory. In any case the idea of using incendiaries at all was simply to cause a diversion, something to occupy the Germans for the ten minutes after the saboteurs had left. If arson was thought to be the object of the operation it would prevent a search being made for the explosives before they began to go up. After that it would be too late.

Besides the main doors, the gallery of workshops were connected by a travelling hoist for transporting the heavy metal from one to another. The overhead rail which carried it passed through tall apertures which had been cut breast high in each of the dividing walls. He posted Harrison to watch through this gap and report on Gringoire's progress. He would be out of the way there and where Maltby could keep his eye on him.

Maltby began to lay the charges. He took off his Sten and laid it beside him so that it was immediately under his hand as he worked.

Henri and the electrician were talking softly together, the low murmur of their voices echoing in the cavernous silence of the workshop.

His mind completely concentrated on what he was doing, Maltby was unconscious of their whispering. He was getting the charges home faster than he had done when he had practised at Birmingham.

He had finished the fifth one and was starting on the next when he suddenly became conscious of a light, a white steady light like a photographer's magnesium flare.

"What the hell——"

"One of the incendiaries has gone off!" Harrison shouted.

Christ, they should not have begun firing for another ten minutes! Gringoire must have made a mess of the fusing. He hadn't had much experience with incendiaries.

"Gringoire all right?"

"Yes. But the fire's been spotted. There'll be all hell let loose in a minute!"

Maltby, fiercely ramming home the charge, heard confused shouting in the distance. One voice was bellowing "Fire". He got up but had to steady himself against the machine. The effort and all the bending he had been doing had made him dizzy.

He found he couldn't get at the seventh point. A collection of spare parts and general junk was in his way.

"Give me your Sten!"

Maltby was lying on his side clawing through the obstacles. He looked up into Harrison's face towering above him.

"Quick! The guards will be here in a minute. I've got to cover Gringoire!"

With a sudden swoop the tall man whipped up the Sten. Maltby dragged his revolver from his pocket. But before he had got it free, Harrison had darted off back to the gap in the wall. He had his back to Maltby, levelling his gun into the next shop.

Maltby dropped his revolver and began to haul on a massive piece of angle iron. He'd got to get it free, got to get the charges in. He couldn't stop. Not now.

"How long are the fuses?" Harrison shouted.

"Half an hour."

They were in fact twenty minutes. But he wasn't telling Harrison that.

He managed to tilt the iron but it caught on its corner. He couldn't get at it properly. Lying on his back beneath a tangle of machinery he managed to get a good purchase on it and hauled. It shuddered and then came away. For a moment everything went black and he thought he was going to faint. But his head cleared. He panted and each breath sent a stab through his side.

But the charge point was free.

He gathered himself together, lying on his back, eyes closed, the charge in his hand.

A voice from somewhere at the far end of the next shop shouted in German and Harrison let out a burst from his Sten.

"Got the bastard!"

Maltby's stomach closed with a bang and for a fraction of a second he stopped ramming at the explosive. He couldn't have done! It wasn't possible! He just didn't believe it! Because——

He got the charge in and crawled out. Scoutier was crouching down behind the machines but the little electrician was standing up, pressing himself against the wall gibbering with fear.

"How's Gringoire?"

"O.K."

There was no trouble with the last charge and he had it in in less than a minute. Running over to the opening below the hoist he looked over Harrison's shoulder.

Gringoire, using the frame which supported the hoist to stand on, was fixing an incendiary in the eaves. On the other side of the shop above another cross stanchion, the bomb which had gone off prematurely flamed brightly. Below it a grey-green figure sprawled on its face.

"Henri! Get the light out. And get ready to open the doors."

"Can't go yet," Harrison said quietly, his eyes on the far door, "leave 'em too long to find the charges."

There was much shouting from the shop beyond the one in which Gringoire was working. Then with a clatter three soldiers appeared in the doorway and Harrison let go another burst. Hurriedly they dodged back into cover as the bullets splayed off the walls around them.

Feet in heavy boots ran along the yard beside the building. As they ran the men shouted to each other excitedly.

"Keep that door shut!" Maltby yelled at Henri. "Bolt 'em and stand clear!"

Stens were snarling outside.

That meant Buchan was in, covering their flank.

He glanced at his watch. Christ, it would be another five minutes before the limpets blew!

Light suddenly spilled in under the double doors. That was the bloody searchlight!

Immediately the half-dozen men in the yard began to shriek in terror, for the searchlight illuminated the Germans and Buchan's Stens went into a crescendo.

They must have hit some of them, too, for though Maltby could see nothing he heard the interruptions in their panic flight to escape from the light and the clash of rifles and helmets hitting the ground as men fell.

Suddenly the light disappeared from beneath the doors.

From behind the far wall the Germans were firing at Gringoire, not daring to make another sally into the workshop. The bullets smashed and ricocheted from the roof tiles.

Harrison fired again, shooting straight down the workshop into the hoist-gap at the other end.

"Can't get 'em," he muttered, "they're too well covered."

"Save it," said Maltby.

He hoped to God Paturin's men had come in. Some of them had because he could hear the distant chatter of their guns. The important ones, though, were on the other side of the factory. They had got to keep the gate watch tower so busy that they would not send any more men round to the yard on this side. If that happened they wouldn't be able to get away.

Some of the rafters had caught fire from the incendiary and smoke was filling the far end of the workshop. It was making it difficult for the soldiers to aim properly at Gringoire. All the same some of their shots were getting very close to him.

"Come back, Gringoire," he yelled, "now!"

Gringoire seemed to shake his head and went on tying the bomb in place. It was difficult for him, for he could only just reach the angle of the eave when standing at full stretch.

A bullet hit the roof just above his hands.

"Leave it, damn you!"

But Gringoire went calmly on. He had just finished and was preparing to jump down when a bullet hit him. He curved backwards on one foot in a grotesque dancing movement and crashed down on to the machinery below.

"Bloody fool," Maltby whimpered, "why the hell didn't he leave it!"

"I'll get him. Here!" Harrison shoved the Sten into his hands. "Cover me."

He slid round the doorway and made a dash for the cover of the first group of machines. A rifle poked through the hoist gap and fired twice. Maltby sprayed bullets into the gap and the rifle was hurriedly withdrawn.

Doubled up, Harrison worked his way towards where Gringoire lay in a crumpled heap, apparently having been knocked senseless by his fall. The further he went the more the soldiers' angle of fire widened and they were able to shoot at him without showing themselves to Maltby. Bullets whistled past Harrison's head, getting so close that he covered the last few yards on his stomach.

Impotently, his finger on the trigger, Maltby watched him, his mind dizzy with thought. It wasn't Harrison! Over and over again it was repeated in his brain. But though he knew now who the spy was, the name would not formulate in his mind.

Harrison pulled Gringoire, still unconscious, down on to the floor beside him. At first he was only able to move inches at a time, for the railwayman was heavy. But as he gained better cover and could get to his knees he was able to drag him faster. The last dozen yards he carried him on his back, while Maltby blazed away over his head.

"Is he bad?"

There was blood staining the left side of Gringoire's overalls. Harrison felt his wrist.

"Dead," he said, letting the limp arm fall back.

Harrison took Gringoire's Sten and ammunition and came to stand next to Maltby.

The roof had really caught now and the fire was licking along from rafter to rafter. Some débris had fallen, setting alight cotton waste or inflammable material of some kind on the floor, and this was sending out thick clouds of smoke that kept blotting out the door at the far end of the workshop. If the soldiers mounted an attack it would hide them completely, Maltby noted uneasily.

The bloody limpets should have blown by now. He'd have to open the door in another minute to see what was happening in the yard.

"You know Hélène's Gestapo?" Harrison asked, speaking softly, almost casually.

Maltby stared at the expressionless, patrician face. So Harrison knew, too. Suddenly he realized that Harrison knew it all, knew all about the game that had been played that night, knew probably even how near he'd been to having Maltby's knife stuck under his ribs.

"When did you know?"

"About a week ago for certain, when I saw her coming out of Gestapo HQ in Caude. But I'd suspected her for months."

He looked down and ran his hand along the barrel of the Sten.

"I'd have told you that day you came to the farm, only——"

He broke off and Maltby saw the same hurt but proud look in his eyes as he'd seen as they'd stood uncomfortably in the yard at the Aigunes farm.

A bell began to ring outside, a loud, challenging alarm bell. For a moment Maltby could not think what it could be. Then he realized it must be the one attached to the electric fence. Buchan must have cut the first strands.

"Get the doors open, Boy!"

The smell of burning was powerful now. The roof would all go now with luck when the other incendiaries burst. Smoke from the other workshop was seeping in thickening the air.

Henri pushed the double doors wide apart. Air, fresh, sweet and wet, rushed in fanning their faces. The rain was swishing down heavily, its steady beat on the paving and the trees beyond the yard a constant background to the firing.

The little electrician, whom Maltby had quite forgotten, let out a cry and dashed through the doors with his arms above his head.

"Don't shoot," he yelled, "don't shoot!"

Suddenly the searchlight swung round, swept across the trees and settled on the yard. The little man screamed and flagged his hands wildly as the light caught him. He ran on for a few more paces before the machine gun on the tower got his range. When it did, the stream of lead first brought him up short, then threw him backwards, like a ping-pong ball on a water-jet, until he hit the ground. There he lay, a silent heap among the puddles.

"Why did he run out? Why? Why?"

Henri was amazed and shocked.

"Panic," said Maltby flatly. "The bloody fool!"

But he was also thinking that they all had to cross the yard within the next ten minutes. With the searchlight on it they'd never make it.

Buchan and his men were firing in short bursts and he guessed they were aiming at the light. If, as was probable, the glass was armoured, their Stens would be as likely as peashooters to put it out.

Peering through the rain, which reflected in the brilliant light looked like a slanting curtain of glass rods, he saw that Buchan had cut out a section of the outside fence. As far as he could see, though, not even the first half of the duck board had been laid over the barbed wire. He supposed Buchan and his men were fetching it when the light had come on.

He looked at his watch. The limpets should have gone up by now. What the hell was the matter with them?

The light was stymieing everything. While it was on the yard Buchan couldn't do a thing. And until he had cut the wire there was no way for them to get out.

In five minutes Maltby saw he would be faced with nothing but a choice of staying where they were and being blown up, and being shot either in the yard or endeavouring to fight their way through the burning workshop. Either way they'd had their chips.

The bloody limpets! Why wouldn't they go?

There was a loud explosion from beyond the wall. One of

Paturin's men had flung a grenade. He couldn't have been near enough to have had any hope of doing real damage with it. But Maltby blessed whoever had thrown it a thousand times, for it upset the Jerries in the watch tower and they hurriedly swung the searchlight round to play on their attackers from the north.

Now Maltby could not see Buchan but he could hear him. Not that Buchan was noisy but Maltby was able to hear the first duck board slap down on the wire. It came to Maltby that it really didn't matter how much noise Buchan made, for the men in the watch tower must be deafened by the alarm bell which they hadn't switched off. Perhaps it couldn't be switched off until the circuit was restored.

Suddenly there was shouting followed by the clumping of heavy boots on wooden steps from the direction of the watch tower.

Thinking this signalled a sortie, Maltby positioned himself on the far side of the doors where he could get the best angle of fire.

"The bastards have got a hose," Harrison shouted from the hoist-gap.

"Won't do 'em much good," Maltby grunted, "but keep 'em on the hop. Blast 'em."

Harrison began to fire short irregular bursts.

The shouting from the watch tower still continued confusedly. But no one appeared in Maltby's line of vision.

Suddenly he saw irregular flames reflected in the trees. The limpets had burst! That was what was causing all the hoo-hah in the watch tower.

And not a moment too soon! But they'd get out now! For the second time that night Maltby felt himself lifted upwards in a great surge of delight. It blotted out the danger which still had to be faced. At this moment, he was not conscious of fatigue or the pain which racked his body. He tingled with excitement like a schoolboy on a scrumping expedition.

The shouting of the Germans had quietened to a single voice which roared orders. He supposed that was the sergeant. He had a flicker of admiration for the man, disciplined enough to fight for order in the chaos into which he had been plunged. The bastards could not know what had come to hit them out of their nice quiet war. From the scale of the attack they must be wondering if a brigade of paratroops had dropped on them.

"Right!"

It was Buchan's voice which came across the yard in a parade ground roar.

"Henri! You first!"

Scoutier leapt to Maltby's side, eager and alert.

"Straight across the yard there's a gap in the wire. Run fast and keep low! Then beat it home. No hanging about, see? Tell Uncle Joe to give you the Order of Lenin. You've earned it."

"Thank you, comrade."

"Off!"

By the dim light of the burning watch tower Maltby was able to follow him as he tore across the yard. He reached the wire before the first rifle cracked. But by the time he was through the machine-gun had begun to chatter.

That was not good. It meant that the Jerries had brought a gun down from the tower and mounted it on the ground. And every second the blazing tower was throwing more light on the yard.

Harrison had joined him at the doors. He drew air into his lungs in great gulps. At the far end of the shop where he had been the smoke was now very thick and acrid.

Maltby took out Hélène's escape packet and stripped off the cover. Snatching out the money and route instructions he pushed them into Harrison's hand.

"The group disperses immediately after we get out of here. Your route is there. Follow it at once. Don't go back to Aigunes. Now get going! The gap's exactly opposite!"

He spoke rapidly, urgently. Getting across those twenty-five yards of open space lit up by the fire was going to be no picnic. The Jerries had recovered from their surprise much quicker than he had allowed for. Another hazard hadn't occurred to him at all. Spent bullets from the fusillades fired by Paturin's men were hissing down everywhere.

A sudden billow of bright flame from the watch tower made Maltby's belly gripe with fear. But it was only for a second. It died away to the flickering torch it had been before.

"Now! Get going, damn you!"

"Not yet. Not safe to leave the charges for another ten minutes," Harrison said calmly.

"They'll blow in five minutes, you bloody fool!"

Harrison glanced down at Maltby's exasperated face and saw he'd lied to him about the fuses. He understood why.

"All right. But you go first."

Harrison was looking out over the yard and Maltby knew what he was thinking. The next one to go would have a better than fifty-fifty chance of making the wire. After that the odds would be high against it, for the Jerries would have found the range.

"You've a lot to do," Harrison added.

"No!"

"All right, then, we'll go together."

A sudden loud explosion came from the top of the yard. Buchan or one of his men had worked their way up along the factory wall and lobbed a grenade towards the machine-gun.

This was their chance. There was no more time for argument.

"Right! Now!" Maltby yelled.

He shot forward. As he cleared the doors the chill rain stung his face. Ducking low he pounded towards the wire with Harrison on his right. The tall man had jinxed round him as they had started.

It was only afterwards that Maltby realized Harrison had done this deliberately to put himself between Maltby and the Jerry fire.

Ten yards from the fence he saw the gap and took hold of Harrison's arm to pull him on course. Harrison began to lurch, and as they reached the duck boards he cannoned heavily into Maltby, knocking him sideways.

"Have a heart!" yelped Maltby, missing his footing and going full-length half on the duck boards and half in the wire.

Harrison had also come down. Heavily.

Maltby rolled clear of the wire, the barbs ripping his overalls and flesh, and lay flat. The machine-gun was going full tilt and bullets whined and whistled above his head as solid as a ceiling.

Harrison did not move or answer when Maltby shouted at him to start crawling.

Buchan flitted over the duck boards like a squirrel. He got a purchase on Harrison's right shoulder. The Jerries were at work with automatics now as well as the machine-gun, and the fences were twanging like harps as the lead clipped the wires.

Another grenade landed in the yard and the firing hiccupped into silence. Together they dragged Harrison across the duck board bridge. They had reached the grass before the machine-gun started up again. In another couple of seconds they were in the cover of the trees.

There was a hole, a mash of blood and bone splinters, behind

Harrison's right ear. There were other holes in him but that was the one which had killed him.

"A goner," said Buchan.

Buchan's soaking clothes were caked with mud and his hair was matted by the rain, but his monocle was still jammed in his eye.

"We'll have to leave him. Gringoire's had it, too."

Buchan nodded.

"I'm off now. Keep it going. The grenades are good. As soon as the first charge goes up, lob all you've got left and beat it. Fast!"

"Damn good show!"

"See you in London!"

"*Merde!*"

That bloody word again!

Maltby stumbled through the undergrowth to where he had left his bike. Quickly the trees threw a screen between him and the rattle of the guns separating him from the battle. He was out of it.

And into another.

He rode without caution, his Sten slung in front of him. The road was downhill all the way and he knew every curve in it. Though the rain whipped his eyes, he drove his feet at the pedals.

His thoughts were not on the factory—except for a twinge of humble awe that he was only on the road because Harrison had shielded him from the machine-gun with his body. He sent up a plea that the tall pansy would forgive him for having behaved like a half-baked old maid that Sunday at Aigunes.

His mind was so far away that he had to adjust it to take in the significance of the boom which reached him as the first charge exploded.

He tried to go even faster but the effort made his head throb. He free-wheeled to let it settle down again and to give some ease to his side.

He was almost dead beat and he knew his only hope was to keep going. If he rested he wouldn't be able to start again. And if he pushed himself too far he'd fold up.

Nevertheless he covered the five miles to Pontrecy in under fifteen minutes. A minute before he rode into the square the last charge blew.

CHAPTER EIGHTEEN

THE square was covertly alive. He sensed eyes peering from behind the black-out and figures deep in doorways.

Pontrecy was awake and heavy with whispers. No one could yet know what had happened but everyone had been awakened by the explosions. And before that the alert would have heard the grenades, perhaps even a faint echo of the crack of small-arms carried on the rain-laden air. But the centre of the square itself was deserted.

Maltby rode straight into it and swung off his saddle in front of the cycle shop. He leapt down so quickly that he twisted his side and had to lean against the wall while an excruciating pain which went through him died down.

What a bloody fool he'd been! She'd risk anything for him, she'd said. And she'd risked not telling the Gestapo about the signal-box because she thought he was blasting it on his own! In case he got hurt! And that was why she was so happy to back him up when he pretended it was Serpier's work. She wanted Schwartzkopf to believe that to save her own neck. But he might have known! Françoise had told him, and he hadn't had the sense to listen. How could he have been such an idiot as to think an acute observer of men like Françoise would ever mistake Sarrut for a Gestapo thug!

Biting his lip and half-supporting himself against the wall he slid along the alley-way. The pain was still bad but bearable. Just. He let himself in quietly and went silently upstairs, entering Hélène's room without giving the signal knock.

The sudden light hurt his eyes and he blinked. Hélène was on the other side of the room and she leapt to her feet when he kicked open the door.

She stared at him, her eyes wide, a bright spark in each reflecting the lamp on the table.

"Harry! You're hurt!"

Blood was caked thick on the back of his hand where he must have caught it when he fell in the wire. The wire had jagged his face, too, for he saw in the mirror above the fireplace one cheek was damply raw. Water dripped from his sleeves and trouser-bottoms on to the floor.

"Stay where you are!"

"What happened?"

"We've wrecked Gibault's."

"Gibault's! The factory! I didn't know——"

"You'd have liked to have known, wouldn't you?"

How was he going to do it? Not a gun because of the noise. He couldn't club her. A knife? Or should he break her neck?

His knees trembled. God, he was weak, weak as a kitten.

"You're all in. I'll get some hot water——"

"Stay where you are, I said!"

It'd have to be the knife. If she struggled he doubted if he had the strength to hold her, so it had to be the knife.

Hélène still stared at him. She was uncertain, troubled.

"What is it, Harry? You're so . . . so strange. You're not badly hurt, are you?"

"No."

He slipped the knife-blade into position.

"Tell me about it. I thought I heard shooting."

"There was some."

Casually he edged his way round the table towards her. He was sure that, needing to touch him as she always did, she would try to press herself against him as soon as he was close to her. It was then that he would strike. Just below the third button of her housecoat, upwards and to the right. He side-stepped a foot or so in order to bring himself into a better position.

"Well, go on. Tell me about it. Tell me——"

She stopped suddenly, head turned, listening. Maltby had heard the car, too. It was driven furiously into the square and squealed to a halt. Directly below Hélène's window it seemed. A front-wheel-drive Citroën.

Hélène, eyes wide, knuckles at her mouth, was stiff with terror. Maltby, the knife already free of his pocket, hesitated.

A fist banged on the door below, two short raps, one long and two short. A signal knock but not the group's! And immediately afterwards the street door was crashed open.

Maltby had just time to get behind the curtain covering the door to Hélène's bedroom before Schwartzkopf entered.

The German came into the room leaving the door open behind him. Maltby got only a glimpse of him through the slit where the curtains joined as he walked to the table and stood looking at

Hélène. His thin features were impassive but his skin was the colour of chalk.

"I'm surprised," he said quietly, "I had not expected to find you here . . . alive. Dead, yes. Or gone. But not here alive."

"Why have you come?" Hélène's voice was trembling.

"Surely you didn't think you could go on fooling me? After tonight?"

"I don't know what happened tonight."

"Not that a raid on the ball-bearing factory at Evine was planned?"

"I knew nothing about it. That's the truth."

"Really? If the British group——"

"They had nothing to do with it. I swear it!"

"Like the signal-box and the bridge at Camaret-Rouge? Only this time we know you are lying. This time all of them didn't get away. Charlemagne was killed."

"I didn't lie"—Hélène was desperate—"I knew nothing."

"They didn't tell you? So big an operation and they didn't tell you?"

"No!"

"It's possible . . . but only if they had discovered you were Gestapo. And in that case they would have killed you before they left Pontrecy."

"No, oh, no!"

There was horror as well as fear in her voice. Maltby took its meaning. She knew now why he had seemed strange to her, knew that he had come to kill her. He tensed. Would she give him away in an attempt to save her own skin?

"Since you are alive it must be they do not know and you are playing the double agent with me."

Behind the curtain, Maltby sweated despite the chill of his water-logged clothes. If she spoke now he'd have to use his Sten. He'd practised the jump from the bedroom window a dozen times and knew he could make it before Schwartzkopf's body-guards could get up the stairs. After that he didn't know. It would depend on how many men Schwartzkopf had brought with him. Without a bike he wouldn't be able to get to Dinville, but it was only his neck that concerned him now.

Hélène did not answer Schwartzkopf but let out a half-stifled sob.

"I'm puzzled why you have not gone with the others,"

Schwartzkopf said thoughtfully. "Or can it be that they have not gone either? That you play this game together and think you can go on fooling me even after tonight? I suppose that is possible, for the English are stupid and you are a woman."

"Why won't you believe me? I tell you I knew nothing about tonight! Oh God, I wish I was dead!"

"That's a wish I think will be granted. Only you have quite a lot to tell us first. Come on, I'm taking you to Caude."

"No, please! I've told you everything I know. Please leave me alone! Please!"

"You can come with me, or I will call my men."

"No. Please, Herr Doktor, not now! I'll come to you tomorrow. If you don't trust me, leave one of your men. I've told you everything I know. I've never done anything against the Party. Never, never! But leave me, tonight . . . please!"

"You little fool!" For the first time Schwartzkopf spoke angrily. "Come on!"

He moved round the table and tried to take hold of her but Hélène held him off.

"No . . . no. . . . Leave me alone!"

Her arms flailed wildly before Schwartzkopf caught them in a firm grip.

"Come on!"

He yanked her towards the door.

"Harry!" Hélène screamed, "Harry!"

Maltby never knew why he did it. Whether it was a reflex action in response to Hélène's appeal, or because he thought Hélène calling his name would warn Schwartzkopf of his presence, or simply because he wanted to kill the Gestapo man. He was only certain that it wasn't, as HQ later insisted, to prevent Hélène being rescued from execution.

As he came through the curtains, the German had his back to him, his attention concentrated on keeping hold of the fiercely struggling Hélène. Maltby drove the knife hard into Schwartzkopf's back, striking from below and upwards. At the same time he swung his fore-arm under the Gestapo man's chin, jerking his head backwards.

Schwartzkopf let go of Hélène and clutched convulsively at the air. Twice more Maltby stabbed him, overarm into the chest. The second time the knife jammed, twisting out of his hand as the German's inert body slid to the floor.

He was standing over the faintly twitching body when Hélène gave a little moan and passed out.

Maltby hauled her up. Small though she was, it was as much as he could do to get her into a chair. He stood in front of her swaying, head dizzy and his side pumping agonizingly.

He'd got to do it now. Could he do it without the knife? Could he get the knife out of Schwartzkopf? Could he do it at all?

Hélène slumped where he had dropped her, limp, unconscious and utterly helpless.

Maltby rubbed his hand across his face. He had no thought but for what he had to do and the sickness it gave him.

"Would you like me to do it?"

Maltby swung round towards the door gripping his Sten. But whoever had spoken had cautiously dodged out of sight.

"Take it easy, boy, take it easy!"

It was Pig-Face!

The big man carefully edged his way into the doorway.

He wore the Gestapo raincoat and trilby Maltby had seen in the square that afternoon. He was smiling.

Hélène moaned softly and Maltby turned towards her.

"Shall I do it?" Tonkin asked again, his voice infinitely gentle. "You're about all in."

No, he couldn't take that. He couldn't stand with his face to the wall while Pig-Face wrung Hélène's neck. That would be something he could never live with.

He took hold of the back of her head and chin in the way they'd shown him at the Assault School. Using all the strength he could gather in his shoulders, he twisted his hands round sharply.

There was a click. But barely discernible. In a panic he twice again wrenched at her head. They'd told him that the sound of the bone breaking was quite loud. But he heard nothing more.

God, he'd botched it!

Panting, he stood back, the blood running up into his eyes from the strain he'd put on his arms.

For a moment Hélène's head remained turned towards her shoulder. Then like a grotesque pendulum it rolled down across her chest.

The next thing he knew he was being sick and B.6. was shoving his head between his knees.

"All right, all right. No need to break my bloody back!"

"Better?"

"Yes."

"Nasty gash you've got on your bonce. Better keep it covered."

Tonkin refixed the dressing where it had broken away from its strapping.

"Can you stand?"

Maltby got to his feet. He felt ghastly and the touch of his stiff and clammy clothes made him shiver.

"Fine. Let's get going!"

Maltby did not look back at Hélène before they went quickly down the stairs.

In the alley-way a body lay in an untidy heap.

" 'I'll lug the guts into the neighbour's room,' " quoted Tonkin macabrely, taking the inert figure by the collar and hauling it into the passage at the foot of the stairs. Shutting the door, he jerked his thumb towards the car.

"Get in," he said, "courtesy of the Gestapo."

There was a youth with nervous, quick-moving eyes crouched over the wheel. Another man was hunched in the back who neither spoke nor moved when Maltby scrambled over him.

Pig-Face got in beside the driver and the car shot forward. Maltby lay back, letting his body go slack, but as they took the road for Caude he shot upright.

"This isn't the way!"

"We're going by the north road. Got to lay a false trail."

It was daft to take the north road but he was too tired to argue. God, but he was whacked! The car travelled fast, throwing him about in his seat. Once he fell on the man next to him and apologized. The man took no notice.

Instead of turning into the lane running parallel to the Dinville road they went tearing along the main road.

"Hoy! You've gone wrong!"

"Get some sleep!" said B.6., adding to the driver, "stop at the next bend."

When they stopped Maltby got out. His bladder felt as though it was going to burst. It was no longer raining but the grass at the side of the road was drenched. As he relieved himself he watched B.6. drag the other man out of the back of the car and prop him up conspicuously beside the road. He was dead.

The youth turned the car round and they got in. This time they turned into the lane.

"This is a damn fool way to come," Maltby grumbled, "we'll run into a road block where this track hits the main Pontrecy road."

"Who'll be holding it? Wehrmacht?"

"More likely Feldgendarmes or Milice."

"Good. Turn your lights on," B.6. said to the driver, adding as the boy opened his mouth to protest, "We're using a Gestapo car, so drive as though there were Gestapo in it."

The boy drove with Gallic dash, accelerating at corners and putting the car at every rut and bump for the sheer joy of feeling the wheel writhe in his hands. Twice Maltby's head was banged against the hood before he found safety by stretching himself almost full length transversely along the seats.

The pain had come again and the agony made him draw back his lips. He'd done it properly this time. Harriet had perforated. Or if she hadn't he didn't want to be around when she did.

"We got the factory tonight."

He spoke for the sake of saying something. Talking, even when it was as difficult as it was in the bucking Citroën, might take his mind off the pain.

"You've done all right, boy."

"I saw you this afternoon in Pontrecy. That Gestapo get-up scared the pants off me."

B.6. chuckled.

"Where the hell did you spring from, anyway?"

In its way, it was quite a story B.6. had to tell. He'd always been suspicious of Hélène. When he got Maltby's description of his first meeting with the group he was convinced she was the spy.

"What? I saw nothing in it."

"When we get back, you read the despatch. You'll see she was the one who tried to winkle out of you the one piece of information Schwartzkopf hadn't got—and wanted. It added up."

So when Maltby radioed that Hélène was in the clear after he and Gringoire had wrecked the signal-box Tonkin felt as though he had trodden on a rake and got the handle in his face. He just didn't believe it.

"You should never play hunches in this game. But I played this one."

That night he took the place of another agent who was due to be dropped in France and started work at the Paris end. The scent was cold and many of the people who could have been most useful were either dead or in concentration camps. But he got enough to convince him that his hunch had been right.

He'd reached Pontrecy that afternoon when Maltby had seen him and had immediately gone on to meet Le Feu at Dinville. There he had seen Maltby's radio that he was going to blast Gibault's that night and ordering Harrison's execution. This last he wirelessed London to countermand and had then returned to Pontrecy to deal with Hélène.

As guide, Le Feu had loaned him the youth, Pierre, who was driving the Citroën. Together they had hung about the village trying to make out what was happening at Evine. Tonkin was certain the operation would be frustrated, and his chief worry was that the dispersal plan had been "blown" and the whole group would be rounded up.

He had heard the firing and this told him the action was in progress. But when, like Maltby, he had counted the explosions and knew all the charges had gone off, he had been completely foxed. He could only assume Maltby had not told Hélène of the raid. While he had been trying to work this out, he had seen Maltby arrive "looking like a blood-stained brigand" and go in to Hélène's.

"There had been no time to tell her. I'd hardly seen her since I was beaten up. In any case none of the group was told we were dispersing until this evening."

"I see. And naturally," B.6. added, to Maltby's astonishment, "having got married while you were in England, you were avoiding her as far as you could."

Had he got glass sides! Could everyone see how he ticked!

When the Gestapo arrived, B.6. continued, it was obvious the time for conjecture was past. He and Pierre had gone into action. And luck had been with them.

"Why did you come, B.6.?"

"Eh?"

"Remember what you told me? We were all dead ducks. Were four dead ducks worth your trouble?"

"I needed the exercise."

"There aren't even four now. Gringoire and Harrison got theirs tonight."

"Many other casualties?"

"Not as far as I know."

"The other two got away all right?"

"They should make it."

Buchan and Lestocq, the two whom Maltby had voted the least likely to see England, home and beauty again. How wrong could you be! And how strangely the luck went. He'd taken Gringoire into the factory with him instead of sending him to cut the telephone because he liked him better than Lestocq. And Harrison would not have been there if Maltby had not come upon him making love to that revolting boy. His affection and distaste had been equally fatal. But for them, Harrison and Gringoire would be alive and in all probability his body would be stiffening in the muddy grass beside the Gibault works.

"What made you use Paturin?"

"I had to. You see——"

"Watch out!" Pierre interrupted, "we're coming to the junction."

B.6. peered thorough the windscreen into the night and laid his Sten across his knees.

"If they try to stop us at the road block we'll shoot our way through. But first we'll see what bluff can do. Keep your foot down hard! And keep going!"

Maltby got his Sten in position to fire on the driver's side. Pierre opened up the throttle and they swept round the next bend very fast.

There was a block. Two lanterns were waving in the air and men shouted to them to stop.

B.6. stuck his head out of the window.

"Gestapo, Gestapo," he bawled.

They now saw that the block was manned by miliciens. As they drew nearer and did not slow down, the lanterns danced more vigorously and figures ran out from the side of the road.

"Gestapo!" B.6. roared, waving his wallet as though it were a pass. "*Schweinhunds!* Gestapo!"

The miliciens hesitated. But the Citroën and B.6.'s porker-like face swung the day. The combination looked too right for its authenticity to be questioned.

The obstacle was pulled aside just as they reached it and they rattled on their way.

Tonkin laughed and slapped his thigh with delight.

"It's our day today!"

Maltby said nothing. He couldn't talk any more. The pain was too bad. He lay across the seats trying not to moan out loud.

"How long now?" B.6. asked.

"About another ten minutes," said Pierre, adding with gloomy relish, "We'll be too late, no?"

"We'll be in time, yes?"

"If the plane came."

"It better had."

All the same the big man leaned out of the window and examined the sky. He was relieved to see the clouds had thinned considerably.

Now they were on the main road the car did not lurch so much, but enough for Maltby to shift his position continually in an effort to ease the knife turning in his belly.

"It's here," said Pierre presently as they came into a long straight stretch of road. "About two kilometres along, a white gate on the left."

They slowed down. Maltby sat up. He could see the gate but there was no sign of maquisards. Braking, Pierre slid the car to a stop. There was still no sign of life and Tonkin put his hand on the door handle.

"For Christ's sake, sit still," Maltby snapped, and B.6. looked round at him in surprise. "Le Feu will fill you with lead. He must think we're Gestapo. If he sees you he'll be sure."

Tonkin nodded.

"Pierre, you talk to him," Maltby commanded.

"Le Feu! Le Feu! It's us! This is Pierre!"

No one answered. They could have been talking to the air.

"All right, you get out, Pierre."

"Le Feu! I'm getting out! Don't shoot! It is I, Pierre!"

He got out and walked round the front of the car into the dimmed-out beams of the headlamps. No one appeared or called out.

"I'm Punch," Maltby shouted as loudly as he could, but he managed no more than a hoarse croak. "I'm coming out now!"

He clambered out and leant with his back to the Citroën.

Three heads appeared out of a clump of bushes beside the gate. "They are mad, these English," said Le Feu, "we nearly shot you when you stopped."

B.6. climbed out.

"You've got yourself a new piece of transport," he said to Le Feu, jerking his thumb towards the Gestapo car.

A man was sent off to the plane with the news that they were on their way. The pilot had been none too pleased when he had found that his passengers were not already on the field when he landed, and Le Feu was afraid his patience might give out and he would take off before they got to him.

It was half a mile to the dropping field from the road, and the path by way of a copse and a strip of ploughland was rough. B.6. made to put his arm round Maltby but his offer of help was rudely brushed aside.

Placing himself at Maltby's elbow, Tonkin set a slow pace. Le Feu hopped around them like a worried sheep-dog. Didn't they understand, he kept asking them, British fliers were all mad and the maddest of all was the one flying their Lysander? He would go unless they hurried.

Even ambling as they were was too much for Maltby. He sweated with the pain in his ribs that began as soon as he started to pant. His head was singing dizzily and he was not so much walking as pitching himself forward. After a hundred yards he was swaying so drunkenly that Tonkin stopped.

"Look," he said, "I've stood for you being about the awkwardest sod it's ever been my misfortune to handle, but I'm buggered if I'm missing this plane because you want to play the hero. Either you let us help you or I'm going to knock you cold. It's something I've wanted to do for a long time, anyway!"

Maltby grinned weakly and closed his eyes. He was too done even to be difficult.

B.6. took one of his arms and Le Feu the other. Half-carrying, half-dragging him, they got him to the plane.

"This isn't a bloody taxi," said the pilot surlily.

B.6. fussed about Maltby.

"We made it, boy. Just a few more hours and we'll have you tucked up in bed."

Maltby's head was dancing and his senses seemed to be leaving him. He had the same sensation of uncontrolled suspension which comes on the edge of delirium with a high temperature.

"All I want is out," he said.

"That's all we all want, boy. And it won't be long now."

"Won't be much different for you . . . going back to coppering?"

"Coppering? What—do you think I'm a policeman?"

"Aren't you?"

"Good God, no. I'm a milliner."

Maltby started to laugh. It came from deep down in him and though it made the pain in his side and belly excruciating he couldn't stop. B.6. took hold of his shoulders and shook him. He coughed and spluttered but he could not stop.

Then suddenly everything went black and he fainted. He did not hear the pilot rev up the propeller or feel the first sway of the aircraft as it took the air.

He was still out when the plane touched down in England.

* * *

They sat on the window ledge in Maltby's room at the Wilberforce, the letter on the sill between them.

Judy, cool and bright in her nurse's uniform, examined him in a soft proprietorial way, tracing his thoughts in her mind. There was a half-moon scar high up on his left cheek-bone where the wire had cut him and the lines running from his nose to the edge of his mouth were deeper. Because his face was thinner, his mud-brown eyes looked even larger and in the last few days they had recovered their brightness. This was the first day he had dressed in his uniform and she, pleased that he looked so handsome, felt very close to him.

Maltby looked out over the hospital grounds, gaunt and bare in the grey late afternoon light. The last of the leaves had fallen from the trees and been swept away. Already the nurses were talking of their plans for Christmas.

He did not mind the winter. It was autumn which always depressed him deeply. For him, the prospect of death was harder to bear than death itself.

Because of the letter, he was thinking of Pontrecy. He had been too obsessed by the need to get well, and too happy to have Judy to nurse him, to do so before. Except as a job which he'd had to do.

Now he thought of the people. Again he was struck by the strangeness that in a matter of weeks he should have come to know the others so well when previously in months he had not known them at all. Was it like this always? Did we always make snap judgments about people and never afterwards see them differently?

The curious thing was that though what he had learnt about

them had mostly been discreditable according to accepted standards, he felt an affection for them all, living and dead, he had not had before. Even for Hélène. He would have liked to know what had made her a Nazi, but considered that less important than that within her small body she had had the steely strength for the dreadful rigour of being a double agent. He felt no guilt for her now. Nor to Judy for Françoise.

Treachery, bigotry, meanness, ugliness, self-interest and corruption were part of the human kind. They were to be found in the bravest and most self-sacrificing as well as the poor in spirit, in the most eminently honoured and the obscurest suburban home. They had taken all the vices with them to Gibault's. And all the virtues, too.

He picked up the letter. It was, unlike the one he had had three months before, a simple summons to HQ. No instructions to meet a cipher in a quiet Mayfair house, no warning to burn the paper after he had read it.

This was the end of the road. He was out. Where did he go from here? If they offered to keep him on in a chair-borne job, should he take it? And if not, what then?

His stomach trembled slightly at the prospect of a future without a precise object. He saw himself as a wheel in a vast machine, neither driving nor being driven. Just spinning without use or purpose.

Judy took his hand.

"Don't worry," she said softly, "there'll be a place for you somewhere."

The butterflies in his stomach ceased to flutter. He grinned down at her, returning the pressure of her fingers.

"You know something, Mrs. Maltby? I think you're right."

TRAIL CREW

Jack Schaefer

From the book "The Kean Land"
published by André Deutsch Ltd.

TRAIL CREW

THE trail herd was bedded on a wide flat finger of plain stretching between long low hills. To the east, out of the hills, the plain spread vast and open into limitless distances. To the west, between the hills, it dropped imperceptibly across the miles to the lower level of an ancient long-dried lake bed.

Large and luminous in the clean depth of sky an incredible number of stars looked down on the wide land and on the dark speckling blotch of the bedded herd and on Monte Walsh riding slowly around the rim serene in saddle atop a sturdy short-coupled dun.

"Keep amoving," murmured Monte. "Want me to fall asleep astraddle your knobby backbone?"

The dun swiveled an ear back towards him and ambled on. It felt him slumping lower into the saddle and slowed to a stop, head drooping. Monte pulled himself awake. "Keep agitating those legs," he said, "or I'll give you a leathering. Personal." The dun sighed and raised its head and ambled on.

Monte stretched erect in saddle and looked around. Off to the left he could see the compact blotch of the cavvy in its rope corral and the dirty-gray blob of the chuck-wagon canvas and the small individual dark blobs on the ground that were others of the trail crew sweetly sleeping. Faintly he could make out the glimmer of the remains of the cookfire.

Off to the right, across the big speckling blotch of the herd, he could see the slow-moving small blur that was Chet Rollins atop a chunky gray. A soft breeze stirred and Chet's voice drifted to him, a melancholy tuneless monotone.

> Now, all you young maidens, where'er you reside,
> Beware of the cowboy who swings the rawhide,
> He'll court you and pet you and leave you and go
> In the spring up the trail on his bucking bronco. . . .

"I've heard frawgs could croak better," murmured Monte. His attention was caught by movement nearby in the herd. The old barren cow, point leader of each day's drive, was heaving to her feet. He stopped the dun with a touch on the reins and watched. Head high and swinging, slow, the old cow tested the air. Slowly she turned until she was facing back over the herd, back down the long finger of plain between the hills.

"Got the worries, old girl?" said Monte. He turned his head to look in the same direction. Clean and cloudless with its myriad stars the sky arched into distance to meet the far horizon. "Nothing back there but sky and a thousand miles of grass," he said. He tilted his head to look up. "My, oh my," he murmured "Time has been footprinting along." He swung the dun and started back along the rim of the herd.

Towards him out of the dimness of dark, easy and comfortable atop gently jogging gray, came Chet Rollins, round stubby pipe poking out of round stubbly face. The two cowponies stopped, nose to nose.

"Quite a man," said Monte. "That braying of yours gave old Gertrude the itch."

Chet extracted a match from a pocket of his open jacket, scratched it on blunt fingernail and applied it to the pipe. Monte nudged the dun forward, reached and pushed Chet's jacket farther open and plucked a small pouch from Chet's shirt pocket. Out of his own shirt pocket came a small paper. Deftly he hollowed this between fingers and poured a portion of tobacco along the tiny trough. In the one easy movement one hand tucked the pouch back in Chet's shirt pocket and the other rolled the cigarette. He raised this to his lips and licked along the paper edge.

"One of these days," said Chet Rollins, "I'll quit buying tobacco."

"No," said Monte aggrieved. "I aint ready to quit smoking." Out of one of his own jacket pockets came a match and flared briefly. "Shucks," he said. "Always carry my own papers and matches, don't I?"

The cowponies drowsed, heads dropping. Monte dragged deep on the cigarette and watched the smoke float from his nose in two tiny streams. "Wonder what's keeping the boys," he said. "The dipper up there's been dipping." He drew again on the cigarette, inspected its shortened length and stubbed it out on stirrup leather. "I'm a growing boy," he said. "Need my sleep."

"Don't be so damned previous," said Chet, amiable, conversational. "They're coming now."

Monte swung the dun to face the night camp. Two dim blurs had left it and were moving towards them. These came closer and were Dally Johnson astride a squat bay and Powder Kent astride a leggy roan.

"Anything doing?" said Powder.

"My oh my, yes," said Monte. "Busy every minute. We had to fight off two jack rabbits and a horned toad."

"Old Gertrude's uneasy," said Chet. "Better keep an eye on her."

In companionable silence Monte and Chet jogged to camp, dismounted, eased cinches and picketed their horses by the others kept ready, saddled, for night duty. Together they pulled blankets from the bed wagon beside the bigger chuck wagon and unrolled these on soft spots earlier picked and claimed. Monte straightened and looked towards the remains of the cookfire. On the tripod over it hung a battered coffeepot.

"Monte," said Chet, low-toned, casual. "Why not forget the coffee tonight. You'll sleep better."

"Shucks," said Monte, starting away. "Gabriel tooting wouldn't keep me from sleeping."

Chet sighed and collapsed down on his blanket. He raised on one elbow, watching.

Over by the chuck wagon Monte pushed a hand under the canvas and pulled it out holding a tin cup. "Good old cookie," he murmured, moving towards the embered fire. "Always leaves me some in the pot." Leaning down, he tipped the battered pot until a dark liquid gurgled into the cup. Squatting back on his heels, he poked a finger into the liquid and yanked it out fast and shook it vigorously. He bent his head and blew into the cup and sloshed the liquid around in it. He tried the finger again. "Just right," he murmured and raised the cup and tilted back his head for a long drink.

"Ow-w-w-w!" yelled Monte Walsh, uncoiling upward like a tight spring suddenly released, spluttering, spitting. Frantic in haste he plunged towards the chuck wagon and tripped over the wagon tongue and went sprawling. Still frantic in haste he scrabbled to the water pail hanging by the wide tail gate and grabbed the dipper. Water dribbled down his shirt as he gulped and spat, gulped and spat.

He stood by the chuck wagon, dipper in hand, and looked around. Not far away, up on one elbow, Chet Rollins regarded him with solemn interest. Elsewhere about lay five other figures, under blankets, quiet, apparently serene in sleep. He reached and let the dipper drop with a clatter into the pail. He waited. No sound, no movement marred the quiet. "Some bat-brained baboon—" he said and stopped. There was a quivering under one pulled-over blanket, a strange small moaning sound. The blanket flipped back disclosing the lean whipcord length of Petey Williams, shaking, knees doubling up.

"Lordy!" gasped Petey. "Oh lordy lordy lordy lordy lordy! Maybe that'll learn you not to come thumpin' in every night clitterin' an' clatterin' an' wakin' us up."

"Why you—" said Monte, starting forward.

"Easy, Monte," came the voice of trail boss Hat Henderson. "Or we'll all take a hand."

Monte stopped, rocking on his toes.

"Not me, Monte boy," came a voice from the chuck wagon. "Anybody like my coffee an' says so like you do kin have all he wants any time."

Monte looked around, calculating the odds. The slender shape of fourteen-year-old Juan Rodriguez, brought along to wrangle the cavvy, did not count. But the wide sloping shoulders of Hat Henderson, sitting up on his blanket, were enormous in the dim starlight. The black-mustached face of Dobe Chavez, sitting up too a few feet away, could have been wearing a hopeful grin. The big barrel body of Sunfish Perkins bulged huge under his blanket.

"Shucks," said Monte. "If that damned pepper hadn't made me feel right puny I'd scramble the whole bat-brained bunch of you." Injured dignity emanating from him, he stalked to his blanket, took off his hat, lay down, set the hat over his face and pulled the blanket over him.

Silence settled on the camp.

"Holy hell!" said Monte Walsh, lifting the hat off his face and setting it aside. "How'm I going to sleep without my coffee?"

"Quit it," came a voice. "Or we'll put you to sleep permanent."

Silence settled again. Monte lay still looking at the myriad stars overhead. He raised a bit and spat to one side. He lay still again. A small quivering began to shake his midriff. "My oh my oh my," he murmured. "Bet I looked like a new-branded calf diving for that water." He began counting stars. At seven he was asleep.

The boot toe against his ribs was hurried, not gentle. Monte Walsh plunged away in the dark grabbing. The thick-muscled leg of Hat Henderson pulled away from him.

"Snap it, Monte," said Hat. "Everybody out. There's a storm coming."

Monte pushed to his feet. High overhead the stars shone, large and luminous in clean depth of cloudless sky. The air was still, soft and still.

"Shucks," said Monte to the retreating back of Hat Henderson. "What's the fuss? Regular spooning weather."

"Not for long," said Chet Rollins, gathering up his and Monte's blankets and stepping to toss them in the bed wagon. "Take a look yonder."

Monte turned to look down the long finger of plain between the hills. Dark and ominous, piling in heavy layers, a great bank of clouds blotted the far horizon. As he looked, lightning played high over them and laced through them and the low mutter of thunder rolled in the dim blackness of distance.

"What do you know," murmured Monte. "Old Gertrude sure has a nose." In the one swoop of moving he picked up his hat, jammed it on his head, and was running towards the short-coupled dun.

He heaved on the cinch, tightening, and behind him heard Chet Rollins gently cursing at the same chore. Other voices floated on the still air, cheerfully complaining, wryly joshing. Over them rose the voice of Hat Henderson, responsibility spurring him, he who was a cold bolt of concentrated action in the midst of an emergency, now as always wailing and worrying in the anticipation of it. "Jeeeeesus, boys! We gotta hold 'em! Those fool cows get araring and arunning out into that open it'll take a week to gather 'em again! Those we can find!"

The cinch slipped in Monte's hands. He grabbed a fresh hold and heaved. The dun, disliking the prospect, sidled away and blew out its sides, eating air. "Go ahead, be smart," said Monte, making it grunt with a knee hard in its distended ribs. "I'll twist a couple of your ears off. Personal."

"Frettin' again, Monte," said a voice above him close by the dun's rump. Petey Williams grinned down from the back of a hammerhead sorrel. "Mebbe you oughta stay an' help cookie lash down the wagons. Feelin' puny the way you do." The sorrel responded to spurs and took off fast.

"I'll puny him," murmured Monte. "Maybe biscuits. Petey's a hawg on biscuits." He stepped into stirrup and swung up to join Chet out to the herd.

The night air hung motionless, still, too still, clinging and oppressive. Silent now, waiting, wearing slickers now, untied from behind saddles, the trail crew of the Slash Y, eight men on eight homely runty tough little cowponies, rode circle around fifteen hundred four- and five-year-old longhorn steers and an old barren cow. And out of the southwest, the long black trail they had traveled hundreds of miles from the wide *vegas* of New Mexico, the great bank of clouds, huge, indifferent, funneled forward between the hills.

Whisperings of wind ran through the bunch grass. The cattle were up, shifting restlessly with rattlings of horns as they pushed against each other. Arching high above, the topmost layer of clouds, driven from behind, rolled forward, blotting out the stars. The first drops of rain, large and irregular, fell with tiny splattings on the dry ground. Suddenly, as if scenting the herd, wind leaped in rushing gusts and wall of rain, swirling, torrential, swept over.

The wind beat in rushing gusts and the rain poured in heavy sheets and the cattle shifted and swayed in frightened mass, trying to work downwind before the storm, individuals and small bunches making frantic dashes to break away. Around them, battered, drenched, sighting by sound and instinct and intermittent flashes of lightning, swinging superb with every twist and wrench of saddles, rode the trail crew of the Slash Y, yielding ground downwind but holding the circle, tough little cowponies as alert, as dedicated, as desperate as the men, squat hard-muscled rumps quivering as they leaped, dashed, pounded to head the runaways, push them, shoulder them, bully them back into the herd.

Abruptly the cloudburst passed. The rain dropped to a steady downpour and this slowly thinned and the air was alive, crackling with electricity. Fireballs hung on tossing horns and little lightnings streaked along the ground. The rain died away and the mutter of thunder dwindled.

"Looks like we make it!" The voice of Hat Henderson lifted out of the dark. "Close up an' quiet 'em down!"

From elsewhere out of the dark rose the voice of Chet Rollins in hoarse tuneless somehow soothing monotone.

> *I love not Colorado where the faro table grows,*
> *And down the desperado the rippling bourbon flows.*
> *Oh-h-h-h-h-h,*
> *I love not Colorado where the card sharp fleeces fools,*
> *And a girlie-girl won't give a man—*

Lightning in one great flare of flame ripped the dark and a steer reared bellowing, outlined in fire, and thunder broke like a cannon shot. Out of the void of blackness following the flash came the heavy rising roar of the herd in motion, a dark tide of panic-stricken animals pouring downwind in relentless onrush.

Above the muffling roar, the cracking of hoofs, the rattling of horns, climbed the shrill yell of Hat Henderson. "Jeeeesus! Ride, you mavericks! Ride!" And Hat and seven other men rode.

Out in front, Dobe Chavez and Powder Kent, caught in the onrush, engulfed by it, surrounded by frenzied running steers, jostled, hit, battered, their horses fighting to hold their feet, ears flat, heads slugging in desperate effort, plunging forward, kicking in stride, taking advantage of every break to work out towards the side. On the left flank Petey Williams and Monte Walsh and Dally Johnson and Hat Henderson, strung out, racing headlong into the dark, ripping off slickers at full gallop, striving towards the head of the herd. On the right flank, Sunfish Perkins and Chet Rollins, dropping back to dash around the rear of the stragglers and drive forward after the others on the left.

"Puny is it?" yelled Monte Walsh, yanking the dun past the tail of Petey Williams' sorrel to join him in smashing in towards the lead steers, flailing at them with his slicker. A horn tip raked across his thigh, ripping through cloth, drawing blood, and he did not know it. The slicker flapped in shreds. Pounding alongside a big steer, he flung the slicker remnants in its face. He pulled his gun and began firing into the ground in front of the foremost steers.

Other guns were out and sounding, flaring in the dark, a barrage angled out across the rushing forefront of the strung-out stampede. The leaders swerved, swinging to the right, the others blindly following. They hit the first slopings towards the hills and slowed some on the climb and, under pressure, swung still more. More, and the herd was running in an arc, a wide U-shaped course. Still more, and the leaders were swinging back into their own tracks, catching up with the stragglers, and the rough flattened circle was closed. The cattle milled around it, gradually slowing in weariness, letting themselves be crowded inward, slowing more to a shuffling walk, slowing at last to a stop, sides heaving, tongues hanging.

Gray and forlorn under overhanging clouds, dawn crept over the great open plain that was miles closer now and slipped down the wide finger between the hills. In the dim half-light the chuck wagon with trailing bed wagon, lurching behind their four-mule span from where the camp had been, stopped a quarter of a mile away. In a few moments the first flickering of a fire showed, fed on wood carried and kept dry under the canvas. From back down the finger of plain a weaving blotch of dark shapes approached, the cavvy coming up.

In the gray growing light the trail crew of the Slash Y left positions around the herd and gathered together, men with eyes bleared and bloodshot, clothes torn and mud-spattered, horses bloody and sweat-streaked, legs quivering, worn close to exhaustion and still standing to whatever more might be asked of them.

"Those bonehead cows aint going anywhere," said Hat Henderson, "Not now for a while anyways. I reckon we can go in and get us something hot."

"Hey, look," said Sunfish Perkins. "There's the horses coming. The kid must a held them."

"Of a certainty, señor," said Dobe Chavez, grinning. "He is of my people. A boy in the years. A man with the horses."

"Damn lucky for us," said Hat Henderson. "We got us a day ahead. I saw a couple bunches break into the draws over there. Must be strays all through these hills."

Silent again, the trail crew of the Slash Y started towards the chuck wagon, horses wearily plodding.

"Coffee," said Monte Walsh. "Aint that a lovely smell? If Petey tries messing with—"

"Petey," said Chet Rollins. "I aint seeing him around."

"Jeeeesus!" said Hat Henderson, rising in stirrups to look about. "Has that fool gone an'—" He stopped speaking and sank down into saddle, shoulders sagging. He spoke again, voice heavy. "All right, boys. Spread out an' look sharp."

Quiet, separated each in his own searching silence, seven men rode back over the wide trampled ground reaching towards the hills beyond. There was daylight now, veiled with stringy gray mists under the overhanging clouds. It was the voice of Powder Kent that called. The others gathered with him on the flat bench a short way up the sloping where a colony of prairie dogs had riddled the sandy soil. They looked down at the sprawled shape, the lean twisted whipcord length of Petey Williams, rain-washed face upturned, strangely white and empty, head awry at grotesque angle. Thirty feet away the sorrel, crumpled on the ground, both forelegs broken, raised its head and whinnied softly at them.

Hat Henderson shifted weight in saddle, turning to see who was closest to the sorrel. His voice was small, tired. "All right, Monte. Shoot the horse."

Monte Walsh stared at the still, twisted shape. He forced his head to turn a bit and stared at the sorrel. The muscles along his jaw ridged and the tendons in his neck stood out taut. "Goddamn it!" he said. "I broke that horse. Taught him his manners."

Fury flared in Hat Henderson, shaking him, shaking his voice. "You soft-brained bitching bastard! I said shoot that horse!"

Monte swung to face the other man, tense in saddle, body muscles tightening towards the blessed relief of motion, action. A shot sounded and, caught, he turned and saw the sorrel's head dropping, the whole body going limp, and turned more and saw Chet Rollins slipping gun back into holster. The muscles along Monte's jaw twitched. A small humorless smile showed on his lips. His head moved in a slight nod, saying what he could not say in words, what he could not even comprehend in words. *Thanks, Chet. That's how it is. You've rode with Petey too. You helped me break that horse. I blow a lot and I strut a plenty and maybe I can ride a horse or two you can't and take on two to your one in any kind of brawl. But dig down to bedrock and you're the better man.*

Slowly, wearily, Hat Henderson dismounted. He moved close by Monte and reached and slapped Monte's leg. He did not look up. "Petey and me run together a long while," he said. "Kind of like you and Chet." He strode forward and scooped up the already stiffening body and came back to his horse and heaved it over his saddle. He took the reins and started leading the horse towards the new camp.

Silent, staring at the ground, the others followed. It was Monte Walsh who carried Petey's saddle in front of him over the tired shoulders of the dun. It was Dobe Chavez who turned back and leaned down in weary but still graceful sweep from the back of his tired bay to pick from the ground the muddied felt that had been Petey Williams' hat.

The fire was little more than a smoking smolder, fighting the heavy moist air. The trail crew of the Slash Y hunkered on heels close by it, scooping food from tin plates. Hat Henderson laid his, emptied, on the ground beside him. "Got to bring in those strays," he said. "That rubs out today. Three days maybe on to the Springs an' that's only a stage stop. I reckon we got to do it here." He straightened. "Dobe. Sunfish. Get a couple of fresh horses and out to those cows. We'll holler when we're ready." He strode to the bed wagon and pulled out two shovels.

The mists had lifted some and rain fell in a thin drizzle. Chet Rollins and Monte Walsh worked on the deepening grave. The cook, limping on old game leg, rigged a canvas shelter for his fire. Young Juan watched in mournful useless silence. Hat Henderson and Dally Johnson and Powder Kent leaned over the stiffened body of Petey Williams. They wrapped it carefully in a blanket. Around this they rolled a trimmed-down tarpaulin. Around this they stretched two bridle reins and tied them.

"Jeeeesus!" said Hat, stretching up from the task. "Aint there anything we can use for a cross?"

The fire burned better under its canvas shelter. Coffee was hot in tin cups. Hat Henderson looked up from his. Out of the drizzle young Juan was approaching, riding bareback on his little roan. He was dragging something on a rope after him, the weathered broken cast-off endgate of an emigrant wagon.

"You're all right, kid," said Hat Henderson. "Dally. Get an iron and stick it in the fire. We'll rig a marker out of that."

The two best boards were fastened together with horseshoe nails to form a crude cross. Dally Johnson knelt on another board, running iron in hand, burning letters into wood. The others watched, silent, intent.

Dally looked up. "Maybe," he said. "Maybe this ought to say Peter."

"Petey," said Hat Henderson, quick, sharp. "That's what he was all the time I knew him. That's what he'd a wanted to be."

Dally reached and laid the end of the iron in the fire. "When was he born?" he said.

Silence. "Damned if I know," said Hat Henderson. "About my age but I never did know exact. We got to leave that go."

Dally took the iron and bent over the cross. "What's today?" he said.

Silence again. "It's April anyways," said Chet Rollins. "That's close enough."

Dally finished and rose to his feet. They all stared down at the crude cross. Near the top of what would be the upright, the Slash Y brand. Under this, on the wider crosspiece, the simple legend:

PETEY WILLIAMS
died on trail
April 1887

"All right, Dally," said Hat Henderson. "I reckon we're ready. Kid, skip on out and fetch Dobe and Sunfish."

"Goddamn it!" said Monte Walsh, kicking viciously at a clod from the freshly dug grave. "That's a hell of a measly marker for a man like Petey!"

Small and alone in the big land they stood around the grave, seven riders and an old man and a boy. Using lariats slipped under, they lowered the rolled tarpaulin into the grave. They stood in an uneasy silence.

"Jeeeesus!" said Hat Henderson. "Aint there anybody knows a few of the words?" The silence held again. "Maybe just as well," he said. "Petey never was much on churches."

"He was a damn good man with a rope," said Sunfish Perkins. "Maybe that'll count some."

"Petey never cussed much," said Powder Kent. "Only when he was mad an' that don't mean nothing."

"He was almighty good company," said Chet Rollins. "Always keeping things lively."

"The long-legged loon was one up on me," said Monte Walsh. "That coffee sure fixed me plenty."

The silence held again. Hat Henderson broke it. "Petey wouldn't want us moping around like a bunch a mangy coyotes," he said. "We got work to do. Cookie. An' you, kid. You can fill this hole. All right, boys. Fresh horses all around. We got to comb these hills."

The herd had grazed part of the day and watered at pools collected in old buffalo wallows. It was bedded again close to where the last night's storm-driven run had ended. In the deepening dusk clouds still hung overhead, blotting out most of the stars emerging in the high clean depth of the sky above. The three dark shapes close by the bedded herd were Monte Walsh on a rat-tailed skittish roan and Chet Rollins on a thick-necked black and Hat Henderson on a big rangy bay.

"Hate to stick you two with it," said Hat. "You're bushed as the rest of us. But it's your watch. Looks nasty and maybe it won't do more'n rain a bit. I'll try an' keep an eye open. Anything happens we'll all come afanning."

Monte Walsh and Chet Rollins watched him jog away towards the camp. "Creeping catfish," said Monte, wriggling inside shirt and jacket. "Feels like I'll never get dry again. Been raining off and on all day."

Chet fumbled in a jacket pocket and found his pipe, in shirt pocket, and extracted the small pouch. He began to shake tobacco into the pipe.

"A hell of a life," said Monte. "Wearing out your backside in a saddle all day, all night, chousing cows that belong to somebody else. If you aint cooking in the sun you're feeling like a cold sponge. A hell of a life."

"Yeah," said Chet. "Aint it." He found a match, scratched it on blunt fingernail and applied it to the pipe.

"Forty and found and break your fool neck," said Monte. He forced the roan to sidle closer to the black and reached and extracted the pouch from Chet's shirt pocket. He fished in his own and extracted a wad of wet gummy small papers. He stared down at these in his hand and in disgust threw them on the ground.

"You'll get to a pipe yet," said Chet, taking the pouch.

"What in hell did we ever come on this damn junket for anyway?" said Monte. "We could of stayed at the ranch. There's that new bunch of three-year-olds to be broke."

"Hat was short-handed," said Chet. He extracted another match, scratched it and tried again on the pipe. "Shorter now," he said.

"Petey," said Monte. "You ever think he didn't even know who he was working for? Who we're working for. Not even a man. Just a goddamned syn-di-cate. A bunch of soft-bellied money-grubbers back east somewhere."

"Yeah," said Chet. "That's right, aint it? But Petey wasn't thinking of that. Petey was just doing what he signed on to do." Chet swung the black and started off around the herd.

"A hell of a life," murmured Monte, starting in the opposite direction. "Seems like I aint slept in a week. Maybe two." The roan shied at a low bush, swinging its rat-tail and skittering sideways. "Quit that," said Monte, clamping down on the reins. "I aint in no mind for games. Just to sit here trying to forget I got wet pants on."

The clouds gathered overhead, moving silently, closing all gaps. Monte Walsh pulled out of a doze in the saddle. Sudden wind rushed in violent gusts down the finger of plain towards the open. He looked around. The cattle were up, beginning to push against each other. Back a bit around the curve of the herd a blur of dark was Chet Rollins on the black, sweeping to head a batch of runaways. Another batch broke loose. Monte wheeled the roan, spinning on hunched hind legs, and lit out after them. He had them back. He snatched a quick look towards the camp. All he could make out was the flicker of the low fire, licking up under the lash of the wind. It was blotted out for an instant as a figure ran past it.

The wind increased in violence and whipped rain with it. The herd shifted and swayed with rattling of horns. Two men on a rat-tailed roan and a thick-necked black dashed back and forth, holding the frightened steers against the hills rising beyond. Over by the camp a sharp crack sounded, and another, and others following. The canvas top of the chuck wagon had ripped loose on one side and flapped up in the gusts like a huge whip snapping.

"Good God amighty!" said Monte, hearing the heavy rising roar of the herd in motion. "Here we go again!" A dark shape rushed past him, Chet Rollins bent low on the black, scudding fast for the head of the rushing herd.

Monte Walsh dug spurs in. The roan leaped into full gallop. "Yowee!" yelled Monte, leaning forward to shout in one of its ears. "You let that fat-faced baboon beat me to the point I'll rip your hide off! Personal!"

Out from the camp in ragged sequence pounded other dark shapes, angling to join them. The trail crew of the Slash Y, seven men on seven tough little cowponies, raced headlong into the rain-drenched dark.

THE MAN WHO
OWNED THE WORLD

Charles Eric Maine

*"The Man Who Owned the World" is
published by Hodder and Stoughton Ltd.*

The Author

A journalist by profession, Charles Eric Maine was born in Liverpool in 1921 and spent the early part of his life in India. During the war he served as a signals officer in the Royal Air Force. He began writing novels in 1952, and since then his work has been published in Britain, America, France, Germany, Italy, Portugal and Japan. He has also done much successful work for radio, television and films. Three of his books have been turned into motion pictures, and two more are to be filmed in the near future. He now lives at Stanmore with his wife and their two children.

FOR

JOANNA

FOR REASONS

WHICH I NO LONGER

REMEMBER

CHAPTER ONE

About ten hours after zero, Robert Carson knew that he was going to die. He digested the information quietly and reflectively, without any positive reaction. Later, in a calm methodical way, he checked the radar and servo instruments to confirm his earlier findings. The rocket was definitely low on its trajectory, some five degrees or more, and the transverse jets which would have brought the projectile back on course were not working. The stacked meters on the instrument panel clearly indicated a fault in the fuel supply, perhaps a fractured feed pipe, or some obscure trouble in the high-pressure pump; in either case an impracticable engineering job would be involved.

He reported the facts to Base HQ, using morse telegraphy because radio-telephone conversation was no longer intelligible. They had been employing electronic computers to verify the orbit of the rocket, and were able to confirm that the trajectory was, in fact, nearly seven degrees low. Unless the transverse jets could be put right, the rocket would miss the moon by more than eleven thousand miles. However, there was a chance, they suggested, that he might be able to use the retrojets in combination with the weak lunar gravitation to deflect the rocket into a long ellipse which would eventually bring him back to within reasonable rescue distance of Earth. It would take eight months, and would require precise timing in firing the retrojets. The available oxygen might last provided he injected himself with somnalin, which would reduce his rate of metabolism to a very low level. The possibility of survival was slender, but there was just a chance. Carson allowed himself to smile grimly.

The control cabin of the rocket was small and cramped, but he was quite comfortable. There was no sense of motion, and only a slight feeling of weight induced by the slow centrifugal spin of the projectile. Air pressure was low, around eight pounds, but he had been conditioned for months to live normally under such circumstances, and he no longer felt breathless. The latex pad on which he lay was soft and resilient, and he could reach everything simply by lifting a hand: the controls and instruments, the oxygen feed valve, the food dispenser, the sanitation device, and the books in the small library which had been provided as an antidote for boredom. More remote, but still accessible, were the dural racks holding the monitoring equipment, the compact television transmitter, the radio telephone, and the apparatus for measuring radiation, magnetic fields, cosmic rays, meteor particles and temperature—and, of course, the gadgets designed to record his own physiological reactions to flight through space. Everything was functioning normally according to prediction, with the exception of the small transverse jets—four of them, positioned radially around the shell of the projectile. On such a point of detail depended the matter of life or death.

The possibility of death in the cold vacuum of space had been foreseen, naturally. During the long months of training before the launching they had overlooked nothing. The team of six men selected for the first orbiting flight around the moon had been under no illusions as to the dangers involved. Carson smiled reminiscently as he remembered the disappointment of his colleagues when he had been finally chosen by the Selection Board. He found himself wondering just how they would feel now, once the news was released that the much-vaunted *Wanderer II*, the first manned rocket planned to circle the moon and return to Earth, was destined to miss its target and become a minor planet of the sun.

I was adequately briefed, he thought, and they talked about death objectively and scientifically. They talked about the big chance of success and the small chance of failure. They talked statistically, mathematically, about the risk involved. If the worst happens, they said, and death proves to be inevitable, then you will have the facility to die as and when you choose, easily and pleasantly. At no time will there be cause for desperation. The entire operation should be completed in ten days, if all goes well, but you will have food and oxygen to last you a month. If anything should go wrong, then you can take somnalin tablets, and in the subsequent cataleptic state you will be able to survive for much longer—six months, perhaps more.

We have taken every possible precaution, they added. *Wanderer II* is the apex of modern astronautical engineering, and you have been singled out by rigorous tests as the one man in the western hemisphere most fitted to pioneer the long trail to the moon.

Dead or alive, Carson had commented sardonically on that day long ago.

He unfastened the straps around his body and sat up carefully, inclining his head to avoid a cluster of metal pipes cleated to the roof of the cabin. He was dressed in a flexible grey one-piece suit with a metallic fitting around the neck to which the space helmet could be securely attached. The cabin was airtight, of course, and he had removed the helmet as soon as he had recovered from the black-out following the take-off. Now he withdrew it from a small locker near the floor, inspecting its transparent surface carefully for any indication of flaw or fracture, then put it over his head, snapping the clips firmly into place. Finally he slung the compact oxygen pack over his shoulders and screwed the breathing tube into place. His thumb pressed a small valve, and oxygen hissed cheerfully into the helmet.

He turned his attention to the control panel, operating switches and moving a wheel. A red warning light flashed solemnly as air sighed from the cabin. The needle of the meter registering air pressure dropped gently to zero.

Satisfied, he walked across the cabin, holding on to a metal rail to maintain his balance against the unsteadying effect of near weightlessness, climbed over a narrow bulkhead bisecting the floor, and advanced cautiously until he reached a circular flanged hatch set in the rear wall. Slowly he unscrewed the heavy locking wheel, then threw back the pressure clips. The hatch opened sluggishly like the door of a safe, revealing a dark cavity beyond.

Clumsily he pulled himself through the hole, then switched on the interior light. He was in the main body of the rocket, surrounded by massive tanks and arrays of pipes and cables, the curved inner shell gleaming dully in the subdued light. He stared blankly at his strange metallic environment for a while, striving to recall the technical information he had absorbed during his period of engineering training. Somewhere among this confusion of equipment and conduits was the pump and its associated feed lines for the transverse jets, but he was not immediately able to orientate himself. He advanced farther into the hull, holding the guide rail.

Even when he finally located the pump he did not at first recognize it. The shape was different, in some subtle way twisted and distorted. Furthermore, the unit seemed to be hanging loose from its mounting bracket, dangling rigidly from bent piping.

It was only when he stooped to inspect the under surface of the pump that he saw the cause of the trouble: a jagged hole torn in the tough steel casing, with thick green oil seeping slowly from the punctured hydraulic cylinder.

Despondently he surveyed the damage, scrutinizing the interior of the pump mechanism and noting the scored piston and the bent cam-rod. The thing looked as if it had been hit by a pick-axe —a sharp pick-axe with a serrated edge—but obviously there could be no question of sabotage. Intuitively he knew the true explanation, and he turned to the curved shape of the hull in search of confirmation. He found the hole in less than ten seconds. It was a big hole, as meteorite punctures went, slightly larger than a penny, and roughly triangular in shape. It was possible to draw, in imagination, a straight line joining the hole with the torn casing of the fuel pump, but, of course, one had to allow for the physical displacement of the unit as it had been jolted and wrenched from its securing bracket. Somewhere in the other side of the rocket hull, diametrically opposite, would be another similar hole where the outsize meteorite, travelling at possibly five miles a second, had made its exit. The damage to the hull structure was relatively unimportant since only the control cabin was airtight, but the wrecked fuel pump was a different matter entirely. It meant the inevitable failure of *Wanderer II*—and death for its pilot.

Carson pouted cynically. In his mind he could hear again the confident, incisive voice of the instructor at the College of Astronautics: *The meteor hazard has been grossly overstated. In fact, the vast majority of meteors in space are mere particles of dust, smaller than grains of sand. The chances of impact with a meteor of appreciable size, say, as big as a marble, are so remote as to be negligible. On a statistical basis, one might expect such a meteor to pass within a radius of a thousand metres of a rocket vehicle once every ten thousand years. As for direct impact—once in half-a-million years, not more.*

"Bad luck," Carson said aloud. The statistics were probably right. Half-a-million years might indeed roll by before another rocket suffered a major meteor impact, but that was little consolation in the here and now. The thing had happened. The *Wanderer II* had been penetrated cleanly, quickly and efficiently at some point after take-off. The transverse jet system was out of action and there wasn't a thing he personally could do about it.

The payload of the rocket had been calculated down to the last gramme, and space didn't allow for the transport of spare fuel pumps and pipelines.

He made his way back to the control cabin, sealing the hatch behind him, and filled the cabin with air, adjusting the pressure to the specified eight pounds. Wearily he removed the space helmet and stowed it in the locker. He sat down pensively and spent fully a minute staring at the grey facia panel of the radio transmitter, not seeing it, but seeing through it with a kind of inner vision, and beyond it was the vast black wilderness of inter-planetary space speckled with burning stardust, and already, it seemed to him, the Earth and its moon were far behind and almost indistinguishable from the phosphorescent cloud of the Milky Way that defined the limits of the galaxy. There was no bitterness or resentment in him, just a quiet and slightly melancholy accept-ance of the situation. The real terror and torment, he realized, were yet to come, but there were ways of dealing with that.

He found his thoughts drifting to people he knew back on Earth, to friends such as Keegan and Brown and Drayton, and his parents, waiting hopefully for each new bulletin reporting the rocket's progress, and the dark-haired beautiful Valerie, the girl he had abandoned for the chance to pioneer the frontiers of space . . . but he snapped his attention back to the radio trans-mitter. Thinking nostalgically about people back home was like looking down from the top of a high ladder: it didn't add to mental stability.

He switched on the transmitter and thumbed the morse key, sending a formal message to Base HQ reporting the damage to the fuel pump and feed lines. The reply, equally formal, came back in thin piping dots and dashes through crackling static. *Stand by for retrojet manoeuvre in about eighteen hours. Com-puting now—will send full briefing later.*

He transmitted an acknowledgement, then switched off the equipment and lay back on the latex pad, fingers interlocked behind his neck. I've no faith in the retrojet manoeuvre, he told himself. There are too many variables and too many unknowns to balance the equation—and the biggest unknown quantity is human life itself. But I suppose they'd like to get the rocket back, even if I fail to survive the long eight-month ellipse. I'd be almost as useful to them dead: they could open me up, and run Geiger counters over me, and study the long-term effects of somnalin on human physiology, and in that way I'd be making things safer for the next sucker who flies a rocket to the moon.

Cynicism trembled acidly in his mind for an instant, then evaporated. He realized that he didn't care much about his fate, and that in the long run one had to take an impersonal view. That was why he had been selected for this assignment: not because of courage, or technical brilliance, or initiative, or IQ, but because he happened to be the controlled objective type of individual, the non-reactive type, the type who would act logically, without much feeling, in whatever circumstances might arise. The human robot, whose brain was bigger than his heart.

Not me, he decided abruptly. I've got a heart, though perhaps I haven't used it much, and there were occasions in the past when I was out of control and swept by passion, or anger, or sheer irresponsible bloody-mindedness. I could have been an ordinary man-in-the-street, working in an office or a factory, with a wife and family. I might have been happier. Even so, I'm not unhappy now—I ought to be, but I'm not. Death is always a little unreal, particularly when it is a predetermined death lying in wait beyond an interval of months. At the age of thirty-four it's difficult to take the idea of death seriously ... and, anyway, the retrojet manoeuvre might prove to be successful, after all. While there is still an atom of hope left, then death is always very far away.

He took four tablets to make sure he stayed awake, then settled down to wait patiently for the moment of the retrojet manoeuvre.

Carson was never quite sure just why the retrojet manoeuvre failed. It may have been due to an error of judgement on his part —a fractional delay in pressing the firing switches in the boost pumps—or he may have forgotten to allow for the interval of time required for radio signals to reach the rocket from Earth. On the other hand, the computers at Base HQ may have been at fault, or inadequately programmed. Obviously it would be difficult for the operators at Base HQ to take into account every conceivable factor that might affect the orbit of the rocket.

The retrojets had responded instantly, at full power, inducing gravitational drag into the free-falling projectile, so that Carson nearly blacked out. He obeyed the radioed instructions from Earth to the precise instant, so far as he was able to judge, and then, when the jets were silent once more, sat back to wait for a report from Base HQ on the *Wanderer's* new orbit.

The message came four hours later. By now the radio signals were so faint that they were almost inaudible above the background level of static. Carson had to break in frequently and ask for repeats of words, but eventually the entire text of the message was written down. It made depressing reading.

Base HQ to Wanderer II—New orbit solar aphelion 250,000,000 miles, perihelion indeterminate, probably 75,000,000 miles. Cyclic period 3·8 years.

About three minutes later there was another radio message, on the fringe of audibility. Mechanically he took it down. This time the words were informal. Authority had finally relaxed.

Base HQ to Wanderer II—Sorry, Carson. We all did our best. Sympathy of entire world with you. History will remember. Radio contact deteriorating rapidly. This may be last message ever. Goodbye. Good luck. . . .

Carson switched off the radio equipment with a sigh. The click of the switch might have been the click of the lock on a steel door; for the first time loneliness began to creep in on him, a black, brooding loneliness that oppressed his mind and made him restless and uneasy. He clenched his fists and rubbed the knuckles of his fingers against his chin, grinding them into the stubble of his rapidly growing beard. What to do, he thought—what to do at this point, when there's nothing left to do but wait. Wait for what? I'm off on a three-and-a-half year orbit round the sun, and at the end of that time I may return to within a few million miles of Earth. By then I'll have been dead three years. I can end it now, or I can drag it out for as long as the food and oxygen last, or I can use somnalin and live unconscious for six months and then die in my sleep. At all events I'm well and truly on my own, and there's no longer the possibility of radio communication with other human beings.

Tentatively he switched on the radio transmitter and sent a call to Base HQ. Minutes passed while he listened to the blank static coming through the receiver. At one point he thought he heard the faint intermittent piping of a morse signal, but it might have been imagination. There was never any discernible reply: Base HQ had been swallowed up by the random background noise of space.

He switched off the equipment for the last time, then opened the small observation shutter in the side of the cabin and peered through the thick armoured glass. The stars rotated slowly as the rocket spun leisurely on its axis. He caught a glimpse of Earth hanging like a tennis ball in the sky, glowing whitely in a first-quarter crescent. A moment later the naked sun swept into view, blinding him momentarily. The moon seemed to be out of sight, probably to the rear of the rocket; if he wanted to see it he would have to use television, but somehow he had no desire to look at the moon, and no further wish to see Earth any more. He closed the observation shutter.

I'll stay alive, he decided suddenly, in a mood of defiance. I'll stay alive for as long as I can, conscious, without using somnalin, but taking drugs to relieve gloom and depression. I'll see the thing through to the end, and perhaps I'll use the tape recorder to make notes of impressions and observations. Some day, in the near or far distant future, the information may be useful to someone. The important thing is to keep my mind occupied during these final weeks. . . .

Carson managed to keep his mind occupied during seventeen long days and nights of harrowing, confined solitude, talking to the tape recorder as if it were a personal friend, reliving and recounting the details of his life as though, in so doing, it were possible to guarantee for himself a kind of immortality beyond death.

Then despair struck him down. In a grim suicidal mood he opened the air valves of the control cabin and allowed the vacuum of space to rush in. He died quite quickly after a brief, violent struggle to suck non-existent air into his collapsed lungs.

Wanderer II continued on its long elliptical orbit round the sun.

CHAPTER TWO

CERTAIN curious phenomena were taking place in the blackness. A purple glow trembled like aurora, then changed colour, moving tranquilly through the rainbow of the spectrum. It vanished abruptly, then reappeared to repeat the performance, and kept on repeating it for an eternity. Somewhere remote a musical tone echoed in a vast invisible hall, then slowly ascended the chromatic scale in a prolonged glissando, rising higher and higher in pitch until it was no longer audible. And there were tentative sensations of feeling: tiny pin-points of physical awareness like the impact of cosmic rays on exposed nerves.

The colours and the tones and the atoms of feeling seemed to merge and coalesce until they became a complex universe of abstract light, sound and touch. They built up to a crescendo in intense sensory experience, then faded slowly over the years until the ebony featureless night returned. In the course of time they came back, but now the colours were broken into jagged patterns, and the tones were blended into harmony and discord, and the points of feeling were harsh and irritating, bordering on the threshold of pain.

These things were happening in a void, and there was nothing in the void that possessed any sense of personal identity, but they were witnessed, and the entity that was witnessing them was able to recognize certain qualities which, though abstract, were intrinsically human. The pain, for instance—that was a subjective thing. In the physical world of nature there was no such thing as pain. It was a psychoneural reaction characteristic of a sentient being. It could not be measured, weighed or analysed, but it was real, nonetheless. There was an awareness of pain, and that implied an awareness of a living body, even though the body existed on a level beyond that of the basic sense data.

The rainbow colours and the musical tones, too, were interesting, for in the world of abstract physics there is neither colour nor music, only frequencies of varying wavelengths in differing media. Colour implied psychoneural interpretation, as did musical pitch. Neither could exist without a living brain.

Something was thinking. Something was analysing the implications of sense data, observing the colours and hearing the tones and feeling the atoms of physical sensation, and that something was in some way independent and apart from the things it was analysing. The simple world of colour and tone and touch had differentiated in a subtle way: now there was the subjective and the objective, and whereas originally the phenomena had been real, now they were no longer real in the same way, but were merely recorded changes in the consciousness of the entity that was aware of them. It was, in a way, the fundamental evolution of life itself, the discreet process by which a simple cell becomes a thing apart from its environment and begins to react to the world around it, so that the cell, although basically an intricate assembly of complex but inert molecules, acquires a quality not possessed by the molecules which surround it.

The sentient being was nameless and eternal, and limited in

function, simply watching the colours and hearing the tones and feeling kinaesthetically the sensations of physical contact. But slowly, almost imperceptibly, the colours hardened and the patterns became static. The tones, settling into dissonant harmony, became congealed and tremulous, persisting like the echo of a strange chord in a minor key. The atoms of touch became penetrating needles, multiplying and spreading over a curved surface.

Suddenly there was consciousness, the awareness of a naked body lying on a cold hard surface, and there was light, and a thin face with deep green eyes, and insupportable pain vibrating in every limb as the atoms of feeling expanded. The consciousness lasted for a fraction of a second, then snapped into extinction. Dense, unfeeling night seemed to endure for a thousand years. There was no more colour or tone or physical sensation.

In the course of time Carson awoke.

Initially he was confused—that was to be expected. The room was bright to the point of incandescence, and detail was blurred. A shadow flitted across an opalescent ceiling, but he was unable to follow it with his eyes because they ached intolerably. It seemed to him that he was lying under a curved transparent shell on a smooth plastic surface, with a network of fine wires covering his naked body. He attempted to move an arm, but the muscles failed to respond, and he was only able to lie motionless in a condition of paralysis, staring straight up at the blinding light.

There were sounds which he could identify: a faint ticking, like a clock, but much slower, and the shallow noise of breathing, quick and irregular. After a while it came to him that he was listening to the sound of his own breath issuing from his lungs. Far away he could detect the murmur of subdued voices, but they were unintelligible.

The shadow moved across the ceiling again, and something came solidly into his field of vision. It was a face—one that he had seen before, mingled with the colours and tones and the atoms of feeling: a thin white face with green eyes and a hairless dome of a head. The eyes stared intently into his for a moment, and then the face disappeared. A moment later the plastic shell above him moved to one side. Cold air swept across his body. The light dimmed slowly to a comfortable level.

Something gripped his limp arm and lifted it. A needle punctured his flesh; almost immediately hot fire raced through his arteries. The face returned and the green eyes scanned him intelligently, as if seeking some kind of response. He attempted to move his lips, to utter a word that would indicate his alert consciousness, but the paralysis still held him in its grip and he was quite powerless.

The face went away again, and now he could hear voices, but they were speaking a tongue that was largely unfamiliar. Here and there he recognized a word, but the articulation and inflexion were different. It seemed to him that he was listening to the English language intimately blended with foreign languages, and spoken with a curious continuity, in which the words were run together to form complete units comprising whole phrases and even sentences. One thing he could understand: a certain subtle sense of academic urgency in the intonation of the speech. He knew they were talking about him, and he realized that he was the subject of anxious, expert attention.

The injection he had received had begun to revitalize him. He found he could move a finger and shift the position of his right leg infinitesimally. His lips were still rigid, but there was a feeling of flexibility about them which suggested that he might soon be able to say something . . . anything to prove that he was alive and conscious.

He attempted to lift an arm, but a restraining hand grasped it firmly.

"Don't move," said a stilted voice.

He stopped trying to move.

"Can you hear me?" said the voice, speaking in a flat mechanical manner, as one might read words from a book of phrases in a foreign language. "If you can hear me, blink your eyes twice."

He did as requested. The fingers relinquished their grip on his arm, allowing it to fall back to the cold plastic surface on which he lay.

"Good," the voice continued. "Listen carefully. You are in a very weak and emaciated state. That is to be expected. You were dead for a long time. You have undergone many surgical operations involving tissue transplantation. Your body is being kept alive electronically, and there are many thousands of wires connected to your flesh and nerve centres for that purpose. You must not move. Do you understand?"

He blinked his eyes again to indicate that he understood.

"You are alive, but only just," said the voice tonelessly. "You must obey every instruction. You will remain here under electronic stimulus for five years. During that time you will gain strength and improve. Afterwards, with care and training, you may be able to live the life of a normal man."

There was a pause. The thin face appeared above him and the green eyes stared into his.

"You must sleep again, for a long, long time. There are more operations to be performed. When you awake, in two years from now, you will be much better, much stronger. You will be able to talk and move, and you will begin to remember. Three years later we shall remove the wires from your body."

The slotted mouth in the face extended into what might have been a smile. "It is a slow process. Death is a difficult disease to cure. Normally we would not take the trouble—but in your case. . . ."

The face turned suddenly to one side. "Hypnomin," said the slotted mouth.

The sharp needle punctured Carson's arm for the second time. Nothing happened for five seconds, and then the face and the room dissolved into an empty void. The sleep was black and dreamless, and lasted no time at all. The moment of coma and the moment of returning consciousness were one and the same. The incandescent light had returned and was burning into his eyes, but now there was energy flowing through his body, despite the paralysis which still persisted and held him motionless.

He gulped air into his lungs and screamed.

They calmed him down with injections, and talked among themselves in the curious flowing language which he found so difficult to comprehend. There were three of them—two men and one woman—dressed in translucent green smocks. The tall man with the thin face and the green eyes was familiar, and he seemed to be the leader of the medical team. The other man was shorter, but still thin, and of swarthy complexion. His head had been shaved, but the scalp was showing a dark area of fine stubble. The woman was gaunt and sharply featured, and her hair had been cropped so that she looked vaguely masculine. Carson, now able to turn his head, was free to observe them, and further, could study the room with its complex equipment.

It was a large room, white from ceiling to floor, with a bewildering array of lights which, he imagined, were intended for irradiation rather than illumination. One entire wall was a mosaic of minute coloured lights which came on and went out individually in an apparently random fashion. He had no idea as to their purpose. He was lying on the same hard-surfaced bed, pinned down by the same complex network of fine wires, but the curved transparent cover had been removed, and he was able to see that the wires from his body were gathered into tied bundles which were connected to a long coffin-shaped metallic object adjoining the bed. There was other equipment, too, lining the walls, but he found it impossible to guess at its function.

After a few minutes the tall man with the green eyes came over to the bed and looked down at him in a professional and slightly impersonal manner, as one might inspect a biological specimen. "There," he said, reverting to the strangely mechanical intonation which characterized his use of simple English, "two years is not so long. Your condition has improved tremendously during that time. In fact, you are almost fully alive."

He turned to the wall bearing the matrix of coloured winking lights and pointed to it with a skeletal hand. "But not so fully alive that you could survive without electronic assistance," he went on. "Here we have a visual monitor panel which shows quite clearly where and when electronic stimuli are fed into your psychoneural system. As soon as a nerve centre begins to fail, the correct revitalizing frequency is automatically applied. The fact is registered by a light on the panel."

He focused his hypnotic eyes on Carson again. "As you gain strength, and as your body learns how to live once more, there will be fewer lights on the panel. One day the panel will become dark and will stay dark. On that day you will be alive in the true sense of the word. We can then disconnect you from the psychoneural stimulator. Meanwhile you must be patient for three years, possibly more. Do you understand?"

Carson nodded weakly.

"You may try to talk if you wish," said the green-eyed man.

Carson moved his lips and squeezed breath from his lungs. The voice was a mere husky whisper, a dry attenuated disused voice, but the sounds and syllables were there.

"How long was I dead?" he breathed.

The doctor regarded him solemnly. "Not long, if one thinks in absolute terms, but certainly long enough to make antimortic procedure extremely difficult." He paused reflectively. "You were dead for about eight thousand years—terrestrial years, that is. Fortunately you died in vacuum, so that your body was quite well preserved. There was a certain amount of internal damage of the kind one would expect under the circumstances—ruptural lesions in the heart and lungs, and some microbiotic decomposition of the abdomen due to anaerobic organisms. However, we were able to replace the faulty parts."

"Replace?"

"Eleven years of transplantative surgery, supervised, I may say, by none other than Dr. Hueste himself, who is probably the greatest living expert in the entire solar system. Of course, we have techniques that you would not know about. Your new heart, for example, is a graft of nylon and other materials of high tensile strength with selected human muscle. It will last for a thousand years. Your lungs are interwoven with synthetic cells to improve their efficiency. Your entire gastric system from stomach to colon was removed for what one might call factory reconditioning. You will find it much superior. The intestines are lined with Raedeker's catalytic enzyme filter, which is quite an improvement on nature. One other thing. . . ."

The doctor hesitated for a moment, and his pale lips seemed to smile a little. He continued: "We also found it necessary to recondition the entire urinogenital system, for reasons which have to do with the structure of our modern society. You will notice a remarkable difference, though you will have to wait three years for the privilege. However, the time will soon go by, and there will be long periods of unconsciousness. But, after all, what are three years in eternity?"

"Eternity?"

The smile persisted as if frozen to the thin lips. "Of course. Time and space have passed you by, and you would not know about these things. There have been great advances in the past millennia, and we know the secret of immortality. You are a privileged man. You were born in an age of birth and death, an age of futility when the accumulation of knowledge meant the passing on of knowledge—the wasted years of learning and teaching and re-learning. Today we have new methods. We have abolished death, and birth is no longer necessary. We have reached the point where man is no longer required to function as an animal, because he is no longer an animal. He has the forces of the cosmos at his command, and the terms of life and living can be controlled by technology."

"Immortality," Carson whispered. "It's unbelievable."

"You were dead. Now you are alive," the doctor pointed out. "We regard death as a curable disease."

"But . . . do you know who I am?"

"Yes," said the doctor crisply. "And that is why we have gone to such trouble to restore your life. You are very important to us, Robert Carson."

"Why?"

"You will find out in the course of time. To explain everything would merely confuse you. For the present, relax, sleep, and allow the natural forces of your body to gain strength and take over from our electronic machines, as they will surely do. You have a great deal to learn, but you must learn slowly."

Carson nodded wearily. Already fatigue was swamping him in the familiar paralysis. The doctor had rejoined his colleagues and was talking once more in the unintelligible blended dialogue which seemed to be the current language of this day and age. He stared at the monitor panel on the wall for a few minutes, watching the tiny lights as they blinked on and off in various colours—red, green, yellow, blue and purple. The lights symbolized his life: they signalled the pulses of energy flowing into his body to vitalize it in a kind of electronic reincarnation. Presently he closed his eyes, feeling soothed and satisfied.

He slept for many months.

CHAPTER THREE

IN retrospect Carson could hardly remember the long years of electronic therapy. There were phases of consciousness alternating with blank intervals of deep dreamless sleep, and he suspected that they were using drugs to lessen his awareness while awake and obliterate much of his memory in the months following. The twinkling lights on the monitor panel blinked into extinction over the years until, one notable day, the panel was quite dark and unilluminated, and stayed that way. He knew then that he was alive, fully and independently, and that he need no longer be sustained by the miracle of psychoneural electronics.

Soon afterwards, within the week, they applied an anaesthetic and removed the wires from his body. He recovered in a different room, a small chamber with amber walls and a luminous frosted ceiling, with simple furnishings in a light metal alloy. There was no window, but from somewhere high on the walls cool air circulated throughout the room. The bed on which he lay was soft and resilient. He observed that he was still naked.

Despite his physical weakness, he made the effort to examine his body. The electronic wires had left a rash of minute red pin-points over the greater part of his torso and limbs, and he could detect a pattern of fine silvery scars across his chest and abdomen where, presumably, he had been cut open for surgical purposes. He put one hand across his ribs to feel the pulsations of his nylon-reinforced heart; the beat was steady, like a machine. He tapped his abdomen experimentally with his fingers and found the flesh firm and strong. Then he lay back to think and reflect.

He tried to recall what it felt like to be dead, but there was no recollection in his mind beyond the final frantic moments in the *Wanderer II* when he had deliberately subjected himself to asphyxiation by vacuum. He remembered the death struggles, the abrupt and urgent change of intention, the irrational desire to continue to live at all costs—when it was already too late. He remembered the tortured desperation of his body, and the black cloud that had engulfed his senses, and after that there had been nothing—just a measureless interval gently disturbed by the rainbow lights and the musical tones. And in that interval eight-thousand years had elapsed.

It will be a different world from the one I knew, he thought. They have told me nothing of what lies beyond these four walls —merely clinical details of fantastic surgery, synthetic body organs, and electronic treatment of the disease known as death. What are they really like, these people, and what do they think of me? After eight-thousand years they must surely regard me as some kind of primitive animal bordering on civilized intelligence. Supposing a Stone Age man had been transported to the London I knew in the twentieth century? On the other hand, the doctor made a strange enigmatic remark: *You are very important to us, Robert Carson.* How can I be important?

He stared idly at the blue fluorescence of the ceiling and allowed his thoughts to ramble, without discipline or direction. Immortality, for instance—that was hard to believe. Even admitting their progress in clinical and surgical techniques, immortality was a faintly incredible concept. They probably knew how to extend life by the replacement of diseased and tired organs, and perhaps the average span of human life had increased to centuries, but complete immortality must obviously be an exaggeration. There had to be a limit, and there had to be a stop; sooner or later even an organism consisting of new and reconditioned parts must fail, or meet with the inevitable "statistical accident", as Shaw had once observed.

And what of the outside world—the London, New York, and Paris that he used to know so well long ago? They must have changed, radically and fundamentally. Indeed, London might well be an eroded ruin blanketed by the soil and sand of time—and New York, too. There might be a new world Metropolis, perhaps in Africa, or Asia. And what of the science of astronautics? After that first abortive attempt to send a manned rocket round the moon, how had humanity progressed in the technology of space flight, or had the whole thing been abandoned in the end?

His mind was too full of questions, he realized, and questions without answers were useless. Knowledge was a matter of fact, not speculation. It occurred to him that information about the outside world might have been withheld deliberately so that he could adapt himself by degrees to the changes that had taken place over the millennia. At all events, they seemed to know what they were doing, and even after eight-thousand years humans were still humans. He was alive and back on Earth, and in an advanced technology the future must be assured, even for himself, a virtual anachronism in an unimaginable new world.

Carson, although he did not realize it then, was quite wrong in every respect.

For the first few days after his return to full life, he was attended by a nurse. She was a woman of indeterminate age, quite attractive in a mature way, who brought him his food and drink and examined him periodically with the aid of unfamiliar instruments. The food was highly coloured but tasteless, and took the form of pressed and processed cubes which dissolved easily in the mouth. The general effect was satisfying enough. He assumed that the food was, in fact, synthetic and occasionally he found himself longing for some ordinary meat with common-or-garden potatoes and greens.

The nurse was uncommunicative. On one or two occasions

he was able to elicit some information from her, but it did not add considerably to his knowledge of his environment. One morning, when she had delivered to him the usual colourful pastiche that constituted his main diet, he said:

"When will I see my doctor again?"

"Which doctor?" she enquired impassively.

"The one with the thin face and the green eyes."

She smiled subtly. "You won't see him again, Mr. Carson. You are alive now. Dr. Wier is a specialist in antimortic pathology, and he has no further interest in your case."

"Then . . . what will happen to me now?"

"You are cured," she pointed out. "There will be a period of convalescence, and after that . . ."

"Well?"

"You will be fit and well. You will become a citizen of the State. Various people will want to see you."

"What people?"

"You will find out in due course."

After a pause he said: "Tell me, nurse, where am I?"

"In a small specialized private clinic."

"What I mean is—am I in London?"

"No."

"Then where?"

She smiled discreetly. "You are too impatient for knowledge. In any case, I am not permitted to tell you."

"Why not?"

"Those are my orders, I'm afraid."

He considered for a moment, then said: "I can't understand your orders. True, I come from an age that has been dead for eight-thousand years, but I'm not an animal, and I have a certain degree of intelligence. Why am I being kept in ignorance of certain basic information? Why should it matter if I know whether I'm in London, New York, Paris or Moscow?"

Her expression became blank for a revealing instant. Abruptly he realized that the names held no great significance for her.

"There are things you will be able to find out for yourself," she said. "You have not lifted yourself from your bed in five years, not since life was first injected into your nervous system. When you begin to walk, you will discover something that will provide you with a certain amount of—basic information, as you put it."

"Such as what?"

"Patience, Mr. Carson. You are trying to run before you can walk."

She removed the tray from his bed and began tidying up. He watched her for a while, and then said: "How old are you, nurse?"

She eyed him sardonically. "A man should never ask a woman her age. How old do I look?"

"I don't know. Smooth enough to be in the twenties, but mature enough to be more than forty."

"I was born nearly a thousand years ago," she said simply.

"I don't believe it," he stated bluntly.

"There are many things you won't believe at first. Don't be impatient, Mr. Carson. You have all the time in the world to learn, and in the end you will believe, because, you, too, will live to be a thousand, perhaps ten thousand. Who knows?"

"One other thing," he said, as she was about to leave the room. "Why am I so important? That's what they told me."

"I must leave that for the politicians to explain," she stated. "There are complications which you do not even begin to suspect."

"You speak my language very well," he observed. "Much better than the green-eyed doctor, for instance."

"I was adequately trained. During the five years of your antimortic treatment I was assigned to study antique terrestrial English. It was difficult enough, but I achieved a fair competence. All those individual words and verbs—the elementary semantics, so complicated because they were so simple. However, so long as we understand each other. . . ."

She went out of the room shortly afterwards, leaving him alone with his thoughts. One thing in particular remained in his mind, something she had said. He struggled to recall her exact words. *When you begin to walk, you will discover something. . . .*

An experimental mood gripped him. I'm alive, he thought. Perhaps I'm not very strong, but I can move my limbs. I could try to walk.

Cautiously he eased himself towards the edge of the bed, then summoned his strength, pushed his legs over the side. Suddenly he was sitting up. Dizziness came and went in a cold wave. He placed his hands firmly on the edge of the bed, then pushed himself to his feet. For an instant he stood upright, but he was unable to maintain the posture and tottered forward helplessly. His legs moved automatically, three steps, four steps. . . . Despite the over-powering sensation of instability he strove to analyse his feelings, noting the long strides and the curious light-headedness. It ended abruptly in a spectacular fall in which he seemed to float to the floor, and the impact was not so hard as he had expected.

Conclusion, he thought, picking himself up lethargically: either I'm extremely light and weak, or gravity is rather low—or perhaps both. But the experiment was disappointing and indecisive.

He went back to bed.

There was no rhythm of day and night in the accepted conventional way, nor was there a clock or similar device by which he could measure the passage of time. All lighting in the room was derived from the luminous ceiling, and periodically the illumination was dimmed to a low level. In this way time was arbitrarily divided up into artificial days and nights, each phase lasting about ten hours, so far as he could judge.

After about a week of such days he was visited by a team of six medical men who examined him thoroughly, as one might carry out a detailed inspection of a complicated machine. They said little, but it was apparent that they were satisfied with his condition. When they had completed their probing they departed in silence, leaving their patient slightly mystified.

About an hour later the nurse introduced another visitor in the form of a Mr. Jaff, who, it seemed, was an official from an administrative department of the government. Mr. Jaff was a rotund man of cheerful appearance (probably not more than a thousand years old, Carson thought whimsically). He was wearing a very brief black garment not much larger than a swimsuit, while from his shoulders hung a silvery cape pierced with a multitude of pockets stuffed with papers. His red hair was cropped in the contemporary fashion. A thick plastic sole seemed to have been glued to the underside of each foot.

Mr. Jaff made himself comfortable on a slender metal chair which seemed too frail to support his ample bulk, and referred to a blue document which he produced in a conjuring fashion from a pocket at the back of his cape. He spoke jerkily, with a lack of fluency which indicated want of familiarity with antique English.

"Medical report good," he said. "Now you go from here to

surface. Three weeks' exercise, training, rehabilitation. After that, normal citizen." He beamed benignly at Carson.

"Surface?" Carson queried.

Mr. Jaff pointed a squat forefinger vertically upwards. "Long time down below," he explained. "Now you have change of view, change of people, time to think and talk. What you call convalescence."

"When?"

"Two hours, three hours."

Carson made no comment.

"Remember, you very important person," Mr. Jaff went on. "Therefore you must obey all instructions. Also you must learn to speak language. No great difficulty. We have psychocerebral techniques."

"All right."

"One more thing. . . ." Mr. Jaff fumbled in his pockets and withdrew a tiny plastic box which he opened carefully, tipping the contents on to his open palm. A small silver cylinder, not much larger than a pea, rolled out.

"Take it," he said, holding his hand forward.

Carson took the object and put it to his mouth. Instantly Mr. Jaff leaned forward and gripped his wrist. "No, no," he declared in sudden alarm. "Not mouth. Ear."

Carson stared at him blankly.

"Put in ear," Mr. Jaff repeated firmly.

Nonplussed, Carson did as instructed, inserting the minute cylinder gingerly into his right ear.

"All the way," insisted Mr. Jaff.

Using his little finger, Carson pushed the thing home. Oddly enough, the metal seemed to be flexible enough to assume the shape of the inner ear cavity, and there was no discomfort.

"Good," murmured Mr. Jaff, smiling with relief. "Now you and me always in contact."

Carson touched his ear lightly and frowned. "What is it?" he asked.

"Just a little transceiver. Radio contact with government wherever you are. Advice and guidance, you see."

"Mm," Carson grunted doubtfully. "How do I get the thing out?"

Mr. Jaff chuckled in high delight. "Never can. Special biometal case will fuse with skin in a few minutes."

He stood up, gathering his cape about him. "Must go now. Very soon they will come for you. We shall meet again after convalescence. Goodbye."

"Goodbye," said Carson with a certain amount of ill grace.

He waited until the other man had left the room, then fumbled in his ear in a half-hearted attempt to retrieve the capsule, but already it had slipped beyond the reach of his little finger. For the first time since his rebirth he felt disgruntled and almost angry. He decided that he didn't like Mr. Jaff very much.

Later, in a more reflective mood, he decided that perhaps the move was justified: the transceiver was obviously a monitoring device by which they could listen to every word he uttered, or that was said to him; at the same time it was a channel of information working the opposite way, enabling authority to pass instructions almost directly into his brain. Such control might prove to be desirable. He knew nothing of his environment and of the people inhabiting this strange world of the future. If, for some unimaginable reason, he was as important as they insisted, then clearly they would feel the need to exercise some control over his conduct and behaviour.

In the long run, he told himself, I can always ignore the radio instructions if I wish, and I can communicate with others by writing, which doesn't make any sound.

They came for him two hours later.

CHAPTER FOUR

"This is Mars," said the blond, urbane young man, pointing through the side of the transparent dome. Carson surveyed the bleak grey and yellow landscape with its irregular outcroppings of orange coloured rock. In the indigo sky a tiny sun burned whitely near the horizon, casting long shadows over the uneven ground. The dome curved above like an enormous glass bubble supported by a fine geodetic structure of slender metallic strips; he estimated that it must have been at least a quarter of a mile in diameter. There were other domes, perhaps half a dozen of them, in the immediate vicinity, interlinked by transparent corridors.

In the dome were two rows of small flat-roofed buildings arranged in concentric circles around a central park area, and here Carson was surprised to see fresh green grass and a variety of cultivated flowers in artistically designed beds. Men and women were walking about, wearing the brief caped costume of the period. The air was warm, and moved gently in a refreshing manner.

"An inhospitable planet," the young man continued smoothly, as if reciting a lecture. "In the early days of colonization there were tremendous problems to be overcome. The land is barren, apart from areas where a simple moss-like type of vegetation grows seasonally. The atmosphere is thin and contains virtually no oxygen, so you see we have to make our own. There are also frequent electrical storms and dust storms of very great violence."

Carson recalled the long ascent in the high-speed elevator that had brought him to the surface of the planet, inside the dome of which he was now standing. He looked around at the people walking near the gardens.

"Do they live up here?" he asked.

"No," said the young man. "Everybody lives underground, where it is easier to control the conditions of survival. The basic rock of the planet is honeycombed with cities, each with its own air and water manufacturing plants. In five-thousand years of planetary engineering we have accomplished a great deal. Even the spaceports are underground—the launching zones are raised up on nuclear powered ramps as and when required."

"I should be interested to see that," Carson remarked.

"You will, in due course. As for this surface settlement, it is purely a relaxation centre. There are perhaps a dozen of them sited at convenient points over the planet, all built to the same pattern."

"You mean—they serve as holiday camps?"

The young man smiled amiably. "In a way. It is not good for humans to spend their lives underground all the time. There are certain undesirable psychological effects. If they choose they can spend rest periods on the surface at intervals."

"And the storms you mentioned?"

"The domes are rugged enough to withstand the most violent of storms, though occasionally . . ." He broke off and touched his chin reminiscently. "A complete settlement was wiped out once, two hundred years ago. Several thousand people were killed. Since then, however, we have tightened up the specifications and the domes are stronger. In the event of a really big storm we have facilities for rapid evacuation to the underground cities."

The young man pointed suddenly to a range of jagged red hills near the horizon. "See," he said. "Low in the sky—a brown cloud."

"Yes," Carson murmured.

The cloud, which seemed to be rising up from behind the hills, looked opaque and ominous against the dark blue of the sky, and even at that distance it appeared to writhe slowly within itself.

"That is a fairly typical small dust storm blowing from the Mestases desert. If it comes this way you will see some fun. There may even be some electrical activity, too."

Carson nodded in silence. They walked away from the edge of the dome towards the gardens.

"It is strange," said the young man, talking idly, "that even after thousands of years humans should never quite be able to adapt themselves to a full life underground. There is a racial memory going back through evolution. Man was always a surface animal. So they like to come here from time to time to look at the landscape and the sun and stars—and, of course, the two moons of Mars, Phobos and Deimos. Then there are opportunities for exploration, but one has to wear an oxygen helmet, of course. We have land vehicles and small aircraft using atomic propulsion units. . . ."

He stood still and listened intently for a moment, then looked up into the sky. Carson tried to follow the direction of his eyes. Now he could hear the sound that had caught the other man's attention—a faint multiple whine of power, growing louder. A moment later he saw the aircraft as it swept above the dome, circling and losing altitude. It was small and dart-shaped, gleaming silver in the pallid sunlight. Presently it disappeared beyond the roof level on the far side of the dome, and the whine faded into silence.

"Probably a sightseer frightened by the approaching storm," remarked the young man. "There is an automatic glide beam which takes over and brings the aircraft in very quickly in cases of emergency. The hangar is actually underneath the dome, with an airlock outside."

"I should like to go outside the dome some time," said Carson. "Perhaps I could take a vehicle or a plane and look around."

"Certainly, in a day or two. For the present there are more

important things to be done. For example, in less than a minute you are going to enter the apartment which is to be your home for the next three weeks, and you will meet the woman who will live with you and look after you during that time."

The young man looked Carson over with humorous eyes. "You are a lucky man," he observed. "Competence was specially chosen by a government committee for the assignment. She is probably the most beautiful and intelligent woman on Mars."

"Competence?" Carson echoed questioningly.

The young man looked puzzled for an instant. "That is her first name," he explained. "It is the custom to use a first name which expresses in some degree our job or personality or function in society. For example, my name is Aptitude Shenn—I happen to be a rather good vocational psychologist. Your Mr. Jaff is known as Mentor Jaff, because it is his job to supervise and instruct. I have a friend named Excision Horther who is an excellent surgeon. Do you understand?"

"Well, yes," Carson admitted doubtfully.

"Your woman's full name is Miss Competence Cayne," said the young man with a mischievous smile. "You will certainly find her most competent in every respect."

Carson made no comment. They continued on their way to the gardens and the inner circle of apartment blocks.

Competence Cayne was all that the young man had implied, and more, Carson decided. In the twentieth century, in wide screen and Technicolor, she would have created immense queues at every box office in the western hemisphere. She was of the right height, and, whatever one's standards, the right shape, and her bronze hair held a fascinating metallic sheen. Her eyes were a lively green. She possessed an indefinable dignity of poise and bearing, and her smile was warm and welcoming. Her costume and cape, styled in the traditional manner, were in green and gold, and she wore gold sandals to match.

Carson, who had also been fitted with a brief costume and cape in pastel blue colour, felt confused and embarrassed in her presence. The urbane young man had left after performing a simple introduction, and they were alone in a clinically white room with a long window and metal furniture.

The girl invited him to sit down, which he did awkwardly, then said in a honey voice: "Perhaps I ought to explain something of the programme planned for you, Mr. Carson. Obviously you must find things rather perplexing."

Carson nodded mutely.

"Basically you are here, under my wing, as it were, for rehabilitation, to enable you to take your place as a normal citizen in our Martian society. There are many things to learn, and one of the most important is language. Inside three weeks we shall teach you to speak as we do."

"You're optimistic," he said sardonically.

"You will find it simple enough," she said smiling, "and probably much simpler than I find your antiquated English grammar. Our modern language is international and agglutinative. We have syllables derived originally from most of the important languages which were in common use on Earth, and they express specific ideas. All we do is join syllables together to make up more complex ideas. A complete thought, a sentence if you like, is expressed in one word. We think in terms of sentences rather than individual words, just as an architect visualizes the structure rather than the separate bricks."

"You must think of me as naïve," Carson said humbly. "Here I am—a man from a past which died eight-thousand years ago. Surely you must look on me as some kind of uncivilized prehistoric . . . well, monster, if you like."

For the first time the tiny transceiver in his ear clicked into active life. Quietly but distinctly the voice of Mr. Jaff spoke into his brain. *Wrong attitude, Mr. Carson. Do not denigrate yourself. You are contemporary human and very important. Speak with much assurance.*

"You don't look like a monster to me," said the girl.

Carson grinned wryly. "Perhaps I was exaggerating. It's just that I feel out of place in this advanced technology. I need time to get used to things."

Better, said the voice of Mr. Jaff.

"You will get used to things very quickly," the girl remarked. "Tomorrow you will meet your instructors who will teach you language, modern sociology, politics, and give you an outline of scientific progress during the last eight-thousand years. Today you can relax."

"I'm relaxing as best I can."

She crossed to a cupboard inset into a wall and opened a sliding door. "This will help you," she said, producing a flask of blue liquid and two ornately cut glasses. She poured a quantity of fluid into each glass, then handed one to him.

"In the old days they used to drink alcohol for its narcotic properties," she explained. "Today we have other uses for alcohol. This is much better, and not so depressing."

Carson held the glass to his nose and sniffed at the blue liquid; the odour was faintly sweet and pungent, reminiscent of chloroform.

"What's it called?" he asked.

"Sonar. Drink it. You will feel better."

Drink it, urged the voice of Mr. Jaff inside his ear.

Carson put the glass to his mouth and tilted it. The blue liquid spread immediately over his tongue like a volatile spirit, and the cloying fumes burned their way into his lungs. He coughed in a sudden spasm. A moment later he was aware of a feeling of warm well-being. He sipped some more, and this time he did not cough.

"Good," he acknowledged. "Very good."

She smiled knowledgeably at him.

His brain spun in search of a topic of conversation: suddenly he felt in a discursive mood. "Tell me about Earth," he suggested. "Are things the same there? And the moon, and Venus. . . ."

"Patience, Mr. Carson. You will learn all in the course of time. Earth has changed considerably since your day. There have been many wars, and for centuries there was universal radio-activity. Earth is a planet of strange mutants, but there are isolated colonies of normal people like you and me."

"And the other planets—Venus, Saturn, Neptune. . . ."

"There is a small colony on Venus surviving under almost intolerable conditions of arid heat, and a research team operating in the twilight zone of Mercury, which is the nearest planet to the sun. The other planets are mainly uninhabited because of extremely high gravity and atmospheres of ammonia and methane. There are expeditions on two of the moons of Jupiter—Ganymede and Io."

"Expeditions . . . from where?"

"From Mars, of course," she said, smiling. "Earth has too many domestic problems to concern itself with long-range space exploration. Apart from routine freight runs to the moon, which is a kind of export exchange centre, Earth has largely abandoned interplanetary flight."

"Tell me," said Carson, with sudden interest, "who governs this network of planets and moons of planets?"

The voice of Mr. Jaff whispered deep in his ear. *Do not ask political questions. All will be explained later.*

"That is a controversial question," said the girl discreetly. "We are hoping that you will help us to resolve it."

Carson, obeying Mr. Jaff's instructions, did not pursue the point, but he filed it in a pigeon-hole of his mind for future reference.

"It seems to me," he said, after a pause, "that the Martian colony has to some extent gained ascendancy over Earth so far as space flight is concerned."

"In every phase of science," she remarked.

"Are there immortals on Earth?"

"No."

He frowned in bewilderment. "I find it difficult to understand. . . ."

"It is simple enough," she explained. "When the first expeditions landed on Mars to establish a bridgehead through space, the majority of Earth's top scientists were sent to the new planet —in particular the biophysicists and psychoneurologists, whose task it was to make sure that the human system could be adapted to survive under alien conditions. Over the course of two or three centuries Mars became the rendezvous for the finest scientific minds that Earth could produce. There were plans to launch expeditions to other planets, and even blueprints for a starship, after Neilsen had developed the photon drive. Then came the big atomic war which devastated the home planet. The scientists stayed on Mars and watched the hydrogen and cobalt bombs exploding through electron telescopes. Miraculously Earth was not entirely destroyed, and in the course of five thousand years much of the damage was undone. The scientists still stayed on Mars, but a number of reconnaissance flights were made to Earth. The reports were depressing."

"Surely things could never have gone so far?"

She smiled ironically. "You are from the twentieth century. You witnessed the beginnings of the ultimate holocaust. You were lucky to be privileged to spend your eight-thousand years of death in the sterile vacuum of space. You missed the carnage."

"And now?"

"And now," she echoed. "Life is tenacious. Even during the

dark ages after the atomic wars the pattern of organized society continued here and there, and the elements of industry and finance survived. Earth is strong again, but it is a very different planet from the one you knew in the long dead past."

"I get the impression. . . ." Carson began, but he never completed his sentence. Outside the building something began to moan and howl with savage intensity. A tremendous echoing crash reverberated in the air. The staccato sound of innumerable tons of gravel rattling on a hollow tin roof assailed his ears. Alarmed, he hurried to the window and stared out, above the skyline, to the great spreading curvature of the dome.

The sky was ebony, but within the darkness beyond the dome something swirled and spun in an incredible dervish dance. Lightning flashed simultaneously in half-a-dozen places. The sharp thunder of the cascading stones increased to an intolerable pitch. Suddenly he was aware that the girl was holding his arm and smiling at him reassuringly.

"Just a storm," she said quietly, "and a fairly normal one at that. Come outside and watch it."

He followed her out of the building to the soft green lawn between the flower beds. Dozens of people were already congregated there, staring upwards through the high ceiling of the dome. Carson looked too.

The storm was an immense area of marbled, undulating blackness, heaving and twisting low in the sky above the dome. From the dark venomous oval, forked branches of incandescent lightning spat angrily at the ground. Like an enormous black beetle prowling the night on legs of crackling fire, the cloud moved forward, hurling unimaginable masses of grit and sand and rock at the smooth surface of the dome. The noise was deafening, and the lightning blinding.

Fear squirmed in his abdomen, and he turned anxiously to the girl, but she was calm and passive, showing only an academic interest in the phenomenon.

"The air spins in a horizontal plane," she shouted above the tumult of the bombardment. "It sucks up the loose top surface of the desert and carries it along, and there's a kind of electrostatic effect, like particles in a vacuum chamber. It will blow itself out within a hundred miles."

The beetle was passing over. Already grey light filtered through the edge of the cloud, and the lightning began to cluster more remotely on the limits of the settlement. Presently the noise and the turmoil began to fade. They went back indoors.

"Impressed?" she enquired, putting her hands on his shoulders.

"Depressed," he countered.

"They are commonplace," she said. "We frequently have two or three minor storms a day, and sometimes we have a really big one that goes on for hours. The lightning can be so bright and continuous that it hurts the eyes."

"Give me the green fields of Earth," he murmured nostalgically.

"For what they are worth here and now, you can *have* the green fields of Earth," she retorted.

Later, after a satisfying meal followed by more of the blue Sonar fluids, the girl introduced him subtly and gently to the refined art of love-making in the 100th century, A.D.

"We are immortal, and there is no longer any need for fertility," she explained. "Consequently the functions of the body, and the nervous reflexes, can be adapted and sharpened in the interest of recreation rather than procreation. When they reconditioned your body they made certain changes which will please you as much as they will please me."

"I'm not sure that I understand," he said hesitatingly.

She kissed him lightly. "Before the night is over you will understand only too well, Mr. Carson.

CHAPTER FIVE

THE next morning Carson received his first lesson in language. He was escorted by the pleasant young man known as Aptitude Shenn to a small square building resembling a clinic, where he was introduced to a gangling youth with aged eyes whose name was Dr. Semantic Groor.

"The essential thing," said Dr. Groor, after the formal introductions had been made, "is to impress on your brain in the form of memory tracks a basic vocabulary of sounds and syllables and their significance, and also to establish a cerebral relationship between syllabic ideas and concepts amounting to what you might call syntax and grammar. This we do electronically, with the aid of a machine derived originally from the electro-encephalograph of your century, but in reverse, if you know what I mean."

Carson nodded dumbly.

"In addition there are ancillary devices—video display of pictures and abstract patterns, synchronized sound from a semantic integrator, and techniques involving hypnosis. In three days you will have a working knowledge of the language. In three weeks you will be fluent, without a trace of accent."

The doctor led Carson into a small adjacent room and ushered him into a deep, inclined chair backing on to a console of electronic equipment. The chair was soft and comfortable, almost embracing. As he lay reclining, Dr. Groor fitted a complicated network of straps and electrodes over his head, pressing home the points of contact so that they pricked his scalp. Carson fidgeted uneasily. Switches clicked behind him, and power surged through the equipment with a faint, throbbing hum.

"Language is communication," the doctor announced, speaking as if to himself. "Music is a language, and so is colour as deployed in art, but they communicate to the senses rather than the intellect. The most perfect language is mathematics. A simple formula can express an abstract idea so complex that it could not be communicated in a million words. I often think it is a pity that humans do not communicate with each other mathematically."

"Yes," Carson agreed politely, "but how would one say 'goodnight' in mathematics?"

In his ear the tiny transceiver clicked admonishingly. *Do not be facetious,* said the reproving voice of Mr. Jaff. *Dr. Groor important semantic scientist. Heed him.*

Dr. Groor, for his part, had ignored Carson's question. He seemed to be dwelling in some remote inner world, and his deep eyes possessed the glazed fervour of the ascetic.

"However," he went on, "we are limited to the sound waves produced by the human larynx, and restricted to syllabic sound formations which owe their semantic meaning largely to imagery in the visual or aural sense. We have to do the best we can with the material available. In any case, our existing vocabulary was established many centuries ago by usage. However desirable it might be to invent a new logical language, it would introduce too many practical difficulties."

Carson made vague noises of agreement.

"So," said Dr. Groor, "I am going to teach you our language, however inferior it might be. I could teach you a new, efficient and greatly superior language, but as you would be the only person capable of speaking it, you could hardly communicate, could you?"

"I suppose not," Carson conceded.

The doctor sighed with ennui. "We shall have to be satisfied with second best. That, I fear, is a characteristic of life—the eternal compromise, the reluctance to break with the past, the adaptation of old ideas in preference to the invention of new. You have one consolation, my friend. The language you are about to learn, bad as it is, is infinitely better than the one which you yourself speak."

"It served me very well," Carson pointed out.

"That was eight-thousand years ago. Advances in technology demand advances in human communication. Even in your day a scientist could hardly have written down the specification of a space rocket or an atomic reactor in Egyptian hieroglyphics."

Carson found himself suppressing a smile. Another switch clicked quietly behind him, and the electronic machinery hummed more insistently. Dr. Groor walked round to the front of the chair and stared down at him intently.

"Are you ready?" he enquired.

Carson inclined his head.

"The first lesson is simple enough. The equipment will impress on your brain the five-hundred basic syllables of the language, with their meaning, and will establish elementary relationships between the syllables so that you can build up more complex words. You will feel nothing, but the syllables will emerge in your mind rather in the way that forgotten memories sometimes arise spontaneously."

The doctor disappeared behind the chair, and Carson settled down to his first session of semantic indoctrination.

Carson bent down and pulled up a cluster of tiny green plants. Examining them closely he observed that each consisted of a transparent globular structure, no larger than a pinhead, mounted on a thin stalk of pallid green. Inside each minute globe was a mass of bright green fronds, almost microscopic in dimensions. He pressed the stalks between his fingers and found them dry and brittle.

"It's really a plant within a plant," explained the girl named Competence. "The fern-like growth develops inside in its own spherical greenhouse, which traps and conserves the warmth of the sun. It also acts as a storage tank for moisture drawn from the deeper levels of subsoil by extremely long roots. Biologists believe that this plant is the final attempt at adaptation to adverse conditions by Martian vegetation. It's the only surviving species."

They were standing on a vast level expanse of Martian plain, on which the green vegetation lay like a thick carpet. A small atom-powered hovercraft waited idly about a hundred yards away. Both he and the girl were wearing oxygen helmets and packs together with a lightweight one-piece suit intended to protect their limbs from the cold bite of the thin Martian air. The sun rode high and white in the dark blue sky, while low on the horizon Phobos gleamed in a three-quarter phase.

From the air the belt of vegetation had taken the form of a strip extending roughly north to south from horizon to horizon, and some fifteen miles wide. Carson had commented on this, using the radio-talk facilities built into the helmet.

Early explorers had been puzzled by this phenomenon, the girl had explained. The vegetation zones formed a criss-cross pattern of intersecting lines, virtually straight, across the face of the planet, fading out at the poles. Between the vegetation belts there was only barren desert. It was not until the geologists and seismologists began to examine the rock strata forming the crust of Mars that the true explanation emerged.

On a planet almost devoid of water, and certainly without seas or oceans, the rocks were of igneous origin, created by fire rather than laid down by sedimentation. As the planet cooled slowly throughout the ages the brittle shell cracked, breaking up the surface into a kind of patchwork pattern. Along the flaw lines some of the internal heat of the planet was able to escape and diffuse into the soil above, raising the temperature by several degrees and creating the bare conditions necessary to sustain life and survival in a primitive chlorophyll-activated type of vegetation.

"So there never were any canals on Mars," Carson had remarked.

"Neither canals, nor any kind of animal life at all, so far as we have been able to determine . . . just this bubble-grass, as it's called."

"And the other planets?"

"Nothing exciting. Several kinds of complex crystalline

molecules on Venus that seem to exhibit some of the properties of life, without actually being alive. They're probably DNA activated. And I believe they found a lowly fungus on Ganymede, but we haven't had samples for analysis yet. It may be of terrestrial origin, taken there in spore form on the expedition ship. We take every possible precaution, but sometimes a spore may slip through the sterilization process."

"It seems strange to me that humans should be able to set up colonies under conditions that are basically hostile to life."

The girl had smiled knowledgeably. "The answer is power and planetary engineering. In your century they were to irrigate and open up the deserts on Earth, build townships in the wastelands, extract minerals and oil. We have done the same kind of thing, but on a much bigger scale, and using immense power which in your day could hardly have been visualized."

For a while they walked arm in arm across the soft carpet of bubble-grass. Several days had elapsed since the beginning of his vacation on the surface of the planet. Already he was conversing in the concisely blended sentences and phrases of the new language, and he was beginning to feel like a veteran Martian colonist. As time went by he found himself drawn more and more towards the girl; worse, he was increasingly aware of an over-powering feeling of possessiveness towards her. It was a subtle combination of her physical beauty and personality, and the exquisite thing they had made of the ritual of love-making, he decided, but he recognized the danger in allowing emotion to gain an ascendancy. There was virtually no emotion among these people; they enjoyed life in a cold-blooded intellectual way, as one might sit down to enjoy a game of chess, and the only apparent motive for seeking pleasure was the gratification that pleasure could provide. Aptitude Sheen had explained, on one occasion, that from the point of view of the inner mind, reading and interpretating the data supplied by the nervous system of the body, there were basically two types of experience: sensory stimuli conveying information about the environment and sensual stimuli recording the body's reactions to the environment in terms of pleasure and pain. Better living, he had suggested, was a simple matter of mechanics: improving the environment, and modifying the bodily response to it—intensifying pleasure and attenuating pain by means of psychoneural surgery. It seemed to work well enough in practice, but Carson had reservations about the ethics and morality of interfering with nature in that way. He decided that he was probably being old-fashioned in his outlook. In the course of time he would probably shake off his twentieth-century heritage and accept fully the standards of this new age into which he had been reborn.

"What happens after the end of this holiday?" he asked the girl.

She eyed him archly as they walked along. "You will return to the city beneath the surface, and I shall return to my duty elsewhere."

"That's the point," Carson said glumly. "It seems so futile that we should come together and then separate. Surely we can continue to meet. . . ."

"You must get used to the fact that people come and go," she advised solemnly. "It is important to avoid affinity and interdependence. We are each of us individual citizens, and in so far as we allow ourselves to become dependent on others, so we fail to give the State the services of a full individual."

"Is the State more important than the individual?"

She smiled reprovingly at him. "The State *is* the individual, and the individual is the State. Our first loyalty is to the society which has given us immortality."

"That sounds suspiciously like a doctrine," he observed. "Just forget for a moment that you are the State. As normal woman, haven't you ever been in love?"

She stopped smiling, but amusement lingered in her green eyes. "As a *normal* woman, the answer is no. What you call love is an obsessive form of compulsion neurosis. It used to be a fairly common disease of adolescents in the days when there *were* adolescents. Now that we have achieved immortality, we have the time to develop into balanced adults. No, Mr. Carson, we do not fall in love, and I strongly advise you to guard against emotional feeling. There are surgical techniques in psycho-neurology for curing conditions of emotional distortion."

For the first time since his rebirth Carson found himself experiencing misgivings about the society in which he was inextricably involved.

Presently they returned to the hover aircraft. The girl took over the controls and flew the machine at high speed towards the surface settlement in its transparent dome. During the return journey the voice of Mr. Jaff spoke quietly into Carson's ear, no longer jerky and staccato, but using the blended fluency of his natural tongue.

Be careful, Mr. Carson. Do not allow the emotional pattern of a dead age to twist your life in this new era. The Cayne woman is merely a part of your rehabilitation procedure. Do not pursue useless affinities. There will be other women in the thousands of years that lie ahead of you. Emotion is for the mortal animal, living under the shadow of approaching death—it has no place among immortals. From the vantage point of eternity one takes a more remote and objective view.

Carson made no reply, but simply studied the girl's enchanting profile as the aircraft sped swiftly through the thin Martian atmosphere towards the settlement.

The spaceport was an enormous cavern buried deep below the surface of Mars. From the entrance it was impossible to see the far wall, and the ceiling, perhaps a quarter of a mile high, was a vast area of liquid light, as if a molten sun had been spread over the solid rock. The air, cool, and refreshing, was generated and circulated by an atmosphere plant beneath the floor on which he stood.

Carson was accompanied by a tall, leather-skinned astronaut named Trajectory Brince, who had been assigned by authority to show him how the Martian colony dealt with the simple matter of space flight. One look at the line of giant space ships poised on their ramps along the length of the cavern convinced Carson that if space flight was simple, as Brince had implied, then it was only so because of the tremendous complexity of the space vehicles. Alongside any one of these ships the old, ill-fated *Wanderer II* would have been a mere cigar.

"These are freighters," said Brince, as they walked towards the nearest ship. "They operate a regular schedule to the moon, where they pick up raw materials and synthetics which we lack on Mars. In return we export finished products and equipment which they can't make on Earth. There is also a periodic run to Venus, and occasional provisioning runs to the expeditions on Mercury and Ganymede."

"Why doesn't Earth send freight ships to Mars?" Carson enquired.

"Because they haven't got any big enough or powerful enough. It takes them all their time to run a shuttle service to the moon.

Also, politics are involved. We can no more land on Earth than they can land on Mars."

"Why not?"

Brince glanced wryly at Carson. "Haven't you been told? Earth and Mars are in a state of war. Quiescent, of course. There hasn't been any actual fighting for more than two thousand years, but the situation has produced a fine crop of restrictions and prohibitions and do's and don'ts—mainly don'ts."

Carson expressed his surprise, and Brince merely grinned.

"It all started when we tried to re-establish contact with Earth after a particularly vicious series of nuclear wars. They were busy trying to rebuild their industries. They wanted equipment and scientists in exchange for raw materials, and they also asked for genetically screened immigrants, men and women, from Mars, in order to introduce unmutated strains into terrestrial human breeding. You've no idea how much trouble mutation caused, and is still causing. If you'd seen some of the monsters that were produced by genetic damage in the atomic wars. . . ."

"Naturally you refused," Carson put in.

"Not immediately. We were prepared to be reasonable. The fact was that not a single man or woman or scientist was willing to return to Earth to live. They didn't care for the high radiation level and the rationing and the disease. So we were forced to decline. The military government on Earth immediately cut off all supply of raw materials, which left us in difficulties. That was the start of the first interplanetary war."

They had reached the enormous space ship now and were walking among the vertical girders of the service gantry. Engineers were swarming over the hull, moving equipment into open ports. The ship was streamlined in the manner of a swallow, with slender swept-back wings. It reared up on its tilted ramp as if ready at any instant to soar upwards through the ceiling and into the vacuum of space.

"Atomic propulsion up to escape velocity," said Brince, "then gravity reactors and photon drive. It's possible to reach speeds in excess of five-hundred miles a second, though we seldom do because of the high acceleration involved. No human could withstand it. Sometimes we cruise at around two hundred miles a second."

"Who started the war?" asked Carson, unwilling to change the subject.

"We did," Brince stated blandly. "We spent about two-hundred years building an armed invasion fleet, then we blasted off from Mars and established a beach-head on Earth, in the Mediterranean area. Took the terrestrials completely by surprise, I can tell you, and held them at bay for half a century. But we had our problems too—mainly logistics. The supply lines from Mars to Earth were too vulnerable, and we lost a lot of ships—and we didn't get much in the way of raw material because of systematic sabotage. With the aid of superior weapons and good communications we managed to hold all the territory surrounding the Mediterranean, but we failed to get a footing in America or Russia, as those countries were known in your age."

"I doubt if the Mediterranean area would be much good to anyone," Carson remarked, "particularly from an industrial point of view. Oil, perhaps, in Africa and the Near East, and some minerals, but not much else."

"True," Brince admitted, "but we had to hold on. Withdrawal would have meant defeat and loss of prestige. In the end both sides came to terms. There was a cease-fire and a trade agreement. Several hundred years of uneasy peace followed. Then there was another war, and after that a third. They all ended in stalemate."

"Did they get their men and women scientists?"

"No," said Brince, shaking his head vigorously. "We compromised by offering a scientific and technological advisory service to help them rebuild their civilization. We have teams of scientists on Mars who try to solve Earth's problems by remote control, as it were. Trade channels were set up, using the moon as a kind of exchange warehouse. Our ships are not allowed to go nearer to Earth than the Lunar orbit, otherwise they might get shot down by a nuclear homing missile."

"It all sounds very unsatisfactory to me," Carson observed sadly. "Why can't human beings get together to solve their problems instead of attempting to destroy each other?"

"They never have throughout history. Earth is governed by a ruthless military dictatorship, and although we exchange commodities and materials we are still officially at war. The next invasion will be the final one. We have learned a great deal in earlier campaigns and we shall make no mistakes. We have the strength, the ships and the weapons—and we have you."

"Me?" Carson echoed, taken aback.

Brince laughed tersely. "You are our principal weapon, Carson. Don't ask me why or how. You'll find out all in the course of time."

After that Brince became relatively uninformative, as if aware that he might already have said too much. He confined himself to conversation about the rocket fleet, answering Carson's technical questions in a facile, expert manner. They watched as one of the freighters, ready for launching, was towed on its ramp by a powerful squat tractor (an iron mule, Brince pointed out) which pulled it onto a huge metal platform level with the floor of the cavern. From afar came the thunder of power generators, and slowly the platform began to ascend towards the distant roof, without support, like a steel magic carpet.

"Gravity reactors," Brince explained. "A controlled version of antimatter. Expensive to operate but it saves having to use a lot of even more expensive elevating machinery."

They waited until the space ship on its platform seemed to disappear into the haze of incandescent light obscuring the ceiling. "There is actually a cavity, but the light conceals it," said Brince. "It's like trying to see a sunspot without a neutral filter. The ship will go right up through the ceiling, then through an air lock, and out on to the surface. We can go up and watch from an observation dome if you wish."

Carson indicated his agreement. They walked back across the floor of the cavern to the main entrance, where Brince ushered him into a small elevator compartment and pressed a wall button. Wind sighed softly around them, and suddenly the elevator was whining upwards through a long vertical shaft.

"Compressed air this time," said Brince. "It's cheaper than antigravity for small loads."

The elevator stopped so quickly that Carson's stomach turned over in a way that reminded him of free-fall in space. They stepped out into a narrow corridor and emerged, beyond an airlock, into a small transparent dome housing control equipment of unimaginable function. Two men were adjusting knobs and switches. Beyond the dome the space ship rested silently on its sloping ramp, awaiting the moment of take-off.

As he watched, the ramp tilted slowly towards the vertical, pushing the nose of the spacecraft high into the dark blue sky. A chronometer impassively ticked off the seconds. Abruptly the jets at the base of the ship exploded into yellow cascading flame.

The great rocket rose tumultuously on its pedestal of fire, gathering speed, then veered off into the darkness of space like an
enormous bird.

"The moon in four days," Brince commented, "or perhaps
less if the pilot feels inclined to give her the full boost."

Carson nodded appreciatively. "It's not so very different, after
all . . . from my own day, I mean. One can still sense a feeling
of nostalgia. The basic procedures don't change."

Brince regarded him shrewdly. "There's more to it than basic
procedure, Carson. And watch out for that feeling of nostalgia
you mentioned. It can be a dangerous thing."

Carson fully expected a lecture from Mr. Jaff on his indiscretion,
but the tiny transceiver in his ear remained silent. Perhaps Mr.
Jaff didn't feel quite so strongly about nostalgia as he did about
love.

CHAPTER SIX

IT was with a feeling of utter desolation that Carson said
goodbye to Competence Cayne at the end of his three weeks
stay in the surface settlement. He knew only too well that he had
allowed himself to become emotionally attached to her to an
undesirable extent, and he could not avoid an overwhelming
sense of personal loss when the moment came for parting. There
was nothing he could say to her; Mr. Jaff would undoubtedly be
listening, and in any case he was forced to admit to himself the
futility of attempting to appeal to her on an emotional level. *Love
is an obsessive form of compulsion neurosis,* she had once said,
and there was certainly nothing obsessive or compulsive or
neurotic about Competence Cayne.

They said their goodbyes quite formally in the apartment.
In a few minutes two official guides were scheduled to take him
back to the underground city. He held her in his arms for a while,
kissing her lightly. She remained passive but amiable, as if already
relaxing now that her tour of duty was almost over. Presently
she withdrew herself gently from his embrace.

"You are now rehabilitated to all intents and purposes," she
said. "I wish you success in whatever assignments you may be
elected to carry out."

"Thank you," he replied solemnly. "Personally, I think I would
prefer to stay on the surface. I was just beginning to settle down."

"One cannot remain convalescent forever. You have learned a great deal about our society and you have learned to speak our language fluently. You must take your place in the scheme of things."

"What do you imagine will happen to me?" he asked.

She shook her head slowly. "Even if I knew, I would not be permitted to say. In time you will know everything, so do not be impatient. Remember you are immortal, too."

Through the window he could see the guides approaching across the green lawn. He kissed her for the last time and said: "Will we ever meet again?"

"Perhaps, in the course of centuries," she answered.

A few minutes later he accompanied the guides to the elevator shaft that led to the city buried deep in the bedrock of Mars. In a sense this was in itself a new adventure, for he had seen practically nothing of the underground city, even though he had spent years in the antimortic clinic. The city, he found, was built in levels, the top level being located about a mile and a half below the surface. This was primarily a residential zone, housing some twenty-thousand inhabitants. There were three other levels, one below the other, accommodating the administrative, commercial, industrial and scientific centres. Each level was an immense horizontal chamber having an area of some four square miles, and cut out of the basic rock strata by the controlled use of atomic explosives. Within the chambers, buildings and avenues were laid out spaciously in a conventional way, but the buildings extended from floor to ceiling, an expanse of some ten storeys. The avenues were lined with miniature flowering shrubs in a variety of bright, cheerful colours, and at road intersections ornamental gardens provided a touch of gaiety. Quaint streamlined vehicles without wheels glided noiselessly along the roads, suspended inexplicably about twelve inches above the surface. Probably antigravity, Carson thought. Warm, even light came from large luminescent panels mounted on the roof. As always the air was cool, fresh and invigorating.

The guides took him direct to the second level and delivered him to an official in a massive block of offices. He was then escorted along corridors to a translucent door with a small metallic panel bearing the inscription: *Mentor Jaff—Department of Co-ordination.* The official pressed a tiny button set in the wall, at which an electronic tone echoed hollowly in the corridor.

The door slid quietly open, disappearing into the wall. Carson entered the room alone.

Tubby Mr. Jaff, his red hair slightly awry, was sitting at a desk of futuristic aspect, watching images on a stacked bank of video screens mounted in the adjacent wall. The office resembled a laboratory and contained, so far as Carson could judge, more electronic equipment than furniture. He remembered the aural transceiver and decided that this must be Mr. Jaff's monitoring centre; at the same time he found himself wondering just how many citizens of Mars were subjected to radio eavesdropping—and video surveillance, too, from the appearance of the active screens.

Mr. Jaff clicked five switches, one after the other, swung round in his chair, stood up and came round his desk to greet Carson.

"You're looking well," he observed affably. "Fit and relaxed. I can see that you made the most of your three weeks on the surface. Sit down, anyway, Mr. Carson."

Carson sat down on one of the slender metal chairs, while Mr. Jaff hovered around portentously.

"Say something," he went on. "Say: the optimistic inhabitants of the refulgent satellite were dedicated to the aesthetic principles of technocracy. Say it in one semantic blended sound."

Carson thought for a moment, then said it. Mr. Jaff beamed in genuine pleasure.

"I can see that Dr. Groor has excelled himself," he remarked. "The accent is perfect—the blending, too, though perhaps just a little premeditated. However, given time. . . ." He waved his hands airily towards Carson. "Now for practical details. We have an apartment for you on the first level—a luxurious apartment, I might say, where you will be well looked after. Anything you need, just ask for. The adjacent apartments will be occupied by a selected team of very attractive women whose duty it is to make sure that you lack nothing."

Carson made a wry smile. "I've already met the woman I would choose to be with . . ." he began, but Mr. Jaff shook his head vehemently.

"Impossible, Mr. Carson—*she* is a very important member of a government research team. You will have to be content with females whose duties to the State have a lower priority."

"I see," said Carson reflectively.

Mr. Jaff's eyes twinkled merrily. "You will have no cause for complaint. The majority of our citizens would wish to be in your privileged position."

"But why should I be privileged? I don't fully understand my place in the pattern of your society."

"At the very top, Mr. Carson," said the other man genially.

"But why?"

"Because you are Robert Carson—the man who sacrificed his life in the first attempt to orbit the moon, using a primitive liquid-fuel rocket. You died in that childish, suicidal gadget called the Wanderer II. You were dead for eight thousand years, and then we gave you back your life. Isn't that a good enough reason?"

"No," said Carson firmly, beginning to feel vaguely irritated by Mr. Jaff's faintly patronizing manner. "You're trying to advance sentimentality as a motive, but I know that sentiment plays no part in Martian society."

Mr. Jaff raised one amused eyebrow and eyed him shrewdly, but said nothing.

"I don't believe this revitalized hero angle at all," Carson continued. "If there's a motive it has to be a good solid motive based on reason rather than sentiment. Hero worship is plainly false."

"How right you are!" commented Mr. Jaff amiably, pursing his lips. "Perhaps I was simply indulging in a little harmless flattery. At the same time, I merely recited fact. In your own day you were a very great hero."

"This is not my own day. Heroism rarely survives a period of eight thousand years. I'll admit that perhaps I have what you might call an interesting case history, and I'm grateful to your scientists for having restored my life. But what I really want to know is, what do you intend to do with me, Mr. Jaff?"

"Nothing. Absolutely nothing."

"But surely . . . ?"

"We have no plans for you, Mr. Carson, other than to make life as pleasant as possible for you. Of course, there may be minor matters of publicity to attend to. Video recordings, interviews and so on. People will be interested in you, particularly those on Earth."

"Earth?" Carson echoed suspiciously.

"Why not? Your point of origin, surely."

Carson sighed impatiently. "I still don't understand. Are you trying to tell me that I am to be kept like some kind of animal in a zoo—as a kind of interesting specimen for the inhabitants of two planets to talk about?"

"Not at all. By merely being alive you are already fulfilling a most important function. Frankly, it would take too long to explain here and now, and there are a number of policy matters to be decided. Military matters, too, I might add. You, Mr. Carson, may well prove to be the means of saving Earth itself. As you know, the Martian colony has on three occasions attempted to take over control of Earth in its own interests, but war across millions of miles of space is an extremely difficult and hazardous operation. More than anything we have needed a symbol, a figurehead to apply a strong psychological thrust to any projected military campaign. It is our belief that you are that symbol."

Carson spread out his hand helplessly. "But I still don't understand why."

Mr. Jaff chuckled. "Of course you don't, but you will. You must have patience. It is all a simple matter of economics. You, Mr. Carson, own the Earth. Just take my word for it. The Earth is yours, and that is why you are so important to us. While we possess you we also possess the Earth in law. That is why we must take good care of you."

He crossed to the desk and pressed a button. "Meanwhile, forget about it. Relax and amuse yourself. Learn as much as you can about our Martian society and technology—it will help you to orientate yourself, and when the time comes for explanations you will understand things more easily."

"I'll try," said Carson wearily.

The door slid open and a smooth, dark-haired young man entered the room.

"Take Mr. Carson to his apartment on the first level," Mr. Jaff ordered. "Introduce him to his women and show him the facilities available."

The young man smiled and inclined his head obediently. Carson pushed himself out of his chair and made his way to the door.

The apartment was certainly luxurious, as Mr. Jaff had stated, and it was also novel. The main room was circular in shape, about twenty feet in diameter, with one oval window overlooking a broad avenue bisected by a central strip of garden. The decor was, if anything, effeminate, as opposed to the usual clinically cold colour schemes in general favour. The furniture was bigger and more comfortable. The floor was covered with a green carpet which, on close inspection, proved to be a miniature and perfectly accurate facsimile of an area of Martian bubble-grass. Three doors in the room opened into a circular passage in which further doors gave access to other rooms. One was a library, but in place of books on the wall shelves there were metallic plaques bearing finely engraved patterns, while nearby stood an electronic reproducing device fitted with an attachment which appeared to be designed to cover the head. Like the language indoctrinator, as he discovered later, this was a machine for injecting visual images direct into the mind, so that one lived the story and, in a dreamlike way, the characters and situations became real. That the library of plaques was mainly erotic in nature did not surprise him.

There was a restfully designed bedroom, and an all-electronic kitchen plus an adjoining cold-store room with frost on the walls; and there was a bathroom with a huge bath in which one could easily swim. Other doors opened into further corridors which connected with other apartments sited concentrically around his own; there were four in all, occupied by the women who had been assigned to look after him.

The women! To meet them all at once was an ordeal, particularly when the memory of Competence Cayne still obsessed his mind. He never did recall their individual names, but Mr. Jaff had evidently used a certain expertise in their selection. They were all young, with an apparent age group of twenty to thirty, though, as Carson realized only too well, physical appearance was no guide to their real ages as immortals, and they all had the same basic shape—the shape which interests a man. The prettiest had auburn hair and quite the pinkest complexion he had seen on Mars; another was a blonde, almost a platinum blonde, with an attractive piquancy of features; the third had long jet black hair and sultry eyes; and the fourth was an ordinary girl with brown hair and blue eyes, but, in some subtle way, the most feminine and beautiful of them all.

Despite the quadruple charm which they exerted on him, Carson dismissed them at the earliest possible moment with as much decorum as he could muster, and retired to the circular room, where he sat by the window for a long time, watching the hovercars flash by on the highway below, lost in his own private world of confused thought.

I'm important, he told himself, and yet all I'm required to do is precisely nothing—just lounge about and amuse myself. Jaff has hinted that I own the Earth, but I don't really know whether he means it literally or not. It's an impossible concept, anyway. How can anyone own a planet . . . particularly a planet ravaged by atomic wars and peopled by mutants, a planet with which we are in a state of suspended war? Jaff is clearly talking nonsense for some obscure purpose of his own. On the other hand, why should I be brought back to life in order to lead a reclusive lotus-eating existence in a compact, highly organized society in which every individual must surely have an allotted duty to perform?

Let's add up the facts, he thought. I'm Robert Carson from the twentieth century, an ordinary sort of character, certainly not a hero. When it came to the point I was terrified of death. Eight thousand years have gone by. Somehow or other they found *Wanderer II* orbiting round the sun, and took my dead body from the rocket and brought me back to Mars. They gave me the full antimortic treatment, and here I am alive. So what happens? I'm sent off on a three-week vacation to learn the language and pick up snippets of information about Mars and Earth and make love to a beautiful woman. Then I'm shut away in a luxury apartment with four more women and told to do nothing. It doesn't add up at all.

Suddenly he remembered the miniature transceiver in his ear. "Mr. Jaff," he said aloud. "Mr. Jaff, this is Carson."

The transceiver clicked faintly. *Yes?* said the resonant voice of Mr. Jaff.

"I want to know what it's all about," Carson said aggressively. "I want to know why I'm being treated like a stuffed specimen in a museum."

Mr. Jaff's voice became silky. *Nonsense. You are being treated as if you were a millionaire—which is precisely what you are.*

"Why am I a millionaire?"

Because you own the Earth.

"Then, if I own the Earth, I shall go there. After all, Earth is my point of origin, as you yourself said."

You will go where you are told to go, Mr. Carson, said Mr. Jaff incisively. *Your orders are to relax and enjoy yourself, and that*

you will do, even if it means using force. Do not be ungrateful.
We have given you your life, and now your life belongs to us.

The transceiver clicked into silence.

"Hello," Carson shouted, as if he were using a telephone. "Hello, Mr. Jaff."

There was no reply.

He stared sullenly out of the oval window at the wide road below, and abruptly he surrendered to a mood of stubborn independence. I'll roam the city, he thought. I'll find something to do somewhere. Not even Jaff can force me to relax and enjoy myself if I don't want to.

Angrily he walked out of the room and made his way down to the highways of the first level.

Within a few minutes he had lost all sense of direction, for the rectangular pattern of the residential blocks was always the same, and the highways were alike enough to make recognition difficult. Each road bore a number, but that did not help, for he had already forgotten the route number of the road in which his own apartment was situated.

He was glad to be lost, and walked on buoyantly, making good speed in the lesser gravity of Mars. Occasionally he passed other men and women, but they took no notice of him apart from a random curious glance here and there. The hovercars fascinated him. Coming suddenly upon a line of them parked at the side of the highway, he felt tempted to borrow one for an experimental attempt at driving, but quickly abandoned the idea as too risky. For the present it was enough to remain anonymous and free.

After walking for about a mile and a half in a direction which he judged to be roughly diagonally across the city, he found himself in front of a small functional building resembling, in certain respects, the Underground railway stations in the London of his own age. A sign, flashed alternately on each side of the entrance, announced in big bright letters: UP—DOWN. He recognized the place as the vertical elevator shaft in which he had travelled from the second level after his interview with Mr. Jaff—perhaps even the same one in which he had made the long descent from the surface settlement. Suddenly he saw the elevator as a further medium of escape: he could descend to the third and fourth levels and roam around the industrial and scientific zones, and. . . . A fantastic idea seemed to explode in his mind. He might even find his way to one of the big spaceports and conceal himself in a rocket bound for the moon, and from there find his way to Earth.

So staggered was he by this thought that he spent fully five minutes walking in circles around the elevator building, trying to see the plan from all angles, realizing the sheer impracticability of it, but fascinated by the possibility of revisiting his home planet. I need time to consider, he told himself—one can't do this kind of thing on impulse. In any case, I don't yet know where any of the spaceports are located. The one I visited is close to the surface settlement, and the settlement is vertically above the city. It's a question of direction rather than distance, but I can't reasonably make enquiries because Mr. Jaff would overhear. It may be possible to get hold of a map, if they have such things outside government offices. At all events, the best thing to do for the moment is explore the other levels and gain a sense of orientation in this strange anthill society.

Men and women were walking in and out of the entrance to the elevator station. He waited until a group of commuters entered in a solid mass, and tagged along behind, following them into the building towards the barrier rail adjoining a small office. At this point he knew he had blundered.

An official at a gate in the barrier, wearing a black cape with a gold insignia across the shoulders, was inspecting cards which the travellers were producing in the manner of season tickets. Carson stopped dead, then turned round and began to walk away. An instant later he was intercepted by another black-caped official.

"Can I help you?" asked the official pleasantly.

"No, no," Carson said quickly. "I've changed my mind."

The official raised his eyebrows in surprise, as if people of the Martian colony seldom if ever changed their minds.

"Which level do you want?" he demanded.

Carson said nothing, but looked around desperately, knowing that Mr. Jaff would be monitoring the unexpected conversation.

"Perhaps I'd better see your social zone assignment card," the official suggested.

"That's the trouble," Carson said with sudden inspiration. "I forgot to bring it. I'll have to go back to my apartment to fetch it."

Without bothering to argue further he walked straight out of the elevator station and lost himself on the highway. Perhaps Jaff didn't hear, he thought. He can't eavesdrop all the time, and there must be moments when he has other things to do. But even as he consoled himself, the transceiver clicked ominously in his ear.

Where are you, Mr. Carson? said the voice of Mr. Jaff.

Carson made no reply, but hurried on his way.

Why did you go to the elevator station? asked the voice.

Silence from Carson.

I'm afraid you are being disobedient, even defiant. You had better return to your apartment.

Carson ignored the instruction and continued to walk on.

I'm ordering you to return to your quarters. Block fourteen on Highway seven.

A further interval of silence.

Mr. Jaff sighed audibly in Carson's ear. *Very well, Mr. Carson. There are ways and means. I'm sorry to have to do this, but you are, after all, being antisocial.*

Seconds passed by slowly. He's given up, Carson thought. He's realized that even a permanent radio link can't force one to obey orders. All he can do is try to hunt me down with security officials. . . .

It happened so suddenly that he was completely taken by surprise. The transceiver in his ear burst abruptly into a nightmarish high-pitched whistle of painful intensity, a warbling discordant whistle way up in the supersonic spectrum. He stopped in his tracks, frantically clutching his head.

Go back, urged a strange new mechanical voice, speaking in metallic tones above the deafening hiss of the whistle. *Go back. Go back. Go back. Block fourteen. Highway seven. Go back. Go back.*

For minutes Carson stood motionless, biting his lips and beating his head with his fists, forcing himself to fight the noise that was boring into his brain like a high speed drill.

Go back. Go back. Block fourteen. Highway seven. Go back.

Passers-by eyed him inquisitively, but did not stop. They knew, he realized suddenly. This was a routine and they were familiar with it.

The whistle increased in pitch and intensity, and always there was the cold, remote voice. *Go back. Go back. Go back.*

"All right," he shouted, unable to stand the torment any longer. "I'll go back."

The whistle stopped and the voice of Mr. Jaff whispered gently into his ear.

Now you're being sensible, Mr. Carson. You see, orders must be obeyed, and we have the means to enforce them. Go back, and do not leave the apartment again without permission.

Humbly, all defiance gone, Carson did as he was told.

CHAPTER SEVEN

FOR several days Carson remained in his apartment, immersed in a bitter, sullen mood. The women fed him and did their best to entertain him, but he resented their presence and made it quite clear that he preferred to be left alone. At night sleep came with difficulty, for his brain was obsessed with the problem of escape. At this stage, although he knew little about the Martian social organization, he recognized the pattern of ruthless dictatorship, the subordination of the individual to the State, and the control of the mind and the will by the application of scientific method. It could be, he thought ironically, that this was the ultimate destiny of the human race, to be welded into rigid social and national units by authoritarian power—the ant-hill society, typified physically by the underground honeycomb of highways and buildings that comprised the city. He had witnessed the beginnings of it on Earth in the twentieth century: the gradual absorption of the individual into the machinery of the State, and the establishment of totalitarian rule, as if, in some incomprehensible way, this were destined to be the next step in the communal organization of the human species. First the family, then the tribe, then the political party, and with the abolition of parties the nation, personified in a single leader; and finally the entire planetary population, directed and con-trolled and governed by an impersonal authority possessing the power to compel obedience.

He was eager for knowledge, but in the absence of books there was only frustration, for he could not ask questions without alerting the ever-listening Mr. Jaff. However, he remembered his earlier thoughts on the subject of communication by writing, and decided to make an experiment. One afternoon he sent for the brown-haired girl who, it seemed to him, possessed more intrinsic sincerity than the others. He motioned her into a chair, then with the aid of a pad of paper and a graphomatic stylus contrived to carry on a written conversation.

I want to ask you some questions, he wrote. I can't talk because I am being monitored by the government. Will you help me?

She took the stylus and pad and wrote her reply.

I'll try.

How long have you lived on Mars?

You mean how old am I?

Yes.

Six-hundred and forty-three years.

Is the government a dictatorship?

I don't know what you mean. We have a technocratic government.

Who is the leader—the president?

The words are meaningless. We have no leader.

But who decides the important issues—life and death, or war and peace?

Nobody. The issues decide themselves. The government is well aware of the climate of public opinion.

Carson sighed, wondering for a moment whether he should abandon his quest. He made one more attempt.

People are forced by scientific means to do things that they do not wish to do. Is that democracy?

How many people really know what they want to do, anyway? They need guidance. And what is democracy?

In your technocracy, who is the leader, the most important man, the one who exercises ultimate control?

She regarded him archly before writing her reply. *You are, Robert Carson.*

Why?

Because you own the Earth.

Carson gave up at that point. It was the same old endless circle, leading nowhere and merely adding to the confusion. The girl had obviously been well briefed, indoctrinated, brainwashed, or whatever you liked to call it. He put the stylus and pad to one side and looked at her in a sour, practical frame of mind.

"Thank you," he said quietly. "I selected you because I like you most of all."

She smiled appreciatively.

"You have intelligence and beauty," he went on. "I've been in an abstract mood for a few days, but now I have decided that I will make love to you." Let Mr. Jaff make of that what he wishes, he thought sardonically.

"I am at your service," she murmured politely.

"What is your name?" he asked.

"Zenna. Sublimity Zenna."

"Sublimity?" he queried.

"Of course," she whispered. "Would you like me to prove it?"

He thought briefly of Competence Cayne; somehow it seemed like an eternity since he had last seen her. Then he thought of plump, devious Mr. Jaff, and on the balance he felt himself to be utterly dispassionate and cold-blooded. They are using me, he thought, and therefore I am entitled to use *them*. They gave me my life, then took it back: now I have the right to do with it as I wish, and if it comes to the point, immortal though I may be, I can always seek death. For the present I shall cut my losses and console myself with Sublimity.

Deliberately, and hating himself, he escorted her to the bedroom.

After nearly a week of frustrating inactivity, during which Carson was confined to his apartment with no news of events in the outside world and was confronted with the discreet reticence of the women, he received two visitors. They were tall, sombre men, wearing the black capes and gold insignia of officialdom.

"Are you the man who claims to be Robert Carson?" asked one, looking him over with cold, expressionless eyes.

"I *am* Robert Carson," he insisted.

"Then I must ask you to accompany us to the headquarters of the Internal Security Division of the Martian Executive Council."

Carson backed away in sudden apprehension. "Now wait a minute. . . ."

"It is a State order," said the official curtly. "You must obey."

"But—is anything wrong?"

"There are a number of questions which you are required to answer."

Carson wondered whether he ought to appeal to Mr. Jaff, but he decided that he was probably behind the move, anyway. He made no further protest, but accompanied the men to street level and sat beside one of them in a small black hovercar while the other took the controls. The car moved forward gently, lifting itself inch by inch from the surface of the road, then suddenly hurtling forward in a burst of high acceleration. Buildings flashed past on either side, and in less than a minute they were swooping into a wide circular tunnel that curved downwards in a long spiral to the second level. He recognized the more massive buildings of the governmental administration zone. Presently the car stopped outside an imposing porch above which a large illuminated sign spelled out the words: *Internal Security Division.*

He got out of the car and was conducted into the building, along a spacious corridor and via an elevator to a room on the tenth storey. Walking between the guards he entered the room, to find himself facing a group of four bleak-faced men spaced around a long table curved in the shape of a horseshoe. In the centre space of the horseshoe was a swivel chair. He was invited to sit down. The officials who had brought him in retired to the end of the room near the door, where they remained standing, taut and erect.

On the table in front of each man was a white plaque bearing a number, and, beyond the table, set high in the wall, was a rectangular translucent panel behind which he thought he could detect a shadowy movement. The men were numbered one, two, three and four, in sequence, and it soon became apparent that number one was the leader of the tribunal, for he took the initiative and did most of the talking.

"You are the man who claims to be Robert Carson," said the number one flatly, referring to a document on the table.

"I *am* Robert Carson," said Carson a little wearily.

"Whether you are, or not, is the subject of this enquiry. At present it is a claim. There is a further claim on record, namely, that you own the Earth."

"I have never claimed that," Carson protested.

"The claim was registered on your behalf."

"Mr. Jaff suggested it. There never was any explanation, and it never made sense to me."

"If you are Robert Carson, then it makes excellent sense. However, it may interest you to know that your Mr. Jaff is under arrest for subversive activity contrary to the interests of the State, and you are implicated. That is why we have brought you here to answer questions."

Carson remained silent while his mind spun, trying to reconstruct his knowledge of Martian affairs from an entirely new angle. Finally he said: "I understood that Mr. Jaff was a responsible government official."

"He was," put in number three ominously. "Subversion is a cancer which can strike at all levels of society."

"For the purposes of this investigation," number one went on, "you will be known as Mr. Zero—a non-entity. If you are indeed Robert Carson, then it is for you to prove it."

"So I'm guilty until proven innocent," said Carson with irony.

Number one smiled fractionally. "It is often as necessary to prove innocence as it is to prove guilt. Tell me, Mr. Zero, what makes you think that you are Robert Carson?"

"The same thing that gives anyone a sense of personal identity. I know who I am. Is that unreasonable?"

"Yes—most unreasonable. Identities can easily be changed with the aid of modern techniques in psychoneural indoctrination. You were in clinic for a long time and your treatment was supervised by Mr. Jaff."

"Then whom do you imagine I am?" Carson asked irritably.

"We think we know. Some years ago a member of one of our astronautical groups disappeared without trace. Later it was learned that he was associated with a subversive organization."

Number two opened a file and produced a photograph, which he handed to Carson. "This is the man."

It was a colour photograph, in some odd way three-dimensional, and, as Carson had anticipated, it was a picture of himself.

"I'll agree it looks like me," he commented, handing it back, "but, in fact, it can't be me, because a few years ago I was dead."

Number one smiled thinly. "How does one know one is dead —particularly in retrospect? Perhaps you were merely unconscious. Perhaps they erased all memory of your former life and substituted the synthetic memory of this Robert Carson."

Carson took time off to think carefully. His initial anxiety and apprehension had given way to something more positive, and now he recognized the subtle intrigue behind the threat, even though he could not understand the motive. The tribunal might be sincere in their attitude, and they might have evidence of a plot to create a substitute Robert Carson by using brainwashing techniques; but he was equally sincere, and absolutely certain of his true identity. Unless. . . .

For a frightening instant the idea entered his mind that they could possibly be right, that he was, in fact, an ordinary member of the Martian community brainwashed into believing that he was Carson. There was no real evidence that he had been revived from the dead, and no proof that his internal organs had been replaced or reinforced. The electronic panel of coloured lights which purported to indicate the increasing flow of his returning life might just as well have been a simple visual gimmick to deceive him while psychoneural indoctrination was effected under the influence of drugs. Dr. Wier, the antimortic specialist, could have been a fake, and perhaps there was no such science as antimortics, after all.

A moment later reason returned. There had to be a starting point in all human knowledge, and the point of origin was the self, and the intuitive awareness of personal identity. Next came memory, in particular the intimate memories of his early life before the fatal launching of *Wanderer II*. No amount of brainwashing could imprint in his mind the vivid, living images of his mother and father which were already indelibly there, and the others, Valerie with her dark hair, and friends such as Keegan and Brown; and all the little trivial incidents of living that so often assumed a sentimental and nostalgic quality in later years. And there were the crowded memories of Earth itself, the blue skies and the white clouds, the rain and the snow, the green fields and the grey buildings and the people—millions of people living out their brief lives with their loves and hates and ambitions and disillusionments.

I can prove I'm Robert Carson, he thought, to the satisfaction of any tribunal, however hostile and prejudiced.

He turned to number one with more optimism and said: "My memory is not synthetic. If you want proof, I can give you proof. I can tell you about my life on Earth in the twentieth century. I can give you details which no Martian colonist could possibly know—which go far beyond the scope of indoctrination."

"Very well," number one agreed. "Say what you have to say, and take as long as you like. We have the whole day before us."

Carson marshalled his thoughts and began talking.

Carson talked for more than four hours, reminiscing fluently, and as the time went on he became more and more absorbed in his recollections. Melancholy crept quietly into his mind. At intervals he was interrupted by staccato questions from members of the tribunal, but he was able to answer without hesitation. He was speaking in the sure knowledge of things remembered, and identifying himself increasingly with the past. The more he talked, the more he wanted to continue talking, but in the end fatigue overtook him. He finished the outline of his early life and said his final words.

Number one stared at him profoundly for a while, then murmured: "Thank you, Mr. Zero. I think now we had better break off for a meal."

The black-caped officials strode forward and escorted him to a room on a lower floor where he ate alone, served by an attractive girl with an impassive face. The food was to formula: rainbow fragments possessing negligible flavour, and there was black, hot fluid to drink, neither coffee nor tea, but slightly piquant and not unpalatable.

Almost an hour later he returned to the conference room and faced the tribunal again. He was aware of a subtle change in the atmosphere; their manner had changed from discerning interest to mild scepticism.

"You have told us a plausible enough story, Mr. Zero," said number one, opening the proceedings, "and it is fairly evident that you have a remarkable memory for detail. Perhaps in the ordinary way we might be convinced, but there are a number of factors which require explanation. We have allowed you to have your say, and you have talked of Earth in the twentieth century and the people you claim to have known. Now, perhaps, you will reasonably let us have our say."

"Of course," Carson said.

"First, a question. Where is the rocket known as *Wanderer II*?"

"I'm afraid I don't know. Presumably it was brought back to Mars, or left wandering in space."

"Would you recognize the rocket if you saw it?"

"I think so."

Number one turned towards number two, who produced a number of photographs from a plastic folder. Carson leaned forward to take them. They were colour pictures, three-dimensional as before, and he inspected them carefully. The first showed a stone plateau or plinth centred in a restrained garden against a background of tall, distant buildings, and poised on the plateau was a rocket, slender and cigar-shaped, which he was able to identify because of certain markings on the stabilizing fins. Superficially it was the *Wanderer II*, apparently erected on its stone plinth of some kind of monument or monolith. The sky in the picture was blue, with striations of white cloud.

The next photograph depicted the interior of the control cabin of the rocket. Carson ran his eye over the familiar array of instruments, each one in its exact place. The definition was so good that it was even possible to read the titles of some of the books on the small shelf which housed the library. They were the same books, undeniably.

The remaining four pictures showed interior detail of the rocket's propulsion and servo equipment, including one close-up of the dislodged and damaged fuel pump which had been responsible for the failure of the transverse jets, but there was something wrong in the finer detail of the photograph, though he was not able to pinpoint it immediately.

He returned the photographs to number one.

"It certainly looks like *Wanderer II*," he admitted reluctantly, "but photographs are deceptive. They can be faked."

"These are not faked," said number two petulantly.

"The pictures you have just seen were taken quite recently," number one explained. "Within the last hundred years, to be precise. They show the *Wanderer II* mounted as a memorial on a stone platform in a park in London, Earth. The platform is actually a tomb, and in the tomb is the body of Robert Carson, enclosed in a transparent coffin. On the tomb is an inscription which reads—In memory of Robert Carson, the first pioneer of space. Born 1932. Died 1966. Posthumous beneficiary of the International Carson Trust, foundation of modern civilization." He paused for a moment, eyeing Carson keenly. "Does that mean anything to you?"

"Not a thing. I don't understand your reference to tombs and coffins. I'm alive, and I am Robert Carson."

"Incorrect," snapped number one. "*Wanderer II* was recovered from its solar orbit more than two thousand years ago by a terrestrial expedition. It was erected as a monument to a brave man, and his body is in its coffin on Earth at this moment, underneath the very rocket in which he gave his life. Great care has been taken to preserve both body and rocket in perfect condition throughout the centuries. Robert Carson is a national hero—

has been for eight thousand years—and the Carson Trust is a functioning reality."

"I still don't understand," said Carson dejectedly.

Number one explained. It seemed that the spectacular death of Robert Carson in the twentieth century had aroused world-wide interest and sympathy. Public imagination, already space-minded as the result of competing satellite projects between the East and West, had seized on the human interest aspect of the tragedy. Here was a man, doomed to a slow relentless death, speeding on an eternal orbit round the sun, destined to return to Earth, but never closer than some seventy-five-million miles, once every three-and-a-half years. Carson's fate supplied news-papers all over the world with headline copy for many months, and there were interviews with his relations and friends, and people who had known him only casually but had an interesting anecdote to tell.

Suddenly, a leading American newspaper, with an eye, no doubt, on its circulation figure, had launched an enterprising campaign. *Bring Carson back,* the headlines had urged. *This man typifies the human being at the peak of his courage and enterprise. Let him be brought back, together with the rocket in which he sacrificed his life for the cause of progress, so that he may be enshrined as an international symbol of peaceful endeavour, and help to bring about the ultimate brotherhood of man working in harmony for the common good.* The newspaper proposed that a fund should be established to finance a space rescue project timed to take place when the orbit of *Wanderer II* next brought it close to the Earth, and as a gesture of goodwill the proprietor of the paper, himself a millionaire, donated half-a-million dollars, which he promptly wrote off against income tax. American indus-try was quick to follow this shining and altruistic example: in a short space of time the fund had swollen to something more than five million dollars—and then it began to snowball. World opinion favoured the idea with its sentimental "bring him back to his own planet for burial" appeal, and contributions began to pour in from all nations. A Carson Trust commission was appointed to supervise the project, and the members of the commission spent their first year of office in merely counting the dollars, and vaguely wondering what to do with them. In less than two years after Carson's death more than fifty-billion dollars in every conceivable kind of currency had accumulated.

Meanwhile, the Soviets had successfully flown two dogs, a monkey and a man round the moon, and the Americans had countered with seven mice, a score of fruit flies and, in a kind of grand slam, three men, all of whom returned alive. Such is human psychology that a living man returning from space attracts less attention than a dead one not returning. Newspaper headlines still gave precedence to the Carson Trust, and made innumerable suggestions as to how the money should be used. All were agreed that a super-rocket should be constructed, equipped with various science-fictional devices designed to home on *Wanderer II*, secure it, and bring it back to Earth. In fact, the problem was not nearly so simple. Back-room boys realized that it is one thing to control a single powered rocket, but quite another to control two when linked together by magnetic grapples. The project, they announced, was certainly feasible, but in the present state of astronautical know-how, faintly impractical. It could hardly be accomplished before the *Wanderer*'s third orbit, in about ten years' time. Meanwhile, the sensible thing to do was obviously to invest the money of the Carson Trust in industry, on an international basis, so that it might increase over the years. And after due deliberation the Trust commission, acting through carefully selected accountants and stockbrokers, invested their fifty-billion dollars in the major industrial enterprises of the world. The preferred industries were those concerned with atomic power, metallurgy and astronautics—and inevitably, armaments.

War broke out three years later, the first of a series of skirmishing wars between East and West, involving buffer territories. It was not an atomic war, for both sides were wary of committing themselves to nuclear weapons, and were suitably deterred, for the time being, by the ultimate deterrent; but rockets and missiles carrying high-explosive warheads were employed in immense numbers, while the industries concerned with the manufacture of nuclear weapons were busily stockpiling their wares against future necessity. Atomics and astronautics boomed; share values rocketed; capital appreciated phenomenally. The Carson Trust, financing these projects throughout the world, doubled, then trebled its value. Fifty-billion dollars rapidly bloomed into a hundred-and-fifty billion.

The tempo of the war increased, and its boundaries spread until there was hardly a nation anywhere on the planet that was not involved. From the Arctic to the Antarctic, industry became inextricably meshed in the ruthless machinery of warfare, and abstract research projects were shelved. Rockets streaked from continent to continent, and low-flying satellites peered through television eyes at enemy installations, but nobody bothered to take a shot at the moon any more. Carson was remembered for a while, but gradually the memory faded. *Wanderer II* continued to orbit the sun unheeded.

Peace came and went like pale sunshine through a rift in heavy storm clouds. The war continued into its second phase, and then the third and the fourth, always becoming more technical and impersonal. With improvements in ballistic techniques, the deployment of armies in the field became a secondary and rather superfluous operation. The true military men were the technicians and the scientists, and nations became personified individually, as it were, simply sitting back and hurling missiles at each other. As damage to property began to add up to a formidable total, so the vital industries were evacuated from likely target areas and dispersed to improbable sites in open country. The Carson Trust, under the stimulus of attack and defence, continued to flourish.

The series of wars dragged on for about two hundred years, with neither side gaining any real ascendancy. In the end it was decided, almost by mutual agreement, to call a halt to hostilities while the war-weary nations licked their wounds and rebuilt their shattered cities. The executors of the Trust fund, conscientiously applying themselves to their task, began to spread their investments into industries which would thrive most under conditions of peaceful reconstruction: building, road-making, and, fortuitously, mining. They gambled on mining because of a leakage of information from government circles which hinted that, while the peace lasted, there would be an all-out effort to build factories, essential offices, and emergency accommodation for important people deep underground, where they would be safe in the event of atomic war breaking out.

The information was accurate. Deep cavities were mined in the Earth's solid bedrock, and the basic techniques of underground engineering and construction, which were to play a vital part in the colonization of other planets in the centuries to come, were established. Vast caverns were excavated below ground, first in America, then in the countries of the Eastern Federation, and finally in Europe. Factories, offices and homes began to move below the surface of the Earth, although the mass of the population still lived, as before, under the sun and the stars.

The age of the automatic factory was well under way, of course. Automation in all phases of industry had taken most of the responsibility out of the hands of the worker, while in the commercial and administrative spheres staffs had been replaced to a large extent by machines and computers. Underground hydroponic farms were started, followed by underwater fisheries into which fish were attracted in their shoals by the use of trace chemicals released into the seas and oceans at predetermined points. Other underground caverns were converted into enormous deep-freeze stores where food supplies could be preserved for centuries, if necessary.

The nations of the world were, although they did not fully realize it, digging in and consolidating their defences for what was to come. Beneath the surface of the Earth a selected survival group could continue the fight with the full potential of a highly industrialized society, even if the mass of the population was wiped out in an atomic massacre. The peoples of the world, slowly and subtly, began to divide into two sections: the few who worked underground, and the many who spent their lives on the surface. It was a division that was later to become permanent.

Defence often provokes attack. Secure in their underground fortresses, the political and military leaders of Earth's opposing hemispheres looked anew at the delicate balance of power in the world, and began to feel optimistic about shifting it in their favour. A cold war began, slowly at first, but building up over the decades into the inevitable succession of conferences, deadlocks and threats.

And then, unexpectedly, using the latest techniques and advances in astronautics and atomic propulsion, the Western Federation shot eight manned rockets to the moon and set up an airlocked base in a lunar crater. This was, they claimed, a purely scientific expedition, but the Eastern Federation denounced the move as an act of military aggression. The political atmosphere became choked with venom.

Nobody was ever quite certain who launched the first H-missile: each side claimed that, having detected by radar the launching of an intercontinental rocket carrying a nuclear warhead into low orbit terminating on a home target, they had promptly taken the only possible reprisal action. The two missiles exploded within seconds of each other, one in the East and one in the West.

The first atomic war had begun.

CHAPTER EIGHT

THERE was an interval of five minutes for refreshment, during which Carson and the members of the tribunal sipped the black, coffee-like liquid and nibbled tasteless coloured biscuits. He reviewed the essentials of number one's narrative, recognizing the familiar pattern of history. That is how it would have happened, he thought, in just that irresponsible way. What is wrong with mankind that his genius should always be channelled into aggression and war?

When the cups had been removed, number one said: "I have told you all this because I want you to see things in the correct perspective. Robert Carson was still orbiting in space while the East and West were fighting out their differences. The first successful landing on the moon had been accomplished."

"What happened to those lunar pioneers?" Carson asked.

"They survived. Despite the atomic war, the Western Federation continued to send more rockets to the moon carrying men and supplies. And, in the course of time, so did the Eastern Federation."

"That must have created a difficult situation on the moon."

"Not at all. The moon project was, in fact, a scientific expedition, and the explorers from the East and West simply combined forces, although they were technically at war. They had sense enough to unite against the common enemy—the vacuum and cold hostility of the lunar terrain. In a way they also united against Earth, but at that time they were not independent enough to set up an autonomous colony. They had to rely on the continuing supply of food, oxygen and materials from the home planet."

"How long did the atomic war last?"

"You mean the *first* atomic war? Long enough to destroy about half the population of the world—those on the surface, of course. The underground people remained underground, safe from radiation hazards. But there were more atomic wars. It became a kind of game in which the opposing forces, secure in their underground caverns, threw an occasional H-missile at each other to register disapproval of their respective political systems. The surface people abandoned the towns and the cities and took to the caves and mountains, where they reverted to a primitive tribal life. Then, after a while, they began to give birth to mutants, and the real horror started."

"I can imagine," Carson said solemnly. "But the wars dragged on, just the same."

"Yes—for generation after generation, with the normal people living comfortably in their underground fortresses, and the mutated monsters struggling for survival on what was left of the radioactive surface of what had once been a green and pleasant Earth."

"But surely there had to be an end. . . ."

"The end came when the Carson Trust commission finally intervened. War is, after all, an industry, and a non-productive industry at that. Industries have to be financed. There came a point when the economic situation of the world was such that the war would have to cease, if only temporarily, in order to permit financial losses to be recouped. The truth was that the commission, having made a long and detailed assessment of Carson Trust assets throughout the world, realized suddenly that they were the legal owners of virtually every industry and property on the entire planet, particularly the underground installations which had largely been financed by Trust investments. The world belonged, in fact, to the dead Robert Carson, and it was his money that was being expended in a futile and expensive war that could obviously never achieve anything other than stalemate. Clearly it had to end."

"I can't quite see how the Carson Trust could exercise what amounts to political influence over two opposing military governments," Carson said.

"They used economic influence," number one pointed out. "A government derives its revenue basically from industry and commerce, and the key factor is productivity. The Carson Trust in effect controlled about ninety per cent of Earth's productivity, and had become a kind of international monetary fund acting as bankers to practically every country in the world. The commission simply withdrew credit facilities, and the wars came to an end."

"I see," Carson murmured. "The commission were, in fact, acting as a world government."

"Precisely. It was a short step from pulling economic strings to pulling political strings. Within a few years the federations of the East and West were united into a world state, with a combined government made up of delegates from all nations. But the real power, which determined policy and economics, was the Carson Trust commission. Robert Carson, dead as he was, had become ruler of the world."

Number one put the tips of his fingers together and paused to consider. "The members of the commission," he continued, "were shrewd, intelligent men, with a profound understanding of human psychology. They realized the importance of a symbol to maintain the stability of a social system. The obvious symbol was Robert Carson himself, still orbiting the sun, whose death so long ago had finally saved the Earth from self-destruction through the medium of the Carson Trust. So they resurrected the legend of Robert Carson, launching what must have been the biggest publicity campaign in all history. Then they announced that the Trust would carry out the terms of its original assignment, namely, to bring back the body of Carson and also the rocket in which he had died. Fabulous sums of money were poured into the science of astronautics, and over the decades space travel became Earth's biggest industry. That was the beginning of true interplanetary exploration, and the beginning of the colonization of Mars."

"And Robert Carson?"

"In due course they recovered *Wanderer II*, with Carson inside, and brought it back to Earth. At this time the surface cities of the planet were being rebuilt, and a national monument was erected in a London park, using the rocket as a kind of obelisk, with the body of Robert Carson entombed in a transparent coffin in the plinth. They had their symbol at last, and the world had a mystical leader, a second Messiah, whose body was on view for all to see."

"Interesting," Carson commented, "but there's one detail which is wrong. I am Robert Carson, and I am alive."

"There obviously cannot be *two* Robert Carsons," number one stated impatiently. "You have heard the facts of history and you have seen the photographic evidence."

"I also have the evidence of my own mind and memories."

"Your mind and memories could have been changed to make you a plausible impostor."

"But why? What would be the point?"

Number one smiled sardonically. "There could be several points. One would be to produce a living Robert Carson who could legitimately claim to own the Earth through the Trust fund. Another might be to seize power on Mars, using Carson as a symbol—an extension, as it were, of the terrestrial system of rule. After all, if he owned the Earth, he could logically deploy the economic resources of that planet to precipitate a crisis on this."

"I know nothing about the politics of the matter," Carson protested. "I died in *Wanderer II* and I was brought back to life eight-thousand years later. If there are ulterior motives and intrigues, I am ignorant of them. I don't want to own the Earth. All I ask is to be left alone to be myself."

"Tell me," said number two, inspecting the colour photographs, "if you *are* Robert Carson, then who is the man in the transparent coffin?"

"I don't know. An impostor, perhaps."

"And the rocket mounted on the plinth?"

"A fake, made to look exactly the same, even to the damaged fuel pump. . . ." Carson broke off abruptly as a memory stirred faintly in his mind. "May I see those pictures again, please?" he asked.

Number two pushed the photographs across the table to him. Carefully he went through them, one by one, trying to pin-point the odd twist in his memory. The full realization came to him as he reached the close-up of the wrecked fuel pump.

"This is wrong," he announced, hardly able to suppress his excitement. "According to this photograph the fuel pump was pierced through the side by the meteorite. It didn't happen that way. The damage was at the bottom, underneath the main cylindrical structure, and the hole was much bigger. The meteorite had come up at an angle."

"In that case," said number one calmly, "will you draw, to the best of your ability, exactly what the damage to the fuel pump looked like, in your opinion."

"Yes," said Carson.

Number four motioned him to the end of the table and gave him a pad of paper and a stylus. Carson then spent some ten minutes making a variety of sketches in diagrammatic form, showing the fuel pump from various angles, and outlining accurately the shape and size of the hole where the meteorite had penetrated. Finally, pleased with his draughtsmanship, he returned the pad to number four, who, after examining the drawings, passed it via his colleagues to number one.

Number one studied the diagrams for a considerable time. When he spoke his voice was quiet and non-committal. "In your view, then, Mr. Zero, the rocket in the national monument on Earth is a fake, and if one could find the real *Wanderer II* the damage to the fuel pump would be exactly as you have drawn it."

"Yes," said Carson positively.

"And you have no idea where the rocket may be?"

"I regained life and consciousness on Mars. I was not told about the rocket."

"But if it were possible to locate it, and the fuel pump proved to be damaged in the manner illustrated in your diagrams, you would, presumably, consider that as proof of the identity you claim, namely, Robert Carson."

"You are the one who requires proof, not me," Carson pointed out.

"Very well," said number one, with an air of finality. "You may go."

The black-caped officials escorted him from the room and down to street level, where they took him in the hovercar to another building in the administrative zone. During the short journey Carson found himself reviewing the details of the strange interview, unable quite to reconcile the manner of the tribunal with the charge of subversive activity which had, in effect, been made against him. He was curious, also, about the mysterious silent movements which he had observed from time to time behind the translucent panel in the wall behind the horseshoe table. Certain aspects of the interrogation seemed inconsistent and out of key, particularly the arbitrary way in which he had been released at the end—if, in fact, he *was* released. As the hovercar stopped outside a grey office block he did not feel so sure.

He followed his guides into the building and along corridors until he came to a translucent door bearing a familiar label: *Mentor Jaff—Department of Co-ordination.* Surprised and confused, he went inside the room to find himself face-to-face with plump red-haired Mr. Jaff surrounded by his video screens and electronic equipment. Mr. Jaff smiled in high humour and offered him a chair with a cordial wave of his hand. Carson sat down.

"Congratulations," said Mr. Jaff amiably. "You did very well."

Carson frowned. "I don't understand. I was told you had been arrested."

Mr. Jaff chuckled with delight. "What was the charge?" he demanded.

"Subversion."

"Excellent!" said Mr. Jaff, shaking with suppressed laughter. "I'm disappointed in you, Mr. Carson, that you should believe such an accusation. You obviously don't know me very well."

"Perhaps I don't," Carson conceded. "I would appreciate an explanation."

The laughter ceased and Mr. Jaff became very serious. "We had to anticipate the kind of interrogation you might receive if you were questioned by sceptical people, or even by the enemy. They would assume that you were an impostor, and it would be for you to prove your true identity. Proof of innocence, Mr. Carson, you understand. You were extremely convincing, and the business of the damaged fuel pump clinched the matter."

"But why all the subterfuge . . . the security tribunal, and so on?"

"Behind a polarized panel on the wall was a battery of video cameras and microphones recording every detail of the enquiry. Later we shall add a final sequence showing expert astronauts examining the interior of *Wanderer II* and confirming that the fuel pump was damaged in the way you described."

"So you *have* got the rocket," Carson exclaimed.

"Of course. It is in a guarded hangar not five miles from this office. And we also have visual records of the entire rescue operation, when a fleet of four Martian space ships spent nearly two years tracking down the *Wanderer*, and finally located it and brought it back, with you inside, of course. There are complete video recordings of the antimortic procedure, the operations to reinforce your internal organs, your first moments of new life—everything. We can prove that you are Robert Carson to the satisfaction of even the most hostile critic. We had to be sure that you could do the same, so we appointed a tribunal to conduct an investigation."

"Which means," Carson said pensively, "that the rocket and the body on show in London are fakes."

"Precisely."

"But—didn't the Trust commission ever attempt to recover the real *Wanderer*?"

"Yes, but it isn't so easy to trace a very small rocket in a vast amount of empty space. There used to be an old saying about a needle in a haystack. Small discrepancies in the predicted orbit added up to a considerable error over a long period of time, and even the best radar devices hadn't adequate range. At its furthermost point from Earth the rocket was some two-hundred-and-fifty-million miles away. The cyclic period turned out to be more like four-and-a-half years. So, all-in-all, the chances at that time were remote. The commission did the next best thing: they had an identical rocket constructed, and found a man bearing a strong physical resemblance to Robert Carson. How the man came to die is a matter for conjecture—it could even be that the body isn't human at all, but is just a synthetic dummy. However, the commission had their symbol, and they were able to abandon the futile and expensive quest for the real *Wanderer*. The population of Earth believes that the fake rocket and body were retrieved from space."

"How do you know all this?" Carson enquired.

Mr. Jaff shrugged. "Partly intelligent guesswork, and partly information received from secret agents operating on Earth. Once we suspected that *Wanderer II* was still in orbit, despite the obelisk in London, we organized an expedition to find it. We were only too successful—and here you are, the original Robert Carson, owner of Earth, alive and well."

"Thank you for my life," Carson murmured, with a hint of irony. "What interests me is—the next step."

Mr. Jaff smiled knowledgeably. "The next step has already taken place," he announced. "Three days ago a fleet of two-hundred of our biggest and most strongly armed space ships took off for Earth. By this time tomorrow the final invasion will have begun."

Carson stared incredulously at the other man.

"We are at war with Earth," breathed Mr. Jaff, savouring his words. "We have been at war before, but this is the final war. We shall restore Robert Carson to his rightful place as owner of the planet." His eyes began to gleam with ascetic fervour. "We shall dissolve the Trust commission and set up a Martian military council to govern the planet, and we shall take over the entire terrestrial economic structure. And you will be the leader, Carson. Ruler of Earth—does the idea appeal to you?"

"No," said Carson tersely. "I don't want to rule the Earth and I don't want to be implicated in war. Nor do I propose to be set up as a puppet dictator as a cover for what you call the Martian military council. I don't want any of it."

"I'm afraid you have no alternative," Mr. Jaff stated coolly. "At all times you must do as you are told. So far you have behaved reasonably well, apart from one small indiscretion at the first elevator station. Please do not spoil your record, Mr. Carson."

Carson sighed wearily. "You can obviously force me to be obedient if you wish. If that is enough, then you will be well served."

"It is enough," said Mr. Jaff, with a brisk nod of his head. "Let me outline briefly what will happen in the foreseeable future, so that you may be prepared. The invasion forces will go in and seize key centres, particularly the major underground fortresses. Reinforcements will arive almost hourly for the next six weeks. We shall seize the moon as a military base, and in due course you, Mr. Carson, will be sent to the moon so that you may be ready, at short notice, to take up your rightful heritage on Earth. Once the civil population is under control, we shall exploit the video recordings as propaganda to destroy any vestige of authority which the Trust commission might still possess. We shall expose the fake Carson, and substitute the real, living legend. With the mass of the people behind us we shall rebuild Earth as a fertile colony of Mars."

Carson laughed. "This man's father is my father's son," he murmured, recalling inconsequentially an old half-forgotten paradox. Mr. Jaff eyed him questioningly. "It's nothing," he added. "Just a private thought."

"Go back to your apartment and your women," said Mr. Jaff. "You will receive instructions in the course of time. One more thing, during your absence engineers have been installing a video screen in your apartment so that you will now be able to keep abreast of the latest news and developments in the inter-planetary situation. Previously, of course, it was necessary to keep you in ignorance for the purpose of the tribunal. Now, however, you can be accorded the privileges of a full citizen."

"Well, thank you," Carson remarked cynically, standing up.

"And don't forget," added Mr. Jaff, "that if you should be

possessed by a foolish, stubborn mood, I can always do this. . . ."

He leaned across the desk and pressed a switch on a narrow panel. Instantly Carson's head exploded into an agonizingly shrill supersonic whistle which lasted for a fraction of a second. He swayed unsteadily, clutching the desk for support, glaring sullenly at Mr. Jaff.

"Goodbye for now," said Mr. Jaff, affably.

Carson made no reply, but walked quickly from the room. In the corridor he was picked up by the black-caped officials and escorted to the hovercar. He returned to his apartment in absolute silence.

CHAPTER NINE

THE video screen was large and rectangular, about eight feet across, and following the curvature of the wall in the circular living room. The material was opalescent and not more than half-an-inch thick, but as it was not connected to any external unit, Carson assumed that the electronic parts were self-contained. One of the women showed him how to operate it by means of a scarcely visible switch on one edge. The picture came on instantly, in full colour and three dimensions; he was amazed at its solid reality.

He watched it for a while in desultory fashion, realizing that he had evidently switched on in the middle of a play concerning frivolous amorous relationships between two men and two women against a background of a biophysical research laboratory. It occurred to him that the pattern of entertainment had not changed much in eight-thousand years, although the electronic techniques of presentation had improved beyond imagination.

At the end of the play the screen darkened for a few seconds, and then, to the accompaniment of lively music, animated letters flashed across the screen spelling the title *News Digest* against a silver-speckled dark blue background resembling a formalized Milky Way.

The music faded and the picture dissolved, giving way to a curious scene which Carson found difficult to identify at first. Recognition came suddenly: he was looking at an enormous fleet of spacecraft, glinting metallically in the hard light of an unseen sun, apparently poised motionless against a backdrop of stars.

As advance units of the first Martian invasion fleet draw near to Earth, said the formal voice of a commentator, *crews are standing by to carry out emergency landing procedure.* A series of quick shots of uniformed men performing various obscure tasks inside the ships followed. Carson was astonished at the quantity of equipment visible in the background, and at the amount of space available for the men to move around in.

New anti-missile deflectors are being used for the first time, together with black-light projectors to give our forces the advantages of initiative and surprise.

Pictures of Earth and its moon taken from a point in space. An animated arrow moving across the screen, splitting into two prongs, the smaller aimed at the moon and the larger towards Earth.

A specially equipped detachment will occupy all lunar bases and set up a missile launching site trained on Earth as a deterrent to counter-attack.

Close-up of Earth, with the big arrow subdividing into a dozen or more tiny arrows curving round to impinge on various scattered points over the globe.

The main body of the fleet will attack selected targets in strategic areas and will then land. Lorentz heat barriers will be set up as a defensive measure. Ultrasonic beams and paralysing coma gas are expected to break down all opposition, particularly in the underground cities, within a few hours.

Now a picture of a Martian spaceport with another vast fleet of spacecraft being raised to the surface on anti-gravity elevators.

Meanwhile the second invasion fleet prepares for take-off. These ships will carry men trained in the administration of occupied territories. Among them may be future members of the terrestrial military government which will be set up as soon as hostilities are under control.

There followed a series of short interviews with military and political spokesmen, commenting on the invasion and its implications. All were optimistic, Carson noted, and all seemed to hold the opinion that the war would end before it had begun. It was to be a short, sharp campaign, using the very latest humane techniques for subjugating the mass of the enemy. Atomic weapons would not be employed unless provoked by the enemy, or unless the circumstances warranted their use (a flexible enough justification, Carson thought). Once the situation had quietened and settled down, Robert Carson, owner of the Earth, would arrive and assume his rightful leadership.

Meanwhile, the commentator went on, *Robert Carson, quietly awaiting the moment of his destiny here on Mars, today voluntarily submitted himself to a searching test of identity before a specially selected tribunal of security officials, and produced new and spontaneous evidence corroborating beyond all possible doubt the truth of his claim. This was the scene in security court number five as Mr. Carson faced his interrogators.*

Carson stared in fascination at a picture of himself answering questions at the interview. The video recording had been greatly shortened but skilfully edited, retaining the hard essence of the proceedings. At the end they had tacked on a sequence showing three experts examining the fuel pump in what was, to all appearances, the original *Wanderer II*, and comparing the damage with that depicted in Carson's drawings. Close-ups of both clinched the argument.

The war news ended and gave way to another item dealing with the construction of a new underground city in some remote region of Mars. Carson switched off the video screen. Turning round, he discovered that he was not alone in the room. The auburn-haired woman was sitting on a chair close to the window.

"How long have you been here?" he asked.

"A few minutes. I am interested in the war."

He smiled sourly. "According to them"—he hooked a thumb at the blank screen—"it will be over in five minutes."

"It will probably take longer," she observed, "but one must be optimistic."

"All this guff about restoring Robert Carson's rightful destiny. . . ." He looked at her resentfully. "It's simply a cover for a pretty ordinary act of military aggression."

The stern voice of Mr. Jaff spoke inside his ear. *Those are treasonable words, Mr. Carson. Be discreet. Do not involve innocent people in your private opinions, or they may suffer more than you.*

He was about to make a defiant remark, but remembered the torture of the high-pitched whistle and remained silent. Looking at the woman he realized the significance of the implied threat in Mr. Jaff's words. Why, indeed, should he involve her, probably against her will, in conversation that might well be regarded as seditious and subversive?

"If you knew the full history of Earth, Mr. Carson," she said, "you would realize just how much they need a strong, rational government. It isn't a question of aggression so much as—how can I put it? Compulsory assistance, perhaps."

He suppressed an acid laugh.

"After all," she continued, "we have developed a superior technology while the terrestrials have been occupied with internal problems—surface reconstruction, the mutants, and so on. They were set back a great deal during the earlier interplanetary wars. What they need more than anything is help and guidance."

"No doubt," he remarked dryly.

"And there is, of course, the practical point of basic economics —the Carson Trust. You are Robert Carson, alive. Sooner or later you would inevitably have to take possession of what is yours by right."

"Posthumously," he commented. "The Carson Trust was set up after my death—does that make Earth mine by right?"

"Of course," she said brightly. "Even the mutants on Earth breathe your name in awe. They regard you as their saviour."

"Me—or the body in the glass coffin?"

"Both, for you are one and the same. For them you will simply have come alive."

"Well," he said resignedly, "I never dreamed, when I took off in *Wanderer II* eight thousand years ago, that one day I should be hailed as ruler of Earth. I suppose it could have happened to anybody."

"Anybody at all," she remarked, smiling. "It is all a matter of economics."

Carson followed the war news during the next few weeks with morbid interest, trying to filter fact from fiction and assess the true situation through the haze of cleverly contrived propaganda. Everything was going well, they said, but terrestrial defences were proving more difficult to break down than had been anticipated. Furthermore, the Earthmen had developed certain new weapons, which had complicated matters, and there was evidence to suggest that there had been a leakage of military information so that they had not been taken entirely by surprise. A number of Martian ships had landed, and a number had been destroyed. A few beach-heads had been opened up, as it were, and the fleet were supporting the landings in every possible way. Severe fighting was in progress on the moon under more difficult conditions of total vacuum, but things were going well, and the unconditional surrender of the lunar bases was expected almost any day. Meanwhile the second and third invasion fleets had reinforced the first, and mass landings were imminent.

In fact, Carson realized, things were undoubtedly going rather badly for the Martian expeditionary force. Reading between the bland, optimistic words of the official communiqués, it was fairly obvious that no major landing had yet been effected; the invasion so far seemed to consist of sporadic raids, with perhaps a negligible piece of territory held here and there. So far there was nothing to suggest that Martian advance forces had succeeded in pentrating any of the underground cities. It will be another of those futile wars, he thought. There will be great destruction and heavy losses on both sides, and nothing will be accomplished.

Carson had underestimated the ruthless striking power of the Martian forces. After the initial setback, the three fleets had hovered in orbit around the Earth, carrying out long-range reconnaissance, and making frequent raids on the ground to keep the enemy occupied. Meanwhile every effort had been made to bring the lunar campaign to a swift, triumphant conclusion. The moon surrendered finally after five weeks of siege, and the Martian colonists moved in and took over. They built their heavy missile launching zones and assembled their big rockets with nuclear warheads. The stage was set for intensive bombardment of Earth.

The bombardment was in the nature of covering fire while the ships went about their business of landing invasion forces and equipment; it served to keep the defenders underground or in hiding while the insurgent forces consolidated their grip on the surface. Here the superior Martian knowledge of anti-mortic surgery tipped the psychological balance in favour of the invaders. Specially equipped hospital ships in the attacking fleets were able to perform miracles of surgical science replacing the organs of those who had been wounded, and cancelling out the effects of over-exposure to radiation. The immortals remained immortal, though there were inevitably a few casualties damaged beyond all repair. The defenders of Earth were far from immortal, however, and so lacked the elementary self-assurance that goes hand-in-hand with courage. In the face of an all-out atomic bombardment from lunar missile bases, followed by mass landings from the three invasion fleets at the principal civilized centres on the surface of the world, the terrestrials sealed themselves in their underground cities, leaving the unfortunate mutants to face up to the horrors of atomic war once again.

It took approximately three months to establish a tenuous occupation of the Earth's surface, and in the meantime further invasion fleets had set off from Mars to supply additional manpower and equipment. The terrestrials, secure in their subterranean caverns, launched a variety of rocket-borne weapons through funnels leading to the surface; the occupying forces, and the mutants, too, had to contend with nuclear bombs, poison gases, germ cultures and self-propagating incendiary chemicals which were exceedingly difficult to extinguish. The occupation of Earth in its early stages was difficult and dangerous, but the men from Mars held their ground and slowly built up supplies as they were freighted in by huge cargo rockets. The moon, apart from its primary function as an orbiting missile base, was developed as an equipment and provisions store, and later, when airtight domes had been set up in profusion, as a transit camp and reserve headquarters for military personnel.

Carson, studying the progress of the war, was astonished at the scale of the campaign. For one nation to attack another was quite a big enough project, involving immense co-ordination of men and materials, but the invasion of one planet by another was an operation which almost staggered his imagination. The science of logistics across millions of miles of empty space offered problems which would have baffled the best military minds of the twentieth century. And yet it was happening, here and now, in a cold matter-of-fact way at unguessable cost. Thanks to the power of the atom and the power of technology in general, Earth was on the verge of becoming a colony of Mars. If it hadn't been true he would have regarded it as sheer fantasy.

Meanwhile life for him continued in a leisurely if rather dull fashion enlivened occasionally by the four women attending him. He had not yet grown accustomed to the liberal amorality of the sterile immortals, and tended to shun the women for long intervals until boredom and a slowly crumbling moral sense impelled him to seek distraction. He was allowed a certain freedom of movement around the city, provided he was escorted by a black-caped official, and in this way he was able to tour some of the big factories and research laboratories on the third and fourth levels. There were occasional vocal interchanges with Mr. Jaff over the aural radio device, but he had given up attempting to resist, and during the early months of the war he remained strictly obedient.

There came a day when a war communiqué tersely announced that the Martian invaders had occupied their first underground city. The operation had been lengthy and costly in terms of casualties, for the attacking forces had tried to avoid damage to property and equipment, so that normal urban life might be resumed as soon as possible after the battle. The defenders, on the other hand, had been prepared to destroy everything as they retreated. The attack had been successfully accomplished by drilling deep shafts to pierce the upper level of the city at several dispersed points and pumping coma gas into the cavern. Troops wearing gravity reactor packs had then leaped down the shafts in their thousands to take control. Despite the coma gas there had been severe fighting, even hand-to-hand, but after three days the defenders surrendered.

The city, located near the eastern seaboard of America, was immediately proclaimed capital of the occupied territories on Earth, and a provisional military government was set up. The Martians then concentrated on their next city, so that, step-by-step, the civilized centres of Earth would surrender to the new ruling authority. The war, it was felt, was virtually over.

On the day the news was announced, Mr. Jaff spoke quietly into Carson's ear. *The time has come for you to assume your full responsibility as ruler of Earth, Mr. Carson. A ship is ready to take you to the moon, where you will await the final call from the terrestrial military government. Are you ready?*

"I'm ready," Carson answered laconically.

Take-off is scheduled in a hundred hours, but we shall come for you before then.

"Whenever you like," Carson murmured.

They came for him the next day.

CHAPTER TEN

THE journey to the moon was swift and without incident. Carson's main reaction, looking out of the observation port of the space ship as it settled gently upon the level surface of a lunar crater adjacent to a group of airlocked domes, was one of irony. Eight-thousand years earlier he had lost his life in an attempt merely to orbit the moon, and now here he was, without effort or fatigue, about to set foot on its dusty surface.

The journey from Mars had taken three-and-a-half days. He had been dismayed to learn that Mr. Jaff was to accompany him on his mission; in fact, the full complement of civilian passengers included some five-hundred government officials, all eager to play their part in the political and economic reorientation of Earth. In addition there were some two-thousand troops bound for the lunar transit camps. The ship, which was enormous by twentieth-century standards, had literally navigated itself across the millions of miles of space, guided by radar and electronic devices. To assist the passengers in idling away their time there was blue Sonar to drink and television to watch, presumably relayed from video recordings somewhere on the ship. But it proved impossible to relax and settle down. Everyone was excited, and they all seemed to know that Robert Carson was aboard, which gave added zest to the trip. Carson, however, had spent most of his time in his private cabin, deliberately remaining elusive so as not to be drawn into conversation. Occasionally he talked with Mr. Jaff and a few other officials, but on the whole he was regarded as a rather mysterious figure.

The moon, viewed at close quarters, was a desolate wilderness of black and white, with harsh splashes of grey. The tops of the jagged mountains surrounding the crater glowed incandescently in the glaring sunlight, but the sun was low on the horizon and most of the crater was enveloped in ebony shadow. The sky was jet black and peppered with silver stars. At zenith hung the great globe that was Earth, in a three-quarter phase, largely obscured by striations of white cloud. The land masses were dark against the phosphorescent glow of the oceans reflecting the sunlight; he thought he recognized the African continent and the elongated blob that might have been Europe, but the cloud concealed detail. Only the poles were clearly identifiable in their dazzling white ice-caps.

They had linked the ship to the nearest dome by means of a flexible tunnel with airlocks at either end. Carson was the first to disembark, closely followed by Mr. Jaff and the rest of the government contingent. Unaccustomed to the weak lunar gravity, he walked warily, keeping his movements under careful control.

The domes, he learned, were in the nature of a temporary encampment. The existing underground caverns on the moon were inadequate to house the large influx of personnel from Mars, having been designed to accommodate a normal staff of about five hundred.

They were welcomed by a group of top brass, including, so far as Carson could judge, high-ranking military officers and administrative executives. There was talk of the progress of the war, with much enthusiasm and optimism. Another city had fallen, this time on the western side of Europe, less than two hundred miles from London, and there was reason to believe that the next assault would be on the underground citadel of London itself. At that point, it was thought, organized resistance would rapidly decay, and the enemy would surrender unconditionally.

"That is where you come in," Mr. Jaff said to Carson. "Already we hold the surface ruins of London, and we have taken care to preserve the Carson monument with its sham rocket and body so that we may demolish it in a formal ceremony with full publicity, and proclaim *you* as the real Robert Carson, the rightful owner and ruler of Earth. On that very spot we shall build a new headquarters for the Carson Trust, and you will be installed in it, with the civil government and security organization to which the military council will hand over its functions when the war is over."

"You seem to have everything well planned," Carson commented.

Mr. Jaff smiled appreciatively. "All action should be the end-product of logical, constructive thought. Action without thought is futile and often destructive. This campaign was planned in great detail for many years. Apart from a few difficulties encountered at the beginning it has worked out precisely as predicted."

Carson looked up through the curved transparent roof of the dome towards the great diffuse globe that was Earth, and suddenly he was conscious of an overwhelming feeling of desolation and nostalgia. If I could have lived my life in the ordinary way, he thought, I wouldn't have asked for more. If I could go back eight-thousand years. . . . He abandoned the idea half-way through. At all events I'm alive, he reflected, and I ought to be grateful. In time I may be able to settle down and adapt myself to this cold, hard society.

"How soon can I go to Earth?" he asked.

"As soon as London surrenders," Mr. Jaff replied.

London never did surrender. The assault was launched within four days of Carson's arrival on the moon. Nuclear-powered ultrasonic drills cut deep shafts through the hard ground to provide access to the underground caverns, and men and weapons poured into the upper level of the city, but the task was more complex than had been anticipated. For one thing, there were eight levels to be occupied, and the city was divided into autonomous units linked by tunnels which were easy to defend and easier still to blow up. It was, in effect, a cluster of about a dozen small cities covering an area of some twenty square miles. Under the threat of attack each sub-city sealed itself off, so that the Martian invaders, under orders to avoid damage to property, communications and essential services, were faced with the prospect of a long and tedious campaign, and the loss of prestige if they failed to achieve a rapid victory.

The military command, anxious to exploit the psychological boost which quick success would provide, decided on a restricted policy. The first aim would be to seize the government and administrative zone and take control of communications, in particular the radio and video networks. Once this had been accomplished, victory would be declared. The residential and industrial zones could then be mopped up in a more leisurely fashion, on a piecemeal basis.

Orders were issued to concentrate the attack in accordance with the predetermined plan, and to abandon temporarily military operations against those sectors of the city not directly concerned with the co-ordination of terrestrial authority. Even so, six weeks went by before the officer commanding the London assault force was able to report success. The nucleus of the city was in Martian hands; victory in principle had been achieved. It was, in fact, check rather than checkmate, but the Martian high command was satisfied.

Mr. Jaff broke the news to Carson, who had been waiting patiently in the restricted space of his quarters in the lunar dome.

"London has fallen," he announced triumphantly.

Carson felt a vague sense of regret, but was careful not to let it show in his expression.

"Earth is ours," Mr. Jaff went on portentously. "This is the first day in the dynasty of Robert Carson—the beginning of a new era in the history of the solar system. Earth is now a colony of Mars."

Carson permitted himself to smile sardonically. Mr. Jaff's eloquence possessed the undertones of blue Sonar.

"When do I go to London?" he asked.

Mr. Jaff waved one hand in a vigorous circle. "At the earliest possible moment—probably within a few hours. Every second's delay represents a serious loss of propaganda value. Already they are installing video cameras at the site of the Carson monument. We have transmitters waiting to blanket the Earth with pictures of the ceremony."

"The enemy don't have to watch," Carson pointed out.

"They don't have to, but they will. I don't mean the ordinary people. The signals will be jammed, of course. I mean the terrestrial politicians and military leaders. They are the ones who matter, whose morale will be broken to our advantage."

Carson considered for a moment. "I always thought it was the morale of the people that counted in the long run. People win wars, not governments."

"Wrong," Mr. Jaff stated decisively. "Morale is a flexible thing that can be moulded by authority. If the government is strong, then the people are strong, too. A weak government breeds a weak, decadent nation. That was true even in your day."

Carson shrugged. "You may be right—I don't know. I've always pinned my faith on the mass of ordinary people. Perhaps they can be moulded up to a point in the short term, but it's the long term that really matters. We witnessed the emergence of strong governments in my century. They didn't survive for long. Somehow the weak, vacillating governments seemed to find a superior strength in times of crisis, and I believe they drew that strength from the common people. After all, a nation of responsible adults doesn't require a strong government; they are already amenable to law and reason."

Mr. Jaff stared coldly at Carson for quite a long time. "That is sedition," he said finally, in an almost surprised tone of voice. "This is the hundredth century, Mr. Carson, not the twentieth. The State is an entity in itself. The government is the coordinating brain of the State, and individuals are merely the cells of a corporate body. A nation of responsible adults may well be amenable to law and reason, but unless they are directed by authority they serve no useful purpose."

"What useful purpose?" Carson enquired. "Waging war on Earth, for instance?"

"Precisely. That is a useful purpose. You must think in more cosmic terms, Mr. Carson. History should be viewed in broad trends rather than isolated incidents. There used to be a fetish for learning the dates of ancient wars and battles, while the important thing, the sociological motivation for war, was overlooked. Wars are merely symptoms of social change and evolution. Nations and planets come into conflict for economic reasons, and it is the economic factors which are important, not the names of the campaigns and the generals who conducted them."

"I see," Carson said thoughtfully. "What, then, is the motivation for this present war? . . . surely not to put Robert Carson on the throne, as it were?"

"The motivation is simple," Mr. Jaff explained. "Raw materials, in particular the radioactive elements such as uranium and thorium, which are plentiful on Earth but hardly exist at all on Mars. And there is a symbiotic motive—the elementary principle that two nations working together for one economic purpose under a single governing authority can increase overall productivity to the prosperity of both. I am not claiming that we are altruistic, but at the same time we are not wholly selfish. We want Earth to prosper under our guidance just as Mars has prospered."

"Meanwhile I suppose Mars will pull all the economic strings through the Carson Trust."

"Not quite the way I should have put it, but nevertheless substantially true."

Carson smiled narrowly. "Well, I'm in favour of prosperity, Mr. Jaff, even though I'm not in favour of war. However, if the one leads to the other. . . ."

"The war is virtually won," pronounced Mr. Jaff. "History will record that the age of terrestrial prosperity started today."

"I hope you're right," Carson murmured without conviction.

The journey to Earth was made the next day. Carson, accompanied by Mr. Jaff and a score of lesser officials, embarked in a relatively small rocket ship which, so far as he could judge, was one of the terrestrial fleet of ferry ships carrying out freight duties between Earth and moon, but obviously it had been converted for passenger-carrying purposes. The journey took six hours, which Mr. Jaff seemed to think was rather slow for a mere quarter-of-a-million miles. As Earth drew near, Carson stared in fascination at its immense rounded surface, slowly assuming colour and detail, always shrouded by intermittent patches of white cloud. He recognized the continent of Europe, but as the rocket spun round the planet on its swept-back wings, America flashed beneath him, and then the Pacific Ocean, followed by the vast stretch of Asia. As Europe mounted the horizon again the retrojets roared and the wings extended. Soon the spacecraft was swooping low over the Mediterranean and curving north towards the small island known as Britain.

They landed at a demolished spaceport some thirty miles north of London. The concrete surface of the landing zone was glasslike and fissured from atomic heat, and the control buildings were gaunt, empty skeletons. Temporary huts had been set up, and here and there Carson could see mobile radar and electronic control units dispersed around the perimeter of the zone. Before disembarking he had to put on a bulky suit which, it was explained, would give ample protection against radioactivity. The entire party was quickly transferred from the rocket into a small fleet of hoverjet aircraft of terrestrial manufacture. Ten minutes later they were flying over London.

The city was unrecognizable, of course. In eight-thousand years atomic bombardment, alternating with periods of rebuilding, had completely altered the geometry and appearance of the place; even the Thames, twisting and turning like a slender silver ribbon through areas of radioactive devastation, seemed to have changed its course at several points. Central London was a wilderness of fused stone and leaning skeletal buildings, blackened and oxidized by nuclear heat flash. The invading forces had prepared their ground thoroughly.

The hoverjets flew west for a short distance. The bleak destruction eased. Buildings were still standing, and green grass glimmered patchily on a wide expanse of open ground that could have been a park—could even have been the famous Hyde Park, though there were no remaining landmarks to facilitate identification. Suddenly Carson saw the monument, with the dark slender shape of the rocket protruding sadly towards the sky. Temporary buildings had been erected around it, and thin, spidery video towers projected vertically from the forlorn landscape.

They landed on the open ground, within a few hundred yards of the monument, and a group of men wearing anti-radiation clothing walked forward to meet the helicopter. Beyond them, on raised platforms, the lenses of complex cameras peered inquisitively at the scene. Oddly, there was music in the air, presumably from an amplified recording. The trend of melody and harmony was unfamiliar: it could have been the Martian anthem, or a specially composed ceremonial work to commemorate the inauguration of the Carson era. In the background, near to the monument, was a large decorated rostrum where, presumably, Carson would be proclaimed owner of Earth and whatever else Martian authority had envisaged for his puppet role.

And then, looking towards the outer fringes of the park, beyond the monument and the rostrum and the cluster of huts, beyond a wire fence, Carson saw the mutants. There were, perhaps, several hundred of them, crowding the wire in an orderly manner, but even at that distance there was something odd and shambling about their appearance; they looked like caricatures rather than human beings. The small ones were indistinguishable against the neutral background, but the tall ones jutted out angularly from the mass in an indefinably incongruous way. For one horrific moment he thought he saw the silhouette of a two-headed man, but the illusion vanished abruptly, and he decided that it was probably a trick of the light. The mutants were, he supposed, the immediate living audience, as opposed to the hypothetical video audience; they were probably denizens of what was left of the surface London, skulking and hiding in cellars and the ruins of buildings, with radioactivity scintillating in every cell of their bodies, if they had not, over the generations, developed a natural immunity to radiation. Depression gripped him for a few moments, but he shook it off and made up his mind to be impersonal and practical about the proceedings which were to come.

He descended from the hoverjet with Mr. Jaff and other officials, and was introduced to the committee of welcome. Under the probing eyes of video cameras he met senior officers of the invading army and civilian members of the military government, and made suitably conventional and innocuous remarks. They, in turn, were cordial but formal in their attitude, as if they knew and acknowledged his puppet status.

"Ten minutes," said Mr. Jaff, sidling up to him through the

throng, "then the ceremony begins. You are not required to say anything at all, not a single word. The monument has been thoroughly mined by engineers—at the appropriate moment it will disintegrate into a million fragments. It is sufficient that you should merely show yourself. It is better psychology. Later there will be opportunities for you to talk to your subjects, once the situation has crystallized."

"Whatever you say," Carson said quietly.

"To be a successful figurehead one must be remote and perhaps a little uncommunicative. Robert Carson throughout the centuries has acquired a certain mystical quality—in the eyes of the populace he has almost the status of a deity. The Robert Carson they knew formerly was a corpse in a transparent coffin, but you are alive. That is why it is important not to present too great a contrast. Act as if you were, in effect, the same Robert Carson brought mysteriously back to life, silent and perhaps still subdued by the lethargy of death."

"I'll try," Carson promised.

Presently they walked over to the solemnly decorated rostrum, Carson leading the way. He ascended the steps to the dais, followed by Mr. Jaff and the military and political leaders. The lenses of the video cameras panned and zoomed.

Carson was never quite sure what happened next. There was a tremendous, hot, concussive blast, and the solid ground of the park seemed to rise tumultuously into the air. He caught a brief distorted glimpse of Mr. Jaff whirling backwards with flailing arms, and then the rostrum had crumbled into fragments of steel and plastic surging upwards on hot turbulent air. The entire world seemed to dissolve into thunder and fire. . . .

CHAPTER ELEVEN

AT some instant before or shortly after the moment of conception, when the woman had been a single cell or perhaps simply an ovum or a gamete, a gene had been destroyed by the impact of a gamma particle liberated from a nuclear source; or the faulty gene might have been inherited through several generations of mutated birth. Whatever the explanation she had grown into what was superficially a half-woman, of normal size and shape, but with one eye and one ear and a small mouth displaced to the right. The left side of her face was blank, and the hair on that side was of a different texture, being dry and limp and almost grey, while the hair on the other side of her head was sleekly brown, with the suggestion of a gentle wave. The rest of her body was quite normal, so far as Carson could judge: she had two arms and two legs, and she wore an ill-fitting garment that seemed to have been crudely fabricated from tarpaulin. The single eye was blue and intelligent.

He recognized the appalling evidence of mutation before he had fully recovered consciousness, and perhaps for that reason he was the less stricken by horror and revulsion. The woman moved away, out of his field of vision. Now he found himself staring at a shattered stone archway, and beyond it a night sky with glittering stars. A cool breeze sighed through the broken masonry of devastated buildings. He was lying in the shelter of the arch, and there was soft fabric beneath his back. Above him moonlight shone pallidly on a cracked wall, but he could not see the moon from where he lay.

A man came into view, a tall thin man with an extraordinarily long neck and wide staring eyes. An odd point of detail seized Carson's attention: the man had eight spindly fingers on each hand, without thumbs. The man stooped low and peered into his face.

"Robert Carson," he said in a toneless, rasping voice. "Are you Robert Carson?" The language he was using was not the Martian semantic blend, but a slurred adaptation of the older English of Carson's own era.

"Robert Carson," the man repeated.

Carson was about to reply when suddenly the man disappeared and the mutated woman returned.

"Robert Carson," she said softly, in a very feminine voice.

"Yes," said Carson.

Abruptly the thin man was there, peering over her shoulder. "I knew it," he said. "I had a feeling about him."

"Where am I?" Carson asked.

"With friends," said the woman. "We will look after you."

"What happened?"

The man interlocked his sixteen fingers nervously. "Reprisal. The norms blew up a first-level residential sector under the park. They must have known."

"The norms?"

"The normal people—those who live underground. They must have known."

"I can see that only too clearly," Carson murmured. "They chose the appropriate moment when the video cameras were focused on the Martian top brass, not to mention the great Robert Carson. The propaganda value must have been enormous."

"You use unfamiliar words," said the woman. "The first level is deep. The explosion was restrained and muffled. There were only four deaths among the immortals."

"Immortality has its limits," Carson remarked. Now that he was fully conscious he was aware of stiffness and pain in his body; his right leg felt numb, as if it were fractured.

"There was an immediate counter-attack. The battle is going on now underground. The norms are engaged in bitter fighting with the immortals to recapture the government zones."

"That means reinforcements will be arriving," Carson said thoughtfully. "And if the norms are counter-attacking with any force they may well push the fighting up to the surface."

"It would be wise to leave London," said the man sadly. "There will be more bombs and missiles."

Slowly Carson pushed himself into a sitting position, encumbered to some extent by the bulky anti-radiation suit. He moved his arms and legs and was relieved to find that they responded normally. The suit had probably protected him from serious damage.

"At least there are no bones broken," he commented. "What happened to the others?"

"What others?"

"The rest of the Martians—the immortals."

The woman said: "After the explosion the mutants broke through the wire fence and tried to help the survivors, then later the survivors were able to help themselves, and they started searching for you, Mr. Carson. But we had already taken you away, and in the confusion nobody saw. Then many hoverjets carrying troops arrived, and we heard that severe fighting had broken out underground. We brought you here."

"Why?" Carson demanded.

"Because, if you own the Earth, then we have a right to talk to you and show you how we live—but we have to seize that right by stealth. It would never be granted in a thousand years."

"What she means is that we're mutants, and mutants have no rights," the man put in.

"You must remember that I represent the enemy. It would not be good for me to fall into the hands of the norms," Carson pointed out.

The woman stroked the smooth side of her long hair in a feminine gesture. "There is no enemy where we are concerned," she said. "There are only norms and immortals—and we mutants. If the norms and immortals choose to fight each other, that is their business. It makes living very difficult for us, but we are not directly involved in the war. We live as we can, where we can. The norms have tried to help us with food and materials and medical supplies, and we are grateful for that, but we are many millions and there is not much they can do."

"I think there's a great deal which could be done," Carson said. "It's about time responsible human beings stopped living underground and started making the surface of the world fit for habitation. This business of mutation is a self-inflicted injury and it ought to be tackled on a priority basis."

"That is big talk," the man remarked, but there was no unpleasantness in his voice.

"There is a solution to every problem," Carson went on firmly. "The immortals have developed very advanced clinical and surgical techniques. When the war is over Martian doctors and scientists will find ways of dealing with mutation. After all, they know how to cure death."

The woman smiled twistedly. "Mutation is a matter of birth, not death."

"It is only a question of time," Carson insisted. "Some of these scientists have been working on researches for a thousand years or more."

"But *we* are not immortals, Mr. Carson. If I live for another forty years I shall be lucky indeed. And I find it difficult to be enthusiastic about the benefits which future generations will enjoy."

Carson remained silent, suddenly depressed. Better for me to go back, he thought, to rejoin the Martian force. These people won't stop me. If I stay here I might get taken by the enemy, and that would be dangerous. One living Carson is better than two dead. When the war is won I can make a point of studying the mutant problem and try to force the administrative people to take some action. After all, there's nothing I can do alone and unaided, other than make idle promises which I may not be able to fulfil.

"What are your thoughts, Robert Carson?" the woman asked presently.

"I think I ought to return," he said quietly. "I do not support war, but now that the thing has started, the sooner it ends the better for all concerned. I am an essential part of the Martian military strategy, and it may be that the war will finish much more quickly if I carry out the duties assigned to me."

The man and the woman looked at him in melancholy disillusionment.

"We had hoped you might come with us," said the woman.

"Where?"

"Outside London. There is a place about twenty-five miles away—a mutant colony—in a valley, with some protection from heat flash if atomic warfare should start again over London. There are caves and tunnels dug in the ground."

"What could I possibly do there?"

"Stay with us for a few days. By then the battle of London will be either won or lost. Nobody will force you to stay if you don't wish to. You can always go back."

"How do we travel? Twenty-five miles is a long journey on foot."

"We have a simple machine—a kind of box on wheels with a geared pedal device for the feet. One can do about eight miles an hour without much effort."

Carson stood up, undecided, and stared across the ruins beyond the arch to the darker skyline of eroded London. Lights moved in the sky. Probably spacecraft or hoverjets, he thought. As he watched, the night glowed white, then crimson, just above the horizon; half a minute later a muffled concussion shook the air around him. He sensed the mutant woman standing by his side.

"They have started already on the surface," she whispered. "It might not be possible to go back. The norms may be in possession of the city again. To stay here would be dangerous."

"All right," said Carson, with an air of resignation. "I'll come with you."

The man appeared before him in the darkness. An eight-fingered hand touched his arm like a spider.

"Thank you, Mr. Carson," breathed the man. "Thank you very much."

The journey to the mutant colony was arduous and trying. The vehicle was of soap-box construction, lashed together from pieces of plastic and metal, with no springs or rubber tyres. They took it in turns to pedal, jolting and bumping over the uneven roads, and occasionally lurching across open country. On the hills they had to get out and push. The entire trip took a little more than four hours, which gave an average speed of some six miles per hour. Better than walking, Carson decided, but only just.

The valley was narrow and confined, with steep sides covered in stunted shrubs which looked as if they had been seared by heat flash at some time. There was little grass, and the ground was damp and sour. They pushed the box-car to the bottom of the valley (the slope was too steep for the primitive brakes) and left it beside a thin, trickling stream. Dawn was grey in the eastern sky, and the countryside was emerging in wan ghostly colour.

He followed the mutants through the scrub to where one side of the valley rose up in an almost vertical cliff face of weathered rock, and here were the caves and the tunnels. Narrow steps had been chiselled at places in the cliff, and here and there crude wooden ladders were lashed into position to provide access to cave mouths.

They began to ascend a ladder, but Carson encountered great difficulty in maintaining his balance, partly because of fatigue and partly due to the anti-radiation clothing, which hindered his movements. Presently, after much effort, he found himself entering an oval tunnel cut in the rock face some thirty feet above the ground. The tunnel, which was quite dark, extended in a straight line for about twenty paces, then opened after a sharp right-angle turn into a large cave, rectangular enough to be man-made. Simple oil lamps burned steadily in the corners, casting a yellow, vapid glow on to the grey rough-hewn walls. There were people in the cave, some standing, others sitting on crude benches. As he entered the room behind the man and woman, all eyes focused on him, and a whisper of dry voices rustled in the air.

Carson. Robert Carson himself. Carson. Carson. . . .

As Carson looked at his audience, his spine chilled, but he fought the horror that spun momentarily in his brain. They were all mutants, of course, in a variety of sizes and shapes—if shapes was the right word. Some, happily, were reasonably human in appearance; others were grotesque nightmarish travesties of men and women. They had one thing in common: intelligent eyes, where there were eyes at all. He remembered once, in the twentieth century, visiting the plastic surgery ward of a military hospital; and, on another occasion, helping to locate charred fragments of human bodies in the burned-out wreckage of an airliner that had crashed: this was the same kind of feeling— the tense, instinctive revulsion conflicting with a civilized determination not to react, not to notice. But more than anything he regretted having come, and he began to understand something of the problems of the underground terrestrial norms, and why they had largely abandoned the world of the surface. When one cannot live with a horror, one tends to escape from it.

"This is our communal assembly hall," said the tall man quietly. "The others got back earlier and told them you might be coming. They have been waiting for hours. They expect you to say a few words to them."

"How do I address them?" Carson asked anxiously. "I mean, as people, or mutants, or terrestrials, or what?"

"They like to be called humans," said the man, without irony. "It helps them to feel . . . accepted."

Carson walked forward into the assembly hall, his mind rapidly formulating the trend of an impromptu speech. They seemed to lean towards him intently.

"Fellow humans," he began, then paused for a moment while he mustered his thoughts. "I am Robert Carson—the real, living, original Robert Carson—the owner of the Carson Trust and, therefore, the economic owner of Earth. Today, for the first time in eight-thousand years, I have set foot once more on the planet on which I was born and raised. I am not a Martian colonist, but I am grateful to the scientists and doctors of Mars for giving me back my life. I am in a sense a man of two worlds, but if Mars was my college, then Earth is my home. My loyalty is to humanity as a whole, whether immortal, norm, or mutant, and I believe that the present hostilities between the two planets will ultimately be resolved for the benefit of the whole human race. The Martian armies must inevitably win, because they have superior weapons and technology. When the war is over, and Earth and Mars are united on a common economic basis, there are certain important tasks to be performed. The first will be to rehabilitate the surface of the Earth, to build new cities and highways and industries, and to bring men up from below the ground. The norms and the mutants and the immortals must all live together as equals, each individual playing his responsible part in the pattern of society. There must be intensive research into the whole problem of genetic mutation, and I am convinced that Martian scientists will find an answer very quickly."

They had listened to him in silence, with such lack of response that he began to wonder whether he was saying the right things. So far he had talked like the average glib politician following a party line. He scanned their weird faces for a sign of response, but could detect only apathy. It occurred to him that they might be past caring; after all, what could that tiny man with the enormous elongated head and the overgrown ears like an elephant's care about the Earth-Mars war, or rehabilitation of the surface, or research into genetic mutation? He had a tragic personal problem, like the rest of them; he was not interested in economics or industry or scientific research, but merely in himself, in his own private hell. To be born a monster or a freak, through no fault of one's own, but because of the folly of a humanity playing irresponsibly with the elemental forces of nature, and to have to live with it, day after day, a normal brain confined within a distorted body, and to be abandoned by the privileged ones, the underground people who had been protected for long generations from the horror of mutation; to live a life of privation on a tribal basis while beneath the very ground from which you sought sustenance efficient automated industries catered for the elaborate needs and pleasures of the hierarchy; to know that on another planet normal humans had conquered death and could envisage a future that had no conceivable end, in which all things were possible. I must be more practical, he thought. These wretched mutants don't want political claptrap or ethereal promises. They want to know what I can do for them —Robert Carson, owner of Earth.

"Humans," he said, making a fresh start, "when the war is over I shall be ruler of Earth, and there are certain things I will do without delay. The first will be to divide the entire wealth of the Carson Trust equally between the two divided sections of humanity—the mutants, and the normal people, whether norm or immortal. There will be two independent governments—a mutant government controlling the world's surface, and a norm government for the people of the underground cities. Norms may live on the surface, if they choose, and mutants may live underground, but they must comply with each others' laws. There will be complete equality of economic opportunity. Above all, the mutants will have the financial basis to develop their civilization in their own way."

Now there was response and a quiet murmur of enthusiastic conversation among his audience. Encouraged, he continued his theme, inventing a programme of terrestrial development from moment to moment as the ideas occurred to him.

"As a basic principle we must accept the fact that, in human values, an immortal is no better and no worse than a mutant, and the norm is the equal of either. Physically we may differ, but the difference is a matter of discreet genetic biochemistry, and the individual remains the same."

Yes, they murmured, *that is so.*

"Well, then, let us face reality. We are one species, all of us, and we have equal rights. . . ."

He broke off suddenly. Deep in his ear the voice of Mr. Jaff said icily: *You are wrong, Mr. Carson. Every mutation is a new species. By the most fundamental of nature's laws they cannot all survive. Only the fittest can survive. Look around you. How many of your mutants are fit to survive, either physically or aesthetically? If you were trying to create a new, perfect Earth, populated by the finest eugenic strain of homo sapiens, how many would you permit to survive?*

Carson knew the answer even before the question was finished. He made no reply, but stared silently at his audience, who were waiting raptly for his next words.

Mr. Jaff continued: *Do not deceive yourself or your mutant friends. When the war is won it will be our task to make a new Earth peopled with genetically perfect humans. The mutants are a phase—a mistake. They cannot be allowed to survive. Humanity was never destined to become a species of twisted monsters. The mutants must die, all of them. In the end the solar system will be peopled by immortals. How many of your mutant friends would you wish to see immortalized?*

The audience was growing restive, wondering why he had stopped talking to them. Frantically he tried to think of something to say, but the firm plausible voice of Mr. Jaff went on and on, shattering the foundations of his arbitrary new world in which mutants and norms and immortals were equals.

Come back, Mr. Carson, before it is too late. We will abandon you if we must, but we still need you as a symbol. The terrestrials have counter-attacked strongly and we may have to withdraw from London for a time. If they capture you they will destroy you without hesitation. Come back before it is too late. The mutants cannot help you. Without us you are lost, and you will very soon be dead.

"But how can I get back?" asked Carson, suddenly oblivious of his audience.

Where are you?

"I don't know. A valley about twenty-five miles south or south-west of London."

Keep talking, ordered Mr. Jaff. *We will use radar direction finders to obtain a bearing and fix on your aural radio transceiver. Keep talking. We shall send a task force in hoverjets to bring you back.*

Carson looked round at the strangely inhuman but rather pathetic faces of his mutant audience, still restless and still waiting for him to make more reassuring words. I could continue speaking to them, he thought, and Mr. Jaff would have plenty of time to pin-point me, and very soon I would be back with the invading forces, among normal human beings, and knowing my precise place in the scheme of things.

But he was aware of an inner stubbornness possessing his mind —a strong conviction that he was right and Jaff, in his autocratic way, was quite wrong. All this talk of genetically perfect humans . . . by what standard could Jaff or anyone else judge the fitness of a human being to survive? Come to the point, Jaff himself was no beauty from a physical point of view, and yet he was immortal. By sheer accident of birth he had inherited the right to survive indefinitely. What supreme authority gave him the right to determine the question of life and death among others who, also by accident of birth, diverged from the standard physical specification of homo sapiens? All physical and mental characteristics were accidents of birth in the last analysis, and no individual had the ultimate right to judge which characteristics were worthy of preservation or justified elimination. Mutation had always been the fundamental mechanism of evolution, triggered by cosmic rays and ambient radiation natural to the soil of the planet; if it had increased because of atomic warfare, then the rate of evolution had merely been accelerated, and it could be that among these horrific mutants were improved variants who might, given the opportunity to survive and reproduce their kind, eventually produce a superior type of human being. In ordering the destruction of the mutants Jaff was, in effect, negating the entire natural basis of biological evolution. He was not prepared to allow the fittest to survive: on the contrary, the privilege of life was to be accorded to those selected by arbitrary eugenic standards.

Rebellion flared in Carson's mind, coupled with the knowledge that he could speak only a few words if he was to avoid location by radar. He held up one hand in a gesture commanding attention.

"I am being monitored," he announced solemnly, "and I can say no more. If it is within my power to help you, then I will. Thank you for listening to me."

Keep talking, urged the voice of Mr. Jaff. *Keep talking, Mr. Carson.*

Carson backed away from his audience towards the entrance tunnel and the mutant man and woman he had first met. They were looking at him anxiously.

Keep talking, Mr. Jaff repeated.

Carson remained silent.

You must obey orders. Keep talking.

"I hope you are not involved in serious political trouble," said the man quietly.

Carson contrived to smile, but said nothing.

Very well, said Mr. Jaff. *If you will not learn to obey, then you must be taught.*

A second of silence followed, and then, with an abrupt click, his brain exploded into the familiar high-pitched whistle. In desperation he clapped his hands to his ears and shook his head to relieve the torment, but the whistle persisted, cutting through every nerve in his body. Over the whistle a resonant, metallic voice called: *Keep talking. Keep talking. Keep talking.*

In a sudden frenzy of unreasoning panic he rushed headlong from the cavern and plunged blindly into the dark tunnel, colliding with the rough wall every few steps, not knowing what he intended to do. Behind him he felt rather than heard footsteps in pursuit, and voices calling to him, but the whistle drowned all awareness of the outside world. He reached the edge of the tunnel mouth in the cliff face without realizing it, and when his stumbling feet stepped upon empty air he was unable to think at all. For a wild instant his legs tangled in the crude ladder, then wood snapped with a dry, splintering sound, and he was falling over and over towards the ground.

At the moment of impact the whistle faded as unconsciousness swooped upon him.

CHAPTER TWELVE

"You are not so immortal that you can fall on your head with impunity," said the tall, grey-haired man in the white coat. "However, the slope of the ground helped to break your fall. Apart from bruising here and there, all is well."

Carson found himself lying flat on his back on a low bed, staring at a white luminous ceiling. The man was doing something with clinical instruments on a shining metal trolley, and beyond him a young woman, also dressed in white, was writing something on a small green card.

"There was severe concussion, of course," the man continued, speaking in a slow, leisurely manner, as if filling in time. "You have been unconscious for four days."

Certain things became apparent to Carson. He was no longer in the hands of the mutants, and, to judge by the windowless room and the evenly glowing ceiling, this was somewhere underground, in one of the buried cities. The man's accent was strange, lacking the semantic blend of the Martian tongue, but more drawling and fluent than the language of the mutants. He was clearly a terrestrial and beneath his white coat he wore grey trousered clothing reminiscent of fashions in the twentieth century.

"Where am I?" Carson asked.

The man glanced quickly at him, half smiling. "In a hospital in a city, but I am not permitted to name the city. You are, I fear, a prisoner of war, Robert Carson—quite the most important prisoner we have yet captured."

"How did you find me?"

"In the simplest manner. Every mutant colony is connected by a radio device to the office of an area commissioner. The commissioner's duty is to look after the welfare of the mutants in his own district as best he can, particularly in matters concerning emergency food distribution and essential medical services. After your fall down the cliff, when it became obvious that you were in a coma and perhaps seriously injured, the mutants did the only thing possible to help you. They called in the area commissioner. The rest was automatic. You were taken prisoner and brought to this hospital for treatment."

"What will happen to me?"

"That is not for me to decide. I am a doctor, not a military officer. My task is to make you well, and that is all."

The doctor took a large envelope from under the trolley and produced an X-ray photograph which he held up in front of Carson. It showed a silhouette of a human skull. On one side, just inwards from the ear, was a tiny rectangular shadow.

"No fractures," said the doctor, in a matter-of-fact voice, "but we were interested in this curious object"—he indicated the shadow with the tip of his finger—"apparently located in the inner ear. On the operating table we found a very small metallic cylinder lodged in the ear, almost in contact with the eardrum itself, but in some curious way the metal casing had fused into the flesh, so that it was impossible to remove the thing without also amputating part of the inner ear, including the drum membrane and ossicles. The result would have been permanent deafness."

"I imagine Martian doctors could soon fit a new ear," Carson commented dryly.

"You may never see another Martian doctor in the rest of your immortal life," the doctor remarked sardonically.

"So what did you do with the . . . thing?"

"Nothing at all. We left it where it is."

"Did you find out what it was?"

The doctor nodded slowly. "Yes, we did. There are ways of using fine X-ray beams to scan the interior of an object and produce a detailed three-dimensional picture. The thing is, of course, a miniature radio transmitter and receiver, powered by one of the smallest atomic batteries it has ever been my pleasure to see. I'm afraid our terrestrial craftsmanship is crude in comparison, but then we have had other problems to deal with in the course of our short lives."

"I wish you had taken it out," said Carson. "The thing is a monitoring device, and they use it for compelling obedience by means of an ultrasonic whistle. I would have preferred deafness."

"You *have* deafness," the doctor pointed out. "If you listen carefully to the sound of your own voice, or if you turn your head while I am talking to you, you will discover that your right ear is inoperative." Carson performed the experiment while the doctor was talking and confirmed for himself that he was indeed deaf on one side. "The radio device still works. It can hear you and me, but you can no longer hear it. All we did was to inject a long-term anaesthetic into the inner ear to paralyse the auditory nerves for a period of, say, three to four weeks."

"But why?"

"To cut you off from radio contact with your Martian colleagues, without destroying the means of communication. We could have drilled into the device and made it useless, but the military authorities had other plans."

"What plans?"

"You will no doubt learn in due course. For the moment you are well, though a little deafer than you used to be, and you will not hear any more ultrasonic whistles—not for some time, at any rate. Meanwhile, you will spend another day or two in hospital until we are satisfied with your condition, after which you will be transferred to another part of the city where you will come under the control of the military."

Carson nodded. On impulse he asked: "How is the war progressing?"

"Fine," said the doctor, smiling. "We are counter-attacking on all fronts, and I'm happy to say that your Martian friends are at present in full retreat."

"I find that hard to believe."

The doctor shrugged amiably. "Suit yourself. For you, personally, Robert Carson, the war is over."

He signalled to the woman, who wheeled the trolley from the room, then, with a final glance at Carson, went out after her.

During the next two days, Carson was able to relax and consider the new situation which had developed. He welcomed the opportunity to rest, for the bruising caused by the fall, coming so soon after the physical shock of being caught up in the explosion, made him feel weary and stiff. He was well looked after by the nurse, and was examined twice by the same doctor. One surprise was the food, which, though largely synthetic, contained certain natural vegetables—peas, for instance, and something that might have been cabbage—no doubt grown in the hydroponic farms.

He tried to visualize Mr. Jaff's reaction to his capture, and how it might influence the policy of the Martian high command. After the fiasco of the initiation ceremony which had literally exploded (Mr. Jaff had apparently been well and truly rescued by the mutants), plus the terrestrial counter-attacks, the capture of the great Carson, owner of Earth, by the enemy, would be a gross insult added to serious injury. The transceiver, functioning all the time while he was unconscious, would have faithfully relayed to Jaff the sounds and voices of the mutants who had saved him, and later the norms who took him to hospital. He would have heard the doctor diagnosing his condition and the experts debating the purpose of the transceiver capsule in his ear. And, if it were allowed to continue functioning, he would in due course overhear the interrogation that would take place when he was eventually delivered to terrestrial intelligence officers. Why the enemy thought this was desirable he was at a loss to understand; it could be that they did not yet fully comprehend the true purpose of the device and intended to question him about it.

At all events, there was nothing in the doctor's manner or conduct to suggest that he would be treated as other than an important and possibly distinguished prisoner. His earlier fears that the enemy might seek to destroy the man who claimed to be the real Robert Carson seemed groundless, though it was too soon to be overconfident in that direction. It seemed more likely now that the terrestrials in their turn would attempt to use him as a major propaganda weapon, thus stealing the psychological initiative from the invaders.

Mr. Jaff and the Martian military and political leaders would be busy enumerating all the possibilities and deciding what action to take in each case on a point-counter-point basis. In particular Mr. Jaff would be frustrated by his inability to communicate with Carson via the transceiver, and by the impossibility of enforcing obedience with the ultrasonic tone. He would be uncertain of Carson's loyalty, knowing that already he held certain ideas and views which were seditious in the eyes of Martian authority, and having heard the manner of his speech to the mutants, which conflicted in its humanitarianism with the official cold-blooded policy of elimination. Jaff would undoubtedly be a very worried man at this moment.

I stand to lose either way, Carson thought. The terrestrials will always think my first allegiance is to the Martians, who restored my life, while Jaff will always suspect me of having terrestrial sympathies. Neither side will trust me fully. In the long run the only friends I may ever have will be the mutants. I may be the theoretical owner of Earth, but that's only a worthless abstract symbol. Without power and the means to enforce that power I own nothing—not even myself. I would be just as useful dead, in a transparent coffin entombed in stone under the shell of *Wanderer II.*

All I can do for the moment is live from day to day, he decided, and assess each new situation as it arises, trying all the time to preserve whatever integrity I can in this strange and rather horrific world. The important thing is to stay alive. For an immortal that is essential: there is no such thing as a dead immortal. In the end the future will depend on who wins the war.

Secretly, hardly admitting it even to himself, he wished that the terrestrials would win.

On the afternoon of the second day, Carson was given his clothes and told to dress. Ten minutes later, after saying goodbye to the doctor and the nurse, he was escorted from the hospital by four uniformed men. In the street outside he was bundled into a large black vehicle balancing itself mysteriously on one wheel centrally located under the chassis. Evidently the terrestrials hadn't got as far as anti-gravity, and the single wheel was the next best thing. Jets hissed quietly, and the car began to move forward, swiftly gathering speed, while machinery hummed faintly beneath the seats—probably gyroscopes for balancing, Carson thought.

Superficially the terrestrial underground city was similar in general construction to those of Mars. Strips of greenery and garden were fewer, however, and the illumination was more subdued; the buildings generally possessed a simpler and more austere geometry. One could reasonably assume that the terrestrial cities were older than their Martian counterparts, and lacking in some of the refinements which a superior technology could provide.

They descended three levels through spiralling tunnels, drawing up finally outside a grey imposing building. Carson, surrounded by his guards, went inside. He was conducted along a wide corridor to a spacious room, coloured restfully in pale green. At a long glass-topped table at one end of the room sat three men—in the centre an elderly greying individual wearing military uniform, and on either side of him a civilian.

The escort halted, then retreated a few paces, leaving Carson to face the committee. As there was no chair, he remained standing.

The uniformed man eyed him with kindly interest. "I'm told that you are Robert Carson," he said.

"Yes."

"That is to say, the original Robert Carson, who died some eight thousand years ago in one of the earlier space rockets known as *Wanderer II*."

"Correct."

The officer stroked his chin thoughtfully. "Well, you present rather a problem to us, Mr. Carson. Technically you are a prisoner of war and an enemy, but if you are whom you claim to be, then you are also the beneficiary in law of the Carson Trust, which makes you in effect the executor of an economic estate which embraces the vast majority of terrestrial property and industry."

"So I've been told," Carson murmured.

"Clearly we have first to establish your true identity beyond all possible doubt, and that will be done during the weeks to come. It could be, for instance, that you are not Carson at all, but a Martian colonist trained and indoctrinated to pose as Carson, quite unknowingly and in good faith. We are well aware that the Martians possess very effective psychoneural techniques. . . ."

"This has been considered before," said Carson, recalling his lengthy interrogation by the security people on Mars. "I was able to prove my identity just the same."

"We have already seen that particular video record," said the officer sceptically. "Our friends from Mars are very liberal in their propaganda efforts. It doesn't really prove anything other than that the Martians tested the strength and efficiency of their indoctrination methods by submitting you to a searching cross-examination, and tried to confuse you by showing you photographs which seemed to refute your statements."

"There was the business of the damaged fuel pump. . . ."

"That could have been contrived. After all, they *had* the rocket, and they must have known precisely how the pump was damaged."

"But I *remembered* it," Carson protested.

"By indoctrination, yes. A half memory, buried deep in the mind so that it could emerge plausibly to the surface when suitably keyed by questions and photographs." The officer smiled shrewdly. "We also know something of psychoneural indoctrination and deep-level hypnosis. There is one point of detail which was never referred to in that video recording—a very important point of detail. When Carson had passed out of radio range of Earth in the *Wanderer* rocket and knew he was going to die, he spent his time dictating memories and impressions into the tape recorder which formed part of the equipment. For seventeen days and nights, on and off, he reminisced, sometimes talking calmly and logically, and sometimes wildly, in a kind of insane desperation. That tape embodies the whole of Carson's life and memories."

"I know," Carson said grimly. "I made that tape. I thought the information might be useful to someone some day."

"It *was*! To you and your Mr. Jaff. It enabled the Martians to create a synthetic Robert Carson with more than enough personal memories and mannerisms to satisfy even the most sceptical unbeliever."

Carson sighed despondently. An idea occurred to him. "How would you know about that tape, anyway?" he demanded. "The rocket was recovered by the Martians, and if they kept it secret, how could you possibly know? I was out of radio contact with Earth when I began recording. Nobody could know what was on that tape until they located the rocket."

"The answer is simple enough," said the officer, smiling. "*We* have that tape. It was stolen from security headquarters on Mars by one of our secret agents, quite recently, not more than two years ago. It happened when we began to learn that a new Robert Carson was about to be launched, if that is the expression, to support another invasion of Earth. Our agent investigated and discovered the tape. He realized that it was being used for indoctrination purposes, and smuggled it to Earth. We made copies, and the original tape was returned to Mars. Nobody had noticed its absence for nearly two weeks, because the psychoneural indoctrination had been completed. The agent is still alive, and still on Mars, working in security."

"That doesn't prove I'm an impostor," Carson said wearily. "I recorded that tape myself. I know what's on it."

"Then why should the Martians be so secretive about it?"

"I don't know. Perhaps they thought people might immediately suspect indoctrination of some kind if they knew such a tape existed. A man might own a small printing press, but that doesn't mean he forges currency notes."

The officer raised his eyebrows in mild remonstration. "It is easy enough to discover whether a currency note is forged or not," he pointed out. "It is far more difficult to prove human identity, particularly when all the circumstantial evidence points to what we might call a forgery of personality, and even more particularly when the prize at stake is economic ownership of an entire planet."

"I'm tired of being asked to prove I'm myself," said Carson heatedly. "I'm not interested in economic ownership of this planet or any other. I didn't ask to be brought back to life, but now that I'm alive all I ask is to be left in peace, to live simply, without ambitions, and without being involved in political intrigue. I renounce all claim to the Carson Trust. I want no part of it."

"You can't renounce what is binding in law. If you are in truth Robert Carson, then you will have to accept your full responsibility. If you are not, then the position does not arise."

Carson leaned forward intently. "I'll go further," he said earnestly. "If it will help matters, if it will put an end to these unending arguments about identity and economics, I'll agree to be somebody else—anyone you like. I'll try to forget I'm Robert Carson. I'll even admit I was brainwashed. All I ask is to be left with the secret knowledge that I am Carson, but I won't ever mention it to anyone."

"No good," said the officer, shaking his head. "If you admit to being an impostor, then you will be summarily executed, immortal or not. In any case, we cannot deal with such an important issue in terms of subterfuge. We have to know the truth. That is why this committee of three has been convened. Our task is to find out exactly who you are, whether it takes hours, weeks, months or years. I am Colonel Ree, a senior officer of terrestrial military intelligence. On my left is Dr. Brant, one of our leading psychoneurologists and a specialist in indoctrination techniques. On my right is Mr. Azan, an executive director of the Carson Trust commission. Between us we shall determine the facts."

He paused, rubbing his fingers together reflectively. "Certain things are already known. The Martians recovered the original *Wanderer II* rocket, long after we had erected our monument as a symbol. Inside they found the dead body of Carson and the tape. Now, either they succeeded in giving Carson a new life— and after eight thousand years of death it sounds highly improbable—or they took the opportunity to *pretend* to bring Carson back to life. They found a man who resembled him physically and gave him a full indoctrination routine over a period of years, reshaping his brain and perhaps parts of his body as well. Meanwhile, of course, the dead Carson would have been incinerated beyond trace."

"You make it sound so complicated, whereas it really is very simple," Carson said. "Whatever the motives of the Martian politicians, and whatever the plans they had and still have for using me as a psychological factor in their invasion of Earth, the truth is that I *am* Robert Carson and there's nothing you or I or anybody else can do about it."

"Don't be too sure of that," said the officer ominously. "There may be a great deal we can do. For example, in a few minutes from now you are going to listen to the tape which you claim to have recorded in *Wanderer II* while we measure your psycho-neural response on special encephalographic equipment. That may tell us something. Always remember—brainwashing can be unwashed. It takes time, but it can be done."

Colonel Ree stood up, and the guards promptly marched forward to take up a position at either side of Carson.

"Escort the prisoner to Room Forty," the Colonel ordered.

CHAPTER THIRTEEN

DURING the next ten days, Carson underwent a harrowing and seemingly endless routine of interrogation and psychological examination, sometimes conscious, sometimes in a comatose condition induced by drugs, but invariably with the electrodes of recording instruments connected to his head. He was forced to listen to his own tape over and over again, and then they would question him minutely, trying to force his answers beyond the information embodied in the tape to particularized, un-recorded details of life in the twentieth century. Always he gave his answers quickly and accurately. The three members of the committee, together with the technical assistants who occasionally helped them, were quite impassive in their attitude: it was as if they had ceased to regard him as a human individual at all, but rather as a complex machine which they were carefully scrutinizing in order to locate some obscure suspected fault.

Obliquely, between phases of questioning, he learned something of what was happening in the outside world, though it was difficult to decide just how much was propaganda. Terrestrial forces, it seemed, had counter-attacked heavily at key points, and the invaders had been forced to withdraw from the underground cities which they had previously occupied. Although the Martians were generally in possession of the Earth's surface, they were vulnerable to missile attack and, in particular, to the use of incendiary chemicals, which were being used on an increasing scale to destroy equipment and food stores. The terrestrials were using guerilla tactics in towns and cities on the surface where concealment was relatively easy, and it was thought that mutants were being employed on sabotage work.

Carson's personal view was that the Martian assault had lost much of its impetus, while the terrestrials had had time to consolidate their defences and launch a series of swift, effective counter-attacks. At no point did there seem to be a long-term positive engagement of the two opposing forces. It was catch-as-catch-can fighting, vicious enough, but indecisive and likely to drag on for a long time unless one side had the strength to steam-roller the other in a fast all-out campaign.

Of one thing he was certain: the Martians could not sustain a long war. The operation had been planned on shock-tactic lines, seizing key centres as quickly as possible, then proclaiming the new order of things with Carson as its figurehead, to be followed by mopping up throughout the world. It had been tacitly assumed that terrestrial resistance would crumble rapidly during the early weeks of the campaign, but the enemy had proved to be more flexible than Martian intelligence had anticipated.

Carson found himself doubting whether the Martians, for all their immense technology and apparent prosperity, could afford to keep sending men and supplies over the tenuous space routes between Mars and the moon. Already, it seemed to him, the invaders had deployed their forces too widely over the planet, with inadequate concentration of striking power, while the real core of the defence remained buried deep in the ground. All they were doing, in effect, was populating the surface of the Earth, vast areas of which were uninhabitable, anyway, because of radioactivity, and relying for their sustenance on food and materials freighted from Mars. That kind of situation could hardly survive for long. To avoid stalemate there would have to be a tremendous concentrated attack from one side or the other.

Meanwhile, the quest for his true identity continued until, in the end, the committee completed its work and went off to consider its findings. Carson was left in peace for three days. The next morning he was summoned to the committee room once more. The three men were sitting at the long table as on the first occasion, watching him with interest as he entered, escorted by the guards.

Colonel Ree, referring to a document on the table in front of him, said: "We have considered most carefully all the data and evidence relating to the disputed question of your identity, and we have referred, where necessary, to other experts for guidance on the interpretation of certain obscure points. We have also used electronic computers to assess the probability of certain specific items of data. As a result of our joint deliberations we have reached the conclusion that you are, in fact, Robert Carson, beyond all possible doubt. Further proof is supported by biological tests, in particular the radioactive level of your bone-marrow, which is much lower than might be expected under contemporary conditions of ambient radiation. The true age of the marrow, according to one of our most prominent biophysicists, is more than five thousand years, and probably nearer eight."

He paused for a moment, eyeing Carson sternly. "In face of all available evidence, this committee finds that you are Robert Carson, beneficiary under the Carson Trust," he announced in formal tones.

"Well, thank you," Carson said a little uncertainly, not knowing quite how he should react. "To me it was self-evident all the time."

"You must realize that this alters your status considerably," said the Colonel. "Perhaps Mr. Azan of the Trust commission will outline for you just what it means to be Robert Carson, here and now."

"Indeed I will," said Mr. Azan, beaming. "I ought to explain first that throughout the centuries terrestrial law has been continuous, and the Trust has survived with the industries and projects in which it was bound up, and with the big international banking houses who administered it under the direction of the commission. It has survived despite wars, and despite attempts made by a number of governments to seize its assets and convert the fund for treasury use. It has survived because it deploys man power and machine power—in other words, planetary productivity—and the commission has always maintained adequate and benevolent control of its labour force. A government might seize factories, but to seize the man power to operate them is to invite political disaster. Wars do not halt productivity. They channel it to military ends, and peace brings a stimulus to even greater productivity. The Trust is stronger today than it ever was."

"I understand," Carson murmured, "but I really don't see just *how* I own the Earth. After all, I was dead when the fund was started."

"An interesting legal point," said Mr. Azan happily, interlocking his fingers and cracking the knuckles loudly. "In fact, as a safeguard, the money was assigned to you, personally, even though you were dead. It was assumed, of course, that you would be dead for ever. Nobody suspected that a later civilization would develop the science of antimortics and restore your life. In law the money belonged to you, and you alone. No other individual or body of men or government could claim one single dollar of it."

"But surely, the commission. . . ."

"Ah, yes, the commission," Mr. Azan continued, holding up a silencing finger. "Obviously a fund assigned to a dead man could serve no useful purpose. It might just as well not exist. The terms of the Trust made provision for investment, the original purpose being to finance an expedition to recover your body in *Wanderer II*. The investment was to be effected by an impartial Commission of economic and industrial experts. It is important to remember that the fund has never *belonged* to the commission—throughout the ages they have merely administered it in your name. The members of the commission have always been men of integrity, internationally chosen with no overriding political affiliations, and they have made their investments wisely. With the aid of the fund they have in the course of time bought the entire planet—and it is all yours, Robert Carson."

Carson stared blankly at Mr. Azan. "But what am I supposed to do with it?"

"Whatever you wish. The commission will be pleased to advise you, naturally, but the fact is that legally all property, industry and assets owned by the Trust belong to you."

Colonel Ree leaned forward, tapping the table lightly with his fingers. "Now you can understand why the Martians took such great trouble to find you and give you back your life. While you were dead the fund belonged to no one, but was controlled by the commission. However, a living Carson is a different matter. He has the legal right to claim all that belongs to him, to dissolve the commission, to hand the planet he owns to somebody else if he chooses—or is made to choose."

"I see what you mean," Carson said thoughtfully. "They never did explain just *why* I was owner of Earth, and they never told me what would happen after the invasion was won—just that I would be installed in a government building, somewhere, as a symbolic ruler. . . ."

"Having legally assigned your rights in the Trust to Mr. Jaff or one of the others," the Colonel put in. "And very soon afterwards you would die, accidentally, in such a way that antimortic surgery would be impossible—and that would be the final, irrevocable end of Robert Carson and the Carson Trust."

"Would they dare to do that?"

"It wouldn't matter once the original terms of the Trust had been abandoned and the trustees dismissed. Law is law, and terrestrials recognize that basic principle. You must remember that for a long, long time the effective ruling power on this planet has been the Trust commission, acting through the appointed government. The commission always acts correctly and in accordance with the highest ethics, and the people recognize its ultimate authority. If the commission should abdicate in favour of a new government, perhaps appointed by you, then there would be no trouble and no revolt. But illegal seizure of power is another matter. It would provoke the strongest possible resistance."

Carson nodded his understanding.

"At present we are fighting the invaders to the best of our ability," the Colonel went on, "and we shall continue to do so while we have the backing of law. The responsibility is now yours, Robert Carson. It is for you to decide what is to be done with the world which you own."

"We fight on," said Carson firmly, "until every single Martian invader is destroyed or forced to return to his own planet."

The colonel slapped his open hand enthusiastically on the table. "Excellent! That is the attitude I hoped you would take. You must be patient for a time while I report to the military command, and then there will be a high-level conference at which you will preside. Meanwhile you will be transferred to new quarters of size and style befitting your status. By tomorrow we shall be ready to formulate new plans."

"I am at your service," Carson said.

The new apartment was situated on the administrative level quite near to the government offices. It was big and comfortable without being ostentatious, as had been the case with the circular room in his living quarters on Mars. Better still, there were no women installed in adjacent rooms ready to serve amorally as and when required. The terrestrials, he judged, had not yet abandoned all principles with regard to sex—or perhaps they assumed that if a man needed feminine company he would have the initiative to seek it for himself, and might even resent being able to turn it on and off like a tap.

Mr. Jaff had obviously presented a distorted view of the terrestrials. If the commission had sought to retain their power they could easily have denounced him as an impostor and destroyed him; on the contrary, they had set out meticulously to determine his true identity by appointing a special committee for that purpose, and having established that he was indeed Robert Carson they were ready to abide by the rule of law and deliver Earth to him as a complete property. That, in itself, was a conception which exceeded the powers of his imagination: to own Earth was a meaningless concept. But he could under-stand the legal mechanics behind it. Equally, he failed to under-stand the opportunist thinking of the Martian colonists, knowing that the Trust commission would abide by the law: *Whoever owns Carson also owns the Earth.*

The picture became clearer in his mind. The Martians had hoped to make a quick invasion strike, seizing power over key centres for long enough to establish through every channel of communication that he, Carson, was alive and had come to claim Earth, according to the law, supported by the armed might of Mars. But the invasion had been too slow, and they had lost the man who owned the world. In effect they had also lost the war.

Without me, he thought, they have no legal right to possess anything. They are operating outside the law. If they want Earth they will have to seize it by force, and, even more difficult, hold it by force—not just for a few weeks or months or years, but for all time. And without the backing of law the entire population of Earth will be opposed to them, using every means of resistance within their power. They will be forced to govern by ruthless totalitarian methods and in the end they will fail, because they will have to rely on their home planet for supplies and reinforcements. It is an impossible project—they cannot maintain the struggle across millions of miles of space. The truth is that there are not enough people on Mars to occupy even half the Earth by force.

He pondered the subject for a while, trying to see his own place in the scheme of things. I am the key, he realized. Terrestrial law revolves around me, and terrestrial economics is based on the ramifications of the Carson Trust—in other words, my money. Therefore I am essential to their purposes, and they will try to find me. At this stage in an invasion attempt that must already have cost an interplanetary fortune, they will use every trick in the book to try to locate me and take me alive. I'm more than a symbol to them—I'm a blank cheque.

He attempted to visualize the policy of the Martian high command, and Mr. Jaff in particular. The transceiver in his ear was still working on a one-way basis, so far as he knew, and Mr. Jaff would have heard everything. He would know now that there was no possibility of further subterfuge—no way of persuading or compelling Carson to return. On the other hand, without Carson the Martian cause was lost.

What would I do if I were Jaff? Carson asked himself mentally. Certain things seemed inevitable. He tabulated the answers in his mind. I'm Jaff, he thought, and I know that the war has reached stalemate, and may even be lost. To force a win by sheer weight of weapons is impracticable. The only possibility of success is to take over Earth within the framework of the law, and that means that Carson has to be found and forced to co-operate.

Problem—how to find Carson. Having found him, the rest is easy. Abandon the dispersed fighting; maintain defensive action only; organize a tough, well-equipped task force to go and get Carson at whatever cost. But, once again, the problem—how to find Carson.

He knew the answer now, and it was absurdly simple. While the transceiver was operating, relaying voices across the radio channel to Mr. Jaff's monitoring headquarters, radar direction finders could orientate themselves on the signal and fix its point of origin with precise accuracy. By now Jaff would already know where he was located and would be mustering a striking force to make the one final important assault. It was only a question of locating the city, and the level within the city. Coma gas and black light would do the rest.

Carson began to feel vaguely alarmed. In his mind's eye he could see the fleets of hovercraft taking off at dispersed surface airports, crammed with assault troops, converging on the city with one single mission to perform: find Robert Carson and bring him back alive.

Anxiously he went out of the apartment, and was relieved to find two guards posted at either end of the corridor. He approached one of them.

"I should like to contact Colonel Ree," he said.

"I'm afraid the Colonel won't be available for some time, Mr. Carson," said the guard. "He's at an important conference. You may be able to get in touch with his deputy, Lieutenant Kier."

"How do I do that?"

"There are facilities in your apartment."

They went back into Carson's quarters where, in the living room, the guard indicated a panel on the wall. He pressed a switch, and a thin shutter slid aside to reveal a video screen which immediately began to glow in fugitive rainbow colours. Within a second the face of an attractive dark-haired woman had materialized in solid three-dimensional colour.

"Security vidar," she announced. "Who do you want, please?"

"It's an internal network for military and government officials," the guard explained quietly. "Just say the name of the person you want."

"Lieutenant Kier," said Carson, as the guard left the room.

The girl's face faded, and the screen remained blank for a

moment. Suddenly a young masculine face with keen eyes was staring at him from the screen.

"Lieutenant Kier . . . oh, it's you, Mr. Carson. Can I help?"

"It occurred to me," said Carson with some urgency, "that the Martians may have discovered where I am by obtaining a radar fix on the transceiver device. . . ."

"Of course they have," Kier interrupted. "There have already been a number of sporadic raids, mainly reconnaissance, to test our defences. We shall have adequate warning when a major attack is launched, and plans have been made for an extremely rapid evacuation of the city by underground tunnels, if necessary. I doubt if it will come to that. This is one of the most strongly defended cities in Europe."

"What city is this?" Carson enquired.

"Didn't they tell you? The name is Atlantis. The city is excavated in the bedrock of the Atlantic Ocean, and is connected by tunnels to the mainland of Europe. It is the most secure city on the planet, and for that reason it is the co-ordinating military and governmental headquarters for Earth as a whole. We are in an undersea fortress. There is nothing to fear."

Carson almost sighed with relief as he savoured the irony of the situation. Water was the one medium with which the Martians hardly knew how to cope, for there were no seas and oceans on Mars. The problem of attacking a city buried beneath immeasurable fathoms of ocean might prove to be insuperable to Martian military technology. Mr. Jaff would be completely baffled and frustrated, wondering how to cope with the new situation.

"You mentioned raids," he said. "How could there be raids?"

"Deep-level submarines. Underwater photography. Contour-sounding by ultrasonics. A few minor undersea bombs to clear the silt and expose the outlines of the city. Eventually they will try to drill through, but it will take time. If they attempt an attack through the tunnels they will be unlucky. We have means to flood them almost instantly."

"Well, thanks for the information," Carson said cheerfully. "Seems I was worrying unnecessarily."

Lieutenant Kier smiled. "You underestimated our technology. In many respects the Martians are ahead of us, but we were the ones to start underground planetary engineering. We have a two-thousand year lead on the enemy in that field."

Carson made a suitable acknowledgment, then switched off the vidar. The terrestrials had overlooked nothing, he decided. If anything, the Martians had under-rated the competence and adaptability of the defenders of Earth.

That night, for the last time, he slept peacefully.

CHAPTER FOURTEEN

EARLY the following morning Carson was summoned to a high command conference in an adjacent governmental building. He found himself sitting at a round table with about a dozen terrestrials, of which half wore the uniforms of senior military officers, while the rest, dressed in civilian clothes, were obviously members of the administrative government. Colonel Ree sat next to Carson, but the man in command of the assembly was a small wiry individual who, Ree explained, was none other than Marshal Haan, the commander-in-chief of the entire terrestrial defence forces.

Marshal Haan made his address in a calm, unhurried manner, keeping it short and to the point. He said:

"Gentlemen, this is a council of war, operating under new terms of reference. Today we have with us the man who in law is the absolute owner of all that we are fighting to defend. I present Robert Carson, beneficiary of the fabulous Carson Trust."

All eyes switched to Carson and for more than a minute there was embarrassing applause.

"I must point out," the Marshal continued, "that while Mr. Carson may in law own the world on which we live, we are nevertheless his tenants. We have certain obligations towards him and towards our planet. He, in turn, has a number of obligations towards us, and the people who live on Earth— the people who, in their several ways, have helped to make the Carson Trust what it is today. The fact is that we all have a vested interest in the Trust. It supplies the amenities of civilized living, while we supply the productivity to provide those amenities. The thing is a self-perpetuating circle, energized by the economic stimulus of the Trust."

A murmur of agreement rumbled diffusely around the table.

"There is one other factor to be considered. Mr. Carson has

one privilege which is denied to the rest of us. I refer to the miniature radio device fused in his ear which makes it possible for him to communicate directly with the enemy. At the moment it is only partly operative, but we can provide ancillary equipment which will make it fully operative, if necessary."

He looked directly at Carson. "In other words, the man who, by established and respected law, is the rightful owner of Earth, also has the power to intercede between the two warring forces."

More sounds of approval, and appreciative eyes glancing quickly at Carson.

"By restoring the two-way function of the aural transceiver, Mr. Carson will have the ability to act as our spokesman and will be able to negotiate directly with the enemy—with Mr. Jaff in particular, which is a desirable arrangement. Naturally it will depend on whether Mr. Carson is prepared to act as an intermediary in this way."

He looked questioningly towards Carson, who nodded slowly and thoughtfully.

"I am fully prepared to act in whatever way is thought advisable," Carson said. "I know Mr. Jaff very well, and he is now aware of my true status so far as terrestrial affairs are concerned. I think Mr. Jaff and I could profitably talk together and negotiate —at least we would understand each other."

"Excellent," the Marshal commented.

"One point, however," Carson went on. "If the transceiver is restored to two-way functioning, there is a possibility that Mr. Jaff may put pressure on me by using the ultrasonic whistle. . . ."

The Marshal raised one hand reassuringly. "We do not propose to restore the device in quite that way. After all, it is functioning normally—it is your ear which is not responding. What we shall do is make a simple adaptation which you can switch on or off, as you think fit. If there should be an ultrasonic whistle, then switch off."

"Good," Carson remarked.

"So we have our intermediary, and our channel of communication with the enemy. All that needs to be decided now is the simple matter of political policy. In other words, gentleman, what are we to say to the Martians?"

A square-jawed officer sitting directly opposite Carson said: "Unconditional surrender."

Another remarked: "Immediate cessation of hostilities, and the complete withdrawal of Martian forces to the moon before any discussion of terms can begin."

Carson said: "I see no necessity for an ultimatum. It will only provoke truculent opposition, and may defeat its own purpose. In any case, would we be able to follow up an ultimatum with effective action?"

"In the course of time, yes," said a voice.

"And in the course of time the Martians will weaken to breaking strain," Carson went on. "They cannot cope with a long drawn out war. Interplanetary logistics is, in the long term, too difficult and too expensive. Sooner or later they must withdraw, but there is a real danger that before they do so they will launch a final goodbye attack in an attempt to wreak as much destruction as possible. At that stage they will not hesitate to use atomic weapons in our underground cities. It will be a final gesture of brutal vengeance."

"We had already considered that point," said the Marshal. "In practice an ultimatum followed by a determined counter-attack might be a wiser policy. At least it would put them on the defensive."

"Why not give them the opportunity to come to terms with honour?" Carson suggested. "As the war has already reached a condition of balanced stagnation, we might propose a truce, during which the military and political leaders of both sides could meet at some neutral place and discuss terms."

"Yes," breathed the Marshal approvingly. "A mid-war conference under the chairmanship of Robert Carson." He added hastily: "Provided they agree, of course. We don't want to be put in the position of making concessions. . . ."

"We will make no concessions. If and when the conference takes place, we can find out just what each planet wants from the other in the way of materials, supplies and products. We can discuss the question of exchange of personnel, of immortality techniques for terrestrials, and other vital matters such as the mutants, rehabilitation of the Earth's surface—perhaps with the co-operation of Martian scientists. We might find that we can do much more together working in harmony than could be achieved by conflict."

"I can see you are something of an idealist," the Marshal said cynically. "You may have lived on Mars, but you obviously do not know the devious Martian mentality. Immortal minds tend to grow twisted and gnarled with age, like the trunks of ancient trees. They become too dry and subtle, and they tend to lack flexibility. I doubt very much if one could do a deal of the kind you suggest with Martian immortals. They are too self-contained. Because of their immense age and experience they tend to take a parental attitude—they possess an urge to exercise a kind of fatherly discipline over those who are not immortals. You might as well talk of a child hoping to strike a bargain with an unscrupulous adult."

"They really have no alternative," Carson pointed out. "The entire success of their invasion depends on me. Unless they can occupy Earth within the existing framework of the law, they cannot hope to occupy it at all. They can produce a striking force, but not a long-term army of occupation. Once they realize that I have changed sides, then their campaign will come to an end."

"You may be right," the Marshal conceded.

"In that case I am ready to talk to Mr. Jaff."

"Very well." The Marshal stood up. "If you gentlemen will excuse me for a few minutes, I shall escort Mr. Carson to the laboratory, where engineers will supply the adaptor to provide two-way radio communication with the enemy."

He walked round the table towards the door. Carson stood up, glanced swiftly round the assembly, then followed him.

The adaptor resembled a small hearing aid, and functioned in much the same way. There were two tiny earpieces, joined by a headband in the manner of a stethophone, and a miniaturized amplifier with a switch, designed to hang round the neck from a looped strap. One earpiece would pick up audio vibrations from the transceiver in the deaf ear, the engineer explained, and after amplification they would be passed to a minute reproducer in the other ear. In this way Carson would be able to hear Mr. Jaff, with the added advantage that he could switch off the adaptor when he chose. Two-way radio contact was established once more, but this time it could be controlled from both ends.

They returned to the conference room and resumed their seats.

Marshal Haan said: "Mr. Carson is now able to talk with

the enemy, and I suggest he does so without delay, so that he can refer to us, if he wishes, for guidance on questions of policy."

The others signified their agreement. Carson nodded, fingering the switch on the plastic case of the amplifier.

"Very well, then, Mr. Carson. . . ."

Carson switched on the amplifier. The faint sound of background static hissed in his left ear.

"Mr. Jaff," he said, speaking slowly and clearly. "Mr. Jaff, this is Robert Carson. I am speaking from terrestrial military headquarters in Atlantis."

An interval of silence—then Mr. Jaff's voice, oddly flat and toneless.

I'm disappointed in you, Carson. I never imagined you would become a traitor and join the enemy—and after we gave you back your life.

"Thank you for my life, but my mind is my own. You can't alter that."

We could have done, but we trusted you. We relied on your sense of integrity and honour. You know that whatever we planned to do was for the ultimate benefit of Earth.

"The ultimate benefit of Mars, you mean. I am no longer so naïve."

We are the immortals, Carson. We are a superior race with a superior technology, and you are one of us at heart. Do not trust these terrestrials. They are using you for their own purposes. When they have finished with you they will destroy you. The Carson Trust has already managed very well for centuries with a fake Carson lying under a fake rocket. Why should they want you alive? For eight thousand years the Trust commission has exploited the economics of the world, and it is because they are trying to interfere with the economics of Mars, too, that this war was begun. Why should they hand over their powers to you? They have nothing to gain and everything to lose.

"They have one thing which you and your henchmen have not got, Mr. Jaff, and that is integrity. They respect the law, as I do. Above all, they are Earthmen, just as I am. This is my planet and it is my duty to defend it against alien aggression."

It is only your planet by virtue of the life we gave back to you. We sponsored your rebirth, and therefore we have the moral right to exercise some control over what you plan to do with your property, just as we also have the right to protect you from terrestrial attempts to seize your power and possessions. You talk of aggression—but is it aggression if one nation tries to raise the level of civilization of another, even if, at the beginning, force is necessary?

At this point Carson outlined the trend of the conversation to the assembly. "They are, at any rate, trying to justify their attitude," he added, "which seems to suggest that they might be prepared to talk things over round a table."

"Try suggesting it to Jaff," said Marshal Haan.

Carson nodded. "Mr. Jaff," he said, "you must know that at this stage force is not likely to resolve the war. Sooner or later there will have to be a cease-fire followed by discussions, or the Martian armies will have to make a full-scale withdrawal. There are certain concessions which both sides can make in the interests of economic stability and progress on both planets. If neither side can force its policy on the other, then the sensible thing to do is discuss the difficulties in a peaceful manner."

We have never been opposed to peaceful discussions, replied Mr. Jaff, *but in the past such talks have always broken down and it has been impossible to reach agreement. There is no point in wasting time in further futile discussions.*

"This time the situation is different," Carson pointed out. "There are three parties to the discussion, and one party has what amounts to a casting vote—and I guarantee to use that casting vote fairly and reasonably on all issues."

I have not the authority to agree to such a proposal without the sanction of high command. That will take time.

"We can wait. We have all the time in the world."

Very well, Mr. Carson. A pause, then: *I make one final appeal to your sense of loyalty. If Earth is yours, you are free to return to us. In your own interests as an immortal, come back now.*

"Even if I wanted to, I couldn't," said Carson with faint irony. "I am still technically a prisoner of war."

In the late afternoon Mr. Jaff called Carson over the transceiver radio link. The conference had been terminated hours earlier on the understanding that he would communicate with Marshal Haan as soon as any positive message was received from the enemy. Obviously Jaff had had a busy day: the mere idea of a truce involving discussion between leaders of the opposing forces was tantamount to an armistice, and therefore, from the Martian point of view, an admission of partial if not utter defeat. Carson had little doubt that top priority signals had been flashing between Earth and the moon, and even between Earth, moon and Mars. Even at this stage, if the Martians agreed to discussions, he suspected that they would try to use them in some subtle way to seize a tactical advantage.

Mr. Jaff's voice, however, sounded sincere enough, if a little weary. It had been agreed, he stated, that key personnel of the Martian military and political invasion force would meet their terrestrial opposite numbers for informal discussions, but any agreement reached would be subject to ratification by the respective governments concerned. Carson himself was to play the role of impartial chairman, without the power of casting vote: in the event of a major dispute over points of detail he would merely offer guidance which both sides could refer back to their governments. The meeting was to take place within three days at a neutral site on the surface, and all military personnel and armaments would be withdrawn from a zone one hundred miles in radius centred on the conference hall. No decision would be binding, but the discussion as a whole would form the basis of a practical programme for further negotiation between the heads of government of the two planets at an intermediate point, perhaps on the moon, or even on a ship in space between Earth and Mars. Meanwhile there would be a cease-fire, as from midnight terrestrial time, and there would be no further troop movements or freighting of military supplies (other than food) during the period of the conference.

Carson relayed the message to Marshal Haan, who made no effort to conceal his delight. "Excellent, Mr. Carson," he said over the security vidar. "It is equivalent to a surrender. If the Martians thought for a moment that they could still steal the initiative and snatch a victory, however slight, they would not hesitate to do so. We'll agree to their terms, so that they will have no possible cause for complaint. I will order a complete cease-fire as from midnight, and meanwhile the chiefs of staff will make the necessary arrangements for the talks. Some isolated place, perhaps in America, or Africa. Let's hope this time we can come to terms with the Martians on a lasting basis."

"I hope so," Carson said earnestly.

He found himself unable to sleep that night, mainly because

his imagination would not be stilled. The cease-fire came into effect promptly at twelve-o'clock, and suddenly peace seemed to descend like a tangible thing. This could be the turning point in the history of the solar system, he thought. It could be the end of war for all time. And it's all centred on me. If, in some way, I were able to return to the twentieth century, they wouldn't believe it—how could they possibly comprehend the things that have happened in the past eight thousand years? How could they understand my present status as owner of the world, and arbiter between two warring planets? And yet, here I am, Robert Carson, like a fish out of water, almost, occupying a fantastic position of high authority.

Around two a.m. he lay on his bed and made a determined effort to sleep. For a long time he pursued fugitive ideas through a world of half-dreams, not fully awake, but never unconscious.

The explosion occurred at precisely ten minutes past three.

CHAPTER FIFTEEN

At first he was merely confused. There was no sense of alarm, nor any premonition of danger. At first there had been a spasmodic shuddering of the room, earthquake-like, and the angry sound of distant thunder; after that he could hear a persistent remote roar, like the noise of a great waterfall far away.

He pressed a switch in the darkness, but the room lights failed to respond. Feeling his way along the walls he found the security vidar, but that, too, was inoperative. He opened the main door to the apartment and went into the corridor. The guards were talking together in anxious tones: he could hear their voices distinctly in the darkness.

"What's happening?" he demanded.

The voices stopped abruptly. Footsteps paced slowly on a hard surface, drawing nearer.

"Is that you, Mr. Carson?"

"Yes. I thought I heard an explosion. There seems to be no power. . . ."

"We've had no information or instructions, sir. There may have been some trouble with the generators."

"I'd like to know exactly what has happened. See if you can find out."

"Yes, sir."

The guards shuffled away in the darkness, and suddenly the corridor was a lonely place. For a while he listened to the background roar, trying to fathom its origin. It seemed to him that the noise was growing louder, and now he imagined he could hear other sounds—a confusion of shouts and screams—but so far away as to be almost imperceptible. Uneasiness gripped him like icy fingers around his heart.

On an impulse he switched on the adaptor connected to the aural transceiver; there was no surprise in him as he heard the voice of Mr. Jaff intoning monotonously in his ear.

Carson, Carson. Can you hear me? Carson, Carson—are you listening?

"Yes," Carson breathed, full of apprehension.

I've been calling for you for a long time. We have sent a special task force to rescue you. They have breached the roof and one of the walls of the city, and the Atlantic Ocean is pouring in. We know exactly where you are. Don't move. We shall find you before the water rises to your level.

"But the cease-fire. . . ."

That was the chance we had been waiting for—to catch the enemy idle and unprepared. We were able to crawl along the ocean bottom in deep-level submarines and blow the top off Atlantis with atomic charges. The power plant is wrecked and there are no communications in the city, but we know where you are. Two hundred men are searching for you on the third level. They will find you within a few minutes.

"No!" shouted Carson in desperation, "you can't do this. It is an act of treachery!"

Mr. Jaff laughed. *It is done. There is no such thing as treachery in war. We are now a big jump ahead of the enemy, that is all. Very soon you will be back with. . . .*

Carson flicked the switch that snapped Mr. Jaff's voice into extinction. The tumult of the rushing water was louder now, and the shouting voices were nearer. Frantically he tried to orientate his mind, to recall the layout of the building. Abruptly he needed to be in the open highways with other people, anywhere away from this black shapeless corridor. He began to stumble forward in the darkness, arms outspread, fingers touching cold walls. Presently he recognized the smooth surface of the sliding door of the elevator. He found the wall button and pressed it urgently, but nothing happened. Warily he advanced, seeking the staircase.

He reached the highway minutes later, but there was only intense night and the threatening roar of onrushing water. He turned, baffled, feeling like a trapped animal. They were all trapped in this sub-oceanic city, every human being from Marshal Haan down, and the chances were that they would all die unless desperate emergency measures were taken . . . but such as what? Surely, he supposed, in a sub-oceanic city they had provisions for escape in the face of this kind of disaster. There had always been the possibility of earthquakes rupturing the outer shell of Atlantis, and skilled planetary engineers would inevitably have taken such factors into account.

A pallid light flashed over his head, flickered uncertainly for a few seconds, then steadied into a gaunt amber glow. Emergency lighting, he thought. Now he could see people hurrying from buildings and running along the highway. He followed until, breathless because of the unaccustomed exertion, he caught up with a man wearing a military uniform. His face in profile seemed familiar, and abruptly he recognized him as Lieutenant Kier, Colonel Ree's deputy, the man with whom he had spoken via security vidar the previous day, who had said: *We are in an under-sea fortress—there is nothing to fear.*

Kier glanced quickly around, saw Carson and stopped running. They stood facing each other in the subdued lighting, gulping deep breaths of stifling air.

"You were right," said Kier. "They have attacked. All the levels from six to ten are flooded. We've lost a great deal of air, but we've managed to close most of the airtight and watertight doors. That should slow things down for a while, though the pressure will win in the end."

"Pressure?" Carson queried.

"The pressure of the Atlantic Ocean at this depth—enough to crush us into unrecognizable pulp. Already the water is compressing the air as it rises. Can't you feel it?"

"Yes," said Carson, realizing suddenly why the air had become so hot, and knowing the reason for his erratic breathing and the throbbing pain in his ears and behind his eyes. "The point is, what can we do?"

"The sensible thing is to make our way to the upper level, which will be the last to survive. There is a certain amount of surfacing gear, if it can be got into use. And there's always a chance that the engineers will be able to pump air back into the lower levels—if they can get the nuclear power plant to work."

"They're after *me*—you realize that," Carson said.

Kier nodded. "The water will hinder them just as much as it hinders us. We'd better get on. The elevators won't be working, so we'll have to ascend the spiral ramp. That's hard work at the best of times."

They continued running along the highway, joining a throng of people, men and women together, all in search of escape. The air became more oppressive and noticeably hotter. Carson found his mouth quite dry and his lungs aching from the heat. Oddly enough, there was no sense of having to gasp for air; the difficulty was in exhaling, as if the lungs of their own volition wished to remain distended. It required a positive act of will to contract the chest muscles and squeeze out the stale air; inhaling was a simple matter of relaxing and allowing the pressurized air outside to rush in, like water finding its own level.

They passed the dark silent elevators and made their way towards the entrance to the ramp. While they were still some distance away it became apparent that a battle of some kind was in progress. In the semi-gloom of the emergency lighting system it was difficult to perceive detail: there was a random crackling and flashing of electrostatic weapons, and a billowing haze spreading through the air above the crowd. Carson thought he could see strange figures encased in metallic pressurized suits advancing through the multitude.

"Coma gas," Kier said urgently. "Without anti-coma injections we don't stand a chance."

There was already a pungent, aromatic smell in the air where they stood.

"What now?" Carson asked.

Kier fumbled in his tunic and produced a small grey pistol of curious shape. "Electrostatic," he murmured. "Quite lethal at close range. I'll get as near as I can. Goodbye, Mr. Carson. I may see you sometime. . . ."

With that Kier plunged into the crowd, forcing his way towards the entrance to the ramp. Carson lost sight of him within half-a-minute.

The crowd in front, nearest to the ramp and the invaders, were attempting to retreat against the pressure of those at the rear who, not understanding the situation, were trying to push their way forward. Carson found himself caught as if in a vice, moving with the mass, quite incapable of independent motion. All the time the coma gas thickened, and the crowd was becoming a collapsing mound of solid humanity as unconsciousness struck.

For a while he struggled furiously to escape from the trap, but was unable to make it. His mind blacked out quite abruptly. Even in this instant of bitter defeat he found himself admiring the ruthless efficiency of the Martian military machine, and, in a masochistic way, he could share the triumph of Mr. Jaff.

"How could you have imagined for one moment that we would be prepared to surrender a costly and ambitious military venture because of one man?" asked Mr. Jaff.

It was a wide circular room with horizontal windows looking out on bleak flat countryside. A stunted tree waved solemnly in a high wind, and purple hills tinted the far horizon. There were half-a-dozen other people in the room apart from Mr. Jaff—mainly high-ranking officers, so far as Carson could judge.

"The operation was simple enough. We used three submarines and not more than two hundred men. We knew precisely where you were located. The wall of Atlantis was breached to give immediate access to the spiral ramp connecting all levels of the city. That gave us complete control of population movement. Our men wore pressure suits, just in case the water rose more rapidly than had been calculated—but, in fact, the operation was completed with plenty of time to spare. I understand the most difficult task was tracing you, Mr. Carson. There were so many bodies that even our portable radar was thrown off balance. However, we got you in the end, and here you are!"

"And the others?" Carson asked dejectedly.

Mr. Jaff spread out his hands helplessly. "The fortunes of war. After all, Atlantis was a purely military and governmental fortress. It was a legitimate target."

"You mean. . . ."

"The water rose, as water will, and the air escaped slowly. It was all over in about two hours, possibly three. There were no survivors so far as we know, though a few lucky ones may have escaped in surfacing equipment from the top level. If so, they are presumably floating around in mid-Atlantic. Perhaps we might arrange to search the area from low-flying aircraft. So far there have been no radar indications."

"It was hardly a legitimate act of warfare," Carson said reproachfully. "After the cease-fire. . . ."

"Is there such a thing as a *legitimate* act of war?" demanded Mr. Jaff. "A cease-fire is for the weak—not the strong. The Atlantis mission has enhanced our military prestige and, incidentally, has deprived the terrestrials of their high command in one stroke. They are now an enemy without a leader, disorganized and unco-ordinated. Already the cities are beginning to surrender—they realize now that they face the possibility of utter destruction. No longer can they assume that our military tactics are based on the principle of avoiding destruction to property and plant."

"You will never hold the entire planet by violence and ruthlessness," Carson protested. "How can you hope to develop Earth as an economic unit if it is run on the lines of a prisoner-of-war camp, or worse?"

"The Earth is yours, Robert Carson," said Mr. Jaff, smiling. "Not even the enemy will deny that. It is for you to act in the best interests of your subjects. After all, as a kind of benevolent dictator, what do you wish to achieve? Rehabilitation of the Earth's surface? This used to be a green and fertile planet, and it can be so again, with the application of science and patience. A solution to the mutant problem? That can easily be achieved, and quite humanely. The one can assist the other: human bodies make excellent fertilizer. Immortality for all normal terrestrial humans? It can be done, as you yourself know from personal experience. Intensive development of planetary and inter-planetary technology for the ultimate benefit of humanity? That is just a question of time and application. We have the knowledge and the power. Sooner or later a race of immortal humans will spread out among the stars and people the cosmos. The ethics of the dream outweigh the ethics of detail. To cure a human virus disease may involve the cruel death of a million tiny animals, but the end justifies the means."

"It has always been recognized that one could gain the Earth by selling one's soul to the devil," Carson said sombrely. "Good may come out of evil, but that is not a justification for evil. Man has the right to live in freedom, even a mutant. . . ."

"Nobody has the right to live," Mr. Jaff stated dogmatically. "It is a meaningless expression. Does the fertilized egg have the right to live while the unfertilized egg has the right to die? If you prune a tree in order to improve its beauty and fruitfulness, are you depriving the sawn-off branches of their right to live? If you were growing a crop of cereal and you discovered part of it diseased and deformed by radioactive mutation, would you hesitate to destroy the bad in order that the good might flourish?"

"We are not trees and plants," Carson insisted. "We are humans, and we have certain rights and responsibilities. We are entitled to live in our homes or countries or planets without fear of ruthless dispossession acting in the name of scientific progress."

"We are entitled to nothing," said Mr. Jaff quietly. "We are born into the world with nothing and we leave it with nothing. There is no profit and loss account. But in the act of living and surviving we all change the world in some way, perhaps infinitesimally, perhaps immeasurably. History will judge our contribution to human affairs, but judgment without punishment is worthless. Ordinary mortal men can act irresponsibly because they will never live long enough to see the final results of their actions. That is why we have mutants on Earth."

"Immortals are still human, and they can act irresponsibly, too."

Mr. Jaff shook his head slowly. "That is not true, Mr. Carson, and in your heart you know it. We, the immortals, can afford to take the long-term view because we shall live and continue to live in the world we are actually creating now. Every act we commit determines the pattern of our future existence and helps to shape the kind of world we shall find ourselves living in during the centuries to come. We can't afford to be humane if we are to create a perfect world, and we can't afford to tolerate the short-term irresponsibility of those who are not immortal, who do not really care what happens to the world after they are dead. You can't plan a perfect world with minds which are only mature for a mere two generations."

"Nor can you plan a world on the basis that individuals don't matter—that they can be destroyed, herded and brainwashed to fit an economic or political pattern. If I am owner of Earth, then I cannot sanction a policy of that kind."

"We can force you to co-operate, if we have to," said Mr. Jaff ominously, "but we would prefer to develop Earth within the framework of terrestrial law. It will make our task easier and will benefit all in the long run. That is why I have talked to you at some length in order to clarify our attitude."

"What exactly is it you want me to do?"

"The world now knows that you have rejoined us. It is widely believed that you yourself organized the rescue mission. As Robert Carson, you are to issue a decree dissolving the Trust commission and appointing a Martian council to administer the Trust. From that point on we shall do the rest."

"The answer is still no," said Carson firmly.

Mr. Jaff uttered a long, patient sigh. "In that case, there is only one thing left for us to do. This is definitely your last chance, Mr. Carson. I appeal to you to make the most of it. Follow me."

Reluctantly Carson walked behind Mr. Jaff to a door in the circular wall of the room.

"In here," said Mr. Jaff. "You can have ten minutes. No more."

Slowly Carson walked into the adjoining room. The door closed behind him with a faint astringent click.

CHAPTER SIXTEEN

THE room was smaller, with fewer windows, but still circular in shape. A woman was standing by one of the windows, her back towards him, but she turned as he entered the room. He recognized her instantly, with her bronze hair and green eyes.

"Competence Cayne," he said.

She came over to him and put her hands on his shoulders, then kissed him lightly. "Aren't you glad to see me?" she enquired.

"Yes and no," he said, frowning. "Why are you here?"

"To try to persuade you to change your mind."

"Not even you could do that."

"No?" She regarded him archly for a moment. "You must not allow your prejudice against Mr. Jaff and his colleagues to poison your feelings for me."

"I thought you didn't favour the compulsion neurosis known as love."

"I favour human relationships," she murmured, smiling mischievously. "I'll tell you a secret. I've been granted a permanent assignment. You."

He said nothing but just eyed her questioningly.

She went on: "You and I can be together all the time. You don't need to worry about the world at all. Leave government and economics to those best qualified to attend to them. You don't

need to be more than a figurehead, Robert Carson, and a figurehead can have a lot of fun."

"Is that the bargain? The Carson Trust in exchange for you?"

"Aren't I worth it?"

He laughed briefly and sardonically.

"After all, what is the Carson Trust worth to you? You may
own a planet in theory, but there's nothing you can do with it."

"I can try to make it a better planet."

"Just how do you propose to do that?"

"Well, I had thought in terms of a kind of coalition government including both Martians and terrestrials. . . ."

"Immortals and norms," she mused. "Mutants, too?"

"Perhaps."

"It would never work. You could never reach agreement on
policy between the immortals, the mortals and the deformed. One
party would dominate the others sooner or later, so why not
start with domination in the first place?"

"Because I don't care for the Martian kind of domination. I
think the terrestrials should be allowed to solve their own problems and build their own future without domination of any
kind."

She shook her head sadly. "You really are being obtuse. You
will co-operate with the Martians, either voluntarily or by force.
The choice is yours. Indoctrination is not pleasant. There is no
way in which you can assist the terrestrials while you remain
alive."

He became aware of some strange quality in her eyes.

"We have just a few minutes left," she said. "Let's go outside."

He followed her to the door, and as they passed through she
quickly put her hand to his right ear and pressed into it a piece
of wax-like substance. "Don't talk," she whispered urgently. "I
have blocked the transceiver, but it can still pick up the vibrations
of your own voice through the bones of your head. Walk naturally
with me and listen to what I have to say."

They went out into the wind, walking across dry barren soil,
keeping their backs towards the building.

"Mars has its own problems," she said quietly, "and there are
many of us who would like to see the end of the military clique
which dominates the government. If the war is lost they can be
overthrown, then perhaps we can come to peaceable terms with
the terrestrials. But now that they have you, they cannot lose,

and they will take good care you do not escape again. There is only one alternative. Do you understand?"

He nodded slowly, saying nothing.

"It will have to be done in such a way that later antimortic surgery is impossible. There must never be another living Robert Carson to be used as a symbol for power politics."

He eyed her gloomily, but her face was impassive.

"This is your chance to save two planets from domination by a military caste," she went on. She produced a slim rectangular canister from inside her belt and handed it to him. "Conceal this in your clothing, perhaps under the belt. When you are ready, press the catch on the side. Wait until you have the chance of wide publicity—the proclamation, for instance. Meanwhile, pretend to co-operate."

"Jaff may suspect," he breathed, mouthing the words almost silently.

Her smile was hard and triumphant. "Don't worry about Mr. Jaff. He is one of us, and he has his own ambitions. But he, too, is monitored, and has to play his part."

Her arms encircled his neck for a moment while she kissed him, but the movement simply disguised the quick manipulation of her fingers as she removed the wax plug from his ear and discarded it.

"Well," she said in a naïve voice, "you have had plenty of time to think. Have you made up your mind?"

"As you said earlier," he replied, "I have no choice. I don't wish to be indoctrinated, and I don't wish to co-operate voluntarily. I'll compromise by choosing you, and bow out gracefully, leaving the future of Earth in the hands of those best fitted to deal with it."

"You are wise," she murmured.

He looked at her for quite a long time before speaking again. Finally he said: "I hope we shall be together for always."

"Of course," she murmured. "After all, we are immortals."

Slowly, arm in arm, they walked back to the circular building.

There was a new quality in Mr. Jaff's eyes and an unaccustomed solemnity in his expression when Carson reported back to him. It was as if he were trying to convey, on some telepathic plane, apologies for past events; as if he were trying to say: "I had to do at all times what they expected me to do, and there was no way of explaining—but now, perhaps, you will understand my dilemma, just as I understood yours."

But there was nothing in his manner or in the tone of his voice to suggest that his attitude was in any way different from usual. He did not react markedly to Carson's statement of his decision, but merely nodded his head tersely, as if he had expected that answer, anyway.

"I knew you would not fail us," he said. "At this point my work is virtually done. All that remains is to plan a suitable ceremony which can be relayed round the world on sound and video circuits. There will have to be a formal, official function, authenticated by legal experts and civic dignitaries, in which you will solemnly dissolve the existing Trust commission and hand over control of the Trust to Martian authority. You can leave the details to the gentlemen in this room," he indicated the officers with a brief movement of his hand, adding: "You will be well briefed and rehearsed, but there will be little to do—sign a few documents and perhaps make a short speech."

"I'll do whatever is required," Carson said.

"For the present you may join Miss Cayne in the other room. She will show you where the residential quarters are located."

"Very well," Carson agreed. He went back to the smaller room where the woman was waiting. She looked at him enquiringly.

"Robert Carson surrendered unconditionally," he stated, with no great enthusiasm. "I suppose it is the only way."

She held up a cautioning finger, then came over to him, producing further wax which she used to silence the aural transceiver device.

"Mr. Jaff can hardly be monitoring," he whispered. "He is in conference with the officers."

"There are other monitors. Mr. Jaff acts as supervisor and is advised by his staff. It is never safe to take risks."

"Tell me about Jaff."

"What is there to tell? He has worked hard to obtain a position of trust, and he has to fulfil his duties meticulously. Like many of the officials concerned with security and administration he, too, is monitored by the military authority. But he has links with terrestrial espionage agents on Mars, and it was Jaff himself who was responsible for stealing the Carson tape in order to have it copied. He will be an important man in the new administration after the insurrection."

"He has ruthless, inhuman ideas."

"Only superficially. He has to reflect official policy, whether he supports it or not." She hesitated uncertainly, anxiety in her eyes. "We cannot talk much longer in this way, Carson. They may be able to hear you, even though you are whispering, and the long silence may make them suspicious, anyway. Tell me, are you prepared to die for the second time?"

He considered the question for a while. "No," he said finally, "but I am acting under pressure. If my death will destroy the Martian hold on Earth, and help to reform Martian government and political policy, then it will be worth while. Perhaps I may achieve a kind of immortality after all." He paused reflectively, then indicated the device located beneath his belt. "What exactly will happen when I release the catch?"

She closed her eyes for a moment. "You will learn soon enough. There will be no question of antimortics, I'm afraid."

She removed the plug from his ear. "You are very silent," she said distinctly. "Surely you are not already having second thoughts about handing over the Trust to the custodianship of Mars."

"No," he agreed reluctantly. "I will do what I have decided to do."

She smiled in a melancholy way. "You won't regret it. Meanwhile, I will show you the temporary apartment in which we shall live for the next few days."

She led the way from the room.

He found it impossible to sleep that night. The thought of imminent death troubled him, even though he realized that it was inevitable. I died once before, he thought, and death itself was nothing, just a deeper form of dreamless sleep. But the moments before death were bad. I would not want to endure them again.

Then, later, conflicting thoughts obsessed his mind. Why should I die? he asked himself. Why should I sacrifice my life for this alien age? Why should I care who rules Earth or what happens to the mutants, and, for that matter, why should I commit suicide so that Mr. Jaff can achieve his ambition in Martian politics? They made me an immortal, and now they expect me to throw it aside for some nebulous interplanetary intrigue. If I choose to live, what can Jaff do about it? I'll sign away the Carson Trust, living in privilege, watching these aliens sorting out their complex affairs without interfering. And if the military clique continues to dominate Martian politics, well, why should I worry? Martian politics were well under way while I was still dead, long before I reincarnated. It is none of my business, and the problems of Earth are even less. I am not responsible for the mutants and the economic difficulties. They say that in Law I am the legal owner of the whole sorry mess, but, even so, what can I do about it? The mutants are not my personal responsibility; it could well be that in deciding to eliminate them the Martians are pursuing a wise course. When the world is reduced to shambles it is better to start again, to begin at the beginning, and remake it, albeit ruthlessly, in the way it should be remade. Who am I, a creature of the long dead past, to decry modern sociological science?

He spent the night in a state of utter confusion, and at one time got up to examine the slim lethal device, which he attached to the inside of his belt. It was of dull metal, slightly curved, about half the size of a cigarette case. The surface was perfectly smooth all over, with no sign of a crevice or crack, and the operative catch was a mere sliding button on one edge. It seemed incredible that so small an object could destroy a man. He handled it gingerly, turning it over and over. It seemed to him that it could hardly contain any appreciable amount of explosive, nor was it big enough to house any kind of imaginable nuclear device. On the other hand, he thought, it could be basically electronic—something that would paralyse the central nervous system.

A new thought occurred to him—supposing the thing were simply a factitious dummy, just a piece of machined metal possessing no lethal properties whatsoever. Supposing this were simply a plot to create a defeatist frame of mind in which he would agree to abdicate his ownership of Earth, and then find himself incapable of carrying out the suicidal act that would undermine the very basis of Martian authority. One could not underestimate the subtlety of Mr. Jaff—or of the very competent Competence Cayne for that matter. He examined the slender object suspiciously. There was only one way to find out if it was lethal or not, and that was to press the catch—but courage failed him. His confusion increased.

I must wait and see, he told himself. If it comes to the point I don't have to sign any documents, and I don't have to make a prepared speech. I can renege on my agreement if I choose. I no longer possess any loyalties in this strange world of the future.

One tends to revert to the basics of nature—ultimately to the problem of personal survival.

Later, in an uneasy frame of mind, he fell asleep.

They had built an immense structure of prefabricated parts on the site where the original Carson memorial had stood. Satellite pylons located round it supported automatic video cameras operated by remote control. A tiered terrace in plastic and timber provided standing space for thousands of terrestrial observers, and already the tiers were full, and the crowds extended beyond the perimeter of the site. Everyone who could possibly come had arrived, it seemed, to witness the inauguration of the age of the living Carson, owner of Earth.

Carson, waiting beneath the wide dais, rehearsed the lines of his speech with a cynical attitude. Mr. Jaff, standing nearby, was looking at him in a solicitous way. There was a sprinkling of high-ranking military officers and politicians among the assembly. Competence Cayne was present, too, but her capacity, it seemed, was simply one of moral support. The beginning of the ceremony had been timed for three o'clock, but there was still more than a quarter of an hour to go. Everyone seemed to be idling impatiently, and Carson himself was growing restive as the minutes dragged by.

Presently the girl came over to him and spoke quietly in enigmatic phrases presumably intended to deceive the monitors.

"After the speech, and before the signing. You know what to do. The speech itself—could be original. . . ."

"It will be highly original, and rather short," he remarked.

She smiled wryly. "I'm glad you're being philosophical about it. In a way, what you are about to do will strengthen the legend of Robert Carson." Her voice dropped to a mere whisper. "You will be remembered as the saviour of Earth, and also the saviour of Mars. You will always be remembered, and in that way you will achieve your own kind of immortality."

"I don't want immortality. I would rather see Robert Carson forgotten—for the world to solve its problems without reference to what is, in effect, a myth. Mr. Jaff said that the only importance of life is in the contribution one makes to human affairs. After eight thousand years what contribution can I possibly make? It would have been better if they had never found my body."